The Bub

STEVEN CLINTON

ISBN: 978-1-958058-05-3

DEDICATION

To Jose Arango, who saw I would be writing for a long time well before I did.

Thank you for your words of encouragement; they remained top of mind throughout this journey.

CONTENTS

Book 1

BOOK 1, CHAPTER 1

"You're an idiot. You know that, right?"

Gavin smiled at Neville's words; Neville had seen that smile before, and it did nothing to quell his anxiety.

"Look, there's no way that you clear the rocks. You're gonna get hurt. You might die."

"Wanna bet?"

Neville frowned. Gavin's grin only grew.

"A hundred Guvernment credits says I make it. Four good strides and I can jump far enough to clear the rocks. I'll drop straight into the cove."

Neville shook his head.

"But why? What good could come of it? What's wrong with riding the stone slide? We've been doing that for years; the Bubble Suits are designed for that."

As he spoke, Neville gestured to the far side of Kingfisher Reservoir, where a stone slide was carved into the dam wall. Gavin shook his head.

"I told you, I'm done with that. We've been riding that slide since we were teenagers, and no matter how great everyone tries to make it sound, it's boring."

Neville drew himself up at those words.

"Now you sound like a revolutionist. Boring never hurt anyone. We live in a perfect society, it's a beautiful day, and we have long, healthy lives ahead of us. Another seventy-seven years, give or take a few seasons. What's wrong with that?"

It had not looked as if Gavin was listening - he was lining up his launch path - but he faced Neville to respond to the question.

"What's wrong with it is that it's boring. I know what you think. I know what they say. But I'm sick of boring - I wanna' feel alive, and this is gonna be epic."

Gavin turned away before Neville could respond. He retreated to the start of his runway and squared himself on his path to the cliff's edge. The sun struck Gavin's Bubble Suit at an angle that turned his face into a mask of light, making it impossible for Neville to see anything but an unruly shock of blond hair. Desperate, Neville mounted a final argument, his voice rising involuntarily to a shout.

"In case you've forgotten, it's against the law."

Gavin shrugged; the sun was no longer in his face, and while he responded in a reasonable enough tone, Neville could see his friend's brown eyes were alive with mischief.

"We're allowed to step off the edge and bounce down the cliffs, aren't we? I'm not jumping - I'm just taking a bigger step - so I'm not doing anything illegal. Anyways, what's the worst that could happen? I'm wearing this thing, aren't I?"

Gavin plucked at the left arm of the Bubble Suit's membrane, pulling back the thin, stretchy material; the membrane snapped back into place as soon as he released it.

"It just doesn't seem like a good idea," Neville muttered, but these words were more for himself than for Gavin.

Neville had known, on some level, that Gavin had some sort of plan in mind from the moment they had picked him up for the drive to Kingfisher Reservoir that morning. Neville also knew, from long experience, that meant the matter was settled; Gavin was decided, his course of action set in stone, as it had been on the precipice of so many other mishaps. Reasoning with him was useless; Neville knew that no matter what he, or any of their friends, might say, Gavin was going to do whatever it was that he had decided to do.

Another desperate impulse seized Neville, but even as he started to shout out a final warning, Gavin took off, exploding from one foot to the other, his arms pumping furiously as he drove himself forward. An inch from the cliff's edge, Gavin planted hard on his right foot and launched himself into the empty air.

For a moment, he soared.

Then, as gravity asserted itself, he began to arc toward the cove.

To Neville's surprise, green and blue lights came to life across the back of Gavin's Bubble Suit, flashing what could only be an alarm; when the trajectory of Gavin's fall changed, and his plummet slowed, Neville realized that the Bubble Suit must have activated built-in safety measures.

As this realization hit Neville, the knot in his stomach unwound; he let out a sigh of relief, thanking Knowledge that the Bubble Suit designers had foreseen such an eventuality.

The day's events were entirely unforeseen - Gavin had been going on for weeks about what it would be like to jump off the cliffs, though Neville had not thought him serious until this morning - but instead of the adrenaline-filled free fall he had talked about, Gavin was floating toward the surface of the cove as gently as a snowflake. Neville doubted that his friend would be happy about that, but that was Gavin's problem; Neville was simply relieved that nothing had gone wrong.

Then, just as Neville started to turn back to the trail that would take him down from the cliffs, the green and blue lights on Gavin's Bubble Suit went out. In the same moment, his fall changed again; Gavin was spinning out of control, accelerating toward the water.

Before Neville could shout, Gavin had crashed through the surface of Kingfisher Reservoir, disappearing in a plume of spray.

BOOK 1, CHAPTER 2

Neville sat in the passenger seat of the car, dumbfounded by what he had witnessed.

His fellow passengers were in a similar state of shock; once Gavin had disappeared with the Emergency Response Team, Neville, Leonard, and Mo had retreated to their self-driving car, desperate for distraction from this onslaught of anxiety.

Fortunately, distractions were plentiful once they were back in the car; without speaking to each other, the three young men tapped the sensors on the right temples of their Bubble Suits, causing holographic monitors to appear in front of each of them.

Neville logged onto the Guvernment Media App and started scrolling through his feed, searching for his favorite reality show. He found it easily enough, but within a few short minutes, he realized that his anxiety was not receding; it seemed that the show would not be enough to distract him today.

The self-driving car had pulled out of the Kingfisher Reservoir's parking area and started its descent through Onyx Canyon, taking them back to Kingston. Neville closed out the Guvernment Media App and shifted his eyes away from his holographic monitor, hoping that he could forget his troubles by watching the passing scenery, the vast swaths of evergreens, the glimpses of the Grand River that he could catch from the roadway, but the view out the window did not prevent the intruding thoughts from entering his mind any more than the reality show had.

As the thought hit Neville, they turned a corner; the changing light caught on the window, allowing him to catch a full view of his reflection in the glass.

The light brown skin.

The dark brown hair, shaved short today, and most every day; Neville rarely altered the settings on his Bubble Suit.

The eyes of the same color, full of a trouble Neville could not recall seeing there before.

Finally, accepting that he could not push his thoughts away, Neville started to turn his attention to face them, but at that moment, salvation arrived in the sound of a soft chime.

Warmth flooded Neville's brain; without hesitation, the fingers of his right hand were at his left wrist, tapping his Bubble Suit's control panel to pull up the message on his holographic monitor.

Do you think he's alive?

It was a new comment from Leonard in an ongoing group chat.

Neville did not need to type to respond; he was able to think out his reply, imparting his message through the brain sensors that were a standard part of a Bubble Suit's operating system. As he did this, the message appeared on the screen of his monitor; response complete, he thought the command *Text Entry Complete*, and followed that up with the instruction *Send.*

It never occurred to him to look at either of his friends as he did this; after all, Neville had known them long enough to picture Leonard's short black hair, button nose, pale skin, and petulant mouth, just as he could envision Mo's freckled visage, the rust-red curls and matching mustache, the bright blue eyes.

Neville's response bounced from the entry window and appeared in the chat window above it.

Probably. He seemed ok when the ERTs got to him. They'll take care of him.

Mo's outlook was less optimistic.

But he had to be running short on time. Remember the footage of the Aeronbald Volunteer Experiment? Some of those folks didn't show signs until they keeled over. That's what they always tell us - in the event of a Bubble Suit breach, seek immediate assistance, because time is running short, no matter how you feel.

Leonard responded.

C'mon, don't be like that. They have the Knowledge to fix this, and Gavin was still alive when the ERTs got to him. Knowledge has allowed for greater miracles than saving Gavin; just look at the utopia it's allowed us to build in the years since The Advent.

Mo's retort came quickly.

Maybe. The ERTs seemed pretty frantic to me. We're lucky the Bubble Suits are rigged to send an alert if a malfunction occurs; if it weren't for that, Gavin would already be dead. We were right at the outer boundary - Kingfisher Reservoir is about as far from Kingston as you can go.

Fine. Our friend is dead, then. You can do whatever you want, but I believe in

Knowledge, and I believe that it will allow the ERTs to save him.

Mo did not immediately respond to Leonard's proclamation; that gave Neville a chance to get a word in.

I'm with Leonard - there's no reason to think Knowledge can't save Gavin. He was alive when the ERTs hooked him up to the machine, at least from what I could see. I'm not worried that the ERTs seemed frantic; I'd have been more concerned if they didn't have a sense of urgency. Time was short; Gavin could have died. It was a stupid thing to do. I told him so, too.

Agreed.

100%.

What's wrong with him, anyways? Why does he always have to push the envelope? We have no reason to be unhappy - when's the last time anything bad happened in The Bubble Society? He's going to get us into trouble one of these days, you wait and see.

Neville stared at Leonard's words for a long time. The message took him back to distant memories of his first interactions with Gavin, back at Kingston Preschool, and the many debacles that had occurred in the two decades since.

No doubt. I can't remember a single problem in my life, if you exclude all the times Gavin has ignored regulations and done something reckless. He's like a brother, don't get me wrong, but he's been pulling these stunts since we were in preschool, and it's putting him in a bad way. I know that he's read The Manual for Proper Behavior - it was assigned reading enough times in school - but I don't think he's processed a word of it.

Mo responded.

Remember when we were little? They gave him quadruple doses of the Focus Solution, and they still had to use the restraints to keep him sitting still.

Leonard posted next.

LOL. Too good. Remember that day when he took off down the hall before they got him strapped in? He ended up trapping himself in one of those old locker things when he tried to hide in it!

Mo added a final thought.

Guess today was inevitable - honestly, I'm surprised it took this long for him to do something this stupid. Anyways, I'm out, gonna watch a show 'til we get back. Peace.

Adios.

Neville was the last one left in the chat. He shook his head as he closed out the Guvernment Messaging App with an aggressive tap of his wrist panel, wondering why Gavin always had to be so headstrong, and where his friend was now. The helicopter's appearance and disappearance already felt like something that had happened in a different lifetime.

Neville sighed, brought the Guvernment Media App back up, and directed his attention to the reality show, determined to find distraction for the rest of the drive down Onyx Canyon; Mo and Leonard had already done the same.

They did not acknowledge one another again until the car reached their apartments in the Andola District, and then, it was only to say a brief farewell before they called it a day.

BOOK 1, CHAPTER 3

Nine days had passed, and Gavin remained tethered in place.

It was for his own safety, they had told him.

But he did not feel very safe.

—

In the nine days that he had been held here, all manner of Knowers had come and gone.

Knowers from the Department of Research and Innovation.

Knowers who specialized in the production side of the Bubble Suits, and Knowers who debugged the software side.

Heck, even the Department of Food and Fluids had sent a delegation, never mind that Gavin's incident had not affected those systems.

In other words, Knowers of every variety had come to see this phenomenon. They poked. They prodded. They expected prompt answers to their inquiries, but ignored any questions that Gavin asked in return.

As it was, the only tolerable period of Gavin's days came at night, when he was left alone, and could find the space to drift away. In the depths of the long, dark hours, Gavin found that he could forget about his restraints, forget about how long he had been held in Kingston Hospital, forget to wonder whether he would ever be allowed to leave.

Instead, he could dream about his jump.

The exuberance that surged through him as he launched.

The weightless feeling he experienced for that brief moment, as he soared over the rocks.

His fury when he realized that the Bubble Suit was taking control of his fall.

The reflection of light off an approaching object.

The thrill of re-acceleration in the final seconds before the surface swallowed him up.

Then disorientation.

Fear.

And in the next heartbeat, when he got his bearings and found the surface above him, relief.

Hope.

Gavin had struck out for the surface, swimming toward the shimmering daylight guiding his way, feeling the water on his skin, a sensation that was not utterly foreign, but that came from a memory so long forgotten Gavin could not say whether it was his or someone else's.

When he broke the surface, he took a breath, too desperate to stop himself, to think about the potential consequences.

It felt so good he did it again; it seemed so natural that he never thought to stop.

After floating on the surface for a beat, Gavin glanced up at the cliff. Neville stood on the edge, pulling at the top of his shaved head through the membrane of his Bubble Suit. Gavin shifted his weight so that he floated in a sitting position, then waved toward his friend. Satisfied that this would reassure Neville that he was all right - and it seemed to Gavin that everything was more or less the same, outside of the fact that he could hear what sounded like a helicopter in the distance - Gavin flipped onto his stomach and paddled toward the small sand beach where his two other friends, Leonard and Mo, waited.

Leonard and Mo had been nearly as frantic as Neville during Gavin's fall, but they were reassured by the fact that their friend was swimming toward them now; by the time that Gavin was wading toward them through the shallows, their panic had largely subsided.

Then, as Gavin stopped on the bank to shake the water droplets off his Bubble Suit, his friends saw something that made them freeze. They stared at Gavin open-mouthed. Their faces might be different - Leonard with his pale white skin, short black hair, and perpetually squinting eyes, Mo with his curly, rust-red hair and broad mouth - but at the moment, their expressions of horror were identical.

Puzzled, Gavin's eyes passed over his friends' faces, searching for a clue, some reason for this reaction. He thought he might already know, but he was not certain, so he asked.

"What?"

For a moment, the pair remained too shocked to speak. Then Mo raised a hand, and pointed at Gavin's neck.

"Your Bubble Suit. It's torn."

Mo had to shout this answer, because the drone of the helicopter engine was almost too loud for them to hear one another, and it was only getting louder; the surface of Kingfisher Reservoir vibrated as the big machine's rotors spun and set the vehicle down on the water's surface. With so much noise, Gavin could only stare at his friends; he had expected them to be startled, concerned, but he had not expected their eyes to bulge in terror this way.

Then again, perhaps he should not have been surprised. On some level, Gavin knew that he should share their concern - after all, it was his Bubble Suit that was torn - and if he had seen it happen to one of them, he might well have shared their sense of suspended disbelief.

But it had happened to him, so he could not quite manage it.

Because Gavin had not needed Leonard's gesture to know about the tear.

He had already known where his Bubble Suit's membrane had ripped.

But he was not that worried.

Why would he be, when he felt perfectly fine?

—

Gavin never got the chance to tell his friends any of that. At the very moment he opened his mouth to shout reassurances, members of the Emergency Response Team swarmed him.

It did not take long for Gavin to question the wisdom of his decisions that day. Or at least, to lament the fact that he had not held his breath until the ERTs had arrived.

If he had held his breath, he might have spent less time on the air replacement machine, a desperately uncomfortable experience that the ERTs insisted was necessary to clear out the noxious fumes that had infected Gavin's system after his Bubble Suit had torn. Gavin objected from the start, trying to tell them that he was fine, but there were six of the ERTs and one of him, and they had him strapped down and hooked up to the machine in short order. The machine did not hurt, exactly, but it did make Gavin feel as if his eyes might pop out of his skull, a sensation that he could have done without.

As the filtered air flowed back into his Bubble Suit, two new figures loomed up in the big helicopter's cargo bay; Gavin was strapped down flat on his back, which meant that he could only observe the pair by staring straight down his nose.

One of the pair announced that they were Suit Breach Specialists, and that they would reseal the hole in the neck of Gavin's Bubble Suit.

This was accomplished with a metal wand, though the positioning of the tear on his neck prevented Gavin from observing exactly what the two technicians were doing. Fortunately, their work went quickly; it took them less than a minute to complete their task, and then they released Gavin's restraints.

Figuring that would be the end of his ordeal, Gavin felt relatively cheerful for the rest of the helicopter ride. He would never have gotten a chance to fly in a helicopter under any other circumstances - the machines were reserved for the Emergency Response Team and official Guvernment business - and he intended to enjoy every moment of the experience.

And so he did, for the fifteen minutes that remained until they landed on the roof of Kingston Hospital. Unfortunately, once the chopper set down, Gavin's wondrous adventure took an abrupt turn for the worse.

Without saying a word, two of the ERTs seized Gavin by the elbows and dragged him backward, away from the window and out of the helicopter. Once they were on the rooftop, they spun him around, then frog-marched him across the rooftop landing pad, pushed him through a door, and herded him down a stairwell.

Three floors down, one of the ERTs opened the door at the landing; two more ERTs waited for them there, a gurney between them. Together, the four of them strapped Gavin down, then the two new ERTs took charge, wheeling Gavin away as his original minders retreated into the stairwell.

A nauseous feeling rose in Gavin's stomach as the ERTs hustled him through the hospital. Once again, his head was strapped back, forcing him to stare straight at the ceiling and watch the banks of lights pass overhead, which only made his mind race more furiously, panic rising as disturbed visions filled his imagination.

Gavin had never known anyone who had been taken to Kingston Hospital. In fact, for most of his lifetime, and all of his memory, nobody in Kingston had been taken to the hospital; the Bubble Suits had rendered the need for such outposts obsolete. It was a remarkable achievement of Knowledge, the crowning success of The Bubble Society, and while the building they still called Kingston Hospital had remained in place, it had been transformed, turned over to the various Knowers who worked on Bubble Suit research innovation, with the exception of a few wings kept for emergencies such as these.

Without knowing why, Gavin felt a sudden increase in his heart rate; he could sense, even before they made the next turn, that they were nearly at their destination.

His gut proved to be dead on; two more ERTs stood flanking a pair of double doors at the end of the next hallway, doors that they pulled open as the gurney approached. Once they were through the doorway, the ERTs pushing the gurney released Gavin's restraints and pushed him into a sitting position, which allowed him to look around the room he found himself in.

It was an operating theater, a circular room with viewing suites overlooking the open space, but by far the most notable feature - and the strangest - was the empty doorframe standing in the middle of the room.

In and of itself, the frame was not strange; to the contrary, it was simple, ordinary: two five-foot metal beams welded to the ground about two feet apart from each other, and a third beam that joined the two beams at the top.

What was strange was what it was doing in the middle of an operating theater at Kingston Hospital.

It was not until the ERTs lifted him from the gurney and started to march him toward the frame that Gavin understood the reason for its presence.

For the first time since they had entered the hospital, he found his voice, and started to scream.

The ERTs acted as if they could not hear him; they turned Gavin around and pinned him to the frame without a word of explanation. Once they had him held in place, one of the ERTs lashed Gavin to the frame by his wrists, ankles, throat, and forehead.

When Gavin was strapped to the frame, another one of the ERTs walked over to a table and selected an especially long needle from a variety of similarly sinister instruments. As the man did this, one of his fellows tapped commands into the wrist panel of Gavin's Bubble Suit, which caused the left arm panel of the Bubble Suit to retract, exposing Gavin's nutrient and fluid injection sites.

The ERT with the needle walked back to Gavin, instrument in hand, and inserted the tip into the fluid site. He compressed the plunger; in almost the same moment, Gavin felt a warm, dreamy sensation flood his body.

As the effects of the drug took hold of him, a pretty young woman in an ERT uniform entered the operating theater. The four ERTs who had handled Gavin to that point faded away to stand at the edges of the room.

The pretty ERT spoke in a soothing voice, assuring Gavin that he would have the very best of care; Kingston Hospital was committed to ensuring that Gavin would not suffer from complications moving forward, and they would spare no expense to ensure that happened.

Gavin heard himself saying something, but he could not make out his own words. The warm feeling was pushing his brain into a fog, but while he could not seem to hear his own speech, he understood the pretty ERT's reply.

"I agree; we're so fortunate to live in The Bubble Society, where the Guvernment takes care of all its citizuns. We've got all the top Knowers scheduled to see you, and I don't mind telling you that they are buzzing with excitement about what they might learn from such a singular incident. You might wind up getting more attention than you want; dozens are clamoring to get a slot on the schedule..."

Gavin faded out of consciousness before she could finish. He did not dream.

—

When Gavin woke a few hours later, his mind still foggy, it was to find a herd of Knowers crowded around him.

It was an unsettling way to begin the evening.

In the hours that followed, a stream of official-looking people came and went, all making notes on various charts as they poked and prodded at Gavin's Bubble Suit. By the time the Knowers started to leave for the night, Gavin found himself agreeing with his vague memory of the pretty ERT's comment regarding excessive attention.

Mercifully, the day did draw to a close, and once the Knowers had fulfilled their daily labor obligations, they seemed as eager as any other sentient being would be to get out of the office.

Surely, Gavin thought, that would be it. They would keep him overnight for observation, then free him in the morning.

But even as Gavin attempted to reason with himself, the words of one Knower from the Department of Research and Innovation continued to penetrate his consciousness.

"This isn't supposed to be possible."

Deep down, Gavin knew what that meant.

His ordeal had only just begun.

—

In the days that followed, Gavin's life became an endless procession of Knowers. They came and went, one after the other, examining different components of Gavin's Bubble Suit, occasionally asking him a question about how it had torn but otherwise ignoring the sentient being within the membrane of the microfilament suit that interested them so greatly.

It was intolerable. Gavin's Bubble Suit took care of all his bodily functions, so he did not even get to break up the day with walks to the bathroom. And to make matters worse, they had disabled the Guvernment Media App on his Bubble Suit, depriving him of his usual distractions when he needed them more than ever.

Gavin complained about the situation, but his complaints, like his questions, were ignored. Since the first day, it had not mattered what he asked, had not mattered what he said. No matter what he did, the Knowers ignored everything about him and continued to circle back to the question that interested them more than any other.

"How did this happen?"

Gavin's frustration grew until he became tempted to answer this question with a blank stare, but at that particular crossroads, his sense scored a rare victory, and he continued to stick to his story.

"I don't know. It all happened too fast. All I was trying to do was bounce down the cliffs, and the next thing I knew, I was in the water, and my Bubble Suit was torn."

His answer was met with skeptical expressions, but Gavin stuck to his version of events through any and all follow-up questions.

Days passed. It was not long before Gavin began to eagerly anticipate the arrival of the orderly at day's end, the signal that the procession of Knowers would stop for the night.

The orderly's work did not take long. He would hook Gavin up to nutrient and fluid packets, empty his waste tank and replace it with a new one, then disconnect the emptied nutrient and fluid packets. His task complete, the orderly would dump the used containers in the trash and leave for the night, shutting off the lights behind him.

Once the door settled shut behind the orderly, an unearthly silence would fall over the operating theater. Gavin could only stand there, tethered upright, murmuring his desperate wish: that Knowledge would send him some relief.

It would not happen all at once; at first, Gavin's mind would fixate on all the Knowers who had examined him during the day, pondering what purpose they might have, wondering whether they would ever let him go.

But somewhere, in the deeper hours of the night, Gavin's mind would leave such questions behind. He would fall into a dream-like state, a trance in which he could replay every moment of his jump. Once he fell into this state, it was easy to replay his adventure, because contrary to what Gavin told his examiners, his fall had not happened quickly. In fact, Gavin felt that nothing had ever happened so slowly; no other experience in his life had imprinted sounds and sights at milli-second granularity, searing the most minute details into his memory.

When he fell into his trance, Gavin could comb back through these memories, re-experiencing the physical sensations that had surged through him as his brain registered the flash of light reflecting off an object hurtling toward him.

Gavin wondered if they had found it.

He wondered if they were looking.

—

By the ninth night, Gavin had grown resentfully accustomed to his routine. But on that ninth night, the fragile rhythm was disrupted.

On the ninth night, he had visitors.

Or at least, he thought he did.

By Gavin's count, there were twelve of them.

They did not come into the theater. Instead, they stood in a suite on the main observation deck, gazing down at where Gavin was strapped to the metal frame in the operating theater below.

At first, Gavin did not know what he was seeing, or if he was seeing anything at all; he had suddenly woken in the dead of night, an uneasy feeling in his stomach, a sense that someone was directing sentient attention at him.

For a moment, he thought that the feeling was merely the ghost of a bad dream, but as he came out of the depths of sleep, Gavin realized that there were figures looking down at him from the opaque window of one of the viewing suites, figures that were visible only as a denser shade of darkness.

In time, Gavin's vision adjusted, and he became sure of what he was seeing.

A group of sentient beings was watching him from the suite.

He could not make out their faces, but he could see their silhouettes walking around, coming close to one another, leaning in to speak to their fellows.

According to the clock on the wall, it was 3:23 in the morning.

Gavin did not understand.

What were these sentient beings doing here at 3:23 in the morning?

Gavin could not say when they left; difficult as it had been to identify the silhouettes when they first appeared, it was even more of a trick to notice when the shadows disappeared into the gloom.

In any case, by the time the clock read 4:17, all of the figures had gone; as he drifted back to sleep, Gavin wondered whether they had been there at all.

—

Were it not for the persistence of the uneasy feeling in his stomach when he woke up later that morning, Gavin might have convinced himself that it was just a dream. But his sense of anxiety, and the desperate desires that now consumed his consciousness, told a different story.

Gavin had no idea how to deal with everything he was feeling; he could not move, could not turn on the Guvernment Media App, could not do anything but be with his thoughts.

It was intolerable. An unimaginable situation for a citizun of The Bubble Society to find himself in.

The Bubble Suits, and the Guvernment that had introduced them, had saved the continent of Acadia, saved sentient life on the planet Shurtain. They had saved the citizuns of The Bubble Society from the terrible fate that awaited all other sentient beings on Shurtain, who had no protection as the planet's increasingly poisonous atmosphere crossed that fatal threshold where it could no longer support sentient life.

Those years had been rampant with panic, full of fear. The population of Kingston had been steadily declining for decades, growing progressively sicker, weaker, and heavier, leaving them less mobile, less able to get around the planet of Shurtain.

And the problem was only getting worse.

The doctors of the day applied the tools of their trade to no avail, sucking the fat out with vacuums, hacking off large hunks of cancerous cells, but more often than not, the fat came back, or the cancer returned, until the doctors were forced to admit that they did not understand the source of all this illness and were unequipped to combat it. The issue was turned over to the research community, but the surge of excitement generated by a Guvernment grant to the newly-formed Dynamic Solutions quickly fizzled out when the company was unable to provide an immediate solution.

For ten years, things only got worse; Kingston's population grew, not only sicker, but more fearful. More and more people began to subscribe to the notion that the end of sentient-kind was near.

Then, in a remarkable turn of events, a researcher at Dynamic Solutions asked the question of whether the atmosphere itself could be changing in a way that made the planet Shurtain inhospitable to sentient beings. When the researcher developed this hypothesis, morale was low across the research community, and though the idea was greeted with considerable skepticism, they had no other ends to pursue, and threw themselves behind this line of investigation.

And as they started to massage the data, they realized they had struck gold.

The researchers could not determine why the change was happening, but they could say, with certainty, that the composition of Shurtain's atmosphere had started to shift some thirty years ago, moving gradually toward a concentration of gases that were ill-suited to sentient life. And based on the trends, things would only get worse; the researchers projected that within ten years, sentient beings would be unable to breathe the air on Shurtain.

Dire as this news was, it also brought hope, because with the source of their problem in hand, the sentient beings of Kingston now had the chance to develop a solution.

The citizens of the day pursued this goal with a zealous fervor; sentient beings across professions provided what expertise they could, but in the end, it was the newly formed field of Knowledge, which sprang up from the research division at Dynamic Solutions, that came to the rescue, Knowledge that delivered insights to the first group of Knowers, the miraculous revelations that allowed those individuals to envision the new technology that would save the sentient race: The Bubble Suits.

It marked a new dawn for sentient life. Not only would the Bubble Suits allow sentient beings to continue living on Shurtain, they would reverse all of the damage that Shurtain's deteriorating atmosphere had done to the sentient beings of Kingston.

And that was only the beginning; the nature of the Bubble Suits meant that their adoption would usher in a new age of society, one where sentient beings were no longer unprotected citizens, but true citizuns of the new utopia that was The Bubble Society, where technology guaranteed the Guvernment could ensure the health and welfare of every one of its people.

This started with the nutrient and fluid ports; as part of the landmark deal between Dynamic Solutions and the Guvernment, every citizun in Kingston would be issued, at no cost, a Bubble Suit, as well as a lifetime supply of the nutrient paste, fluid packets, and waste pods necessary for the Bubble Suits to function. This was possible, in part, because Dynamic Solutions had developed the Bubble Suits to allow sentient beings to run on a more efficient diet, which meant that, with the introduction of the Bubble Suits, starvation and hunger would fade into distant memory.

There was more; in addition to filtering air so that it was breathable for sentient beings, and streamlining the process of nutrient intake and waste excretion, the Bubble Suits regulated every aspect of a sentient being's body, protecting the wearer from illness and disease, which would become distant memories, things of the past.

Miraculous as this achievement was, it did cause one notable complication; according to all of the projections from Dynamic Solutions, sentient beings could live indefinitely in Bubble Suits without their bodies suffering any deterioration.

Or, to put it in more grandiose terms, the citizuns of the utopia that was The Bubble Society would be immortal.

It was an incredible turn of events; before Knowledge had provided them with the Bubble Suits, the people of Kingston had faced their imminent demise. Now, thanks to the bounty of Knowledge, they were left to debate how they should Guvern a utopian society whose most pressing concerns were with the downsides of immortality.

In the end, it was agreed that one hundred years made for a long, ripe life on Shurtain. This would be especially true after the introduction of the Bubble Suits, which would allow the Guvernment to guarantee that every day of those one hundred years would be spent in comfort and safety. No citizun need feel worried, or desperate, or scared; in The Bubble Society, such emotions would be eliminated from the sentient experience. As the Knowers so rightly asked, what sort of sentient being could reasonably object to ending their life after one hundred years in such a paradise?

Nor would the impact of the Bubble Suits stop at life-and-death matters; the Bubble Suits allowed the wearers to regulate details such as eye, skin, and hair color at a touch of their control panel. The same was true of clothes, jewelry, and other accessories, which would no longer exist, at least in the physical sense. In The Bubble Society, such adornments would only exist as holograms overlaid on the membrane of the microfilament suit.

And because the Bubble Suits would regulate body composition, it was speculated that it would be impossible for a sentient being to have bad teeth or blotchy skin, to go bald, or to become obese. With such vanities as musculature and healthy skin eliminated from the equation, every sentient being in Kingston could be comfortable in their appearance.

In short, the Bubble Suits allowed Kingston's Guvernment to structure society in such a way that its citizuns would never want for anything; so long as they behaved according to *The Manual for Proper Behavior*, there was no reason for a sentient being in Kingston to experience anything unpleasant.

Of course Gavin, who consistently struggled to adhere to the rules laid out in *The Manual for Proper Behavior*, had experienced his share of unpleasantness in life, but, as the adults around him had always pointed out, that was Gavin's fault, not The Bubble Society's.

Even so, at least the torture of going to school, or work, had always ended in the afternoon; Gavin had never been held overnight, much less held overnight for days on end. Now, as he thought about everything that had happened over the past ten days, every cell in his body seemed to scream in unison, though he knew better than to give voice to the sound.

Until then, he had been frustrated, bored, irritated.

Now, he was desperate. And that felt very different.

Gavin knew he needed to get out of this room. And he needed to do it before they discovered the part that he had avoided telling them.

BOOK 1, CHAPTER 4

An alarm screeched three times, jerking Gavin from his uneasy sleep. The clock on the wall read 7:20; his nighttime visitors had disappeared just a few hours earlier.

Blinking his eyes, Gavin looked for the reason for the alarm.

It was not difficult to find.

A lone man stood in the operating theater.

Gavin recognized this man; how could he not? And with that recognition, he understood why the alarm had been sounded, why he had been woken. Out of force of habit, Gavin attempted to raise his right hand in a salute; there was nothing else to do, with The Guvna' himself standing in the room.

Of course, Gavin's attempted salute only reminded him that his wrist was tethered to a metal pole, but The Guvna' did not miss his attempt at movement.

"Don't wurry 'bout dat. It's just you and me, no need fer pomp 'n circumstance."

Even as he neared his mid-sixties, The Guvna' remained remarkably handsome; the color had started to fade from his sandy blond locks, but his hair remained thick, and while his skin might be a bit more lined, a shade less tan, his lean jawline, thin nose, and bright blue eyes remained the same as ever.

The Guvna' stopped a few feet in front of Gavin. An uneasy silence ensued as he looked Gavin up and down, a bemused smile playing at the corner of his lips. Finally, The Guvna' spoke.

"Been speaking to da Knowers. Dey tell me ya don't recall da details o' yer fall."

Though Gavin had heard The Guvna' speak on several occasions - always on the Guvernment Media App - so he was familiar with The Guvna's accent, but still found it jarring. Gavin knew the accent had its roots on the coast of Western Acadia, and that the accent, like the cities that had once stretched up and down Acadia's western seaboard, was fading into oblivion, particularly as so many who were forced to move to Kingston in the final years of the Economic Era had done their best to ditch it.

The Guvna' was not such a man; he stuck to the accent, which happily truncated opening syllables of some words and skipped over the ends of others, all in a comfortable drawl.

"No. It all happened too fast."

The Guvna' nodded. Gavin could not say for sure, but he got the sense that The Guvna' found something about this situation quite amusing.

"Summa our Knowers reckon ya weren't just trying ta' bounce down da cliffs. Dey think ya jumped."

Without hesitation,Gavin shook his head.

"I wouldn't do anything like that."

The Guvna' allowed his smile to spread.

"Know what da black box is, Gavin?"

Gavin frowned, shook his head again. The Guvna's use of his name made him feel uneasy.

"Well, yer not da only one. Precious few know 'bout da black box - it's classified 'less yer high 'nuff up in da Guvernment. Dat'll be one thing ya get outta dis adventure o' yours: a bit o' classified information dat almost nobody in Kingston has ever heard. Knowledge Knows ya deserve summin; I can't 'magine being trussed up da way dey got ya here."

The Guvna' winced as he looked over Gavin's restraints, then shifted his gaze back to meet the younger man's eyes.

"Ya see, every Bubble Suit has what dey call da black box, tho in reality, it's not a box, nor black. Any case, da black box, it's a chip, records everything happening to a Bubble Suit, and uploads da information in real-time."

"Most times, da data is anonymized; it's why we don't gotta tell folks 'bout it. But in yer case, da team had to pull yer personal data; to understand what had happened, ya see?"

Gavin felt cold; the air seemed to be going out of the room, and his mind felt foggy. Some of this must have shown on his face, because The Guvna' chuckled.

"Now, don't get yer'self worked up son. Here, let me get you outta dis contraption, everyone who wanted to see you has already been by. There ya go, steady now."

The Guvna' dipped a shoulder under Gavin's armpit as he released the straps, helping the young man to steady himself when the tethers were free.

"Ya may not believe it, but I was yung, once 'pon a time. Hadn't seen da harder sides o' life yet. So I know what it's like to make a bet."

It took Gavin a moment to process The Guvna's last words; when he did, his face froze in horror. The Guvna', who had been stepping away from Gavin as he said this, laughed at the younger man's expression.

"Now, don't go wurrying yerself, da voice data is normally scrambled so da folks studying it don't know whose it is. Again, had'ta make a special 'ception in yer case. Sure you'll understand; trying to keep ya alive, weren't we?"

Gavin nodded slowly.

"Ya see, dat's how we know ya aren't lying. Bout it all happening too fast to remember, at least. Because we heard everything ya said to yer friends after."

For the first time since The Guvna' had entered the room, Gavin felt some of the tension in his body release. Unfortunately, the relief was short-lived.

"Something dat troubles us, though, is what ya said to da 'Mergency Response Team. Dat ya dinnit need da air replacement machine. Dat ya felt fine."

Caught off guard, Gavin replied with an honest answer.

"Yes, I did. I did feel fine. Actually, I felt great."

The Guvna' looked at him, a deep frown on his face.

"No, son. Ya dinnit, and if ya did, it's probably 'cuz ya were suffering from delirium. All da reports showed yer body was on da verge of death when da ERTs got ya hooked up to da oxygen replacement machine. Air's poisoned. You ought to know dat, everyone in Kingston knows dat. It's full of viruses, germs, all manner of disease, and who knows what else. If ya felt fine, it only means yer brain was misfiring. Telling ya stories, as it were."

Gavin started to argue, but The Guvna' shook his head.

"No use arguing, son. Ya remember da video of da Aeronbald Volunteer Experiments you saw in school?"

Gavin blinked.

Of course he remembered the Aeronbald Volunteer Experiments. How could anyone forget?

The viewing of the Aeronbald Volunteer Experiments was a monumental coming of age for students in their first year at Kingston High, one of the days they had looked forward to for years of their young lives. When the day arrived, the students approached it with a shared nervous excitement, uncertain of what they would see, but eager to be able to say that they had witnessed it.

The video had not lasted more than eight minutes, but what it lacked in length, it made up for in horror.

Even now, as the images flashed back through his mind, Gavin felt sick. The Guvna' looked Gavin in the eyes, his expression solemn, and nodded.

"Some o' dem folks swore dey was fine. Right up to da last second, dey claimed dey was fine. One man swore he was fine with his dying breath."

"But it dinnit matter what dey claimed. Because sentient beings can't survive on da planet Shurtain without Bubble Suits."

To take some of the harshness from his words, The Guvna' clapped a hand on Gavin's shoulder. This surprised Gavin, rare as it was for sentient beings on Shurtain to touch one another; the Bubble Suits made it safe, of course, but the Suits also blunted the sense of touch to the point that most sentient beings had given up on it. This was different; despite the Bubble Suits, The Guvna's friendly grip on Gavin's shoulder cut through, conveying the desired message, causing the younger man to straighten up, and an unconscious smile to briefly cross his lips.

"Now, don't beat yer'self up. As I told'ya, I was yung once, and 'round yer age, I was more'n a bit wild myself. Of course, dat was a different world back den, but even if things hadn't changed, time woulda shown me life ain't all fun and games. And in da world we live in now, trying to hang on in dis inhospitable environment…"

The Guvna's voice trailed off. Gavin took a step back from the man, putting a few feet between them, allowing Gavin to meet The Guvna's blue eyes with his brown ones.

"We're gunna release ya, but I need two things from ya. Think ya can help me out?"

Gavin nodded.

"Good. First off, if you 'member anything - anything at all - 'bout what happened with da fall, you come tell us straight away. It's very important, you see; da Knowers dinnit believe dis could happen, a Bubble Suit breach o' dis magnitude, and dey need'ta learn everything dey can 'bout da issue to make sure it neva' happens again. It's a safety issue fer our whole society, ya understand, so it's very important dat if ya 'member anything, ya tell us. Not fer yerself, but fer da rest o' da sentient beings in Da Bubble Society. Fair 'nuff?"

"Of course."

The Guvna' grinned at Gavin, showcasing his thousand-watt smile.

"Good. Now, da second thing. Already talked 'bout it, but ya dinnit feel fine after da Bubble Suit tear, did'ya?"

Gavin shook his head.

"Good. Can't have ya going about spreading dat nonsense. We get sentient beings questioning whether da Bubble Suits work, and there'll be panic in da streets. Everyone will think we're all 'bout to drop dead."

Gavin started to voice a question, but The Guvna' cut him off.

"Now, everyone in Kingston already knows what happened. I 'splained it all on da Guvernment Media Broadcast, announced dat we've identified da problem dat caused da malfunction, dat it's all been resolved, dat there's no reason for concern. Now, you wouldn't say anything to dispute dat, would ya?"

The Guvna's smile had vanished; he was not quite frowning, but his face had taken on a far more serious expression as he awaited an answer. Gavin's response came in a hushed whisper.

"No. Of course not."

The smile returned.

"Good. Now let's getcha outta dis place, and back to yer duties. Da Bubble Society needs every citizun healthy and contributing, as ya well know."

BOOK 1, CHAPTER 5

Gavin stood inside his apartment door, contemplating the day ahead. It was the morning after his release from the hospital, and he was scheduled to return to work, but as he reached for the doorknob, he hesitated.

Gavin had never had a problem summoning the will to report to his job at the Department of Media Productions before - or at least, he had never had this much of a problem - but now, as he tried to get back into his routine, a sense of helplessness flowed through him, drowning out the desire to say or do anything.

He stepped back from the door and retreated across his apartment to the couch. He took a seat and put his head in his hands, trying to get his bearings. He had time - there were still ten minutes until he had to be at the bus stop - but first, he needed to find a way to get moving; otherwise, he would have to skip work.

Gavin shuddered as he registered the last thought. He knew he was no Saint - Gavin was all too aware that he had never met, or indeed, come close to meeting, the standards of a model citizun laid out by *The Manual for Proper Behavior* - but even he knew that a lackadaisical approach to work was one thing, failing to appear for duty quite another, for in The Bubble Society, there was no illness, no unexpected deaths, no excuse at all for a citizun to not fulfill their duties to the society that provided sentient beings with life itself.

That left Gavin with little choice, except to do something that would get him out of this funk. Making his decision, he stood, and crossed to the small room that served as both bathroom and kitchenette.

There was no toilet in this room, nor were there any cooking appliances. Instead, there were shelves stocked with nutrient pastes, fluid injections, and empty waste pods, all generic issue, as well as Gavin's personalized supplements.

It was the supplements that had his attention; Gavin disliked the twitchy, amped-up feeling that the Focus Solution gave him, but he could not deny that it shifted his mind into a more docile state, and it was readily apparent that he needed that now.

Gavin's prescription called for him to inject four vials of the Focus Solution each morning, a dosage that he had built up to in his days at Kingston Elementary. It had not taken long - less than a day, in fact - for his kindergarten teacher to decide that she could not possibly cope with the young Gavin in his normal state, and to insist that he be administered the compound. It was not an unusual request - teachers often resorted to this tactic when their young charges showed a lack of interest in sitting and listening to their lectures - so it was carried out without question.

And so began Gavin's morning routine of starting his school day with a visit to the nurse, and an injection of Focus Solution.

As an adult, he had no such oversight in place, so Gavin rarely took the stuff, even though it was delivered to his doorstep three times each season. More often than not, Gavin ended up dumping the unopened packages of the Focus Solution down the trash chute, but he always kept the latest shipment on hand in case of a day like today.

Gavin used his right hand to tap in commands on the control panel of his Bubble Suit, which rested over the inside of his left wrist; as he finished the command sequence, the cover on his upper left arm slid up and exposed his intake ports. Next, Gavin took a syringe from the medicine cabinet, pulled out a vial of the Focus Solution, and filled the syringe with the clear liquid. He spun the prepped syringe in his hand, caught it between his middle and pointer fingers, and readied his thumb. Then, with a deep breath, he inserted the needle into his fluid intake site and depressed the plunger.

The effects of the Focus Solution hit Gavin before the needle was out of the port; a warm, luminous sense of contentment bloomed in his mind, slowing his thoughts and refining his focus as every other aspect of his physical being sped up.

And just like that, it no longer mattered that Gavin's job was boring, or that his life felt pointless; he was ready to be a productive member of The Bubble Society.

As if on autopilot, Gavin strode back to his apartment door. This time, he did not hesitate when he reached for the doorknob; instead, he turned it, pushed the door open, and stepped into the hall beyond. He did not bother to lock the door behind him; in fact, there was no lock, because in The Bubble Society, it was against the law to steal.

Gavin turned left and made his way down the hallway to the stairs - the

Focus Solution was hitting him in full force now, which had Gavin too amped up to wait on an elevator - but as he proceeded down the stairwell, passing under the watchful eyes of the security cameras positioned above each landing, he realized that something felt different; he could feel an uncomfortable sensation creeping over him, a sense that he was unclean, that some malignant eyes had focused their attention on him.

Irritated that he should have to grapple with such unpleasant feelings, Gavin shoved the thoughts aside. He returned his mind to the day ahead as he reached the ground floor and pushed through the exit, stepping onto the sidewalk outside. The corner bus stop was only half a block away from the apartment building; as he approached, Gavin could see that three others who regularly took the bus at this time were already waiting.

Percy Levenstein stepped out to greet Gavin as he approached; the elderly gentleman acknowledged Gavin with a slight bow, and Gavin mirrored the gesture. This was customary; though the Bubble Suits eliminated the risky skin-to-skin contact involved in a handshake, the time of the Advent had seemed an apt occasion for the sentient beings who would form The Bubble Society to set themselves apart from the unenlightened beings who had lived Before Knowledge. One change had been to replace the handshake with a bow, which, according to *The Manual for Proper Behavior,* was an altogether more elegant gesture.

As Gavin and Levenstein straightened back up, the older man spoke.

"Gavin, lad, can't tell you how much we've missed you. Such a shock, such a shock. You'll never imagine how relieved we were, after the news of your dreadful accident, to learn that you were none the worse for the wear."

Gavin nodded politely at Levenstein's words, but made no further response; he had never felt comfortable with Levenstein's overly formal bearing, a trait that was as apparent in his dress as in his speech.

Levenstein dressed as a gentleman, alternating each day between blue and grey three-piece suits. To accessorize, he projected a matching top hat onto his head, but that was only the start; Levenstein also adjusted the hologram settings on his Bubble Suit so that the thick gold chain of a pocket watch appeared to snake out of his tailored suit, and, even more outlandishly, had set the Bubble Suit to make it appear that he was holding a thin black cane in his right hand.

Of course, there was no watch concealed in Levenstein's pocket, because there was no pocket for a watch to be in. The cane was no different; Levenstein affected the air of using it to walk, but the cane was not real in a physical sense, so it could not make contact with the ground to provide support. Even if the cane had been solid, it would have been unnecessary; the Bubble Suits controlled a sentient being's balance, posture, and mobility, which was well Known, as the Suits had eliminated the need for canes, walkers, and wheelchairs as anything but ornaments.

"Mr. Levenstein speaks for all of us; it was dreadful, the thought that something so terrible could happen to a citizun of Kingston. It's all anyone has been talking about; what were you thinking?"

Sheila Bovoski, a short, middle-aged woman with red cheeks and redder hair, spoke in a voice that was somehow both shrill and booming at once. As always, Sheila carried her dog, Terror, which was built to resemble a Frenchie.

Dogs were an oddity in The Bubble Society, a fancy of those who had lived part of their life before The Advent, in the years Before Knowledge. This generational gap stemmed from the fact that, since The Advent, the dogs living aside the sentient beings in Kingston were not actually dogs; those animals had been filthy creatures, prone to spread all manner of disease and dirt. They had to go, and they were not the only ones: cats, rodents, lizards, and birds had all needed to go to the same place at the dawn of The Bubble Society.

This process had posed difficulties, however, because the sentient beings who lived Before Knowledge had emotional attachments to their animals, and would not willingly turn them over to the Guvernment for its "relocation" program, no matter how wonderful the wildlife sanctuary on the coast might sound. When met with this resistance, the Guvernment realized that some substitute would need to be offered for Kingston to transition smoothly into years After Knowledge.

Fortunately, Dynamic Solutions swept in to solve the problem. They devoted an entire department to the issue, and within a season, the Department of Pet Development was cranking out robotic animals of every variety, all of them powered by an artificial intelligence considered highly preferable to the whims and fancies that the animals of old had possessed. It was widely lauded as the perfect solution; the animals from Dynamic Solutions did not shed, go to the bathroom, or exhibit any willful or undesirable behavior. The advertisements claimed that the pets acted exactly like "a real dog" or "a real gerbil" or "a real kinkajou", though as Gavin had no memory of ever seeing a "real animal", he could not say one way or the other.

In any case, Gavin and his friends did not try to understand any of this; they simply made fun of the "animal people" and wondered why anyone would want some yappy piece of machinery following them around.

"Did you hear me, young man? I asked for an explanation of what you were thinking."

It was a long moment before Sheila's shrill voice penetrated Gavin's consciousness; when her words did reach him, he started suddenly, then began to sputter as he tried to think of a response. Fortunately, the third regular at the bus stop, a young woman named Annette, chose that moment to join the conversation.

"I think it's dreadful that they ever let anyone go up to Kingfisher

Reservoir. We're lucky that nobody died. The one good thing about your misadventure is that it put an end to that dangerous nonsense."

That got Gavin's attention.

"What do you mean? Put an end to what?"

Annette turned her protuberant grey eyes on Gavin, who suppressed an urge to shudder. Annette had moved into the neighborhood a few years after Gavin, and had invited him to socialize with her and her friends once or twice, but Gavin had always declined; he had no idea what her friends would be like, but while Annette was nice enough, something about her presence made him feel uncomfortable.

Annette was several years younger than Gavin, part of the generation born After Knowledge in the Department of Infant Development, and while it was impossible to fall ill in a Bubble Suit, Annette gave off a sickly air that Gavin suspected was the reason for the discomfort he felt around her. There was also the fact that her skin was forever fading to grey, and that Annette was obviously aware of it, regularly adjusting her Bubble Suit to bring her skin tone back to baseline, only for the color to fade away once again.

And it was more than the sickly aura and the skin oddity; Annette's skeleton appeared, to Gavin's eye, to lack proper form. Even in the rigid structure imposed by the Bubble Suit, her body sagged in on itself. Annette would live to one hundred, of course - everyone did - but Gavin could not help but wonder what she would look like by then.

"The reservoir access, of course," replied Annette in an irritated tone. "They've closed down Kingfisher Reservoir, as well as the other outdoor recreation areas that were still open on the outskirts of Kingston. It's sensible; after all, you caused all this trouble for something you could have experienced with a virtual film."

Gavin stopped himself from issuing a cynical retort, but it was a close thing. He knew all about virtual films - he was on his way to edit them for eight hours, after all - and he knew what he had felt after his Bubble Suit was pierced.

But if Annette thought that was the same, it was not Gavin's place to correct her. She seemed, perhaps not happy, but content in her ignorance, and more importantly, even Gavin could recognize that this was not a point he should press.

Not after his conversation with The Guvna'.

To Gavin's relief, the bus rounded the corner at the end of the street, so he did not need to respond to Sheila and Annette's remonstrations; instead, he nodded absent-mindedly in their general direction and stepped back to let them board the bus first.

Like the cars in Kingston, the buses were self-driving. Riders scanned their wrist panels on a device mounted where a driver would have sat, which simultaneously deducted credits from each of their Guvernment-issued bank accounts and tallied the ridership statistics for the Department of Transportation.

Mr. Levenstein, Sheila, and Annette scanned their wrist panels, then took their usual seats near the front of the bus. Gavin repeated the action as he passed the ticket stand, then he stepped past the others, making for one of his preferred spots near the back. The last two rows were deserted; Gavin took a seat in the back corner, where he turned to stare out the window.

His fellow passengers were no different, were they?

Gavin thought back over the past few weeks, but could not think of any noticeable differences in Mr. Levenstein, Sheila, or Annette, much less all three. Even so, Gavin now felt a compulsive need to run from them, a primal instinct to get away from these model citizuns of the Bubble Society.

It made no sense. But no matter how much he tried to reason his way out of the situation, Gavin knew that the thumping of his heart was very real; if his neighbors had not changed, it meant that he must have. As Gavin came to this uncomfortable conclusion, he felt his heart beat even faster.

Recognizing this, he took a deep breath; he knew that he could not behave like this, that he needed to calm down and conceal his inner turmoil, or he would find himself back under the Guvernment's watch. Gavin did not like to think where he would find himself strapped down - or locked up - if he violated additional protocols from *The Manual for Proper Behavior* the day after his release.

The bus, which had picked Gavin and the others up in southeastern Kingston, was traveling west on the Southern Corridor toward the Brick Bridge, one of three overpasses that spanned the Grand River in Kingston's city limits. The majority of Kingston's population resided on the west side of the river, with the most luxurious living in the northwest part of the city, in the Amada District to the west of Capitol Square. For his part, Gavin preferred the Andola District, particularly the side of the Andola District where he lived, which was situated on the east side of the Grand River. Out there, on the outskirts of the city, was about as close to the Cadillac Mountains as you could get while still living in Kingston. Gavin liked that; he also liked that he was close to the intersection of Riverside Parkway and the Southern Corridor - his bus stop was at the turn where the north-and-south bound Riverside turned, and became the east-and-west bound Southern Corridor - particularly because from that juncture, it was a straight shot north on Riverside to reach Kingfisher Reservoir.

Of course, Gavin had to figure this was no longer the perk it had once been; not after what Annette had just told him about the reservoir closing. And in any case, he was not going to Kingfisher Reservoir today; he was heading west, along the Southern Corridor, across the Brick Bridge, then up Central Boulevard to the Center of Industry.

Gavin's favorite part of this journey was crossing the river; the Brick Bridge looked out over Kingston, offering up a magnificent view of the valley to the west. From where he sat, Gavin could see the turn onto the northbound Central Boulevard started, the Academic Campus, and the Center of Industry.

As Gavin looked out at the Academic Campus, imagining students from the ages of three to eighteen scurrying to classes, his mind drifted back to his own years in the Kingston school system. He had moved on to occupational training some five years ago, but sometimes, it felt like he had never left; he still woke up with the same nightmares.

For most individuals in Kingston, the years they spent in school were undemanding, comfortable; in a word, easy. Gavin's personal flaws had made his experience different, but for well-adjusted sentient beings, school was meant to be enjoyable. There was no unemployment in The Bubble Society, no poverty, no reason at all to fret about the future, so academics need not be rigorous, and certainly not competitive. Why should they be, when the lives of sentient beings were orderly, safe, and predictable from conception to death?

It had been so since The Advent; in the world After Knowledge, the lives of sentient beings started at the Department of Infant Development, where Knowers took sperm and egg from two sentient beings, fertilized the egg, and placed it inside a starter Bubble Suit to begin the growth process. Of all the engineering marvels that went into the Bubble Suits, this feature, the ability to accommodate the development process by expanding as the fetus grew, was perhaps the most impressive; after three hundred days, or three-quarters of a year on the planet Shurtain, the child would be sufficiently developed to leave the growth pods, and the Department of Infant Development would release the child to their Guvernment-approved parents.

Of course, the Guvernment did not forget Kingston's children once they were sent home with their parents; on the contrary, the Guvernment provided generous support to parents, paying for the cost of childcare from the day they went home, freeing up the parents to be productive members of The Bubble Society. The infants would start at Kingston Daycare, then transition to Kingston Preschool at three, Kingston Elementary at five, and Kingston High at twelve before moving on to occupational training at the end of their final year of standard schooling, when they would be eighteen or nineteen. Occupational training could last anywhere from weeks to years, depending on the nature of the work; those slated for basic security details trained for weeks, while those selected to become Knowers would move on to the Academy of Knowledge, where they would do at least another half-decade of study. But no matter the occupation, once the sentient beings of the Bubble Society completed their training, they worked in their field until the retirement age of eighty; after that, they were entitled to twenty years of leisure until they "made their transition" out of life on the day after their one-hundredth birthday.

"Gavin?"

Gavin jumped at the sound of his name. He turned to find Neville and Leonard looking at him.

"Oh. Hey guys. Sorry, I was thinking about something."

Neville and Leonard took the seats in front of Gavin, exchanging half-exasperated smiles as they did. Were it anyone else, the startled reaction would have been disconcerting, particularly because the two of them had joined their friend on the bus at this stop every day for the past three years, but Gavin was Gavin. On a normal day, they might have left him to his daydreams, and kept any communication to the Guvernment Messaging App, but after Gavin's lengthy absence, Neville and Leonard wanted to speak directly to their friend.

"No worries. How you been? We tried to get in touch with you, but you never responded to our messages."

"I never got them. They shut off all communication on my Bubble Suit while I was in the hospital. Disabled my linkup to the Guvernment Media App too. No television, no movies. And when I came back online, the backlog of messages didn't get delivered."

Neville winced; Gavin nodded knowingly.

"It was brutal. Bad enough that I would have killed to read an e-book, but they even disabled that part of the Guvernment Media App. So it was just me and my thoughts for a week and a half."

"Did it take that long to fix the tear?" Leonard asked.

"No, they fixed the tear quick enough. But all sorts of Knowers wanted to see my Bubble Suit first-hand, so they can make sure nothing like this ever happens again."

Neville and Leonard exchanged a glance at Gavin's words, then turned back to their friend, their eyes wide.

"Do they know what caused the tear?"

Gavin shrugged.

"If they do, they didn't tell me, but with all the Knowers who saw me, I'm sure they'll have it figured out. We're fortunate to have so many people working on behalf of Knowledge; I tell you, it was impressive to watch them at work, even if I wasn't happy to be there."

Gavin thought that this statement squared with The Guvna's cautions on what he should and should not say, and was pleased with himself for remembering the warnings. A bemused smile crossed his face as he congratulated himself, but Neville and Leonard did not notice; they were looking at one another and nodding, relieved by this reassurance of the certainty that the Bubble Suits afforded them in life.

"Well, I suppose this will finally put an end to your hijinks, whether you like it or not. They closed Kingfisher Reservoir, you know."

There was a note of accusation in Leonard's words.

"I know. I messed up."

Leonard's posture softened when he heard the remorse in Gavin's voice.

"Hey, don't worry about it. I didn't think it was a great idea, but I never guessed any of this would happen. We'll find other ways to pass the time."

Gavin nodded.

"For sure. I'll try to think of something; plenty of time to consider some alternatives now that we're stuck here for eight hours."

Neville and Leonard did not appear reassured by Gavin's words, but they did not have time to respond; as Gavin had indicated, the bus, which had turned north on Central Boulevard some minutes ago, had entered the Center of Industry, and was approaching the Department of Media Productions, where all three of them worked.

The bus stopped. The young men stood, exited the bus, and said their good-byes as they started down the paths to their various destinations. Gavin's route took him through the middle of the Media Productions campus to the Department of Video Editing, where he worked out of a cubicle on the third floor.

Wes had not yet arrived, but Tanya and Mel, Gavin's other cubemates, were already at their desks. They waved to Gavin as he approached, and after a brief greeting, chided him about all the trouble he had caused. Evidently, they had spent the bulk of their time since Gavin's misadventure editing Public Service Announcements about lessons learned from his incident.

Their conversation tailed off after a minute or two; everyone on the floor understood that while productivity was not measured, the citizuns of The Bubble Society were expected to work diligently during their daily labor hours, and to postpone their socializing for the hours that the Guvernment had set aside for relaxation.

Gavin settled into his seat as Tanya and Mel disappeared behind the walls of their cubes. There was no computer at his desk, nor any sort of papers; instead, Gavin tapped on his right temple, calling up his holographic monitor, and pulled up the queue on his Video Editor App. A quick scan of his scheduled tasks revealed that little had changed during his absence; there was no pileup of tasks, no overflowing inbox.

Instead, his usual daily workload awaited him.

For a moment, Gavin wondered about that. Nobody ever got sick in The Bubble Society, and the Department of Infant Development had eliminated the need for female sentient beings to carry children and give birth, so no citizun should ever have to miss a day's work. This had caused Gavin to worry about how his absence would be handled; after all,

Kingston's Guvernment never missed an opportunity to remind everyone how The Bubble Society needed every citizun's contribution, whether that contribution came from a common laborer, a Knower, a member of one of the Halls of Parliament, or The Guvna' himself.

However, despite the many times that Gavin had heard this mantra repeated, every indication was that his lengthy absence had not affected anything; his cubemates had not said anything about an increased workload, which seemed to indicate that the videos Gavin had not been there to edit simply had not been edited.

Gavin shrugged, pushing these thoughts from his mind; the Guvernment must be referring to more important sentient beings than him, he thought. The Bubble Society did not really need Gavin, did not really need every citizun to maintain their utopia; they merely said that to be polite, to make him, and others like him, feel some sense of importance.

That was fine with Gavin; in fact, it was a relief to realize he was not as important as he had been led to believe. He had never completely accepted the idea that The Bubble Society would come to a screeching halt if he failed to edit a few videos, but despite his doubts, it seemed that part of Gavin's mind had somehow transformed his meager responsibilities into a disproportionate weight on his shoulders; he had not realized that until now, but it was a relief to feel the burden lift.

Gavin settled back into his seat and pulled up the first task on his docket, which required him to insert transition frames into a children's anime. He began to work, falling into his routine.

An hour later, Gavin felt his attention start to wander; he realized that the Focus Solution was tapering off, and that in its absence, the questions that he had tried to push to the side were once again knocking at the edge of his consciousness. The knocks were faint now, but they were persistent, and he knew they would only grow louder.

At least it was easier to refocus at work, Gavin thought, moving to the next task in his queue. On the day after his release - which Gavin had spent holed up in his apartment - there had been nothing to stop him from returning to Kingfisher Reservoir.

Nothing except for The Guvna's words, and the idea that it would be wiser to lay low, because if they were watching him, Kingfisher Reservoir was the last place that he should go.

But then again, they might not be watching him; he might have misinterpreted The Guvna's words.

Those dueling arguments had tortured Gavin's mind during his day in the apartment. The idea that he might be denying himself his greatest desire - a return trip to Kingfisher Reservoir - for no reason at all was enough to drive him half-mad.

Gavin shook his head and returned his attention to the holographic screen; using his thoughts, he "clicked" on the clip he was supposed to work on, and to his surprise, found himself reading the Safety Decree that Annette, Leonard, and Neville had all mentioned.

Bubble Society Safety Decree #28

Henceforth, no citizun of The Bubble Society shall visit any of the outdoor recreation areas previously sanctioned by the Guvernment. Knowers have determined that the risks involved are a great threat to stability in The Bubble Society, which needs all of its citizuns operating at full capacity to produce the greatest good in our utopia.

The Guvernment thanks you for your compliance.

Praise Knowledge.

Gavin leaned back in his seat, a flood of emotions coursing through him. Hearing about the new Safety Decree had been one thing, but it was another to see it in print. Gavin could not quite believe that he and his friends could never go back to Kingfisher Reservoir; the fact that it was his fault made the situation even more difficult to stomach.

Then, quite suddenly, an idea struck him, an idea so exciting that it drove all traces of disappointment from his body. Why had it taken him so long to think of it?

Gavin jumped to his feet, crossed to his manager's office, and walked through the open doorway, knocking on the frame to get the man's attention.

Felix Podmore looked up, surprise evident on his face. His skin was a deep bronze, his eyes brown, his hair black and thick. He kept his cheeks shaved, but had a thick mustache and sideburns to go with his prominent eyebrows, which rose as Gavin entered.

"Boss? Do you have a minute?"

Podmore nodded, striving to conceal his dismay. He had an "open-office" policy - he considered it one of his managerial strengths - but that was because it sounded impressive without requiring any extra effort. Podmore had never thought one of his subordinates would come to him with a question; it was quite outside of the standard decorum outlined by *The Manual for Proper Behavior.* However, given how much he had gone on about this policy during the interview for his post, Podmore decided he ought to have a go of it.

"Gavin, of course. Should've called you in earlier, in fact - how are you, lad? You gave us quite the scare."

"Oh, I'm getting on all right. A bit better each day. I do apologize for my absence, I know that The Bubble Society needs all its citizens working at full strength."

Podmore waved a hand.

"Don't worry yourself. We got on all right, bang on schedule, as we always are, though we missed you, of course."

Gavin nodded.

"Thanks. So, the reason I wanted to talk to you is the latest assignment in my queue. I've got some ideas for the project."

Podmore, whose expression had relaxed as they exchanged pleasantries, raised an eyebrow.

"Indeed? Well, I must say, that's a lot of initiative for an associate video editor to take."

Gavin nodded, oblivious.

"I don't mind. Anyway, what I was thinking was, I've got this Safety Decree #28 to splice into several programs, and it would be a lot better to have some live footage with it. To help, uh, show the dangers involved. I'd know better than most - in fact, I was thinking I could go shoot it. To make sure we get the most effective angles to educate folks, you know?"

Podmore was staring at Gavin as if he had grown a second head.

"Could you close the door, lad?"

Caught wrong-footed by Podmore's lack of enthusiasm, Gavin stood and shut the door, uncomfortably aware that Podmore was staring at him with deep concern on his face.

As Gavin sat back down, Podmore straightened up. He slid forward to sit on the edge of his seat, set his hands on his desk, and steepled his fingers.

"Now, lad, you've been a fine worker since you joined us, and I'm inclined to give you some latitude after what you've been through. But this idea of yours…I must be blunt. I don't think I've ever heard anything so daft."

Gavin's face fell, but Podmore was only getting started.

"For one thing, you are not a videographer. There's precious few of them left now that the industry is able to produce such outstanding images with the computer, but in any case, videographers are the only ones with the Guvernment's leave to perform that duty. For Knowledge's sake, lad, can't you see the havoc that would ensue if sentient beings could choose their own profession, or jump from one occupation to another willy-nilly, with no permission, no administrative oversight? It would be pandemonium."

Podmore shook his head.

"For another thing, if the Guvernment were to make an exception for someone, it would not be you. First off, you're the reason that Safety Decree was put in place. Second - well, ordinarily, I would never bring this up, as it has no bearing on your pay or job security - but we do have a record of every piece of content we produce. So we could measure productivity, if we wanted to."

"Again, it has no bearing on anything, but I have reviewed the numbers, and you, Gavin, are the least productive associate video editor that we have on staff."

Gavin frowned, and started to voice an objection, but Podmore rode over him.

"In fact, you're the least productive associate video editor I've seen in my five years as a supervisor, and according to historical records dating back to The Advent, you're the least productive editor of all time. The day before this incident at the reservoir, you turned in two pieces of content, and based on what I could tell from the security feed, you spent the rest of the day staring off into space, with the exception of one hour when you were switching the pants on your Bubble Suit from jeans to cut-offs and back again."

Gavin felt a bit of heat rise in his neck as he recalled the day in question. He glanced over his shoulder at one of the surveillance cameras that monitored the floor, then turned back to face Podmore, whose expression had softened.

"Now, I'm only a bit older than you, but someone needs to talk some sense into you. You need to understand how our labor force is structured and fall in line. We are assigned to an industry, and we work in that industry, and only that industry, until the retirement age. Everyone Knows that the Guvernment does not allow for exceptions in such matters."

"Knowledge has given us a utopia; all you have to do is sit back and enjoy it. You, like every other being in the Bubble Society, are fed and happy. Perhaps you'll ascend to my role one day, or the role above that, but it doesn't really make a difference, because no matter what, the Guvernment will see you are taken care of. You've got a good, long life ahead of you. So sit back and enjoy the ride. And don't come to me with any more of this nonsense about filming live footage."

Gavin nodded stiffly. Podmore, seeing that the young man was not satisfied, continued.

"I'll tell you what, knock off early today. You've had a lot going on, go get your mind sorted. I'm sure you'll be back to normal by tomorrow. I'll call the timekeepers, tell them to make you an exception for the day."

Gavin perked up at the suggestion. He thanked Podmore, who dismissed Gavin from his office with a wave of his hand.

BOOK 1, CHAPTER 6

Gavin continued to feel out of sorts as he wandered away from the Department of Media Productions, heading east on a path that took him out of the Center of Industry and through the Academic Campus on the way to the southwest gate of Kingston Park. He had walked the route thousands of times before, either from the Center of Industry or the Academic Campus, but like everything else today, something about the walk felt different.

He had to cross Central Boulevard to reach Kingston Park, but this was easy enough, as a tunnel ran beneath the Boulevard, allowing pedestrians to cross without having to wait for traffic. As Gavin ascended the ramp that took him back up to ground level, the archway that served as the southwest entrance to Kingston Park came into view; the archway, which stood where the hedges that bounded the park would have intersected, was ornate, wrought of iron, and shaped to form the words *Praise Knowledge.*

It was not the only way into Kingston Park - Gavin had used all of the entrances at some point over the past decade - but he preferred the southwest entrance because of the archway; he always felt a sense of importance when he passed beneath the impressive motto. At least that part of the day was familiar; a small smile crossed Gavin's face as he passed beneath the words.

The paved walkway continued deep into Kingston Park - it ran all the way across to the northeastern corner, and intersected many other paths along the way, which led to various parts of the park - but Gavin had no intention of following those sanctioned pathways. Instead, he took a detour after a few hundred yards, stepping off of the path onto the turf lawn and crossing to where the ground gave way to the trees.

The Manual for Proper Behavior explicitly stated that stepping off the paved walkway in any park was prohibited, but The Villa was just on the other side of the creek that ran through this wood, and the shortcut saved Gavin half an hour in each direction, which made it an easy decision. In any case, Gavin did not think he was hurting anything; as far as he could tell, the turf in Kingston Park sprang back just fine after he stepped on it.

Gavin took his time on the path through the trees, enjoying the feeling of being engulfed by living greenery - the trees were the only real plants in Kingston Park - and of being invisible to the world around him.

Before his stay in Kingston Hospital, Gavin would have taken a few hard strides and jumped across the small creek, but he was more cautious today, uncomfortably aware that this would be an unacceptably bad place for his Bubble Suit to malfunction. He did not think that would happen - it seemed unlikely that there would be any unidentified flying objects in this secluded section of Kingston Park - but still, if his Bubble Suit did tear, or did something else to set off an alarm, he did not want it to happen in a restricted area.

Fortunately, Gavin crossed the creek without incident. He emerged on the far side of the wood on a rolling turf lawn; from there, it was an easy walk to The Villa, which stood on the crest of the hill, overlooking the Grand River, which ran along the eastern border of the property.

The sight of the estate up on the hill brought a familiar swell of emotions and memories in Gavin. He pushed the emotions aside - he was practiced at that - but the full film had already played back in his mind, the images flickering through his consciousness in ultra fast-forward.

—

The film started shortly after Gavin had turned eleven years old.

It started on the day that they had come for his parents.

They were Guvernment Officials.

Officials from the Society for the Promotion of Laureates.

They were not cruel about the matter. Their leader, a middle-aged woman, explained to Gavin that his parents had been called by Knowledge, selected to pursue a higher calling, which was the reason they were increasingly unable to function in the world they had once shared with their son.

The woman was kind.

The woman was sincere.

But when Gavin protested that he liked living with his parents, and did not want any of them to move, she was firm.

"I'm dreadfully sorry; truly I am. As wonderful as it is to bring new Laureates to The Villa, to help them live out their purpose, it is as difficult to tell the families."

"But I am afraid there is no alternative. For The Bubble Society to thrive, we must put all of our citizuns toward their most useful function, and when Knowledge is good enough to bless our citizuns, we must heed its call and move them to a space where they can focus on their visions. For how is Knowledge to help us advance, if we do not have the Laureates to listen to its message?"

"Of course, it creates difficulties for the families, but the Guvernment has not overlooked that; after all, what sort of a utopia forgets its children? To make it easier on all involved, housing was built on the Academic Campus - I'm sure you're familiar with the buildings - so that the children of the Laureates are free to continue their education in comfort and security until they are ready to leave school as productive citizuns of The Bubble Society."

Gavin blinked; he had barely heard the second part of what the woman had said.

He was familiar with the housing she referred to.

In fact, he was so familiar with that housing that the very mention of the buildings they called The Barracks was sufficient to make the full gravity of his situation hit home.

Gavin knew some of his peers who lived on the Academic Campus.

The ones who lived in The Barracks.

They were the Wards.

The Wards of the Guvernment.

The Wards of The Bubble Society.

That was what he was now.

He, Gavin Owens, was a Ward.

The thought made him shudder.

Gavin had known for a long time - years, really - that something was happening to his parents, that things would have to come to a head someday. But he had never imagined that this would be that head.

It had started slowly; at first, Gavin did not understand what was happening when his mother got lost on her way home from the park, or when his father would spend whole nights cleaning the house. All Gavin knew was that he felt a knot in his gut when his parents got into these states, and that it could not mean anything good.

The Guvernment Official had stopped speaking. Gavin acted as if he had been listening, acknowledging her words with a meek nod of his head. Then, staring at the middle-aged woman's shoes, he spoke in a hushed voice.

"I thought they were getting sick. Like in the stories about Shurtain, and Kingston, before The Advent. They say that Before Knowledge, before the Bubble Suits, sentient beings got sick all the time. Only I thought my parents were getting sick in their brains, instead of their bodies."

It was an effort for the Guvernment Official to suppress her smile.

"No, of course not. Nobody gets sick in The Bubble Society; you should Know that by your age. Even so, I'm sorry we weren't notified earlier; I realize how confusing this must have been for you. But rest assured, Knowledge put an end to illness and disease years ago."

"And as there is nothing wrong with your parents, there is no need to fret about them. In fact, you can sleep easy knowing that there is something very right with your parents, take comfort in the fact that they will be at The Villa, doing important work alongside the other Laureates, work that allows us to build a better, stronger Kingston."

The woman sighed. The transformation of her features shocked Gavin; he would never have imagined that this middle-aged woman, whose expression had been so dour until now, could possibly wear such a distant, dreamy look.

"I can only hope that I will join your parents and the other Laureates one day; they are the dreamers. But only so many receive the gift."

The woman shook herself, and her dour expression reappeared.

"As for you, you will move to the Academic Campus full-time, where you will continue your studies. You and your parents will both be doing your part for The Bubble Society, and one day, you will emerge as a happy, healthy, and productive citizun in our utopia."

The woman made the prospect sound wonderful for all involved, but Gavin did not believe a word of it; he had engaged in too many interactions with the Wards to be excited about the latest lot that he had drawn in life.

And that misery was only on his end; after his first visit to The Villa, he thought that his parents might have it even worse.

As far as Gavin could tell, the life of a Laureate did not match the descriptions painted by the Guvernment, nor were the Laureates the portrait of serene wisdom that Gavin's teachers at Kingston Elementary had conveyed while educating their charges about the Laureates and The Villa.

In fact, the contrast was so stark that Gavin had to take pains to remind himself that he was an ignorant schoolboy, and that all of the Knowers, and all of the knower-reviewed papers, agreed with the Guvernment's official stance. Whatever Gavin observed did not matter; he was uneducated in these matters, unfit to render a judgment. After all, he had not even graduated from Kingston High yet, and without that certificate in hand, how could any sentient being hope to Know anything about the world around them?

But while Gavin regularly reminded himself of this particular bit of Knowledge, which was laid out on page 577 of *The Manual for Proper Behavior*, he could not help but wonder why, if the connection between Knowledge and the Laureates was so divine, that same Knowledge would drive his mother to touch every fence post they passed while walking around their apartment complex, or cause his father to regularly forget the names of people that he had known for years.

Gavin had considered raising his questions during his first visit to The Villa, but by some miracle, his sense, transient as it was, had stepped in on this occasion, convincing him that it would not be wise to question the story the Knowers had told him, especially as they were so certain of their narrative.

But no matter how many times he told himself to stop thinking of questions, Gavin's regular visits to The Villa often left him wondering if the Knowers might have missed something. It was a dreadful conundrum; Gavin already felt bad enough about his perpetual inability to behave in accordance with *The Manual for Proper Behavior*, which his teachers reminded him of at least seven times a day, and he knew that having such questions bubble up in him flew directly against *The Manual*, which clearly stated, right on Page 1, that Knowers could not be wrong about anything.

That was what made them Knowers.

Yet Gavin could not stop the questions arising, even if he had the sense not to voice them; ultimately, he resigned himself to the fact that this was one more aspect of *The Manual for Proper Behavior* that he was unable to comply with, one more reason he would never be regarded as a model citizun in The Bubble Society, one more reason for him to feel guilty.

—

At least The Villa was in a beautiful place. Gavin walked up the sloping lawn, doing some rough math in his head, trying to calculate how many times he had visited the place over the past twelve years. Thousands, at the least; painful as the trips could be, Gavin made it a point to visit his parents several times a week.

Gavin smiled when he saw that George stood at the door. Gavin knew all of The Villa's security officers - they always seemed happy for a chance to speak with him on his visits - and today was no different.

"Gavin! Good'ta see ya lad, good'ta see ya, you've had us all in a right state. Was just saying to Jenkins the other day, when're we going ta see 'ol Gavin 'round again? Right scared you were done 'fer, we were."

Gavin grinned; he had not liked his fellow commuters bringing up his situation, but George was different.

"Ah, it wasn't so bad, George. You know how things go in Kingston, something out of the ordinary happens, and it's quite the attraction, but I'm getting on fine."

"Shook things up 'round here, that's for certain. Well, I won't keep ya, I'm sure yer parents 'bin worried silly, wondering 'bout you."

Gavin's stomach clenched at those words, but he did not bother to correct George; he merely nodded as the man held the door for him.

The moment he crossed the threshold, Gavin found himself face-to-face with a Laureate, a middle-aged woman who stared at him through vacant green eyes. Avoiding eye contact, Gavin nodded politely to the woman, then stepped around her to the front desk. The woman's absent look was common among the Laureates, but no matter how many times Gavin visited, he still found it unsettling to meet the empty stares; he could not imagine how the staff coped.

Aubrey, a young woman with short blond hair, was at the front desk today. Though not technically a caregiver, she was dressed in a similar uniform, her Bubble Suit set to project light blue scrubs and a white nurse's hat.

Aubrey looked up from her tablet at Gavin's approach. Her features were as lovely as ever - high cheekbones, long, straight nose, and gleaming white teeth - but her green eyes were hazy with exhaustion, and her slumped posture suggested that the weight of the world's problems rested on her narrow shoulders. She addressed Gavin in a lethargic tone.

"Hello, Gavin. Good to see you again. Check in here."

She indicated a tablet on the front desk. Gavin reached over and ran his Bubble Suit's wrist scanner over the surface.

"Are my parents in their room?"

"There, or in the dreamer's studio. Outdoors time is over, and it's another hour before everyone gathers in the Dining Hall for their nutrient tanks."

Gavin thanked Aubrey, then stepped around the front desk and into the spacious room beyond, which was a blend of library and coffee shop. It was a pleasant space, full of comfortable furniture and books, though the various volumes were only for decorative purposes; for all Gavin knew, the pages inside the elegant covers might be blank, as any actual reading in Kingston was done via the Guvernment Media App on the Bubble Suit's holographic monitors.

There were not many Laureates using the space at the moment; the exceptions were two men sitting in a pair of armchairs, chatting as their mugs steamed in front of them. Gavin did not stop as he walked past the men, but he did smile at the sight of the mugs, which, like the robotic pets that some sentient beings carried around, were props, a relic of another age. Nobody actually drank from the mugs - the heat of the liquid, the possibility of contamination, the need to expose one's mouth to the outside environment - all of these factors made drinking from a mug an absurd proposition. Even so, the Department of Research and Innovation's early trials had shown that while sentient beings were somewhat aware of the effects when coffee was injected via the fluid system, the experience was enhanced when the subjects could see steaming liquid in front of them. This effect was amplified further when the liquid was the proper color, or if the subject found the mug particularly appealing, and as it turned out, the impact was not limited to visual cues; it carried over to the other senses. Sending airborne molecules that smelled like coffee into the Bubble Suit's air filtration system enhanced the experience even more than the visual effects, and combining visual and olfactory effects was still more potent. Given their efficacy, these practices were widely adopted, and it was thought that they would become a permanent fixture in The Bubble Society.

As it turned out, the children produced by the Department for Infant Development, who had spent their whole lives in Bubble Suits and had no memory of another world, were not interested in the accessories that the older generation used. For these children, receiving an injection of coffee was not *like* drinking coffee; it *was* drinking coffee. They had never done it any other way, and they saw no need for a mug, or a stand-in liquid, to enhance the experience.

Though old enough to have been born outside of the Department for Infant Development, Gavin and his friends had been caught in the middle, young enough to adjust their behavior rather than take on the habits of the "olds." So when Gavin and his friends drank, they did not use props, and just as they laughed at people who owned robotic pets, they found it hilarious to observe the "olds" who clung to their props.

It was different in The Villa, however; Gavin had noticed that the Laureates enjoyed these trappings more than most in The Bubble Society, and he had no wish to bother these men, who smiled and waved amicably as Gavin passed them. He reciprocated; it always gave him a good feeling when he saw Laureates who seemed happy.

Gavin reached the rear of the room and passed into the Dining Hall, a vast space capable of housing all of the Laureates at once. Many staircases led out of the room; the one that Gavin sought was much like the others, constructed of broad, deep stairs and covered with non-slip rugs.

The rugs were another thing that Gavin had asked about on his first visit; it had struck him as odd that so many of the Laureates appeared to have trouble with their balance, since the Bubble Suits were supposed to regulate all aspects of movement, but one of the caregivers had explained this, telling Gavin that certain Laureates would get so swept up in their visions that they lost track of this world, and often lost their footing as a result.

That had seemed plausible to Gavin at the time.

Or at least, he had not bothered to question it.

Lost in his thoughts, Gavin was almost surprised to find himself on the third floor; a few strides down the hall and he stood outside his parents' room. Gavin knocked, wondering if they would be there. He got his answer immediately.

"Come in."

Gavin smiled at the sound of his mother's voice; no matter how lost she and his father were to him, there was still that, the unchanged sounds of their voices. He pulled the door open.

"Brent, dear, come to the door, we have company."

Gavin took two steps inside the doorway.

His mother approached him, the joyful smile that she always wore these days plastered across her lined, pale face, but her brown eyes, once so like his own, were as lost as ever, and when she looked at Gavin, there was no recognition.

His father appeared behind her a moment later. He gave a start at seeing Gavin, and his green eyes seemed to spark, but then they returned to their usual dull state. This was not a surprise; Gavin had mentioned the recurring phenomenon to the caregivers, but they had written it off as a coincidence.

"Well, this is a pleasant surprise. It's not often that we get visitors. What brings you here, young man?"

Gavin's stomach clenched as he found a way to smile at his father.

"I hoped to interview you, sir. You and your wife; I wanted to learn more about your lives, and all your notable accomplishments."

Brent and Amelia beamed at him.

"Well, come in, come in, make yourself comfortable. We'd be happy to tell you whatever we can."

—

As soon as he shut the door behind him, Gavin sagged against the wall, letting the cascade of emotions that so often accompanied his exits wash over him.

His parents seemed happy; at least there was that. Gavin's years of visits had shown him that certain Laureates were not as fortunate. Many of them seemed haunted, tormented by mental demons, at least as far as Gavin could tell.

However, when he mentioned his suspicions to the staff during one of his early visits, they laughed off his concerns, telling him that Knowers had determined that the Laureates with more volatile moods were actually more likely to have visions; it was a worthy sacrifice to serve Knowledge in such a way.

Still, whether or not they seemed happy, it was difficult to accept your parents forgetting you. It had never mattered much to Gavin that Knowledge had called them, or that the life of a Laureate was considered the noblest of pursuits. All that mattered to him was that when his parents became Laureates, it had meant the end of his family.

After a time, Gavin straightened up and started down the hallway. A young woman with red hair, perhaps two or three years older than he was, appeared on the landing as he approached.

She was very pretty, Gavin thought, with her creamy white skin and dark red hair. The people of Kingston had hoped the Bubble Suits would strip away the vanity of beauty - the Suits did a great deal to adjust physical appearances, after all - but Gavin still found himself drawn to certain features. Bright, intelligent eyes or a mischievous smile made his heart beat faster, even though he was well aware that *The Manual for Proper Behavior* plainly stated, on Page 17, that sentient beings should not be concerned with the physical appearances of others.

Chalk it up as one more thing that Gavin could not get right.

Excitement rose in his chest as the young woman approached him, but then he saw her eyes, and a horrible mixture of disappointment and dread flooded him.

The young woman was a Laureate. There was no doubt; her vacant green eyes told the story.

"Hello there. My name is Lucy. I don't believe we've met before."

Gavin smiled, then inclined his head in a polite bow.

"It's a pleasure. I'm Gavin."

"Lucy."

Gavin nodded patiently. At that moment, a caregiver appeared on the landing and approached the two of them. Lucy turned to face the woman.

"Hello there. My name is Lucy. I don't believe we've met before."

The caregiver's mouth turned up at the corners, but that was as far as the smile went.

"No, I don't think we have. I'm Maria; wouldn't you like to go back to your room, Lucy?"

Lucy nodded eagerly. Maria indicated that they should go down the hallway. When Lucy turned, she caught sight of Gavin again.

"Hello there. My name is Lucy. I don't believe we've met before."

An uncomfortable wave of pity coursed through Gavin, but he forced himself to smile and nod at her again.

"No, I don't believe we have, but it's a pleasure. Weren't you going to your room, Lucy?"

Lucy gave a start, then nodded eagerly again.

"Yes, I was. Well, it was nice to meet you!"

Lucy allowed Maria to lead her down the hallway. Feeling wretched, Gavin stood and watched as Maria opened a door further down the hall and ushered Lucy inside. Once the door was shut, Maria walked back toward Gavin, her exhaustion obvious.

An urge to ask a question seized Gavin as Maria approached him; it had been years since he had asked this particular question, and he doubted whether the official answer would have changed, but he felt a need to voice it again.

"Maria? Are you sure that the Laureates have had their minds called by Knowledge? It seems to me that their minds and memories are failing them."

Maria's expression remained exhausted, but a genuine smile crossed her face at Gavin's question.

"No, no. Of course, I'm not the one to ask such questions. You should really ask one of the Knowers we have on staff. I thought the same as you, when I first came here, but the Head Caregiver explained it to me. Knowers settled the matter long ago; they did knower-reviewed studies, you know. I don't know exactly what that means, but they say it's…what was it that the Head Caregiver called it…an incorruptible instrument to divine Truth, that's it."

"In any case, all of those studies showed that the Laureates' condition is the result of a connection to a higher calling, a direct link to Knowledge itself. That's all it can be, in any case; as you Know, sentient beings in The Bubble Society can't get sick."

Maria shook her head.

"I know how it might appear to you and me. Even after the Head Caregiver explained it all to me, I was unable to see the Laureates the same way that the Knowers do. But that's why we're in our positions, and why the Knowers are in theirs. After all, if we left it to sentient beings to figure things out for ourselves, we would end up in a very bad place indeed. That's why we have the Guvernment."

Gavin nodded at her, uneasy.

It was the same answer he had gotten years ago.

It was also an answer that he had accepted more readily back then.

Now, another question occurred to him; Gavin would not have dared to ask it to any Guvernment Official, but he did not think it was dangerous to ask Maria.

"But who are the Knowers? Who works for the Guvernment? Aren't they sentient beings themselves?"

A puzzled expression came over Maria's face.

"Why, I can't say that had ever occurred to me. I suppose they are, but they aren't sentient beings like you and me. They're cut from a different cloth; The Guvna' himself appoints them, you know."

"But if they're all just sentient beings, how do they Know what we're supposed to do?"

Maria laughed out loud at that.

"Why, that's the sort of thought that you and I don't need to bother with. Knowledge itself tells them, I expect. All we need to Know is that Knowledge gave us a utopia. Life in The Bubble Society is as good as a sentient being could hope for, so as far as I'm concerned, the leadership is getting the right message."

She smiled at Gavin, who decided to nod in agreement. He did not want to raise any suspicions, but it was difficult to keep the uncomfortable squirming in his guts from showing in his expression.

"Well, I suppose that's true enough. It was good talking with you,

Maria. I appreciate you calming my concerns."

Maria returned his smile. Gavin nodded, turned away, and started down the stairs.

—

Though he was not conscious of it, Gavin's brown eyes often took on a placid, distant expression after he left The Villa. That was the case today; rather than chat with George, Gavin only waved absent-mindedly in the security guard's direction as he exited the building.

Thankfully, something about following the path through the woods worked as a salve on Gavin's soul; by the time he emerged from the trees to rejoin the paved walkway on the other side of Kingston Park, Gavin's eyes were a bit more active, and he was starting to reconnect with his surroundings.

As it turned out, this was all relative; Gavin remained distracted enough that he did not see the young woman coming along the path until after they had collided.

Gavin staggered back a few steps but kept his balance; the young woman was not so fortunate. Gavin had thought the impact minor, but she went sprawling and landed on her backside. She was quick to voice her displeasure.

"Geez, walk much?"

The young woman scowled as she glared up at Gavin, her fierce hazel eyes framed by tumbling blond curls.

Gavin did not know what to say. He recognized the young woman; how could he not? Anyone in Kingston would have recognized her, but as Gavin had only been two years behind her in the Kingston school system, he was more familiar with her than most.

"Help me up, at least?" asked Tesla, an exasperated note in her voice.

Her words jarred Gavin back into action; he reached out a hand and pulled Tesla up. There were so many questions streaming through his mind that the strangeness of her request never occurred to him; even with their Bubble Suits, sentient beings typically avoided touching one another unless it was strictly necessary.

Questions exploded like fireworks in Gavin's brain, but one stood out: What was The Guvna's youngest daughter doing at Kingston Park, which was so far away from her family's sprawling estate in Capitol Square? The Guvna's Mansion stood in Capitol Square, which sat adjacent to The Guvna's Park, and had far more expansive grounds than Kingston Park.

Gavin barely knew Tesla, however - in fact, he did not know her, he only knew of her - and such a question would have been too familiar.

"I'm sorry, I didn't see you there. My mind was somewhere else, I guess."

Tesla sighed, her exasperation obvious, but then recognition flickered in her eyes. For the briefest of moments, Gavin sensed that this flash of recognition might have been contrived, but her question drove that suspicion from his mind before he could really consider the matter.

"You're Gavin Owens, aren't you?"

Before he could answer, she was nodding.

"Of course you are. I'd recognize you from school even if you hadn't been the subject of half a billion news segments the past two weeks."

Gavin opened his mouth to speak, but found he had to swallow. He was surprised that Tesla had known who he was; it would have surprised him to find out that she had known who any boy his age was, for that matter.

"You remember me from school?"

It was the only thing he could think to say.

Tesla rolled her eyes.

"There weren't that many people with us at Kingston High, Gavin. We also overlapped at Kingston Elementary; I remember most everyone who was ever in school with me."

Tesla grinned; her impish eyes hinted at some sort of purpose.

"In any case, I've heard an awful lot about you lately."

Gavin found himself confused again, then realized what she must mean.

"Oh ya. The news. I guess everyone has heard a lot about me."

"Not just the news. You're about the only topic of conversation at The Guvna's table these days."

Gavin gaped at her.

"You're surprised? I'd have thought you might have guessed. How many visits to Kingston Hospital do you think my father typically makes in a year?"

Gavin shrugged.

"I dunno; I've never thought about it."

"The answer is zero, Gavin."

Tesla arched an eyebrow, looking him over.

"You don't get it, do you?"

"Get what?"

Tesla shook her head.

Was it pity in her eyes? Disdain?

A little of both?

"You're breaking convention, according to *The Manual for Proper Behavior*."

Gavin stood very still.

"Because of the cliff jumping?"

"And the ideas you put forward at work this morning."

Gavin blinked.

"How did you find out about that?"

Tesla smiled.

"I found out. And that should be enough for you to worry about who else is aware of that."

She paused, glanced around, then turned back to Gavin.

"Actually, I don't suppose it hurts to tell you. The Guvna' was notified of your proposal shortly after you left work. That sort of issue is typically monitored by people far down the chain of command, but there have been special orders issued about you after the incident at Kingfisher Reservoir."

Gavin did not respond at first. He looked Tesla over closely, trying to puzzle things out, but he could not begin to think what to ask. In the end, he kept it simple.

"Why are you telling me this?"

Tesla smiled.

"Can't you guess? I want to find out how you did it."

BOOK 1, CHAPTER 7

Gavin sat next to his apartment window in a straight-backed chair.

Through the window, he could see the festivities in the streets below; through his holographic monitor, which he had set in picture-in-picture mode, he could see the crowd gathering at the gates of Capitol Square, waiting for them to open up the grounds for the night's revelries. It was Day 400 of the Year 20, A.K., and nearly all of The Bubble Society's citizuns were out to celebrate the anniversary of The Advent and the start of a new year.

That the start of the year coincided with The Advent was no accident; the dawn of The Bubble Society had been such a momentous event that the newly-branded citizuns had drawn a line in the sands of time, separating old from new. Everything before The Advent became Before Knowledge - B.K. - and everything to come would be After Knowledge - A.K.

They reset the calendar, proclaiming the day after The Advent to be Day 1 of the Year 1, A.K. The length of a year remained constant - regardless of their machinations, it still took 400 days for the planet Shurtain to orbit its sun as that star hurdled through the Syrian Galaxy - so the span of a year remained the same, but the counting took place on a reset calendar.

Gavin had never thought much about that - in past years, he was always too busy celebrating to consider such matters - but as he sat in his apartment, contemplating the night ahead, it struck him that it had taken some gall for the sentient beings of the time to reset the calendar. And there was a certain irony in this observation, for while he did not consciously recognize it, Gavin had started a new calendar in his own mind, one that started on the day after the long-winded end of the cliff-jumping incident, on the day of his release.

By that measure, it was Day 4 of the Year 0, A.R. - After Release.

Day 3 of the Year 0, A.R. had gone smoother than Day 2, the day when Gavin had first returned to work. Day 3 had been the final day of the work week, and with the celebration of The Advent so near at hand, the sentient beings of Kingston were far too excited to devote much attention to their work, whatever was written in *The Manual for Proper Behavior.* That collective distraction allowed Gavin's to get through his day without incident; his acquaintances at the bus stop did not express any further interest in his misadventure, and his manager, Felix Podmore, gave no sign that he and Gavin had exchanged anything but polite conversation in their meeting the previous day.

On the outside, it appeared that things were back to normal.

On the outside, nobody could see that going through his daily routine was suddenly tearing Gavin apart.

He had gotten through Day 3; now he waited, marking the progress of Day 4. Any moment now, a lone firework would launch from Kingston Amphitheater, giving the signal for the crowd to make its way to Capitol Square for the formal celebrations, which would continue past the usual midnight curfew and into the early hours of Day 1 of the Year 21, A.K.

Before his confinement, Gavin would have been eager to join them. As a child, The Advent had been the best day of the year; Gavin could remember struggling to fall asleep, then waking at dawn, wired with a sense of anticipation for the festivities and goodies, particularly the free-flowing sugar-water tanks.

Now, all of that felt like something that had happened to someone else.

Someone in a different life.

A different world.

The Gavin of today felt no urge to join the celebrations in the streets below, and he had no intention of going to Capitol Square for any of the other festivities. This had surprised his friends, but Gavin had put them off, using his recent ordeal as an excuse, claiming that he needed rest.

The lone firework appeared in the distance, provoking a roar from the crowds. Gavin watched as the great mass started to meander through the Andola District toward the Brick Bridge, where shuttle buses were waiting to take them the rest of the way to Capitol Square. They raised cries of "Long Live Knowledge" as they made their lethargic progress; with plenty of daylight remaining, and plans to party into the night, there was no hurry to reach the festivities.

Gavin's movements could not have struck a greater contrast; at the sight of the firework, he jumped to his feet and began pacing his apartment, no longer able to keep still, anticipation coursing through his body as he counted down the time, forcing himself to wait ten minutes for the crowd outside his building to clear.

As soon as the time was up, Gavin was out his door and into the hallway.

He took the stairs instead of the elevator.

It was not out of the ordinary for Gavin to do this, so it should not spark suspicion if anyone was watching the security cameras. But while it was not outside of his usual routine, Gavin's decision to take the stairs this evening was far more deliberate than usual; tonight, the choice to take the stairs was a necessary precaution, a way to ensure he would not run into one of his neighbors.

He could not afford a delay.

As Gavin started down the concrete stairwell, her face swam back to the front of his mind, as it had so often over the past two days, and he found himself replaying the final part of their conversation, the bit that had led him to employ so much caution on this expedition.

—

"Did what?" Gavin had asked.

Tesla's hazel eyes danced with excitement.

"How you got out of your Bubble Suit, of course."

Chills ran down Gavin's spine. Though they had been in school together, Gavin did not think he had ever been this close to Tesla, and there was something different about that; a palpable energy emanated from Tesla's being, and when she turned her full stare on Gavin, she sent the gears in his head spinning.

Feeling wrong-footed, Gavin cleared his throat.

"I didn't 'get' out of my Bubble Suit. Something happened. Something got me out of my Bubble Suit."

"What's the something?"

Gavin felt the heat rise in his neck. He could not look away from Tesla's eyes; they had him in a sort of trance. A small voice told him that he should be careful, that something was off here, but a much louder voice screamed that Gavin should do anything - absolutely *anything* - that Tesla wanted him to do.

Then, just as Gavin started to give an honest answer, his self-preservation instincts, such as they were, sprang into being, setting off alarms that drowned out everything else in his mind.

Tesla was The Guvna's daughter.

She lived in The Guvna's Mansion at Capitol Square.

She probably sat down with The Guvna' each night for the evening nutrient intake; she had already said as much. She might even have been sent here on her father's behalf to get this information from Gavin, since he had kept it from all the Knowers.

"I don't know what the something is. I wish I did - trust me - because then I'd know how to make sure it never happens again. I don't want to go back to Kingston Hospital."

Tesla shrugged, the mischief in her eyes brighter than ever.

"But you got to breathe fresh air, didn't you?"

Reluctant to continue down this path, Gavin nodded, never stopping to consider what a strange question it was.

"What else happened?"

"Well, I touched water - it got in through the tear in my Bubble Suit - and when I was falling, just plummeting down, out of control, it was the best…"

Gavin stopped. Tesla was nodding, her eyes locked on his, encouraging him to continue. But in that moment, Gavin realized she was exerting her influence over him again, and that he was about to say something very foolish. He shook himself.

"Uh, the best way to show how well the Bubble Suits work. And how lucky we are to have Knowledge watching over us, what a miracle it is that we have all the Bubble Suits to protect us. I can't imagine life without them."

Tesla raised an eyebrow.

"The best way to show the Bubble Suits work? Really?"

Once again, Gavin was struck dumb. He did not like this; no matter what he said, Tesla seemed to know how to keep him off balance.

"Well, sure. Because I was dying. Once the Bubble Suit stopped working."

"That's not what your vitals say."

Gavin hesitated. When he spoke again, his tone was measured.

"How do you know what my vitals said?"

"That doesn't matter. But your Bubble Suit wasn't damaged badly enough to stop tracking your vitals. The tracker is mission-critical infrastructure, since that monitoring system dictates everything that the Bubble Suits do to meet the body's needs as they arise. So I know you weren't dying."

This piece of information made Gavin even more uncomfortable. He thought back to his conversation with The Guvna', thought about the contrast between The Guvna and Tesla's respective takes on the situation. Gavin also wondered how Tesla knew all of this, but then it struck him that she was an aspiring Knower, studying at the Academy of Knowledge, and that Gavin's case must have come up in her studies.

But that made no sense; if all of the students at the Academy of Knowledge had been told that Gavin had not been dying, then why would The Guvna' have gone out of his way to ensure Gavin would tell the world he had been in terrible pain?

"It was your dad who told me that I was dying. That I was moments from an unavoidable death. Are you saying that he was wrong?"

Tesla grinned. She opened her mouth, but then her eyes shifted to look at something on her holographic screen; it seemed that she had suddenly remembered something.

"Dammit. I'm late. I need to go, or I'll be missed."

The hazel eyes snapped back to Gavin.

"You're going to see me again. I know I surprised you this time, but next time, you'll be ready to tell me everything. Won't you?"

Gavin nodded, dazed. Tesla grinned, and then she did something else that surprised Gavin; she reached out, took his hand, and squeezed it. As she did, she bit her lip, her eyes meeting his from under her long blond lashes. Gavin felt something warm in his chest. Just as quickly, her hand was gone, but the feeling lingered.

"See you soon, Gavin."

Tesla gave him a last smile, then turned and disappeared up the path. Gavin stood there, staring at the spot where she had vanished.

Their Bubble Suits prevented any actual contact, but even through the microfilament membrane, Tesla's grip had been both personal and sensual. Gavin had always been told that sentient beings did not need this, that there were countless other ways to feel good; after all, they lived in a utopian society, so why would anyone want to risk their health for something as fleeting as touch?

Gavin had never questioned that. But as he directed his attention to the warm glow inside him, attempting to hold it in place, he found that he had one more question about life in The Bubble Society.

—

Gavin had reached the bottom of the stairwell. He paused for a moment, letting the memory of Tesla's touch steel his mind for what was ahead.

No matter the potential repercussions, Gavin knew what he needed to do. He thought that he had been careful enough. He had made mistakes on his first day back in The Bubble Society, but there was no fixing that, and he had done nothing to draw suspicion since.

Now, with everyone celebrating The Advent, Gavin did not think that the Guvernment would have the manpower to watch him. At least not for the next few hours.

Gavin stepped out of his doorway and crossed the street to a rack of electric bikes. He passed a seemingly identical rack as he went, but despite appearances, Gavin knew that the two racks were not the same, that the one across the street was malfunctioning.

That made it ideal for Gavin's purposes.

If the rack had been working, it would have required Gavin to scan his

Bubble Suit's identification code to unlock the bikes, which would not have been ideal for what he had in mind tonight. Fortunately, this rack had stopped scanning for identification a few weeks earlier, and had not been repaired; Gavin had checked earlier in the day to make sure.

Gavin pulled a bike off the rack, threw a leg over, and kicked the electric motor into action. Taking a deep breath, he settled himself on the seat, then pressed his right thumb to a lever. The bike jumped forward.

Gavin steered north onto Riverside Parkway, on his way to Onyx Canyon. The route would stay well clear of Capitol Square, never crossing the Grand River; Gavin would be on the east side of the waterway the whole way.

He was going back to Kingfisher Reservoir.

Back to the Cadillac Mountains.

—

Knowing what he did about Safety Decree #28, Gavin had expected that the Guvernment might erect barriers along the road, perhaps multiple barriers, that would make it more difficult to access Kingfisher Reservoir.

Instead, there were two sawhorses, striped orange and white, arranged haphazardly next to each other partway up Onyx Canyon on Riverside Parkway. Gavin did not bother to slow his bike - the barriers were so loosely arranged that a car could have fit between them - or to read the signs on top of each barrier (which were headlined by the words *Safety Decree #28)* as he slalomed through.

When he reached the entrance to Kingfisher Reservoir, Gavin paused; eager as he was to start his search, he could not help but take a moment to turn back for a glance of the wide-open view. Gavin could not see the origins of the Grand River from here - its source was in the peaks of the Cadillac Mountains - but he could observe the mighty river's journey down Onyx Canyon, through the city of Kingston, and into the Badlands Desert beyond.

It was everything he had ever known; Gavin's world started and ended in that valley. Of course, he had heard legends of the world beyond, of what had existed in decades and centuries past, but with the planet Shurtain now a lifeless wasteland outside of Kingston, life as a citizun of The Bubble Society was all he would ever know. He might dream of following the Grand River southwest through the Badlands Desert, where the river dove into Lawrence Canyon to complete its route to Yacha Bay and the Nicaean Ocean, imagine what it would be like to follow the Grand's main fork, the Gatsby, south from Kingston to the Gulf of Gian, wonder what it would be like to strike out east and stare off the coast across the Sister's Break, where they said you could glimpse the continent Alexandria on the far side of the Amphitrite Ocean.

But he could do no more than dream. Gavin had seen videos of all these places, yet that was something unsatisfactory in that, perhaps because he knew first-hand how easy it was to fabricate images and videos.

Perhaps the places had changed.

Perhaps they had never been.

Gavin took a last moment to savor the view, then dismounted from his bike and approached the shores of Kingfisher Reservoir. He stopped at the bank.

Gavin stared at the small sand beaches at the water's edge, at the tree-lined hills and cliffs surrounding him; he was suddenly overcome, not by the beauty of the place, but by the hopelessness of his task. A glance up at the sun told him that there was not much daylight left to him.

That much daylight…to search all of this.

And what was he even looking for? A flash of light?

He did not know, not really. He could only hope that he would recognize whatever it was on the off chance that he found it, assuming the flash had not been a figment of his imagination.

Gavin shook himself. He could not think this way. He had to get to work, had to think productive thoughts. He knew it had been more than a flash of light; that flash had been light reflecting off something.

What had it been? A pin? A nail? A spear?

Gavin decided to start by searching the banks of the reservoir, hoping that the object had washed to shore. It was a monotonous process, sifting through pebbles and sand, but Gavin kept at it diligently, satisfying himself that each area was thoroughly cleared before he moved forward. He scuttled over the ground, crawling at times, getting down on his knees if an area demanded a particularly close examination.

The lack of results bred a dull frustration in the back of his mind, but when those thoughts tried to butt in, Gavin focused on the fact that he was a little bit closer to the end of the search, and that even if he did not find the object, he could not have found a better place to watch the sunset.

By the time that he reached the opposite shore, the eastern sky was deep purple, the western horizon faint pink. Gavin continued to work tediously in the fading light, searching at a juncture where one of the small sand beaches faded into the woods.

He was on one knee, sifting sand between his hands, when he glanced up.

Gavin's initial reaction was to look back down to the sand. It was as if his brain wanted to skip over what he had just seen, to write it off as a glitch in the program and continue on with his life.

It did not work.

Gavin froze.

Slowly, as what he had seen penetrated his consciousness, he lifted his gaze.

An old man stood at the edge of the wood, his posture stock-straight, his hands clasped behind his back. He was watching Gavin through dark brown eyes.

The old man's grey beard was tangled, chest-length; it swayed in the evening breeze. His hair was pulled back in a top knot, so Gavin could not tell how long it was, but at a glance, he guessed it would hang halfway down his back. His skin was deeply tanned, weathered by the years.

The old man was dressed simply. He wore a hooded overshirt that was a darker grey than the pants he wore. Both garments were made of the same material, a fine, flowing fabric that rippled in the breeze. His sandals were similarly straightforward: a single strap that wrapped his ankles and threaded in between his first and second toes.

Though the man was old, he was not frail. Quite the opposite; Gavin could make out the musculature of the man's body as the soft cloth of his garments rippled against him.

All of this passed through Gavin's mind in an instant, but none of it registered consciously, because he was far too preoccupied with the most distinctive detail about the old man to think about anything else.

The old man was not wearing a Bubble Suit.

Gavin blinked. He waited for the vision to disappear.

It did not oblige.

Instead, it walked toward him.

Still, Gavin's mind insisted that it was just that - a vision.

A hallucination.

A bad dream.

Then, when he was mere feet away, the old man stopped, and spoke, the sound of his voice shattering Gavin's remaining hope that this was a figment of his imagination.

"Looking for this?"

Gavin looked down. The old man held something in his open, upturned palm. Gavin knew, even before his eyes fixed on the thing, what he would find.

A silver spear, perhaps six inches long, rested in the old man's weathered palm.

—

Gavin looked up from the spear and met the old man's brown eyes. His eyes flicked back down to the spear, as if to reassure himself it was there, then they returned to the old man's lined face.

"Who are you?"

The old man smiled.

"A friend."

The old man's face changed suddenly; he frowned, and looked past Gavin to a point across the reservoir. He scanned the horizon, quickly at first, then more deliberately. In the end, he shook his head and looked back at Gavin.

"Are you real?"

The old man chuckled.

"I think so. But I suppose there's some subjectivity to that question."

Gavin did not know what to make of that.

"But if you're real, how are you…how are you…"

"Breathing?"

Gavin nodded.

"The same way I always have. It's not special. You can do it, too."

The old man's smile broadened.

"I think you already know that, though."

Gavin did not like this. What the old man said was true, but Gavin's brief experience breathing after his Bubble Suit had torn was one thing; encountering a sentient being who was simply not wearing a Bubble Suit was another thing altogether. His whole life, the adults around Gavin had praised Knowledge. In their history classes at school, Gavin and his peers were taught that the Bubble Suits had provided sentient beings with a new lease on life, a chance to extend their time on a planet that had turned inhospitable to their kind, and *The Manual for Proper Behavior* stated, in no uncertain terms, that it was accepted Knowledge that sentient beings could not survive on Shurtain without a Bubble Suit; it was written in bold font on Page 22.

Yet now this old man stood in front of him, not wearing a Bubble Suit, and he was not just alive; he was vibrant.

The implications of what his senses were telling him stretched Gavin's consciousnesses, pressing against it like a bowling ball carving out a path across a strained sheet of tissue paper. The heavy ball exerted its will, straining the paper, pressing ever further at the membrane, until it finally started to tear…

Gavin stumbled forward. As he fell to his knees, his head spinning, he felt the old man's hands catch his shoulders. And then, overriding the Bubble Suit implant meant to eliminate the gag reflex, Gavin retched.

The vomit rebounded against the Bubble Suit's lining, spraying Gavin in the face. The smell was intolerable; Gavin was no longer consciously registering his state, but if he had been, he would have been overjoyed to recognize his approaching blackout.

Anything to escape the smell.

—

Gavin's face was wet. His whole body was wet, but the breeze playing on the bare skin of his cheek brought his focus to his face.

The breeze…

The bare skin…

His face…

Gavin jolted back to life, his eyes snapping open as he sat up. He scrambled to his knees, looking around in a mad panic. He realized that he was still at Kingfisher Reservoir, that the lighting had not changed, that very little time could have passed.

Then he looked up, and found the old man. All other thoughts were driven from his mind.

"Calm down, Gavin. Take a deep breath."

It registered, in a distant corner of Gavin's mind, that the old man had used his name, but he had no bandwidth to consider that now.

His Bubble Suit…HIS BUBBLE SUIT!!!

Gavin tried to get up again; he had no idea where he was going, but his raw impulse to survive urged him to move, to go somewhere, anywhere. He could not move, though; the hands on his shoulders were firm.

"It's alright…you're going to be alright."

Gavin's head continued to spin.

"I need you to hear me, Gavin. We have more than enough time if we act with conviction, but we can't wait here much longer."

Gavin blinked. He looked down at his bare chest, traced his fingertips gently across his skin. Yet even as he touched the skin, and took in steadying breaths of air, the absence of the Bubble Suit was setting off alarm bells in his head. He looked up at the old man, who understood Gavin's concerns at a glance.

"I had to cut you loose. Sorry to do it so abruptly, I would have waited until we had talked about it, but you were suffocating on your own vomit. Figured in for a penny, in for a pound, so I cut the Bubble Suit off and got you in the water to wash you clean."

The old man glanced up at the horizon, then back at Gavin, whose expression remained alarmed.

"It's ok, you don't need the Bubble Suit. But cutting it open will have sounded an alarm. By now, they are coming."

Gavin shook his head. He opened his mouth to ask a question, but burped up a bit of water instead.

It was at that moment that he realized he was naked.

Of course he was; his Bubble Suit was gone. As the realization solidified in his mind, the old man handed him a towel. Gavin wrapped himself with it; as soon as this was done, the old man caught him by the chin and turned Gavin's face so their eyes met.

"You have to make a choice. If you want to stay here, you can pull the remains of your Bubble Suit back on. There will be difficult questions, especially after last time, but there's a chance you will come out of it all right."

Gavin gaped at the old man. He knew that was no choice at all; he could not, would not, go back to Kingston Hospital. They might never let him leave.

"You have another choice, though. You can follow the impulse that led you to jump off that cliff. You can leave all this behind, and come with me. But you can never go back. It is not my rule; it is theirs. And it is ironclad."

The old man looked into Gavin's eyes.

"You have to decide. Now. There is no time to waste."

Gavin nodded. Fear threatened to overwhelm him, but scary as it was, the idea of following this old man was also exciting beyond words, while the thought of returning to the hospital was intolerable.

Yet Kingston, The Bubble Society, The Villa, his parents, his friends… that was all Gavin knew. That was his world. And while part of him - the thinking part of his brain - recognized the peril he would be in if he stayed, another part of him screamed not to go, that it was too dangerous, that no sentient being could survive without a Bubble Suit.

It would have been so much easier to stay.

But that door was closed to him, if it had ever been open at all. The unknown awaited, and while Gavin could not see what lay before him, he realized that nothing lay behind. He had to trust that this stranger could guide him.

"I'll go."

The old man nodded, his expression solemn. He pushed a bundle into Gavin's arms.

"Then stand up and put these on. Quickly."

Gavin pulled on the clothes, which were similar to the garb the old man wore, though there were shoes and socks in place of the sandals. It was awkward - the mechanics of pulling the clothes on came to him out of a different life - but the garments were simple, and Gavin accomplished the task in short order. Once he was dressed, he looked up at the old man, who was looking at Gavin with a solemn expression on his face.

Gavin looked back at Kingston; in the distance, beyond the edge of hearing, Gavin saw lights rising over the city in the night sky, recognized the lights as belonging to a helicopter. He shifted his gaze back to the old man.

The old man turned, and led Gavin into the woods.

—

From her spot behind the rocks, Tesla seethed with indecision. Gavin and the old man were about to disappear, but she could still catch them if she hurried.

If only the old man had not glimpsed her; Tesla had been moving along the far shoreline when his gaze had pierced her, pinning her down. She had taken shelter behind some boulders on the shoreline, only peeking back up when the old man's attention had left her. After that, she could watch, but she could not get closer.

Tesla shook her head, frustrated. Following Gavin had been easy - he was completely oblivious - but the old man was a different animal.

Time slowed down as she weighed her choices. She was not prepared, and it was an effort to set aside her frustration at finding herself in that unfamiliar position. She had not thought it would happen on the first visit - she had thought she had more time - so she had not arranged matters so she could disappear.

Dammit Tesla.

If she did not go now, she might lose them, but if she did, there was so much that would be left undone…

They were at the edge of the wood. And then they were gone.

The distorted moment was over. For better or worse, she had made her decision.

Her world back at full speed, Tesla took a deep breath; as she exhaled, she heard the distant sounds of the approaching helicopter.

Tesla straightened up, her eyes alert. She tapped her right temple with a finger, bringing up her holographic monitor. She swiped across several screens, then entered a series of passcodes on her left wrist panel. She did all of this in less than five seconds, moving with remarkable speed and precision.

When she was done, a wall of monitors flickered in front of her. Tesla zoomed in on the different screens, noting the various alarms that had gone off. She saw, through the confused transcripts, that the Capitol Guard, the City Watch, and the Emergency Response Team were only now starting to coordinate on the situation, and that was only because their respective units had encountered each other on their way to Riverside Parkway.

So much for the consolidation of power leading to efficient communication.

Tesla smirked at the thought as she finished reading the relevant transcripts and trackers. The various information sources indicated that she had almost eight minutes before the members of the two units would arrive.

Tesla tapped in another command, enabling a hidden feature on her Bubble Suit; this allowed her to override the Bubble Suit's base movement package, and to take off at a sprint down Riverside Parkway.

After a quarter of a mile, Tesla stepped off the roadway, disabled the sprint feature, and started to pick her way through the trees, forcing herself to take long, deep breaths. She continued into the forest, disappearing into the night, until she found the spot where she had concealed an electric bicycle. The bike was custom-built, much more powerful than the flimsy community models of the sort Gavin had taken from the public bike racks. Tesla had upgraded the bike with phat tires, which allowed her to ride off-road without fear of puncturing a tire.

Now she waited. Tesla considered bringing up the image of the room again - she could put it in picture-in-picture mode - but she decided against it. Instead, she tapped on her right temple and called up a small digital clock in the top left corner of her holographic monitor, which allowed her to monitor the time without obstructing her view of the road.

Tesla consciously slowed her breathing as the first headlights appeared; they were followed by two dozen more. Tesla decided to give it thirty seconds to make sure no other vehicles were following.

While she waited for the digital clock to turn, she tapped her temple again, calling up the feed of the room to make one final check on the alerts. There were no surprises there.

Tesla decided that she had waited long enough. She engaged the bike's motor and took a final glance at the digital clock, which told her this delay had caused her to stay a bit too long. She was running late for the Closing Ceremonies, but not by much; she could make up the time.

Tesla turned off her holographic monitor; then, her eyes on a path that only she could see, she sent the bike surging forward. Small branches snapped under the phat tires as she dropped into the gully and shot up the far bank, where she swerved back onto the road.

Book 2

BOOK 2, CHAPTER 1

"It was a long time ago," said the first voice.

"It was not so long ago," replied the second.

"It was in a different world," said the first.

"It was in the same world," retorted the second.

"Of course it was," interjected a third. "How could it not be, when time and space are relative?"

—

Salomon Cahn woke before dawn on the Last Day. It was his habit, and he saw no reason to break it today.

He slipped out of bed, padded silently across the room, and closed the door behind him. His wife never stirred.

Salomon did not bother with the lights - he knew the layout of the house intimately - and he also knew that it amused Santino to stalk him through the shadows. He made his way to the kitchen in darkness.

The stove stood next to the sink on the far side of the kitchen. Two glass bottles of water waited for him there, along with a pair of small wooden cups.

Salomon poured one bottle into a kettle, lit the stove, and set the water to boil. He took the second bottle, uncapped it, and poured half into one of the small wooden cups before taking a long draw directly from the bottle.

After his drink, Salomon set the bottle down and scooped the cup up. Then he turned to greet Santino.

Santino stood stock straight, delight on his face as he gazed up at his grandfather with the sort of wide-eyed admiration that only a four-year-old can muster. Salomon laughed, and handed the boy his cup of water.

As Santino drank from his cup, Salomon's gaze drifted to the window. Outside, the Cadillac Mountains towered overhead, visible only as a denser shade of darkness in the pre-dawn hours. Salomon inhaled, using the mountains to set his perspective, reminding himself of the fleeting nature of existence, the fragility of sentient life in the face of such forces.

Salomon picked up the bottle of water, took another sip, and set it back on the counter. His eyes flicked in Santino's direction; the boy's eyes met his, and he set his cup down.

Quite suddenly, Salomon let himself topple forward, falling face-first toward the ground, where he caught himself in a push-up position. Santino mirrored the movement.

Salomon could not help but smile as he pressed himself up and down, one eye on his second child's second child as they moved through their practice. It would not last forever, he knew; he had already watched Coreen and Sao outgrow this stage, while two others - Coreen and Sao's younger sister, Leanna, and Santino's older sister, Tina - had never attached themselves to their grandfather as the others had. As for the grandchildren in other cities, their time together was too limited to fall into such a rhythm.

But that was all right; it would have been all right if none of them had ever joined him. In fact, it would have been expected, and Salomon was duly grateful that so many of his grandchildren had joined him in his morning rituals; after raising four children of his own, he did not underestimate how quickly life passed, how easily the years ran together, how rapidly childhoods disappeared.

And today?

Today, it could all disappear, if their plans did not succeed.

The kettle hissed. At the apex of his next pushup, Salomon launched himself up and pulled his feet forward, finishing in a standing position. He turned the stove off, poured the first round of boiling water over a cone of coffee grounds perched over a glass beaker, and continued his exercises, pausing intermittently to pour more water over the grounds.

Even the pouring was part of the exercise regimen; once the coffee was primed, Salomon balanced on one leg and pressed the sole of his raised foot to his inner thigh as he traced more water over the coffee. Santino did not have a kettle to hand, but he mirrored every aspect of the movements exactly, remaining silent all the while, a blend of yogi and mime.

Salomon's exercises concluded as the last of the coffee drained into the beaker. There was still a bit of boiling water left; Salomon poured it into the second wooden cup, added half a scoop of his wife's hot chocolate mix, and gave it a moment to cool before he handed it to Santino, chuckling at the way the boy's eyes widened in anticipation. Santino made a small sound of delight, then thanked his grandfather in a quiet voice, a bright smile on his face. If Salomon had not known that his grandchildren could cajole Eleanor into giving them a mug at any time of the day, he might have believed the cocoa was the real reason his grandchildren joined him in the morning routine.

Their reasons, of course, were not so simple; as such, Salomon did not devote much thought to wondering what moved his grandchildren. He could no more say what drove their desires than he could explain where their personalities came from; nor could he say why Santino, who would be sprinting around, shrieking and shouting, an hour from now, had never needed to be told to gentle his voice and movements during this morning routine.

Salomon pulled the beaker of coffee from beneath the grounds and poured the steaming contents into a mug, then extended his free hand to Santino. His grandson took it, and together, they stepped onto the porch, where they sat in the early dawn, sipping their hot drinks and staring at the moon.

As the sun started to peek up over the mountains, Salomon finished the last of his coffee and set the mug down. He stepped onto the mat that he kept on the deck and started a sequence of yoga postures.

Others might have skipped the routine on a day such as this, but Salomon felt that it was wiser to keep his mind present; it would be all too easy to allow thoughts of the day ahead to overwhelm his consciousness. Everything was ready; they had laid their plans over seasons, years. He could only overthink things now.

Once Santino finished his cocoa, he set his cup down and started to emulate his grandfather's movements on a small mat of his own, though his attention was starting to wander, and he did not mirror his grandfather as precisely as he had in the kitchen.

Still, Santino always stayed with his grandfather until the end of the practice, so he was there with Salomon when the young man appeared on the horizon. The world was fully lit by then, and Salomon and Santino could see the young man coming a long way off, though this hardly mattered; his arrival was anticipated.

The young man approached in silence; he had practiced yoga with Salomon on many occasions, and knew the old man was nearing the end of this particular set of postures. He could wait until then to speak.

Santino was not so patient. He uttered a war cry when the young man was a few yards from the deck, then he charged, little fists raised, bellowing "Anton" over and over, bursting into raucous laughter when the young man scooped him up and spun the two of them in a circle. When they were facing the porch again, Santino perched in the crook of Anton's arm, they found Salomon looking at them, hands clasped behind his back.

"Everything ready, Anton?"

The young man nodded, setting Santino down on the porch as he did.

Anton's blond hair was short, freshly cut. His face was clean-shaven, the bushy beard he had worn a day ago gone. Were it not for his eyes, his appearance might have been youthful; there were no shadows, no wrinkles, but something in the depths of Anton's hazel eyes, in the way they fell away to tunnels, spoke of immense age.

"Went smoother than I hoped. They don't know - no sign that's changed. I even made one last stop by the family house, as you insisted, and spoke to the old man. He knows I'm leaving, but he'll keep that between us; in any case, he thinks I'm going alone. Told him I'd rather adventure to whatever end than join him. He gets it, says he'd go with me if it weren't for the rest of the family. But no sign that he, or anyone else around him, has a clue that there is any sort of organized defection planned."

A curious expression appeared on Salomon's face at this point; Anton did not have to ask what it meant.

"I didn't see any of them. It's been more than a decade, so it wasn't worth getting into, especially since I've never met the new kid. Santino might like her though, she's about his age."

Santino's eyes lit up at the mention of his name; he smiled as he looked between his grandfather and Anton, hoping that the two men might tell him more. Instead, his grandfather turned toward him and sank down to his haunches. He beckoned, and Santino stepped toward him.

"Thank you for joining me, Santino. I enjoyed your company; it's kind of you to make sure your old grandpop isn't lonely in the morning. Can you go see if your grandmum is up? If she isn't awake yet, you can jump on the bed next to her."

Santino's grin stretched to his ears at his grandpop's last words; he darted around Salomon and shot through the open door into the house. When Salomon turned back to Anton, the young man had an eyebrow raised.

"Seems like a way to make sure you don't reach that fifty-fifth anniversary."

Salomon chuckled.

"Ah, that's where you're wrong. Eleanor will have me on my toes for weeks after this, and even if I'm looking out for it, she'll get me at some point. Nothing like taking a drink from your water after a long run and realizing someone dumped half a bag of salt in it. Adds a different element when your girlfriend bursts out laughing as soon as she sees your face contort at the taste."

Anton's smile was tinged with skepticism.

"Eleanor did that?"

"Oh ya. I deserved it - obviously - but that's a story for another time.

You checked that all of the guides are in place along the trail?"

"Last thing I did before I came here. The way is well marked; the guides will make sure we don't walk into anything blind."

Salomon nodded. Anton could see approval in the old man's placid green eyes, but that was nothing new; Salomon had relied on Anton for the better part of a decade now, and over the past year, they had rarely gone more than a day without speaking, unless one or the other was in the heights of the Cadillac Mountains.

"And your unit?"

"Ready to roll. I'll rejoin them as soon as we're done here."

"So we're off to a good start."

It was a statement, not a question, but Anton only shrugged.

"Won't matter much if things go sideways in an hour. I still say we should have sent part of the group ahead. Everyone who wouldn't have been missed. We're going to be shepherding quite the herd."

Salomon shook his head.

"We spent enough time discussing this before we made our decision. That sort of move might have been noticed, no matter who we sent ahead. There is little danger of that today; the rest of Kingston's population will have their attention captured by a very different sort of day. They won't notice our departure."

Anton frowned. His eyes were out in the distance, on the Cadillacs.

"I can't believe it's come to this. Through all our planning, all our preparations…on some level, I still harbored hope that the rest of Kingston would wake up in time. What do you think it will be like?"

Salomon shrugged.

"For us? Or for them?"

Anton laughed.

"Both."

Salomon smiled.

"For us? Challenging. Difficult. But if successful, ultimately satisfying. For them?"

Salomon paused, and for a moment, a great sadness filled his eyes.

"They are building a bridge to nowhere. Even if they succeed in their vision, what will they have built? Can you succeed if your aim is in conflict with your nature? Can you win if you play the wrong game?"

He shook his head.

"I think they would do well to slow down, to consider what they are hurtling toward, but they will not. The idea of an examined life is foreign to them. But I've said all of this before; it does not bear repeating."

"You never know. Maybe they're right. Why live an examined life when you could acquire stuff? Why live a life of uncertainty, when Knowledge allows for a world of certainty?"

Anton wore a wry smile on his face. Salomon gave a dry chuckle.

"Ah, of course. For we sentient beings have so much control over Nature. We aren't fragile beings on a rock orbiting a star as that star hurtles through space; Shurtain is the center of the universe, the sun revolves around us, and we have complete control of our destinies, the power to pass through this experience in total comfort."

Salomon shook his head again.

"As wiser beings than I have said, uncertainty is an uncomfortable position, but certainty is an absurd one."

Anton grinned.

"Eleanor is going to have those words carved on your headstone. I agree though, it's something else, everyone who believes that these Knowers can save them. Where do they think these all-knowing sentient beings came from? A few weeks ago, they were merely our neighbors. And why do they believe it should be possible to eliminate all the causes of suffering in the first place? As you're so fond of saying, even an exceptional sentient being is still a sentient being. We're not an omniscient species - we're not even close."

Salomon nodded; Anton continued.

"And the difficulties don't end there. Every thinker who has added something valuable to our stores of information has been mistaken about some other ideas; for Knowledge's sake, to use their words, even the sentient being who formalized special relativity failed to solve some of the problems he challenged himself with. The grains of wisdom that we've accumulated came as a result of painstaking trial and error, of pushing half-correct ideas against each other, not from a pre-ordained Knowledge of the Universe."

Salomon shrugged.

"History leaves no room for debate. But the majority will always find a way to believe that we are the exception, that while every other iteration of sentientkind has been an evolving entity, a work-in-progress, we, the sentient beings that exist in this moment, are the end product, the final, glorious result of this grand design. The lessons provided by history no longer apply, for the sentient beings of the past had an inexact understanding of Nature, and The Bubble Society has conquered that shortcoming. Their understanding of the cosmos is now exact; they have Knowledge, after all."

Salomon shrugged.

"You can understand why so many are eager to accept this notion, why they embrace it without question. Sentient beings want to be comfortable, they want to be safe, so they embrace the promises that these Knowers offer, no matter how preposterous, misguided, or inaccurate their so-called Knowledge might be."

"And remember, it didn't happen by accident. Those who grew up in the orthodoxy were carefully educated so that they would never raise questions. Count yourself fortunate; if you had lived the life that so many of them have lived, you might believe in the infallibility of the Knowers, and find yourself at the head of the line for a Bubble Suit today."

Anton turned up his palms in mock surrender.

"It always comes back to the same argument, doesn't it?"

Salomon ran a hand over the fringe of dark hair that remained on his balding head, a broad smile on his face.

"An old one, but difficult to defeat. Like me, I hope."

Anton smiled at that.

"I think you've got some time left. I'm counting on it - we need you to lead the way."

—

The way was up Onyx Canyon.

With so many on foot, the journey would be a long one, but that was not important today. Today, all that mattered was that they get beyond Mesa Outcrop, an overlook roughly five miles past Kingfisher Reservoir. The view from Mesa Outcrop provided a last glimpse of Kingston, way down in the valley below - or the first look, if you were descending rather than ascending - but most of the travelers did not look back at their former home as they passed the Outcrop. There were many miles ahead, and with thousands in tow, it was hardly a good time to pause for sight-seeing.

There were exceptions: a dozen who stood out on Mesa Outcrop, watching. From their perch, they could observe the progress of the pilgrimage as the people snaked their way up the trails.

More importantly, they could ensure that nobody followed them out of Kingston.

These dozen took pains to seem at their ease, attempting to make it appear that they were merely enjoying the day as the rest passed them. This had been planned for the sake of the young ones, though that hardly seemed necessary now; the children in the crowd were lively, running about when the trail was flat enough to permit it. They seemed to think this a jolly lark, a magical adventure, and saw no reason to concern themselves with the dozen standing watch on Mesa Outcrop.

That was a good thing, Anton thought, standing at the head of the dozen. It beat the hell out of a panicked flight. And it was an adventure, even if it might not turn out to be so magical.

As Anton watched the pilgrimage pass him by, he realized it was the adults, not the children, who they should have been worried about. They, at least, understood the gravity of the situation; many of them watched Anton's units with wide eyes as they passed, the presence of his dozen reminding the crowd that they were not yet clear of peril.

Salomon led the Rear Guard; as such, he was one of the last to reach

Mesa Outcrop. When he did, he indicated to his lieutenant that the rest of the unit should continue on, and broke off to speak with Anton.

Anton did not look up as Salomon approached; his attention was on a rectangular video screen, which played a feed of the action back in Kingston. His unit had used six of the tablets to monitor activity in the valley throughout the day, but the rest had been packed up as the Rear Guard approached.

Without a word, Anton handed Salomon the remaining tablet, then knelt down to where several rocks held a tarp in place and jerked the cover free, revealing a cache of weapons. With the tarp clear, Anton and the rest of his unit began to collect their weapons and break them down.

Salomon addressed Anton without taking his eyes off the screen; similarly, Anton continued his task as they spoke.

"Any surprises?"

"Not a one," answered Anton. "Ceremonies started at noon, just as they planned. It's all recorded; you can rewind, go back to where The Guvna' gets the day started."

Several sets of eyes flicked uneasily in Anton's direction at the mention of The Guvna', but Salomon's were not among them. He followed the younger man's suggestion and rewound the broadcast to the beginning.

The Advent had opened with theatrics: a fireworks show, accompanied by a thick fog that engulfed the stage beneath the pyrotechnics. When the fog cleared, The Guvna' stood at a podium, flanked by ten of Kingston's most infirm citizens. All ten of these sentient beings either leaned on walkers or sat in wheelchairs; it was obvious to anyone who glanced at them that these ten were at death's door.

"People o' Kingston," started The Guvna', his voice amplified by the microphone, "Welcome to da first day o' da rest o' yer lives! Y'all Know why we're here; without further ado, let's step into da future!"

At The Guvna's words, a delegation of Knowers walked onto the stage, waving and smiling, drawing roars from the crowd. A herd of maintenance technicians followed close on their heels, each of them carrying a Bubble Suit. The crowd's fervor picked up at the appearance of the Bubble Suits; it was the first time that the citizuns of The Bubble Society were getting to see the miraculous technology that Knowledge had granted them.

They gasped.

They shrieked.

They hooted in delight.

The sounds died away as the technicians approached the ten, Bubble Suits in hand. The crowd waited in hushed apprehension as the technicians helped the ten frail individuals into their Suits; this did not prove to be a particularly dignified exercise, especially for those in wheelchairs, but they got it done in the end.

Once the process was complete, the technicians stepped back, and the

Knowers stepped forward to examine each of the patients. When they had confirmed that the Bubble Suits were correctly in place, the Knowers nodded to the technicians.

As the Knowers stepped out of the way, the technicians stepped forward, each of them drawing a wand from a holster on their belts.

The crowd held its collective breath.

The technicians sealed the Bubble Suits.

They holstered their wands, then motioned for the Knowers to rejoin them. As they did, The Guvna' stepped back to the microphone.

"For da last years o' der lives, 'til dey reach da age o' one hundred, dez sentient beings won't hafta wurry 'bout sickness, nor da uncertainty o' death! Dey will have years o' peace ta enjoy da utopian society we're building here, dis Bubble Society o' ours, and not only dat, dey get ta enjoy it in style, moving 'round Shurtain in ways dey believed was lost to 'em!"

The Guvna' turned to the Head Knower, who stood off to the side, overseeing his team's work. After exchanging silent glances with each of them, the Head Knower looked at the Guvna' and nodded.

The Guvna' turned back to the microphone.

"Alright, let's show every'un what it's 'bout!"

The ten in the Bubble Suits exchanged quick glances, their fears that it might all be too good to be true evident on their faces; then, as one, they started to move, releasing their walkers, stepping out of their wheelchairs.

The ten sentient beings, who had all required support to stay upright moments earlier, did not fall. They stood tall and proud; then, giving the mute crowd what they were waiting for, a few of them started to walk around the stage.

They moved without issue.

The individuals in the Bubble Suits appeared as stunned as anyone. The Guvernment had leaked selective rumors about the Bubble Suits, and those had spread like wildfire, but the miraculous claims had seemed too good to be true. How could these Bubble Suits eliminate the need for walkers and wheelchairs? How could they take over the physical body's role of moving a sentient being through the world? How could they eliminate disease, or guarantee lifespan?

But as the people stood there, staring at the ten previously infirm individuals moving around on the stage, even the most incredible dreams seemed possible.

As the crowd stood watching, too stunned to make a sound, General Bill Hitchcock, one of the ten who had donned a Bubble Suit, stepped to the front of the stage. Hitchcock, a decorated veteran of the Old War, was as recognizable a sentient being as there was in Kingston, though in recent years, his heavy lean on his walker had become as ubiquitous as his silver mutton chops.

That heavy lean was gone now; Hitchcock stood stock straight as he approached center stage.

For a moment, he stood still.

Then, with a wild look in his eyes, Hitchcock raised his fist in the air.

The crowd's roar was immediate and deafening; the sense of wonder had burst, replaced by unbridled exuberance at what they were witnessing.

The Bubble Suits that Knowledge had delivered to them were nothing short of a miracle. But as raucous as their reaction to Hitchcock had been, it was nothing to the fever pitch that the crowd reached a moment later, when The Guvna's family joined him on the stage.

While The Guvna' had ultimately insisted that Kingston's most infirm be the first to don the Bubble Suits, it had been a hard-fought debate. Many, both in the Guvernment and in the public at large, would have preferred that the decision had gone the other way; after all, the people of Kingston were attached to Andrea, The Guvna's oldest daughter, who had become the poster child for the Bubble Suit movement over the past few years.

Andrea was not the only sentient being to suffer from the unexplained diseases that had spread through the population in recent years. Nor was she the only child to be stricken with these illnesses - far from it - but because of her father's position as The Guvna', Andrea was a publicly visible figure, and her case had drawn a sympathy that bordered on obsessive; she was a constant reminder of all that sentient beings had to lose.

The crowd's excitement peaked as The Guvna' gathered behind Andrea with his wife, Kelli, and his two younger daughters, Rachel and Tesla. The Head Knower stepped in this time, overseeing the process as a technician helped Andrea into her Bubble Suit.

This time, the technician handed his wand to The Guvna'. His face full of emotion, The Guvna' held out the wand so that his wife could put her hand over his.

Together, they sealed Andrea into her Bubble Suit.

When the girl stood, the crowd erupted all over again; their excitement was such that it was difficult for The Guvna', even with the assistance of the speaker system, to make himself heard. Once he calmed the crowd down sufficiently, he announced that the people of Kingston should report to their pre-assigned Bubble Suit distribution locations; in a few hours, once all the newly branded citizuns of The Bubble Society were suited up, they could return to Capitol Square to safely celebrate The Advent in all its glory.

In the present, that celebration was upon them; even as Salomon finished watching the replay, fireworks went off in the distance. As he watched them shower Kingston in a cloud of falling stars, he knew it was done.

The Bubble Society had come into being.

BOOK 2, CHAPTER 2

Twenty-one years had passed since the Last Day, but the path from Kingfisher Reservoir to Mesa Outcrop remained largely unchanged. Indeed, the night sky itself was similar; Shurtain's two moons, Shylan and Aphrodite, were in similar spots as the canvas of purples and blues shifted to inky darkness.

The old man would know; he had been there, after all, tagging along with Salomon and the Rear Guard, one of thousands of newly-christened Acadians on their way into the Cadillac Mountains.

Twenty-one years later, and the old man was one of two, the young man at his side a far cry from the young men who had left Kingston on the day of the Advent.

After two decades of relying on a Bubble Suit, Gavin's body was ill-equipped to move without it; his posture was stooped, his balance poor, his stumbles regular. The old man did not blame Gavin - the boy had no say in his development, had not chosen to grow up in The Bubble Society - but the old man withholding judgment did not cause Gavin to move any better, or make their present situation any less dangerous. The old man was not surprised by Gavin's physical state - he had anticipated it, to some degree - but he had planned to cut Gavin free of his Bubble Suit higher in the Cadillac Mountains, closer to the Elevation Limit. Once they crossed that boundary, they would be in the clear, and could proceed at whatever pace Gavin's body could handle.

But they were not clear of the Elevation Limit.

And at Gavin's present pace, they were not going to get there anytime soon.

Broad, flat stones had been laid as steps along the steeper stretches of the trail, but most of the ascent was loose dirt and gravel, which made the going more difficult. The trail twisted and turned, passing under trees, over creeks, around boulders, always climbing; in the eerie silence of the wood, Gavin could almost imagine they would pass through some glimmering sheet, a doorway out of Shurtain into another world, a world where sentient beings could live without Bubble Suits.

Nothing of the sort happened, but they did reach a ledge that provided a spectacular view of Kingfisher Reservoir, as well as a distant glimpse of the city of Kingston and its twinkling lights.

Gavin did not know the name of the place, but he was standing on Mesa Outcrop, in almost the same place that Salomon Cahn had taken his final look at Kingston on The Last Day.

"Can we take a break? Please?"

Gavin's words came between labored breaths.

The old man shook his head.

"Soon. But not here. We need to get higher, to an elevation above the functional range of the Bubble Suits, before…"

The old man trailed off. His eyes had fixed on something in the distance, but when Gavin tried to follow his gaze, all he saw was the distant reservoir, and the seemingly still night.

"Wha…"

"Ssh."

Gavin's pulse quickened.

"You hear it?"

Gavin glanced around.

"Hear what?"

The old man did not answer. His eyes were darting about, taking in things that Gavin could not see.

"We need to move. Hurry."

Gavin stumbled after the old man. His body had felt ungainly from the start; now, as he tried to push it harder, he was hit with an onslaught of unpleasant physical sensations: his lungs seared, his legs burned, his entire body wailed in protest.

Gavin ignored it all, and kept his eyes on the old man's back, intent on catching back up to him. The trail, which had taken them out in the open as they passed Mesa Outcrop, dove back into the trees, on a course for the heart of the Cadillac Mountains.

A few yards ahead, at the base of a bluff, the old man made his move; he took two hard steps and launched himself to the top of the rock wall, catching the top of the ledge with his right hand. Nimble as a monkey, the old man found footholds and scrambled over the edge.

His disappearance was short-lived; an instant after his feet vanished, the old man was back, leaning out over the edge, reaching for Gavin with his right hand and holding himself to an anchor point up on the ledge with his left.

"Reach up, and take my hand. Quickly."

Gavin started to reach. Then he heard the sounds, and froze.

There were footsteps.

Voices.

People coming their way.

And, faint in the distance, the whir of a helicopter.

Memories of Kingston Hospital flooded Gavin's mind. He wanted to run, to dart into the trees, but when he tried, he found himself paralyzed, rooted to the spot by panic.

"Reach up, now. You have to move - they'll kill you."

The last words prodded Gavin into action; he reached for the old man, who grasped Gavin's wrist and yanked him over the edge with surprising ease. Once Gavin was up, he saw that there was a shallow cave worn into the rock wall that bounded the ledge; he and the old man shuffled into it, to a spot where they could see, but not be seen by, their pursuers.

They were a party of four, all of them using the built-in flashlights in the wrists of their Bubble Suits to light the way along the trail. All four were focused on the ground lit by their flashlights; they did not spare so much as a glance at anything above them.

After the foursome disappeared around a bend in the trail, the spotlight of a helicopter appeared in the darkening sky. Its sudden appearance stopped Gavin's heart, but when he turned to get a better look, he realized the chopper was miles away, lighting up the slope on a different part of the mountain.

"Well, not quite how I planned it, but we should still get out all right in the end. Lucky it was the night of The Advent; I'd thought they'd be on us a lot quicker than that."

Gavin turned to look at the old man.

"How long are we going to wait here?"

The old man shrugged.

"Until those four come back. It won't be long; this trail ends in a dried-up waterfall, and unless you know the way, you wouldn't guess that anyone could climb out, especially if you've spent twenty years living with the limitations of the Bubble Suits. They'll be back sooner than later."

The old man sat down and leaned against the cave wall; Gavin watched him, a wary expression on his face.

"Why are they following us?"

The old man stared at Gavin from behind his long grey beard, a bemused expression on his face.

"Not too quick, are you? There was a Bubble Suit breach - what did you think would happen?"

Gavin reddened slightly.

"Ya, well, it's hard to think right now. There's a lot going on."

The old man did not respond. Gavin stared at him, taking in his appearance once again, noting the frenzied energy behind his brown eyes, how it seemed to pulse even as they sat in the cave.

"Who are you, anyways?"

The old man shook his head, then pressed a finger to his lips. Gavin understood why; he could hear the voices returning.

"There's no way he went any further. We found the Bubble Suit down near Kingfisher, didn't we? This whole search is pointless - he's drowned and sunk to the bottom of the lake, mark my words."

"But Wes, we have orders, and…"

"That's Captain to you, Officer Conley. If you're going to undermine my decisions, you could at least do me the courtesy of addressing me by my title."

The man said this in a half-jesting voice, one that invited the woman to continue.

"You're the one undermining decisions, *Captain*."

The man chuckled at the woman's retort.

"Look, Maya, if you want to go rooting around in the dark, be my guest. I'm not wasting my time, and as long as none of us goes ratting out the others, there's no way for anyone to know where we did or didn't search, because there isn't anything to find. If we start back for Kingston now, we might get there in time to rejoin the celebrations."

The search party's discussion fell out of Gavin's hearing as they continued down the trail. For a time, the old man did not move; instead, he sat watching the distant helicopter, breathing in a soft, rhythmic pattern.

"Ready?"

The question startled Gavin, who had fallen into a lethargy, but he nodded once he processed the old man's question. The old man stood and offered Gavin a hand; the young man bit back a groan as the old man pulled him to his feet.

"We'll follow the ridge for a bit. There's a spot up ahead with an easier way down."

The ridge was a tangle of stones and branches. This was no problem for the old man, who picked his way along the path with ease, moving lightly from one foot to the other, but Gavin's clumsy movements were hazardous on this terrain; he used tree branches to help his balance where he could, and crouched down on all fours to guard against falls when there were no branches, but that did little to loosen the knot of anxiety in his gut. The way was exhausting, and Gavin felt a great sense of relief when he saw the old man stop and turn to the edge.

"There is a sort of ladder cut into this chimney. It's a short climb down to the trail."

The old man crouched down and swung himself over the ledge. Gavin followed more cautiously, sliding along on his backside until he was at the edge, where he turned over on his belly. Unwilling to look down, he fished along the rock face with his feet until he found the first jagged step in the ladder. Gavin let himself glance around then, and found the old man staring up at him, his lips twitching as if suppressing a laugh. Ignoring this, Gavin turned his attention back to the ladder and made his way down the five rungs to the ground.

From there, it did not take long to reach the end of the trail; when they did, Gavin understood why their pursuers had given up. They were facing the dried-up waterfall the old man had alluded to earlier; as the old man had indicated, there did not appear to be a way up. A chimney was carved out where the waterfall had once flowed, but the walls were polished smooth. Even after seeing the old man scramble up to the rock ledge, Gavin doubted whether anyone could climb this wall without sliding back down.

"I'm going up. I'll pull you to the top after; wait here."

Gavin started to object, but before he could say anything, the old man was scrabbling up the face of the wall, his hands and feet deftly catching creases invisible to Gavin's eyes. He was over the top in short order, and a moment later, a coil of rope sailed back down, the bundle landing hard in the dirt next to Gavin.

As he stared down at the coil, Gavin knew, without question, that the old man must have had all of this prepared. His suspicion mounting, he took hold of the coarse weave with both hands.

"Tie it around your waist first. I wouldn't trust your grip yet."

Gavin did not bother to look up at the old man, but he did obey his words, tying a crude harness around his hips and groin before gripping the rope with both hands and bracing himself. A tug came, the rope grew taut, and then it began to pull Gavin up and over the edge of the cliff.

The knots Gavin had tied to construct the harness were sloppy, but they held; as he approached the wall, Gavin stuck a foot out to keep himself off the cliff face, and without planning it, found himself walking up the wall, his hands tight around the rope to keep his torso from falling back to the ground.

As he made the ascent, his body parallel to the ground below, Gavin felt, to his great surprise, the tension of the pursuit dissolving, passing out of his body into the night sky. Part of him insisted, in rather loud tones, that he should be consumed by terror, but Gavin ignored those thoughts, preferring to lose himself in the experience, enjoying himself so much that he found he was smiling by the time he reached the top of the waterfall.

Then he was over the edge; the sight of the old man cut through his sense of elation, bringing all his suspicions rushing back to top of mind.

Neither of them said anything as Gavin tried to untie the harness, a process that went rather poorly. Gavin felt his face growing red as he attempted to disentangle himself; when he finally gave up on untying the knots and tried to jerk the whole harness down, it caught around his hips, causing him to lose his balance and fall flat on his ass.

"Easy there, easy there."

He felt the old man's hand on his shoulder, saw the knife in his free hand. The blade sliced deftly through the ropes at several spots; when the old man straightened up, Gavin was free.

Face glowing, Gavin got back to his feet, dusted off his new clothes, and looked the old man directly in the face. He did not thank him for cutting him loose.

"Who are you? Why are you doing this?"

The old man frowned.

"When you jumped off the cliff, I figured you were showing the world what you wanted. I thought you deserved some help getting there."

Gavin considered the explanation and found it wanting. He frowned and shook his head.

"That doesn't explain it. Why are you so interested in me? Why are you taking this risk?"

Then, as the old man looked at him with those brown eyes, Gavin realized that he had seen two sets of eyes very similar to them, and knew, without thinking, where he had seen them before.

One of the two pairs had been dull and lifeless for years. The other pair, he only saw in the mirror.

The old man shrugged, a grin appearing on his face as he watched Gavin putting it together.

"You're my blood. My niece's son, and the last of our family's line. I thought, if you wanted to escape, that you deserved that chance."

BOOK 2, CHAPTER 3

A volley of fireworks went off over Kingston Amphitheater as Tesla sped clear of Onyx Canyon. She grinned at the sight; she had made better time than she hoped.

The Stone Bridge was the first crossing of the Grand River south of Onyx Canyon, a massive structure with foundations that reached the depths of the riverbank; wide slits were carved into the granite to allow the river a frothing passage beneath. Tesla made a hard right when she reached the bridge, revving the bike's motor and leaning into the turn until her right leg skimmed the asphalt. It was unwise to attempt such a risky maneuver, especially when she was pressed for time; Tesla knew that, but she was having a difficult time burning off her frustration, and she knew she needed to compose herself by the time she reached her destination.

She followed the Stone Bridge west across the Grand River, keeping to the main roadway, which was empty aside from herself, Once she was across the Stone Bridge, at the point where the road became the Northern Corridor, Tesla swerved suddenly to the right, popping her bike's phat tires up the curb onto the sidewalk; an instant later, she corrected course, straightening her bike out and proceeding on the walkway for fifty feet or so, until she turned hard onto another pathway that took her into The Guvna's Park.

The spiraling concrete pathway descended on a steep grade, depositing Tesla in the park grounds just west of the Grand River. A mile later, the path split into three forks: one that went west, parallel to the Northern Corridor, another that went northwest, directly toward Capitol Square, and a third that ran along the banks of the Grand River on as north a course as was possible, given the river's curve.

Tesla took the rightmost path, the one that ran north along the river. Had she followed the route to its end, it would have taken her to a point where a large platform offered Kingston's citizuns a spectacular view of the point where the Grand River surged out of Onyx Canyon in a wash of white froth.

However, Tesla was not going that far tonight; she was not interested in sight-seeing. Her eyes darted around the hilly terrain, ensuring that she was alone, that she had not stumbled across any wayward citizuns, or worse, been followed.

When she was certain that nobody else was in the vicinity, Tesla dismounted, and with a tremendous force of effort, forced her Bubble Suit to lift her bike over her shoulder. She ignored the shrill beeps that went off in her ear as she stepped off the sidewalk, making for the trees.

Tesla did not have to carry the bike far; once she was beyond the first stretch of trees, she set her ride down, no longer worried about tracks. The shrill beeping ceased as soon as the bike was back on the ground; mouthing a silent prayer of thanks, Tesla re-mounted her bike and re-engaged the throttle.

As she moved forward, Tesla sensed a familiar frustration bubbling to the surface; it irritated her to no end that the premier Bubble Suit innovators had failed to develop a satisfactory "enhanced strength" mode, even though that feature had been near the top of the Guvernment's priority list for decades. Tesla was only one girl halfway through her graduate studies, and her own efforts on that front were miles ahead of the industry's best efforts.

But miles ahead did not mean she had anything to deploy, so until Tesla finished that particular project, she would have to deal with the Bubble Suit's warning signals, which went off whenever a sentient being engaged in an action that could cause system failure in the Bubble Suits; in this case, it had gone off because the Bubble Suits were not designed to carry external loads. Kingston's citizuns were regularly reminded that they should cease all activity at the sound of the alarm, but Tesla knew better; she had done the calculations, and knew that, in the case of the bike, her Bubble Suit would allow her to carry the extra load for two minutes and sixteen seconds before she was truly at risk of any system failures.

Tesla wound her way up the hill, snaking back and forth, keeping to the most favorable terrain, slowly but surely drawing closer to The Old Capitol. She continued that way until she reached a massive boulder, a slab of rock at least three times her height that stood on a section of the hill that had been leveled off to flat ground. It was obvious that this had been done by sentient beings - Tesla knew nothing in Nature could have sheered off the straight drop from the natural slope of the hill down to the leveled portion - though she could not imagine how they had gotten the rock, which was closer to a hill of its own than a mere boulder, into place.

Tesla dismounted. Bushes had grown up in the gap between the boulder and the sheer wall; Tesla made her way to a spot where there was some give, then pushed her bike through the foliage until she reached the back of the formation.

There, hidden from view, a steel door was built into the side of the hill. Tesla glanced at the digital clock in the corner of her holographic monitor; noting that she still had fifteen minutes, she tapped on her wrist panel to shut off the clock, then punched several more commands into the panel to engage her Bubble Suit's night-vision setting. When the world turned green around her, Tesla pushed the door inward; it swung smoothly on its hinges. She grinned, remembering the horrible screech it had made the first time she had opened it, back before she had oiled the hinges.

Tesla pushed her bike through and pulled the door shut behind her. There was a small alcove to her right; as usual, she stood the bike up there, then continued down the pitch-black tunnel.

The first few years she had used this passage, Tesla had used her Bubble Suit's built-in flashlight to find her way, but she had never liked having her vision restricted to that narrow spotlight. These gloomy passages were not the place for it; the hallways were the sort of place where the imagination could get the best of someone, even someone like Tesla. She hated the sense that something might leap at her out of the dark, which had made downloading the night-vision software package a powerful temptation once she discovered its existence.

In retrospect, her hesitance to download the software to her Bubble Suit seemed laughable; Tesla had assumed that the security around military-grade software would be top-notch, but nothing could have been further from the truth. The upgrades were not even password-protected; apparently, nobody at Dynamic Solutions, or in the Guvernment, had considered the possibility that anyone would think to acquire such upgrades outside of the usual protocols.

Once she got past her initial shock, however, Tesla decided that this was not particularly surprising; she had been eleven at the time, old enough to have seen enough of life in Kingston to understand that such oversights were typical of the city's apathetic workforce. There was always some possibility of discovery - the night-vision software was installed on her Bubble Suit's operating system, after all - but the eleven-year-old Tesla had concluded that there was not much reason for concern.

She had been right not to worry; fifteen years had passed since Tesla downloaded the night-vision package, and she had never heard a peep about it, nor about any of the other restricted packages that she downloaded from The Bubble Suit repository over the years. The only disappointment, once Tesla had installed the night-vision package, was that there was nothing to see in the hallways; her imagination in the dark, shadowy places had been just that: imagination.

Tonight was the same; the first hallway was empty, and Tesla crossed to the door at the far end without issue. She pulled that door open and stepped into another dark room.

She was in the basement of The Old Capitol now; it had been officially replaced with The New Capitol on the day of the Advent, which Kingston's leaders had determined was an apt occasion to replace the outdated architecture of The Old Capitol with modern construction. The Old Capitol was spared, left standing next to The New; in another age, or another place, the building might have remained so that people could appreciate the beauty of the dated architecture, but that was not the case in The Bubble Society. Instead, the old edifice was allowed to fall into disrepair, left standing as a reminder of how much better off sentient beings were thanks to the grace of Knowledge, of the great improvements they had made to create the utopia that was The Bubble Society. It was also a reminder of the foolish tastes of the sentient beings of the past, who had wasted time and resources on useless decorations when they could have been striving for efficiency; after all, any sentient being with half their wits could see that The Old Capitol did not need its great spires, and that it had been a wasted effort to paint such spectacular murals on the ceiling when a sentient being could simply call up a picture of a painting on their holographic monitor and overlay it on their display.

And so The Old Capitol had fallen into disrepair; the main floors remained open for tours, but the basement, and sub-basements, had fallen out of use, left totally abandoned.

Or they had been, until Tesla moved in.

The way in had been easy enough to find; Capitol Square had become Tesla's backyard roughly two seasons before the Advent, when her father and the rest of the family had moved into The Guvna's Mansion. By that time, Tesla was old enough that her mother's attention had refocused almost entirely on her sickly elder sister, while her father's new role as The Guvna' left him little time to monitor what his youngest daughter was up to.

For a young girl with a dangerously active imagination, it was a dream come true.

Guvernment Officials, who might have been called servants in a less enlightened age, were set to keep an eye on her, but Tesla was well up to outwitting them; she could escape her minders whenever she liked, which freed her up to explore Kingston to her heart's content.

And what places there were to explore, now that they lived in Capitol Square.

The Guvna's Park, which surrounded Capitol Square: rolling miles of green that stretched to the Grand River in the northeast and the Cadillac Mountains in the north.

Kingston Amphitheater, which had stood even longer than The Old Capitol.

The Old Capitol, and its basements, and sub-basements, and the tunnels that connected it all.

The New Capitol, which stood to the north of The Old.

And next to The New Capitol, The Guvna's Mansion, with all of its secret entries and exits, which were by no means the same.

Tesla was not thinking of any of that at the moment, however; she was on a tight schedule, and had to move quickly through the bowels of The Old Capitol.

Her footsteps took her to the far side of the building; she was now directly beneath the main entrance. Were she two floors up, on the ground level, she would have been looking out the open front doors of The Old Capitol, to where Kingston Amphitheater stood on the other side of Capitol Square.

However, while Kingston Amphitheater was Tesla's ultimate destination, her way was down, not up. She knelt, grasped an iron ring in the floor, and pulled a trap door open.

A circular hole in the floor awaited: in the gloom, it was difficult to see the eighth of an inch of ladder that extended over the lip, but Tesla's night-vision made it easy for her to find the steel rungs and begin her descent. When she reached the bottom and stepped back onto solid ground, Tesla grabbed a rope pull and yanked on it. The rope, which was strung through a system of pulleys, snapped the trap door shut above her.

With the trap back in place, Tesla turned away from the ladder. Once again, she found herself at the end of a long tunnel; this one was lined with stone, as silent as the last, yet the energy here was different, far more still, silent as the tomb.

Tesla knew the reason for this; at the moment, she did not have time to examine the painted walls, or to look into either of the holding cells that stood to her right and left, but it had not taken a genius to figure out what this tunnel had been used for, back when Kingston Amphitheater was the greatest structure on the Acadian continent, back when it had been known as Kingston Coliseum.

Tesla whispered a few words, paying her respects to the doomed souls who had stood in this place, waiting to meet their fate. Once she had said her words, she crossed to the far end of the hall; when she reached the door, she paused and tapped on her wrist panel again, putting in the commands that would shut down her night vision.

For this, she needed a more natural light.

Tesla tapped a few more buttons on her wrist panel. A white orb came to life on the shoulder of her Bubble Suit, lighting up the door, the small alcove to the side of it, and the mirror that stood waiting there.

The customized version of the Bubble Suit's flashlight software was another feature Tesla had added to her suit, though she had developed this software herself rather than illicitly downloading it; the standard Bubble Suit came with a generic flashlight that allowed sentient beings to shine narrow beams of light from the bulb under their right wrist, but while that did a good job of mimicking the hand-held flashlights of old, it was not much use to Tesla when she needed her hands free.

Tesla turned her attention back to the mirror, which seemed entirely out of place in the tunnel. It was not ornate by any means; rather, it was an unframed rectangle that stood propped against the wall, almost as if it had been left there by accident.

Or at least, Tesla hoped that was what it looked like; as far as she could tell, she was the only one who had entered these tunnels since The Advent, but if anyone ever stumbled across the mirror, Tesla did not want it to look as if anyone were actively using the place.

Tesla positioned herself in front of the mirror and glanced at her appearance, then reached to the control panel on her left wrist to tap in more commands. In the blink of an eye, Tesla's blacks were replaced by the lavender evening gown she had worn earlier that night, when she walked out of The Guvna's Mansion at her father's side, proceeding along the red carpet that had been laid out across Capitol Square for the family to make their way from The Guvna's Mansion to Kingston Coliseum in style.

That had been several hours ago, well before the festivities at Capitol Square were open to the public. Once inside, Tesla was able to excuse herself from The Guvna's Box under the pretense that she wanted to celebrate The Advent with her friends, but she was expected to be back at her father's side for the Closing Ceremonies at the end of the night.

Another series of taps, and the imitation grease she had smeared across her cheeks was replaced by blush, eyeshadow, and red lipstick. A moment later, her skull cap disappeared and her blond locks fell loose, her Bubble Suit shifting to accommodate her curls as they tumbled to her shoulders.

Tesla looked at herself critically, appraising the effect. She looked the perfect portrait of a debutante, she thought, and could not help but roll her eyes at that. She stuck her tongue out at herself and laughed as she shut off her flashlight, plunging herself into total darkness.

Standing in the dark, Tesla tapped her right temple to bring up her holographic monitor. She navigated to the portal she needed; as always, she felt a sense of frustration at the way her connection lagged in the tunnel, but despite that delay, it was less than a minute before she had accessed Kingston Amphitheater's security system. Tesla ran her eyes over a series of video feeds, then tapped her temple again.

The security camera feeds were replaced by a view of a dark, monitor-filled room: the same room that Tesla had checked in on from Kingfisher Reservoir. She zoomed in on the left-most computer, then brought the text on the bottom half of the document into greater resolution; once she could read the text, she zeroed in on one of the access codes she had not used that night. A tap of her wrist later and Tesla was back on the security screen, entering the credentials. Once authenticated, she navigated to the surveillance controls, disabled the camera outside the doorway, and logged out.

The clock in her head started to tick. It was not urgent - there was no need to hurry - but Tesla did need to move efficiently, or the auto-reset would kick the security camera back on before she was clear of its frame. Tesla tapped on her temple to shut down her holographic monitor, then pushed through the door into the disused storeroom beyond. The room was cluttered, but Tesla knew the way well; she picked her way through the shadows to the far end of the room with practiced ease and climbed four flights of stairs to a doorway. She emerged in the night air at the juncture of a switchback ramp between the first and second levels of Kingston Amphitheater, the disabled camera directly above her.

Tesla moved swiftly as she strode through its frame; once she was clear, she slowed to a more relaxed pace for the rest of her ascent to The Guvna's Box. Upon reaching the Box, she nodded politely to the two men who stood on either side of the suite's double doors. They returned her nod, and the one on the right pulled the door open for her.

The Guvna's Box was well-appointed, a roomy suite with two rows of seating in front and a full bar in the rear, though nobody was taking advantage of the comforts at the moment; they were all on their feet, gathering around The Guvna' as they prepared to make their exit. The man himself beamed when his youngest daughter appeared.

"Now 'en, just as I was startin' to wurry, here she is. Cutting it awful fine, 'lil lady."

The Guvna' smiled as he said this; Tesla returned the smile, then glanced beyond her father to where her middle sister stood. She tried to meet Rachel's eyes, but Rachel looked furtively away in the direction of their mother, who had a firm hold on their older sister, Andrea.

Without saying a word to the others, Tesla fell in at her father's side, her eyes twinkling up at him.

"C'mon, Guvna', you don't actually need me. I didn't want to leave my friends, I was having fun."

The Guvna' chuckled at that.

"Don't need'ya? Tesla, can'cha see how worn down yer old man's looking these days? If I dinnit have ya at my side ta take da 'ttention, there'd be whispers in da streets 'bout how Da Guvna's gunna drop dead, dat he'll be da first in da history o' Da Bubble Society who fails ta live ta one hundred."

His eyes were playful as he said this. It was far from the truth - her father was as handsome as he had ever been, even if he looked a bit more distinguished than he had in his younger years - and Tesla could not help but smile. Then, almost involuntarily, she looked over her shoulder, to where her mother and sisters trailed behind them. When she turned back, her father was looking at her, a sad smile on his face.

"Don'cha worry 'bout dem tonight. Tell me, who's dis every'un you been celebrating with?"

His voice was cheerful enough as he said it, but Tesla noticed that the gleam in his eyes had gone, that his gaze had turned circumspect. She smiled as she answered, injecting as much cheer into her voice as she could muster.

"His name's Derek, Daddy. That's ok, right? I mean, you're not expecting me to live at home forever?"

The Guvna' shook his head.

"Course not. It's good ta hear; terrific, in fact. Now, let's go get dis damn 'nouncement taken care of. Den you can get back ta yer fun, and I can get my ol' ass ta bed."

BOOK 2, CHAPTER 4

"Up and at 'em. Time to get going."

Gavin came to at the sound of the voice; when he opened his eyes, he found the world was still dark.

Stiff and sore, he wished he could have laid there longer, but he pushed himself up to an arm.

"Why are we getting up so early?"

The old man did not answer. Gavin glanced around and realized that he was not there; he must have gone to retrieve their mounts.

But he was not just the old man anymore.

His name was Clarence Barnett.

And he was Gavin's great-uncle.

—

Clarence's pronouncement had hung heavy in the air. It took Gavin a moment to find his voice.

"You're what?"

"Your great-uncle. Your mother, Amelia, is my niece. Name's Clarence - Clarence Barnett."

The old man extended his hand. Gavin reached for it, feeling dizzy.

His great-uncle.

This old man, who did not wear a Bubble Suit, was his great-uncle.

The world started to spin as Gavin's hand moved toward his great-uncle's; he thought that if he could just grasp it, then the world would right itself, but when the warmth of the old man's flesh met his own, wild thoughts smashed into his consciousness, making things even more unsteady.

None of this was real.

The old man could not be real.

Gavin had been out of his Bubble Suit for more than an hour now, and that could not be real.

He should already be dead.

It was impossible that he was not dead.

Because if he was not dead, then everything he had ever learned, everything he had ever been taught to think, the underlying beliefs that informed The Bubble Society's structure and purpose, were abject nonsense, complete bulls…

Gavin started to fall; dazed as he was, he barely registered it when he started to stumble, but Clarence caught him by the shoulders and guided him to the ground.

When the sensation passed, Gavin found himself in a seated position, the taste of water fresh in his mouth. He realized that he must have blacked out again; his mind felt foggy, and his thoughts had a different weight to them, an almost fuzzy feel as they passed through his consciousness.

It was as if he were seeing the world for the first time; on this side of the blackout, or whatever it had been, Gavin observed the absence of his Bubble Suit with a calm indifference.

He knew that he had not been wearing a Bubble Suit for more than an hour.

And he knew that nothing bad had happened.

He did not have a certificate to verify this observation, no written guarantee that this was Knowledge, no permission from the gatekeepers.

Yet he knew it all the same.

Gavin took a deep breath. He let the air out, and took the sound of his exhale as confirmation that he was still here, still alive, still having an experience.

Whatever life was, he still seemed to be living it.

He turned his bare hands over slowly, staring at them as he let these new thoughts wash over him.

It was real.

He was out of his Bubble Suit. And alive.

Having that conscious thought triggered another violent reaction in his being; all the old beliefs were suddenly on the horizon, preparing to swarm his being and reconquer the headspace that had once been theirs. Gavin felt his body tense as he registered the incoming thoughts, but he did not black out this time; without knowing why, he took the deepest breath he could and held it. And to his surprise, he found that as he expelled the exhale, he felt a deep sense of control; ready, he turned the full weight of his attention on the thoughts massing at the edge of his consciousness.

Somewhere in his mind, the old tenets shattered, broke apart as the ground they stood on collapsed in on itself. Gavin could see the end of the confrontation playing out as clearly as if it had been happening in the physical world around him; his newly freed consciousness sprang, transforming itself, adapting for battle, crashing down on the enemy's army like a wave on a sandcastle.

When the wave receded, there was nothing left but smooth ground. The foundations, the materials, the very ground that Gavin's belief system had stood on had washed away, leaving fertile, virgin land in its place. Those ideas that had massed at the gate, which had stood up so convincingly in their protected environment of theory and controlled experiment, could not survive in the face of Nature.

The old man's weathered hand appeared in front of Gavin's face. Gavin took it; his great-uncle pulled him to his feet.

"Sorry," Gavin muttered.

"Not a problem; it's a lot to take in. You all right?"

Gavin nodded.

"Well, let's keep moving then. Should help you shake this off, and it's only a mile or so to the Elevation Limit; I tied our mounts up just beyond there."

The mounts turned out to be a pair of big-horned sheep. The rams were imposing in their own right, and would have prompted caution from any sentient being, but for Gavin, who had never seen more than a picture of any animal, the beasts might as well have been dragons.

"These are tame?"

Clarence chuckled.

"I don't know about tame, so much, but trained. Rex here is one of a few who will put up with a saddle; you'll ride him."

"Rex?"

"That's right. Have to call them something, and they never bother to tell us their names. Other one's called Bruce."

Clarence approached Rex from the side and stroked his neck gently, then motioned for Gavin to join them. The old man continued to murmur to the beast, stroking its neck with one hand while he used the other to indicate how Gavin should mount.

There was nothing graceful about this process; Gavin's foot slipped out of the stirrup twice before he finally managed to get a firm base. When he did get his leg up and over the ram, he would have toppled off the other side if Clarence had not grabbed him. Rex snorted.

"Might be awkward at first, but you'll figure it out. By the time we reach Trepani, you'll be an old pro."

Satisfied that Gavin was situated, Clarence mounted Bruce bareback and nudged the ram with a heel, setting the beast in motion. As the two came even with Gavin and Rex, Clarence gave Rex a slap on the rump, and the ram lumbered into motion.

The path they followed out of the clearing narrowed to a single-file, tree-lined track; they followed the trail for an hour, ascending steadily all the while, their way lit by the bright glow off Shylan and Aphrodite. When they had gone as far as they would for the night, Clarence turned to find Gavin asleep in the saddle. Clarence touched him on the shoulder; Gavin jerked awake.

"We'll camp here; the rams were tied up a bit past the Elevation Limit, so there's no chance of anyone getting close enough to bother us here."

Gavin nodded wearily, but tired as he was, he still had enough energy to be curious about his great-uncle's phrasing. He had mentioned the Elevation Limit during their flight, but Gavin did not know what he meant by the phrase, and he had not thought to ask at the time.

"What Elevation Limit?"

Clarence raised an eyebrow.

"Didn't anyone ever tell you? The Bubble Suits only function in a certain range of elevations; not enough oxygen up here for the air filtration system to keep a sentient being conscious. If anyone in a Bubble Suit reaches an altitude it can't tolerate, an internal alarm system will go off, and the safety features will disable the Bubble Suit's movement abilities unless the wearer reverses course."

Gavin frowned.

"If there's not enough oxygen up here to survive in a Bubble Suit, how are we ok?"

Clarence chuckled.

"Because your body was designed by Nature, not sentient beings. Stunning as it may seem, the Universe has a bit more intelligence at its disposal than sentient beings, Knowledgable or no."

Gavin raised an eyebrow.

"What are you saying? Sentient beings are the most intelligent beings on the planet; we control our destinies."

Clarence laughed uproariously at that, throwing his head back to emit a deep, full-bellied chuckle.

"They say some very funny things down in Kingston. Organisms on a rock spinning through space, following the course of a star without a firm understanding of how we got here, or where consciousness emanates from, and we are the ones in control?"

"As to intelligence…well, I suppose it's what type of intelligence you value. Sentient animals have the capacity to think, no doubt, but we often use that power to produce thoughts that are unfathomably stupid. Non-sentient animals don't create the way sentient ones do, but they also deal with far fewer problems of their own making."

"But it's too late for such talk now; the day's been too long already. Morning will be here soon enough."

—

Now it was morning - dark or not - and Clarence was re-emerging from the trees, the rams in tow.

Their appearance shook Gavin from the last remnants of sleep; he crawled out of his sleeping bag, pulled on his shoes, stood, and walked stiffly to the edge of the clearing to relieve himself on a tree. As he listened to the sound of his stream, Gavin thought about the strangeness of being in sync with his bodily signals. Color rose in his cheeks as he remembered the previous night, when he had first felt an urge in his bowels; Gavin's distant childhood memories had been insufficient to handle the situation, and Clarence had been forced to direct Gavin, a full-grown man, in how to take a shit. Clarence was clinical about the process, but Gavin had still been highly embarrassed. Drinking had been another novel experience, though the sheer delight of that consumed Gavin so thoroughly that he forgot to feel any shame at his ineptitude, even after he turned the skin up too high and poured water up his nose.

His bladder empty, Gavin shook himself off and tucked himself in, thinking that, despite his soreness, he was excited at the thought of the new experiences that the day ahead had in store.

Mounting Rex was not the ordeal it had been the previous night; once he was seated, Gavin realized how sore his ass was, but the discomfort was driven from his mind when Clarence passed him a water skin. Gavin drank eagerly; when he passed the skin back, Clarence offered him an open pouch.

"It's shredded jerky. Suck on it for a while before you chew on it. When you do chew, take your time, and go slow. It's soft, but you haven't chewed anything in twenty years, and you need to give your teeth time to adjust. They should be fine from a structural standpoint - the Bubble Suits guarantee that much, at least - but they would fracture if you bit down on something hard now, and it'll take some work to build them up. And watch your tongue; a few years back, a defector damn near bit his off during his acclimation period. Don't need you doing that now."

Gavin looked down at the pouch. When Clarence saw him hesitate, the old man reached out, took a pinch with two fingers, and put the loose clump of meat in the side of his cheek.

Gavin mirrored him.

The sensation was immediate; a pleasure unlike anything Gavin had experienced surged through his brain, the smoky smell and savory taste of the meat waking up circuitry that had lain dormant for decades. Gavin sucked the juices from the meat, igniting another surge of pleasure in his brain.

Clarence prodded the rams into motion. As Rex and Bruce made their way up the trail, a question, briefly driven from Gavin's mind by the taste of the meat, returned to the surface.

"You said a defector almost bit his tongue off. What's a defector? I've never heard that word before."

Clarence chuckled.

"No. You wouldn't have. A sentient being becomes a defector when they abandon The Bubble Society, and the existence of such individuals is not acknowledged by your Guvernment."

Gavin stared at his great-uncle open-mouthed.

"You mean I'm not the first?"

Clarence grinned.

"The first? Far from it. There were folks who knew that we were leaving on The Last Day - what you in Kingston call The Advent - who elected not to join us. They were a minority, those few who were in on the secret but decided against taking the risk, but they existed."

"Yet, as The Bubble Society blossomed, some of those individuals came to regret their decision. They started to plot their way out, and whispered to others that there might be an escape. It was tricky - first, they had to find a way to cut themselves free, which meant stealing a Spike - but once that first group made it, and we learned what metals were in the tip of the Spike, there was a way out."

"They started to come. Not in a mass exodus, but in trickles, twos and threes, sometimes as many as a half-dozen. After all, most sentient beings eventually wake up to the price they pay to be a citizun of The Bubble Society, and when they do, it's a hard thing to unsee."

BOOK 2, CHAPTER 5

Dire as the times had been, there were few moments in its history that the city of Kingston had been as alive with excitement as it was during the last season before The Advent, that intoxicating period when the Bubble Suits had been approved and the manufacturing had begun. The end of their suffering was finally visible on the horizon, a tangible place they were approaching rather than some fantastic dream that would never be fulfilled.

This would have been the case without any promotion, but the Guvernment, in partnership with Dynamic Solutions, had done more than its part to stoke the fire.

There were mockups of the Bubble Suit, in-depth interviews with recently ordained Knowers, feature-length films about what life would be like on Shurtain in the years After Knowledge, when every citizun in Kingston would be protected by the wonders that were the Bubble Suits. The Bubble Suits would filter the planet's air, but that was only the beginning; to build a suit that could sustain a sentient being, the team at Dynamic Solutions had to develop an intimate understanding of the sentient body, and their research revealed that Nature had made a remarkable number of mistakes in its design. Fortunately, all of that could now be corrected with the wonders of Knowledge.

It was truly a miracle; the team at Dynamic Solutions had been able to correct nearly all of the health conditions that had emerged as Shurtain's atmosphere became poisoned, conditions that had grown steadily worse as the atmosphere grew more toxic. Obesity, heart disease, diabetes, cancer: the introduction of the Bubble Suits would wipe out all of them in one fell swoop.

This meant that, with every individual set to receive a Bubble Suit at The Advent, the transition to the years After Knowledge would mark the end of disease. As if that were not enough, the Guvernment, in partnership with Dynamic Solutions, was guaranteeing a lifetime supply of nutrients and fluids for every sentient being in Shurtain, which would mean an end to hunger. Throw in the massive labor needs projected by Dynamic Solutions in their project roadmap, and Kingston would never again have to worry about unemployment; if anything, The Bubble Society would need more sentient beings to fill the necessary roles as they fulfilled their vision of a utopia.

The dreams were so fantastic that life in the present hardly seemed worth living; everyone wanted to hit fast-forward, to end the pain, end the suffering, and get to life in their Bubble Suits.

Unfortunately, life did have to be lived in the interim; under the circumstances, the people of Kingston, those future citizuns of The Bubble Society, drifted into a state of lethargy, doing little as they speculated endlessly about what life would be like on Shurtain in the years After Knowledge, wondering whether crime would continue in a society where the Guvernment could guarantee full employment, if jealousy could exist when everyone had the same clothing options, or whether sentient beings would still gather for meals when they took their nutrients and fluids through injectable tanks.

As to the last question, most continued in their habits; those who had eaten alone, or on the go, continued to do so, and those who gathered to take time over meals did the same.

For the Mancini family, that meant gathering for dinner. As far back as Tesla could remember, to her first home in the Andola District, Donnie and Kelli Mancini had insisted that the five of them share time over their evening meal. The Andola District felt like a different lifetime to Tesla now, but even as her father's promotions had moved the family to the Axios District, the Amada District, and finally, The Guvna's Mansion, her parents had continued to prioritize the evening meal.

Tesla smiled as she remembered those years; given his inauspicious beginnings, Donnie and his wife had never expected to find themselves in this position.

Donnie Mancini found that he was not the only apathetic clerk working in the office after he took his first job with the Guvernment, but unlike the majority of his peers, who saw their post as a stepping stone to higher offices, Donnie Mancini had no ambitions of being promoted; in fact, the only reason he had taken the post was that Guvernment employees got to work a half-day at the end of each week, which meant that Donnie could beat the traffic on the road out of the city to enjoy some time in Nature with his family.

Their family was the reason that Donnie and Kelli had moved to Kingston; as a young couple, the pair had lived on the road together, cruising the coast of Western Acadia for six years, the last three with the new addition to their family in tow. Donnie could have lived that way forever, but as their son started to near school age, Kelli insisted that they needed some sort of stability.

So they left Western Acadia and its scattered beach towns. Left Calipso, the city on the northwestern peninsula of Acadia where, if your eyes were good, you could just make out the continent of Thysion on the western side of the Ambaric Passage.

It was a difficult decision to leave their home behind, but Western Acadia's population had been dwindling for years; the coastal cities were the last holdouts on a continent that had seen its midwest gutted over the past decades. But while the signs might be obvious, it did not make it any easier for the people of Western Acadia to abandon their roots, no easier than it had been for the people of Central Acadia to give up on their homes.

For the young couple, those roots ran deep; Donnie's father was from Thysion, the first in his family to cross the Ambaric Passage to live in Acadia, and Kelli's family had come to Acadia a generation before Donnie's, her maternal grandparents returning to Thysion before her birth, which meant that Kelli had grown up visiting the neighboring continent once or twice a year.

In those years, the cities of Western Acadia had thrived; from Quincy in the south to Nederland, which stood midway along the coast, to Calipso, Western Acadia did not lack for beautiful places to live.

But as years rolled by, the troubles with the rail lines, and then the crop yields, had taken their toll, wiping out the central cities, making the overland shipping routes nearly impassable, and, in time, cutting off those Western cities from the continent's main hub in Kingston. It did not happen all at once, but slowly, the populations of Western Acadia melted away, leaving ghost towns on the outskirts of what had once been thriving cities.

By the time Donnie and Kelli were in their twenties, Quincy was the only one of Western Acadia's cities to retain much of a population, and that number was less than a twentieth of Kingston, the only thriving city on the Acadian continent.

Any way they looked at it, employment was harder to come by in the coastal towns, and by the looks of it, things would only grow even meaner. Ultimately, Kelli determined there would be more opportunity for their family, and their son, in Kingston.

So, Donnie's reluctance aside, they left, and Donnie took up his position as a Guvernment clerk.

His first fifteen years in the Guvernment were not distinguished.

Donnie performed his job adequately - or at least, nobody had ever told him he was doing anything wrong - but he had no interest in his responsibilities, no ambitions of moving up the ladder.

Perhaps, with more time, Donnie would have developed at least a passing interest in his work - it was unlikely, perhaps, but stranger things had happened - yet that was never to be.

Fate saw to that.

For Donnie might never have overcome his reluctance to move up the ladder, were it not for the dramatic change in his and Kelli's life that had occurred six years after they had moved to Kingston, the birth of a daughter that would cause them more sleepless nights and worry than they ever could have imagined.

Tesla glanced across the table, where her mother fussed over Andrea, who was gazing past Tesla with a vacant stare on her face. Rachel, the middle sister in the Mancini family, sat on the other side of Andrea, hunched over as much as her Bubble Suit would allow. Tesla looked away from the three of them. Her insides squirmed, but that was nothing new; Tesla had long ago mastered the art of compartmentalizing the feelings related to her older sister's troubled health. She did it now, pushing the anxiety away and turning to look at her father.

Usually, The Guvna' would have been watching Andrea, but his mind appeared to be elsewhere tonight; he was staring vaguely at the far end of the table, his mouth set in a slight frown, the bags under his eyes adding to his air of exhaustion. Tesla had an idea of what was bothering him - she had read all of the most recent Guvernment reports, after all - but it surprised her that the recent events should weigh on her father's mind when so many other happenings had failed to affect him during the two-plus decades that he had served as The Guvna'. Tesla's plan had been to wait until after the nutrient packets had been served to broach the topic, but she decided to take the plunge now.

"So, how was your day, Guvna'?"

Tesla's voice transformed her father's aspect; as Donnie's eyes shifted toward his youngest daughter, he straightened up, and a smile spread across his face. Tesla returned it, enjoying the little glow of satisfaction she always felt in these moments. For all the tricks she had taught herself, her ability to pull her father out of his preoccupations was her favorite; it was the skill she had possessed since memory, the one that was uniquely hers, the one that she could never teach to another.

"Neva' gunna stop wit' dat, are ya? Even afta' I'm retired and outta office, you'll go on calling me dat, won'cha, lil' lady?"

Tesla smiled, aware of the twinkle in her eyes.

"Well, you are The Guvna', aren't you?"

Her father rolled his eyes.

"So dey tell me. Three more years 'til dey let me step down, but den again, dey told me it'd only be three years at da start, and here I am, seven terms later."

He shook his head.

"Don't s'pose it matters - hafta do something 'til I hit da retirement age - but on days like this, I gotta admit, I wish I was in a senior advisor role by now. None o' dem advisors got hundreds o' people clamoring to get in front of 'em. Meeting afta' meeting, all o' da greatest urgency."

The Guvna' paused. Tesla nodded, encouraging him to continue. She knew that her father was happier to remain Guvna' than he let on - Tesla strongly suspected that Andrea and Rachel, who should have joined Kingston's workforce years ago, would be sent to live at The Villa if it were not for his influence - but she was more interested in other matters at the moment, and did not want to distract her father from his musings.

"You 'member dat yung fella who had da Bubble Suit malfunction a few weeks back?"

Tesla nodded. She more than remembered Gavin Owens, but there was no need for anyone, her father included, to know what an active interest she had taken in his case.

"Well, seems he had some new malfunction last night. Darned fella was up at Kingfisher again, never mind da Laws. Just can't protect some people from demselves - too reckless for us ta Guvern. Can't say I blame 'im, seein' as I wussint so different at his age, but even so, howdya help someone who don't want no help?"

The Guvna' paused, the frown returning to his face.

"So? What happened to him?"

"Oh, right. Dat's da trouble; nobody knows. Found da Bubble Suit up at Kingfisher, but dat's all dey found. Seems dis Gavin disappeared entirely. Dat's what all da meetings, all da damned phone calls were about, Knowers from dis department and dat department calling ta tell me da same thing, dat dey dunno what happened."

He let out a deep sigh.

"Da Head o' Suit Development dunno how da Suit could've come open. Da Head o' Filtration dunno why dis Gavin ain't dead ten feet from his suit, cuz he didn't take da filter, and he can't have survived long on open air. It's a big mystery, to hear dem tell it. Hell, I even had da Head o' Suit Innovation come in person ta tell me he dunno why da Bubble Suit dinnit reseal itself, as he claims it should."

The Guvna' snorted.

"I swear, da way Knower Galvenstein went on, you'da thought we hadn't gone through da same song 'n dance two weeks ago. Da clown even brought da same damn slideshow he showed me last time; he just replaced da word "partial" with da word "full" wherever he referred to da tear."

The Guvna' shook his head and met Tesla's eyes, then continued in a slightly calmer tone.

"I tell ya, when ya decided ta take up Suit Innovation as yer field of study, when you had yer choice o' pursuits at da Academy, I had my concerns. Dunno why, in retrospect - shoulda known yer too damned smart ta fall fer summa da nonsense Galvenstein passes off as fact - but I worry 'bout da rest o' yer classmates sometimes. Bright 'nuff, certainly, lot brighter'n yer old man, but it don't do no good ta teach an intelligent person nonsense, 'specially when ya defend da ideas with da sort o' fervor a fellow like Galvenstein brings ta da table."

"Don't get me wrong; da Bubble Suits are a miracle, and we need ta be grateful for 'em. But I ain't so stupid as ta believe dis resealing mechanism dat Galvenstein goes on about *should* work when da only evidence he can provide comes from tests he designed in his lab."

Tesla nodded. She could not imagine what the reaction would be if she, or one of her classmates, voiced such a thought at the Academy of Knowledge - expulsion would be certain, imprisonment likely, and dismemberment possible - but Tesla also knew that over the past twenty years, there had been tens of thousands of, not tears, but "wrents" in the Bubble Suits, where the microfilament of the Bubble Suit membrane either folded in on itself or split open.

In theory, those wrents should fix themselves.

In theory, even a full tear should reseal itself; the Bubble Suits had a perfect track record of achieving this result in the lab, results that were thoroughly documented in the knower-reviewed journals.

In reality, the wrents did not reseal themselves.

In reality, every one of the tens of thousands of wrents that had occurred in the history of The Bubble Society had required the manual intervention of a Bubble Suit Technician to repair the damage.

Those results, of course, were not documented. They were anomalous events, random occurrences, unrelated to how the Bubble Suits were supposed to function.

"Between da two o' us, if it was up ta me, I'd call off da damn search, and tell all da Knowers ta stop bothering me. Dis Gavin is dead somewhere, and da resealing mechanism on da Bubble Suits don't work near as well as Galvenstein and da others would have us believe. What's so hard 'bout dat?"

The Guvna' turned his hands up in exasperation.

"O' course, dey want more answers den dat - demanded a full inquiry - so dat's what dey get. Da Board has ta be appeased, afta' all."

Tesla blinked. She glanced down the table at her mother and sisters, but they were lost in their own world, and had not reacted to what her father had said. Her eyes returned to The Guvna', who continued to speak as if what he had said was not the least bit extraordinary. Tesla took in the bags under her father's eyes, and realized how tired he must be; she also wondered if he had hit the liquor before dinner.

For more than twenty years, her father had maintained the pretense that the "they" he spoke of was the population of Kingston. Tesla had always known better, of course, but she had never let on to this fact. It was an effort to hide her shock now, but she kept her expression neutral and returned her attention to her father's words.

"...ain't getting worked up over it, though. More o' a nuisance 'n anything, ta tell da truth. And I'm a bit miffed I wasted my time, goin' outta my way ta try'n talk some sense ta da yung man, as he don't seem'ta have listened to a word o' it. Now he's lying dead somewhere, mark my words, and it's his own damn fault. He'd be just fine if he'd been celebrating Da Advent like a model citizun."

The Guvna' stopped speaking; the dining room doors had opened.

Two Guvernment Officials entered, wheeling in nutrient tanks on silver serving carts.

The first part of the dining process was seamless; the family had swapped out their waste disposal tanks before coming to dinner - waste excretion did not involve genital exposure in The Bubble Society, but sentient beings still generally avoided dumping their load in front of their fellows - so everyone sitting at the table was prepared to take in the contents of their nutrient packets without engaging in that less tasteful task.

The Guvna', Kelli, Rachel, and Tesla all tapped the controls on their wrist panels, causing the covers on their upper left arm panels to retract. The two Guvernment Officials serving them moved efficiently through their task, inserting the needle on the end of the tanks into the nutrition ports of each diner seated at the table, then moving on to the next diner as the tanks emptied.

The absorption process did not take long; it was an area of constant improvement in the Department of Research and Innovation, and they had gotten the time down from fifty-three seconds to twenty-nine in the years since the Bubble Suits were introduced. From her studies, Tesla knew that the latest trials indicated that the twenty-five-second barrier might be broken within a year.

In her mind, it was too little, too late; the Knowers would need to get the time down under ten seconds for it to consistently matter in the Mancini household, and Tesla knew that by the time that happened, she would be out of the house.

Under the circumstances, she had resigned herself to riding the emotional roller-coaster each evening; while her own nutrient tank was draining, Tesla wished it would take forever, so they would never get to what came next, but once it was empty, her failed wish would transform into a fervent desire that the nutrient absorption process could be instantaneous, so Andrea would not have to suffer.

On a conscious level, Tesla had been able to recognize the lunacy of this thought pattern since she was six or seven.

But that awareness did not prevent her stomach from clenching every night as her nutrient tank emptied out.

After one of the Guvernment Officials had removed the empty nutrient packet from his injection site, The Guvna' stood. He walked around the table to Andrea's chair and placed his hands gently on her shoulders. Andrea smiled when her father's hands touched her - or rather, when he touched her Bubble Suit - and then her mother and sister took her hands. Andrea loved these moments, when she was surrounded by her family; Tesla cringed as she watched the smile continue to spread across her sister's face.

The smile always appeared.

Because she never remembered.

As Andrea smiled, her mother furtively dialed in commands on her daughter's wrist panel; the panel on Andrea's upper arm retracted, exposing her nutrient and fluid intake ports. One of the Guvernment Officials approached Andrea from behind, a nutrient tank in her hand; as the woman prepared to insert the needle, Rachel started talking animatedly to Andrea, causing her older sister to turn away from the woman.

As soon as the needle was into Andrea's nutrient intake port, the clock in Tesla's mind started counting down. It was a concerted effort not to let the count speed up; she knew that counting faster would not accelerate time, but her insides were desperate for the moment to be over, for the meal to pass without incident.

With four seconds left, she thought it might.

Then, for no obvious reason, Andrea turned from Rachel back to her mother. Tesla saw Rachel's eyes widen in panic, saw her bite her lip the way she always did on the nights that she did not keep Andrea distracted until the process was complete.

Andrea's dull eyes found the nutrient intake tank attached to her arm. There was a moment when she froze, then another where she seemed to realize what was going on, light surging into her eyes. Then the clarity disappeared, and Andrea started to scream, howling like a wounded animal as she attempted to reach for the needle.

Rachel held tight to her sister's right arm; before Andrea could make the move, her mother pressed a button on the side of the chair. Bindings sprang from the arms and legs of the seat; Andrea's limbs were strapped down, and she screamed all the louder for that.

The tank was empty now; one of the Guvernment Officials removed it, but that did nothing to calm Andrea, who continued struggling, trying to free herself. For her part, Tesla stared into her lap.

At least the nutrient tank had been close to empty tonight. As soon as the Guvernment Official had collected the nutrient tank and stepped away, Kelli pushed the button again, releasing the restraints on her oldest daughter, then put an arm around her and started to sing in a gentle tone.

It was no more than a minute before Andrea calmed down, but to Tesla, it might have as well have been a lifetime.

When her oldest daughter was quiet, Kelli's tired eyes moved to meet her husband's.

"I think we'll call it a night. It's been a long day."

The Guvna' nodded. He leaned down and gave his oldest daughter a one-armed embrace, then moved back to his seat. Kelli and Rachel rose, then helped Andrea to her feet. At least she was calm again, Tesla thought, noting the small smile on Andrea's face as she turned to leave the room. When the dining room doors shut behind them, her father slumped back in his seat and closed his eyes.

"Is it really better now?"

It had been years since she asked the question, and Tesla did not know why she asked it again now.

The Guvna's eyes opened slowly.

"Better? Oh, lawd's yes, it's better. Back before da Bubble Suits, when you were five, and Andrea was thirteen, you were on pace ta pass her in weight by da end o' da year. No knock on you - you were right on track - but more often n' not, it took hours o' convincing ta get yer sister ta eat anything. And some days all dat effort went fer naught."

He shook his head, a dejected expression on his face.

"Yer sister wouldn't be here without da Bubble Suits. Her, and all da other ones who were too sickly ta survive once Shurtain's atmosphere started going ta hell. It's a miracle dey developed da Bubble Suits in time; gotta thank Knowledge fer dat one."

Tesla nodded, still uncomfortable, but then her father shook himself and turned his attention back to her. Tesla smiled when he did this; all her life, her father had always taken pains to set his troubles over Andrea aside when he engaged with his youngest daughter. Tesla recognized this, and loved him for it; it was not that she blamed her mother and sister for getting sucked into Andrea's world, with the amount of time they spent caring for her, but the young Tesla had adored the moments where her father found the space to spare her his undivided attention.

"In any case, we was talking 'bout da damned search. As I say, I'd call it off. He's dead, and it ain't worth da manpower ta keep looking. Knowledge is well established on da point; ain't no way a person can survive without da Bubble Suits for more'n a few minutes. We've dragged Kingfisher Reservoir, turned over every stone in da woods 'round there…if they were gunna find him, it woulda happened already. It's a sad story, but we oughta accept it, and move on with our lives. Dat's what I say, at least."

Tesla nodded, her eyes on her father.

"Makes sense to me. Like you say, there's no way he could have survived without his Bubble Suit; how many knower-reviewed studies have the Knowers published in the knower-reviewed journals to prove that Knowledge?"

Her father raised his palms to the sky in mock exasperation; re-engaging with Tesla had washed away any frustration he felt over his work, once again allowing him to joke about the lunacy of Guvernment operations, as they had done so often over the years.

"Ya got no idea how many times I said da same. Hundreds o' knower-reviewed trials conducted in da first year da Bubble Suits were introduced, all showing da same result."

"Not to mention the Aeronbald Volunteer Experiment."

The Guvna' stopped short at Tesla's words. He opened his mouth, closed it, then licked his lips before he spoke again.

"O' course. Though I don't like'ta speak o' dat if I don't hafta, 'lil lady, as you well know."

He paused.

"It was turrible. Just turrible. And it dinnit hafta happen. If it weren't for all da conspiracy theorists, all da campaigns disseminating nonsense, all da whispers dat da Bubble Suits might not be necessary…"

He trailed off, shaking his head.

"Da Aeronbald Experiment snuffed dat out quick 'nuff. We couldn't just silence all da whack jobs, not in a Democratic society, but we couldn't let 'em go on with their stories."

Tesla nodded.

"They broadcast it live, didn't they?"

"Broadcast it live? 'Lil lady, da Aeronbald Volunteer Experiment was da Guvernment's first Mandated Media Missive. Course, you didn't watch it then - no kid under twelve did - but Kingston Amphitheater was packed to the gills, and the video feed o' da Aeronbald Experiment was forced onto da holographic monitor o' everyone o' age across Kingston. Every one o' us was forced ta watch dem sentient beings suffer and die."

"Those folks weren't out o' der Bubble Suits more'n a few seconds before dey was in da utmost agony. Not a one lasted more'n five minutes, and two o' da fourteen died in two minutes flat. All o' dem screaming like nothing sentient, some o' dem jerking 'round on da ground…"

The Guvna' shuddered.

"What dey got for their nonsense beliefs, I s'pose. All prominent critics o' da introduction o' da Bubble Suits, claiming da Guvernment helped ta rig da Knowledge in da knower-reviewed studies. Talk for da loony bin; how could anyone cheat da knower-review system? It's foolproof, everyone knows that. Dey claimed there'd been payoffs; as if a Knower would accept a payoff. Like saying a priest woulda done summin' corrupt, back in da years way Before Knowledge, when dat religion stuff was all da rage. Pure foolishness; blasphemy ta even suggest dat such a thing could happen. But there's nothing you can do fer fools who don't acknowledge da power o' Knowledge and da fury o' its wrath."

Tesla nodded.

"An important lesson for us all to remember."

The Guvna's eyes flicked to his oldest daughter's empty seat. As his gaze rested on the restraints, Tesla squirmed.

"Yer not kidding, lil' lady."

BOOK 2, CHAPTER 6

Gavin had thought that he was sore when he woke up that morning.

By the end of the day's march, when he toppled off Rex's back to land in the muddy shallows of Turquoise Lake, he knew he had been wrong.

Hell, he had known he was wrong for hours by then; every inch of him had some sort of complaint.

His back ached.

His legs cramped.

His chapped ass burned.

And to add to it all, he smelled bad enough that he was surprised Rex had not tried to buck him off.

All of this, after one day out of his Bubble Suit.

Given his myriad other complaints, Gavin found that lying in the mud was not particularly objectionable; the cold muck soothed his skin, and nothing could have made him feel more soiled than he already did.

When he heard the sound of a body entering the lake, Gavin gathered his energy and pushed himself to his knees. His great-uncle had left his clothes on the shore and disappeared into Turquoise Lake, the ripples on the blue-green surface the only sign that he had entered the water. Gavin watched the ripples widen across the clear, still surface of the lake, which reflected the Cadillac Mountains from the far shores as clearly as a mirror would have, the reflection of the peaks pointing back at Gavin while the mountains themselves pointed to the heavens. Everything about the Cadillac Mountains was surreal, but Turquoise Lake, and the valley that held it, were spectacular even by those standards.

The first hint of the majesty started at Turquoise Falls, which toppled fifty meters from the cliffs at the western edge of Turquoise Lake to a churning, frothing pool below, which fed the continued progress of the Grand River. Gavin and Clarence had made the climb with the roar of the waterfall in their ears, an all-consuming experience in its own right; when they had reached the summit, and stood on the edge of the ridge, the valley that cupped Turquoise Lake on one side, the plummet from Turquoise Falls on the other, Gavin had felt transported. For an instant, he forgot how sore he was, forgot his sense of exhaustion, forgot everything but the moment.

Half an hour later, when they had made their way down to the shores of Turquoise Lake, that feeling had not entirely dissipated, even if Gavin's physical complaints had made themselves heard again.

Even from his seat in the mud, life was spectacular out here. From here, Gavin could see more animals, more life, than he would have seen in a lifetime in Kingston, and while Clarence had not proven much inclined to discuss anything else, he was more than willing to introduce Gavin to the wider world; his great-uncle had identified every animal, and many of the plants, that they passed on their journey, speaking at length about their various characteristics and attributes.

Now, as he sat on the shore, Gavin could distinguish ducks from loons, and loons from geese, as the birds swam across the water. He knew the difference between the chipmunks and squirrels scrabbling around the trees, could even identify the pine marten sitting on a limb that stretched over the surface of Turquoise Lake. He recognized the beast lapping water in a distant cove as a bull moose, the early growth of its velvety rack hovering over the lake as the animal dipped its muzzle to drink; Gavin and Clarence had seen a moose earlier, shortly after they had passed a herd of elk resting in a meadow near the Grand River.

The sound of his great-uncle resurfacing took Gavin's attention away from the moose; Clarence's head was the only thing to reappear, and it was only there for a moment. When his great-uncle disappeared back beneath the surface, Gavin let out a sigh, and decided he ought to get on with it.

He could sense, without touching Turquoise Lake, that the water was cold, which was the cause of his hesitation. Unfortunately, it seemed there was no other way to get clean; when Gavin had complained of his stink earlier, his great-uncle had told him that he would be able to wash at Turquoise Lake. Clarence had also told Gavin that his body would get used to moving, and that as he shed old layers of himself and rebuilt from better materials, the stink of his odors would not be so bad.

"Can't say I know precisely what goes into that nutrient paste you survive on down in Kingston, but essentially, you built the current version of your physical body out of garbage, and it takes time to turn those cells over. It's not just you - every defector goes through this process - but for a while here, your breath, sweat, and shit are all gonna stink like nothing natural."

As Clarence re-surfaced for a second time, Gavin pushed himself to his feet and started to strip off his clothes. He threw the bundle next to the one Clarence had left on the bank, and, forcing himself not to think about it, took a few hard strides and dove into Turquoise Lake.

The pain was immediate, all-consuming; it felt as if burning needles were piercing every pore of his body, and the overwhelming sensation was all the worse because he had not expected it and did not know what to do about it. Panicked, Gavin opened his mouth and sucked in water, which he spewed out as quickly. He might have drowned then and there, in five feet of water, but an arm wrapped around his torso and pulled him above the surface. When Gavin blinked his eyes open, still sputtering, he found Clarence's head bobbing next to his, the old man's grey beard floating on the lake's surface.

"Easy there. There's still snowmelt feeding the rivers and lakes; even if you hadn't spent your life in a Bubble Suit, it would be a shock. Keep breathing; your body will adjust."

Clarence swam them the few yards back to the bank. Gavin shivered as they waded to shore, where Clarence retrieved towels from Rex's saddle bags.

Gavin wrapped himself in one of the towels and sank down in a huddle, trying to warm himself, but his great-uncle dried off quickly and started to dress. Gavin was about to ask about a fire, but as soon as Clarence had his sandals on, he was off, without a word of explanation, taking a path along the bank and plucking leaves from a variety of plants as he made his way.

By the time his great-uncle returned, the sun was setting; Gavin had warmed up since donning a fresh set of clothes, but he worried that their campsite would be in shadows before the old man thought of a fire. The plunge into the icy waters had left him feeling clean, and washed some of the ache from his bones, but such blessings were difficult for Gavin to appreciate while he was preoccupied with thoughts of freezing to death.

Unfortunately, Gavin did not seem destined to get any quick answers on that front; ignoring his great-nephew completely, Clarence approached the rams, who were grazing nearby, and offered Bruce a handful of the plants and herbs he had collected on an upturned palm. Gavin was not sure whether the beast would even notice - Clarence was standing several feet to the side of the ram - but Bruce immediately caught the scent and abandoned the grass on the ground for the concoction that Clarence had prepared. By the time Bruce had eaten his share, Rex was standing next to them, waiting for his turn.

Clarence rubbed Bruce's muscular neck and muttered a few words to him, then relieved him of his packs. The beast returned to the grass while Clarence repeated the process with Rex, feeding him the mix of grass and herbs before he removed the animal's packs and saddle.

Gavin was eager to ask what Clarence had given them, but before he could voice that question, or ask about a fire, his great-uncle was off again, wandering off into the trees. When he returned this time, Gavin felt a rush of relief; his great-uncle's arms were full of wood.

It took the old man less than five minutes to have the fire started; once the flames were going, Clarence started to rummage in one of the packs that he had removed from Bruce's back. He set a few things to the side - more jerky, some fruit, a bag of nuts - and put everything else back in the bag. Food in hand, he took a seat next to Gavin, positioning himself on a flat rock near the flames.

"Help yourself."

Gavin took an apple; as he took a bite, he watched the black and silver loons swimming on the water, taking turns disappearing under the surface for minutes at a time. His observations of the birds, his wonder at their ability to submerge themselves for minutes at a time, reminded Gavin of a question that had crossed his mind earlier in the day; the thought of it made him shudder. He turned to check whether Clarence had noticed, but the old man's attention was on Turquoise Lake.

It struck Gavin that for all the trouble Clarence had taken on his behalf, his great-uncle had not shown a great deal of interest in him, or even spoken to Gavin much, unless you counted his monologues about the plants and animals around them. However, that did not seem important right now; at the moment, Gavin's question was the pressing matter.

As Gavin voiced his inquiry, images from the video clip that he had watched with his classmates at Kingston High rose up in his mind. The images were so sharp, so real, that Gavin almost felt as if he still had his Bubble Suit's holographic monitor in front of him.

"Do you know about the Aeronbald Volunteer Experiment?"

Clarence turned to Gavin, a curious expression on his face, and nodded.

"Certainly. We've kept an eye on The Bubble Society; not me specifically, but some of the other Acadians. Our technology allows us to pick up Kingston's media broadcasts, which keeps us apprised of the goings on down below, or at least, the Guvernment's narrative of what's happening."

Gavin opened his mouth to respond, but Clarence continued before the younger man could speak.

"The Aeronbald Experiment; I assume you've seen the footage?"

Gavin nodded.

"Grim stuff," Clarence observed.

Gavin shook his head, not in disagreement with Clarence's assessment, but as an attempt to express his internal battle, the debate that twisted his guts as it played out in his mind.

"That's why…that's why this can't…this doesn't make any sense. I saw them screaming. I saw them die."

Gavin turned to his great-uncle, and the two men made eye contact. As they looked at each other, the footage from that terrible day played back in each of their minds.

It had been a season and a half since The Advent.

Everyone in Kingston wore a Bubble Suit. No citizun had a say in the matter; the handful who held out had been knocked out with tranquilizer darts, and woke up wearing Bubble Suits, with no way to reverse the process.

But that fraction of the population, the resistance, did not go down without a fight. They were a small group, to be sure - most who embraced such beliefs had abandoned Kingston on the day of The Advent - but a handful stayed behind, so that for every ten thousand sentient beings in Kingston praising Knowledge, there were one or two who remained committed to living life without a Bubble Suit.

And that minority group, now trapped in Bubble Suits against their will, would not give up.

Instead, they started to search for a way to free themselves. They tried to cut the Bubble Suits. They tried to pull the microfilament apart, stretching it so far that it would have to snap. They procured lasers and tried to use the beams to shear through the Bubble Suits.

When all of that failed, a few brave souls resorted to a blow torch.

None of it worked. None of it did a thing.

When that became apparent, their outcries started.

The Knowers were not gods, they cried. They were merely sentient beings, and even the most learned sentient beings were not omniscient, or anything close to it. Like every other sentient being, these Knowers could not explain where sentient consciousness had come from, why sentient beings were on Shurtain, or where sentient consciousness was going, and on the collective level, sentient beings' understanding of their own bodies and their environment was appalling; at the time of the Advent, sentient beings were the only animals on the planet who had "figured out" a way to create widespread obesity, which did not strike the dissenters as any great mark of their species' wisdom.

The dissenters were shouted down, their character smeared, their arguments belittled. Nobody claimed the Knowers were gods; such spiritual nonsense was the stuff of a primitive age. The people of Kingston only claimed, correctly, that the Knowers spoke for Knowledge, and that meant that anyone who spoke against them was a liar, a denier of Knowledge, a denier of Truth, a threat to the prosperity of the community and state, the utopia that was The Bubble Society.

And still, the dissenters would not be silenced. They continued to claim that the Bubble Suits were unnecessary, a farce forced upon the citizunry by the Guvernment to exert their control on society.

In the end, the Guvernment decided that they could not allow the problem to persist. These deranged lunatics were going to get someone hurt; the loudest voices had to be dealt with, but in a Democracy like The Bubble Society, the Guvernment could not simply disappear them.

So the Guvernment decided to give the dissenters what they wanted.

They decided to give them an opportunity to prove the Knowers wrong.

Two seasons after The Advent, at the time when all of the knower-reviewed papers agreed that Shurtain's atmosphere had passed the point of no return, the dissenters were given their chance.

They held the event in Kingston Amphitheater. It was a fitting choice; it was the same place that they had held their celebrations on The Advent, the place where The Bubble Society had been born. Now, with The Aeronbald Volunteer Experiments, it would be the place where The Bubble Society cemented its place in history.

The event was open to the public free of charge, and while attendance was not required, any citizuns of age who did not attend the event in person would have the broadcast streamed onto their holographic monitors.

Of course, very few of The Bubble Society's citizuns had any desire to miss such a momentous event; the sentient beings of Kingston packed Kingston Amphitheater to capacity, excited to see the heretics fail, to see proof of Knowledge's might, and to celebrate the victory afterward.

The Guvna' did not oversee the event; instead, Knower Ancel, the Head Knower at Dynamic Solutions, was given emcee duties.

Ancel's speech was straightforward and brief; he announced to the crowd that fourteen individuals were being given their opportunity to prove the Knowers were wrong, to show that the Bubble Suits were a farce, an unnecessary invention. Ancel reminded the crowd that the volunteers had been educated, over and over, about the dangers of what they were about to attempt. They had all insisted that they be given this opportunity, the chance to prove the truth of what Knowledge had deemed heresy.

Knower Ancel's announcement complete, the fourteen were directed to walk onto the stage.

Each of them carried a silver needle.

Knower Ancel announced to the crowd that the needles, known as Spikes, were specially designed to destroy the microfilament membrane of the Bubble Suits in a way that nothing else could.

And then, once they were free, the heretics could prove the truth of their claims.

The crowd held its breath as Ancel turned to the fourteen.

"You are certain you wish to attempt this?"

The fourteen nodded, resolute. Ancel shook his head, his eyes downcast.

"Then there is nothing I can do. But I cannot bear to watch."

Ancel strode off the stage.

When he was gone, the fourteen plunged the Spikes through the membranes of their Bubble Suits.

As Knower Ancel had promised, the Spikes cut through the membranes of the Bubble Suits like nothing else could. Smiling, some of the heretics made longer cuts, peeling off portions of their Bubble Suits.

And then they started to fail.

They failed miserably.

They failed painfully.

And they failed publicly.

They never even got all the way out of their Bubble Suits.

The fourteen started to writhe, to scream. Some raked at their faces in terrible pain; others fell to their knees in their agony. The first heretic to die did not last a full minute, and after he fell, the others started dropping like flies.

Within a few short minutes, they were all dead.

When the last body hit the stage, a pin drop would have been heard in the packed amphitheater. Then, as the certainty that all fourteen were dead spread through the crowd, the roar started, and swelled, the triumphant cheers of the zealots bellowing out acknowledgments of the power of Knowledge.

His eyes on his great-uncle, Gavin shook his head.

"It was terrible. The worst thing I've ever seen."

Clarence nodded.

"I agree. Well, I've been alive a long time, so perhaps it wasn't the worst. But it was as bad as the worst."

"But if they died, then how are we alive? How are we able to breathe, when we're not wearing Bubble Suits."

Clarence let out a grim chuckle.

"It's pretty simple, actually: we haven't been exposed to the pathogens they used to tip those Spikes."

BOOK 2, CHAPTER 7

Tesla was restless.

For others, the frenzied push to get ready would have been the difficult part.

For her, the opposite was true.

Her preparations were made, but Tesla could not relax; her whole body felt tense as she sat in the lecture hall, compulsively scrolling through a series of video feeds to distract herself from Knower Maddox's meandering monologue.

Unfortunately, the video feeds she was watching were not providing much in the way of distraction. An uninitiated observer might have even wondered why she did not switch over to a selection from the Guvernment Media App, but Tesla was not interested in any of that; she was interested in the video feeds from the cameras that she had set up during her preparations.

She had only gotten a few hours of sleep each night - some of the work, such as going up past Mesa Outcrop in the Cadillac Mountains to install surveillance cameras, was best done under cover of darkness - but the efforts had been worth it. Her own eyes now extended far past those of the City Watch and Capitol Guard, whose surveillance network ended at Kingfisher Reservoir.

But worth it or not, the effects of the sleepless nights were catching up to her; Tesla felt the exhaustion coming on, and could not have paid attention to Knower Maddox's lecture if she wanted to.

As it was, she did not want to; if it were up to Tesla, she would be asleep with her head on the desk right now, but she knew that Knower

Maddox would not react well if an aspiring Knower fell asleep in her class.

It was unfortunate; Tesla needed the sleep, and she did not need to listen to any of the noise coming out of Knower Maddox's mouth, except to keep up appearances. In any case, exhaustion was a small price to pay to feel prepared, particularly after the way things had played out on the night of The Advent.

Her dash back to Kingston Amphitheater that night had served as a brief distraction, but as soon as Tesla had exited the stage with her family, the voices returned to her mind, berating her for her lack of anticipation, for missing the opportunity that she had dreamed of for so many years. Her recent prep work had served to burn off some of that frustration, given her time to find perspective, to recognize that the night of The Advent would not be her only opportunity. The sight of the old man had confirmed that the whispers were true, that there was life outside of Kingston, outside of The Bubble Society.

And if any of those others came down from the Cadillacs again, Tesla would be ready; she would know it before they were at Mesa Outcrop, and she would be prepared for whatever would come next. The surveillance system had been the first step, but it was not the last; Tesla had also packed, and oddly enough, it was difficult to say which task presented the greater obstacle. Setting up the cameras was exhausting, and had severely depleted the cache of cameras, remote controls, and night-vision lenses that Tesla had "borrowed" from the Department of Media Production a few years earlier, but to pack for her journey, Tesla had to obtain items that nobody in The Bubble Society had any reason to possess.

—

Tesla had been five at the time of The Advent, old enough to vaguely remember shopping trips with her mother in the years before the Bubble Suits negated the need for material possessions.

In those years, racks of clothes had filled the floors of department stores. At the time, Tesla had been more interested in hiding in the clothes than anything else; now, she wished that she, somehow, could have set aside just one of the thousands of outfits that had been available back then. In those years, she could have acquired a complete set of clothes in less than an hour, and it would not have raised an eyebrow.

Now, it was difficult to find so much as a sock, new or used.

The frenzied celebrations that broke out after the Aeronbald Volunteer Experiments had seen to that. That night had turned into an exceptionally rowdy celebration in Kingston; flush with victory after watching Knowledge strike such a decisive blow against its enemies, the citizuns of The Bubble Society had flowed out of the Amphitheater, through Capitol Square, and into the streets of Kingston beyond, where they filled up the bars and public squares, which were all open for trade well past their usual hours on this magnificent night.

The fervor continued to build; fueled by alcohol, the fiery emotions sparked by the night's events only burned hotter as the people reveled in the wake of Knowledge's decisive victory over the heretics.

It was about midnight, hours after the conclusive end of the Aeronbald Volunteer Experiments, that those emotions spilled over, and the burnings began.

It started innocently enough; a middle-aged woman named Annie Fleming, who lived in a third-story apartment in the Axios District, tossed her computer and its accessories out of her apartment window; these items were quickly followed by a television set, and then a microwave.

That might have been the end of it, but the falling debris narrowly missed several children in the street below, and with so many people out and about, the near-miss drew a crowd.

The crowd's anger vanished entirely when Annie Fleming stuck her whole torso out of her window and declared, in a booming voice, that she had no need of the old technology, the garbage that sentient beings had produced in the years Before Knowledge. Her Bubble Suit came from the real Knowledge, was the only true technology on the planet Shurtain, and that was all that she needed; all the rest was trash, fit to be burned.

Perhaps Annie Fleming did not mean for her words to be taken literally; regardless of her intentions, one young man in the crowd took the opportunity to run into his own apartment to grab a lighter, a keepsake from the days back Before Knowledge, when he had still been able to smoke. The lad's initial attempts to set the television on fire were unsuccessful, but when a friend from the neighborhood ran up with a can of gasoline tucked under his arm, the situation changed dramatically; within a quarter of an hour, all manner of debris was being hurled into the streets all over Kingston, acrid black smoke billowing up where citizuns were piling the junk and setting it aflame.

Computers and televisions were not the only casualties; as more and more citizuns joined in, the flying debris expanded to include kitchen appliances, washing machines, even the clothes that sentient beings had worn before the Bubble Suits. And everywhere the debris landed, there was a crowd ready to light it.

The frenzy spread from the Axios District, first east to the Andola District, and then, as the citizuns in the Amada Districts became aware of the fervor down south, up to that district of luxury, whose residents were determined to demonstrate that they were the true model citizuns, even more committed to The Bubble Society's ideals than their neighbors in the downtrodden areas.

By the time the sun rose on Kingston, the crowds and fires had finally died out; the burned-out hulls and the acrid clouds of smoke that had yet to dissipate were the only remaining signs of what had happened.

The Guvernment's clean-up crew started work early that morning; by the time they were finished the next evening, the evidence of the riots was gone, and with it, nearly all of the trappings of sentient life in Kingston from the era Before Knowledge.

It was a story that Tesla was well familiar with; she had been too young to be clued in on what was happening on the night in question, it was impossible for anyone who looked out at Kingston the next day not to realize something dramatic had happened the previous night.

Even so, Tesla would not let herself believe that there were no clothes left in Kingston; too many sentient beings, both women and men, had harbored deep attachments to their wardrobes. They would never have willingly fed them to the flames, even in the frenzy of the night that had followed the Aeronbald Experiments.

To start, Tesla scoured the Guvernment's inventory lists, but when that failed to turn up anything, she decided that she would need to target specific individuals who might have held onto their clothes.

This was an unappetizing prospect; Tesla had no qualms about breaking into Guvernment institutions, but the idea of creeping someone's home was not an appealing prospect.

Fortunately, after hours of profiling potential targets, an idea had struck her, one that was so ludicrously simple that she wondered why she had not thought of it straight away.

Her mother had not joined the post-Aeronbald riots; on the night in question, Kelli Mancini had accompanied her husband to Kingston Amphitheater to witness the spectacle, then returned to The Guvna's Mansion immediately after. Tesla knew that for a certainty; she remembered the night well, remembered the air of tension as a group of Guvernment Officials had monitored her and her sisters during their parents' absence.

Once Tesla had the idea that her mother might have held onto some of her clothes, it was not hard to find them. The master bedroom, which was situated on the top floor of The Guvna's Mansion with the rest of the family's living quarters, featured large, walk-in closets on either side of the canopy bed.

As it turned out, her mother's closet was perfectly preserved; Tesla had waited for a time when she knew her mother would be busy with Andrea, which gave Tesla time to sort through the clothes at her leisure. Images of her childhood swam up as she went through this process, moments when she had carefully observed her mother dressing for formal occasions, making herself up and picking out dresses.

Those were rare moments, moments when Kelli had not been hovering over Andrea, moments when she could be present with Tesla, and laugh with her youngest daughter; it was strange for Tesla, who thought back on what her mother had looked like to her then, and realized, with a shudder, that she had grown up to look remarkably like her.

So like her, in fact, that Tesla wore all the same sizes, and had her pick of Kelli's old clothes.

Those clothes were now stowed in a rucksack, which sat next to her bicycle in the basements of The Old Capitol, along with a few other items she thought she might need.

There was only one thing left to find, and she did not think she would need it, since the people she intended to seek appeared to possess them. That would make things easier, because if there was one item that Tesla might find it difficult to steal from the Guvernment, it was a spike.

—

Now all she had to do was wait. Her surveillance system was rigged with motion detectors and accompanying alerts; even so, Tesla found herself passing the time by scrolling through that feed, wishing that she could be out in the open on this sunny day rather than sitting in this stuffy auditorium, listening to Knower Maddox drone on.

Knower Maddox's class was dull at the best of times, though this had little to do with the woman herself; Tesla found the majority of her classes at the Academy of Knowledge to be insufferable. Between her exhaustion and her frustration, she found the need to sit here and keep up appearances particularly galling today.

The worst thing about the Academy of Knowledge, she thought, was their bizarre assumption that if one had to learn a huge volume of information, the best approach was to sit still and passively absorb that material during hours of lectures, never mind the reams of research on how to optimize informational intake blocks with periods of free association, or leveraging studies on how movement, nutrition, and sleep impact memory formation. Even in the times that research had been done, back in the years Before Knowledge, such considerations were generally disregarded; educators charged forward, insisting that if students - even the youngsters at Kingston Elementary - could not sit still for hours on end, it was a problem with the student, not the system. And of course, there was no alternative; after all, if children did not learn to sit still and learn from what others had written in digital books, where would they go for an education?

Lived experience?

Shurtain itself?

Such considerations were utterly preposterous; how could the planet Shurtain award you a certificate? And if you lacked a certificate, how could other sentient beings judge your value? Relying on sentient beings to make such judgments on their own, without the benefit of a certifying body, was as absurd as the idea of learning something outside of a classroom.

Of course, Tesla ignored those nonsense beliefs, engrained as they might be in Kingston's wider consciousness as established Knowledge, settled fact. It did not matter how deep others tried to dig their heads in the sand, or how often the Knowers claimed that the Knowledge they put forth was truth; Tesla had been alive long enough to determine that Nature would continue to produce evidence to the contrary. It was out there in the Universe for anyone who cared to look, proof that the knower-reviewed papers were far from infallible; like all sentient beings, Knowers acted in accordance with sentient nature, and like any being acting according to sentient nature, they could be corrupted by the base indulgences all sentient beings are vulnerable to.

Greed.

Envy.

Lust.

There were others, but they were superfluous; Tesla was well aware that most Knowers would be persuaded by one of the three. Of course, Guvna's daughter or not, Tesla dared not say this out loud, not even when she was joking in private with her father; most in The Bubble Society were fervent believers in the orthodoxy, and would not take kindly to the idea that a fact put forth by Knowledge could be wrong.

This adherence to the orthodoxy predated The Advent; in fact, it was the growth of the belief in Knowledge and the wonders of technology that had created the conditions for Kingston's population to accept the transition to the Bubble Suits in the first place. To the true believers, it was obvious that Knowledge could cure all the woes of the sentient condition; the planet Shurtain might be a veil of pain and suffering, but Knowledge had the power to correct these errors in Nature's design, to create a utopian society, a world without discomfort, and a new dawn for sentientkind.

—

Tesla's parents, Donnie and Kelli were among the converts; under different circumstances, the couple might have been ambivalent about the steady rise of Knowledge, but everything changed with the birth of their oldest daughter. When the Bubble Suits were delivered, it was nothing short of a miracle; for the first time in their lives, the couple did not go to sleep wondering whether their daughter would be alive when they woke up the next morning.

Perhaps it was inevitable that Tesla would embrace alternative views, but as it played out, her journey to a new awareness had started a few weeks before her third birthday, back in the years Before Knowledge, when sentient beings did not have a direct interface with a computer through their Bubble Suits. As it played out, this awakening would coincide with her father's unexpected - and rapid - rise to The Guvna'ship.

On the day it all began, her father returned home with a new laptop computer under his arm, which he had dumped unceremoniously in an armchair as soon as he walked through the door. His boss had issued Donnie the machine in case he ever needed to do work at home, but given that Donnie rarely felt inclined to do work when he was at the office, he could not imagine what would possess him to work when he was at home.

Neither of Donnie's older daughters showed any interest in the machine, and Kelli was far too preoccupied with Andrea to bother with it, but the young Tesla took to the computer immediately. Her parents were surprised, but pleased; it was a huge weight off Kelli's shoulders, as trying to juggle an over-energetic two-year-old with a teenager in perpetual struggle was wearing her nerves raw. Anything that distracted Tesla for five minutes, let alone for hours on end, was a welcome relief.

As far as her parents knew, Tesla used the computer to play games and watch television shows. They were unaware that she could do anything else; Donnie used a computer to send messages and type reports at work, but he did not have much interest in the machines and had never learned anything about what they could do beyond what he needed to know, which meant that he had no inkling of the possibilities the computer offered his daughter.

For her part, when Tesla found it, she had not known what the laptop was, or what it was supposed to do. She simply found the box in the armchair and opened it up, with no expectations, no mental constraints on what the computer was, and what it could - or could not - do. A remarkable reader for her age, Tesla was able to follow the instructions, and quickly had her new toy working. And once she had it running, she found that it did all sorts of interesting things.

The first thing Tesla figured out was, as her parents expected, how to play games and watch shows. But as she continued to explore, she discovered instructional courses that showed her how to write her own programs, which allowed her to make the computer do whatever she wanted to - more or less.

Tesla loved it. She would spend hours lost in the machine, occasionally using it for the purposes her parents imagined, but more often building new programs, pushing the boundaries of what she could create. It was all wonderfully exciting from the start, but it was some weeks later, when Tesla was really getting familiar with the computer, that she had a realization that made her machine all the more interesting.

From the time she had started to use the computer, Tesla noticed that a gear would appear in the top right corner of the screen and turn for twenty or thirty seconds at roughly the same time each evening. At first, she had no idea what was happening, but as the weeks wore on, she realized that the gear icon must appear when her father shut down his desktop computer at the office; the gear was turning to indicate that his work computer was updating the Guvernment servers.

And as soon as it finished, it meant that the laptop had access to those servers.

Once Tesla figured this out, she was able to look through her father's files.

And that was not all.

With a bit of exploring, she found that she was able to look at everything in the system.

Absolutely everything.

In the decade that followed, Tesla would come to understand what an egregious security flaw this represented, but at the time, she had no idea that it was a mistake, or that the Guvernment's computer systems were full of similarly basic errors. It was her first lesson regarding the cracks in The Bubble Society's foundation; the population, comfortable and safe in their utopian society, was generally indifferent about the work they did, and in that culture, errors and shortcuts sprouted like mushrooms after a hard rain.

Tesla had not known of any of this when she started, and by the time she realized that her access to the Guvernment servers was due to an oversight, it was too late; by then, she had learned what the word "hacker" meant, but when she had finally come across the formal term, she was in so deep that she had laughed out loud at the thought of stopping. Nor did she think it was her fault that she ended up in this situation; on the day she had crossed the line onto the Guvernment's servers, she was just a three-year-old who had found a new way to use her toy.

Nothing more.

Nothing less.

But it had turned into so much more; it was how Tesla found her first clues that everything in The Bubble Society might not be as it appeared. In time, those hints would lead to a more thorough search, one that would lead her to design field experiments, which led her back to more papers, more documents, more knower-reviewed studies, and, in time, to the sealed-off library in The Old Capitol.

The journey had taken years, and in those years, it was not just Tesla's life that was affected by the computer.

Three weeks after he had brought the computer home, Donnie Mancini was called into his supervisor's office. Thinking that this could mean nothing good, Donnie had trudged into the office, wondering how he would feed the three children under his roof if he were fired.

Instead, to his utter astonishment, Donnie was informed that he was getting a promotion. His ears seemed to fill with a sort of buzzing; once he shook off the sensation, he heard his supervisor, Tad Richter, going on about how impressed he was with the hours Donnie was putting in at home. Donnie had no idea what Richter was talking about, but it seemed best to nod along as Richter lauded Donnie's willingness to race home and get back to the grind. Richter expressed that his only wish was that everyone else in the department was as committed to the job as Donnie.

All of this was utterly perplexing to Donnie, given that he considered himself to be the least committed member of Richter's team. His peers often pontificated about the contribution they made to Kingston by working for the Guvernment, but in Donnie's view, their entire department was a grift off the rest of society, just like 98% of the Kingston Guvernment. This did not bother Donnie; the department would exist whether or not he was there, and he had to feed his family somehow, but he had no delusions about his work providing any actual value to society.

If Donnie had asked Richter a clarifying question, or if he had realized that the computer was connected to the Guvernment servers, he might have made the connection between Tesla, the laptop, and this meeting.

But Donnie Mancini never made this leap in logic; his only concern was getting out of Richter's office without having to speak. He was also wondering how on Shurtain he would handle the responsibilities of his new position when he had never bothered to figure out what he was supposed to have been doing in his old one, which he had held for a decade and a half.

Fortunately, his new duties proved no more onerous than his previous ones, a pattern that continued to hold true as Donnie Mancini moved up the ladder. As far as he could tell, most of the folks working for the Guvernment did very little work; in fact, as he continued to receive promotions, it seemed to Donnie that more and more of his responsibilities consisted of talking to other senior Guvernment Officials about the work that folks in lower positions were supposed to be doing.

This rise, which saw Donnie receive another two promotions in as many seasons, started to expose him to some of Kingston's most influential private citizens; private citizens who stood to become even more influential citizuns if their plans for The Bubble Society came to be.

And these private citizens, who took a strong interest in Kingston's politics, became downright giddy when they discovered that Donnie Mancini, an exceptionally handsome man with a long history working for the Guvernment, had no political opinions or ambitions whatsoever.

From there, his rise no longer depended on confused managers drawing ill-formed conclusions; to this influential group, Donnie Mancini was the perfect candidate for Guvna'.

—

As Tesla sat there, wondering how much longer she had to endure the noise coming out of Maddox's mouth, she wondered what would have happened if her father had stuck the computer in his closet, or dumped it in the trash on the way home. Neither action would have been out of character for him.

It would have been a different world.

Her family would never have been able to live the life that they did.

And Tesla would never have developed a desperate desire to break free, and leave it all behind.

BOOK 2, CHAPTER 8

They reached the place late in the afternoon.

Gavin and Clarence had departed Turquoise Lake three days ago; now they stood on the rim of the last valley between them and Trepani, looking up to where the churning white froth cascaded over the edge of the mountain ridge, the point where the Western Grand began its voyage across Acadia.

For his part, Gavin was still getting used to the idea of a Western and Eastern Grand; as he and Clarence nudged the rams into motion and started to make their way across the valley, he remembered all of the times that his teachers, reading straight out of the books of Knowledge, had described the Grand River as a single entity, one that flowed from the peaks of the Cadillac Mountains to nourish The Bubble Society. The Grand River was *theirs*; Knowledge had designed the world so that Kingston, and only Kingston, would have access to the great water supply.

Gavin shook his head, thinking back to everything else that they had taught him.

Was any of it true?

Or had the Knowers decided all of it?

The ascent ahead of them was steep; switchbacks had been carved into the mountainside, a winding path through towering evergreens that grew on the north side of the river. Gavin glanced over the trees, noting the gaps in the forest that marked the path ahead, then shifted his eyes back to where the Western Grand flowed over the mountainside. As he did, he saw the silhouette of a sentient being at the top of the ridge; it was gone as quickly as it had appeared.

"Did you see that?" Gavin asked.

Clarence nodded, but his next words had nothing to do with Gavin's question.

"I'm excited for you to see Trepani. Don't spend much time in the city myself, what with all there is to do out in the wild, but it will be good for you. Get you around some folks your own age."

"Does anyone my age live close to your house?"

Clarence frowned at the question.

"Err, no. Don't have a house. As I say, I'm out in the Wild most of the time. When I am in town, I board at one of the lodging houses."

"Is that where we're going?"

Clarence shrugged.

"Maybe. We'll have to see."

The old man did not offer further clarification, and Gavin did not think it worth the effort to pursue the matter; like as not, his great-uncle's mind had already darted off to some other thought.

This had become a theme over the past few days: both the lack of clarification and his great-uncle's perpetually distracted nature. After his years living as a Ward on the Academic Campus, Gavin was not bothered by the lack of attention, but the more time he spent around Clarence, the more apprehensive he grew about what sort of welcome they would receive in Trepani. The old man was eccentric - to say the least - and it would not surprise Gavin to discover that more than a few folks had a more negative take on his great-uncle's behavior.

They continued on the trail for another ten minutes, Rex and Bruce making steady progress all the while. When they reached a clearing in the trees, the rams stopped.

"All right, time to unload," Clarence announced, dismounting.

Gavin looked around the clearing, confused.

"What do you mean? We aren't riding all the way up?"

"Nah, we don't keep the rams in Trepani - they'd wreak havoc if we tried to keep them cooped up - and it's easy enough to go the rest of the way on foot, there's a stone staircase built into the hillside up ahead. The rams can take care of themselves; we leave them to their own devices most of the time."

Gavin had taken over the saddling and unsaddling of Rex over the past two days, and he continued to handle those duties now, unburdening his ram as Clarence did the same for Bruce. Once they were done, they fed the rams a few more handfuls of their preferred mixture of herbs; the beasts snorted contentedly, then turned and trotted away into the trees.

"How do you get them to come back?" Gavin asked.

Clarence grinned at the question.

"That same mixture of grasses and herbs, or something similar," he replied, his eyes bright with energy as the topic shifted to Nature. "Sweetgrass, sage, a few other things…nothing the rams can't find on their own, but they have no way of mixing it in the ratios they like best. You come down here with a few handfuls, and the rams will come quick enough. Rex is usually the first to arrive, loves the stuff. Comes checking anytime sentient beings pass through, and if you've got what he wants, he'll smell it, and know you want him to approach you. Eager to trade, if you will."

Gavin was on the verge of replying, but as he started to speak, a young man appeared on the far side of the clearing. Gavin knew without asking that this was the silhouette he had seen at the top of the ridge.

The young man appeared to be about Gavin's age, and they were of a height, but that was where the similarities ended. Gavin was pale, the other swarthy; Gavin had a messy mop of blond hair that stood on end from all the times he ran his hands through it, while the other had meticulously barbered black hair, a curly black afro on top with a skin fade on the sides that gave way to a thick, sculpted beard at his jawline. Both had brown eyes, but Gavin's were round where the others were almond-shaped, a light brown where the other's were nearly dark enough to blend into his pupils.

And those were the least of their differences.

The stranger was dressed in shorts and sandals, his shirt hanging from his belt, which allowed Gavin to take in the young man's physique; as he did, he became far more aware of the flabby pale skin that his own clothes concealed. His counterpart was sculpted like some of the statues Gavin had seen in the films; though no more than six feet tall, Gavin guessed that the other must weigh well over two hundred pounds, and nearly all of it was muscle. His sculpted pectorals bulged over clearly defined abs, and swollen quadriceps peeked out from beneath his high-cut shorts.

Gavin continued to stare at the stranger, but the stranger was not looking at him; as that registered, Gavin's senses zoomed out, taking in the new arrival in his entirety, and he realized that while the young man was physically imposing, his expression was friendly, his brown eyes gleaming with amused interest as he looked at Gavin's great-uncle.

"Clarence. It's good to see you made it back safe."

Clarence looked at the young man with an eyebrow raised.

"A pleasure to see you as well Santino, though I'm surprised to find you waiting for me. I assume that's what you were doing."

Santino shrugged, then motioned back in the other direction.

"Shall we walk and talk? I imagine it's been a long couple of days, and you'll want to get up to town sooner than later. I can grab the saddle if you like."

Without waiting for an answer, Santino picked up the saddle and one of the packs, then started up the trail. Clarence grabbed two of the remaining saddle bags, leaving the last one for Gavin, and stepped past his great-nephew to match Santino's pace.

"You haven't answered my question; why were you waiting for me?

That is what you were doing, isn't it?"

Santino shrugged.

"Curiosity? And I wouldn't say I was waiting for you, though others are. I just decided to take my post-work run along the ridge, knowing that there was a chance you would arrive today. Lucky timing, I suppose."

"But how did you know I would be coming?"

Santino looked surprised.

"I'd have thought you could answer that. I know the night you left Kingston, and I know roughly how long it takes to get back to Trepani on a ram. It was no great trick; I'm certainly not alone in figuring it out."

"So you know where I've been?"

"Everyone knows where you've been, Clarence. Everyone knows what happened. It's all good with me, I'm not here to argue with you; if I was watching for you at all, it's because I wanted to meet Gavin Owens, the most famous defector in history. The only famous defector in history, for that matter. Which has an awful lot of people upset."

Santino turned to Gavin and shrugged the saddle up onto his shoulder so he could extend an awkward hand, which Gavin shook.

"Santino Vincente. Pleasure to meet you; it's been a few years since we had a defector close to my age. It's gonna be fun showing you the ropes."

Gavin started to respond, but Clarence interrupted.

"When you say an awful lot of people are upset; what do you mean, exactly?"

Santino shook his head.

"Do you remember the Town Gathering we had two weeks ago? The Ethics and Conduct Debate? The one that you participated in after the first incident at Kingfisher?"

"Certainly," Clarence responded.

"Well, this might surprise you, old friend, but so does everyone else. We all listened to you give your reasons for that first stunt with Gavin's Bubble Suit, and if you've forgotten, you didn't convince a whole lot of people. Almost everyone in Trepani agreed with The Council's argument then, and their opinion hasn't changed; from their perspective, there isn't a good reason for anyone to alert The Bubble Society to our presence. I don't think they ever imagined a disturbance on this scale."

"I'm an adult sentient being. The Council does not have the power to control me unless my actions are directly against another sentient being or their property."

Santino shrugged.

"That may be, but they're calling for you to defend yourself again after this latest incident; you're going to need to answer some questions when we get to Trepani."

"The Council…"

"It's not the Council, Clarence. It's a bunch of mothers and fathers who want an explanation for why you're stirring things up with Kingston when the leaders of The Bubble Society have ignored us for so long. People who are very uncomfortable with the fact that the Kingston Guvernment's Media App is now full of broadcasts about the search for Gavin Owens."

Clarence frowned.

"When do they mean to question me?"

"Now. As in, right when we get over the ridge and step into Trepani. There's been a group standing vigil for two days now, taking shifts to make sure there will be a crowd when you arrive; they've been at it day and night. By the time you get done explaining all this, Anton's unit may be back from their hunt, and they only left two days ago."

Clarence bristled at that.

"Is that any concern of mine? Is Anton someone I should fear now? He has no more authority than the Council to control my behavior."

"No. He doesn't."

Santino said this last part as if it did not matter very much, but he did not elaborate on the subject; instead, he glanced over his shoulder at Gavin.

"So, Gavin, you lived in a Bubble Suit until four days ago? Freaking wild. What was that like?"

Gavin opened his mouth, trying to decide how to answer. As he did, it occurred to him that he had not introduced himself.

"How do you know my name?"

Santino's eyes swiveled between Clarence and Gavin, a bemused grin on his face.

"You two really are family, huh? Brotha', the name Gavin Owens had already been on The Bubble Society's news non-stop for the last two weeks, and since you disappeared a few days ago, the coverage of the search to find you has been wall-to-wall. That's what I was telling Clarence, just now, while you were walking next to us; I thought you might have heard me. But in any case, you're famous in Trepani, and every other Acadian city. Everyone's seen your picture, everyone knows your name."

Santino chuckled when Gavin's eyes widened.

"Anyways, how you liking life on the other side? Journey up here treat you all right?"

Gavin grinned; after his time with Clarence, Santino's friendly manner was a welcome change.

"More or less. Sore, but that's ok. I never imagined I'd ever get to see any of this, everything we passed on the way up here. Down in Kingston, they told us all of the animals were dead."

Santino roared with laughter.

"I've heard about people in Kingston believing that. They got you too, then?"

The words could have been delivered harshly, but they were not; on the contrary, Santino sounded deeply amused. Gavin nodded, a grin on his face.

"Yep. The only animals I can remember before this were computer-programmed robots."

Santino shook his head. His eyes flashed to where two squirrels chased each other up and down a tree on the trail's edge.

"As kids, we'd hear about all that, and just laugh. We couldn't wrap our heads around it, a world where they denied the existence of animals, especially since there had still been animals in Kingston when we left."

He shook his head again.

"Then you get older, and learn there really aren't any animals left in Kingston. Same thing with the Bubble Suits; if it weren't for the Guvernment Media App, I don't think I would have believed that the sentient beings down there really live like that. After all, it's a strange thing to believe, when you're out here and can see that everyone can breathe the air just fine."

Gavin nodded, unsure of how to respond; despite Santino's good-natured tone, Gavin was starting to wonder whether his new acquaintance was mocking him. After all, Gavin had believed all of this until a few days ago. Santino seemed to read his thoughts.

"No worries brotha', I'm not criticizing you. If I'd been born into your life and had your experiences, I'd have grown up believing everything you did. Or at least, that's what my grandfather would have said."

Unburdened by Santino's words, Gavin found his voice.

"You have no idea. I couldn't believe it when I saw my great-uncle, standing there without a Bubble Suit. It felt like my brain had gone haywire."

Santino shrugged.

"Nothing out of the ordinary, from what I understand. Most defectors struggle with the transition, but they can't help but settle into their new awareness with time. They're immersed in it, after all, and once you're out in the open, breathing the same air they claim is too toxic for sentient beings, it's impossible to keep believing all the Knowledge they insist is truth down in The Bubble Society."

Gavin did not respond. Santino's words had sent his mind back to the shores of Turquoise Lake, where he had sat next to the fire with Clarence.

Back to their conversation.

—

"Pathogens?"

Clarence nodded.

"Lethal pathogens."

Gavin mirrored his great-uncle's nod, though he did not really know why. His eyes floated over to where the last rays of the setting sun reflected off the surface of Turquoise Lake; the night was clear, the sky a glowing tapestry, oranges and reds fading into deep purples, the first hints of the coming darkness.

That the world could be so beautiful made it even harder to understand.

"Why?"

"Why what?"

"Why would they do that?"

"Now," Clarence said, settling back. "That's a story."

He was not looking at Gavin; instead, Clarence stared into the fire, his eyes seeing something far away as he started his story.

"There's a funny thing about what you in Kingston call Knowledge. Your Guvernment would have you believe that sentient beings understand everything about the Universe, about Nature. The way they tell it, the introduction of the Bubble Suits marked the completion of Knowledge; that's what they meant, when they designated the present era as 'After Knowledge' - as in, After Knowledge was settled. After generations of struggle, sentient beings had finally taken hold of their destiny, had become masters of the Universe."

"Perhaps it wasn't a lie, per se. Perhaps they really did believe it themselves. It is a comfortable notion, after all… but it is utterly absurd."

"They aren't the first. They come in different forms, the overlords, but whether they use religion, prophecy, or reason to convince you, there will always be those sentient beings who insist that they should have control of others, who believe that they alone should make decisions for society, that they alone know what is right, and what is wrong, what is true, and what is false. On some level, they act as though they are omniscient - though they cannot see it themselves - but regardless of what they believe, the passage of time has yet to produce the sentient being who transcended sentient nature. In the end, we are all flesh and blood, destined to return to dust and ashes, but the powers-that-be rarely act in accordance with the ramifications of that truth."

"For instance, in the Scientific Era, it seemed that once or twice a generation, a group of scientists would put forth the argument that science was nearing completion, that all of the mysteries of the Universe had been unraveled. It was a tale nearly as old as science itself; no matter how many times their predecessors made fools of themselves, there was always a younger generation of scientists ready to believe that they would be the ones to transcend reality, who believed that they were the chosen ones, the sentient beings who would reach the promised land, rather than yet another generation that would make progress, and hold up the flag for another generation to carry forward."

"Far from being even vaguely correct, such pronouncements were often the harbinger of breakthroughs that undermined the science of the day, rearranging our understanding of the Universe. Instead of discovering the last piece of the puzzle, those using the scientific method to better understand the world would instead find a piece that did not fit, a discovery that, rather than simplifying our understanding, opened our eyes to new mysteries about the nature of reality, new depths to plunge."

"The truth is that we understand next to nothing about the experience that we call life. Perhaps we understand 1% of the Universe…we might be generous and give ourselves 2%…but what would that even mean? We understand, to some extent, how to operate on our planet, in our time, in our galaxy…but what is that to Nature?"

"In the end, it led to the end of the Scientific Era; over and over, the most famous among them would fall victim to this hubris, convincing themselves that they were different, immune from the types of mistakes that the sentient beings of the past had made. They promised the people the stars and both moons, but they had no way to make it happen."

It was full dark by then; Clarence had taken on a new aspect as he told the story. He continued to stare into the fire, his eyes a thousand miles away, then shook his head.

"It's a remarkable thought, really. The idea that we could completely understand," Clarence turned his gaze to the stars, "all of this."

Gavin mirrored his great-uncle's movement and looked up into the night; startled, he fell back where he sat. Pure awe washed over him for a moment, and then he found himself wondering how he had never seen this before.

Understanding came a moment later.

On the previous night, after their escape, Gavin had been too exhausted to focus on anything but the trail in front of him.

And that had been his only other chance to see this phenomena, because this was not the same sky that he saw at night in Kingston; in Kingston, he could see the moons, and perhaps a few dozen stars, if there were no clouds and the moonlight was dim.

This was something else entirely.

Some of the stars were familiar to him, but even those looked strange. Not only were they brighter than he could have imagined, but rather than floating out there on their own, they were a few amongst many, whole clouds of sparkling lights strewn across the sky, coming together to form a world that he had never seen. A shooting star streaked across the backdrop, then another, both there and gone before Gavin could do more than gape.

"Finally, it became too much; they left one too many promises unfulfilled, and public confidence in science - or what science had become - shattered."

"There was a moment in time when it appeared that there was nobody to fill the power vacuum; it seemed there was nothing left for society to build around. Before the Scientific Era, the Church had reigned supreme, but their leaders had lost their credibility during the Evangelist Era, when - in the name of the endless love and compassion of their Lord - the Church developed an unfortunate habit of hunting, torturing, and killing any heretics that they perceived as not being sufficiently devoted to their cause."

"Those were grim times, and the history, as well as the myths that sprung up around it, remained prominent in the minds of many as the Scientific Era collapsed. So while the leaders of the Church - or what remained of it - hoped that they might step in to fill the power vacuum, the population had no interest in subjecting themselves to that authority again."

"With so many shattered idols, and no other entity to fill the void, the people of Kingston gravitated towards the worship of money, to the pursuit of material possessions. To facilitate these desires, they turned themselves over to the guidance of the economists, that select group of individuals who promised that they could create unprecedented prosperity on the planet Shurtain if given license to lead. They claimed that they had figured out how to avoid the rises and falls of the trade market that had plagued sentientkind since trade had begun, and that by taking control of the treasury and managing the money supply, they could ensure the consistent production and trade of goods, year after year."

"And so began the Economic Era."

"It might not have been so bad, had their goal actually been to improve the standard of living for your average citizen - this was back in the days before The Bubble Society made citizens citizuns - but the economists were not interested in that. First and foremost, the economists were concerned with enriching themselves, and the influential individuals who kept them on the throne. They made great claims about the virtues of free markets even as they rigged the markets, turning whole industries into monopolies and oligopolies, strangling the free market power that they claimed was the source of so much good."

"For a time, things were not so bad; thirty years in, the Economic Era actually looked quite promising. But as time wore on, the impacts built up, eventually causing catastrophic collapses in the trade markets with impacts that reached far beyond Kingston."

"At the same time, new waves of illness and disease were spreading across the Acadian continent, illness that could not be explained."

"Those were the decades that saw the collapse of whole towns and cities across the Acadian continent. And though many could not see it, all of the issues emanated from Kingston, where the population continued to swell, the desperate and frightened across the Acadian continent abandoning their homes to come to the one city that had not been impacted by the economic downturn."

"Unfortunately, the people of Kingston were as plagued by health troubles as the rest of Acadia, and as the people packed in, the problems grew worse. Fear spread, slowly but surely, gripping a population that came to believe its extinction would come sooner than later."

"That was the world that opened the door for The Bubble Society."

Clarence paused, his eyes back on the fire and a deep frown on his face. Impatient to hear the rest of the story, Gavin prompted him, asking again about the pathogens.

"Ah, yes. Well, with the failure of their vaunted economists, Kingston's Guvernment, which had amassed a great deal more power by overseeing all of the regulations implemented during the Economic Era, was scrambling to save face. Unfortunately, they were not particularly capable, or competent, when it came to managing the situation. They needed help. And that's where Dynamic Solutions stepped in."

"Precisely when Dynamic Solutions was created remains a mystery, but from what we've pieced together, a small group of influential individuals had long been pulling the strings in Kingston, pivoting from one era to the next, working to retain control through the ebbs and flows of time. Of course, they were well aware of the inner workings of the moves the economists had made, and they understood that there would be a time, in a few years, or perhaps a decade, when chaos would engulf Kingston. And in that moment, they would have an opportunity to strike."

"With the benefit of time, they studied what had doomed the ruling bodies of old, took time to understand why previous authorities had failed to maintain their hold on power. This cabal, which was led by the man who would become The Director of The Board at Dynamic Solutions, took steps to ensure that their new control mechanism - Knowledge - would never be challenged, its figureheads never threatened."

"This, of course, was no simple matter. Kingston had been a democracy - ostensibly - since the beginning of the Scientific Era. As such, when the newly branded citizuns of The Bubble Society began to argue against the need for the Bubble Suits, there could not simply be a silencing, or a disappearing; that would have been too much a reminder of the stories from the Evangelist Era."

"The Board had to find another way to deal with them. A public way to end any further claims that the Bubble Suits were unnecessary. A way to prove that what Dynamic Solutions was doing, in partnership with the Guvernment, was a purely magnanimous gesture, a heartfelt gift from two great organizations that were sacrificing their own interests to uplift the masses, suffering profound hardships in order to ensure the people could live a better life."

"So the Aeronbald Experiments…" Gavin started.

"Weren't what they appeared," Clarence finished. "When they used the

Spike to cut open the Bubble Suits, the subjects got more than they had bargained for. The needles were tipped with pathogens, and those Spikes were designed so that if someone used enough force to pierce a Bubble Suit, they would have to leave at least a small prick in their skin."

"So they didn't die of atmospheric poisoning?"

Clarence shook his head.

"No. We didn't know exactly what had happened at the time, but one of the Knowers who had been charged with altering the Spikes defected shortly after the Experiments - he was the one to steal the first Spike - and we got the full story from him, along with the information we needed to build our own versions of the Spikes. Minus the pathogens, of course."

"As convenient an explanation as it was for all of the health problems that plagued sentient beings during the Economic Era, you can still breathe the air on Shurtain. In fact, we Acadians are fond of saying that the air on Shurtain is blessed; after all, the air in our atmosphere, the air we all share, is the only air in the Universe that sentient beings can breathe at all."

—

Now, as they made their way toward Trepani, Gavin drew in another breath, savoring the taste of it, the cool crispness of the air, which was so much fresher than the product that flowed out of the vaunted air filtration system in the Bubble Suits.

"I think I'm there. I'm past the sense that this isn't real."

Santino smiled at that.

"That's good. I expect it will only get better; I'll be interested in what you have to say a few days from now."

They hiked in silence for a time, steadily gaining altitude as the trail snaked through the evergreens.

"What's on the other side?" Gavin asked.

Santino grinned.

"He didn't tell you?"

"Well, I know that we're going to Trepani. But all I know is the name of the place."

Santino nodded.

"Well, you're about to see for yourself; we'll reach the top of the ridge soon. But I can tell you some of the things you can't know by seeing. First thing to know is, Trepani is our principal settlement."

"So it's the Capitol?"

Santino shook his head.

"No. We don't have a Capitol. In…"

"But then where does your Guvernment rule from?"

Santino chuckled at Gavin's interruption, amused by the panic that had risen in his companion's voice.

"Remember how I said I'd be interested in what you think of the transition a few days from now? Well, this is one of those things that defectors tend to struggle with."

Gavin opened his mouth to interject, but Santino held up a hand, indicating that he would explain.

"The outright lies are the easiest to right, because those are indisputable. Once you're out in open air, and you don't fall over twitching and foaming at the mouth, your conscious brain is forced to reconcile the disparity and accept that you can breathe the air on Shurtain. Such moments are profound, and you come out of them with your belief system irreversibly transformed."

"That part is straightforward; rewriting your beliefs about the stories that sentient beings tell themselves is a different beast. It's objectively false that sentient beings need Bubble Suits to survive, which makes it easy to demonstrate that the alternative is true. But convincing someone who grew up in Kingston that a Guvernment with top-down control of sentient beings is neither necessary nor practical is another matter altogether; it requires a different sort of approach, a different sort of argument. The same goes for arguing that The Bubble Society's primary aim, the guarantee of a certain future, is not achievable in this experience we call reality, which is inherently uncertain."

Gavin found himself nodding along as Santino spoke, but when his new companion paused, Gavin shook himself, and looked the other young man up and down.

"How old are you? You sound like some old man, but you don't look much older than me. Where'd you come up with this stuff?"

Santino laughed.

"You got me there; the thoughts aren't my invention. I spent a lot of time following my grandfather around as a child - sort of a family tradition - and he was full of this stuff. He died when I was five, but by then, I was pre-loaded with his recordings, as my old man likes to say."

"In any case, we don't have a Guvernment like the one you have in Kingston. We don't have rulers, because if we'd had rulers, we never would have survived."

"Why not?"

"There was too much to do. Any sort of oversized, top-down bureaucracy would have slowed us down, made us too inefficient to adequately prepare for the first Winter. There was a loose leadership structure, but its primary purpose was to facilitate communication; there weren't layers of managers attempting to run things from the back. Those who led did so from the front. Everybody worked. Everybody contributed. Fortunately, sentient beings are made for that; we benefit from working together, but we are smart enough to make determinations on how to best complete our own tasks."

"Anyways, that's too long a story to tell now; the steps are up ahead, we're almost there."

Santino said this as they rounded a final switchback, onto a portion of the path where the trail pitched up sharply; as he had promised, a series of rectangular stone steps, roughly hewn and jagged, were set deep in the ground of the incline.

The stairs began in a patch of open sunlight but were quickly swallowed up by the evergreens; the trees grew close here, letting little light through their canopy, making the path feel like a tunnel. Gavin tried to count the number of steps on the staircase, but he lost count at seventy-seven, and, on his second attempt, at forty-six. He would have asked Santino, but something about this place, and the quiet that engulfed it, gave Gavin the feeling that he should wait until they reached the top of the ridge to ask any more questions.

In time, the end of the staircase appeared, a patch of daylight that grew steadily larger as the three men climbed. When they stepped through that daylight, they stood at the top of the ridge; dozens of peaks towered above them, and below, sprawled out across the valley from the northern banks of Grand Lake, was Trepani.

Trepani was laid out on clear gridlines, the steep wooden roofs of its dwellings spaced evenly along the slope of the valley, the buildings following the arc of Grand Lake's edge. Gavin could not see the whole of the settlement - Grand Lake bent to the right at the far end of the valley - but he could see that, in addition to all of the homes, the city of Trepani boasted several larger structures. From where he stood, he could see a towering wooden building with an expansive stone patio on the lakeside of the building, the stone pit of a sort of lakeside theater, and, right at the point where the bend of Grand Lake took the rest of Trepani out of his view, a stone spire that stood at least twice as tall as any other building in his vision.

Gavin continued to gaze around the valley, drinking in the scene, but his companions had their focus elsewhere. Santino's attention was on Clarence, and the old man's reaction to the crowd that waited for him in the valley below. Santino was hard-pressed not to laugh; from the look on Clarence's face, it seemed that his grandfather's old friend had somehow failed to anticipate that something like this would be coming.

Santino had known Clarence as long as he could remember; the old man and his grandfather had been close friends, and Santino had often been underfoot on the occasions when Clarence, a recluse who lived up in Onyx Canyon, ventured into Kingston for a visit. The young Santino was endlessly amused by Clarence; quirky, and quick to laugh, his grandfather's friend had been happy to let the young Santino tug at his long beard, which was going to grey even in those days.

As Santino grew older, and came to understand that Clarence did not exist for his personal amusement, he had wondered aloud why his grandfather spent time with such a strange man. His grandfather had ruffled the young Santino's black hair, and told him not to let the packaging prevent him from seeing the gifts a sentient being has to offer. He pointed out how naive it was to rely on appearances, to allow the external to prevent one from seeing the consciousness in another sentient being. It was not only a disservice to the individual being observed; it was a disservice to the observer, a self-inflicted wound, a failure to appreciate all that the Universe had to offer. His grandfather told Santino that he should not be put off by those who did not conform to society's demands; it was the ones making the demands who were the real danger.

It was a message Santino had never forgotten. But his grandfather had also implored Santino never to take life so seriously that he could not smile at its absurdities, so Santino smiled now, allowing himself to marvel at how Clarence could have possibly thought his actions would not draw this sort of reaction, that they would go unremarked upon by the people of Trepani.

After a few minutes on the ridge, Santino broke the silence.

"Well, Clarence, I believe that's your welcoming party. I suppose we ought to meet them."

BOOK 2, CHAPTER 9

"You haven't found the body?"

The Guvna' leaned back in his chair, frowning as he considered what seemed to be a question.

At least, Tarissa Cross had voiced her words as a question, though The Guvna' could not have said why. Like every other member of The Board, Cross was receiving hourly updates on the progress - or more accurately, the lack of progress - via her secured version of the Guvernment Messaging App, so she knew very well that the Guvernment's search parties had not recovered the body.

Taking a breath, The Guvna' reminded himself that Cross's question should not come as a surprise. He should have realized what was coming when he got a call from The Director, announcing that three members of The Board had been dispatched to meet with The Guvna' in his office at The New Capitol. He should have mentally prepared himself for the duel of words that inevitably defined his interactions with Tarissa Cross.

Cross was second-in-command on The Board at Dynamic Solutions, which meant that she held the title of Viceroy. The Guvna' thought this an absurd title to apply to anyone, but he supposed that Cross was the perfect fit to fill an office with such an ostentatious name. He decided that, on the balance, it was better to play along with Cross today, and to answer her question as if it needed answering; that would give him the best chance of getting out of the office before the sun started to set.

"Nope, haven't found da body. And not fer lack o' resources, as I told yer boss when he called earlier. We've kept da search parties going day n' night, just as Da Director insisted."

"But you haven't found the body?"

As always, Tarissa Cross's dress was immaculate, a stylish blend of professionalism and taste; today, she had set her Bubble Suit to project a dark blue suit over a white blouse. Her shoulder-length black hair was brushed back, highlighting the most prominent aspects of her features: her dark brown eyes and smooth tan skin.

She was accompanied by two others; Reginald Klaus, an older man with a bald head, pale skin, and watery eyes hidden behind tortoiseshell glasses, and Yvonne Delverta, a platinum blonde with bright blue eyes and creamy white skin, who stood respectfully behind Cross as their superior addressed The Guvna'. The Guvna' was familiar with the pair - he had met with them many times over the years - and he could not recall sharing an enjoyable moment with either of them.

Still, that was part of filling the role as The Guvna'; when The Director of The Board at Dynamic Solutions asked you to receive an audience, you received the audience.

"What I jus' said, innit? No, we haven't found da body; far as anyone can tell, damn thing's vanished. It's a mystery, I'll give you dat, but not one dat needs solving; wherever Gavin Owens is, he's dead."

Cross's mouth tightened at his response; behind her, Klaus and Delverta exchanged a meaningful glance, as if Cross's presence in the foreground would prevent The Guvna' from noticing the look that passed between them. The Guvna', of course, did not miss this - he was not blind - but he did not have the bandwidth to wonder what it meant at the moment. Tarissa Cross took enough of his attention.

"We see it differently. The Board has decided that it is essential that we recover the body for research purposes. Knowers might glean Knowledge of tremendous importance by studying the remains, and grim as this may sound, the recovery of the body will serve as a reminder to the rest of the population."

"A reminda' o' what?"

"Of the terrible dangers of suffering damage to a Bubble Suit. Of what can happen when sentient beings stray out of bounds and disregard the safeguards that the Guvernment has put in place to ensure our utopia will continue to flourish."

The Guvna' shrugged.

"Well, it's a reminda' o' da dangers o' being young and reckless, I'll give you dat. But I dunno what ta tell ya - if it were in my power ta 'ppease y'all, I'd do it - my track record speaks ta dat. But I don't got da body, and I dunno what ta do except keep da searchers working. I ain't 'bout to go looking myself, I'll tell you dat."

"We weren't going to suggest that. Reginald, Yvonne?"

The Guvna' watched as Klaus retreated to the doorway, his attention on the light switch. As Klaus moved to submerge the room in darkness,

Delverta set a small black box with a projector lens on a table in the middle of the room.

The Guvna's stomach clenched; he held up a hand.

"No, no. You don't need ta bother wit' any o' dat; you can jus' send me da slides, I'll read 'em on my holographic monitor later, and in da meantime, you can jus' tell me what da Knowers concluded."

Cross turned and nodded at Klaus and Delverta, who stopped setting up the theater experience for their presentation; Klaus turned on the lights, and Delverta switched the device off, then they returned to their original positions.

Relief flooded The Guvna'. It was not that he doubted whatever they were going to tell him - it was Knowledge, after all - but after more than twenty years, he could not bear the thought of another Knowledge-based presentation from anyone at Dynamic Solutions. There would be reams of data, uncounted graphs and figures, stacks of evidence from knower-reviewed papers, all to confirm what anyone should have Known without asking: that the Knowledge was correct.

Her presentation scuttled, Cross turned to continue addressing The Guvna'.

"Very well, I'll give you the short version. Some of our Knowers have grown concerned that this Gavin may have survived long enough to get clear of the Elevation Limit before he died. The Director - and The Board - have unanimously agreed that we must find a way to expand the limits of our search."

The Guvna' was about to object, to point out the lunacy of the idea that the young man could have gotten from Kingfisher Reservoir, where his Bubble Suit was found, to the Elevation Limit, but Tarissa Cross was in full stride, and he never got the words out.

"Due to this new need, The Board has crafted a proposal; in accordance with proper Democratic procedures, you will pass this proposal along to Moderator McKenzie, who will put it to the Halls of Parliament tomorrow morning."

"What sorta' proposal?"

"A proposal for the creation of a new prize: the Elevation Upgrade Prize."

"Dat's da best name y'all could come up with?"

Cross ignored The Guvna's remark.

"The Board has determined that the limitations of our Bubble Suits - namely, their inability to function at high altitudes - is an issue that must be remedied immediately. We have great faith in Kingston's Knowers, but even so, a little extra incentive will not go amiss; a million Guvernment credits, and a home in the Amada District, will provide powerful motivation for anyone who might be able to solve this problem."

"To avoid the appearance of impropriety, The Director has determined that the Academy of Knowledge will establish the prize. They need not put up the funds, of course - Dynamic Solutions will provide that - but we will need their cooperation in all else."

The Guvna' frowned; he did not like to directly dispute The Board, but this plan made absolutely no sense to him.

"All dat ta find one fellow who went missing? Ain't it a lot o' bother? Once we retrieve da body, we'll have no reason to employ da upgrades again; afta' all, everything beyond da Elevation Limit is dead. Nuthin' but trees up there."

"As I've told you, we consider it essential to Knowledge that we retrieve this body, and learn all there is to be learned from this poor young man's unfortunate demise."

For the briefest of moments, The Guvna' thought of pressing Cross, but then he glanced at the clock, and realized the day was getting away from him. He shrugged.

"If ya say so. Good 'nuff, I'll have ma team make da necessary arrangements; I assume Moderator Montenegro has already been read in on this, so he'll have dis on da floor for da East and West Halls of Parliament tomorrow morning. Should be passed by da afternoon."

Tarissa Cross frowned.

"Of course Montenegro Knows about this, but not in his official capacity. You still need to make the call and meet with him this afternoon. Democracy is the bedrock of our utopia; we must ensure we continue to respect it above everything, and that means following proper procedures. So there must be a public record showing that you delivered this proposal to Montenegro."

Cross started to turn away, then paused. This did not surprise The Guvna'; Cross was a poor actress, and she had also employed this particular tactic on several other occasions.

"One last thing. If anyone asks, you will tell them that Knower Antonius came up with this idea, and passed it along to you."

The Guvna' nodded.

"He's da fella who was up fer Head Knower after ol' Ancel died, right? One who lost out to Head Knower Mallion in da replacement proceedings?"

"One of a few, yes. He's over at Dynamic Solutions now, the Head of the Department of Atmospheric Sciences. The Director - and Head Knower Mallion - thought him a credible source for the suggestion."

"Fine by me."

Cross nodded in response.

"Wonderful. Well, Guvna', I thank you for the audience. I'm certain The Director will be pleased to hear how our conversation went; we look forward to tomorrow's announcement."

BOOK 2, CHAPTER 10

As he sat next to Santino in the steaming pool, watching the sun set over the western peaks, Gavin found it hard to believe he had experienced so much in a single day.

The final stretch of the hike.

The Western Grand.

And now, Trepani.

Of course, not everything about the day had been good. Or at least, not everything about the day had been good for his great-uncle, though on the whole, Gavin figured things could have gone worse.

—

"Well, Clarence, I believe that's your welcoming party. I suppose we ought to meet them."

Clarence frowned.

"You're sure they're not here for Gavin? That's who you wanted to meet, isn't it?"

Santino shook his head.

"No, Clarence, they're not here for Gavin."

"How do you know?"

"They told me, Clarence. When I was on their side of the ridge. Less than an hour ago."

They stood in silence, Clarence gazing down at the crowd with his eyes narrowed, scratching at his beard as he took in the scene.

"Well, so be it."

Clarence started down the hill without another word; Santino gave a slight start at the old man's abrupt movement, then shrugged his shoulders and followed, Gavin a step behind them.

"What are you going to say?" Santino asked.

"I'll figure it out. Right now, I need to think."

They made the rest of the descent in silence. Gavin felt a certain sense of anxiety for his great-uncle, who was tapping the tips of his fingers against his thumbs in a compulsive pattern as they made their way down the trail. He thought Clarence might attempt to duck away from the crowd, but to his surprise, his great-uncle did the opposite; as Clarence, Santino, and Gavin turned onto the final leg of the trail, coming out from behind a last stretch of tree cover to find the crowd waiting before them, Clarence sprang forward and held up a hand for the few dozen people awaiting their arrival. Before anyone else could say a word, Clarence drew himself up, and began to speak.

"Greetings, my fellow sentient beings. I am delighted that you have all come out to welcome me on this joyous occasion."

"You will be pleased to learn that, at great risk to myself, I, Clarence S.Q. Barnett, have extracted my great-nephew Gavin from the clutches of The Bubble Society."

Clarence gestured toward Gavin with a sweeping motion of his arm, then caught him by the wrist. Gavin turned to meet his great-uncle's eyes; with a slight nod of his head, Clarence indicated that he wanted Gavin to step forward with him.

Gavin felt the heat rise in his face as his great-uncle raised Gavin's arm up over his head, as if he were the victor of some great contest. It occurred to Gavin that he ought to say something, but Clarence beat him to it.

"Now, my fellow Acadians, Gavin would like to express how excited he is to join us, but it has been a long journey, and he needs to begin his recovery, so we really must be off. Again, we thank you for being here to greet us this evening; I couldn't have imagined such a scene, nor dreamed up a better way to show my great-nephew the kind, welcoming nature of the Acadians who call Trepani home."

Unsure what to think of his great-uncle's pronouncement, Gavin glanced at Santino, who, to Gavin's surprise, was trying not to laugh. Before Gavin could say anything about this, Clarence dropped his hand and started toward the crowd, his strides long and purposeful. Santino fell in stride with Gavin and tapped him on the shoulder, indicating that they should follow.

Gavin saw more than a few angry expressions in the crowd and heard discontented murmurs increasing in volume, but even as a few of the crowd opened their mouths to address Clarence, his great-uncle boomed out, "Too good of you, too good, I'm really much obliged. No time for questions now, but I shall be at Nately's Public House later this evening, once I have my great-nephew situated, and I would be pleased to let you all buy me a pint or two in congratulations then."

That turned a few faces bright red, but for the moment, most in the crowd appeared more confused than angry; at the very least, there was enough hesitation in the mob that they allowed Clarence, Gavin, and Santino to pass by and continue into Trepani without actually saying a word to them.

When they were further along the footpath, headed toward a stretch of houses on the edge of town, Santino broke the silence.

"You'll have to face them eventually."

Clarence shrugged.

"Perhaps. If I put them off another day or so, they might forget. It's hard to say what twists and turns life will take."

Santino rolled his eyes; Clarence did not appear to notice. Gavin trailed behind them, too preoccupied by everything around him to pay their exchange much mind.

There were a handful of people outside their homes, but at the moment, Gavin's attention was consumed by Trepani's animal population. A great variety of creatures roamed the streets, yards, and pastures around him; Gavin was pleased that he could identify several species, but for every one he had seen along his journey, or in a film, there was another that he had never encountered.

He recognized the cows roaming the pastures, but not the long-necked, curly-haired, hump-backed creatures that shared the fields with them. He also knew the long-billed ducks, but not the feathery, sharp-beaked creatures that pecked at the ground next to them. The cats and dogs were relatively familiar from his time in Kingston, though Gavin could tell, without asking, that not one of these was a robot.

Gavin was too lost in the newness of it all to realize how much attention he was drawing from the people he passed. Defectors were always a curiosity - their unhealthy pallor, stooped postures, and droopy musculature made them easy to identify - but Gavin was recognizable for a different reason. He was famous, the only defector to ever enter Trepani with any sort of recognition or notoriety, and as he passed, people stared, or rushed back into their houses to call out the rest of their families so they could all take in the spectacle.

After a couple of miles, Clarence and Santino paused to let Gavin catch up to them. When Gavin turned in the direction that his two companions were facing, down a wide boulevard that ran to the shores of Grand Lake, he knew that he was looking at their destination; down near the water's edge, the wooden building that he had noted from the ridge loomed over the homes around it. It was built of the same wood as the houses, but was at least ten times as large, standing four stories tall with a footprint that took up half a block.

"Well, there it is. The Hot Springs."

Santino turned to Gavin, who nodded uncertainly.

"What's in there?" Gavin asked.

"In there? A couple pools, several rooms for physical rehabilitation work, a gym. But we're not here for what's inside, at least not tonight. We're here for what's outside."

They crossed the remaining distance to the building and approached a doorway on the north side of the structure, opposite Grand Lake. Santino got there first; he pulled the door open and held it for the others.

A young woman waited inside, standing behind a greeter's podium at the mouth of a cavernous room. She was on the verge of addressing Clarence and Gavin, but then Santino stepped inside, and she shifted her attention to him.

"Got the timing right then, did you?"

Santino nodded, his eyes flashing in Clarence's direction.

"I had good information, what can I say?"

Elsie smiled at Santino, brushing back a few strands of black hair from her mocha skin as she did. Then she turned to Gavin.

"So you're the defector?"

Gavin nodded, feeling awkward.

"Nice to meet you. Eleanor is waiting for you out by the Hot Springs; we shouldn't keep her waiting."

Elsie turned and indicated they should follow her. As they crossed the hall, she fell into stride beside Gavin.

"So, what's it like being back in your skin?"

"Back in my skin?"

"Oh, you know what I mean, being able to feel the world through your skin instead of those Bubble Suits. Being able to touch things. I mean, I don't even like it when I have to wear gloves in the winter; I can't imagine being trapped in one of those things."

Gavin was about to retort that the Bubble Suit's technology actually enhanced the ability to feel things, but even as he opened his mouth to say so, he stopped; he almost laughed as he realized that this bit of Knowledge was still lodged in his mind, clinging to life despite all the evidence he had seen to the contrary. Gavin dismissed the nonsense thought and turned his mind to Elsie's question.

"Nothing like it. At least, not in Kingston. I'm sore - not as sore as I was on the first day - but that's ok. It's better than feeling nothing, and that's about what you get in the Bubble Suits; a total lack of sensation."

Elsie nodded. They had reached the far side of the room; Elsie pulled a door open and stepped down onto a winding staircase. The group followed her; after descending twenty or thirty steps, they reached a black iron door. Elsie reached for the handle, turned it, and pulled the door in, revealing a small deck attached to a staircase that led to the steaming pools below.

A woman waited for them on the deck; Santino stepped forward.

"Gavin, allow me to introduce my grandmother: Eleanor Cahn."

The old woman stepped forward, a glowing smile on her lined face.

"Welcome, Gavin. It's a pleasure to meet you," she said, holding out a hand.

Eleanor Cahn held herself upright with a certain effortlessness; she was tall, with dark brown eyes that might have once matched her hair, though the latter had gone to a grey that contrasted sharply with her light brown skin. Uncomfortable with her familiarity, Gavin nodded and shook her extended hand; he did not know what else to do under the circumstances.

"And how was your journey? Clarence managed to keep you alive, I see."

"It was good. I'm glad we're here - I'm pretty sore - but it was worth it. I never imagined anything like this," he answered.

Eleanor nodded, smiling.

"That's good to hear. Well, Gavin, I regret that I only have a brief moment to greet you, but as your great-uncle has managed to find his way past his greeters, there are several matters I need to discuss with him. However, I did want to take a moment to welcome you to Trepani, and to let you know what to expect in the days to come. If my grandson didn't tell you, I oversee operations here at the Hot Springs and the attached center. For the most part, we provide services to the community as a general healing and wellness clinic, but we also have a specialized program for defectors making the transition out of their Bubble Suits. You are twenty-three, correct?"

"Twenty-three?"

Gavin was caught up short; it took him a moment to realize what Eleanor meant.

"Oh, ya, I turned twenty-three this year. Why does that matter?"

Eleanor smiled.

"You'd be surprised; the fact that your physical body had several years to develop before you put on the Bubble Suit makes a tremendous difference. And more importantly, it means that you grew in a womb, with a direct connection to another sentient being - your mother - and through her, the wider planet of Shurtain. You were not grown in one of the hermetically sealed pods created by the Department of Infant Development."

Eleanor paused to appraise Gavin.

"He made the journey by ram?"

She kept her gaze on Gavin, but the question was directed at Clarence.

"That's right. I had the rams tied up near the Elevation Limit, so there was a bit of a hike."

Eleanor nodded.

"Well, you seem to have come through unscathed. There are several obvious issues that I can see at a glance; poor hip alignment, pronounced stoop in the shoulders, and appalling bone density, but all of that is to be expected. The fact that you made it here alive indicates that your body still has some measure of metabolic flexibility, which is certainly not a given after twenty years of living on that nutrient paste. It's one of the reasons it's so dangerous to defect without a proper escape plan in place."

Eleanor's eyes flicked in Clarence's direction as she spoke her last words, but the old man did not react to the comment.

"In any case, it looks like you'll survive; no, don't look so shocked, it's only an old woman's joke, you look just fine, all things considered, and your health will improve markedly in the weeks to come. Santino will oversee your acclimation in the first stage of the program; he has worked with a defector or two in his time working here, so you will be in good hands."

Eleanor turned to Clarence.

"As for you, Clarence, I look forward to sharing a meal with you. There is a great deal of unrest in Trepani, and the concerns have spread to the other Acadian cities. With so many moving parts, and you in the middle of it, I think we ought to take some time to discuss the best way forward."

Clarence appeared uncertain about this invitation, but while she had spoken in a soothing tone, Gavin noticed that Eleanor had not actually asked Clarence if he would join her. Her demand had been polite, but it was, unquestionably, just that: a demand.

Eleanor turned back to the two young men.

"Well, Santino, Gavin, enjoy the Hot Springs; I trust I'll see you again soon."

Eleanor crossed to the black iron door and pulled it open, disappearing with Clarence and Elsie close behind her. Santino and Gavin turned their attention back to the steaming pools below, and started down the stairs toward two small buildings that served as changing rooms.

"How was all this built?" Gavin asked, marveling at the way the clouds of steam rose out of the pools, submerging them in mist as they descended to the ground level.

Santino laughed.

"Built? I wish I could say. I wasn't consulted on the design plan, nor do I know anyone who was."

Gavin glanced over his shoulder to the building, then turned back to Santino, confused. Santino got the message.

"Oh, I can tell you how the building was built. Everyone knows that. But the Hot Springs were waiting for us to build around them; you'd have to ask Nature how the pools got here, and it's not real quick about answering."

BOOK 2, CHAPTER 11

"Jimbo, would you please, please slow it down? There isn't anything to find."

Jimbo Kerns, who had once again wandered off the trail to stick his head in a grove of trees, looped back to the group as quickly as his Bubble Suit would permit. The man's pale blue eyes, slightly distorted by the moonlight reflecting off his Bubble Suit, were manic with excitement.

"Whaddaya mean? We gotta find dis guy quick; he's already in real trouble. Heck, he's been missing weeks now; we gotta git'em ta da hospital."

Ariel Montez shook her head. She took a moment to glare at Bennett, her unit's supply chief; she could not believe this had happened again, particularly right at the start of a fourteen-hour night shift.

"Jimbo, if we find him, we'll have to get him to the morgue, not the hospital. He's been missing for weeks, and he's been dead just as long. Nothing can survive out here without a Bubble Suit. So please, *please*, take a deep breath and relax."

Jimbo nodded as if in agreement, but his eyes had continued to dart around as she spoke, and Montez knew he had not listened to a word she had said. She also knew, from the jerky manner of his movements, that Jimbo had gotten into the amphetamine supply again.

The City Watch had first issued the drugs on the night that Gavin Owens disappeared; when hours of searching did not turn up their quarry, the quartermaster authorized the release of the stimulants to all members of the Watch so that they might continue the search.

At the time, it had been a one-off, a way to fuel the City Watch as they continued their efforts into the early hours of the morning.

But they had not found Gavin Owens.

And while utter exhaustion forced the officers of the City Watch to allow the foot soldiers to get some sleep the next day, the rank and file woke up from their brief reprieve to learn they would be working extended shifts until the young man's body was recovered.

There was an upside to this, in the eyes of a few; when the members of the City Watch reported to Kingfisher Reservoir to continue the search, a more than ample supply of all manner of stimulants was waiting for them.

Montez could not have known it at the time, but as it turned out, that supply of stimulants would create a nightmarish scenario for her; she had her sights set on a promotion to Captain, and she would do herself no favors by admitting to a superior that she needed help reigning in one of her direct reports.

But on some level, Montez recognized she needed help, because she had proved utterly incapable of managing Jimbo Kerns.

At least, ever since he got into the amphetamines.

Jimbo had never struck Montez as a particularly steady individual, but after three weeks on speed, the man's wildly erratic behavior had become untenably problematic. Montez blamed Bennett, who she was starting to think had no business being in charge of anything, much less the unit's medical supplies.

Of course, she had no power to stop Jimbo taking the amphetamines, not as long as the City Watch was supplying them, but she had hoped that she could keep his dosage under control by reasoning with Bennett, trying to appeal to the medical side of his training, to cajole him into seeing that this could not possibly be healthy for Bennett. She even planted the suggestion that the City Watch ought to create a soldier assistance program; that way, she would have somewhere to shunt Jimbo off to.

Apparently, that had not worked; whether he got the stuff from Bennett or somewhere else, Jimbo was high as a kite tonight, which meant that the next fourteen hours would alternate between disconcerting bursts of energy and periods of total despondence, during which Jimbo would walk so slowly that he put the unit at risk of falling under their minimum movement speed, which would send an alert to their superiors that Montez had no wish to explain.

As she stood there, trying to figure out what to do, Montez once again wondered why they were out here at all. When the Unit Commander had gathered them for a meeting earlier that day, she had been sure it was to announce an end to the search; instead, the Commander had informed them, once again, that their pointless task would continue until the body was recovered. It was essential, he told them, that the body be retrieved so that the Knowers could examine it, and fully detail the damage that Shurtain's atmosphere could do to a sentient being.

Aware that this would not sit well with his charges, the Unit Commander had reminded them - warned them, really - that any one of them could be the next to tear their Bubble Suit, and if they were, they would want the Knowers to have the latest and greatest Knowledge at their disposal.

Montez was not sure about the others, but as she watched Jimbo dart off into the bushes again, she thought that the search was more likely to cause the next Bubble Suit tear than it was to turn up Gavin Owens.

As she resigned herself to another hellish night, Montez wondered whether anyone really cared, or if this search was allowed to stretch on because the City Watch had, until now, had so little work to do over the past two decades. Perhaps the politicians in the Halls of Parliament simply felt that they should do more to earn their keep.

But for some reason, she did not think so. And Montez could not help but feel uneasy at that idea.

—

The boardroom's occupants watched as Montez's search party passed out of the camera's lens.

Once the camera detected that the frame was empty, the image on the screen changed, automatically turning over to another camera, which showed another one of the City Watch's search parties. Those with an eye on the screen did not watch it with any concerted attention; the meeting was scheduled to begin shortly, the images on the screen merely a distraction as they waited for their fellows to arrive.

The early arrivals acknowledged Tarissa Cross with nods or lazy waves when she entered the room. They did the same when Reginald Klaus and Yvonne Delverta trickled in some minutes later, and as the rest of their colleagues arrived in twos and threes, until they were twelve.

The reaction was far more formal when the last man entered the room.

The twelve each moved into position behind one of the sleek silver chairs surrounding a long table of the same design. They stood at attention until The Director had taken his seat at the head of the table; this was tradition at Dynamic Solutions, and at Dynamic Solutions, tradition was everything.

This Director was nearing eighty years of age; were it not for the Bubble Suits, he might have been forced to retire years ago, but the very Bubble Suits that The Director had been so instrumental in pioneering had dramatically slowed his aging process. It was a source of mounting frustration to the other Board members, as it meant the end of The Director's reign was not yet in sight.

The Director had a big frame; as a young man, he had developed that foundation, building an impressive musculature during his time on athletic fields and in weight rooms. Were it not for the Bubble Suits, The Director's physique would have faded decades ago, but that was immaterial; The Director did have a Bubble Suit, and his frame was as imposing as ever.

The Director's hair and mustache were black everywhere except the fringes, where he allowed a bit of grey to creep in. Not so much that he would appear aged - that would not be fitting of his office - but enough to make him look distinguished. The same was true of his onyx black skin; the Director had set his Bubble Suit so that the skin would show a few wrinkles, enough signs of age to make it plain he was no schoolboy without hinting that he had entered the winter of his life.

Once The Director was seated, the others followed suit.

As Viceroy, Tarissa Cross was the Director's second-in-command; as such, she occupied the seat directly across from The Director, at the far end of the table. When all thirteen members of The Board were settled in their seats, Viceroy Cross nodded at Yvonne Delverta, who got back to her feet.

"As Chief Consul, I, Chief Consul Delverta, propose we begin Session #4768 of the Dynamic Solutions Board."

Delverta sat as soon as she was finished. Her words had been directed at Viceroy Cross; they always were.

By way of answer, Cross got back to her feet, turned to Reginald Klaus, and asked, "Are all of the thirteen in attendance?"

Cross sat down again as Klaus stood.

"As Secretary of the Dynamic Solutions Board, I, Secretary Klaus, verify that all thirteen of our members are in attendance."

Klaus sat. Cross nodded, then stood again.

"We are ready to take the minutes?"

This question was not directed at anyone, and Cross did not anticipate an answer. She had to say the words - The Board Guidelines stated that clearly - but nobody at Dynamic Solutions wanted records of these meetings, and the practice had been abandoned long ago, if it had ever been followed at all.

After a brief pause, Cross nodded.

"Very good. I, Viceroy Cross, turn the floor over to The Director."

The Director was deliberate as he got to his feet. He had a name, once, but he had left his old name behind when he ascended to the top post; in turn, one of the other twelve Board Members would take his office, and shed his or her name. It did not matter which of the twelve; or at least, it did not matter for the future of Dynamic Solutions, though it mattered enormously to each of the twelve. They all wanted the position desperately, but regardless of who was selected as the next Director, the company would march on, for while the Board Members had been carefully selected for the diverse aesthetics of their physical vehicles, it would have been impossible to find thirteen sentient beings on the planet Shurtain with a more monolithic belief system than the thirteen in the boardroom of Dynamic Solutions.

"I hereby convene this meeting of the Dynamic Solutions Board. We are here today to continue our discussions regarding the recently identified threat to The Bubble Society. Viceroy Cross, did you have your audience with The Guvna' this afternoon?"

The Director remained standing after he finished speaking. This was another formality of the Dynamic Solutions Boardroom; once the Director convened a meeting, he or she was obliged to remain standing until the business of the day was complete.

As Viceroy, Tarissa Cross did not have to stand, not now that the openers were complete, but she returned to her feet anyways. Cross had her gaze firmly fixed on the Directorship - a manic desire to acquire power was a prerequisite for Board membership - and she saw her speaking opportunities at these meetings as a chance to audition for the top role.

"I did. The Guvna' has been briefed on the proposal. He will put the matter before the Halls of Parliament first thing tomorrow morning; everything should be signed and sealed by lunch. Board Member Montenegro will oversee the process, with his usual assistance from Board Members Garcia and Johnson."

Cross paused, inclining her head to acknowledge the Board Members she had mentioned.

"Once the Elevation Upgrade Prize is officially approved, there will be a ceremony at the Academy of Knowledge. Knower Antonius is scheduled to give a speech to announce the prize and to detail the objectives of the Knowers who will pursue it."

Montenegro, who sat halfway down the table, spoke up.

"Antonius is not going to announce the full objective to all of Kingston, is he?"

Cross adjusted her body slightly so that she could turn the full weight of her stare on Giuseppe Montenegro. The man had set his Bubble Suit so that the tips of his spectacular black mustache twirled up at the ends, the effect so dramatic that most noticed nothing else about his face. Tarissa Cross took the time to look beyond the mustache and connect with Montenegro's beady dark eyes before she responded.

"No, Giuseppe. The Director's plan is a bit more nuanced than that."

Montenegro's eyes flickered to the far end of the table, but The Director said nothing of their exchange; Cross continued.

"Knower Antonius will tell the population the same thing that I told The Guvna' today: Gavin Owens wandered beyond the elevation limit after the incident that caused him to lose his Bubble Suit - he was delirious, no doubt - and we need to recover his body so the Knowers can study it. To do that, we must expand the capabilities of the Bubble Suits. The explanation is plausible, in the Director's view, and I am inclined to agree."

Around the table, heads nodded in agreement.

"Did Knower Antonius provide any estimate of when we might expect Knowledge to deliver the Bubble Suit enhancements?"

The question came from Nessie Hunter, a small woman with piercing brown eyes and olive skin, who had set her Bubble Suit to pull her sleek black hair into a ponytail today.

Cross shook her head.

"No. Knower Antonius is only announcing the project. He only learned of it today, from The Guvna', of course, as the Guvernment will be putting up the prize. Once the contest is announced, we will communicate with the more advanced research teams to get estimates on timelines."

"If that is the case, perhaps we ought to return to our previous discussion of simply stealing the Knowledge from these…"

Hunter paused. She said her next word with severe distaste.

"*Savages*…that we have concluded must be out there. After all, we have shown our devotion to Knowledge for years, and it has never delivered us the technology that allows these others to live at such absurd elevations."

Cross shook her head.

"We come back to the same problem: how would we go about stealing this Knowledge? The air filtration system that the Savages possess allows them to live at elevations beyond our reach; unless one of them comes within our boundaries, we have no way of acquiring any of their technology."

"It must be a wonder," mused Montenegro, recovered from his earlier misstep. "It has kept me up nights, wondering how small the system is, and where it is installed. My money is still on a small ventilator over the mouth and nose."

Cross shrugged.

"Who Knows? All that our surveillance cameras showed was that the old man who abducted Gavin Owens wasn't wearing a Bubble Suit. If the imbeciles monitoring the system had been paying attention, perhaps we would have realized what was going on in time, but nobody noticed a thing until the alert went off from the torn Bubble Suit. When we reviewed the footage from Kingfisher, there wasn't enough detail to determine who the Savage was, much less where he carried his alternative air filtration system."

"It doesn't hurt to wonder," said Montenegro, his tone conciliatory.

"Maybe on your time. Not mine," snapped Cross.

The Director raised a hand; the argument subsided at once. After the Director had looked at Montenegro, Hunter, and Cross in turn, he nodded.

"Viceroy Cross, continue with the briefing."

"Yes. Well, more to the point, we will shortly have most of our Knowers working on developing the technology we need to reach these Savages. Once it is working, we can discuss capturing whatever technology it is that the Savages use, assuming that our own Knowledge does not outstrip theirs by then."

"Until then, we have instructed the Capitol Guard, and the City Watch, to remain on high alert. We have not told them why - we can't tell the rank and file, or even the officers, that these Savages exist - but we can ensure that the defenders of our boundaries remain vigilant. If another one of these Savages is so bold as to venture into our territory again, we will capture it alive, and then its secrets will be ours."

BOOK 2, CHAPTER 12

"Inhale. Exhale. Fully in, let it go."

"The inhale is a full-body experience. Let your body expand, oxygenate yourself from head to toe, then release. No pause between inhale and exhale. There you go, just like that. Fully in, let it go."

"You're almost there. Five more breaths."

Santino's words streamed through Gavin's mind; he did not think about them. There was no time to think about them; he simply obeyed.

Fully in.

Let it go.

"Remember, let your body relax on the last exhale…just like that, now, stay calm, and hold your breath. The mental grip should be loose, but you need to hold fast. Let your body settle into the sensation; surrender to the experience."

Gavin held. In the next instant, he witnessed the first thought rising on the horizon, a whisper that he ought to breathe. Gavin dismissed it as nonsense; he smiled as he sensed the thought floating on by.

He felt he deserved the smile. After all, until he met Santino, Gavin had never considered the possibility that he did not need to engage every thought that came into his head; he had never stopped to think about the fact that most of his thoughts were nonsense.

Gavin's expression settled back to neutral as more thoughts crested on the horizon, hurtling toward his consciousness from the source of thoughts, wherever that might be. He could hear Santino's continued encouragement, but the longer Gavin held his breath, the more it sounded as if Santino's voice were coming through a badly tuned radio.

"The thoughts are like water. Each is but a molecule, so minuscule that the particle would go unnoticed if it fell in isolation. But as molecules group together, they become drops, then a stream, and we suddenly perceive that stream as its own thing, rather than a collection of its components."

"Thoughts work in much the same way. They can appear to be a single stream, and when they do, they can overwhelm. But as soon as you break that stream, you can see through it, see each thought on its own. They are not so powerful that way; you can turn the thoughts back, or let them pass by, off to wherever it is that unengaged thoughts go."

"Remember, the thoughts are liars, and no matter how loudly they protest, if you can still hear me, you are just fine."

Santino's words provided Gavin a momentary sense of relief, but he was deep in the battle now, his primal urge to breathe making itself increasingly loud as he cleared the minute-and-a-half barrier. Still, Gavin let those thoughts pass by, unheeded; he knew that a sense of relief would come when he cleared the next wave.

It had been on the night of Gavin's arrival in Trepani, as they dried off after soaking in the Hot Springs, that Santino had first spoken of the benefits of the breathing practices that he would teach Gavin in the days to come. Despite all that he had seen on his journey through the Cadillac Mountains, Gavin's initial reaction was to assume that his new friend, regardless of his positive qualities, must be slightly mad. The very idea of a breathing practice was odd - breathing was something you just did, not something you actively engaged in - and Gavin seriously doubted whether a person could significantly alter their body's state with a few minutes of breathwork.

The skepticism must have shown on his face, because Santino had started to laugh.

"C'mon, you believe us about the Bubble Suits, you're out in the open air, and this is too much for you?"

He shook his head.

"No need to worry. It's not like I was going to make you do it without proving it first."

At that, Santino sucked in a single inhale and held.

Gavin watched in silence, unsure of what to do.

A minute passed.

Gavin felt sweat beading on his forehead.

Then another.

His skin was starting to feel clammy.

By the time Santino crossed the four-minute threshold, Gavin felt terribly dizzy, and then, much to his dismay, the walls started to close in on him, darkness wrapping from behind his eyes, tightening his field of vision, and there was nothing he could do to stop i…

Santino noticed Gavin start to sway and grabbed his shoulders to hold him upright, laughing as he released his breath.

"It's all right, brotha'; you're going to pass out way before me, I was at about half my best time. Didn't mean to freak you out."

And so they began.

Gavin's initial efforts went poorly - he could barely hold his breath for five seconds, much less five minutes - and as he labored through the exercises, he had wondered why anyone would subject themselves to such an uncomfortable experience.

As he laid here now, five days into his training, a warm glow spreading through him as he held his breath, he more than understood.

"Be still. Ignore the nonsense. If you can still hear me, you know you're ok. The body will scream. It will tell you that you need the air now, this very moment. It tries to force the message through every cell of your being. But it is a liar. You know it is a liar, because it has already screamed that you need to breathe, and you ignored it, yet here you are. Your body is strong, and you are spurring adaptation by transforming your environment."

"You are past two minutes. It's only practice, we can always try again, but we learn more by pushing our limits than by living in them."

Gavin could barely hear Santino now; in his mind, the protests had swelled to the collective roar of a crowd, drowning out the outside world.

All at once, his will broke, and Gavin inhaled as deeply as he could.

"Good, good. Now hold that for fifteen seconds…yes…yes. Enjoy the sensation of oxygen flooding back into the body. We breathe all the time, never thinking twice, but as soon as you take the breath away, force the body to delay its gratification, a simple inhale becomes a moment of ecstasy."

"And now, release that breath. That is three rounds; now we rest."

Gavin exhaled through his nose. His world, which had felt increasingly panicked the longer he held his breath, had been replaced by a sense of serene calm.

"That was an excellent effort; your strongest attempt yet, I would say."

Gavin gave a slight nod of agreement, too deeply settled in his thoughts to offer any further response. It took a few minutes for the feeling to fade; Gavin felt as if he were floating back to Shurtain, gently passing through a veil that divided the serene world he had briefly visited from the one he had known all his life.

As the feeling settled, Gavin blinked his eyes open and sat halfway up. Santino was sitting on a table in the corner of the room they worked in, his legs swinging as he looked out the window. When Santino saw that Gavin was sitting up, he turned to him and smiled.

"Not bad. Not bad at all. Another couple of weeks, and nobody will ever know you ever wore a Bubble Suit."

Gavin knew this was an exaggeration, though he appreciated the sentiment; he had made significant progress, but his days in Trepani had shown him that the differences between his body and Santino's went far beyond aesthetics, and that it would be some time before his physical vehicle functioned as well as Santino's. The differences in functionality were stark; Santino moved through the world with an ease foreign to Gavin, cruising through his experience on Shurtain in a top-end all-terrain vehicle. He also spoke of his body with a disconnect Gavin could not comprehend, referring to it on various occasions as a meat machine, an avatar, a biological vehicle, and an intention craft. Santino made it clear that he viewed his body as something that his self was controlling, rather than an aspect of his self, an idea that, on one occasion, he relayed to Gavin by pointing out that down in Kingston, sentient beings could get into their self-driving cars to travel without becoming a permanent part of the machine. The comparison struck Gavin as far-fetched, but he did not doubt Santino's sincerity.

At any rate, Gavin had come to the conclusion that, at present, his own physical vehicle was totally unsatisfactory. When they met, he had envied Santino's external appearance for the sake of aesthetics, but after a few days in Trepani, he no longer cared about that; as he lurched around in his meat machine, and determined that it balanced too poorly, moved too slowly, and fatigued too quickly, Gavin began to envy the bodies of the sentient beings in Trepani for entirely different reasons. He marveled at Santino's ability to walk the hills around Trepani without tiring, to squat down to his heels and pick things up from the ground, even the ease with which he got up and down from a sitting position. And it was not just Santino; in his time in Trepani, Gavin had been struck by the fact that the Acadians were almost universally fit. Even the elderly population moved around well; his great-uncle and Eleanor were not unique in that regard.

As thoughts of his great-uncle surfaced, Gavin found himself staring at the ceiling of the room that he and Santino were working in, wondering how the old man had fared over the past few days. Santino had assured Gavin that Clarence was fine - there were plans for the two of them to visit the old man that night - but while he was not under arrest, precisely, he and Eleanor had come to an agreement that he ought to stay near Trepani, but out of sight, until the situation could be addressed at a Town Gathering.

Gavin had no standing to object, but it did bother him that, as far as he could tell, his great-uncle was being held prisoner ahead of trial; he did not like that Clarence should have to suffer on his behalf, because whether or not the Acadians were happy that Clarence had freed Gavin, he was ecstatic to be here.

Life in Trepani was unlike anything Gavin could have imagined, his enjoyment of the experience heightened by the sense that he was only getting started. If not for the physical exertion of the days leaving him utterly exhausted, Gavin doubted whether he would have been able to sleep, because even when his physical body reached its limits, his mind continued to race, processing all the novel experiences from his new world.

After the breathwork at the Hot Springs, there had been dinner with five of Santino's friends; Gavin and Santino met Ruby, Renee, Tessa, Raul, and Titus at Nately's Public House, which stood along the shores of Grand Lake. Santino's friends had a table on the deck; they got to their feet as Santino and Gavin approached and extended their hands to greet Gavin.

For a moment, this caused Gavin's insides to clench; his great-uncle and Santino had both touched him over the past few days, but that contact had been more incidental, Clarence grabbing Gavin's shoulder to steady him, or Santino grasping his hand to pull him from the Hot Springs.

Nothing so formal as this.

Gavin stared at the five hands. They were different shapes, sizes, colors; two black, two brown, one white, two with painted nails, three without…

Through his panic, Gavin darted his hand out like a drowning man reaching for purchase. Almost at random, he seized the black hand with the orange nails and gripped it hard, as if clinging to life.

His world righted itself; when it did, Gavin lifted his gaze from the hand and found the face of a young woman with long black hair fighting back a laugh.

"Doing all right?"

Gavin nodded, shaking himself.

"I think so. It's just…different, is all."

"I bet. I'm Ruby, by the way."

"Gavin."

Gavin released Ruby's hand, and she proceeded to introduce him to the rest of the group. Once handshakes and names had been exchanged all around, they sat back down.

Initially, Gavin was so distracted by the people around them that he found it difficult to pay attention to the table's conversation. Nately's was busy, and everywhere Gavin looked, he could see sentient beings touching one another. Gavin's work as a video editor had occasionally exposed him to ancient works of art or film, creations from the age Before Knowledge, so the happenings at Nately's were not entirely beyond his imagination, but he had never thought that he would witness such a scene first-hand. His eyes found a young couple walking with their daughter between them, each holding one of her hands and swinging her through the air on every third step, the girl shrieking in delight. As the family disappeared back around a corner, Gavin's eyes passed over a pair of middle-aged women looking out at Grand Lake with their hands intertwined, then a jumble of twenty-somethings even younger than himself, six of them draped over one another on a bench meant for four, all in danger of spilling their drinks on the others.

When his gaze returned to their table, Gavin noticed that Tessa and Raul's hands were intertwined. He stared for a moment, then took a deep breath, reminding himself that everything was fine; whatever he had been told in Kingston, it did not appear that all of this touching was the precursor to an outbreak of plague.

As the thought drifted through Gavin's mind, Santino's voice shocked him out of his reverie.

"Eh, Gavin, you back with us yet? We've got questions for you; I was just telling the others that you've got some wild stories about life in Kingston. Tessa and Raul are particularly interested in the Department of Infant Development - they're about to start trying to have a kid - and while we've all heard about the differences, we'd love to hear it from your side."

Santino's words left Gavin more confused than he could remember being at any other point during his years on Shurtain.

"Trying to have a kid? What do you mean? Don't you just submit your application papers to the Guvernment, then go to the Knowers to have them extract your reproductive material?"

There was an uncomfortable silence, a little oasis of incredulous speechlessness that existed even as the rest of the crowd at Nately's carried on. Then Ruby let out a giggle, and after that, Tessa could not contain herself; with the awkwardness broken, the rest of the group joined in. A moment later, they were howling with laughter, drawing interested stares from the crowd around them.

Raul was the first to regain his composure; after assuring Gavin they were not laughing at him, but at what passed for Knowledge in Kingston, he proceeded to explain to Gavin where children came from in Trepani.

This explanation left Gavin as embarrassed as he could remember being, far more embarrassed than when Clarence had instructed him on how to take a dump.

"You're telling me the infants grow *inside* the mothers? Not in a pod? Isn't that unhygienic? And uncomfortable?"

Santino, for one, could not respond. He was slumped over the table, crippled by laughter. Tessa answered this time.

"Well, uncomfortable or not, it's how sentient beings have produced children for the entirety of our history, save the last twenty years in The Bubble Society. That's some crazy new experiment, and from what we've heard of those children, not a particularly successful one."

Tessa paused, put a second hand over Raul's.

"And parts of it are said to be uncomfortable, yes. But parts of it are supposed to be wonderful, an experience beyond anything I can imagine, or so my mom would have me believe. She says she's never forgotten the first time she felt me kick inside her, and that those seasons together did more than a little for the bonding process."

The conversation turned to less weighty topics from there, the group eager to hear Gavin's accounts of The Bubble Society. Gavin enjoyed himself so much that he forgot to feel uncertain when their meal was delivered, and carried on telling stories of the robotic pets as he enjoyed his food. The process of chewing and swallowing his food had quickly become second nature; it was almost as if he had been born to do it.

From Nately's, Gavin and Santino had gone to the home that Santino shared with two of his cousins. Gavin, who had no siblings or cousins, no family beyond his parents, and apparently, his great-uncle Clarence, was surprised by this; he asked Santino if those were his only cousins.

"Hardly," Santino responded. "There's a dozen of us on my mom's side of the family, and I've got six more on my dad's. Bruno and Paulo, my roommates, are from my mom's side; they're twins, my Aunt Lyra's two oldest. She and my uncle live in Kirfi, same as my parents."

Santino introduced Gavin to Bruno and Paulo that night, but they did not spend much time talking; it was late, and Santino planned to have Gavin up at the crack of dawn.

The pair of them spent the next two days hiking the hills around Trepani, carrying their lunches and only returning for the evening meal. Santino told Gavin that all of the walking would prepare him for the next phase of his mobility program, and it also gave Santino time to tell Gavin about the history of Trepani, how the Acadians had come to settle there, and in the other towns that were scattered throughout the Cadillac Mountains. In telling that history, Santino offered Gavin more context about his great-uncle's present situation.

"Clarence is in a murky area. You see, when we abandoned Kingston, our people took great pains to establish a society where adult sentient beings would not have the right to tell other adults what to do unless their actions directly harm others. The line in the sand, on its face, is simple enough; it is illegal to commit a crime against another sentient being's person or property. And in the same way that nobody else has the right to impose their will on your life, you can't force yourself on others."

"Of course, while the guideline is meant to be simple, the interpretation is, like everything else, made through the unique perspective of each sentient being, which means that the law, such that it is, is read in countless shades of grey."

"That's where your great-uncle sits right now: somewhere in the grey. His actions did not harm another sentient being or their property, unless you count him destroying a Bubble Suit, and nobody in Trepani is going to care about that. But while his actions did not cause any harm at the time, there's no getting around the fact that the downstream effects of his decision could change life for every Acadian, and that's where the interpretation gets tricky."

"Our founders anticipated this, and decided that, in such a case, both sides would present their cases in a Town Gathering. The hope was that it would offer a chance for both sides to consider the opposition's thought process, to understand why the other side took the stance that they did, which would open the opportunity to find common ground, or for one or both sides to shift their perspective. But that's not a cure-all; the Town Gathering after the first incident with your great-uncle didn't stop Clarence continuing to meddle down in Kingston."

Santino shook his head.

"That time around, an elder from The Council put up an argument in favor of the greater good, of considering the ripple effects of one's actions, and the wisdom - or lack thereof - of drawing attention to Trepani after so many years of peace and tranquility."

"On the other side, your great-uncle presented a straightforward argument that every sentient being has the right to be free, and that he was simply opening the door for you to seize that right, if it was what you wanted."

"Clarence's defense has been used in the past, but while Acadians agree with the principle as a general guideline, there are also persuasive arguments against interfering in The Bubble Society."

"The main objection raised is that there were sentient beings who knew what we were doing ahead of the Advent, sentient beings who made the choice to stay behind. As sovereign individuals, they had every right to make that decision, and given that they made their choice, who are we, as Acadians, to impose our beliefs and preferences upon them now? Throw in the fact that more than a few people have found their own way out of Kingston in the years since the Advent, and it becomes difficult to come up with an effective counter; if they want to get out, they can."

Santino paused, shook his head, and continued.

"Clarence's reasoning did not sway the crowd, but of course, Clarence was not obligated to change his mind. Obviously, he didn't. He'll have his chance to state his case again, however; my grandmother will see to that. I don't know if she agrees with what he did, but she does believe in his right to defend himself in reasoned debate. After all, she sat on the original Council during the development of Trepani and helped to draft those guiding principles."

"Is that why you believe in them so much?"

"To a degree. But it started with my grandfather. He taught me all the arguments, all the history, that led him to adopt stoicism as a life philosophy. He would speak of the Logos, the source of all intelligence, and how a shard of the Logos exists in each sentient being, giving us our consciousness, making us equals, no matter the differences in our external appearances, our manner of speech, or place of birth. We each have a bit of the Logos within us, and that is what makes us sentient, what sets us apart from the other animals on the planet. In any case, the foundations of our society's structure were heavily influenced by that philosophy."

They were hiking the hills on the northeastern outskirts of Trepani as they had this particular discussion; their conversation had brought them to an overlook of Grand Lake, where Santino and Gavin could look down at the still waters from hundreds of feet above.

"Your grandfather?"

Santino nodded, sadness etched on his face.

"My grandfather."

"Is he Eleanor's husband? Or your grandfather on the other side? Where does he live?"

Santino shook his head.

"He was Eleanor's husband, but he's gone. Died years ago, in the first winter, out in the wild on a hunting expedition with Clarence, Anton, my uncle Marcus, and a few others."

"Died?"

For Gavin, there was a long moment in which his words seemed to hang in the air. He knew, on some level, that Santino was probably too young to have a grandfather who had reached the age of 100; this realization caused a moment of disbelief, and then a bit more of life in Trepani sank into Gavin's consciousness.

"I'm sorry."

He did not know what else to say; Gavin had been lost in the ecstasy of life up here, and had not stopped to consider that the price of experiencing that joy was an uncertain lifespan. His years growing up in The Bubble Society had cemented the idea that sentient beings lived to one hundred into his mind.

Santino nodded.

"Me too. Don't get me wrong, things in Trepani are great…but the first few years were hard. Much harder than they would have been with him. And I don't think this place ever became what my grandfather had envisioned, back when he was laying the plans to leave Kingston."

The two young men stood in silence for a time, looking down at the sun's rays reflecting off Grand Lake.

"What was his name?"

Santino blinked; it took him a moment to register Gavin's question.

"His name was Salomon. Salomon Cahn."

Gavin nodded, then turned his eyes from Santino to look out over Trepani.

It was registering, somewhere in Gavin's being, that the uncertain lifespans of the Acadians now applied to him, that living out here meant there was no longer a guarantee that he would reach the age of one hundred.

But as he looked out over the sweeping scene below, he decided that this did not matter.

Or at least, not enough to reverse the trade he had made.

He turned to Santino.

"Well, maybe it could have been different, but I love living in Trepani. They can keep their Bubble Suits; I hope life here never changes."

Santino smiled, but for once, the grin did not extend to the rest of his being.

"That would be nice. But as my grandfather used to say, life only changes. Nature continually turns one thing into another, and we ought to avoid becoming too attached to any one state, any one idea."

"We've been lucky. For the past twenty years, things have become fairly steady in Trepani. But if my grandfather is to be believed, that won't last forever - because nothing ever does."

BOOK 2, CHAPTER 13

Ostensibly, they were the best and brightest in Kingston, the future of The Bubble Society.

But The Bubble Society was a utopia, so there was nothing to improve on.

Nothing to aspire to.

No possible improvements that could be made.

So, best and brightest or not, Tesla's peers showed little initiative in their academic pursuits.

Of course, it was unlikely that they would have been motivated even if Kingston were not a utopia, because the vast majority of Tesla's peers were not there because the work interested them; they were there because, once they had their degrees, the living arrangement they would receive from the Guvernment was more likely to be in the Amada District. Most folks in Kingston lived in the Axios and Andola Districts, which were perfectly comfortable, perfectly safe - The Bubble Society was a utopia, after all - but the Amada District was the shiny carrot that ensured that the best and brightest in Kingston pursued the most important careers.

It might have struck some as unfair that certain citizuns got to live in the Amada District while others did not - it could even have created the prospect of competition, which was unheard of in The Bubble Society - but, fortunately, one of the Guvernment's Knowers had pointed out that genetics predetermined which sentient beings were the best and brightest, so the housing assignment process was not unfair at all, but a predetermined end result of Knowledge.

This observation was the primary reason that the Guvernment took such pains to ensure that the pipeline of the best and brightest remained functional; it was obvious to those in power that if they did not actively recruit this group, they would only get candidates who were passionate about the work, and as several Knowers had pointed out, those folks were likely to be a brain-dead group of morons. Expecting such individuals to become Knowers, or even researchers, was preposterous. It would never happen; no matter how much time those people devoted to their studies, effort and passion could never trump talent. After all, sentient beings did not have much power to change.

Early in her life, Tesla had believed all of that; like all small children, she accepted what the adults around her told her about the world.

Then she had turned four.

And as Tesla had continued to work at her computer, she changed, and her world transformed.

It did not register consciously; not at first.

Then she found the list.

The list on the Guvernment servers that assigned students to their academic track.

The reasons were listed.

The patterns were clear.

The decisions were about favors, not genetics.

And even at that age, Tesla could understand.

She wanted to tell somebody - more than anything, she wanted to tell somebody - but even then, she sensed how dangerous it would be to share her findings with the adults around her.

Because what Tesla had found in those files ran contrary to everything she had been told about the world.

Witty, energetic, and beautiful, the young Tesla had made friends easily at school, but after that day, everything started to change. It was not all at once - in fact, it would be years before Tesla consciously recognized how far she had drifted from her friends - but as her silent understanding of their world expanded, it became harder and harder for Tesla to find any connection to the girls who still believed every bit of the lie.

The breaking point had occurred sometime in their teens; these days, Tesla Mancini only maintained her friendships for camouflage. On some level, she thought the other girls must realize this, but if they did, they did not complain. They loved being around Tesla - she was The Guvna's daughter, after all - and it was entirely possible they did not actually notice Tesla's distance, given the state of self-assured indifference that they lived in.

And why not? Her friends lived in total comfort, riding along on life's conveyor belt as it took them toward all of the milestones that their parents, their teachers, and their Guvernment had laid out for them. Each of the girls knew that she would celebrate a special birthday to mark her transition to womanhood at 17, graduate from Kingston High the year after, go on to study and work in a profession, find a husband, ask the Guvernment for children…and on, and on, and on, until they reached the end of their lives at the ripe old age of 100. Life was something that happened to them, a play that offered the heroine some latitude in how she delivered her lines, but no choice at all in what she said or when she said it, much less an opinion on the premise or the plot.

Once in a while, Tesla wondered what would have happened if her father had not brought the computer home that day, or if he had tucked it away somewhere high, somewhere she would not have stumbled across it. Were it not for the computer, she might have wound up just like her friends. It was the computer that had granted her access to those lists of future career paths, and the understanding that came with it; in the years that followed, it was the computer that allowed her to delve into other secrets, the lab results and financial records that told the true story of The Bubble Society, and the Guvernment's alliance with Dynamic Solutions.

Tesla knew, no matter what the Knowers said, that The Bubble Society had not sprung up out of nothing simply because Knowledge had granted the proper insights. Sentient beings had made this happen; the going had been slow, the progress measured in decades, but sentient beings had laid the foundation for The Bubble Society with their thoughts, words, and actions, and subsequently realized their vision with the same tools. They had been able to make The Bubble Society happen; they had been able to construct a hermit kingdom, shutting off their citizuns from the outside world, prepared to use brutal defensive measures against any sentient beings who dared approach the city of Kingston, whether they be from Acadia or another one of Shurtain's continents.

And if they could make something happen to life, then so could she.

Tesla's perspective was completely at odds with that of her peers, which was one of the reasons that Tesla could hardly stand to be around them. The girls were nice, certainly, and polite, but sometimes Tesla felt as if she were talking to a bunch of computer programs, forms of intelligence that could predict the next word they ought to say based on the latest Knowledge, but who were incapable of forming their own interpretation about the world they lived in.

Still, appearances had to be kept up, and it was not difficult for Tesla to mouth empty pleasantries to the other girls as they passed the time between classes at the Academy of Knowledge. Thankfully, it was only during gaps between classes that she had to put up with this; if Tesla had to give up her free time to socialize, that would have been a different matter, but there was only so much that one could do in the fifteen minute breaks between their lectures.

The bell rang; Tesla started. She had not been listening to Knower Peraux's lecture, but her surprise went unnoticed by the girls around her, who had been sitting through the lecture with similar indifference.

Thea, Anna, and Shannon glanced at Tesla; once the girls had made eye contact, they stood and exited the room. There was no need to discuss their destination; as usual, they were headed for a spot in the Academy's front courtyard.

Thea and Anna, identical twins, were an inch shorter than Tesla. The pair was blond, blue-eyed, and depending on the settings of their Bubble Suits, quite tan. Shannon, a red-head, had bright green eyes and was the tallest of the four; a good three inches taller than Thea and Anna, she loomed over Tesla and the twins.

The girls reached their spot in the courtyard and took their usual seats on the low stone wall. Tesla suppressed a grin when she saw Anna start to fiddle with a setting on her Bubble Suit; her friend was making her adjustments between covert glances at a young man across the courtyard. But that was nothing new; Tesla was well aware that her friends did not select this spot because it had a good view, but because they would *be* the view.

Assuming that the break would pass like any other, Tesla took a deep breath, willing herself to relax; it made the shock even greater when Shannon said something of substance.

"So, what do you think about this Elevation Upgrade Prize they announced? Should we go in for it?"

Thea and Anna exchanged a quick glance; Tesla could tell from their expressions that the idea had not occurred to them.

"Us? What do you mean? How could we make that happen?"

Tesla knew the *that* they referred to was the proposed upgrade to the Bubble Suits, an enhancement that would allow the suits to function at higher altitudes.

Thea shared her twin's skepticism.

"Anna's right, Shan. It will be a Knower, not an academy student, who makes the breakthrough. Some of the Knowers have been showing their devotion to Knowledge for decades; if Knowledge is going to grant the insight to any of us, surely it will be an established Knower. We're still learning about the basics of the filtration systems in our lectures."

"And if it's not a Knower who makes the breakthrough, then it will be one of the Laureates who sees the solution, and gives it to the Knowers to implement," Anna chimed in.

Shannon shook her head.

"But what if we did? I mean, it would be AAAmazing. We'd be famous; everyone in Kingston would know who we are. What do you think, Tesla?"

Tesla managed to keep the frown off her face, but it was a close thing. As it happened, she had devoted a good bit of thought to the challenge that Knower Antonius had announced earlier that week, and she knew, on some level, that she could develop a solution if she wanted to. But as it was, an improved air filtration system was the last thing that Tesla wanted to see come into existence; she had zero interest in anyone in Kingston figuring out how to allow the Bubble Suits to reach higher altitudes.

Of course, it would not do to tell her friends this.

"I think Thea and Anna have a point, Shan. I mean, of course it'd be amazing, but what makes you think we could be the ones to figure it out?"

Shannon frowned.

"Easy for you to say. You're already famous."

Tesla sighed. It was an old grievance, one that her friends, Shannon in particular, picked at continually.

"I'm not famous. My dad is famous. There's a difference."

Shannon shook her head stubbornly.

"There are e-magazines with you on the cover and in the center spread. Articles about you. Documentaries about your family. When I put your name in the Guvernment Media App's search bar, endless pieces of content come up, most of them going on about how beautiful you are. That doesn't happen if you put my name in, or Thea's, or Anna's."

Tesla shrugged.

"So? What can I do about it?"

"You could help me win this prize, for one."

Thea and Anna burst out in laughter; the sound broke the awkward tension building between Shannon and Tesla.

"C'mon, Shan, lay off. Tesla might be the best in the class, but that doesn't make her a miracle worker. And she's right, there's nothing she can do about her father being The Guvna'."

Shannon bristled, but gave no verbal response. Thea changed the subject.

"Why do you think the Academy of Knowledge announced this prize? It's an odd goal, isn't it? Everything we need is right here in Kingston; why would anyone want to go to higher altitudes? They say they want to recover that Gavin Owens's body, but that seems like a strange reason to create a prize like this."

"One of the Laureates must have had a vision. They don't always announce that information to the public, but don't they say that it was a Laureate's vision that inspired the Bubble Suits?"

Tesla was hard-pressed to suppress a snort at Anna's response; her friend's story was the official line, but it was one of the more brazen lies that the Guvernment regularly told, given that the Laureates had not existed before The Advent.

"That must be it," Thea agreed. "What else could it be? Like I said, there's nothing outside of Kingston, so no normal person would think of doing such a thing. It had to have been a dreamer; it had to have been a Laureate."

Shannon was nodding along.

"That makes sense. Gosh, it's amazing how lucky we are to have the Laureates; if it weren't for their visions, we might not be sitting here today. They might have never figured out why so many people were getting sick."

Thea and Anna mirrored Shannon's nod.

"Do you think it will be long before someone wins the prize?"

Anna's question hung out there for the group to answer. Finally, Thea broke the silence.

"Who Knows? But we've got an awful lot of sentient beings devoted to Knowledge in Kingston; my guess is that we'll be rewarded sooner rather than later."

BOOK 2, CHAPTER 14

Knower Ludquist felt as if Knowledge itself were shining a spotlight on him as he stood in the center of Knower Robinson's office, making his groundbreaking announcement.

So he felt more than a tinge of disappointment when his words were greeted with silence.

Ludquist had expected applause, praise, perhaps a wringing handshake from a superior who had leapt out of her chair in exuberance; after all, he had just announced a tremendous triumph for sentient beings, a new day for Knowledge, an oversized, glossy feather to stick in the Department of Research and Innovation's cap.

Instead, Knower Robinson remained seated, her expression deeply skeptical. There were reasons for her hesitation; she had set their team's initial regroup for the end of Week 3, and that was only supposed to be an early planning session. Nor had the rest of the team's lack of progress been much of a surprise; until a few weeks ago, Robinson's team had been focused on The Bubble Suit's nutrient intake system. They had only shifted their focus to the air filters after the Elevation Upgrade Prize was announced, when Dynamic Solutions informed its employees that all Knowers would work towards this goal until the prize was claimed.

Yet despite all that, here Ludquist was, far beyond those initial steps, claiming to have something close to a complete solution. He even claimed to have run successful trials on a test model.

Most sentient beings would have understood that Robinson's skepticism was warranted, but Ludquist was not most sentient beings, and he was growing impatient as his superior sat there, surveying him. A quirky fellow, Ludquist rarely collaborated with other members of Robinson's team; instead, he would take charge of one aspect of the team's assignment and handle it as an individual project. More times than not, that area was the strength of the project once it was integrated into the whole, but while Ludquist would work with others to implement his solutions, he refused to team up with anyone else while he did the actual work.

This project was no different, except that Ludquist was working on the full problem rather than one aspect of it; since the announcement of the Elevation Upgrade Prize, the man had been lost in his own world, diving into the challenge and ignoring everyone else entirely.

Which meant that Ludquist was wholly unaware that the rest of the Knowers on the team had come up with precisely nothing in the weeks since the announcement of the Elevation Upgrade Prize.

Nada.

Zilch.

Not so much as the beginning of an idea.

So Knower Robinson, fully aware that the rest of her team intended to come to their meeting with their hats in hand, had trouble believing the oddball Ludquist when he stepped into her office and declared that he had devised, tested, and implemented a solution that would allow the Bubble Suits to filter air at significantly higher altitudes, and that he would like to claim the Elevation Upgrade Prize.

But as Robinson sat there, processing what Ludquist had said, and continuing to listen as he detailed the experiments and the alterations he had made to the existing equipment, her skepticism disappeared, and a warm glow of excitement started to blossom within her.

"This is excellent - EXCELLENT. Close the door and take a seat, Ludquist."

Ludquist did as Robinson asked, then watched impatiently as she leaned back in her chair and tapped her temple to bring up her holographic screen. Robinson tapped a few commands into her wrist panel, then said "Knower Robinson, Department of Research and Innovation, Leader of Air Filtration Team Number 14, reporting a Code 137. I request transportation from the Department of Research and Innovation to the secure location so that I can relay information in accordance with the new procedures."

Ludquist had no idea what was happening on the other end; Robinson sat listening intently for almost a full minute, a smile growing on her face as she heard whatever was said. Finally, she nodded and tapped her temple to shut off her monitor; she rose from her chair, indicating that Ludquist should do the same.

"Our car has been dispatched from the garage. It will be waiting outside by the time we get downstairs."

Ludquist nodded; he had imagined this scene in his mind thousands of times since The Elevation Upgrade Prize had been announced, but he had never dreamed that things would proceed so quickly.

Ludquist was a small man with pale skin, short black hair, and a matching mustache. He was thin, twitchy, and as much a recluse in his social life as he was at work. For that reason, Robinson had always done her best to avoid her subordinate, but any thoughts of Ludquist's peculiarities were out the window now; he had all of Robinson's attention as they exited her office.

Ludquist had worked on Robinson's team for nearly two years now, with no reason for applause or complaint. He had no particular opinion about his superior, who was a few years older than him, an attractive woman with glowing black skin and intelligent brown eyes. Her most distinctive feature was her hair; Robinson always had her Bubble Suit set to style her long black locks in braids, but she also added a color to certain strands of the braids, which she changed daily. Today, it was bright red.

As they strode down the hall and stepped into the elevator, Ludquist walked Robinson through the story of his discovery again, all of the experiments, minor and major, that he had used to test and sharpen his ideas. By the time the elevator reached the ground floor, Robinson was up to speed, and each of the Knowers had moved on to other thoughts, Ludquist lost in fantasies of how his life was about to change while Robinson, like any good manager, devoted her attention to determining the best way to claim as much credit as possible for Ludquist's work.

When the elevator doors opened, the ceiling-to-floor windows on the other side of the atrium offered a view of their ride; a black limousine sat waiting for them in the roundabout at the Department's main entrance.

As they got into the vehicle, which had automatically opened its rear passenger door as they approached, Robinson continued to marvel at her sudden change in fortune; until ten minutes ago, her impression had been that the project was going incredibly poorly. That the team had previously focused on a different area was only part of the problem; until the recent announcement, the Bubble Suit had always met every needed specification, and for the past twenty years, no research and innovation had needed to be done on any part of the Suits, the nutrient intake system included. So, like most of the top-line research teams in Kingston, Robinson's department devoted themselves to designing experiments that would further validate the quality of the current systems and publishing knower-reviewed papers to add to the body of evidence granted to them by Knowledge.

After so many years of following this routine, Robinson's team had proved ill-equipped for the challenge when the Academy of Knowledge announced the Elevation Upgrade Prize; they were so overwhelmed by the idea of having to devise a creative solution that they could not figure out where to start. The prospect of mapping out such an ambitious project had reduced two team members to tears, caused eleven to take leave for general anxiety, and inflicted three others with such severe bowel distress that their waste tanks had to be changed every quarter of an hour, severely curtailing their productivity.

All of these mishaps meant that Robinson's team of twenty-five was essentially reduced to nine - eight, once you accounted for Ludquist's disappearance - and those eight had not produced results despite the tremendous pressure Robinson had applied to them. She had tried everything in the book; she had deprived them of sleep, she had emotionally berated them, she had even gone so far as to suggest they had lost their devotion to Knowledge and might need to be put under the scrutiny of the City Watch.

None of it had worked; given these failures, Robinson was profoundly grateful to find herself riding in the limousine on this wave of success.

The limousine featured a mini-bar; Robinson watched as Ludquist selected a small vial from the variety of liquors on display in a glass-fronted case and tapped in the commands to make his arm panel retract. He glanced in her direction, then back at the vials; Robinson shook her head, rejecting the implied offer.

Ludquist shrugged, and inserted the vial's needle into his fluid intake port; even as he depressed the plunger, he felt his body relax. That feeling was enhanced as the aroma of hot apple cider and smoky-sweet whiskey penetrated his nostrils while the tendrils of the alcohol burned through his body. It was remarkable, Ludquist thought, that Knowers had been able to pack such an experience into one little vial.

He felt perfectly content; or at least, he did until the self-driving limousine, which was traveling north through the heart of Kingston on Central Boulevard, reached the traffic circle where the Boulevard intersected the Northern Corridor.

Ludquist had expected them to continue north through the circle, straight through the roundabout and up the drive to the gates of Capitol Square.

They did not; Ludquist stiffened as the self-driving limousine passed that exit and instead took the next one, which put them west on the Northern Corridor, headed towards the heart of the Amada District.

"Does the vehicle know where we're going?"

Robinson smiled at Ludquist, a superior look in her eyes.

"Of course. But the Elevation Upgrade Prize Committee doesn't do business in Capitol Square."

Ludquist could tell that Robinson wanted him to ask her where the Elevation Upgrade Prize Committee did do business, and decided he did not want to give her the satisfaction. He tried to relax, to enjoy the views of the sweeping lawns and sprawling mansions of the Amada District, to imagine what it would be like once he had claimed the Elevation Upgrade

Prize and moved out of his quarters in the Axios District, but despite his best efforts, he could not help but feel uneasy as the car continued through the Amada District with no signs of stopping.

His misgivings multiplied when they reached the outskirts on the far side of the district.

Quite suddenly, when they were no more than a mile from where the Northern Corridor would turn south and become the Western Highway, the limousine jumped the curb and drove down a small gully, wheels spinning on the green turf that covered the ground between the road and the forest beyond.

Ludquist felt his bowels turn to jelly as they accelerated toward the edges of the Northern Woodlands, hurtling toward the trees. He shut his eyes, bracing for the crash, wondering what in the name of Knowledge could have caused such a horrible vehicle malfunction on the greatest day of his life.

The crash never came.

When Ludquist opened his eyes, he found that they were on a road in the forest. Not a dirt track, or a trail, but an honest-to-goodness, paved road. He spun back quickly, in time to catch a glimpse of the point where the pavement began, a few yards into the tree cover.

Ludquist wondered what he had gotten himself into; he tried to keep his cool, but found it difficult. They had left the city behind, and were driving through the Northern Woodlands into the Cadillac Mountains on a hidden roadway. He could no longer remain quiet.

"Where is it that we are going, Knower Robinson?"

"They call it The Retreat. It is only Known to individuals of a certain rank, but the most important individuals in Kingston, such as the members of the Elevation Upgrade Prize Committee, have a facility out here where they can go when they need to focus on their work. They are able to get more done when they leave the distractions of Kingston behind; the extra travel time is a great inconvenience, but those tasked with carrying out the projects that merit access to The Retreat bear that hardship for our sake."

Ludquist did not understand why Robinson would be privy to this information, if only the most senior individuals knew of the place. Robinson seemed to see the question in his expression, or perhaps she simply anticipated the follow-up; in any case, she answered Ludquist's inquiry before he voiced it.

"I only learned the details on that phone call; on the day that they had Knower Antonius announce the Elevation Upgrade Prize, Head Knower Mallion told me, and the heads of the other top R&I teams at Dynamic Solutions, that if our team did produce a winning idea, we would be shuttled to a secure location to convey our findings."

They drove for another quarter of an hour, the limousine snaking through the trees, passing through alternating pools of shade and light, until they reached the open clearing where The Retreat stood.

The Retreat surprised Ludquist; from Robinson's talk of the inconvenience to the members, he had expected something modest. Now, as he stared up at the ultra-modern structure looming over him, he wondered why he had expected anything but opulence; Kingston's leaders would not actually inconvenience themselves for the greater good, whatever story they tried to tell the public.

The Retreat was five stories tall, built of a silvery material with floor-to-ceiling windows on each level, an ultra-modern building that clashed horribly with its surroundings in the Northern Woodlands. A few dozen cars were parked out in front of The Retreat; Ludquist and Robinson's limousine drove them past the parked cars and stopped at the front gates, where the vehicle spoke in a monochromatic voice.

"Thank you for riding. I will be waiting for you when you are ready to return."

Robinson thanked the self-driving system. The two Knowers stepped out of their vehicle and approached the front entrance, an archway that rose out of a knee-high lattice fence, framing the walkway that paved the path to the front doors. The burnished bronze doors swung inward as Robinson and Ludquist approached, revealing the luxurious room within.

Two figures awaited them.

Neither of the figures was more than four feet tall, and while one was noticeably shorter, their difference in height was no more than an inch. The pair shared the same hair, curly locks gone mostly to grey, contrasting sharply with their black skin. The male, the taller of the two, had a beard, and the female wore her hair a bit longer, but there were few other differences between the pair. The short creatures were aged - it showed in their lined faces - but neither appeared to lack energy for that; their identical brown eyes shone with bright curiosity as they took in the new arrivals.

Or perhaps it was mischief.

All of this Ludquist could gather from observation; what he could not tell was whether these two were sentient beings, or something else entirely. They were wearing Bubble Suits, which was a point in their favor, but even so, they were much smaller than any sentient being he had ever seen.

"Welcome to The Retreat. I trust you had a comfortable journey?"

Ludquist blinked; their male greeter had spoken.

"Who are you?"

Ludquist's tone was blunt, but the pair ignored his rudeness, instead smiling as if delighted that a visitor would take the time to inquire about them. It was the female who answered, in a voice that was surprisingly warm.

"I am Penelope Kastner, and this is my husband, Cornelius. We are the caretakers of The Retreat, and have been for some years. It would be lovely to tell you more - perhaps there will be time later - but as my husband mentioned, many important individuals await your arrival, and we should not keep them waiting."

Their greeters turned and started across the room, gesturing for Ludquist and Robinson to follow. With their longer strides, the two Knowers quickly caught up to the two caretakers; when they did, Penelope turned to look at Ludquist.

"We understand that you are the Knower who received this inspired idea from Knowledge."

Ludquist nodded. Penelope beamed.

"Very good sir, very clever, you are to be congratulated. We are not the type to build such things, of course - Cornelius and I are hard-pressed to keep The Retreat in order - but we can tell from the prize committee's excitement that this is a monumental achievement indeed."

Ludquist returned Penelope's smile; whatever he had thought of them on first glance, he was quickly warming to the pair. The more Penelope spoke, the more certain Ludquist became that she and her husband must simply be short sentient beings; she was too intelligent for there to be any other explanation.

The luxurious room gave way to a sweeping staircase; as they climbed, the environment changed, every step taking them a bit closer to the daylight flooding in through the windows above, a bit nearer the sounds from the string quartet playing above them, a bit further into the intoxicating aroma of freshly blooming lavender.

Ludquist and Robinson looked around with mouths open as they stepped into the second-floor ballroom, a cavernous chamber with towering ceilings that stretched to the fourth floor of the building, where a chandelier the size of a small house glittered magnificently in its heights. Below the chandelier, the room was filled with well-manicured individuals who had set their Bubble Suits to project dinner jackets and evening gowns; they milled about listlessly, occasionally plucking a cocktail vial and or a nutrient packet of hors d'oeuvres from the servers circulating through the room. Ludquist was oblivious to the attire, but Robinson wished she would have thought to change the settings on her Bubble Suit; she felt horribly underdressed, but it would have been considered gauche to adjust her suit's clothing settings after arriving at such an event.

Most of the well-dressed individuals did not react to their appearance, but as Penelope and Cornelius led Ludquist and Robinson to three people near the front windows, the group broke off their conversation and turned to greet the Knowers.

Tarissa Cross had updated the settings on her Bubble Suit, swapping her blue suit and white blouse for a black and tan combo, but her deeply tanned skin was still smooth, her shoulder-length black hair still styled so that a few strands hung across her forehead. Cross's companions, Yvonne

Delverta and Reginald Klaus, were at her side. The pair stood silent behind Cross as she addressed the arrivals.

"Penelope. Cornelius. I take it these are our esteemed Knowers."

"As you requested, Ms. Cross," Penelope answered, a matronly smile on her face. Cross responded with a dismissive nod and turned her attention to the Knowers.

"A pleasure to meet you," said Cross, inclining her head to Robinson and Ludquist. "Allow me to introduce my colleagues, Yvonne Delverta and Reginald Klaus. We are eager to hear your report; we just need to gather the rest of the Elevation Upgrade Prize Committee. We will convene in one of the conference rooms to hear your report; Penelope and Cornelius will show you the way."

Penelope and Cornelius nodded, then turned to lead the Knowers across the ballroom to one of the many hallways running out of the room. It was not long before they found themselves at an elevator; Robinson and Ludquist paused at the doors, but Penelope and Cornelius continued past them to a stairwell.

"No need for the elevator; we're only going up one floor," Penelope announced.

The pair disappeared into the stairwell before either Knower could say anything; they followed, catching up to Penelope and Cornelius as they reached the second floor, where they exited the stairwell and turned down another hallway. The door they sought was the third on the right; Cornelius stopped in front of it and pulled it open.

"Make yourselves comfortable," said Cornelius, ushering them into the room with a bow.

Penelope and Cornelius retreated once the doors were shut, leaving Robinson and Ludquist to enjoy the lavishly decorated room. Plush executive chairs were gathered around a table of polished dark wood, but rather than take their seats, the two Knowers crossed to the refreshment bar on the far side of the room, where they each took a fluid tank of mineral water.

Robinson and Ludquist had just finished disposing of their empty tanks when the doors opened again, revealing the members of the Elevation Upgrade Prize Committee. Tarissa Cross was at the head of the group, flanked by Klaus and Delverta. Seven others filed in behind them; Cross waited for her fellow prize committee members to find their seats before she took her own.

"Well, I think this is all of us. First of all, I want to thank you, Knower Robinson and Knower Ludquist, for visiting us today. I speak for all the members of the Elevation Upgrade Prize Committee when I say how excited we are to hear of your progress."

It was Robinson who replied.

"Thank you, Ms. Cross; we appreciate you taking the time to see us. It was my colleague, Knower Ludquist, who came up with this innovation, so I will leave it to him to share the details of our plan."

Robinson nodded to Ludquist, who began to describe the novel design that he believed would allow the Bubble Suits to function at higher altitudes.

Unbeknownst to Ludquist, the members of the Elevation Upgrade Prize Committee were not the only ones listening to his explanations. Several stories above, in the rooftop penthouse of The Retreat, The Director sat in a throne-like chair, watching a video feed of the conference room on a theater-size holographic screen.

The Director was not alone; four others watched the projection with him. Penelope and Cornelius stood in front of the throne-like chair, their backs to The Director, their eyes on the feed, while two full-sized sentient beings in crisp black uniforms flanked The Director on either side.

The Director listened patiently as Ludquist described the enhancements to the Bubble Suits, but when the Knower started to speculate about tests they might be able to run in the Cadillac Mountains, The Director typed a few commands into the panel on his left wrist. He watched as Tarissa Cross received an alert and tapped on her control panel to pull up his message on her holographic screen; once she had processed it, Cross interrupted Ludquist's monologue.

"We are glad you are thinking of future experiments, Ludquist, but let's keep the focus on the technological capabilities for now. Plenty of time to discuss what field experiments we might run once we have prototypes of the upgrade ready to test."

Ludquist reddened slightly.

"Of course, of course. I'm a bit excited, you understand. It's been a lengthy process testing out the concept, and I kept it a secret, lest I get everyone excited over a red herring. It's gratifying to be able to share the results of my work with others."

Cross nodded.

"And we appreciate your enthusiasm. As to the current work, you say your calculations indicate this process might allow the Bubble Suits to function two thousand feet higher than they do at present. Is there any prospect that this upgrade could exceed that?"

Ludquist's face fell at her words.

"Exceed? Ms. Cross, Kingston sits at an elevation of four thousand five hundred feet. This two thousand foot gain represents a forty-four percent increase in viable functionality above sea level, which I would say is quite significant; it gets us well past the current Elevation Limit, in any case. How high do you want to go?"

"We should like to see a Bubble Suit that functions up to twelve thousand five hundred feet."

Struck dumb by her words, Ludquist could only gape, open-mouthed.

For her part, Robinson was blinking as if she could not comprehend what Cross had said.

"Twelve thousand feet?"

"Twelve thousand five hundred feet, Knower Ludquist."

Ludquist shook his head slowly.

"But...but only the highest peaks of the Cadillac Mountains are above that elevation. You're not going there, are you? The mountains are a death trap. Everyone Knows that."

Cross fixed her attention on Ludquist, a patronizing smile on her face.

"Knower Ludquist, I do not need you to school me on what *everyone* Knows. Of course we don't intend to go into the peaks of the Cadillacs, but as long as we are doing the work, The Guvna', and the members of Parliament, think it best that we do the work the right way. And they have concluded that means building a Bubble Suit that can function anywhere on Shurtain."

Ludquist nodded slowly, trying to make his feigned agreement appear sincere, but his eyes gave him away. They flickered from Cross to Robinson and back again, making it obvious to everyone in the room, including Cross herself, that Ludquist thought she was quite mad.

"Now, don't take me the wrong way, Ludquist. This is a remarkable start, and it is not my intention to disparage the progress you have made, which more than exceeded the requirements that were set for this initial Elevation Upgrade Prize. You, along with Knower Robinson and the rest of your team, will be celebrated at a Kingston-wide event within the week. But understand that this committee intends to announce a second Elevation Upgrade Prize at that event, a prize that will be awarded to anyone who can expand the capabilities of the Bubble Suits beyond what even you have achieved. You will, of course, be eligible for this second prize; in fact, we will see to it that you have any and all resources you might need as you attempt to take your work to the next level."

Ludquist and Robinson both smiled at that, questions about the project requirements vanishing in the wake of visions of glory. Satisfied that she had deflected their attention, Cross continued.

"I will contact The Guvna' about the details as soon as we are done here. He will be very pleased by the progress; overjoyed, in fact. But because I think he will ask, can you give me your best guess of whether your method might push us past a two thousand foot increase, or share any other ideas on how we might accomplish that feat?"

Ludquist did not answer at first; he was quiet, clearly thinking.

"I think we could do better. I'm not an expert in the mechanics of Bubble Suit hardware design, so there could be further improvements in that process, and my software code is not yet optimized. Perhaps we get from forty-four percent up to fifty on those clean-ups."

Ludquist shrugged.

"Not quite the one hundred seventy-seven percent increase you're ultimately looking for, but fifty percent gets us up to six thousand seven hundred and fifty feet."

Cross nodded in approval.

"Over halfway there, in terms of the elevation we ultimately need to reach."

Cross glanced around the room at the other members of the Elevation Upgrade Prize Committee. It was the first time she had paid them any attention, and the moment allowed Ludquist the opportunity to do the same. In his brief survey of the room, it struck him that many of the committee members wore disinterested, glazed expressions; the exceptions were Klaus and Delverta. Cross's subsequent question was directed at them.

"Very well. Any questions from the Elevation Upgrade Prize Committee, or shall we approve the design for trials?"

There were no objections.

"Lovely. Well, I don't suppose there's much else to say. Knower Ludquist, Knower Robinson, do feel free to enjoy the refreshment bar before you head back to the city. Knower Ludquist, please put all of your conclusions, as well as your proposals for prototype testing, into a report as soon as possible. We will want to get this design over to the Department of Manufacturing so they can start to build prototypes for testing. After all, Knowledge will not bless us without the requisite sacrifice of energy."

Robinson and Ludquist bowed in acknowledgment of Cross's final words. Cross nodded, then turned and exited the room, Klaus and Delverta close behind her.

BOOK 2, CHAPTER 15

For two switchbacks, he could still see glimpses of her back.

On the next, he caught a heel disappearing around the turn.

Then, she was gone.

As he realized this, Gavin's pace slowed a few ticks. He had chased Coreen as far as he could; now it was time to throttle down to his pace.

The trail was a moderately easy one by Coreen's standards, a gradual incline on the northeastern outskirts of Trepani. It was hard-packed earth, with the odd rock here and there, good to run on, and wide enough for two to pass. The early part of the trail had been flat, which was part of the reason Coreen had picked this route; it gave her a chance to launch herself off the bigger rocks on the trail's edge before they really got going. Gavin did not join her in that; though pleased by his progress, he could not imagine he would ever casually veer off from his trail run, spring off a rock, turn it into a tight front flip in the air, and hit the ground running.

Coreen did all of that as if it were the most natural thing in the world; when Gavin asked her where she had learned to move that way, she had laughed, and replied that she could not remember, but according to her parents, she had started gymnastics when she started to walk, turning her first stumble into a clumsy tuck and roll. The stumbling quickly turned into running, the tuck and rolls into flips.

Gavin had reached the steepest portion of the trail, but with his pace dialed in, he was able to enjoy the world around him as he climbed, one eye on the magnificent views out over Grand Lake, the other on the trail. It was amazing, he thought, that even as he continued to run, the heat buildup in his legs was dissipating, leaving his muscles feeling, if not fresh, then at least game to make the rest of the climb.

Still more amazing, he had anticipated his recovery; the ebbs and flows of such sensations no longer surprised him. Experience had been a good teacher.

—

Three weeks earlier, after their evening meal, Santino had announced to Gavin that it was time for him to start training with Coreen.

"You're coming along, but there's plenty of work left to do. You need to keep printing better versions of yourself, replace the part of you that is dying each day with a stronger, healthier foundation. Coreen will help you do that."

They were at Santino's house, sitting at a table with Bruno and Paulo, empty plates in front of them. Bruno and Paulo were identical twins, two years younger than Santino and a head shorter than their cousin, but far broader in the shoulder. Though identical, the twins distinguished themselves by wearing their hair in strikingly different styles. Bruno's curly black hair was grown out into a bushy afro, while the only evidence of Paulo's curls was in his brother's locks; his own hair was sheared short on top with a high skin fade on the sides.

It was Bruno who responded to Santino's announcement.

"Or she'll just end up killing him entirely."

Santino and Paulo chuckled, but Gavin felt too nervous to join in.

"What do you mean?"

Santino raised his hand in a mollifying gesture.

"Bruno exaggerates. You don't have to worry, Coreen has settled into her current role, but she's a bit…"

"Loco?" Paulo supplied in his baritone voice. Santino ignored him.

"Intense. She's the oldest cousin on this side of our family, and she's awesome, used to travel in the wild with Anton, only spent maybe three weeks out of the year in Trepani. But that meant it took some…"

Santino trailed off, at a loss to find the right words.

"Adjusting?" Bruno chimed in, his voice as deep as his twin's.

Santino nodded.

"… adjusting when she got back here."

Gavin nodded.

"Ok. But why can't I keep training with you?"

Santino shrugged.

"You could. But it's not my choice - they've got me set to go back on my usual teaching schedule at the Hot Springs - and ultimately, it's not best for you. Coreen is going to push you; after you go through her program, you can decide what level of fitness you want to settle in at, but you want to hit as high a peak as possible coming out of your situation, get everything in your body working as well as it can. That's Coreen's province;

she's the perfect person to help you print out better versions of yourself."

Gavin raised an eyebrow; it was the second time Santino had used the phrase.

"What do you mean, print out a better version of myself?"

Santino shrugged.

"Printing, generating, replacing. Whatever you want to call the process of cellular death and creation that our bodies are undergoing every moment."

"A printer isn't a bad comparison," Bruno opined. "A 3-D printer, at least."

Gavin still looked confused. Paulo provided a more complete explanation.

"See, every moment, countless cells in your body are dying off. If everything is functioning, they are replaced by new cells. And on an even more fundamental level, atoms are rearranging themselves at a faster rate than a sentient brain can comprehend, though that's a bit beyond the point here."

"In any case, the new cells can be stronger or weaker than the old; it depends on a wide variety of factors. Everything you do in life - your thoughts, your relationships, your movements, your environment - helps to inform your body about the design of what needs to be printed next. And the physical building blocks - nutrients, fluids, air, everything we take in - are like the ink and paper, if you will."

"That bit is critical, because you can create a great design for what needs to be printed and provide all the best behavioral inputs, but if you try to build your body out of garbage, you're not going to get a quality end product. All the exercise and rehabilitation work that you're doing would have some effect if you were eating that nutrient junk y'all subsist on down in Kingston, but it wouldn't have nearly the impact that it does when you're eating the way you have up here."

Gavin had no arguments on this last point; it had been Bruno's night to cook, and Gavin's mouth had started to water as soon as he had walked through the door. That was nothing out of the ordinary; whether it was fish, venison, or some other game, the meat and vegetable dishes that Bruno, Paulo, or Santino prepared for dinner each night were consistently a sensory delight.

But while Gavin had no arguments, there was much about what the others were saying that did not make sense to him. It took him some time to gather his thoughts, but eventually, he found the words for his question.

"I don't understand. I thought my body burned food to produce energy. Sort of like the way that cars burned up fuel to produce energy, back before they converted to electricity."

Bruno shrugged.

"Not really. I mean, there's some truth to it, but it's leaving out a lot of important points. Your stomach isn't an incinerator that burns food for fuel. Food provides energy, sure, but it also contains the components needed to replace the old cells in your body, to facilitate all the chemical reactions that need to take place for your body to function properly. Cells in your body are constantly dying, and the replacements have to be built from something. It's not as if we're robots with fixed parts who burn food for energy and dump the charred ashes."

Santino chimed in then.

"And in any case, food isn't the only way for a sentient being to get energy. Some of us can spin it up out of nowhere."

Paulo grinned at that.

"Why tell him? He'll see for himself when he meets Coreen."

—

So, with the previous night's conversation in mind, Gavin had followed Santino out into the early morning hours to meet Coreen, their breath rising in the frigid morning air. When they reached the trailhead they stopped, watching and waiting, listening to the chatter of the birds as the world came to life.

Gavin sensed her before he heard her; her footfalls were that soft.

Perhaps he never would have heard her; as to the sensation, Gavin might have said that he felt a sort of charge, or vibration, enter the clearing.

Santino felt it as well, though he did not give it away until he was certain Gavin had recognized it for himself. Then he turned around to smile at Coreen.

"Morning cuz'. Have a good run?"

Gavin mirrored Santino's turn. As he did, he wondered what Santino had meant by the question. Then his eyes found Coreen, and everything else was driven from his mind.

Gavin stared.

Coreen was tall, a couple inches over six feet. Her long brown hair was tied back in a braid, making her bright green eyes all the more prominent. Everything about her was lean; she had angular features, a sharp jawline, and a thin nose. A sheen of perspiration shone on her olive skin, which only added to the glow emanating from her.

Coreen did not appear to have an ounce of fat on her, but Gavin would not have called her thin; that would have implied a frailty that was completely at odds with the ropy musculature of her body. And then there was the way she carried herself; Coreen moved like a ballerina, light on the balls of her feet, her head held tall, her posture perfect, not in a rigid sort of way, but as if she were floating through the world around her. When she stopped in front of them, and put one hand on her hip, Gavin thought her the very image of an ancient conqueror.

But none of that was why Gavin stared.

He stared because he had never been around another sentient being with energy like Coreen's before, never been around someone whose presence was so undeniably palpable. And when her green eyes turned in his direction, he found an intensity, a presence, a focused force of will beyond anything he could have imagined. There was something disconcerting, even frightening, about those eyes; Gavin knew at a glance that he would not want Coreen to come after him with bad intentions.

Gavin shook himself back to reality as Coreen answered her cousin's question.

"The run was good enough, given how much sleep I got. I heard all about the terrible twos, but nobody warned me that three-year-old Carly would decide to climb out of bed to attack the cat in the middle of the night. In full superhero costume, if you can imagine; the racket was unbelievable. But I still got in ten this morning."

Coreen turned her eyes on Gavin. Santino made the introduction.

"Gavin, my cousin, Coreen Jokofski, who was once known as Coreen Cahn, back in the days before ol' Ollie."

Coreen's eyes warmed at that, which quelled Gavin's apprehension. She extended a hand; Gavin took it briefly, then, still feeling slightly dumbstruck, he asked the question that had stuck in his mind.

"Ten what?"

Coreen raised an eyebrow and exchanged a quick glance with Santino, then realized what Gavin meant.

"Ten miles. And it's nice to meet you too."

Gavin blinked, staring past her to the steep trail beyond, then realized Coreen was looking at him expectantly.

"Oh. I'm Gavin. You're saying you ran ten miles? Up that?"

Coreen laughed.

"Well, five up, and five down. Or close enough."

She saw the look on Gavin's face and continued to laugh.

"It's no great feat. Kiddo, I've spent most of my adult life traveling with Anton, and every day in the Wild presented greater challenges than my hardest workout in Trepani."

Gavin frowned, irritated that Coreen would call him kiddo, but she continued before he could voice his displeasure.

"Anyways, I'm told that you were two at the time of the Advent?"

Gavin nodded, confirming the implied answer to Coreen's question.

"Well, we caught a break there. You would have been up and walking around, getting into more advanced movements, before you got into the Bubble Suit. All that experience, all those falls, some trace of them is still in your body's memory."

"Does that matter?"

"More than you can imagine. I've been at this for four years, and when

I started, they had me working with defectors right out of Kingston, the ones who had only just shed their Bubble Suits. I saw plenty of folks who were in rough shape, but the ones grown by your Department of Infant Development were their own type of disaster."

"What was wrong with them?"

Coreen shook her head.

"Everything. This is the short version, but most of the space in a sentient being's brain is devoted to movement skills. Or at least, it's supposed to be, because movement is an amazingly complex task. But apparently, when an egg is fertilized in a Bubble Suit, and the Bubble Suit handles all movement from the fetus stage and on, the portion of the brain that is supposed to be devoted to movement doesn't develop properly. The theory put forth by some of your Knowers, when the issue came to light, was that this might cause a leap forward in sentient consciousness, as all of that vacated brain space could be turned over to creativity and reasoning."

"I don't know what happened, but it sure wasn't that; the defectors I worked with who had spent their whole lives in a Bubble Suit were as dull as you can imagine. They have to learn their movement skills from scratch, and while we now have examples who show that it can be done, that isn't an easy process. Add in the fact that those sentient beings were never given opportunities to develop mental fortitude, and it takes something close to a miracle for them to overcome the obstacles in front of them."

Coreen shook her head again.

"They're here, so something has to be done with them, I suppose, but what a nightmare."

"As you might have guessed by now, there's a reason Coreen got reassigned from that initial posting," Santino commented.

His cousin grinned.

"In my defense, I always kept it in check - or did my best - when I was working directly with the defectors. But I won't deny that it was a relief when our grandmother pointed out that I might not have the temperament to work with that group. It had only been two weeks, so I didn't want to bail, but that was a long ways from traveling with Anton. Too big of an adjustment, regardless of my intentions. This has been much better."

"And what is this?" Gavin asked tentatively.

Coreen's smile grew.

"I'm going to make you forget you ever wore a Bubble Suit. More directly, I'm going to make your body forget it ever wore a Bubble Suit. You won't need to keep up this regimen after we're done, not if you don't want to, but for your long-term health, it's critical we put your body through a series of stress tests to make sure everything is working again."

"But don't worry - we'll start slow."

Starting slow had been a two-mile run up the mountain trail. Gavin had only made it a quarter of the way before he had been forced to stop, his breaths desperate heaves; Coreen told him to keep moving, to walk if he had to, to get his wind back, to continue to push forward.

By the time they returned to the bottom of the trail, Gavin's whole body was cramping, and it was only after several bottles of mineral water and a series of stretches that he was able to hobble back to town.

Once they were back in Trepani, Coreen took him to the Hot Springs, where Gavin soaked for an hour before meeting Coreen for a lunch of river trout and vegetables. As they ate, Coreen explained the reasoning behind the inclusion of each spice and vegetable in the dish, as well as the amino acid profile of the protein in the fish, highlighting the reasons it would promote muscular recovery and growth.

The meal marked the end of their work for that day; Coreen left Gavin with instructions to meet her at a trailhead in northwest Trepani an hour after sunrise the next day.

Three weeks had passed since then, and each morning, Gavin had met Coreen to run a trail. Occasionally, Santino, or another cousin, joined them. But on most mornings, Gavin and Coreen ran alone.

With so much going on, it was not until the second week that Gavin took any notice of the small duffel pack Coreen wore around her waist, or the holstered items beneath it, but once he did, he realized that they had always been there.

"Is that a gun?"

Coreen no longer laughed out loud at Gavin's blunt questions, but they still drew an amused smile.

"Yes, it's a gun, Gavin. And a canister of bear mace, and a knife."

"But why?"

"Because there are mountain lions, and wolves, and bears, and all sorts of other things out here. They tend to stay away from Trepani, but if I get attacked, I'm not trying to fight a wild animal with my bare hands. There's no getting out of that unscathed, and there might not be any getting out of it at all. This pistol has as much stopping power as you can pack into a handgun, and I still put in my time on the range a couple of nights a week. Just have to wear good ear protection. My hearing has always been superb, and I'm not trying to lose that; if anything comes for me, I want to get the jump on it."

Gavin's eyes widened in alarm as she spoke, but Coreen continued undeterred; in fact, after weeks of mounting amazement at Gavin's ability to move through life with such placid unawareness, she was glad that something finally seemed to have gotten his attention.

"Ya. Sometimes, when you're out here, life gets real like *that*."

Coreen snapped her fingers as she said the last word; Gavin flinched.

"So I'm not trying to run into anything, but if I do, you better believe I'm still going home to my daughter."

They had not run into any mountain lions, or wolves, or bears, however, and for that, Gavin was profoundly grateful. He had enough on his plate with the workouts, which, in many cases, went well beyond running. As Coreen explained, Gavin could build endurance with miles, but it was more efficient to build muscle - and speed - with other work. Running hills was a start, but it was only a start. So they did squats and push-ups, dips and up-downs. They did pull-ups when they found good tree limbs to use, lifted heavy stones when they found them, pressing them up over their heads and throwing them as far as they could. Several days a week, they went to Coyote Run trailhead on the eastern end of Trepani, where Coreen had assembled a selection of boulders in the clearing; they would strap themselves to the stones with harnesses and drag them, walking both forward and backward, across the flat surface of the clearing, or up the hill next to it. And at the end of each day's work, Coreen would lead Gavin through sequences of yoga postures, expanding his body's range of motion across all planes, as she put it.

Through it all, she kept him in high spirits, reminding him that the sensations he was feeling should be welcomed.

"Burn is good. Sensation is good. Those are unmistakable signals that we aren't wasting our time here. They are your feedback loops, validating the work that is happening. Keep breathing, and keep going. That signal is not pain. Burn is not pain. If you feel pain, you will know it. Don't let your mind tell you that burn is bad. The burn is signal, and the more signal we send to the body, the more it will respond when we finish and you begin your recovery."

During their first week, Gavin had not been sure whether to believe this. His initial progress had been dismal; on the first two days, he had overestimated his endurance, and with his legs searing, found his body collapsing into a sitting position before they were halfway up the trail. On the third day, he pulled back his pace so much that it took six hours to cover the distance, and on the fourth, he over-adjusted so violently that he found himself vomiting on the side of the trail after half a mile.

But those difficulties had passed, and now that Gavin had a better feel for his body and its capabilities, he was able to move up the trails at a steady pace; as Santino and his cousins had put it on the night before he started with Coreen, it was as if the Universe had printed a new version of Gavin into existence, a more functional model that ran longer, more efficiently, and with a greater capacity for high-end output. Even his mind felt better; Gavin found himself thinking faster and clearer, noticing details that had previously eluded his consciousness as he went about his life.

Gavin came around the last switchback and found Coreen at the top of the trail, staring out over Trepani. The settlement housed a notable population - Santino had told Gavin it was close to fifteen thousand - and from where they stood, partway up one of the northern peaks, they could see all of it.

The sentient beings below, moving like ants through the streets of the town.

The spattering of small islands near the bend in Grand Lake.

The sunlight glittering like diamonds on the water's surface.

The beginnings of both the Eastern and Western Grand, the two rivers that flowed out of Grand Lake, in direct contradiction to Kingston's Knowledge.

Yet as Gavin stood next to Coreen, catching his breath as he took in the scene, he was not thinking about the Knowledge he had learned in Kingston. He was thinking about his trainer, and how Coreen had become what she was.

"Can I ask you a question?"

Coreen turned, a grin on her face, her green eyes shimmering.

"Strange of you to be so formal. Sure, you can ask me a question; you usually ask about a hundred a day."

Gavin was undeterred.

"Why don't you dress like a girl?"

Coreen raised an eyebrow.

"And what does a girl dress like?"

Gavin was caught off-guard by this. It seemed obvious to him; in Kingston, women set their Bubble Suits to project dresses, or pants and shirts of a distinctively feminine style, and from what he had seen, it was not so different in Trepani - many of the women wore clothing similar to the imitations the women in Kingston projected through their Bubble Suits - but when Gavin and Santino had come across Coreen with Ollie and Carly one evening, Coreen had been wearing a black t-shirt and sweats of an indistinct cut. It was no different when they trained; everything Coreen wore had a generic cut to it.

Gavin had barely finished processing these thoughts when Coreen threw another argument his way.

"In fact, given that I'm a girl, and I dress like I do, then isn't dressing the way I do dressing like a girl?"

Gavin could only gape; the gears in his head felt like they were starting to smoke. Coreen was obviously having fun with this, but she relented when Gavin continued to look bewildered.

"Don't worry, I know what you mean. It's just a more amusing way to answer the question."

"The straightforward answer is that I don't subscribe to your notion that I have to do anything because of the body I was born into. The I that is me, my unique consciousness, emanates from the source, the creator, the Logos, whatever term you prefer, which is neither male nor female, but something greater, encompassing all things."

"So yes, it's true that on the whole, most girls dress a certain way. But that doesn't mean any individual has to do anything, and if you let generalizations bleed over into your assessment of an individual, you're ultimately handicapping yourself. You miss out on the opportunity to see that being for who they truly are."

"I have this body in my present experience, but at heart, I am a warrior. My physical traits meant I had to express that in a different way as part of Anton's troop, but I, and the other women who have traveled with the hunting parties, had our own strengths to contribute. For instance, nobody in our troop could match me in distance running - especially once we got up over fifty miles - and my weight - or lack thereof - allowed me to climb ice spears that a larger sentient being might have brought crashing down."

Seeing that she had tied Gavin's mind in a knot, Coreen tried to lighten the mood.

"I do appreciate you calling me a girl, though; motherhood is taking its toll on me. Soon enough, you'll be asking why I don't dress like an old woman."

The thought was so implausible that Gavin burst out laughing.

"I know, you're imagining this version of me with a grey wig, perhaps a walker that I'm forcing myself to stoop on?"

She shook her head.

"Don't fool yourself; nobody lives forever."

Gavin nodded slowly, processing everything Coreen had said. His instincts told him to look for the flaw in her argument - in Kingston, identity and external appearance were one and the same - but he could not find one. Instead, he shared another thought that had bubbled up in his mind.

"You mentioned the Logos; Santino talked about it too, when he was telling me a story of your grandfather. His name was Salomon, wasn't it?"

Coreen nodded.

"It's too bad about the accident. Santino told me about that; it's a shame he died so early. I suppose that's why nobody in Kingston goes into the mountains. All the adults always told me it was too dangerous."

There was a certain sadness in Coreen's eyes at the mention of her grandfather, but the smile that bloomed on her face was all the more beautiful for that.

"Dangerous? Sure. But too dangerous? In exchange for all of this?"

Coreen's eyes swept out over the landscape beneath them, Grand Lake, the people of Trepani going about their day, the clouds hovering over the peaks in the distance.

"Life has its sorrows, but that doesn't mean you huddle up in a hole and cling to your treasures, forsaking the chance to live your life in the hopes that the inevitable never catches up to you. Risk is unavoidable; death is the price of being born, after all. And it might be an end, or it might not be; I've never spoken to anyone who can provide definitive proof of what happens after this."

"In any case, to give up this experience to hide out in a sanitized environment and hope that nothing bad happens to you…well, that doesn't make much sense to me. And it's impossible in any case; uncertainty may not be a pleasant condition, but certainty is an absurd one."

Gavin raised an eyebrow.

"But in Kingston, everyone lives until one hundred."

Coreen burst out laughing.

"Yes, and every citizun of The Bubble Society is happy, for they live in a utopia, and have no reason to be unhappy. That's the Guvernment's line, isn't it?"

There was a giddy playfulness in Coreen's eyes as she leveled her gaze on Gavin. He would never forget that look, never forget that moment, the instant before Coreen said the words that shook him to his core.

"I know what they say in Kingston, Gavin. It's not true. Almost nobody in Kingston lives until one hundred. What do you think happens to the ones they call the Laureates? The ones they claim are called by Knowledge?"

BOOK 2, CHAPTER 16

She sat at a table, using a set of hand tools to attach an extendable arm to a camera. Her headlamp, an extra upgrade she had installed in her Bubble Suit, put a miniature spotlight on the objects in question.

The rest of the room was lit by the eerie glow of the television-sized monitors mounted on the front wall. Seven of the nine monitors were given over to her surveillance system; the remaining two displayed the output of critical programs spitting out lines of green text to verify their execution.

A grim expression on her face, her eyes narrowed in concentration, Tesla lifted the camera and tested the extendable arm, pushing it in and out, first by hand, then with the remote control sitting on her desk. The arm moved as expected; with a small nod of satisfaction, Tesla stood and walked to the back of the room, where she set about mounting the camera on the wall next to two others.

It was overkill, she knew; her primary camera, the one that she used to monitor her lab's computers through her holographic monitor, had never failed, nor had the backup she had installed next to it. But Tesla had little else to occupy her time at the moment, and of late, she found herself filled with more anxiety than usual, particularly when she had to attend classes at the Academy of Knowledge; she thought she might have a stroke if her camera feed of her lab went down during a lecture.

Tesla's Lab was deep in the basements of The Old Capitol, occupying a room off the same hallway where she stored her bike, the same hallway that provided access to the steel door that opened into The Guvna's Park. She had started work on her lab when she was seven; by that age, it had become intolerably frustrating to have her work confined to one computer monitor.

And there were other reasons to go underground; by that time, two years After Knowledge, it had become exceedingly odd for any sentient being, much less a seven-year-old, to use any sort of external computer, much less a setup with the specifications Tesla desired. After all, the Bubble Suits had a built-in computer, and sentient beings with jobs that required more computing power could hook up to the Guvernment's cloud via their holographic monitor.

Tesla had no interest in that option, and even at seven, she knew better than to draw the sort of attention that assembling her lab in The Guvna's Mansion would have brought. Her bedroom, of course, was not safe; against any objections she might have, the Guvernment Officials tasked with cleaning The Guvna's Mansion insisted on straightening Tesla's room.

Fortunately, Tesla had been exploring Capitol Square for over two years by then; she had never thought of her adventures as scouting assignments, but as soon as she decided that she needed to build herself a lab, she knew that the bowels of The Old Capitol would be perfect, especially if she could get that rusty-hinged steel door on the hillside to open again.

Every bit of hardware from Tesla's original laboratory was gone by now, replaced in her upgrade cycles, but while the only thing that remained constant was the room itself, it still had the feel of home; Tesla loved spending time in her lab, and it made her sad to think of the steps she had taken to prime it for destruction in recent days.

For a long time, she had debated whether this was necessary. Her plan was to disappear forever, one way or the other, but even with no plans to return, the thought of destroying the lab had been too much to bear.

That was until a few days ago, when, in her boredom, Tesla had decided to take a closer look at the second challenge announced by the Academy of Knowledge, which had announced three additional Elevation Upgrade Prizes open to anyone who could figure out a way to build on the work of the famous Knower Ludquist.

Tesla had started her reading of Knower Ludquist's paper with her usual sense of arrogance, but as she took in the abstract, her heartbeat accelerated, and by the time she had completed the paper, she felt faintly ill. A few rough calculations confirmed it, or confirmed it as far as Tesla could without testing her new idea in the field.

Before Tesla read Knower Ludquist's paper, she assumed that he would have used the same methods that had occurred to her in her original review of the problem. But he had not; Ludquist's approach was completely different from her own.

And the two methods were not incompatible. In fact, they would complement each other.

They would get the Bubble Suits to the peaks of the Cadillac

Mountains.

After that, the decision to eviscerate all traces of her lab was easy, even with the inconvenience of having to disarm the explosives whenever she wanted to get back in. Tesla was resigned to the fact that, with so many sentient beings devoting attention to the problem, someone would eventually reach the same conclusions that she had, but she was not eager to leave any clues that might help the Kingston Guvernment on their way.

Especially not when there were already looming signs of what that could mean.

On that front, the signs were blatant; the City Watch had recently increased its activity, putting more officers in the streets of Kingston, all of them in full dress uniform. There were similar changes at her home; the Capitol Guard had officers walking security patrols around Capitol Square in addition to those guards who stood vigil at the standard posts.

Tesla was not the only one to notice this; the change was too dramatic for anyone in Kingston to miss. It was even remarked upon by her friends at school; for the first time in years, Tesla genuinely wanted to join their conversation, to share everything she knew as Anna, Thea, and Shannon speculated on the change in the City Watch, and why it had happened the morning after Knower Ludquist received the Elevation Upgrade Prize.

But that was impossible.

Or at least, Tesla could not be honest if she joined the discussion, because her friends - and the rest of Kingston - could only connect the increased activity of the City Watch with the celebration the previous night, when the Elevation Upgrade Prize had been presented at Kingston Amphitheater. Nobody could say what the two things had to do with each other, but it was hard to miss the fact that the City Watch had appeared in the streets the morning after the celebrations.

Yet no matter how much they puzzled over it, they could not establish a reason for the connection, because Tesla's friends - and the rest of Kingston - only knew half of what had happened that night.

—

The presentation of the Elevation Upgrade Prize had been an occasion for celebration, a moment for the people of the city to congregate at Kingston Amphitheater.

So in a roundabout way, Knower Ludquist's findings were the reason that Tesla was on the roof of the Department of Infant Development. One could even go as far as to blame Ludquist for Tesla's break-in - she certainly did - even if Ludquist was sitting at Kingston Amphitheater, waiting to go on the stage to receive his prize from The Guvna'.

As for blaming Ludquist, Tesla did not honestly put her actions at his feet, but his discovery had certainly forced her hand. Were it not for Ludquist, Tesla could have continued to wait, continued to hope that someone would come down from the Cadillac Mountains to offer her a way out.

Now, with The Bubble Society one step closer to extending its domain, Tesla no longer felt she had the luxury of waiting.

She needed to be able to dictate the terms of her exit, if it came to that.

She needed a Spike.

Her heart had been in her throat as she scaled the side of the Department of Infant Development, though she was more concerned about being spotted than about falling; Tesla had added a "grippy fingers" package to her Bubble Suit in her mid-teens. A "grippy toes" addition had followed shortly after; together, they allowed her to move easily up any building in Kingston, and her understanding of the city's surveillance system allowed her to select spots where she would not be seen by any cameras.

She wished she could say that she designed the features with a less criminal enterprise in mind, but it would have been a lie; as Tesla pulled herself onto the roof of the Department of Infant Development, she found herself reflecting that she had spent her whole life preparing for tonight.

Tesla went straight to a cluster of vents, lifted the cover off one of them, and crawled in. She had the blueprint of the ventilation system, downloaded from the Guvernment servers, locked into her mind; in the mental image, she had highlighted her route through the twists and turns in a glowing blue light. The path would take her, in a convoluted way, to the room where the Spikes were stored.

She did not encounter difficulties as she navigated the vents, but she did linger when her route took her directly over the Infant Staging Theater. She could see down into the theater through the slits in the vents, see the cavernous space filled with pods, all of them glowing softly in the darkness, the next generation of sentient beings who would enter Kingston.

It gave Tesla the creeps; she could hardly imagine what life would be like as one of the two technicians who sat in a small box at the top of the bowl, monitoring the vitals of the infants on the overnight shift. After observing the room for a time, Tesla pressed on, her mind shifting back to her objective.

Like so much else in her life, the theft turned out to be easier than she could have dreamed; she did not need to disable the cameras in the room that housed the Spikes, because they were not turned on, and when she dropped into the room through the ceiling vent, she found that the case where they stored the needle-like objects was unlocked. Kingston's workforce was truly pathetic; she supposed that was what two decades of complacency got you.

Even so, Tesla did not want to push her luck, so she moved quickly as she put a Spike in a protective sheath and dropped it into the shoulder bag she had brought along. She climbed back through the vents, descended the wall of the building, retrieved her bike from a nearby alley, and returned to the hillside door, where she stowed her ride and hid the Spike in her lab before re-entering Kingston Amphitheater.

Everything went so smoothly that Tesla dared to hope that the theft would go unnoticed.

The appearance of the City Watch on Central Boulevard the next morning dashed those hopes; complacent they might be, but it seemed that while the keepers of the Spikes could not be bothered to turn on their cameras or lock their cases, they could still count to twelve. Tesla thought it was a shame that there had not been more of the Spikes; if there had been hundreds in the case, nobody would have noticed a thing.

Still, it did not matter much. Tesla had her Spike sitting in its sheath on the desk in front of her, and there was no sign that anyone suspected her, no indication that any of her activity had been unmasked. As to the response, it was hardly a surprise; to the contrary, it was a predictable, tired reaction to anyone or anything that challenged The Knowers, The Board, The Director, or any other instrument of The Authority, at least for anyone who knew the true history of how The Bubble Society had come into being.

Then again, those individuals were few and far between; certain moments, such as The Advent, and the Aeronbald Volunteer Experiments, were imprinted in the population's collective consciousness, forming their creation myth, but the truth was that those moments were only a small part of the story, dramatic as they might have been.

In some cases, other bits of the story were known, but only in a twisted form; one example was how Dynamic Solutions had responded to one of the greatest challenges that they had faced on their road to conquest: the continued existence of pests, the rodents and insects that stubbornly remained alive in Shurtain's atmosphere despite the proclamations of the Knowers. The large animals had been easier; they were easier to count, easier to identify, easier to hunt. In fact, Dynamic Solutions had used the large animals to their advantage, pointing to their accelerating disappearance as evidence of the deteriorating atmosphere even as they carried out the killings.

It was the rodents and insects that were the real problem; if Dynamic Solutions was to be believed, they would not be able to survive in Shurtain's new atmosphere. But how to eradicate the innumerable tiny creatures that cohabitated Shurtain with them?

The solution had been to "disinfect" the ground. Dynamic Solutions contracted with the Guvernment to design a chemical disinfectant that would work by killing every living organism in the ground, directly destroying most of the pests and depriving the others of their nutrient source.

The downside was that the solution would kill all of the natural landscape in Kingston, but the Knowers at Dynamic Solutions did not see that as a particularly significant problem; in fact, killing off the landscape, which would necessitate some sort of replacement, simply created another profit opportunity. Dynamic Solutions spun up a division to create artificial grass and landscaping, and, once the ground disinfection was complete, set about replacing the dead areas with what was widely considered a superior substitute; after all, fake flowers would not attract bees, and fake grass would not require water.

The solution was a microcosm of The Board's attitude toward anything that questioned their narrative: if it put the lie to The Bubble Society, it must be destroyed.

For twenty years, The Board had not needed to employ such tactics.

But Gavin Owens had changed all of that.

Gavin Owens - and his abductor, if that was the right word for the old man - had forcibly reminded the members of The Board that a threat to their power might still exist, and if the increased activity of the City Watch was any indication, The Director's instincts for handling threats had not changed much over the years.

It was what had convinced Tesla, more than anything, that she was on the right path. The Board would continue ruthlessly on their quest to make the Universe conform to Knowledge, and sooner or later, that path would lead them to Tesla's Lab.

So, right, wrong, or indifferent, Tesla knew she had no choice.

When the moment came, she would have to run.

BOOK 2, CHAPTER 17

Coreen had not known.

Coreen could not have known.

But the information that she had shared with Gavin had shaken him to his core.

He had always had a sense, deep down, that something was off with his parents.

He had attempted to share that belief with the caretaker, Maria, on his last visit.

And Maria had known, just as he had known; they had simply allowed themselves to be convinced otherwise.

So why, when something was so obviously wrong, did everyone in Kingston insist the Laureates were called by Knowledge, and that everyone should regard them with reverence?

Why did the Guvernment pretend that they were living to 100? Why did they claim that they Knew this?

His roommates could sense that something was off with him, but Gavin did not feel comfortable confiding in Santino, or either of the twins. With no idea of what was bothering their new friend, the cousins could not offer much in the way of support.

When he had left Kingston, Gavin believed that he had decades to return and see his parents, to say a last goodbye to them. Half a century, really; everyone in The Bubble Society lived until 100, and Amelia and Brent Owens were a long ways off from that age.

—

"The truth is that almost nobody in Kingston lives until one hundred. What do you think happens to the ones they call the Laureates? The ones they claim are called by Knowledge?"

The comment had been offhand, had clearly assumed that Gavin shared whatever insights Coreen already held, but for Gavin, it was an effort to keep his breathing steady as he answered her question.

"I don't know."

Coreen turned on him, an eyebrow raised.

"Well, you do know what's wrong with them, right?"

Gavin shook his head.

"They have dementia."

Gavin blinked.

"Dementia?"

"Sure. The Bubble Suits do all sorts of things to cover up dysfunction in the body, but they don't address the root causes, and inevitably, that has to manifest somewhere."

"They've been able to put most diseases out of the picture, but the result wasn't a downtick in the rate of infirm people. Instead, the rate of dementia skyrocketed to compensate for all the reductions. The only reason that The Villa isn't overflowing is that once a patient is diagnosed - or a Laureate is discovered, as they would say - the expected survival is ten to fifteen years, tops."

A cold hand closed on Gavin's insides.

Ten to fifteen? But that would mean…

He did not allow himself to finish the thought; he knew how it finished.

His parents had been taken away eleven years ago.

—

Had Gavin shared his concerns with Coreen, or any of the others, they might have convinced him that his sense of guilt was unreasonable. More importantly, they might have pointed out that Gavin's desire to say a proper farewell to his parents, however heartfelt, was an impossibility. As painful as it was, there was nobody left for Gavin to say goodbye to; just the abandoned vessels that had once been the vehicles of his parents' consciousness.

But Gavin did not see it that way.

He was so consumed by his thoughts that he barely listened to the lively discussion that Santino, Bruno, and Paulo engaged in that night, even though they were speaking of his great-uncle Clarence, and the latest updates on the old man's troubles.

Despite the hopes Clarence had expressed after redirecting the mob upon his arrival in Trepani, nobody who had shown up to meet him had forgotten about the danger his actions had put them in. Emotions continued to run high across the settlement; the angry feeling against Clarence was not universal, but those who were angry tended to be highly animated, and nobody was stepping up to take Clarence's side, to try to argue that his actions were some sort of example to follow, or in any way a good idea.

Clarence was not in a prison, but he was not free, either. Eleanor Cahn had reasoned with those calling for immediate action against him, convincing them to accept an agreement where Clarence would be held at a house on the outskirts of Trepani until they could have a Town Gathering. It was not a prison sentence, precisely - Clarence would be offered every comfort and freedom of the property - but he would not be allowed to leave Trepani until the others had a chance to hold him to account.

Gavin had visited his great-uncle on two occasions, but he had not found Clarence in a talkative mood. The old man did not seem overly concerned with his situation, and showed no interest at all in Gavin's acclimation to life in Trepani; in fact, Clarence seemed annoyed that Gavin's presence was taking him away from the latest volume off the stack of books assembled in a corner of his room.

Unsure of what to make of this, Gavin was purposely vague about a third visit, and had not gotten around to returning. Something about the situation was off - he would have expected his great-uncle to be incensed at being held captive until the Town Gathering, and interested in how Gavin was enjoying the life Clarence had risked so much for him to have - but the old man seemed content to sit and wait for his day in the Town Square, making no inquiries of what was going on outside of the property that he was held on.

That was probably for the best, because he had a long wait. When Trepani's Council met to discuss Clarence's situation, it quickly became clear that all present believed that the situation affected all Acadians, not just those in Trepani, and that it had the potential to impact all of their fellow Shurtainians.

It meant they needed to hold something more significant; an Acadian Summit.

The Summit had been announced weeks before, but there were plans to be made and distances to travel, both for the messengers and the responding delegations, which had kept excitement in check when the event was initially announced. But with the day fast approaching, Trepani was abuzz with speculation; the air was charged with the excitement of it, and until Coreen's revelations, Gavin had been as eager as anyone to discuss the notable figures who would make the journey to Trepani.

But now…

As Santino, Bruno, and Paulo discussed the impending arrivals, Gavin found he could not engage, could not pay attention to their words. It all felt so distant, so meaningless, compared to the painful thoughts that had embedded themselves in his being, the gut-wrenching anxiety he felt as he reproached himself for his past mistakes. But while he could not find the space to listen, Gavin did hear what they said.

Like the rest of Trepani, the cousins were highly excited by the upcoming event. There was regular commerce between the different Acadian cities, but groups of travelers were typically small, and it was rare that so many would descend on Trepani at the same time. In fact, the last time the cousins could recall such a gathering had been over a decade earlier, when all of the Acadians had come together in Trepani to celebrate ten years of life in Nature.

From their discussions, Gavin had learned that there were three major Acadian cities besides Trepani: one to the south, and two to the northeast. He had passed the route to the southern settlement during his voyage with Clarence; in fact, his great-uncle had pointed out the route to Giota as they departed Turquoise Lake, but with so much going on, Gavin had forgotten until Santino described the place.

The two other cities, Kirfi and Larissa, lay to the northeast. Kirfi was another mountain dwelling, the second-largest Acadian settlement, and the closest to Acadia; Larissa was much further away, the only Acadian settlement at sea level, sitting on the northeastern coast of the continent. From Larissa, it was a short sail across the Sister's Break to the neighboring continent of Alexandria.

Larissa was said to be unique in many ways, not least of which was that it was the only Acadian settlement in the functioning altitude range of the Bubble Suits; like Trepani, Kirfi stood in the peaks of the Cadillac Mountains, and Giota was built in the cliffs of Acadia's southeastern peninsula, overlooking the Amphitrite Ocean from towering bluffs.

However, Larissa had a different type of protection from The Bubble Society; there were obvious ways to reach Trepani, Kirfi, and Giota by land, but to reach Larissa, the people of Kingston would either have to pass through Trepani and Kirfi on a route through the Cadillac Mountains, or they would have to sail around Acadia. Two routes existed - they could either go south out of the Gulf of Gian, sail around the Southeastern Peninsula, and turn north to cross the Amphitrite Ocean, or they could sail northwest through Nicaean Ocean, following Acadia's western coastline through the Ambaric Passage, where they would turn east to sail along Acadia's northern coast through the half-frozen Larean Ocean - but while the routes existed, the citizuns of The Bubble Society were no seafarers. They feared the open waters as much as they feared the heights of the Cadillac Mountains; they would not make the voyage to Larissa.

That had meant Larissa was safe.

Until now.

Which was why people were coming from Kirfi, from Giota, from Larissa, even from Alysanne, a city in Alexandria, the continent that loomed to the east of Acadia, the only continent on Shurtain that was larger than Acadia.

For the others, the anticipation of so many visitors translated to palpable excitement, but Gavin could not share that feeling. It did not matter to him that Coreen's father, Marcus Cahn, was leading a delegation up from Larissa. It did not matter that Alabaster Minteran, who had once been Salomon Cahn's chief lieutenant, was leading another group from Kirfi, that Gweniviere Holt was leading the people of Giota, or that someone named Anton was set to come in from the Wild with his troop, and several other bands of their ilk.

Gavin did not know any of these people, but he knew his parents. And he could not pay much attention to anything else while he was consumed by the idea that they were slipping away, standing on the crumbling precipice of the beyond; it barely even registered that the arrival of a delegation from Alexandria put the lie to The Bubble Society's claim that there was no life on any continent but Acadia.

What was on Gavin's radar was that he needed to find a way to get back to his parents. He needed to find a way to make things right. To say a proper goodbye.

It should only take a week. Three days down on Rex if they went fast, a day to find the right opportunity to visit his parents at The Villa, and three days back up. Then, proper goodbyes said, Gavin could get on with enjoying his new life back in Trepani.

Easy enough.

BOOK 2, CHAPTER 18

"And as you will all recall, we must always consider the hypothetical interactions of the hypothetical compound with the Bubble Suit's nutrient and fluid feeds. In this hypothetical example, the hypothetical compound presents no concerns, so, in theory, we would be able to proceed to trials, if we still lived in a world where there was any need for novel medications."

Tesla suppressed a yawn; she was aware that Knower Hunt, a prickly woman, would take offense at the slightest sign her audience was not captivated by her words.

And with Knower Hunt's endless qualifiers to spice up the Knowledge she spewed, how could anyone fail to be captivated?

Knower Hunt taught Hypothetical Pharmacology, and while the vast majority of the courses conducted at the Academy of Knowledge were a waste of time, Tesla had always thought that this one took the cake.

The powers-that-be - the Guvernment, the Academy of Knowledge, and Dynamic Solutions - refused to acknowledge that the Bubble Suits were anything less than perfect, which put them in something of a bind whenever an obvious need for improvements became evident.

Fortunately, the great minds governing those institutions had used Knowledge to develop some ingenious workarounds. For instance, in the first year, when frequent "wrents" - small cracks in the Bubble Suit membranes that were supposed to self-seal, but in reality needed to be repaired by a technician - forced Dynamic Solutions to spin up a new division of the Emergency Response Team, they did not record any of the Bubble Suit wrents as malfunctions, but instead credited them to "user error", a term that proved to be incredibly flexible, and thus, incredibly useful.

And that was not the only time that the intelligentsia of The Bubble Society was called upon to deal with a knotty problem; far from it. Mere weeks after they had resolved the wrent issue, it became apparent that the problem of cognitive decline had persisted After Knowledge, and had perhaps accelerated.

Fortunately, the Knowers assigned to the project devised an elegant solution; they simply coined the term "Laureate", loudly proclaimed that these infirm individuals were called by Knowledge, and moved them into The Villa. When the individuals grew too sick to function, a select few from the staff - who kept silent about their activities under threat of death - dumped the bodies in a trash chute that led to the basement furnace.

Problem solved.

But it was in the face of persistent day-to-day physical complaints from their citizuns - which, in the view of Knowledge, required pharmacological intervention - that the Knowers claimed their greatest victory.

They invented the Department of Hypothetical Pharmacology, which carried on doing the type of research they had done Before Knowledge, and applying it to the Bubble Suits.

Hypothetically, of course.

And if a new compound needed to be introduced - which would never happen, because the Bubble Suits were perfect - then Dynamic Solutions would produce records showing that the drug had been patented during the creation of the Bubble Suits back before The Advent, and that they were only now entering the period where the drug needed to be put into use.

The Focus Solution was one such example; when Kingston's teachers complained that the children in their classes wanted to get up and move around from time to time, Dynamic Solutions stepped in, supplying them with the drug and loudly announcing that it had been designed years ago as part of the Bubble Suit blueprint.

Tesla could not say if Knower Hunt and the others would have gotten more done if their constant qualifiers did not extend their speech by 50%, but somehow, she doubted it; the woman seemed far too comfortable with the idea that there was someone, somewhere, who Knew better than her.

Someone who Knew why sentient beings were on Shurtain.

Who Knew where sentient beings went after they died.

Who had an exact understanding of Nature, who had the perfect plan to end sentient suffering, who could explain what consciousness was and why this whole experience on Shurtain existed.

Who Knew exactly what every member of sentientkind should do next.

Tesla pitied her.

She pitied all of them.

Because of her father's position as The Guvna', she had been exposed, at one time or another, to nearly all of the figures in Kingston's power structure, and many of the more prominent Knowers besides. And of course, her education had exposed her to all the great minds teaching at the Academy of Knowledge.

They were incredibly unimpressive, a flock of lemmings whose greatest accomplishment was setting their Bubble Suits to project fancy clothing, which created the illusion of competence.

There were a few exceptions - sentient beings such as Knower Ludquist - but from Tesla's observations, these exceptions were often considered weirdos by their peers, shunted to the sides of Kingston's society until they were needed.

Tesla did not believe that it had always been this way; she had a fierce sense that life was not supposed to be like this, a sense of injustice at the very idea that anyone else should tell her what to do, what to think, or how to act.

And she understood that her father would not be The Guvna' forever.

That Kingston would not always be safe for her.

But she also believed there had to be more sentient beings somewhere, more sentient beings who believed in the world that she did. Sentient beings who believed in an internal locus of control, in their ability to steer their own ship, in the possibility of making incredible things happen.

They were not the ones guverning The Bubble Society; that much was for certain. Whatever Knower Hunt and the others might tell themselves, the Kingston Guvernment and Dynamic Solutions did not have all the answers. Nobody did, and sooner or later, that reality would come to light. In fact, if the rate of Laureate admissions continued to increase at its current pace, and the affected age groups continued to creep downwards, with more and more individuals sent to The Villa in their twenties, and even their teens, the clever facade that the two institutions had patched together would soon come undone.

It was all inevitable; Tesla had come to that conclusion a long time ago. It was the only possible outcome of bowing to leaders who cared, not about making Kingston a better place, but about creating the illusion that they were making Kingston a better place so they could advance their personal interests.

Her realization regarding the possibilities for the Elevation Upgrade Prize had been a line in the sand for Tesla, but since she had stepped across it, she had realized that if it had not been that, something else would have happened. She had come to accept that her life had always been hurtling towards this moment.

There was no sense in worrying; it was time to meet what would come.

Barring any unexpected developments, today would be her last day at the Academy of Knowledge. This would be the last time she had to listen to Knower Hunt drone on; in two days' time, at the end of the weekend, she would exit stage left.

Whatever awaited her in the beyond, Tesla was ready to make the jump.

Book 3

BOOK 3, CHAPTER 1

"Less than an hour to go," Gavin thought.

The last wisps of the sunset had faded from indigo to darkness an hour ago, but that was not a problem; with Shylan and Aphrodite both nearly full, the moonlight was more than enough to light his way.

Gavin was making good time; he had passed Turquoise Lake early that morning, and at his current pace, he expected to reach Kingfisher Reservoir before midnight. He thought he might catch a few hours of sleep, and then, before the sun was up, he would sneak into Kingston, visit The Villa, and say his goodbyes to his parents. Getting out would be trickier - it would be daylight by then - but even if he had to wait it out for most of the day, Gavin figured he should be on his way back to Trepani by nightfall.

There was, unfortunately, a flaw in this plan, one that even Gavin had recognized, though the issue had not struck him until he was halfway down the Cadillac Mountains.

Gavin did not have a Bubble Suit. And it had occurred to him that there was at least a chance somebody might notice that, and that it might cause some consternation amongst The Bubble Society's citizunry if they did.

However, Gavin refused to let this potential pitfall bother him; in fact, he had convinced himself that there was a chance he would find a Bubble Suit before he reached Kingston, and that, once he suited back up, he would be able to enter the city unnoticed. Gavin did not much like the idea of getting back into a Bubble Suit, but he thought he could tolerate it for a few hours if it meant a chance to say goodbye to his parents; never mind the fact that there had not been a single time in his life when Gavin had seen a random Bubble Suit lying around.

However, aside from the lack of a Bubble Suit, everything else about Gavin's scheme had gone according to plan. He was thankful that Rex knew the way so well; when he had slipped out of Santino's house in the dead of night, a pouch full of the ram's preferred grass and herb mixture tucked in his pocket, Gavin's main concern had been that he would not remember how to get back to Kingston. Fortunately, his memory had served him well enough, and whenever he reached a point where he was not sure which way to go, Rex was happy to make the decision. The more times the ram picked the right path, the more confident Gavin became that the ram would get him to Kingston, that he would not live out the nightmare of getting lost and dying alone out here.

Had he possessed more sense, Gavin might have realized that he could die without getting lost; there was every chance of that happening on the trail, particularly for a lone traveler. Perhaps it was just as well that he was oblivious to his danger; whether it was because of Rex's presence, or some higher power, the predators that observed the young man traveling alone on a single ram had, so far, elected not to make a meal of them, and Gavin was far happier riding along in blissful ignorance.

He dismounted when they reached the top of the dried-up waterfall, tethered Rex to a tree, and fed him another handful of grasses and herbs.

Once Rex was settled, Gavin set about securing a second coil of rope to a different tree. Thanks to some lessons during his time in Trepani, Gavin's knots were efficient and neat, far easier to work with than the rat's nest of a harness he had tied his last time through; he rappelled down the waterfall face without the slightest fear that his anchor would come undone.

—

Tesla was getting into bed when the alarm went off.

Adrenaline surged through her, eviscerating any trace of weariness; she touched a finger to her wrist, disabling the shrill sound in her ear.

If only she could tame the beating of her heart so easily.

Tesla felt unnaturally jittery as she tapped on her temple to pull up the video of her lab on her holographic monitor.

She zoomed in on her surveillance screens.

She froze.

She knew the sentient being on the screen.

Tesla had imagined this moment thousands of times, but in her visions, it had always been a stranger, or strangers, who appeared on the horizon.

She had never imagined that Gavin Owens would be the one to trip her surveillance system.

Tesla shook herself.

Gavin's identity was immaterial at this moment.
The clock was ticking.
She had to move.

—

The going was slower without Rex, but Gavin was so high on the exhilaration of the descent, so pleased that he had not killed himself rappelling down the waterfall, that the walk down to Kingfisher Reservoir seemed to fly by.

It was incredible to think how far he had come since his disappearance; the last time Gavin had been on this path, he had been fresh out of his Bubble Suit, barely able to navigate through the world around him. Now, his legs felt strong, his steps felt springy; heck, if someone came looking for him, he thought he could even match his great-uncle's evasion tactics and scramble up a cliffside, though he did not anticipate any such problems.

Pleased to be on the home stretch, happy to know that he would be on his way back to Trepani sooner than later, Gavin started to whistle a tune. He was not much of a whistler, and he only half-remembered the notes from the first stanza of *When the Saints Go Marching In*, but nevertheless, he was giddy at how well his plan was working, and felt a need to express his exuberance. It would be good to see his parents again, good to let them know he was happy, good to say a final goodbye.

Gavin continued to whistle the tune - at least the parts he knew - until he reached Mesa Outcrop. The view from there was not right for whistling; he grew silent as he took in the bright lights of Kingston in the valley below. Realizing how far he had come, and finally seeing his destination in sight, he let out a sigh of relief; he could hardly believe how well this was all going, and he picked up his whistling with a fresh exuberance as he started down the switchbacks toward Kingfisher Reservoir.

It was when he rounded a final turn, bringing the reservoir into clearer view, that Gavin felt his first misgivings.

Kingfisher Reservoir was transformed; a chain-link fence, ten feet tall and topped with barbwire, surrounded the body of water, surveillance cameras on top of each fence post.

Gavin almost stopped to think, but then he remembered that he was in a hurry, so he skipped over that process and concluded that none of this was a problem; he was going to The Villa, not Kingfisher Reservoir. It was a shame that his friends could not even sneak up here to enjoy the area, but it was not as if Gavin planned to spend any more time here.

His momentary dismay discarded, Gavin started walking toward the reservoir, picking up his whistling again, thinking that he could simply walk along the edge of the fence to get to Riverside Parkway on the other side.

At that moment, a hand clamped over his mouth, and an arm caught him across the chest; before he could mount a defense, Gavin felt himself being pulled into the trees.

—

"Shut up. Right now."

Even in his shock, Gavin recognized the voice. He glanced back, and confirmed his suspicion; it was Tesla.

And she looked furious.

"*What* are you doing?" She hissed. "Could you make more noise? Don't you realize…"

She did not finish.

Gavin did not have to ask why.

The whir of helicopters was rising in the distance.

—

"C'mon, we have to move. Back the other way."

Gavin could barely process what was happening, but Tesla had taken hold of his wrist and was dragging him up the trail. He followed her for a few steps, then shook his head and stopped.

"No. You don't understand. I came to say goodbye to my parents."

For the briefest of moments, Tesla froze, her face a mask of incredulity. Then she spoke, not bothering to conceal her disbelief.

"Are you *insane*? You think they would let you go waltzing through Kingston with no Bubble Suit on?"

Now Gavin was the indignant one; Tesla was speaking to him as if he were some sort of idiot.

"No, I figured I'd get in and out while it was dark out, so nobody would notice. And I know the staff at The Villa well; I didn't think they'd say anything about it."

Tesla snorted.

"Well, somebody noticed. And if you don't believe me, those helicopters should be enough to convince you. The only thing that saved you from being taken unawares is that I knew you were coming before they did. But that's not going to matter unless we move. NOW."

With that, she turned on her heel and started back up the trail, moving with a purpose that suggested she did not care one way or the other whether Gavin followed her.

Gavin stood there, frozen, Tesla's words filtering through his mind; then, with a jolt of panic, it all slammed home. Gavin realized that Tesla was right in every regard. He started after her, no longer whistling, his heart pounding in his chest; he wanted to run, but Tesla would not be able to match him. Should he abandon her? How could he, after she had saved him?

But that question raised another: why had she saved him? How had she known he was coming before the City Watch did? And what was she doing up here now?

Fear kept his feet moving as he distilled all of these questions into a single inquiry.

"Why are you doing this?"

In answer, Tesla reached into the side pocket of the backpack she wore. Gavin had not noticed the backpack until then, but now he realized how strange it was for her to have such an item; nobody carried possessions in Kingston, so there was no need for any sort of bag.

Tesla's hand emerged holding a thin, metal Spike, similar to the tool that Gavin's great-uncle Clarence had shown him on the banks of Kingfisher Reservoir.

"I'm coming with you. We're escaping together. And then you're going to show me the way to wherever you've been."

—

Tesla noticed Gavin's surprise at her words, but she did not acknowledge it. After all, they had to keep moving; she had a head start on the City Watch, but that was evaporating faster than she liked to think.

She reached down to her wrist panel and tapped in a series of commands, pushing her Bubble Suit into overdrive and accelerating her pace to a jog. She saw Gavin blink in astonishment when this happened, but he did not ask questions; he simply increased his own pace to match Tesla's. They continued in silence for nearly ten minutes, Tesla pushing her Bubble Suit to its max capacity as they climbed the switchbacks toward Mesa Outcrop. All the while, the drone of the helicopters grew louder, but neither Tesla nor Gavin made any mention of this. There was no time to look back; they could only take the next step, and the one after that.

They ran past Mesa Outcrop without bothering to look back at Kingston, their eyes on the tree-lined path ahead of them, Gavin in the lead, showing Tesla the way. When they reached the trees and entered the passage beneath the dense canopy, Tesla felt the tension in her guts loosen slightly. She was starting to believe that they would make it.

Then the unthinkable happened.

Tesla's Bubble Suit froze.

It felt as if she had slammed into a wall; the Spike clattered to the ground, her hands no longer possessing the dexterity to hold anything. Tesla was frozen mid-stride, one foot off the ground, unable to move in any direction.

In that instant, there was only one thought in her mind.

They know.

—

Gavin had only taken two strides when he realized Tesla was no longer with him.

When he turned back and found her frozen in place, his guts clenched.

"What the…"

But Gavin did not have time to finish his thought. His brain felt frozen; he had no idea what to do. Fortunately, Tesla had the presence of mind not to panic.

"The Spike," she hissed. "It's there, by that rock on the trail. You have to get it and cut me free."

Gavin obeyed without question. He snatched up the Spike and went to work; he wished he had been conscious when his great-uncle had cut him free of his own suit, so he would know how Clarence had done it, but by cutting long, vertical lines down the body of Tesla's Bubble Suit, he was able to free one arm, then the other.

He paused when he reached her back, a question occurring to him.

"What about clothes? Shoes? You can't go naked where we're going."

"There are clothes in my bag. Just keep cutting, and don't stare. If you do, I'll sock you in the jaw when we get out of all this."

Gavin kept Tesla's warning in mind as he cut lines down the back of her skull, along her back, over her buttocks, and down her legs, though in his panic, he barely had the bandwidth to focus on making the cuts, warning or no warning.

The cuts across her back left Tesla free from the waist up; once she had use of her arms, she started rummaging through her bag, pulling out items of clothing and dressing as quickly as she could.

Then her legs were free, and underwear and pants went on, followed by a pair of tennis shoes.

The whole process had taken less than two minutes.

But those two minutes had been enough for the spotlights from the helicopters to come into their field of vision, and for the flashlights of those pursuing them on foot to become visible on the switchbacks below. They could not hear their pursuit over the sound of the helicopters - not yet - but that would change soon unless they did something.

This time, it was Gavin who took charge.

"Hop on my back. We need to go fast, put some space between us and them, and if you're anything like I was, your body isn't going to be ready to run at the moment. But it's all right; I've been training for this."

—

Pleased as he was to test his recently acquired strength and not find it wanting, Gavin was relieved to round the corner that brought them into sight of the dried-up waterfall; his legs burned with the effort it took to run with Tesla riding piggyback style. It had been worth it, though; they had made good time, and their pursuit had not caught up.

Gavin stopped when he reached the rope. He allowed Tesla to dismount, then closed his eyes, taking a few deep breaths to steady himself. When he opened his eyes, it was to find Tesla looking at the rope, and the dried-up waterfall, with a searching gaze. He could not have known this, but Tesla was wishing that her Bubble Suit would have kept working for a few more minutes; she had been here before, back when she had rigged up her surveillance, and her grippy fingers and toes feature had made the climb easy on that occasion.

That was no such help available now.

"How do we get up?"

Her question came in an urgent, slightly panicked tone.

Gavin shook his head, hating what he had to do. He needed to climb up first and pull Tesla up behind him, but how could he leave her down here?

Fortunately, she reached the same conclusion, and unlike Gavin, she did not hesitate.

"If you have to go first, go. I'll be fine, just pull me up after. Just go - and go fast."

Gavin nodded; with a certain reluctance, he started up the rope.

—

Gavin's hand was on the top of the waterfall when a shout boomed out from below.

"You there! Stop where you are, and come back down the rope. We are armed; if you do not comply, you will be executed."

Gavin glanced over his shoulder, and with a swoon of dread, saw what was happening below.

There were seven of them, standing well away from Tesla, guns raised. From the way they were cringing away from her, Gavin knew that their pursuers had not failed to notice that Tesla was not wearing a Bubble Suit; it was as if the officers from the City Watch expected her to topple over and start spewing some noxious gas at any moment.

Gavin thought he could probably get over the ledge safely, but then what? Tesla would be exposed to fire if he tried to haul her up, and he could not count on them missing from such close range.

In his mind, there was no decision.

He started to descend.

—

The night seemed to have been nothing but unpleasant surprises, but this was the worst; Tesla's heart caught in her throat the moment Gavin kicked away from the wall and started to rappel back down.

She wanted to scream at him.

But that would have given up the game.

Instead, she stared in disbelief as Gavin returned to the ground.

Their pursuers might have each gotten a shot off at him if he had scrabbled over the ledge, but Tesla knew that none of these seven had ever fired a weapon in a live combat situation before. The odds of one of the officers actually hitting Gavin would have been next to nothing; moreover, she had given herself at least a fifty-fifty chance of surviving her own climb up the wall. Her first reaction, when she had seen their pursuers appear in the clearing, had been to think of evasive maneuvers she could use, ways that she could swerve up the rock face once Gavin started pulling her up the wall.

Instead, this idiot - Tesla could not find another word for him at the moment - was coming back DOWN the wall, dropping his own survival odds from ninety-nine percent to zero, and throwing away whatever chance Tesla had in the bargain.

She forced her mind to slow down. Her eyes darted around, searching for an escape, but it was pointless; even if they made it to the trees, she knew they would not get far. There would be more members of the City Watch arriving soon; these seven would have relayed their location as soon as they had visual confirmation.

It was unbelievable. After all her years of caution, of meticulous planning… it had all been undone by Gavin's decision to waltz down into Kingston.

She would not let them take her alive; she had prepared for that. She would not be subjected to the same confinements as Gavin had been. But even so, Tesla felt sick with guilt; she knew what her being caught might mean for her father, and what his losing the Guvna'ship could mean for her sisters.

—

Gavin's expression was downcast as he reached the ground and turned to face their captors. The reality of the situation was hitting him.

Gavin had not seen any flaws in his plan until he started to execute it - if he had, he would have stayed in Trepani - but with this outcome in hand, it was occurring to him that at least some aspects of his scheme might have been poorly considered.

He turned to look at Tesla, his apology etched in his expression.

It was as if she had slapped him full across the face.

Gavin had not known what to expect when he met Tesla's eyes - he thought he might see fear, or desperation, or even surrender - but in the instant when her gaze pierced him, Gavin got the message, loud and clear.

Tesla was not finished.

—

Unit Commander Blaire was uncertain of how to proceed.

Blaire kept his weapon trained on the pair as he tried to think, but to do that, he had to look at his targets, and that was not helping anything.

What was this? Knowledge bless it, what the hell was going on?

Blaire glanced over his shoulder to check that his six subordinates had their weapons trained on the target. They did not - their weapons hung limply by their sides - and Blaire could see, from the mixture of horror and revulsion on their faces, that they felt as sick as he did about what they were about to see.

But as the seconds stretched into minutes, Blaire started to wonder. He did not have a watch, of course, and had not set his Bubble Suit to monitor the time, but he did not need a timepiece to know it had been way more than two minutes since his unit had found the cut-up, discarded Bubble Suit on the trail.

Yet neither one of his targets was writhing on the ground, desperate for air. Neither seemed in imminent danger of anything like that.

Blaire reminded himself of the Aeronbald Volunteer Experiments, trying to ground his racing heart, to slow his frantic mind.

Any second now, he thought, sighting his weapon again.

Blaire was glad that he had sent in their location; he could hear the helicopters hovering somewhere in their vicinity, dropping more members of the City Watch on open ground. Someone else would be here soon. Someone who would Know what to do about this; it would not be more than ten minutes.

It was then, lost in the river of his thoughts, that Blaire heard a pair of thuds and a quickly strangled cry. The sounds came from behind him, from where his officers stood; he started to turn, but at that moment, he felt a weight press into the back of his head, heard a loud click in his ear.

Tonight was the first time Blaire had taken his weapon into the field, and he was not particularly familiar with firearms, but even so, he recognized that sound; the instant he heard it, he froze.

"That's right. Let the gun fall to your side. Set it on the ground and get down on your knees. Now."

—

Gavin shifted his eyes away from Tesla's blazing gaze to look back at their pursuers.

The seven Capital Guards were all looking at them, but only one had his weapon at the ready, and even he appeared reluctant to approach them. He glanced over a shoulder at his backup, then returned his focus to the scope.

Gavin blinked, not believing, when the first apparition stepped from the trees, but before he had time to decide whether it was real or not, two more figures appeared - the two largest men he had ever seen in his life - and then, a fourth, and a fifth, that he knew: Coreen and Ollie.

All of them moved without wasted movement, without sound, but even as they did, Gavin could not see what the five could hope to do against seven, particularly when the five were not armed with the type of weapons that the seven held.

Then, moving more suddenly than Gavin would have believed, the two huge men each snatched a pair of the City Watch officers by the backs of their necks, wrenching them bodily off the ground and smashing their skulls together. The four bodies fell limp to the ground when the big men released their grips, leaving the numbers even for the rest of their side.

Coreen and Ollie fell on two others at the same moment, each of them taking their target to the ground. Gavin could not follow what happened next, but within seconds, Coreen was on one man's back, her right arm wrapped around his throat, her left arm sliding behind the man's head as she tightened her legs around his waist and stretched out her body, locking in her choke as Ollie strangled his target with the man's own arm, which had somehow ended up wrapped around his throat.

As all of this happened, the first man to step from the trees, the blond man with the thick beard and hazel eyes hard as flint, made his move. He was tall - as tall as Ollie, though both men appeared small next to their massive comrades - and he closed the distance to the Capitol Guard's leader in three strides, exuding a force unlike anything Gavin had felt in his life, a presence that was even more overwhelming than Coreen's.

And suddenly, as that final thought passed through his mind, Gavin understood who the man must be.

—

Unit Commander Blaire did not move.

He stared straight ahead, trying to process his situation.

This could not be happening.

It was impossible.

He was part of the City Watch, one of the elite individuals selected to defend Kingston, the Kingston Guvernment, and Knowledge itself. The best of the best, the deadliest fighting force on the planet Shurtain.

Whoever had the gun to his head could not possibly be as capable a fighter as he, Blaire Knew. And Blaire had another advantage; as long as he kept his sights on the young couple until the last moment, his foe would not expect Blaire's counter-attack. Blaire also determined, in the brief moments he had available to him, that his foe could not be all that bright; he was trying to rescue two sentient beings who were about to expire of their own accord, the same way the heretics had died in the Aeronbald

Volunteer Experiments.

Blaire moved suddenly, pivoting to his left, trying to swing the long barrel of his rifle to face his would-be-captor. He hoped that, if his fellows were also held at gunpoint, they would follow his lead.

But a curious thing happened when Blaire turned; he found that his foe was no longer behind him.

Or at least, he was not in the spot that he had been before Blaire turned.

Then, as Blaire's momentum continued past where he had thought he would find his target, he tripped over what felt like a bony branch sticking out of the ground; as he tumbled to the ground, his weapon spilling from his hands, he realized that his foe was still behind him.

By the time understanding hit Blaire, his left arm was pinned to the ground and his right arm had been wrapped, against his will, back around his own throat. The man - for by now, Blaire knew it was a man - was pressing his head into the ground with one hand while he controlled Blaire's wrist with the other.

The man on top of him issued what sounded like a curt command, though Blaire was too disoriented to process his words. Then the man was moving himself and Blaire again, Blaire with no idea what the man might be trying to accomplish until they were lying on their sides, the man on Blaire's back, a massive arm wrapped around his throat.

Blaire tried to struggle, but there was no getting away. He felt the man's knuckles against his chin; Blaire winced, thinking the man was lining up a punch, but his foe only nudged his chin a bit. For half a second, Blaire felt relief, his only focus on the punch that had not come; then the coil around his throat tightened, blackness crept in on the edges of his vision, and everything was gone.

—

Gavin stood frozen as the blond man extricated himself from the body of the City Watch's unit commander. All of their would-be captors had been dispatched, though the pair that Coreen and Ollie had choked out were already starting to stir.

The blond man got to his feet and approached Gavin.

There was no warmth in his eyes.

No smile on his face.

The man stared at Gavin with unmistakable dislike.

"Gavin Owens?"

It was asked as a question, though the man had to have known the answer. Gavin nodded mutely.

"Up the rope. We'll have company soon."

Gavin started for the rope, but then he stopped; the man was turning to Tesla.

"You, on my back, and hang on tight. We can't waste time pulling you up."

Tesla did not hesitate; as she jumped on the man's back, Coreen, Ollie, and the two others sprang into action, using handholds to scrabble up the dried-up waterfall, just as Gavin's great-uncle Clarence had so many weeks before.

For his part, it took Gavin a second to get into motion. His delay was not long; by the time the man and Tesla were halfway up the waterfall face, Gavin was pulling himself up the rope.

But even as he climbed the waterfall, his mind remained on what he had realized in the moment that the man had turned to Tesla.

Tesla's eyes had not hardened as the man's had, did not appear nearly so old.

But they were the exact same hazel color. The exact same shape.

Tesla and Anton had the same eyes.

Book 4

BOOK 4, CHAPTER 1

"What do you mean, you don't Know how many of them there were?"

Unit Commander Blaire sat on a four-legged stool, sweating under all the attention.

He did not like being in the spotlight.

And there was, quite literally, a spotlight in the otherwise darkened room, a spotlight that illuminated Blaire and nothing else. He was certain that there was at least one other person in the room with him - hers was the voice questioning him - but beyond that, he could only guess, though he sensed there were others hidden in the shadows of the room.

It was highly disconcerting.

Blaire sighed wearily before he responded; they had already gone over this point, but it was becoming apparent that he did not Know the proper answers to satisfy his questioner.

"I mean what I said; I dunno how many of them there were. Don't think it coulda'been just one, because the rest o' ma crew got taken out too. But all I can say fer certain is that it was one man who got the drop on me."

"You are a Unit Commander in Kingston's City Watch, the finest fighting force on Shurtain. How could one man have gotten the drop on you?"

Blaire bristled at that.

"Hey, you dunno what it was like. We dinnit get no warning we were going after a couple o' freaks. And come to think o' it, I don't think the man that attacked me was wearing a Bubble Suit either."

That prompted a pause; after a long moment, his inquisitor posed her next question.

"I see. And did you, in the course of this catastrophic failure, at least manage to notice what type of air filtration device your targets were using?"

Blaire was confused.

"Air filtration device? I dinnit see any air filtration device. Just The Guvna's daughter - Tesla - and some fella' bout her age, standing out in the open air, like nuthin' natural. Gave me the creeps."

His questioner was close to him now; Blaire could make out her silhouette, a denser shade of darkness just outside his circle of light.

"No. You are mistaken in that regard. Knowledge has demonstrated, over and over again, that such a feat is impossible. They must have been using some sort of filtration device; you were simply too dull-witted to notice it."

Blaire started to object, but the woman's voice rode over him.

"You're certain you didn't see anything? Some sort of mask, or a respirator over the nose and mouth?"

"No, I dinnit, 'cause neither one of them was wearing anything like that."

"Of course they were. It's the only plausible explanation, and if the City Watch hadn't made an imbecile like you a Unit Commander, then we would have one of those devices in our possession, and could be reverse-engineering it at this very moment."

"Or maybe yer just wrong."

Blaire said the words without thinking, goaded by the woman's condescending tone. They were met with a stony silence, a silence that was broken by the click of a light switch, readily audible in the stillness of the room.

Blaire blinked furiously to adjust his eyes to the light; when the room came into focus, he wished that he could have remained in the dark.

There were more than a few others who had been hidden by the gloom; Blaire's eyes swiveled around, counting, and confirming the number.

There were thirteen of them in total.

Twelve sat in chairs, forming a semicircle around Blaire.

The thirteenth - his questioner - stood in the center of the arc.

Yet it was not the questioner who drew Blaire's attention; it was the man in the center of the semicircle, who sat stock-straight in the room's largest, most luxurious chair. As Blaire took in the man, he felt the knot in his stomach tighten; even without the throne-like seat, Blaire would have been able to tell that this man was the one in charge.

The man was the oldest sentient being in the room. Blaire could see it in his eyes, even if the rest of the man's appearance did not betray him; old he might be, but the man's thick black hair and mustache held only a hint of grey, his cocoa brown skin was well preserved, and his imposing frame had yet to give way to the forces of time. Blaire sensed that this man would have his own question, or questions, sooner or later. But that would have to wait; the woman was addressing him again.

"*I* might be wrong? Did I hear you correctly, U.C. Blaire? You think that *I*, the Viceroy of The Board at Dynamic Solutions, could be wrong about something? You think that Knowledge would permit such a thing?"

Blaire felt heat rising in his cheeks, and knew that his round face was turning as red as his hair. He swallowed.

"No, 'course not; though I neva' heard o' a Viceroy or a Board 'fore now. I only meant that..."

"What you meant is not important; you ought to think before you speak. Haven't you ever bothered to read *The Manual for Proper Behavior*?"

Blaire cringed back, certain that the woman was about to strike him; she was not an imposing figure, but the half-crazed gleam in Tarissa Cross's eyes was enough to make him nervous.

Cross hissed her next question through clenched teeth.

"I will ask you again, U.C. Blaire: What sort of device were they using?"

Blaire sat, trying to force his brain to think. Even as he did it, he resented the task; ever since The Advent, and for years before it, he had been a model citizun, following *The Manual for Proper Behavior*, working for the Guvernment, contributing to the utopian society that existed in Kingston. He had turned his life over to The Bubble Society, and in return, The Bubble Society was supposed to take care of him, to guarantee his future against losses and injuries. As part of that bargain, Blaire - and the rest of the sentient beings in Kingston - had been given to understand this meant they would no longer have to do any thinking. Kingston's leaders had certain Knowledge about the Universe, and with it, all the answers necessary to shape sentient destiny.

Strangely enough, Blaire found that he resented that part of his situation more than anything else that had happened that night.

More than encountering those freaks cavorting about in open air.

More than hearing the click of the gun and getting choked out.

More than being dragged to this room without his consent, without a question about his well-being.

No, it was the fact that he was being asked to think, the very thing that Kingston's Guvernment had promised he would never have to do again, that really stuck in Blaire's craw.

It was a viciously uncomfortable experience, the thinking.

"Well...well yes, I s'pose, based on what yer saying, that it musta been a very small device indeed. I was o'erwhelmed, couldn'ta been thinkin' straight, but even so, I don't think I coulda missed it if both o' them were wearing a gas mask, or something like that. I mean, I remember seeing their faces."

Blaire paused - he could feel the heat building in his brain as the gears whirred - but before he was forced to elaborate on his story, a different voice spoke up.

"Perhaps the filter is inserted directly into the nostrils; did you notice anything like that? A silicone insert, perhaps, that prevents the toxic air from getting in through the nasal passages?"

Blaire felt a rush of relief at the words; back in familiar territory, he responded eagerly.

"Uh, ya, that was it. Yes, I recall now, there was some sorta clear putty in their noses. Probably how the man was able to get the drop on me; I couldn't hear him breathing through the device."

The individual who had made the suggestion, a man with his Bubble Suit set to twirl up the ends of a spectacular black mustache, nodded in satisfaction. His beady black eyes on Blaire, Giuseppe Montenegro continued his musings.

"Yet what of the air that comes in through the mouth? Surely, these sentient beings must open their mouths sometime."

"Perhaps not," interjected Nessie Hunter. Her Bubble Suit had pulled her black hair back in a complicated knot today, making her piercing brown eyes all the more prominent. "Perhaps they have invented novel devices that allow them to live with their mouths shut."

Hunter paused and gazed around the room. When she saw that she had the rest of The Board's interest, she continued.

"It's easy enough to imagine; they aren't wearing Bubble Suits, so they would carry some sort of device that allows them to translate their thoughts into communication. Similarly, they must have found a way to consume nutrients and fluids without using their mouths, something similar to the system in our Bubble Suits."

Blaire felt a twinge of unease at this. He hoped nobody else in the room would overlook the flaw in this explanation, and nearly said a prayer before he remembered that only heretics worshipped anything other than Knowledge since The Advent.

Unfortunately, things did not go Blaire's way; a pale woman with platinum blond hair spoke up and dashed his hopes.

"But U.C. Blaire told us that his attacker spoke to him. How could his attacker speak, if these others do not open their mouths?"

"A voice box hooked up to a brain chip, perhaps?" Montenegro suggested, but the others appeared skeptical. The man seated next to the woman with platinum blond hair, a pale man with a bald head and watery blue eyes obscured behind tortoiseshell glasses, offered an alternative.

"I think not, Giuseppe. It is too complicated; if we start from Ms. Delverta's observation that the attacker spoke, and use the principle of Knowledge's Razor, we can surmise that a simpler solution is at play."

Reginald Klaus paused for effect.

"I think it far more likely that they have developed a throat implant, a device that neutralizes any malevolent humors as they enter the body. It is a far simpler explanation, and fits better with these nasal plugs that Unit Commander Blaire observed the Savages using."

"A throat implant?" Tarissa Cross's implied question dripped with sarcasm. "You think they could eat with a throat implant?"

Klaus bristled.

"Perhaps, if my imagination were so limited, but it is not; my thought was that the implant would hook up to a feeding tube that passes nutrient pastes and fluids into the stomach. Is that so absurd?"

"You really think these Savages could create such a thing, or put the machinery in place to produce that type of device on a mass scale? For all we know, these people wear animal skins for clothes. They lack the wit to create such a device."

Blaire was not stupid enough to voice the question this stirred in him, but apparently, he was not sufficiently adept at concealing his facial expressions; Tarissa Cross did not miss the spasm that crossed his mouth at her response.

"You have a question, U.C. Blaire?"

Wishing that one of the others would speak up, Blaire shook his head.

"Well then, what is it that you have to say? Is there something about this conversation that you find amusing?"

Blaire spluttered, trying to find the right words.

"Well, it's just…they got themselves these air filtration devices, right?"

"Yes. The ones that you saw them wearing, the silicone nostril implants."

The tension in Blaire's brain cranked up a notch.

"Yes. The ones that I saw them wearing, the silicone nostril implants."

He could not think what else to say. He wanted Cross's gaze to go somewhere else, anywhere else.

"Well?" Cross prompted.

"Well what?" Blaire replied in what he hoped was a friendly tone.

"Well what is it about this conversation that you find so amusing? You think that something funny could happen in as dignified a setting as this? You think it appropriate to smirk at the proceedings of The Board of Dynamic Solutions?"

"No."

"I should think not. This assembly consists of the best and brightest sentient beings ever produced by Knowledge. We are the pinnacle of sentient evolution, the perfected end product that our species dreamed of through countless generations of stumbling and bumbling through existence, and it is your good luck that we have dedicated ourselves to making Kingston a utopian society. There is nothing funny about anything that happens here."

Blaire stared at the floor, silent.

"I'm still waiting," Cross hissed.

He could see no way out of it.

"It's just…I'm having trouble understanding why ya think these Savages can't build a throat implant if they came up with the silicone nostril implants. As you pointed out, those certainly exist; I saw 'em ma'self."

"They must have stolen them. Or they stole the Knowledge needed to create them."

"From who?"

"U.C. Blaire, I will remind you that I am the one asking the questions here."

"Actually, Tarissa, I think that time has passed."

Cross froze, then turned to The Director, who was getting to his feet. He gave a slight nod to indicate that Cross should take her seat, then approached Blaire.

"You have nothing else to add?"

The question came in a conciliatory tone. Physically imposing as the man might be, Blaire thought that he saw a softness in the dark brown eyes, a sentient kindness that had been notably absent from the proceedings until now. Wanting to please this man, Blaire racked his brains, buying time by looking at his new questioner, taking in the old man's features in closer detail.

He had nothing.

"No, I've told ya everything. I'm awful sorry I dinnit catch 'em."

The Director nodded.

"As are we all."

Blaire heard the doors open behind him; he turned to find two burly men, their Bubble Suits set to project uniforms of all black, entering the room. Blaire knew every uniform worn by the various units of the City Watch, as well as the uniforms worn by their counterparts in the Capitol Guard, and this was none of them.

He turned back to The Director, ready to ask for an explanation.

He never got the chance.

The Director was already speaking, his eyes looking past Blaire to the new arrivals.

"The incinerator for this one. Dump the ashes in the river."

BOOK 4, CHAPTER 2

She sat on the balcony in the predawn chill, drawing warmth from her mug of steaming green tea as she took in the view, looking past The Lodge at the Hot Springs to where the moonlight reflected off Grand Lake.

It was an ideal spot; from here, Eleanor Cahn could hear her great-granddaughter breathing in her bedroom. That gave Eleanor the leisure to ponder her thoughts without letting Carly out of her awareness; after the events on the first night of Carly's stay, Eleanor had no intention of letting that happen again.

Eleanor smiled at the memory of her great-granddaughter leaping down on her from the top shelf of the closet; the shock had nearly killed her, but between Carly's peels of laughter and Eleanor's relief at finding the girl, the unannounced game of hide and seek had been a welcome reprieve from her concerns.

The girl was certainly Coreen's daughter.

Eleanor wondered at that, how Carly could be so like Coreen when Coreen was so utterly unlike her own mother. Eleanor adored her daughter-in-law, Renee, but where Renee was the type to radiate kindness as she gently pulled the front door open, Coreen and Carly had always been more inclined to come crashing through the window.

The aftermath of Gavin Owens's disappearance had been a reminder of that.

Coreen had been the first one alerted to the situation; she was scheduled to meet Gavin at a trailhead on the northwestern outskirts of Trepani, and he never showed. She gave it half an hour, assuming that he had been delayed, but when he did not appear, she had started back to the settlement. Because of the trailhead's location, and the nature of the situation, it had made sense to stop at Jerry and Darlene Brown's property, where Clarence Barnett was being detained.

It was there, as she spoke with the old man, that Coreen shifted from curious to alarmed.

She left Jerry and Darlene's property at a run; by the time she reached her cousins' home, she was in full operator mode, and when her repeated knocks were not answered, she did not hesitate to kick in the front door.

Hours later, after Coreen had taken off with the others, Paulo had bemoaned that particular detail of the afternoon's sequence of events, complaining bitterly about the fact that Coreen had not bothered to check the door, which was unlocked, before she destroyed the frame and handle.

On the whole, Santino agreed with Paulo, but he did not plan to raise the point with Coreen; he had no interest in provoking a disagreement with the woman who had shown up at the Hot Springs, eyes blazing and hackles raised. Santino had been leading a small group through a series of breathwork exercises when his cousin had suddenly appeared, and, taking no notice of the students, demanded to know where Gavin was. Santino told her that, as far as he knew, Gavin was training with her; shaking her head, Coreen told Santino to follow her, then started up the stairs toward the black iron door that opened into The Lodge.

Santino had not thought to question Coreen, nor did he find it necessary to offer an explanation to his students; he could tell that she scared them just as much as she scared him. He followed his cousin up the staircase at a run; there had been no breath to spare for questions, but Santino wondered what had put his cousin so on edge. Surely, there could be an innocent explanation for Gavin's failure to appear at a workout.

He learned more once they were on the open roof of The Lodge, where, as was her habit, Eleanor was coordinating the day's activities from her seat at a table beneath the rooftop gazebo. Without so much as a hello, Coreen had started laying out the situation for their grandmother, explaining that she had already stopped to see Clarence, where she learned that Gavin had recently visited the old man. Clarence told her that, among other questions - all of them concerning - Gavin had asked him where he could get the mixture of grass and herbs that he had used to attract the rams.

And apparently, Clarence had done better than answer the question; he had handed Gavin a pouch of the stuff.

From the moment Clarence told her that, the kicking in of Santino's door had been inevitable; Coreen had determined that Gavin had decided to go back to Kingston, and that he could have as much as twelve hours head start on her. That she was going after him went unspoken; neither Eleanor nor Santino had to ask what Coreen meant to do.

As unfavorable as the situation seemed, a silver lining appeared in the time that Coreen laid out the situation to her grandmother, some fortune that caused Coreen's arrival on The Lodge's rooftop to coincide with the appearance of a band of travelers on the western ridge of the valley.

Coreen saw them first, and stiffened; she could tell, even from a distance, who was in that group. She reacted as if it were a pre-arranged signal, crossing the rooftop to the stairwell and descending with her grandmother and cousin trailing behind her. Coreen continued her debrief as they went.

"From everything that Clarence told me, my guess is that Gavin is on his way back to Kingston. I think it might be my fault; I told Gavin things he didn't know about the Laureates sometime last week; I had no idea that his parents were at The Villa until Clarence told me this morning."

Santino's eyes widened at that.

"They are?"

Coreen glanced over her shoulder, though she did not slow her pace.

"You didn't know?"

Santino shook his head.

"No. He's never said anything about his parents, now that I come to think of it."

"You're certain you don't know when he left?"

Eleanor had asked the question; it was directed at Santino.

"No. If Bruno or Paulo had heard anything, I'm sure they would have told me. I saw both of them at breakfast this morning; we just assumed that Gavin had gone out early to meet Coreen."

They were back on the ground floor now, Eleanor moving with an ease that belied her age as she kept up with her grandchildren, which was no mean feat given the pace that Coreen had set. Once in the streets, they started moving northwest through Trepani, but their progress met a brief interruption when they turned a corner and Coreen let out a shout.

"Brock! Al!"

As Santino and Eleanor caught up to Coreen, they saw who she was addressing: a group of two dozen men ascending the steps to Orr's Pub.

Brock and Al were easy to pick out amongst the two dozen; for one, they had turned at Coreen's shout, and for another, they towered over the men around them. Caught wrong-footed by the tone of Coreen's shouts, both wore confused expressions as they took in her sudden appearance.

"Coreen?" Replied Al Nierland, a red-headed man with skin so freckled that he appeared tan. "What's up? Good to see you, we only got in late last night, bout to get a nip. Care to join?"

"No, I'm on my way out of here. We've got a situation; if the two of you are up to it, I've got to get down to Kingston. I'm going at a dead run. If you're not up for it, I get it, but I could use the he…"

"We're going," interrupted Brock Lukavsky, a square-jawed, swarthy man with piercing brown eyes and close-cropped black hair. "Lead the way."

Coreen nodded, then turned to her grandmother.

"Take them straight to the western ridge and intercept the others. I'll meet you there in five minutes tops."

And then she was gone, sprinting down the street and swerving into an alley between two houses.

"Gentlemen," Eleanor said, stepping to lead them down the street at a more measured pace.

As they went, Eleanor and Santino explained the situation to Nierland and Lukavsky, everything that they thought was going on. They had nearly reached the outskirts of Trepani before Nierland raised a question.

"You're telling me this is the same kid that Clarence cut out of the Bubble Suit? The one we're having this whole Acadian Summit about? The reason we were all called in from the Wild?"

Eleanor and Santino nodded. Nierland rolled his eyes.

"Well, this should make the Summit more interesting. And Coreen wants to run him down?"

"She hopes to catch him before he reaches Kingston, yes."

"Well, that part makes sense. But why did she tell us to keep walking? Why didn't we stay with her?"

Eleanor did not need to answer; at that moment, Nierland saw why Coreen had told them to keep walking.

A band of hunters, similar to the units that Lukavsky and Nierland led, had entered Trepani. At their head, walking between a young woman and a middle-aged man, was an individual with hazel eyes as hard as flint, a man whose thick blond beard was a shade darker than the long locks on his head, which were tied back in a top knot. As Lukavsky and Nierland raised their hands to greet Anton, the sounds of footsteps behind them caused them to turn around.

Coreen had caught back up to them, and she was not alone; her husband, Ollie, was at her side, their daughter, Carly, riding on his back, both adults carrying a pair of backpacks in addition to the one Coreen had already strapped on.

"Glad we keep these ready," said Ollie as he tossed a pack to Anton, who had already stripped off his larger backpack and passed it off to the man at his side, who immediately began removing weapons and critical tactical gear from his commander's pack, preparing to hand them back to his leader as soon as Anton had the smaller pack strapped on. Coreen tossed her extra packs to Lukavsky and Nierland, then took Carly off Ollie's back.

Coreen kissed her daughter as Ollie slung his pack on, gave Carly to her father for a quick goodbye, and took her back for one more hug before she handed her to Eleanor.

"Get back quick," was all Eleanor said.

And then they were gone, Anton in front, leading the others back over the western ridge of Trepani.

—

That had been three days ago. By Eleanor's estimate, that meant that, if all had gone well, Anton and the others would have run Gavin down by now. That assumed a great deal - that Gavin had survived, for one, and that he had not reached Kingston before his pursuit caught him, for another - but even so, she could hope.

Of course, if all had gone well, she doubted that she would find out today. Anton and the others had not taken any communication equipment with them, so Eleanor would only get an update if it came from Kingston's media broadcasts, and if it happened that way, it would mean that Gavin Owens had made contact with The Bubble Society.

Eleanor hoped against hope that would not come to pass, but she had to concede that it was a possibility. She sighed, losing herself to despair for a moment, wondering, not for the first time, what Salomon might have said about all of this, and why the Universe had seen fit to take him from this world.

As if hearing her question, the wind picked up, swirling, then howling, and then, as abruptly, ceasing entirely, leaving the world in perfect stillness as a flower drifted down towards the balcony. It was brilliantly colored, with a burst of yellow in the center that faded to orange before the pedals abruptly changed to a deep purple. Eleanor turned a palm up to catch it; as she did, color came into the eastern sky, lighting the world with a soft glow of red.

She wondered what it meant.

BOOK 4, CHAPTER 3

He sat there in disbelief, his guts clenched with emotion.

He wanted to see his wife.

He *needed* to see his wife.

But this was not the moment to entertain such thoughts.

—

Donnie Molinaro had struggled to fall asleep the previous night, so he had been half-awake when the red bulb in the right palm of his Bubble Suit lit up. He had reacted immediately, acknowledging the alarm with a tap of his control panel, turning it off before it issued a shrill whistle that would have woken Kelli. His heart in his chest, he slipped out of their four-poster bed and padded silently across to the double doors of their bedroom, which he opened and closed as he stepped into the antechamber, making certain that the doors were shut tight behind him before he turned on the lights.

Donnie looked at himself in the mirror, at the deep bags beneath his eyes, at all the other signs of exhaustion. The Bubble Suit could conceal most of it - all it would take was a few taps on his control panel - but Donnie Molinaro was not bothered by his appearance. He was tired, and he was getting older; he saw no reason to try to convince the world otherwise.

With a weary shake of his head, he started tapping commands into his wrist panel; a moment later, his t-shirt and shorts were swapped out for a three-piece suit. Shaking his head wearily, he pushed through the doors that led out of the antechamber and stepped into the hallways of The

Guvna's Mansion.

The place was quiet as The Guvna' descended from his family's living quarters on the top floor. It felt odd - The Mansion was usually full of energy, bustling with all manner of Guvernment Officials - but in the dead of night, it was silent as the tomb.

The Guvna' veered off the staircase at the second floor, turning right to walk the short distance to a glass-faced door that opened into a small, well-appointed office. The Guvna' entered the office, shut the door behind him, and pulled up his holographic monitor.

On the screen, next to the standard "phone call" icon, was a red version of the graphic with a silver lock over it. A password screen appeared when he selected the application; concentrating on each of the numbers in turn, The Guvna' used his thoughts to enter his four-digit identifier.

The application was programmed to dial one number, and one number only; the call was answered on the first ring.

"Your immediate presence is required at The Retreat. We await your arrival."

The call ended with an audible click. This was the first time that The Guvna' had used the emergency line, so he had not known what to expect; the instructions did not surprise him, but the high-pitched voice that had issued them did, even if it was a voice that he knew well. Shrugging, The Guvna' pulled up his standard phone application and made the necessary calls; by the time he exited his office and started down the stairs to The Mansion's entryway, a self-driving limousine was pulling up the front drive.

He made the journey alone. It was cold outside, but his Bubble Suit regulated his temperature, allowing him to remain comfortable as he reclined his seat and retracted the panoramic sunroof to take in the few stars that were visible through Kingston's light pollution.

It was not the first time Donnie Molinaro had wished that he could leave all of this, that he could pick up and go back to Western Acadia, back to all the nights he and Kelli had spent under the open sky, first together, and then with their son, needing nothing but freedom, content to make enough to get by so long as they could continue their adventures on the road, cruising up and down the coast.

And as long as he was wishing for things, Donnie might as well wish to fly to Shylan and Aphrodite, to visit both moons in turn, and to lose himself in the stars afterwards; it was every bit as realistic as returning to their past life.

He did not understand how it could all feel so far away.

How it could seem so long ago.

His musings ended when the limousine jumped the curb to cut a path across the turf to reach the hidden roadway in the forest. With his destination close at hand, The Guvna's mind turned from his foolish dreams to what he ought to expect when he arrived at The Retreat.

—

It had not been this.

The somber expressions on Penelope and Cornelius Castner's faces - the former of whom had been the one to answer The Guvna's call - had confirmed Donnie Molinaro's suspicions; this summons meant nothing good. When he walked into The Director's Audience Chamber, and saw what the members of The Board were wearing, his feeling of dread only increased.

The Board had adjusted their Bubble Suits to project a standard uniform: purple robes with an ornate "N" embroidered over the right side of the chest and a matching "K" on the left side, both of the letters stitched in white. The Guvna' could hardly remember the last time he had seen The Board don these particular costumes - if memory served, it had been back around the time of the Aeronbald Volunteer Experiments - but as absurd as they looked, The Guvna' had a hard time finding any humor in their appearances.

The situation was far too grave for that.

The Board sat in a semicircle, all of them facing the one empty chair in the center of the room. The Guvna' took it, drawing a deep breath, wondering why they had summoned him here in the dead of night.

When they first told him, he did not understand.

Then, when he understood, he did not believe.

As far as he knew - or thought he knew - Tesla was at home, asleep in her bed. It was difficult to wrap his head around this development.

"Abducted?" He repeated the word in a croaky voice.

"Unfortunately, yes. It is a violent attack on the rights of the sentient beings of Kingston. A true outrage, an affront to The Bubble Society, and we mean to treat it as such."

The Guvna' was not particularly interested in how Tarissa Cross, who had gotten to her feet as she laid out the situation, would treat anything. He was trying to understand what this meant for his daughter.

"But why wussint da City Watch dispatched? Why aren't dey out there now, workin' ta bring her in?"

Several Board Members exchanged glances at his question, but Cross took it in stride.

"Unfortunately, these Savages have taken your daughter beyond our reach. They have crossed the Elevation Limit."

The Guvna' shook his head, trying to grasp what Cross was saying.

"Whaddaya mean, dey crossed da Elevation Limit? I thought Knowledge had shown dat da Bubble Suits can't function past dat altitude."

"Guvna' Molinaro, I do not need to be reminded what Knowledge has shown. Nor do I need you to tell me what it is to be Noble."

In case The Guvna' had not understood the reference, Cross took a moment to indicate the two letters embroidered on her robes.

"As it is, your daughter is not in her Bubble Suit. She…"

Cross was still talking, but her words had become garbled; blood thumping in his head, Donnie Molinaro gripped the arms of his chair very tightly, trying to hang on to something in his physical experience as blackness crept in on the edges of his vision. It felt as if he were spinning; he wanted to be sick, but even as he had the thought, he felt a pressure in his chest, the implant meant to prevent sentient beings from vomiting in their Bubble Suits moving into action.

"Guvna'? Are you listening to me?"

Tarissa Cross now stood directly in front of him; her expression was irritated rather than concerned, but it was obvious that she had realized something was wrong. The Guvna' shook his head in an effort to steady himself.

"So she's dead? Tesla? But then why'd'ya tell me she was abducted?"

This time, Cross was caught up short; she glanced back at The Director. When he nodded, she continued.

"No, we do not believe that she is dead. We do not have all the details yet, but it appears that these Savages have stolen the air filtration technology from our Bubble Suits, in violation of any number of patent laws, and adapted it to work without the Bubble Suits, and at higher altitudes."

The Guvna' could only gape.

"Of course, we already have plans in motion to respond accordingly. The Bubble Society will not tolerate such an assault on the intellectual rights of our citizuns, nor will we permit these Savages to abduct sentient beings from our midst."

There was a great deal of nodding from the rest of The Board as Cross said this.

"Guvna' Molinaro, The Board has decided that The Bubble Society is going to war against the Savages. All other aims will be abandoned; the full focus of The Bubble Society will be devoted to building the machinery of war, everything that we need to right this terrible wrong. We will turn all of our offerings to Knowledge, all of our thanks toward this request, this need, and Knowledge-willing, our wishes will be granted."

The Guvna' sat in stunned disbelief, trying to think what to say. Under ordinary circumstances, he would have liked to ask Cross about a billion questions, as he found her explanation to be exceptionally confusing.

Why did The Board believe the technology had been stolen if it was so superior to their own?

How on Shurtain had these Savages been living out in the Wild for so long?

And - most importantly - how many of them were still alive?

An image flashed through The Guvna's mind at the last question, the vision of a face, decades older than he had ever seen it.

But he had to push all that to the side for now; none of those questions would get him back to The Guvna's Mansion - and to Kelli - any quicker. At the same time, there were some things that he did need to know.

"Wut else did'ya find out 'bout who took Tesla? Besides dem being Savages, I mean."

Cross frowned.

"Unfortunately, very little."

"So wut makes ya so sure she's still alive?"

Cross paused.

"Because we do Know at least one thing about your daughter's abduction. Gavin Owens was there; as he's still alive, it stands to reason that Tesla also survived."

BOOK 4, CHAPTER 4

Never, in his wildest dreams, had Gavin imagined he would miss the company of his great-uncle Clarence.

By the time the sun started to set on the day after his unsuccessful return visit to Kingston, that had changed; by then, Gavin would have been quite pleased to have the old man at his side. True, he and Clarence had not spoken much, but that was because his great-uncle was distractible, preoccupied with the world around them.

It was different than being actively ignored.

Which was what was happening now, as Gavin trailed some yards behind the rest of the group on their way back to Trepani.

—

Initially, Gavin assumed that Anton and the others would be happy that they had saved him and Tesla.

They were not; or at least, Anton was not.

Gavin had gotten his first hint of this at the top of the waterfall, when Anton cut off Gavin's attempt at a thank you, curtly telling him to shut up until they were clear of The Elevation Limit.

Unfortunately, Gavin had not taken the hint in Anton's tone; once they were clear of the Limit, Gavin expressed his gratitude in a louder voice, directing his words at the blond man.

"Hey, did you hear me? I said thank you."

Anton turned around then, a hard look on his face. He considered Gavin for a moment, then, without saying a word, stepped toward him and hit him across the face with a backhand that sent the younger man sprawling to the ground.

"It's fine, it's fine. I'm done."

Gavin struggled to all fours, his vision shaky. He spit out a glob of blood and ran his tongue over his teeth, which felt loose along the right side of his jaw.

When he turned his head back, it was to find that one of the two huge men, the red-headed one, had a hand on Anton's shoulder; Anton shrugged it off as he fixed his eyes on Gavin.

"Thank you? That's what you've got to say to us? You ought to be *apologizing* to us."

The words hurt almost as much as the blow; Gavin could not believe the injustice of what Anton was saying.

"Apologizing for what?"

Anton's jaw hardened, the skin at the edges of the hazel eyes growing taut; the effects were subtle, but they were enough to send Gavin scooting backward in his seated position, eager to put a bit more distance between the two of them.

"For what? Where should I start? When Al and Brock intercepted me and my troop coming back into Trepani, I was looking forward to a hot meal and some sleep. Instead, I find out that some idiot had wandered off to Kingston, that Coreen and Ollie were coming with go-bags, and that they had gear for me, if I wanted to join in the chase to run you down."

Anton paused, shaking his head as he glared at Gavin.

"If we had caught you in time, you'd have owed us an explanation. But that doesn't matter now, because this expedition was a catastrophic failure; we were trying to catch you *before* you made contact with anyone in Kingston. They didn't capture you, so they can't question you about the details of Trepani, or the rest of what you've seen in your time away, but that's the only positive in this."

"Who are they?" Gavin asked.

Anton ignored his question.

"And apparently, that's just the start of it. I don't even want to ask how she got involved."

He gestured toward Tesla.

"She's The Guvna's daughter," Gavin responded, nonplussed.

Anton stared at Gavin, incredulity mixing into his hardened glare.

"I know that she's The Guvna's daughter, you fucking nitwit; what did you think I meant when I said I didn't want to ask how she got involved?"

He shook his head.

"I don't know what's going on in Kingston right now, but I can promise you that none of it is good for us. They're going to be furious about this abduction, and trust me, they will call it an abduction. They might not have cared all that much when you disappeared, but I promise you, they're going to care about her."

Gavin blinked.

"Your actions have put everything - the lives of every Acadian - in danger."

Nobody else had spoken to Gavin that night. It was more of the same the next morning; as the others trooped ahead, Gavin naturally fell to the back of the pack.

Anton stayed at the head of the group, pushing the pace with his long strides, all four of his fellow rescuers joining him at various times, in ones or twos, or as a whole group. But no matter who joined Anton at the head of the group, the tone of the conversation was urgent, serious.

Tesla, who was riding Rex, spent most of the day with Coreen at her side. The younger woman's need to re-familiarize herself with her bodily functions had necessitated the relationship, but the two appeared to have hit it off, and chatted animatedly as they made their progress up the Cadillacs.

Gavin watched all of this from the back of the column. The only break in his solitude on that first day of travel came around midday, when Coreen had slowed her pace to fall in stride next to him. She acknowledged him with a slight nod of her head, but it was a few minutes before she spoke.

"Did it not occur to you?" She had finally asked, "That it might have been a good idea to consult Santino, or one of my other cousins - or even me - before you ventured off?"

Gavin did not answer right away. He had not known what to expect, but he had never imagined he would hear Coreen speak with so much weariness in her voice.

"I didn't think you would understand."

Coreen had looked at him then, a sad little smile on her lips.

"Wanting to see your parents again? We would have understood that."

She paused.

"We also might have pointed out that it was an impossible dream. You would never have gotten to Kingston's city limits, much less all the way to The Villa. And we also could have reminded you - and I say remind because I assume you already know this - that no sentient being who has spent ten years in The Villa would be mentally present for you to say good-bye to them."

She shook her head.

"I'm sorry for that. I really am. But it doesn't change the damage that you've done. Your reasons won't stop The Bubble Society from going to war."

Gavin had been left to his own thoughts since then. As his solitude stretched from one day into two, he mulled it all over, but could not understand what Coreen meant. Why would anyone go to war over this?

Kingston was a utopia, so why should they be bothered with what went on up in the Cadillac Mountains? He and Tesla had both gone willingly; why should that affect The Bubble Society?

He woke up thinking about those questions on the third day, and thought that they might haunt him until they got back to Trepani; with only one ram, and the five who had chased him down profoundly uninterested in hustling back up the mountain, that might be a good many days.

But something changed on that third morning; when they set out, Tesla, who had spent about half of the previous day on foot, let Rex go ahead with the others and fell into step with Gavin. He looked at her, surprised.

"Something the matter?"

Tesla shook her head.

"No. I've just been thinking, over the past couple days, and I realized I should thank you. For your help the other night. I might not have agreed with everything you did, but when my Bubble Suit froze, and I was in trouble, you helped. When they caught up to us, you didn't leave me behind. I'm still not sure what to think about that - you should have kept going - but I appreciate that you didn't want to leave me."

Gavin was not sure what to say to this, so he said nothing. After a brief pause, Tesla continued.

"I do have a question, though. What made you think you could get back to The Villa? Your plan didn't make any sense. How did you think that the Guvernment would let you walk through Kingston without a Bubble Suit on?"

Gavin considered the question.

"Well, I didn't think they would *let* me. I just thought that I could get in and out without anyone noticing, and…"

He trailed off, sighed.

"I didn't know that there was anything wrong with the Laureates. I mean, I did, but I never imagined anything like what Coreen told me."

He shook his head.

"Once she told me that Laureates don't last more than a decade and a half, and I realized how little time my parents have left… I dunno. They've been gone for so long, and it was hard, not being able to connect with them, but even so, The Villa was my refuge, in a way. At least, it gave me a break from being penned up all those years that I lived on the Academic Campus."

Gavin trailed off; Tesla let the silence stretch, waiting for him to proceed. She vaguely remembered Gavin joining the Wards partway through their schooling, but he had been a stranger in all but name, one fellow student among many, and she had no idea how it had affected him.

"It was the only excuse that would get me out of solitary. And I was in solitary an awful lot once they stuck me with the Wards."

"Solitary?"

Gavin nodded.

"Probably don't hear about it, unless you're a Ward, but that's what you get if they feel like you haven't been punished sufficiently during the school hours. Which, for me, was always. Most weekends, the only reason they would let me out of the detention cells is if I was going to visit The Villa."

Tesla smiled at that.

"What was it that you were doing?"

Gavin, catching her expression, gave a sheepish shrug.

"It was never any one thing. I didn't try to be a problem… it's just, I don't like sitting around, y'know? I never liked being herded into a room and being forced to sit at a desk for hours on end, whether it was at school or work. I never figured out how to follow *The Manual for Proper Behavior,* no matter how many times I read it."

He paused.

"And now that I'm out here, and seeing how the Acadians live, I'm starting to wonder why so many people insist it has to be that way."

Gavin blinked, caught up in his epiphany; until the words had come out of his mouth, he had not recognized the thought, but now that he heard the words, he realized how true they were. He felt a smile spread across his face, and for a moment, thought Tesla might be impressed with what he had said - he certainly was - but when he turned back to her, she looked less than awed. She was grinning - sort of - but she had an eyebrow raised, and her eyes held an expression of suspended incredulity as she spoke.

"Well, it was a roundabout answer, but I guess the answer is that you didn't think much about the plan, or whether it made sense; you just locked in on the end result you wanted. I have to say, though, I don't understand how some of this wasn't obvious to you. You've been living out here for more than half a season, right?"

Gavin nodded slowly. He had no idea where Tesla was going with this; it felt like their first meeting back in Kingston Park, when she had been several moves ahead of him, leading him by the nose as they went through their exchange.

"So you know that sentient beings don't need to wear Bubble Suits, right?"

Gavin nodded again, a nervous tension in his guts. Tesla's expression suggested that there was some obvious conclusion to jump to, but he felt more confused than ever.

"Ya, I know that…" he said slowly, trailing off as he realized that was all he had to say.

"So how do you think the people who devised the Bubble Suits would react if someone came rolling through Kingston and showed they were unnecessary?"

Gavin blinked, startled by the question.

"I dunno; I've never thought about it. But… they'd be happy, right? I mean, if the people down in Kingston don't need the Bubble Suits anymore…they'd be pleased to find that out, wouldn't they?"

He turned to Tesla, satisfied with his conclusion, but even as he saw her start to shake her head, a memory came to him, a memory of what his great-uncle Clarence had told him about the Aeronbald Volunteer Experiments as they camped next to Turquoise Lake.

"Anymore? Gavin, nobody ever needed the Bubble Suits."

He blinked again, not understanding. He started to respond, but Tesla cut him off.

"And, given that a few people went to incredibly elaborate measures to convince the people of Kingston that they needed the Bubble Suits in the first place, they would be the opposite of pleased if someone pointed out - or worse, if someone showed - that sentient beings don't need Bubble Suits to survive on Shurtain."

BOOK 4, CHAPTER 5

The Guvna's day had not improved since his early-morning wake-up call.

It was nearly midday now, and he stood off-stage in Kingston Amphitheater, waiting for the signal to take his place behind the podium, where he would deliver the first Declaration of War in the history of The Bubble Society.

He wished that someone else could have handled these duties. So many people would have been excited to be in his shoes - Tarissa Cross, for one, and the rest of The Board, to make it a dozen - while he just wanted to go home and be with his wife.

He could hardly believe that Kelli would find out this way. Part of him prayed that she would have picked up on Tesla's absence, that she would somehow know that something was amiss, but deep down, he knew that was folly; it was not unusual for them to go weeks at a time without seeing Tesla outside of the dinner hour, and contrary to the announcement he was about to make, there had not been any visible signs of a disturbance at The Guvna's Mansion.

Or at least, there had not been signs of a disturbance at The Guvna's Mansion when he had left that morning; Tarissa Cross had been exceptionally busy in the past few hours, and it would not surprise him in the slightest if he were to return home to find The Mansion in shambles.

—

The Guvna' had missed the first part of Cross's planning session - The Director had kept him behind after dismissing the rest of The Board - so by the time The Guvna' arrived in the conference room, Tarissa Cross had already dispatched most of the other Board Members to their duties. The only remaining members were Gina Townsend, Nessie Hunter, and Corwin McKenzie, but while he had not heard their instructions in person, that did not mean that The Guvna' could not guess what those missing Board Members were up to; he knew the score well enough to take a good guess at that.

Giuseppe Montenegro, Astrid Johnson, and Sofia Garcia would be on their way to the Halls of Parliament, where they would formally announce the Hall's support for the Declaration of War in their roles as the Democratically elected Moderator and Speakers of the respective Halls.

Yvonne Delverta and Reginald Klaus, Cross's most trusted lieutenants, would have been dispatched to inform the Head Knower and the Chief of the Capitol Guard about the latest developments. Delverta and Klaus would have split up, but neither would not have gone alone; in all likelihood, Delverta would be accompanied by Odin Arbuckle, while Reginald Klaus would have Zuri Mwangi in tow.

The final Board Member who was not in the room - Mateo Fernandez - was a wild card.

The Guvna' did not join the Board Members at their table; instead, he took a seat near the door, angling his chair so that he could take in the faces of everyone in the room. Of course, his entrance did not go unnoticed; on his arrival, Cross stopped speaking and turned in his direction.

"Ah, Guvna', perfect timing. Our preparations are coming along beautifully; I was about to dispatch Board Member Townsend to round up your daughter's friends, but she has rightfully pointed out that they may not be enough to create a sufficiently rich backstory. We must spare no expense on that end; your daughter is a beautiful young woman in the prime of her life, a glowing example of why we work so hard to maintain our utopia. Surely she must have had a consort, some handsome, love-stricken young man who has had his future snatched away by these filthy Savages."

The Guvna' glanced at Gina Townsend, a green-eyed brunette whose Bubble Suit could not quite conceal the unhealthy pallor of her pale skin, nor the sagging jowls of the heavy face straining at her microfilament wrapper. He shrugged.

"Nobody I'm aware of. Least not anyone regula'."

Cross frowned at that; Townsend's expression was similarly dissatisfied.

"Well, what about someone who wasn't regular?"

The Guvna' thought back, wondering. The truth was that Tesla spent the bulk of her time alone - in fact, there were times when he worried about her near-constant isolation - but he knew that Cross and Townsend would not want to hear that.

Then, as he struggled to decide what to say, a memory came to mind.

"There was a Derek. Tesla mentioned 'im at da last Advent."

Cross nodded, a satisfied smile spreading across her face.

"Terrific. Derek who?"

"Oh, dunno 'bout dat. She dinnit mention a las' name."

Cross's smile vanished.

"Not much of a parent, are you, Guvna'?"

Donnie Molinaro did not dignify that with a spoken response; his expression did not change, but his eyes went cold as he met Tarissa Cross's gaze with a deadpan stare. It was one of the few times Donnie could recall taking anything that anyone had said to him in his role as Guvna' without a heaping of salt; protector of his family or not, he had to draw a line in the sand somewhere, and a shot like this from the childless Cross was a step too far with what he and Kelli had endured too much to support Andrea over the past decades. He maintained his gaze until Cross looked away, picking up the discussion to pass off her discomfort.

"Yes, well, I don't suppose it matters. We'll round up all the Dereks in Kingston in a six-year range, everyone between three years younger and three years older than your daughter."

Cross paused; from the change in her expression, The Guvna' guessed that some problem had struck her.

"Is he handsome, this Derek?"

The Guvna' blinked.

"Hansum? Heck, I dunno, I never seen 'im. Don't know nuthin 'bout 'im 'cept dat Tesla mentioned his name once. And when I say once, I mean *once*."

Cross nodded.

"Hmm…well, I suppose if he isn't, we could pick a different Derek who is. That's very important, that our forlorn lover be handsome; nobody is going to care if an ugly person had his partner abducted. In fact, to be safe, we'll round up all the Darrens, Damiens, Dantes, Devins, Deacons, and Deons in Kingston as well. That should give us a large enough pool to find a suitable candidate."

The Guvna' thought she might be joking, but Townsend, McKenzie, and Hunter were all nodding in agreement; Townsend half-rose from her seat as she asked, "Shall I put things in motion?"

"I think so, Gina. We still have more than six hours until curtain call; if you can have the candidate pool ready when I arrive at Kingston Amphitheater in two hours, we should have more than enough time to make our selection."

Townsend nodded and left the room. Tarissa Cross leaned back in her chair, sighed, and allowed herself a half-smile as she exchanged a glance with Corwin McKenzie. The man's white hair and mustache looked as if they had been trimmed with a slide rule, a sharp contrast against skin so tan it looked like leather, a relic of the early decades of McKenzie's life, which he had spent in the Badlands Desert of Southwestern Acadia.

"It's an exhausting business, running a utopia, but we do it for the people, no?"

McKenzie responded to Cross's words with a sanctimonious nod.

"And they are grateful for your sacrifice, Tarissa. If your role were more public, more widely understood, you would not be able to get anywhere in Kingston; the citizuns of The Bubble Society would be throwing themselves down at your feet, overwhelmed by gratitude. That you are humble enough to operate in the background, and leave so much of the public praise to the Guvernment and the Halls of Parliament, speaks volumes about your character."

Hunter nodded in agreement, her piercing brown eyes filled with a fervent gleam. Cross smiled. Then she turned back to The Guvna'.

"Now, Guvna'. We need to talk about your speech."

—

They had talked about the speech. Or rather, Tarissa Cross had provided The Guvna with a summary of what she had written into his speech.

Now it was time; at the signal, The Guvna' strode across the stage and took his place behind the podium. But as he stepped to the microphone, his mind was not on the speech Tarissa Cross had written, which he had projected onto his holographic monitor in picture-in-picture mode; it was on his wife, and how badly he wished he could have spoken to her before he was ushered into Kingston Amphitheater.

Unfortunately, Tarissa Cross had been adamant; anyone who did not absolutely have to be in on the planning would not hear a word of the news until the Declaration of War. The more people who were in on it, the greater the chance of a leak, and Tarissa Cross would not allow anything to take away from the shock and awe of this moment; it was *her* moment, after all. She had scripted every bit of this Declaration of War, and she would not have it ruined so that Kelli Molinaro could find out that her daughter had been abducted a few hours earlier; she could get the news with the rest of Kingston.

What difference would it make?

The Guvna' disagreed, but that was nothing new; it was not the first time that he had shouldered a distasteful task to protect his family. He had learned long ago that a man must accept certain indignities, if he and his family were to survive in Kingston.

The Guvna' cleared his throat, preparing to begin the speech, but as he looked at the words projected on his holographic monitor, he seemed to see Tesla's face floating in front of him. Tesla's, and another's, the second from so long ago.

It felt like The Advent all over again. And once again, here he was, about to give a speech.

It made him feel inexpressibly old.

The audience was waiting. The Guvna' shifted his thoughts to his second child, remembered why he had to do what he had to do. The visions disappeared; focus back, The Guvna' cleared his throat, and began his speech.

"Ma' fella' citizuns, I come before y'all today with da most t'urrible news."

The script indicated that he should pause for effect; The Guvna' acted accordingly, letting a silent count to three pass through his mind before he continued.

"Last night, for da first time in our history, Da Bubble Society came unda' attack. Da Guvna's Mansion was ransacked by a band o' Savages, and it looks like dis is only da beginning."

As The Guvna' made his statement, the many video boards strewn throughout Kingston Amphitheater came to life, displaying vague silhouettes depicting their enemy: the Savages. The silhouettes had a sentient being's shape, but there were notable differences; for instance, none of the sentient beings in Kingston had slanted red eyes, nor did any of them have blood dripping from mouths full of sharp, pointed teeth.

"Da Savages are too cowardly ta fight us face-to-face like civilized sentient beings, so instead, dey came in da dead o' night, and stole da best o' our young people right from our midst. Dey abducted ma' youngest daughter; dey took Tesla."

There had been a growing murmur in the crowd as The Guvna' shared this news, but his final words stopped that in its tracks; a stunned silence gripped the crowd.

"Dat's not all. From da intelligence da City Watch and da Capitol Guard have gathered, it seems dat da Savages have stolen our Knowledge ta build a variation on our air filtration devices. It's a gross violation o' patent law, a truly disgusting act dat shows da contempt dey have fer Da Bubble Society, and fer our utopia. Da Savages can't stand dat we got it so good in Kingston."

This statement drew a different reaction; the crowd remained silent, but more faces appeared confused than outraged. This was not a surprise to The Guvna' - even Board Member McKenzie had agreed that this part of the speech was too convoluted - but Tarissa Cross had been adamant. She wanted to establish the debauchery of these Savages, to lay out every sullied detail of the case in front of Kingston's full citizunry, and from Cross's perspective, the theft of Knowledge from the Guvernment, and Dynamic Solutions, was every bit as despicable a crime as the abduction of Tesla Mancini.

Unfortunately, the crowd did not seem to share Cross's view, or to even understand why The Guvna' had brought up the point, but no matter; The

Guvna' had an ad-lib prepared.

"Da whole thing is a grand injustice. Truly despicable; dey showed da contempt dey have fer Da Bubble Society by stealing Tesla, not jus' from me and ma' family, but from her friends, from her significant otha', from all of y'all. Da Savages, dey can't stand da happiness we got here in Kingston, can't stand dat we live in a utopia as dey huddle under animal skins out in Nature, scratching and clawing ta' survive."

"Dey mean ta take our utopia from us, da Savages, and to dat I say, OVER MY NON-FUNCTIONING BUBBLE SUIT!"

With the speech back on familiar ground, the crowd reacted as expected; the angry buzz that had filled the arena as The Guvna' spoke turned to a roar as he shouted the last words, the crowd venting their outrage at the despicable behavior of their enemies, these Savages. Amidst that outrage, any questions of where the Savages had come from were left to the side. After all, their origin, their backstory, their history, did not matter; all that mattered was that these Savages wanted to take their utopia from them.

The Guvna' was well aware that all of this was misguided, that he was leading the sentient beings of Kingston down a garden path, but even so, he found himself choking up at their show of support. He had not expected such a widespread, organic reaction - he was too focused on keeping all the lies in this storyline straight - but it struck The Guvna' in that moment that the people of Kingston were a good lot on the whole. Kind, and willing to step up to help others, willing to help his daughter, willing to follow whatever directions their Guvernment gave them to help make Shurtain a better world.

The Guvna' shook himself, pushing those thoughts to the side; he had a speech to complete.

"I thank ya', ma' fella' citizens. Da people o' Kingston are too kind, truly. And it pains me ta say dat we may have ta dispense with some o' dat kindness for what lies ahead, because da Savages don't deserve a lick o' it."

The crowd grew quiet at these words; every face gazed at The Guvna', their eyes full of apprehension.

"Da crimes o' da Savages have affected every one o' us in Kingston. Da theft o' our Knowledge is a crime against Da Bubble Society, a crime against Knowledge itself, a truly disgusting act. As'fer abducting my daughter; well, it'd be a problem any way you slice it, but da fact dat dey had da gall to break right into Da Guvna's Mansion, to disrespect our society's most hallowed institutions, makes dis more'n a crime against one citizun. It's a shot across da bow fer all o' us, and you can bet we heard it."

"You're bout ta hear from a great many people, sentient beings who knew Tesla personally, and who wanna speak ta da type o' person da Savages have stolen from us. But before they speak, I wanna assure everyone dat yer Guvernment will not take dis lying down."

"As I speak, our best Knowers are at work, partnering wit' da City Watch and da Capitol Guard ta track da Savages. We got every member o' da Watch and Guard deployed; we're running down every loose end, turning over every rock we can find, until we figure out where da Savages have taken Tesla."

"By da time we get da location, we will be ready ta act. As o' dis morning, the Halls of Parliament have passed a new Resolution, Resolution 4446, giving me full authority to shift Da Bubble Society into preparations fer war."

"I don't care fer any o' dis - I'd prefer ta avoid war at all costs - but we did not start dis war. Da Savages did, and we can't ignore it. Dey did it because dey hate our utopia, and more attacks are certain ta come, because da Savages will do anything they can ta bring us down."

The Guvna' paused to take a deep breath, steadying himself for what he was about to say.

"Da situation leaves us wit' only one option."

"To ensure our security, we must destroy any'n'all sentient beings living outside o' Da Bubble Society, wipe out any foothold where a neighboring society might begin to grow. So, on dis day, I am here as Da Guvna' of Da Bubble Society, with powers granted ta me through da representatives o' da citizuns in Resolution 4446, ta make a Declaration: a Declaration o' War."

"Da fighting will not begin tomorrow. It may not begin dis week, o' da next. But rest assured, all our resources will be devoted ta da effort. Da Bubble Society will not accept dis insult, and Da Bubble Society will not be defeated; Knowledge will see ta dat."

"It will mean sacrifice. It will mean hard work. But those are traits dat da citizuns o' Da Bubble Society possess in abundance; we are da sentient beings who created da Bubble Suits, afta' all, da pinnacle o' sentient evolution, da ones dat were promised ta so many generations who came before us, da chosen people who have been blessed by Knowledge."

"So on dis day, I ask fer yer trust, and fer yer renewed commitment ta our utopia. Ain't no people truer than da citizuns o' Da Bubble Society, and we will show dat in da seasons to come. We will win da war; we will destroy da Savages."

BOOK 4, CHAPTER 6

The Eastern Grand's path away from Grand Lake was gentler than the sheer drop that started its Western counterpart; where the Western Grand crashed off cliffs to a waterfall-fed pool, the Eastern rolled over a lip on Trepani's outskirts to begin its descent down the sloping hills.

"It doesn't change much, does it?"

"Oh, it does. We just don't live long enough to see it happen."

Marcus Cahn paused, and turned to face the man at his side: his brother-in-law, Harlan Brinson.

"Mountains rise and fall, even continents shift, and we men are such little things. That's how your old Acadian saying goes, isn't it?"

Marcus laughed.

"One of many. But I'd wager Alexandria has its own version."

"You'd win. Though we say it's the valleys that rise and fall, and the oceans that shift."

Marcus shook his head.

"No way to invert the last?"

Harlan smiled, revealing a set of gleaming white teeth behind his closely cropped black beard. At six-foot-two, Marcus was not a small man, but it was hard to tell next to his brother-in-law, who stood two inches taller than Marcus and was half again as wide. It was one of many ways they differed; Marcus's skin was olive, where Harlan's was the bronze common among the sentient beings born on Alexandria's western coast. The stubble on Marcus's beard was growing in black - he would shave it when they arrived in Trepani - and he only left the hair on his head a bit longer, where Harlan grew his beard thick and let his matching hair fall to his shoulders. To complete the contrast, Marcus's eyes were a pale green where Harlan's were a dark brown.

"Not at the moment, but perhaps something will occur to me later. I'm looking forward to a nap once we arrive."

Marcus raised an eyebrow.

"No apprehension about this Summit, brother?'

Harlan shrugged.

"It's in what, two days? Let Tyene worry about it, if anyone from Alexandria is going to worry about it; she speaks for our people, after all. I'm only along for the ride because I married the pretty girl from across the sea."

They glanced back to where Mykala Brinson - Marcus's youngest sister and Harlan's wife - walked at Tyene Medrana's side. Mykala's skin was a deep tan, her lively eyes a brighter shade of green than her brother's, her brown hair pulled back in a ponytail. Tyene, like Harlan, had the bronze skin and black hair of western Alexandria; both women were slender, but Tyene was much taller, and while Mykala's face held a certain playfulness, Tyene had strong, stoic features that brought to mind the statues of former heads of state, which she might very well become.

At forty-two years of age, Tyene Medrana was in her sixth year as the Elected Representative of Alysanne, the fourth-largest city in Alexandria, and by far the most populous city on the continent's western coast. She was not universally revered in Alysanne - such political leaders only existed in the imagination - but nearly all of her constituents respected her, and at the very least, they trusted that her actions would match her rhetoric when she went to speak for their interests in the Alexandrian capitol. There had been questions about this early in her tenure - at thirty-six, Tyene was one of the youngest sentient beings ever elected to her office - but the young woman had shown a fierce sense of principle from the first opportunity, and it was widely speculated that she would pull an overwhelming majority of the Western Alexandria vote were she to run for the top job in the capital city.

Almost as importantly, her people trusted her to maintain the strong relationship that had developed over the past twenty years with their sister city, Larissa, over on Acadia's northeastern coast.

Previously little more than a fishing outpost, Larissa's population had exploded in the decades since Marcus Cahn had led some eight hundred down from Trepani after the first Winter. Those eight hundred had been enough to develop a more established settlement, but it was a small number in other regards; with a long journey between Larissa and the Acadian settlements of Kirfi and Trepani, it was only natural for the people of Larissa to establish relations with the city across the sea. After all, on a clear day, it was possible to see the continents from one another across the little channel of water known as The Sister's Break, where the

Amphitrite Ocean hit its northern boundary, and transformed into the Larean Ocean.

The relationships between Larissa and Alysanne had been strong during that first decade and a half, but they had flourished with Tyene in charge; like her predecessor, Tyene Medrana was sympathetic to the circumstances that had driven the Acadians east, and more than willing to establish ties with the blossoming city. So while it was not required, it would have been a surprise, given their connection, if Marcus Cahn had not invited Tyene Medrana to attend the Acadian Summit; the other Acadian cities were well aware of Larissa's commerce with Alysanne, and the fallout from their discussions would affect the planet Shurtain well beyond the borders of Acadia.

For Tyene - and the rest of Alexandria - it had been an easy decision to accept. She had even reached out to the rest of Alexandria's leaders to gauge whether they wanted to send a more significant presence, but all were in agreement on what needed to be done, and Tyene had been trusted to carry that word. In her view - and the view of Alexandria's other leaders - it was long past time that the Acadians do something about the pestilence that had been festering down in Kingston for so many years.

"Even so, you might be apprehensive, or even concerned. Who knows what we're going to find."

Harlan shrugged.

"The Bubble Society is a hermit kingdom. I know, they stockpiled powerful weaponry during their Economic Era; so did we. If you give the go-ahead, Alexandria can have an army on the Acadian Continent in a few weeks, tops; we'll run the people of Kingston off the field."

"Easy to say when you don't have to live on the field after. Larissa might be safe enough, but I'll wager these folks up ahead don't want to see Trepani reduced to ashes."

Marcus indicated the welcoming party that had appeared at the top of the ridge. He and Harlan were just close enough to make them out; at the head of the group was Eleanor Cahn, striding toward them at the head of a dozen or so sentient beings, her great-granddaughter, Carly, in her arms.

Harlan smiled at this, but as Marcus took in the group, he saw, not who was there, but who was missing.

When that realization came, he wondered what it could mean.

"You'll excuse me," Marcus said to Harlan. Without waiting for an answer, he detached himself from his brother-in-law and strode out ahead of the column. As he went, he glanced over his shoulder, and found his wife, Renee, extricating herself from a companion to do the same; he knew from her expression that she had made the same observation as him.

Carly shrieked in delight when she recognized her grandparents; Eleanor set the squirming girl on the ground, and she sprinted to Renee. As Renee scooped Carly up, Marcus looked at Eleanor, his expression grim.

"It's good to see you, Mother. Tell me; where is Coreen?"

BOOK 4, CHAPTER 7

The Guvna' did not stick around for the rest of the show.

When he walked offstage, he found that Board Member Townsend had her back to him - she was issuing final instructions to Anna, Thea, and Shannon, who were the next act up - and that Tarissa Cross was nowhere in sight. The Guvna' did not hesitate to take advantage of his opportunity; he strode to a rear door of Kingston Amphitheater, pushed through the exit, and started to circle back across Capitol Square, on a course for The Guvna's Mansion.

Capitol Square was empty aside from a few members of the Capitol Guard, who were spaced out across the cobblestones, standing sentry in blue uniforms with high-peaked caps. None of them acknowledged The Guvna' - they were too well-trained to break protocol - but still, The Guvna' felt their eyes on him as he made his way across the courtyard.

Getting back to Kelli was the priority, but The Guvna' did not want to miss the rest of the drama, so he pulled up the Guvernment Media App on his holographic monitor and put it into picture-in-picture mode. He did not need to search for the broadcast; The Declaration of War was the only show in town.

As he made his progress, one eye on the screen, it suddenly struck The Guvna' that, outside of that brief glimpse backstage a moment ago, he had not seen Tesla's friends in years. It felt strange; he had recognized all three girls without issue, but it was now hitting him that, in his mind, Anna, Thea, and Shannon were still girls, children of ten or eleven.

And now, as he thought about seeing them backstage, dressed to the nines for their moment in the spotlight, it struck him that he had never seen pictures of the girls getting ready for dances and the like in their teenage years.

Tesla had never mentioned anything of the sort.

But he knew those events would have happened; Andrea had not participated in anything of the kind, of course, but even Rachel had gone to dances when she was in school at Kingston High.

Tesla had never brought it up.

He wished he could pretend that he wondered how he missed that.

But he did not have to wonder; he could not pretend.

He knew what had happened, where all the years had gone.

"Fuckin' a', Donnie."

He found Kelli in the home theater room, with the broadcast up on the projector screen. Donnie tapped his temple as he stepped through the doorway, shutting down his holographic monitor to take in the proceedings with his wife.

Kelli did not turn around, but he knew she felt his presence. He crossed the room and wrapped his arms around her shoulders, felt her head sink into the crook of his shoulder.

"So sorry. Got blindsided; had no idea Tesla wussint here when I left dis morning. Dey've had me in da dog n' pony show since."

He felt her nod against his chest.

"Don't worry. I knew. I knew you would have told me if you could have."

Donnie wrapped her up tighter.

"Da other girls 'round here?"

"Up in their rooms. I asked Dolores to take charge of Andrea."

Kelli choked back a sob as she said it. Donnie turned her and pulled her in, closing his eyes as he touched his chin to the crown of her head.

"What happened?"

Donnie waited, holding her for a few breaths. Then he shifted his body, gently pushing Kelli back so he could meet her eyes.

"Jus' wut I said in da Declaration. Da Savages abducted Tesla, right outta Da Mansion here."

Kelli's expression did not change, but the look in her eyes told him that she understood.

"It's an unimaginable act, truly despicable. Ain't a bit o' decency in da Savages, it seems. Make ma' skin crawl."

Donnie shook himself theatrically.

"We need ta get out, get some sunlight; I been indoors too long today. But first, there's summin' I wanna see here."

He indicated the projector, where Tesla's friends were waving to the crowd as they exited the stage. Kelli frowned.

"More of this? What for? Those girls have been going on about how upset Tesla's abduction has made them and how unjust it is that they should have to feel distressed in a utopian society. It's nonsense; let's go for a walk."

"Jus' a minute. I promise, dis next part'll be worth it."

Kelli was about to ask a follow-up question, but as she opened her mouth, a handsome young man strode onto the stage.

"Who is that?"

Donnie shook his head.

"Dinnit you catch wut I said in da opener? Bout significant others?"

Kelli turned to stare at her husband, a frown on her face.

"That's Tesla's fiancee."

"Her *what?*"

"I'll tell you soon as he's done. Like I said, this'll be summin."

—

"I don't understand."

Tarissa Cross's mouth twitched at the young man's response.

"What is there not to understand, Derek?"

They stood in an empty room in the bowels of Kingston Amphitheater. Darwin Thompkins was looking at Cross, frank bewilderment etched on his face as all of the other young men filed out of the room. It was not the best look for his handsomely carved features; Cross thought that she might have picked someone else, had he looked like this during the selection process.

"Why ya can't remember my name, for one; I've told ya, it's Darwin, not Derek. And I only know one Tesla, I'm sure not engaged to her, and I think my girlfriend would be awful sore to hear ya say that."

Cross looked at the young man as if he had belched at the ball.

"Your girlfriend?"

"Ya, my girlfriend."

Cross considered him for a moment.

"Do you enjoy attending the Academy of Knowledge, Derek?"

The young man stared at her, his expression now exasperated rather than perplexed.

"Well enough. And the name is *Darwin*."

"Not anymore. What if I told you that you could be allocated a house in the Amada District with no further study or effort; your time at the Academy of Knowledge would end, and you would move into your new role full-time."

Darwin blinked.

"That sounds good, I guess, but…"

"In that case, there are a few things you need to do. For one, you are to call this… this *girlfriend* of yours immediately, and break up with her. Tell her you can't recall why you started dating in the first place, that you've been seeing someone else on the side, and that in your mind, it's been over for years."

"What? Listen, lady, I gotta think about that. I might stay at the Academy if…"

"You won't be staying at the Academy. If you turn down this assignment, Derek, then you will be reassigned to a janitorial team in the bowels of The Villa and living quarters in the Andola District, effective immediately."

Shocked into speechlessness, Darwin could only stare at Tarissa Cross. But as he considered how his morning had started - with members of the City Watch smashing down his unlocked apartment door to wrestle him bodily from his bed - he realized what decision he had to make.

It was not that difficult; there was only one path forward.

Only one person to be.

Derek nodded.

"All right. And what comes after that?"

—

"We should never have come east. We should have stayed on the coast forever, or crossed over to Thysion."

Donnie and Kelli sat together in a rock alcove, Kelli in Donnie's lap, leaning back against his chest, her eyes closed. From her position, she could not see her husband smile, but she could feel it.

The alcove that they sat in was part of the wall of Onyx Canyon.

The path to it was nearly invisible, at least, for those who were not looking.

And very few people had a reason to go looking for out-of-the-way paths that would take them to this secluded stretch along the Grand River.

The path wound northeast through the forests of The Guvna's Park, the forest that marked the northern edge of Kingston, a forest that grew progressively wilder the deeper one ventured.

On the other side was this place, this bend in the Grand River. And at this bend, there were caves carved into the walls, the fallout of frothing waters rushing past, wearing down the rock over eons.

Some caves were impossible to reach, and others had crumbled to nothing over the years, but a few - such as the one that Donnie and Kelli currently occupied - were relatively easy to reach, at least for sentient beings who knew their way around Nature.

Donnie had found the place during his wanderings in the first year after the move to The Guvna's Mansion. It was one of the few times that he was without his staff, the one time he insisted he needed to clear his mind, to think things through without a tail of guards.

That was true enough, but there was more to it; whatever his wanderings were on the surface, Donnie's true purpose was to conduct some basic reconnaissance work that he considered essential.

It had become one of his top priorities in the years leading up to the move, back when he had been watching the workers of Kingston construct The Guvna's Mansion and The New Capitol, understanding it was his destiny to inhabit the one and work in the other for the foreseeable future. He could never have imagined that he would still be The Guvna' so many years later, but that made it all the more fortunate he had the foresight to imagine some way to slip outside of the Guvernment's plans.

To some, it might have seemed strange that The Guvna' would be working to slip the Guvernment's plans; in fact, if Kingston's Guvernment was working as well as its operators hoped, every one of Kingston's citizuns would have found it strange to learn that The Guvna' would be working to slip the Guvernment's plans, because according to *The Manual for Proper Behavior,* it was The Guvna', in collaboration with The Halls of Parliament, that set the Guvernment's policy.

Of course, in his role as The Guvna', Donnie Molinaro knew that what was written in *The Manual for Proper Behavior* was pure nonsense; the plans that Dynamic Solutions was carrying out in concert with the Kingston Guvernment had been in full swing by the time he took over as The Guvna', and he had no say whatsoever in where those plans were going. His only role was to ensure that these processes continued to run smoothly, or at least, to The Director's standards.

It would have been a bitter irony, had he been seeking the throne for its own sake, but Donnie Molinaro had never seen it that way; to him, this was a job, just like his original position as a Guvernment Clerk had been a job. He understood that he was merely there as a handsome face to repeat the line of the day and maintain the status quo, but it did not bother him; he had more pressing concerns in life than how it was that the Kingston Guvernment actually functioned.

Perhaps that was why he had been left in the role for so long.

However, while The Guvna' might not dictate Guvernment policy, Donnie Molinaro's figurehead role did mean that his presence was required at a great many meetings.

Meetings where important plans were discussed.

Meetings where the people responsible for designing Guvernment policy issued orders to the people who would carry out the instructions.

Donnie Molinaro was no genius, but nor was he a stupid man, and it did not require any sort of significant intelligence for an individual in his position to read between the lines and figure out the big picture behind the plans that The Director had laid out.

The Director - and the rest of The Board - were perfectly open about the fact that the Bubble Suits they had dreamed up would have built-in monitoring systems, and that both The Guvna's Mansion and The New Capitol would be heavily wired for surveillance. It was all about safety; the monitoring systems in the Bubble Suits would ensure the wellness of the wearer, while the cameras in The Guvna's Mansion and The New Capitol would ensure his protection, the protection of his family, and the protection of all the Guvernment Officials who would frequent the two places.

Or so they said.

Donnie Molinaro knew better.

He knew that the work on The Guvna's Mansion and The New Capitol had only begun after the completion of another structure, a much grander structure, tucked away from the prying eyes of Kingston's citizens. They had not told him this directly, but Donnie's access to the meetings of Kingston's power brokers allowed him to figure out a great deal more than The Director ever disclosed to him. So whatever he told Gavin Owens decades later, Donnie Molinaro knew damn well, even before The Advent, that the voice records recorded by the black box in each Bubble Suit would not be anonymized. Far from it; why else would they have built The Retreat, if not to establish an observation post?

By the time Donnie Molinaro was preparing to move his family into The Guvna's Mansion, and to help the Kingston Guvernment usher in the beginning of The Bubble Society, he understood that if he ever wanted to have an honest conversation with his wife, one where both audio and video of their interaction was not being actively recorded, he would need to find a secure location to do it.z

Fortunately, that part was easy; indifferent as he might be to his Guvernment duties, Donnie Molinaro was in his element getting around Nature. And he had learned enough to understand that if something blocked the transmission between the Bubble Suits and the satellite system that The Bubble Society ran on - something like the walls of a stone cave - then nothing could be recorded.

Donnie and Kelli did not come to their refuge too often - life put so many demands on their time - but they never went more than half a season without finding an hour or so to get away from it all, to be in a space where they could be open and honest with one another in a society where speaking your mind posed such grave risks.

"Maybe. Woulda made fer a good few years, but where would dat have left us at Da Advent? And what would weh'uve done if Andrea was born back when we was living on da road?"

Kelli sighed.

"You can let me dream, can't you? Let me imagine something other than…this?"

Donnie made no reply except to tighten his arms around his wife.

"Do you think he's alive?"

Donnie did not answer right away; there had not been a day since The Advent when he had not asked himself the question, but as time had passed, as Shurtain's atmosphere had become steadily more poisonous, any hope he had held out had faded to the faintest of glimmers.

This morning had changed all of that. For better and for worse.

"I think so. I always wanted ta think dat I would know it - feel it - if he had passed outta dis world. I never said it aloud, even ta you; I'd started ta think I was crazy ta believe he coulda survived all dis time."

"But now?" Kelli prompted.

"Now? Now I ain't feeling so foolish. Da Savages, as Da Board calls 'em, certainly exist, and by all appearances, dey are organized enough ta have some advanced technology. Could be a different group, but we always knew dat Anton dinnit just go off on his own. Why shouldn't da Savages be da group dat he left with? And if dey survived, why not Anton?"

He felt Kelli's head nodding in agreement.

"I still can't believe he left. I have dreams sometimes, dreams where our family is together, for a meal, or an evening. But then I wake up, and remember that he's gone... that he never even took the time to meet Tesla."

Kelli stifled a sob.

"I know," Donnie whispered, tightening his grip around her.

They sat there for a time, silent in each other's embrace.

"And now she's gone."

Donnie did not know what to say to that.

"That bit about her fiancee; absurd as it was... some part of me wishes it were true. That she was here, and happy, and engaged to be married."

A sad smile crossed Donnie Molinaro's face at that.

"It's summin' else. But I do admit, dey'd make a hansum couple, Tesla and dat young man."

Kelli snuggled up to him.

"Well, maybe she'll find someone out there. If I could get one of these air filtration devices that these Savages have, I'd be tempted to join her; having you for a husband just isn't the same in these stupid suits."

For the first time that day, a genuine smile crossed Donnie Molinaro's face. As it did, Kelli twisted around so she could meet his eyes, mischief in her own.

"Yer not kidding, lil' lady."

The sleepless night was taking its toll. Donnie closed his eyes, content to sit and breathe with Kelli for a little while.

BOOK 4, CHAPTER 8

Neville hustled down the street, stretching his strides as far as he could, wishing that his Bubble Suit would allow him to run.

The proceedings were about to begin, and he was late.

He rounded a corner to find Mo and Leonard sitting at the outdoor bar of Bailey's, a seat saved between them. Neville crossed through the crowded public square, pointed at his friends as he passed the hostess, and stepped around the waist-high fence that separated Bailey's from the rest of the plaza. As he did, he pulled up his Guvernment Messaging App on his holographic monitor, and thought out a question to drop in the group chat.

Did I miss anything?

No, you've still got a minute…

Leonard had responded. Neville had one eye on his friends, one eye on the oversized television monitors mounted behind the bar. These televisions were not strictly necessary - all of the patrons at Bailey's could have projected the broadcast on their holographic monitors - but watching on the same screen promoted a sense of camaraderie, which was why people came to Bailey's; to socialize. As Neville looked around for the bartender, he heard a soft chime, and saw that Leonard had expanded on his original message.

They're about to get started - all the elected representatives of the Halls are assembled - but the Speakers haven't entered yet. You've still got a minute.

Neville nodded. At the same moment, he caught the eye of the bartender, and she approached him. Without a chatroom established to communicate, Neville was forced to speak to order his drink, and found himself stuttering as he asked the attractive - *no, not attractive, that was a prohibited term in The Manual for Proper Behavior* - the competent young bartender, who had set her Bubble Suit to project a slinky black top and booty shorts, for a whiskey sour. The young woman pulled out a flat-bottomed vial from a cooler and set it in front of Neville, needle up. He turned red as he thanked her and glared at Mo, who was grinning in Neville's direction as the bartender scanned his control panel to credit his account.

Neville had a response for Mo ready, but the whiskey sour came first; he injected the vial and allowed the sensation to hit before he thought out his message.

Laugh all you want; Leonard and I don't work in a place where we speak to each other. All we do is exchange messages on the Guvernment App. So soooory if I'm a little awkward…

Mo continued to smile - as a laborer in Kingston's Department of Infrastructure, he spent plenty of time outdoors, working with an older generation that had not adopted the Guvernment Messaging App as readily as the young men and their peers - but before any of them could say anything else, the cavernous room on the television screens came to life.

Sessions of the Halls of Parliament were always broadcast on the Guvernment Media App, but this was the first time that Neville, Leonard, and Mo had ever watched; from the brief clips they had seen in the past, it was typically a dreary, boring affair.

Tonight promised to be different; tonight, they had moved the proceedings of the Hall to prime time and shut off all other programming so that the whole of Kingston could tune in.

There was a simple reason for this change; tonight's proceedings in the Halls of Parliament would be the first official update from the Guvernment to the citizuns of The Bubble Society since Tesla Mancini's abduction and the subsequent Declaration of War.

The broadcast shifted to an angle shot from the front of the Hall; the camera was centered on the red carpet path that the chief dignitaries would walk to the Chamber Floor. As the doors of the Hall were pulled open, the camera zoomed in; three figures stood there, waiting to make their entrance.

Giuseppe Montenegro, the Moderator of the Halls of Parliament, stood in the middle of the trio, his brilliant black mustache freshly waxed and curled. On Montenegro's right was Astrid Johnson, a blond woman with green eyes who stood nearly as tall as Montenegro; she spoke for the East Hall of Parliament. To Montenegro's left was Sofia Garcia, a black-haired woman with brown eyes who was two inches shorter than Johnson; she spoke for the West Hall of Parliament.

In the tradition of Parliament, the three dignitaries entered the chambers arm-in-arm, Moderator Montenegro in the middle, both women smiling as they used their free hand to wave to their respective delegations, who had filled the rows of benches on either side of the aisle. The attendees understood what an effort this was for the two Speakers - the East and West Halls of Parliament despised each other on principle - but the two sides of the Hall also held great respect for the traditions of Parliament, and so their leaders entered in customary fashion, with all the dignity of their office. Everything down to the arrangement of the group was tinged with meaning; the Moderator stood between the two Speakers to symbolically bridge the gap between Kingston's two political factions, and to remind all in the Hall that he was there to bring them all together, no matter how great the differences between the two sides, and to ensure that their utopia would continue in perpetuity.

There were other theatrics built into the entrance; to express their joy at the opportunity to guvern over a utopia, the trio broke into a sort of jig when they were halfway down the aisle, skipping and swaying, their arms still interlinked, deranged smiles painted across their faces. Then, a few feet from the small gate that blocked access to the Floor, they stopped, putting on solemn features as they adopted a measured pace, a reassurance to all in attendance that the Speakers and the Moderator understood the gravity of their responsibilities.

For the young men, who had never witnessed this entrance before, and who had no understanding of the intricate symbolism, it was an utterly bizarre display.

They don't always start these meetings like this, do they?

Leonard had dropped the message into the group chat.

Why would they start any of their meetings that way? Have to be touched in the head to do it once.

Neville sniggered at Mo's response as he returned his attention to the video feed; a Guvernment Official was opening the small gate to allow the two Speakers of Parliament and the Moderator onto the Floor. Speaker Garcia and Speaker Johnson took their places at their respective podiums while Moderator Montenegro strode to the platform in the front of the Hall and took his place behind the center-stage podium.

"Honored members of Parliament, it is, as always, my pleasure to welcome you to another congregation of this distinguished delegation."

By tradition, Montenegro paused here, allowing his words to receive their proper applause.

"Thank you, thank you. Now, you know why we are here today. We are here to discuss the threat the Savages pose to our society, and to… yes, Speaker Johnson, you have something to say?"

Johnson's hand had shot up midway through the Moderator's words; her blond hair swayed as she nodded in response. Montenegro ceded the floor with a curt bow of his head.

"Thank you, Moderator Montenegro, for giving me the Floor. Following days of discussions, and no shortage of committees, the members of the East Hall of Parliament have determined that the term *Savages* does not accurately describe these monsters. We are talking about animals - I will not call them sentient beings - who were low enough to come into our utopia, to steal our technology in violation of innumerable patents, and to abduct the brightest gem in our society: Tesla Mancini."

"No, Moderator Montenegro, it simply will not do. The East Hall of Parliament demands, as one, that you refer to them as *dirty Savages* forthwith; nothing else will suffice."

Montenegro nodded; his mouth was slightly open, but besides that, he did a reasonable job concealing his irritation. Astrid could have easily brought this up an hour ago, when they were running through a dress rehearsal of the proceedings, but as Montenegro had often warned The Director of late, Astrid Johnson and Sofia Garcia had become far too fond of filling their public personas in recent years.

"Very well, Speaker Johnson, that seems quite reasonable, I can certainly…"

Montenegro stopped short. Nobody had to ask why; Speaker Garcia had shot out of her seat, her own hand in the air. She did not wait for Montenegro's ok to start speaking.

"Moderator Montenegro, the West Hall of Parliament vigorously objects to this type of egregious mis-labeling. We, too, have spent the past four days discussing the matter, and unlike the East Hall of Parliament, the committees that we formed were blue-ribbon units, certain to render a superior judgement to any flim-flam committees the East Hall may have assembled."

The skin around Speaker Johnson's eyes grew taught at these words, but Speaker Garcia was not finished.

"We, in keeping with the decorum of this Hall, had intended to wait until a more appropriate moment to breach the topic, but we also object to the use of the term *Savages*. However, *dirty Savages* did not make the top five on our list of alternatives. The West Hall of Parliament has determined that we should call these animals *filthy Savages*."

"Filthy?" cackled Johnson before Montenegro could respond. "How absurd. I suppose that only the West Hall of Parliament could overlook the fact that these are sentient beings, and that no matter the circumstances, it is beneath us to use the word *filthy* to describe another sentient being."

Garcia was ready with a retort, but Moderator Montenegro beat her to it this time.

"Speaker Johnson, you said yourself, not two minutes ago, that you would not call the savages sentient beings; you called them animals."

"Yes, but that was different."

"Why?"

"Because I was the one making the point then."

Montenegro waited for Johnson to offer some further explanation, but none came. He looked between the two women, trying to prevent his left eye from twitching; he had not even made it through his opening remarks, and already he felt like a man who had just heard the *click* of a land-mine priming beneath his foot.

Yet the show had to go on. He had to lift his foot.

"Well, the terms don't strike me as mutually exclusive. In fact, they seem to be reasonably similar…"

"Are you comparing our suggestion to their suggestion? They're nothing alike!"

"Not a bit!"

Garcia and Johnson's voices boomed out over Montenegro's as they pointed fingers at each other. Montenegro raised his hands in a conciliatory gesture.

"Ladies, I'm not comparing anyone to anyone else. I merely thought that, perhaps, we might use the term *dirty filthy Savages* so that everyone…"

"Preposterous!" Shouted Johnson.

"Absurd!" Screamed Garcia.

Montenegro closed his eyes as he took a deep breath.

"All right, then, not *dirty filthy Savages.* Might I suggest we table this discussion? It would seem that you both have unanimous consent on your respective sides of the Hall, which leaves me with the deciding vote, and I shall have to give the matter some thought."

Thoughts as to how I avoid losing my mind while we put on this charade.

"Very well."

"Fine."

"All right then," said Montenegro, struggling to remember where he had been before remembering that he had barely started the speech. He decided to skip over references to the *Savages* wherever possible; he wanted to get home sometime today.

"Yes, well, as you all Know, we passed Resolution 4433 into law some time ago, establishing the inaugural Elevation Upgrade Prize. Later on, we came together to pass Resolutions 4446, 4447, and 4447A. That was on the morning after the abduction of Tesla Mancini by the Sa…er, our enemies."

"Today's order of business is to vote on Resolutions 4448, 4449, and 4450 as follow-up measures that would strengthen the legislature we put into action at our last gathering."

"As you all Know, Resolution 4447 established three more Elevation Upgrade Prizes for anyone who can achieve a two thousand foot increase over the established standard. Thanks to the efforts of Knower Ludquist, we have already pushed the Bubble Suit's elevation limit from four thousand five hundred feet to six thousand five hundred feet. Once the remaining three Elevation Upgrade Prizes are claimed, each of them expanding our limit by another two thousand feet, our Bubble Suits will be able to filter air in the peaks of the Cadillac Mountains. These achievements will make us masters, not only of our utopia here in Kingston, but of the planet Shurtain itself."

"This delegation also introduced Resolution 4447A as an addendum to Resolution 4447 with the aim of determining how our enemies gained access to the Knowledge that allowed them to engineer their mouth filters. To that end, the City Watch and the Capitol Guard are using the emergency powers we granted them to investigate by any means necessary, and we are optimistic Knowledge will soon reward them for their efforts in this inquiry. As you will all recall, we made this an addendum to Resolution 4447, because if we discover how our Knowledge was stolen, then we should be able to replicate the air filtration device that the Sa... that our enemy is using, which would eliminate the need for the Elevation Upgrade Prizes established by Resolution 4447. Unfortunately - and though we remain optimistic - neither Resolution 4447 nor addendum 4447A have achieved the desired outcome as yet, despite the timely and competent work of the sentient beings in this chamber."

"As a result, we are here today to introduce Resolutions 4448, 4449, and 4450, which we hope will expedite these processes. I received these Resolutions just before entering the Hall; I will now read them aloud. We will also make them available via your holographic screens so you can familiarize yourself with the details before we take our vote."

"Resolution 4448 is an Emergency Measure that allows the Guvernment's Department of Occupation to redistribute the workforce as they see fit. Our old model worked perfectly during peacetimes, but we are no longer in peacetimes, and it will not do to have every sentient being in Kingston continue in their present occupations indefinitely. Not when the next attack from the Savages might come at any moment."

Montenegro winced as he realized he had uttered the word Savages again - he had not thought about it in time to avoid it - but mercifully, both Speakers remained quiet.

"Resolution 4449 is an Emergency Measure to extend the work day by one hour. This hour will be taken out of each sentient being's social and sleep time in an equal split. Each individual will wake up half-an-hour earlier, arrive at work half-an-hour earlier, and depart for the evening social time half-an-hour later."

This reading drew mutters of consternation; understanding the reason for the concern, Montenegro went off script.

"While Resolution 4449 will apply to all sentient beings in Kingston, I have been assured that it is primarily for our Knowers, who we all need to work a little harder if we are to accomplish the aims of Resolution 4447 in a timely manner. As for the members of this chamber, the time will be added to the morning greeting and afternoon farewell sessions."

A sense of relief swept across the Hall at these words; Mo, Leonard, Neville, and the rest of the patrons at Bailey's had a rather different response.

They know that they're on camera, right?

They must think that we're idiots.

What are they talking about, an extra hour of work?

"And, finally, we have Resolution 4450, which grants Emergency Authorizations to the City Watch to create a new surveillance division. This division will be tasked with ensuring that all of The Bubble Society's citizuns - particularly our Knowers - are working as hard as possible toward achieving Resolution 4447."

"All of these measures fall under the purview of The Bubble Society's Coordinated Defense Plan, and as I can't imagine that there is anyone treasonous enough to vote against the defense of our utopia, I think we can vote on all three measures at once."

Montenegro exchanged brief nods with Speaker Garcia and Speaker Johnson.

"Very well. As is tradition, we put it to the East Hall of Parliament first; on Resolutions 4448, 4449, and 4450, who votes aye?"

Speaker Johnson, and every sentient being in the rows of benches on her side of the hall, raised their right hands in the affirmative.

"Excellent. And the West Hall of Parliament; on Resolutions 4448, 4449, and 4450, who votes aye?"

Speaker Garcia, and every sentient being in the rows of benches on her side of the hall, raised their right hands in the affirmative.

"Terrific. Resolutions 4448, 4449, and 4450 are all law. That is it for the business of the day, so I suppose we ought to return to this debate regarding which term we ought to apply to the Savages…"

Neville, Leonard, and Mo had stopped watching; all three had exited their group chat and turned to stare at one another in shock.

Just like that, their work days had been extended by an hour.

And given that they did not actually get paid - instead, the Guvernment allocated goods, services, and housing to every citizun in The Bubble Society, along with Guvernment Credits that could only be used on discretionary spending in the social hour, which had just been cut - it did not seem that there was any upside to this situation.

Neville broke the shocked silence; the moment was strange enough that he spoke to his friends, rather than pulling up his Guvernment Messaging App, his words coming in a shaky, uncertain voice.

"Well…I suppose this is what you do in wartimes."

Leonard nodded, but Mo only frowned.

"You don't think so?"

Mo shrugged in response to Neville's question.

"I dunno about the wartime stuff. But I don't trust these people - bunch'a doofuses - and the more they talk about this air filter technology the Savages stole from us, the more questions I have."

BOOK 4, CHAPTER 9

"You've been busy since our last meeting."

"Not so much lately. They've had me pinned up here."

Marcus Cahn smiled at Clarence Barnett's response. He did not answer immediately; instead, he took a puff from a long-stemmed pipe, blew out a smoke ring, and paused to watch it drift away.

"And yet, my mother would have me believe that you did not argue against your present arrangement."

Clarence scratched his beard as he rocked in his deck chair, his brown eyes on the horizon, taking in the Cadillac Mountains. After a moment, he shrugged.

"Well, once it was clear that freeing Gavin had caused such a ruckus, it seemed best."

"And that's what you were trying to do? Free Gavin?"

Clarence did not respond. Marcus shrugged.

"Have it your way, then. I can draw my own conclusions; I remember how much time you spent with your family back before The Advent."

Still, Clarence did not respond. Marcus shook his head.

"They've told you of the coming Acadian Summit?"

Clarence nodded. Marcus waited for some further response; when none came, he continued.

"It will mean war. Kingston has already made their own declaration."

Clarence finally turned to look at Marcus, who met the older man's brown eyes with his pale green ones. After a pause, Clarence shrugged.

"It could."

"Could? Whose forbearance are you counting on, Clarence?"

"I'm counting on time, not forbearance. Tempers are running hot now, but war is not imminent; no matter what The Bubble Society might want to do, they're still stuck down in Kingston. Short of firing missiles blind into the mountains, there's not much they can do for now. And there are those on our side who can advocate for patience. You, for one."

"One amongst a few; we will stand against many. This will not go well for us; besides determining how to respond to Kingston's Declaration of War, the Summit is still proceeding with its original purpose of figuring out what to do about your situation. And now your great-nephew will sit trial next to you."

Clarence frowned.

"That last bit, I didn't anticipate."

"And the rest?"

Once again, Clarence did not respond. This time, Marcus did not let it pass by; he set his pipe on a side table and clasped his hands as he fixed his eyes on the old man.

"When I last saw you, you'd been in Elysia with the Shamans for two or three seasons, and you came back to shore in Larissa raving about a revolution. The next thing I hear, you'd been actively meddling with sentient beings down in Kingston - how it happened to be your great-nephew is beyond me - and no more than a moon's turn after that, we get word that you had helped your great-nephew in his exceptionally conspicuous exit from The Bubble Society."

Marcus paused.

"I know that much. So why not tell me the whole of it?"

Clarence smiled.

"Because, as you yourself pointed out, you will be heard at the Acadian Summit. In any case, there's no plan; just some things I figure might happen. So it's better if we keep our thoughts separate; you play your role, and I'll play mine."

Marcus frowned.

"Your old man didn't know every thought in my head, either. We saw, from the time we made our journey together, that we would play different parts in life. Salomon was the statesman. Theodore… well, Theodore was Theodore. And I had my role."

"And I am the statesman now?"

"You're well suited to it. But that's up to you. Little about your father's vision has gone the way that he - that we - thought it would. Yet the idea lives on."

Marcus blinked.

"And it's still the same vision? My father died twenty years ago, Clarence."

The old man shrugged, then abruptly changed the subject.

"You say Coreen, Gavin, and the others made it out safe?"

Marcus frowned. He seemed to make a decision to let Clarence's evasion pass; in any case, after a long moment, he nodded.

"We haven't heard directly from them, but the announcements out of Kingston made it clear. Somehow, The Guvna's daughter - the youngest Molinaro kid - got roped into all of this."

Marcus shook his head.

"I don't understand that part anymore than I understand your great-nephew being the one who was up at Kingfisher Reservoir. But in any case, Kingston's Guvernment is furious, and they've been quite vocal about that in the media broadcasts we've intercepted; if they had captured any of us Savages, had any good news to report, they would trumpet it far and wide."

Clarence's smile widened.

"An apt title. And it was Gavin who went down and caused all this?"

Marcus nodded again.

Clarence chuckled, shaking his head.

"Well, as you've guessed it, I'll give you this one; it surprises me that the fates brought my grand-nephew into the mix. I didn't even know he was my great-nephew, not until after I returned to Trepani after the first incident, and saw the recorded broadcasts from down in Kingston. I just needed someone, and I figured someone doing a bit of cliff-jumping would fit the bill right enough. Seems to me I was right."

BOOK 4, CHAPTER 10

"GOOD MORNING KINGSTON! It's time to RISE AND SHINE with Malachi and Simone! I'm your host, Malachi Quarley, and with me is Simone Collister. How are you this morning, Simone?"

The blare of sound, forced in through his Bubble Suit's sound system, woke Derek from his brief slumber. It had been a long night at the studio, but the morning wake-up call was expected; he had been part of recording this nonsense, and as Tarissa Cross had reminded them a few dozen times throughout their work, their program would be pushed onto everyone's Guvernment Media App as a wake-up call the next morning.

But he had not realized they would crank the volume so loud.

Derek kept his eyes shut, knowing precisely what would be projected on his holographic monitor if he opened them, wishing he had a way to block out the sound as Simone Collister read her response to Quarley's opener.

"Well, I don't know about you, Malachi, but I'm ready to RISE AND SHINE, GET UP, and GET GOING on this glorious day in Kingston. Seven more days, and we will be at the 100th of Spring, on the precipice of Summer. As you might expect, today's weather is set to be simply beautiful, weather worthy of a utopia such as The Bubble Society; Knowledge-willing, the weather will be the same all week, and the first day of Summer will kick off in similar fashion."

"Knowledge be praised, Simone; what a blessing it is to have such weather. Knowledge continues to provide us with unrivaled gifts, and such gifts require a great sacrifice, which means that we need every sentient being in Kingston ready and eager to meet the coming day. We live in a utopia now, but as you all Know, we were recently reminded that we need to remain vigilant if we wish to continue living in a utopia tomorrow."

"That's right, Malachi. The abduction of Tesla Mancini was a crime against us all, and every citizun in The Bubble Society should Know that the Savages do not plan to stop there. That is why we need to fight back, and fight back now; if we allow the Savages to abduct one of our number, they will feel emboldened to abduct a second, and a third. Before you can blink, they'll have abducted the lot of us."

"Indeed, Simone, and none of us wants to imagine what that would be like. We Know these Savages are vicious creatures, indescribably violent, soulless beings who rose up from the depths of hell. We are fighting the children of darkness, a spiteful band obsessed with ruining the civilization that we have built. They hate everything about The Bubble Society - they hate our utopia, hate our Democracy, hate our happiness, hate our freedom - and they will stop at nothing to tear us down."

"Well said, Malachi. Now, we Know that all of Kingston's citizens have duties that they are eager to attend to, but before you begin your day, we want you to remember why we must be diligent in our pursuit of our goals. We want you to remember Tesla Mancini."

Derek groaned as he heard the first notes from a piano; if he opened his eyes, he would see a picture of Tesla graduating from Kingston High. Four other photos would follow, the pace of the piano picking up as flashes of Tesla's life were put on display. After that, Tesla's three closest friends, Anna, Thea, and Shannon, would come on screen for their bit.

It was the part after that he dreaded. Derek remembered the other bits of the spectacle reasonably well, having sat on the sidelines watching them film it, but it was his lines, which came last, that he remembered best; even as Anna's voice poured into his speaker system, Derek could hear his own voice, reading the script that Tarissa Cross had written for him.

Had it been up to Derek, the program, or commercial, or whatever the hell it was, would have been burned, and he would never have had to watch it. Instead he lay here, in a king-sized four-poster bed in a huge home in the Amada District, less than an hour into an uneasy sleep that had begun when he finally got back to his place at the break of dawn.

Realizing that he was not going to get back to sleep, Derek finally surrendered and opened his eyes to see one of the twins on his holographic monitor. He put the image in picture-in-picture mode and tuned out Anna's monologue as he swung himself out of bed to pad across his bedroom. Yet even with his eyes open and the broadcast in picture-in-picture mode, Derek found different images running through his mind, memories from hours before, the behind-the-scenes version of Anna's seemingly flawless monologue.

—

"CUT."

Tarissa Cross, who was occupying one of three high-perched chairs on the set's edge, was on her feet again.

"It's wrong, all wrong."

Anna flushed.

"What's wrong? I read every word of the speech you put on the teleprompter."

"Yes, but you need to read it better."

Anna blinked.

"What do you mean? Did I miss a word, or something like that?"

"No."

"Well, do you want me to get up out of this chair while I say all this? I tried to tell you, it's awkward to sit in; I feel like I'm going to slip off the front."

"No, I love the chair, Board Member Townsend and I spent hours picking it. It's a work of art, a masterpiece; don't you have the Knowledge to see that? The chair stays."

"Ok, well do you want me to add an actual story about me and Tesla? I've told you, we were friends for a long time, and it might be more authentic if I tell true stories instead of all this stuff you've made up. I mean, this story about how I wanted to go on an adventure wandering outside of Kingston, only to be saved by the Knowledge that Tesla read to me out of *The Manual for Proper Behavior*...it doesn't make sense. Anyone who ever met Tesla, or me, will be able to tell it's not true; if anything, it would have been the other way around."

"No, the script is perfect. And if you Knew anything about *The Manual for Proper Behavior*, you would have come to that conclusion yourself, because you would Know that Kingston's leaders are in direct contact with Knowledge, which allows us to perfectly shape sentient destiny. You just need to read your lines better."

Anna turned to exchange a glance with her twin, who stood offstage with Shannon. Thea shrugged, and Anna turned back to Cross.

"All right, I'll try again. And I'll do it better this time, I guess."

"Don't guess. *The Manual for Proper Behavior* does not encourage guessing; Know."

Anna started again. Derek, who was sitting in the background, observing the proceedings as he waited to record his bit, could not help but notice the gnawing discomfort taking hold in his gut.

On the morning of Kingston's Declaration of War, Derek had been too shell-shocked by the City Watch breaking down his door to think much about Tarissa Cross's selection process for his role, or anything that had been proclaimed during The Guvna's Declaration.

But those turbulent times had passed, and he now had time to consider the developments. This was hardly wasted time; before he became Derek, Darwin had been a reasonably thoughtful young man.

And as a thoughtful young man, he was starting to conclude that Tarissa Cross was some sort of idiot, but that did not stop Board Members Townsend and McKenzie, who occupied the two high-perched chairs next to Cross, from applauding every decision that the woman made. It seemed that the more preposterous Cross's ideas became, the more devoted Townsend and McKenzie were to defending them; their echo chamber could have made anyone deaf to sense.

It all struck Derek as strange. There was a lot about the situation that he did not understand - why Cross called Townsend and McKenzie Board Members, for one thing, and what Board they were a part of, for another - but he did recognize that all three seemed dangerously arrogant about the certainty of their Knowledge, and that whatever lip service Tarissa Cross paid to the Kingston Guvernment, she, and this Board that she was part of, were the ones who really ran the show.

Derek stepped into the closet-sized room that served as the bathroom, a sterile room with a small trash chute in the floor. He remembered the bathrooms of his youth, how much the young Darwin had enjoyed the feeling of hot water running over his skin, massaging his muscles on the days he woke up stiff and sore. His family had not had much - they had been some of the last holdouts in southwestern Acadia, living in the coastal town of Quincy until the bitter end, when the city was finally abandoned - but while the young Darwin had only had a thin mat to sleep on back in those days, he found himself missing that home now.

As much as the Guvernment talked about the comforts and conveniences that Knowledge had provided Kingston, it did not seem that sleeping in a four-poster-bed and never having to take a shower was doing much for Derek on the happiness front.

Nor did it make him feel much like a sentient being.

But that was life on Shurtain After Knowledge, after The Advent; you could either get on board, or depart this life for the next.

Derek cringed as he heard his own voice over his Bubble Suit's sound system; it was even worse than he had imagined. He did not want to look at himself on the screen, but he could not help himself from glancing at the picture-in-picture window. He heard himself talk, heard a voice that did not sound like his own, heard stories that anyone who had attended Kingston High or the Academy of Knowledge would recognize as pure nonsense.

Unable to look away, he listened, but even as he did, Derek's mind shifted to something else; somewhere in his imagination, or hallucinations, he could see a pair of brown eyes - Tarissa Cross's eyes - staring at him through his mirror, full of an intense fervor.

Always watching.

Never ceasing.

Omnipresent.

He thought about reporting this odd phenomenon, of seeking the medical advice of a Knower; then, as quickly as the thought had appeared, Derek burst out in laughter.

If he had hallucinations of red-eyed, sharp-toothed, blood-thirsty Savages, the Knowers would probably have been pleased that Derek had the Knowledge to take the threats to The Bubble Society so seriously.

But his hallucinations were not of the Savages.

And he did not think it would be wise to bring such hallucinations to anyone's attention, much less a Knower's.

Not unless he could find a way out of all this.

BOOK 4, CHAPTER 11

"Carly! Get down from there, right now."

Coreen turned away from the pot of the stew and crossed the kitchen, stopping in front of the tall cabinet where her daughter had perched herself. The little girl smiled, her blue eyes open wide. Instead of retreating, she crawled further along the top of the cabinet, then turned herself toward the kitchen table as she shifted to a crouched position.

"Don't you *dare*," hissed her mother.

Carly only smiled; then, with a shriek of glee, she jumped, her momentum carrying her to the far side of the kitchen table, where she tucked her shoulder and rolled through her landing, staying well out of her mother's reach.

Tesla, who was chopping vegetables at the kitchen's island, had set down the heavy knife in her hand to put her full attention on the spectacle. She could not help but smile; the first time she had seen Carly jump off the living room banister, her heart had gone into her throat, but the panic subsided when the little girl tucked and rolled, then burst into peals of raucous laughter on the floor.

Today was the same. Carly lay on the floor, laughing, until her mother started to come around the table; then she was up, darting behind a kitchen chair. Coreen took a step toward her, but Carly had anticipated this; the little girl shot past her mother, ducking a shoulder as she went and shooting back into the hall. Coreen shook her head and returned to the stew.

"I'm surprised you can't catch her," said Tesla. "I mean, what with everything else you can do."

Coreen shook her head.

"I used to be able to. It was sometime last season that she started to get some wins, and now I've got no shot. She's trained against me since she could walk; I guess it's only fair to expect she'd get me timed up. I can't imagine how my grandmother manages when she takes her."

Tesla turned back to the vegetables, but did not immediately resume her task; Carly had appeared in the yard, and Tesla could not help but smile as she watched the little girl stalking toward her father, who was giving the chickens and goats their evening feed.

Even with Carly running around, Coreen and Ollie's home, situated well up a slope on the western end of Trepani, was serene. The kitchen, which faced south, featured oversized windows that offered an incredible view of Grand Lake and the valley below. The property was about as far to the outskirts of Trepani as anyone had settled, and afforded them a good bit of space for the little farm that Ollie maintained.

Eventually, Tesla stopped watching Carly and returned to her task. Once the last of the vegetables were chopped, she set the knife down and picked up the cutting board. Coreen stepped aside as Tesla approached; once Tesla had the board in place, Coreen used a long wooden spoon to scrape the freshly chopped vegetables into the stew.

"That should do it. Another half-hour, and we'll be ready to eat."

It was their second evening back in Trepani, the end of a long day of work. The sun was starting to set, shifting the colors on the horizon; Tesla took a deep breath, enjoying how beautiful the scene was, a watercolor brought to life with a twist: a small girl climbing up the side of the chicken coop, where a cat, black as the night with glowing green eyes, was perched, observing the little girl's approach.

"Has she always been like that?"

Coreen, who was pulling a bottle of wine from a cabinet, glanced out the window at Tesla's comment; she sighed and shook her head, then turned her attention to uncorking the bottle.

"Since she could walk. Ollie says it's my fault, that if it's not purely genetic, then strapping her to my chest as an infant and taking her with me on runs and climbs did it. It's terrifying, but she's healthy, that's for sure, and that's a blessing. I do look forward to her being big enough that she can't climb up the furniture like a monkey, but that's going to be another couple years."

Coreen's expression changed, and she turned her attention back to Tesla.

"What about you? Have you always been like this?"

Tesla raised an eyebrow, but there was a smile on her face.

"Like what?"

"Like you are. You're the best trainee, or student, or whatever, that I've ever worked with."

Tesla grinned.

"What can I say, you're teaching something that I'm interested in. It's not always that way; I don't think any of the teachers at Kingston High or the Knowers at the Academy of Knowledge would agree with you. Don't get me wrong - they would never say anything bad about The Guvna's daughter, particularly not when she makes perfect marks - but my ambivalence annoyed more than a few of them."

Coreen rolled her eyes.

"I was out before The Advent, so I can't really say, but I imagine ambivalence is the best I could have mustered; I hated my time in school when I did live in Kingston. I don't know where people got the idea that young sentient beings should go sit in a box to learn about the world when the actual world is right outside. I understand that it makes sense for learning certain concepts, but spending the bulk of your waking hours as a child sitting at a desk? It's a way to brainwash and propagandize, pure and simple. Plus, you have to sit still, and sitting still for too long is horrible for the sentient body; you've been able to overcome all those years of stagnation quick enough, but you're the exception, not the rule."

Tesla grinned at the compliment. She knew it was true, but it also had not been difficult, not from her perspective; as soon as Tesla had realized how awkward she felt moving in her body, training had become her new obsession.

It had started with Tesla's complaints about her body on that first morning after the rescue at the waterfall; Coreen, who had been the natural option to guide Tesla as she acclimated to her body, had listened to Tesla describe all of the new sensations she was feeling with a small smile.

"Don't worry. Can't say I've been there myself, but plenty of defectors have. It always passes."

Tesla had frowned.

"How does it pass? What do I have to do?"

"You have to use your body. The more you use it, the faster you'll adapt."

From that moment, Tesla had zeroed the considerable weight of her focus on engaging in any and all physical activities that Coreen suggested, pushing it all to the *n*th degree.

When Coreen told her that walking for a half-mile would be a start, Tesla walked two.

When Coreen said that submerging herself in the frigid waters of Turquoise Lake would activate her system in numerous ways, Tesla completed Coreen's suggested time on her first attempt, then went back for, not only seconds, but thirds, fourths, and fifths before she finally slept.

When Coreen woke in the morning, it was to find Tesla back in the water, using the breathing exercises Coreen had taught her to extend her time in the lake.

And when Coreen said that recovery would be as essential as training, Tesla put her focus into consuming as much protein as she possibly could, and on getting to sleep before the others, skipping the campfire conversations for extra recovery time.

Her body responded; halfway through their voyage up the mountains, Tesla was ending her evenings, not exhausted, but with extra work, engaging in a series of lunges that Coreen had suggested to strengthen her legs.

And upon their return to Trepani, after Tesla had a full night's rest in a bed, the younger woman insisted that they double up on the training Coreen had planned, and return to the trails in the afternoon for Round Two.

Coreen loved it. She had upped the intensity this morning, but even that had not been enough; not only had Tesla once again demanded a second session, she was now picking Coreen's brain as they prepared the meal, asking about the properties of every ingredient that they added to expand her understanding of optimal recovery practices. Earlier, when Santino had stopped by to ask if Tesla would like to join him and his friends for dinner at Nately's Public House, Tesla had politely declined, telling Santino that she would be happy to meet them all another time, but that until her body was moving the way that she wanted, she needed to focus on her training and recovery.

"What can I say? I love moving; even when I had my Bubble Suit, I was constantly working to install upgrades, upgrades that would let me run, or lift things the way I could have without it."

Coreen shook her head; Tesla had told her a good bit about the different projects she had worked on in her Lab during their training sessions.

"I'm still amazed by all that. Given how oblivious Gavin seems about The Bubble Society, I'd have thought you'd be equally in the dark. It seems remarkable that you could have lived in The Guvna's Mansion without succumbing to the propaganda."

Tesla shrugged, but Coreen did not miss the uncomfortable frown that crossed the younger woman's face.

"There's something to that question, isn't there?"

"I suppose. It's more thinking about how close I was to falling into that trap. If I hadn't taken to that first computer the way I did, if I never got into the Guvernment's systems...I don't know what I would believe."

"I know what I've seen since - I mean, I was able to notice early on that there were far fewer people living at The Villa than their admittance numbers would suggest - but I don't think I would have been asking those types of questions if I didn't know the real story beforehand. At the same time, some of The Bubble Society's actions are incredibly transparent. At the Academy of Knowledge, we took courses in Hypothetical Pharmacology. They called it Hypothetical Pharmacology because ostensibly, the Bubble Suits have already eliminated all diseases, so they can't acknowledge any need for additional exogenous molecules, or any other upgrades at all; whenever they do, they have to concoct some sort of story to explain it away. It was enough to fool most of my peers, despite the fact that more than a few students in those classes had been taking shots of the Focus Solution since they started at Kingston Elementary. You'd sure think they would be able to put two and two together. But then again, maybe they just didn't want to see it."

Coreen nodded.

"Or they never had a reason. If a sentient being trusts that their Guvernment is the engine of all that is good - preposterous as that notion might be - then it's more likely that they will create a story to accommodate the narrative rather than a question to challenge it."

A small frown appeared on Tesla's face as she considered the thought.

"I'd never thought about it that way… but it makes sense. We don't judge the story on its own; we judge who is telling us the story, and adjust our credulity accordingly."

"Yes and no," Coreen responded. "I think, in most cases, it's more of a feedback loop. We adjust our opinions, both of individuals and of entities, based on the claims they make. If someone builds up significant credibility with you, then you might believe a lie, but once you realize it is a lie, they lose some of that credibility, and if it happens enough, they lose all of it."

"For some people," said Tesla, laughing. "But I think you also just described exactly why Gavin is the way he is: there's no feedback loop there. From what he told me, someone has always had an issue with his behavior, but rather than changing, or stopping to ask questions about the authority figures who are berating him, he just keeps going. He says that he feels bad about it, but I wonder what he even means by that; he seems to forget most of the things he feels bad about almost immediately, and then he just charges on with whatever he's going to do."

Coreen rolled her eyes.

"Well, he's got time to think about it now; I wonder how he and Clarence are getting on."

Tesla frowned at the mention of Gavin's imprisonment.

"Me too… I'm just glad that it won't be long until this Summit. Gavin might be reckless, but I don't think he deserves to be locked up. Or maybe I just don't want to see it; he might be an idiot, but he's a friendly idiot. Much friendlier than my *dear* brother."

A pregnant silence followed these words; both women had returned to the memory of their second night on the trail.

—

The group had halted for the day an hour earlier. There was a fire burning; Anton had a haunch of venison on a spit. He turned it while the others attended to other matters.

Tesla's approach had been direct.

"You're my brother, aren't you?"

Anton had not looked up from the meat.

"We have the same parents, yes," he responded, his face expressionless.

"They told me that you died. That you disappeared years ago, back at the time of The Advent, and that you must have died."

No change.

"Well? Don't you care that you're meeting me? Are you going to ask about our parents?"

Anton had turned his gaze on her then. It was those eyes that had first given rise to Tesla's suspicion - none of the others had seen fit to tell her Anton's identity - but while their hazel color was the same as her own, her brother's eyes were hard, tired, where she knew her own sparkled with excitement.

"No. As far as I'm concerned, you all died a long time ago. Same as I had died, as far as you were concerned. We might share blood, but you're a stranger to me."

That was it; Anton returned his attention to the fire. Tesla stood there for a moment, waiting to see if he would say anything else. Realizing that he would not, she had shrugged, turned on her heel, and gone to join Gavin in collecting more firewood.

—

It was the only time they had spoken, though Tesla kept a close eye on her older brother for the remaining five days of their journey, wondering if his attitude might shift.

It did not; Anton restricted his discussions to conversations with his fellow hunters and treated Gavin and Tesla like cargo.

Coreen broke the silence.

"It's not personal, you know. Anton is distant with everyone. The mothers of his children included; all three of them."

Tesla snorted.

"He sounds like an asshole; why do so many people respect him?"

Coreen sighed.

"That's a long story - one that goes back to The Advent - but the short version is that Anton led our survival efforts in the First Winter. It wasn't just him, but he was our most forceful leader, the most magnetic personality among those who had to chart a new course after my grandfather died. For that, and for his prowess as a hunter and a warrior, he is admired by most Acadians. Many of our young men - and some of our young women - aspire to be like him. They may not want to become hunters - though some do - but they do want to be strong, fierce, courageous. Anton represents all of that, and he's handsome and tall in the bargain."

"Anyways, I would know; I held that type of admiration for him once. I've known Anton my whole life - he was close with my grandfather - and I thought he was a god, or something close to it, though that changed during my time in his crew."

Coreen paused.

"Don't get it twisted; I still admire Anton in many ways. His physical prowess is real; he and Ollie are about the same size, and Ollie is younger, but my husband would tell you without hesitation that Anton is different… that Ollie would face long odds in a confrontation with Anton."

"There's value in that, but I've learned there's a lot more to life - a lot more to sentient beings - than how hard we are when we go out in Nature. Anton might be a great hunter, but he also has three daughters - one in Giota, one in Kirfi, and one in Larissa - whom he rarely sees. He fathered all three of them in the dead of winter, when the snows forced him and his unit - the only unit that hunts close to year-round - to take shelter. He might be a decent enough guy whenever he's around the girls, or their mothers, but they're lucky to see him two days out of the year; he shows no interest in being part of their lives."

She shrugged.

"He is what he is. Hard as iron, with no sense of humor whatsoever. I don't know if it was like that before my grandfather's death, but since that happened, Anton hasn't been big on anything that doesn't contribute directly to our collective survival. It's part of why he's revered - he takes nothing for himself - but it's not like it was in that first Winter. We're fine - or we were, until Clarence stirred things up - but he continues to hunt like a starving wolf."

"I still respect him, but once you spend years around a person, the idea that they are infallible goes to the wayside. Anton is remarkable in many respects, but like my grandfather used to say, he's a sentient being, so he's inclined to do the sorts of things that sentient beings tend to do."

Coreen looked out thc window; Ollie was trying to convince Carly, who was now standing on top of the chicken coop, doing her best imitation of a rooster, to jump down to him.

"I'll take Ollie myself. He might not have as much sway at the Acadian Summit, but that's all right; I couldn't dream up a more patient, loving father if I tried. He helps balance me out."

Tesla replied with a small nod, but even as she watched Ollie and Carly, her mind was on Anton; Anton, along with Gavin and his great-uncle Clarence.

“What will happen? At the Summit?

Coreen shook her head.

“I don’t know. The Bubble Society has issued a Declaration of War; I expect more than a few from our side will want to respond in kind. Anton, for one, will want blood.”

“Don’t you agree?”

Coreen pondered the question for a time.

“No, not really. As I see it, The Bubble Society is almost entirely comprised of people who have been duped into thinking a certain way. There aren’t hordes of terrible sentient beings down there; for the most part, it’s just a bunch of people doing their best to survive, sentient beings who are too consumed with the day-to-day to ask probing thoughts about existence.”

“At certain times in history, the masses have done great good, or great evil, but I don’t think that it’s because the sentient beings in these groups were particularly good, or particularly evil. They lacked critical thinking skills, they lacked personal agency, and that made them susceptible to propaganda, so they wound up following a leader who directed them to behave in a certain way. Those people make decisions in their lives, but only to a certain degree; they aren’t setting the agenda any more than your bones inform your brain what to do. They’re just along for the ride.”

“From that perspective, it’s hard to want to go to war against anyone except the people calling the shots, and the people running things are far too self-important - or cowardly, take your pick - to meet us on the battlefield. Instead, they’ll send sentient beings who, in their minds, don’t matter. They’ll send weapons of war at you, bomb you from afar, but they would never engage in a tactic that requires them to risk their own precious skins. As if their lives aren't as brief as the lives of any other sentient being, in the grand scheme of things.”

Coreen shook her head.

“I’m not afraid to fight, but war isn’t that simple. We won’t meet The Board in hand-to-hand combat; if that were the case, I’d lead the charge.”

“Instead, we would face Kingston’s machinery of war, and for all of their shortcomings, The Bubble Society still holds a stockpile of artillery from the Economic Era. And there’s every possibility that their leadership decides it’s a good idea to simply wipe out Trepani.”

Tesla looked surprised; Coreen did not miss the expression.

“Don’t you agree?”

Tesla considered the matter.

“I don’t know…if they wipe out Trepani with that type of weapon, it could destroy the flow of the Grand River. Without the river, Kingston will shrivel up and die by mid-Summer.”

Tesla shook her head.

“I don’t think much of them either, but I can’t imagine them being so short-sighted as to not realize the problem that could cause."

Coreen shrugged.

"You have more faith than me. Foreseeing that outcome would require a basic understanding of Nature, not to mention a little bit of respect for it, and I'm not sure any of them have that anymore. They're too locked in on the idea that they can control Nature, and with it, sentient destiny. It seems to be a heavy burden to bear; they can't even pick up their heads and see what's right in front of them."

BOOK 4, CHAPTER 12

His was a spacious office, with a fine view of The Guvna's Park and the Grand River beyond it, a view that was especially fine as the sun set on the first day of Summer.

In seasons past, The Guvna' had scheduled his days so that he could slip out the glass-paneled door at the back of the room, the one that opened onto the terrace of The New Capitol, and stroll through the grounds as he took his calls. It was a far more pleasant way to pass the time, especially as he had little interest in any of the topics discussed in Guvernment meetings.

That was before; now, The Guvna' was trapped in his office, forced to be there in person to receive endless updates, constant demands for progress, and worst of all, the seemingly innocuous status requests. The Guvna' had gone so far as to requisition three extra Guvernment Officials to answer his phone calls; it had simply gotten to be too much for two people to handle, but while this eased their load, it did not change the fact that a great many people were clamoring to see The Guvna' in person, that some of them were arriving at The New Capitol without an appointment, and that many of them could not be ignored.

Today's meeting was one that could not be ignored; as far as people he would like to spend time with, these folks ranked near the bottom of The Guvna's list. It was difficult to think of a worse group to spend time with than Tarissa Cross, Giuseppe Montenegro, and Zenus Mallion, yet here he was, surrounded by the Viceroy of The Board, the Moderator of the Halls of Parliament, and the Head Knower.

Nor were they alone; at least, not really. The Bubble Society had recently undergone another round of upgrades to maintain their status as a utopia, dramatically increasing the surveillance in the city for everyone's benefit; in the course of installing cameras all over Kingston, it had been no trouble at all to install a few cameras in The Guvna's office.

Not only was it no trouble, it was a priority; The Director had conveyed as much to The Guvna' when they met alone on the morning of Tesla's disappearance.

"You understand my predicament, of course," The Director had said, his tone suitably grave as he laid out the situation for The Guvna'. "We must, at all costs, avoid the appearance of impropriety. The people must believe that The Bubble Society is a Democracy, that the elected officials they place in the Halls of Parliament speak for the people, that they have some say in plotting our future. Without that illusion, there is no telling what anarchy might ensue."

"And yet, we all Know how important it is for our plans to proceed. We Guvern for the greater good, make sacrifices so that all the citizuns of Kingston can live in freedom, live in a utopia. They do not understand the price of their happiness; it is left to people like us to calculate that price, and to ensure that the price is paid, over and over. And if that means installing surveillance so that nobody steps out of line, then that's what will happen; it's simply the price of living in a free, Democratic, utopian society."

"To that end, it is imperative that I be assiduous in my duties during the seasons to come, and for that, I need all relevant information at my fingertips. It would raise eyebrows if I suddenly set myself up in your offices, or alerted the population to my presence in any way, so instead, we will install cameras; that way, I can monitor the discussions in real-time from The Retreat as you conduct business from The New Capitol."

The Guvna' had nodded in agreement.

In his position, there was nothing else to do.

But the arrangement, like everything else about his meeting with The Director, had given Donnie Molinaro the creeps.

"I'm having trouble understanding this, Knower Mallion. We turned over full control of the workforce to you. We increased the work hours and installed surveillance to ensure that all of our workers are operating at full steam. Why is it that, after two weeks, you still have no progress to report?"

Zenus Mallion bristled. He was a few years past sixty, with dark brown hair and darker brown eyes that were half-hidden behind thick, perfectly round spectacles. He wore a coarse beard, which he tugged at through the membrane of his Bubble Suit when agitated; he tugged at it now.

Mallion had never liked Tarissa Cross; he had been Head Knower for ten years now, and she had never treated him with the respect owed to his position. Since the day he had taken office, Mallion had quelled crisis after crisis, starting with that most essential requirement that Mallion construct some plausible explanation when his predecessor, Head Knower Ancel, died at the age of ninety-eight back in 12 A.K., two years short of the requisite age of one hundred.

It was Mallion who concocted the plan to cast the blame on the idiot sentient beings who had lived Before Knowledge, Mallion who had come up with the idea to claim that the details of Ancel's birth entered into the record Before Knowledge were wrong, Mallion who had suggested that they forge birth records indicating that Ancel had been born in 88 B.K. rather than 86 B.K., and Mallion who had thought to change the place of birth from Quincy, the coastal town in southwestern Acadia, which some citizuns still remembered, to Sarisota, the first of the great midwestern cities to collapse, a city that few could recall.

Yes, in that time of crisis, it had been Mallion who forged the explanations that put the citizuns of The Bubble Society back at ease, and while he had been suitably rewarded by The Director, he was still forced to contend with Tarissa Cross whenever she saw an inch of ground to be gained.

"Ms. Cross, if you will recall, it took Knower Ludquist nearly four weeks before he was granted the Knowledge that allowed him to win the first Elevation Upgrade Prize. Our Knowers are investigating every possible avenue, making every possible sacrifice, but it is difficult to say when Knowledge will reward their work. It is, after all, a novel problem."

"I didn't ask for your explanations, Mallion."

"Actually, you did."

Cross was caught up short at that; she quickly took another tack.

"All I Know is that when I tell Moderator Montenegro to get a law passed, he gets the law passed. He has passed Resolutions 4446, 4447, 4447A, 4448, 4449, and 4450 in the past few weeks, and none of them took more than a day."

"Moderator Montenegro's tasks are rather more straightforward. Whenever you put forth a resolution, both Halls of Parliament either vote in lockstep, keeping Moderator Montenegro out of the process, or they disagree vehemently, reminding the population how different our two parties are, before each side votes as one, resulting in a tie that allows Moderator Montenegro to swing the result your way."

"Thank you for explaining how Democracy works, Mallion. I was so unfamiliar with the process."

"Well, however Democracy works, this is Knowledge we speak of, and Knowledge is not always so easy to manipulate."

"I don't see why not. We are the greatest sentient beings who have ever existed, the chosen ones who transcended the endless failings of past generations to exist After Knowledge. We control the planet Shurtain."

The Guvna' could not help but chime in here; the days had been too long of late.

"Y'know, Viceroy, from summa' wut I seen, it's gravity dat controls Shurtain. Nature, if ya'will."

Cross's eyes narrowed as she turned to look at The Guvna'.

"I won't," she spat. "If gravity ever threatens The Bubble Society, it will find out its place, the same way the atmosphere did before it."

The Guvna' grinned; Cross elected to ignore this, and instead turned her attention back to Mallion.

"The team at General Dynamics went out of their way to form the new Department of Air Filtration Construction, and they are eager to begin assembly work. We have already reassigned over a thousand workers from other industries and trained them; they are now on standby, ready to start rolling out these advanced mouth filtration devices. Are they supposed to do nothing?"

Mallion sighed.

"As I have told you from the start, there was no reason to make that move until after we had a viable product to build. You have full control of the workforce; you could have waited until we were delivered the necessary Knowledge to make the shift, allowed these people to continue in their current roles in the interim. I also remain deeply confused as to why you told them that they will be building mouth filtration devices; where did you get that idea? Knower Ludquist's solution uses the same platform as the current Bubble Suit."

"Because, Knower Mallion, that's what these dirty, filthy Savages have built with the Knowledge that they stole from us."

Mallion closed his eyes. For his part, The Guvna' quite enjoyed watching someone else suffer through an exchange with Cross; after twenty years, it was a welcome change.

"Viceroy Cross, as I have told you, on numerous occasions, we have no record of this supposed Knowledge, nor do we have any evidence that any Savages, dirty, filthy, or otherwise, stole anything from us."

"Perhaps you ought to devote more effort to that investigation."

Mallion threw up his hands.

"Devote more effort from where? I have every available Knower at Dynamic Solutions and the Academy of Knowledge working on the Elevation Upgrade Prizes. I have, with the help of our partners at the City Watch and Capitol Guard, created a surveillance network to ensure that our Knowers are putting their noses to the grindstone. Now you want me to divert the resources focused on discovering this Knowledge to an investigation into a theft that might have occurred?"

"Might have occurred? How else would a bunch of dirty, filthy Savages create such a device, Mallion? Surely you don't believe such a breed of beings could build anything on their own."

"Ms. Cross, I do not purport to have any Knowledge on what these

Savages might, or might not, have built. All I Know is that I do not have the workforce hours to conduct this investigation without slowing down the search for new Knowledge."

"Fine."

Cross swiveled to Moderator Montenegro.

"Giuseppe."

Montenegro, who had started to doze as the exchange dragged on, jerked to attention at the sound of Cross's voice, the tips of his magnificent mustache quivering as his Bubble Suit resettled itself.

"Viceroy?"

"You are to pass another Resolution. Get in touch with Speakers Johnson and Garcia as soon as we are done here. Resolution 4451 will increase the workday by another half-hour."

Cross turned back to Mallion, a triumphant smile on her face.

"There are your precious workforce hours, Mallion. I will have the results of the investigation. And I will have the design for these mouth filtration devices."

She got to her feet.

"If I don't, then General Dynamics might be looking for a new Head Knower sooner than you would like."

BOOK 4, CHAPTER 13

Gavin slept in a comfortable bedroom and woke up to a spectacular view of the Cadillac Mountains. He ate well, had leave to stroll the grounds around the big house and the little farm, and between his great-uncle and the owners of the property, Jerry and Darlene, he had enough in the way of engagement.

But eight days in, imprisonment was starting to take its toll on him.

Perhaps someone else would have expected it. Perhaps someone else would have realized that his troubles had only begun, that Anton's backhand was not the formal punitive action that would be taken against Gavin.

They had not bothered to take him all the way into Trepani; Jerry and Darlene lived on a plot on the northwestern outskirts of the city, and when they had reached the waterfall that fed the Western Grand, Anton had instructed Al Nierland and Brock Lukavsky to take Gavin up the back way.

"I don't want to deal with fighting our way through a crowd, if one is waiting. There will be enough problems to deal with; we don't need someone losing their shit and tearing this kid limb from limb."

The imagery of Anton's words caused Gavin to shudder, but beyond that, his instructions led to a marked improvement in the final hour or so of Gavin's journey; as it turned out, Nierland and Lukavsky were not nearly as angry with Gavin as Anton, or for that matter, angry with him at all. They did not dispute the significance of his actions, but they were not the type of men to let a little matter like an impending war affect their dispositions; they said as much once they were clear of Anton's hearing, making their way through the trees on a twisting dirt path.

"So, you thought you could walk through Kingston without a Bubble Suit on? Bold strategy, that."

Even after their days together, Gavin found it disconcerting to look up at Nierland's freckled face, and uncomfortable besides; he had to twist his neck to an odd angle to meet the man's brown eyes, as Nierland was at least a foot and a half taller than him. At least hearing was not an issue; Nierland had a voice to match his size.

"I was hoping the darkness would help. That nobody would notice."

Nierland roared with laughter at that. Gavin glanced at Lukavsky to check the other big man's reaction, and found the swarthy, black-haired man smirking. When he noticed Gavin looking at him, Lukavsky spoke, his tone markedly reserved in comparison to Nierland's booming tones.

"A fine idea. But you should have given yourself the powers to turn invisible rather than relying on the shadows. Could have just stripped your clothes off and gone waltzing naked through Kingston."

Nierland continued to laugh.

"Suppose it was all inevitable, whether or not you involved yourself," Lukavsky continued. "Things have been stagnant for too long, and from what I understand, there are enough things starting to go haywire in Kingston that they were going to need an external force to blame, sooner or later."

Gavin frowned.

"What do you mean?"

Lukavsky exchanged a brief glance with Nierland; the red-headed man nodded, and Lukavsky continued.

"I understand your parents are Laureates - my condolences - but they are the crux of it all. The number of people moving to The Villa is increasing in Kingston, the dementia becoming more and more ubiquitous. They don't speak of it publicly, of course, but the condition is creeping in two directions; it is affecting sentient beings at younger and younger ages - we have heard rumors of teenagers showing symptoms - and it is affecting an increasing percentage of the population at every age."

"They're keeping up appearances, but beneath the surface, everything in Kingston is going to rot. When The Board set about devising this utopia of theirs, they failed to consider sentient psychology, basic things like how an internal or external locus of control impacts a sentient being's happiness, sense of purpose, and productivity."

Gavin frowned.

"What does that mean? Locus of control? And why does it matter?"

Lukavsky grinned.

"Loosely put, it's whether or not a sentient being feels like they have some say in their destiny. Not ultimate say, of course - need Shurtain to keep spinning and all that - but our spirits need to feel as if they have some agency in this realm. It can be as small as having the freedom to do your assigned duties as you see fit - from there, it turns into a mindset issue - but top-down control and micromanagement tend to shift a sentient being's sense of control from internal to external, and that's where things start to go off."

"How so?"

"You take a whole population of people and assign them to industries. Sure, some of them will be happy with their placement, but even among that group, the very fact that they did not get to make the choice on their own will breed some level of resentment in certain individuals; that's sentient nature, hardwired into us."

"Then you ask those same sentient beings to work in their assigned occupation for years on end. They'll do it - they need to do it to meet their survival needs - but they aren't likely to do it with any great enthusiasm, and lacking that, it's hard to find much in the way of focus."

"Over a year or two, that might not matter much, but over decades? The planet Shurtain has been here as long as sentient memory, but the city of Kingston did not come pre-assembled; any man-made infrastructure must be constantly maintained, or Nature will swallow it back up. As I say, everything looks fine on the surface in The Bubble Society, but our best guess is that Kingston is, at best, a few years away from catastrophic collapse; given the state of things, their leaders might even welcome this war and the distraction it would provide from all their other problems."

Gavin squirmed uncomfortably at that.

"You're sure it will be war, then?"

Nierland laughed again. Lukavsky's half-smile returned.

"You don't understand your old society particularly well, do you? Do you really believe The Board will tolerate anything, or anyone, that exists outside of their control?"

They crested a hill as Lukavsky said this, bringing Jerry and Darlene's property into view, so Gavin never got a chance to answer the question. Gavin was familiar with the place - he had visited his great-uncle here - but it felt altogether different approaching this way, and not only because the path itself was different; this time, Gavin would not be allowed to leave.

Jerry and Darlene saw them coming and met them at a gate on the edge of the property. Jerry was about six feet tall, with a short fringe of hair going to grey and a mustache that had started to do the same. His dark brown skin showed similar signs of age, long wrinkles that were more prominent when he smiled, but he retained an athlete's build and moved with an easy grace. Darlene was nearly as tall as her husband, even leaner than he was, with black skin that remained smooth despite the years.

Gavin knew from past experience that his hosts were friendly enough; even so, he found himself in sort of foggy unreality as he shook their hands.

He could not quite believe that he was under arrest.

True, his stay in Kingston Hospital had been a sort of imprisonment, and he had never really been free when he lived as a Ward on the Academic Campus, but it had never been put to him in those terms.

As they parted, Lukavsky reminded him of that.

"All of this is new to us - we aren't in the practice of jailing non-violent offenders - but if I were you, I'd consider the possibility my situation might be made worse. Al and I argued hard to let you stay here with your great-uncle until the Summit, but if you go wandering off again before we can settle this, they are going to find you different accommodations, and from what Anton suggested on the trail, they wouldn't be as comfortable as these."

Lukavsky glanced at Nierland as he said this; Nierland shook his head.

"Psycho, that one. We can keep him in check, to some degree, but as Brock says, it'd be better if you don't push things. Just wait it out until the Summit; this isn't a bad place to be."

With that, the two hulking men had left the property, exchanging a quick word with Jerry and Darlene before they loped off toward Trepani.

Yet even after they had passed out of sight, and Gavin had turned to find his way to the room that now served as his cell, their conversation lingered in his mind, Lukavsky's last question repeating itself over and over.

"You don't understand your old society particularly well, do you?"

With a squirm of his insides, Gavin remembered his last visit to The Villa, remembered meeting Lucy, remembered thinking, before he had seen her eyes, that she was a potential companion, had they gotten along; after all, she was about his age, and more than pretty enough.

He had always understood there was something wrong at The Villa, but could Kingston's Guvernment, the same group that oversaw the utopia they called The Bubble Society, the same body that ensured every one of its citizuns were taken care of, really be as dangerous as Lukavsky said? He could not believe it; he had met The Guvna', after all, and he had seemed like a good man.

But even as Gavin thought of The Guvna', another thought found its way into his consciousness.

What does his daughter think about all this?

Gavin shivered as he flashed back to his conversations with Tesla in the latter stages of their journey.

It wasn't a mistake…

Even now, as he sat back, replaying her explanations, he could not quite believe everything she had told him.

—

"Anymore? Gavin, nobody ever needed the Bubble Suits."

He blinked again, not understanding. He started to respond, but Tesla cut him off.

"And it wasn't a mistake."

"What do you mean, it wasn't a mistake?"

Tesla sighed, shook her head.

"Look, this all goes back to way before you and I were born, so I'm going to need to string some things together, but it'll take a minute, and interruptions will slow us down."

"How do you know about it all, then?"

Tesla stared at him for a long moment; when Gavin finally realized what he had done, he reddened slightly.

"Gotcha. You'll tell me."

"Thank you. To start, we have to go back decades before The Advent, back to when something shifted, and the health of sentient beings started going to hell."

"Even then, the source - or sources - of the problems were known, even if they weren't thoroughly understood. They were complex, certainly, multi-faceted, but as bad as the overall health of the sentient being population got, there was always a significant percentage of the population that remained healthy; exceptions to the rule."

"Yet even as they co-mingled with those exceptions, the vast majority of the population did not take the time to question why the exceptions existed, and instead became convinced, not only that the sentient race was getting sick for reasons outside of their control, but that there was nothing that they could do to stop the decline."

"The truth was less complicated. Back before The Advent, roughly around the same time the Acadian continent started to have so many problems with its rail system, some of the most influential individuals in Kingston - the Oligarchs, as they were known - started to perform wild experiments on Nature, convinced that, in their infinite wisdom, sentient beings could correct what they judged to be errors in the grand design."

Tesla paused to shake her head.

"In reading back through their accounts, it's hard not to notice how many of the errors they identified in Nature were rooted in the lack of profitability. There was nothing wrong with the animals of the past, per se, but you could make more money on them if they were fatter. The same could be said of the corn and the wheat, the fruits and the vegetables; it all served its purpose, but not as profitably as if they could produce more of it at lower cost and find ways it would never expire."

"Of course, on some level, that's a reasonable way to look at things. But when you take it a few steps further, and start running experiments with chemicals and genetic mutations… well, things appear to get a bit more complicated there, and regardless of what the experimenters of the past *thought* they were doing, there were nearly always impacts that they did not anticipate or intend. They even found a way to edit the genetic code, and became convinced, not only that their method was precise enough to work as well as they imagined, but that they had the know-how to fully anticipate the myriad impacts of editing that code. They thought it would be simple, straightforward; a snip here, a snip there, and away you go. They claimed they had figured out how to make the changes in exactly the same way that Nature would; as if the Universe couldn't spot a counterfeit."

"Based on the downstream results, they were wildly mistaken; the food products they created, for instance, turned out to cause all sorts of unanticipated health problems. But the products were profitable, and in the Economic Era, back in the years Before Knowledge, profit ruled Kingston. Ruled its politics, ruled its population; in a way, you could say the pursuit of profits had taken the place of religion as the guiding light of sentientkind."

"Unfortunately, as profitable as those methods might have been, they left Kingston's Oligarchs with a problem. They were making money in the short term, but it was becoming obvious that they would soon run into problems; the spread of disease was slow at first, but they were well aware of it even then, and understood it was a long-term threat to their venture, assuming they did not find an off-ramp."

"So, rather than cut off any income stream, the Oligarchs devised a new plan. They would create a second profitable venture to correct the issues caused by the first profitable venture; thus, rather than impoverishing themselves in the course of saving the population, they would enrich themselves, which, as they saw it, was the only just arrangement, given that they were the ones saving the population, never mind that they were the reason the population needed saving."

"From there, the idea for the Bubble Suits was born, and with it, the idea of restructuring Kingston's Guvernment to partner with Dynamic Solutions."

"After that, it was easy. The Oligarchs pulled some atmospheric data that allowed them to create their narrative, and they were off to the races. You can make numbers say whatever you want if you massage them; it gives you a lot of power if people assume that your projection models are an accurate depiction of the future, rather than a guess that a sentient being built with a computer that may - or may not - have some degree of relevance to reality."

"What's scary is how little resistance they faced. They were clever, the Oligarchs - they understood that it is sentient nature to seek out comfort and easy solutions - and they played on those desires; but even so, I would have expected some level of skepticism from the public."

"In time, that same public who had bought the explanations for the decline in sentient health would buy into the narratives surrounding the Bubble Suits with next to no questions. The Bubble Suits seemed to check every box; they would ensure that every citizun in Kingston lived a long, happy life, and as far as profitability went, they were a dream come true."

Tesla paused. Gavin caught her eye; seeing the confusion on his face, she nodded, letting him know he was free to ask his question.

"Profitability? The Bubble Suits aren't profitable, are they? The Guvernment provides them for free."

Tesla laughed.

"The Guvernment also claims to provide the people of Kingston with housing, as well as the nutrient and fluid tanks you need to survive, for free, but they don't pay any of the workers in Kingston outside of the meager allowance of credits that citizuns can use at Guvernment-owned establishments in the city. So, what exactly do you think you're getting for free?"

Tesla shook her head.

"If you think the people running things aren't taking something off the top of every one of those transactions, then you don't know much about sentient beings. Everyone else works while the politicians sit back, talking about how wonderful they are, and paying themselves exorbitant sums to carry out tasks that they assigned to themselves, or to one another, without any thought of whether or not their actions make things better or worse for the citizuns of Kingston."

"The Guvernment pulls most of the value out of what would be your paycheck, pays Dynamic Solutions grossly inflated prices for the muck that they pass off as food, and shells out an even greater premium for more specialized compounds, such as the alcoholic drinks, or the Focus Solution, that Dynamic Solutions produces. There is no free; the cost you are paying is for a select group of people to live their utterly grotesque lives. Those sentient beings live in opulent luxury, but those are only the trappings of powers; it's the power itself they lust for, and more specifically, the power to control others."

"It's gross, when you think about it, the idea that any sentient being should feel, not only a right, but a responsibility, to tell another sentient being what to do with their time on Shurtain. As if any of us actually knows what we are doing here, or where we are going, as our planet orbits a star that is hurtling through space."

She shook her head.

"I wish I could say it's all a game to them, but it's worse than that. To them, it's all too real, and they have convinced themselves that they are doing something good by exerting their twisted control over the rest of sentientkind. They see themselves as a cut above the masses, as the masters of the Universe, and there is nobody in a position to stop them. They delude themselves into believing they are working for the greater good, and ignore any and all evidence to the contrary; those at the top do not bother themselves with the ashes that are dumped into the Grand River from The Villa's basement each night, do not care about the souls whose remains are flushed away without a word of acknowledgement."

"And if you did something to threaten their enterprise, those same sentient beings would kill you without a second thought. If you had made it to The Villa, and shown everyone that a sentient being can survive on Shurtain without a Bubble Suit, then you never would have made it out of Kingston alive."

—

The memories of that conversation were troubling.

They were troubling because, deep down, Gavin believed Tesla, and those feelings were resonating, slowly but surely, on the surface of his consciousness.

He had never had any great liking for the Guvernment. Not when he had started to attend school, and been subject to its rules. Not when his parents had been taken away. And not when he had been consigned to the ranks of the Wards.

Then again, this was more infinitely troubling than anything he could have imagined.

He shook himself back into the present, and upon doing so, noticed, from the light filtering into the room, that the sun was setting. He got up from the edge of his bed and exited the room, heading for the front porch, where he would be able to watch the sun sink over the western Cadillacs.

Gavin found his great-uncle doing the same; Clarence sat in a rocking chair on the porch, facing the sun.

For a time, neither man said anything. Finally, Gavin broke the silence.

"The Summit is tomorrow."

Clarence nodded, his eyes still on the horizon.

"And our trial."

Clarence shrugged.

"High time, if you ask me."

"Aren't you worried?"

Clarence shifted his gaze to take in Gavin.

"Not particularly. I expected I would encounter this sort of difficulty, somewhere along the way. It had been a busy time before all this, and I think there will be busy times to come. The time to rest is welcome."

Gavin's face scrunched in confusion; he ran a hand through his blond hair, pulling it up on end.

"But when we arrived in Trepani, you seemed surprised when Santino told us there were people waiting for us. When I visited you, before they brought me here, you seemed resentful that they had you cooped up in this place."

The old man smiled.

"Sometimes it's easier to keep up appearances. I've been here on Shurtain a year or two; if I wear a mask to minimize my difficulties, I will not forget who I am."

Gavin chewed on that for a while.

"So you don't think they will convict us, or whatever you would call it, tomorrow? You think they will set us free?"

"Oh, no, I'm fairly certain they will convict us, and sentence us to some sort of confinement. There will even be those who call for our deaths, but the moderates should reel them in."

Gavin stared at his great-uncle in disbelief.

"Then how on Shurtain can you be so calm about all of this?"

Clarence considered the question for a moment. He glanced around the porch; once he was certain they were alone, he shrugged, and told Gavin exactly how he could be so calm about everything.

BOOK 4, CHAPTER 14

The Town Square was built for moments like this.

Situated at the bend in Grand Lake, the lowest structure on the hill, the Town Square was a stone-bottomed pit, the benches on its three sides carved out of the rocky hillside itself and smoothed from two decades of use and weather.

The seating did not end there; at the top of the benches, Trepani's Town Square gave way to a boardwalk of various eateries, all of which had patios and upper-deck seating with a view of the courtyard. Yet even with all the seating, the place was overflowing; the whole of Trepani's population had turned up for today's event, many of them coming in from the outskirts to witness the Acadian Summit.

Eight individuals had been selected to participate in the Summit; most were there as the representatives of Acadia's cities, others to supply critical information, or to facilitate the discussion.

Two more would join them in the courtyard; throne-like stone chairs had been arranged in a circle in the pit of the Town Square, one for each of the ten who would be in the arena.

Tyene Medrana, the representative for the city of Alysanne, and the wider continent of Alexandria, made her entrance into the Town Square first, emerging from a gap between two of the boardwalk eateries and making her way down the staircase to the cobblestones below, brown eyes flashing in the sunlight as her long legs carried her to the courtyard. She took the seat that faced directly out at Grand Lake.

Gwynivere Holt, who spoke for the city of Giota, the Acadian settlement in the peaks of the continent's southeastern peninsula, was next; half-a-foot shorter than Tyene Medrana, Gwynivere looked a small thing making her entrance to the Town Square after the woman from Alexandria, but she held herself high as she descended the staircase, the lively intelligence in her eyes a reminder that time had not yet touched her energy, even if it had left her skin wrinkled and her hair grey. She took the seat directly across from Tyene Medrana.

Gwynivere Holt was followed by Ruby Jones, a tall, slender, red-headed woman of nearly fifty years, who would speak for Trepani; Ruby's bright blue eyes sparkled as she entered the Town Square, her eyes on Grand Lake as she made her descent. She took the seat to Tyene Medrana's right.

With the three female representatives in place, the three male representatives entered in quicker procession. Marcus Cahn, who spoke for the city of Larissa, took the seat to Gwynivere Holt's right. Anton Molinaro, who spoke for the hunters, took the seat to Tyene Medrana's left. And Alabaster Minteran, a small man with keen green eyes, dark brown skin, and a neatly trimmed beard shot with white, who spoke for the city of Kirfi, took the seat to Holt's left.

Next up was Darlene Brown, who was there to facilitate the discussion; Darlene had come alone to the Town Square, leaving her husband to escort their two guests. She took the seat to Anton's left.

That left three seats in the circle; Tesla Mancini was not one to get nervous, but even after years of entering Kingston Amphitheater in celebratory processions, descending the stairs into Trepani's Town Square felt different.

Tesla was there to reference the significant stores of Knowledge - as well as the actual knowledge - that she had accumulated in a lifetime living in The Bubble Society. It had been Coreen's idea, one that she had insisted on after hearing more and more stories from Tesla's past during their training sessions.

But while nobody had instructed Tesla to do anything more than supply information on Kingston, she entered the Square with an innate understanding that, ironic as it might seem, she may need to speak for the people down in the valley, who had no other voice than the young woman who had helped to cause all this with her decision to run away.

Tesla had been instructed to take the seat between Darlene Brown and Marcus Cahn - it was one of the few direct instructions they had provided her - but as innocuous as the request seemed, she was half-tempted to ignore it, and to sit more or less directly across from her *dear* brother. She decided against it; there were matters of greater importance at the moment.

The crowd began to clamor as those matters came into view; nobody seemed likely to take a run at Clarence Barnett or Gavin Owens, not with Al Nierland and Brock Lukavsky escorting them down the stairs into the courtyard, but as they entered, every neck in the Town Square craned to get a glimpse of the pair who had conspired to create the present mess the Acadians found themselves in. As she watched them descend the stairs into the courtyard, Tesla noticed a stark difference between the two men; Clarence appeared calm, rested, almost bored, while Gavin was the opposite, his brown eyes darting all around, his messy blond hair standing more on end than usual.

Nierland and Lukavsky stopped at the bottom of the staircase, allowing Clarence and Gavin to proceed to their seats without escorts. It was a small thing, but an important one, meant to indicate that the two men were not yet condemned; the Acadians had clear rules about directly harming others, but even those who were fervently in favor of some sort of imprisonment for both Clarence and Gavin did not deny that this situation was not as black and white as the usual question of whether one sentient being had directly harmed another.

Yet that question of what to do with Clarence, the original reason for the Summit, was more or less an afterthought, even with his great-nephew joining him on trial.

Instead, as the Acadian Summit began, the chief concern was very different; the Acadians needed to determine how they would answer Kingston's Declaration of War.

—

"So, here we are."

The crowd was settled, the speakers in place. Darlene Brown had gotten to her feet; now she stood in front of her chair to address the audience.

"You all know the generalities of why we are here, but as we will be making formal decisions today, I will begin by laying out the details of what has happened over the past seasons; or at least, the details pertinent enough to merit inclusion in that narrative."

Darlene re-told the story, but Tesla found she was not really listening; her insides were squirming, her mind racing as she anticipated the moment she would have to tell the crowd the news it would not want to hear. She desperately wished she did not have to be the one to deliver it, but a lie would not do; the secrets Tesla held mean that the current obstacle facing The Bubble Society, their inability to reach the altitudes where the Acadians dwelled, could be overcome any day now.

The Acadians needed to know that; it was too critical a piece of information to leave out of their planning.

As her eyes absently roved the crowd, she felt somebody's gaze on her; she shifted her focus to where Gavin sat next to his great-uncle.

Tesla was surprised to see that her fellow defector no longer appeared particularly distressed; in fact, as she took in Gavin's appearance, it occurred to her… but no.

At that moment, Gavin realized Tesla was looking at him. He met her eyes, smiled, and gave her the thumbs up before returning to his crowd-watching.

Tesla could not believe it.

As she ran back through her perspective of the proceedings, she realized that Gavin's eyes had not been darting around during his entrance because he was anxious; they had been darting around because he was *excited.*

As if the Acadian Summit were a movie, and he was just sitting here enjoying it, rather than one of the two on trial.

Tesla almost laughed; as the tension in her stomach loosened, she found herself wishing that she was sitting on the other side of the circle.

Then her eyes moved to Clarence, and her sense of wonder increased; she realized it was the old man that had been watching her, his gaze she had felt.

The brown eyes smiled in acknowledgment when Tesla met them. Tesla could not quite describe the expression in those eyes; it was not the interest she often drew from men, nor the judgement of an authority figure assessing whether anything needed correction, but a different way of looking at things all together, a keen curiosity, as if she were some sort of marvel.

She wondered what that meant.

But there was one thing she did not have to wonder about.

From Tesla's perspective, Clarence ought to have been highly concerned that he was about to be imprisoned for the remainder of his life. But from everything she could see, he was not; Clarence did not have the look of a man on trial for his life, or any sort of demeanor close to what Tesla had anticipated when she imagined this scene in her mind.

Clarence confirmed that suspicion when, catching Tesla's eye, he gave her a wink, then closed his eyes and bowed his head, evidently ready to nap until the proceedings took a more interesting turn.

She wondered what was going on.

—

"And that all brings us to our present circumstances."

Tesla's eyes moved back to Darlene Brown as the woman concluded her retelling of the events.

"I will now turn the floor over to others, who will voice their views on how we ought to proceed in light of the developments down in Kingston. The Bubble Society has never given us trouble - not since we were forced to leave Kingston - but it would appear that time is fast closing, and we must decide how to respond."

"We will open with our guest from abroad: Tyene Medrana."

Tyene Medrana rose to her feet as Darlene sat.

"Thank you, Darlene, for your introduction."

Tyene paused, taking in the crowd with her bold brown eyes.

"I want to begin by saying what an unlikely ally the Acadians, particularly those Acadians in Larissa, have become over the past decades. I was too young to be in power during the run-up to The Advent down in Kingston, but I was old enough to follow the conversations back home in Alysanne as we observed their progress. Even then, there was talk of action; our relationships with our neighbors across the sea may have frayed during the Economic Era, but we were still tied in enough with those individuals living in Larissa at the time to get word of the direction that Kingston's society had taken."

"In the end, we stayed our hand; we could not see how our people, across the ocean in Alexandria, were going to convince a whole civilization that their core beliefs, the underlying set of convictions that govern their day-to-day experience in this reality, were complete and utter nonsense. It was an errand for fools, as they said. And yet… our leaders could not ignore how dangerous the ideas forming the foundation of this new society could be. There was a thought that we should snuff it in the cradle, end the experiment before it could begin. But it would have meant war… and blood… and so our leaders watched, and waited."

Tyene smiled.

"A funny thing happened then. The Acadians - your people - emerged from Kingston, and proved to be, not a threat to the wider world, but an honest partner, looking to collaborate in good faith. If you know your history of this planet, you know how rare that is, for two peoples to work together with no thoughts of one population taking advantage of, or even toppling, the other party."

"And in proving yourselves such good allies, you did another thing; you cemented the decision to forestall any action that we might have taken against Kingston. With the Acadians spread through the Cadillac Mountains, controlling the eastern part of the continent, we in Alexandria had fewer concerns about the goings-on in The Bubble Society. The buffer you provided seemed sufficient to ensure nothing terrible would happen too suddenly."

"Yet, while we in Alexandria never took action, we did not forget. As we have watched The Bubble Society evolve, our views have only hardened."

She paused.

"In light of this Declaration of War from The Bubble Society, we think the time for patience has ended. We need to engage them before they can develop the enhancements to their technology that would allow them to leave Kingston."

"As it stands, we can pin them down, take the fight to them on their home soil. They sit on an impressive arsenal, but we can match them in that exchange, and the damage would be contained to the valley that holds Kingston. The rest of Shurtain would be spared."

Tyene stopped again, taking a long moment to look at the others in the circle, and a longer moment to sweep her eyes over the crowd, which sat hanging on her every word.

"The people of Alexandria stand ready to join you in this; say the word, and we will have as large an army as you require at your disposal. The process is already taking place; on the same day that The Guvna' issued Kingston's Declaration of War, the leadership in our capital city of Ulysses called up all reserve troops in the Alexandrian army, declaring that they should engage in battle-readiness exercises."

"It is not our continent - that is why we are eager to work in concert with you - but nor is this a problem that my people can ignore. If The Bubble Society steps outside its boundaries, and hunts down the Acadian people, it will not stop there; they will have to open their eyes to what lies beyond, and when their leaders see that, they will have to destroy it. They have no other choice; they can't allow our existence, not if the population is going to remain convinced that they need the Bubble Suits to survive."

"It is the preference of most back in Ulysses that the Alexandrian Army strike hard and fast; I tend to agree. We believe, if properly done, we can wipe The Bubble Society from the face of Shurtain before that malignancy has a chance to spread to our continent."

There was no response at first, only stunned silence. Then, as Tyene's eyes scanned her counterparts in the courtyard, a voice boomed out from the audience.

"WHAT ABOUT PEACE?"

To an outsider, this might have seemed unacceptable, but in the Acadian Town Square, it was expected behavior; persistent, or pointless, interruptions were frowned upon, but the expectation that spectators could voice their questions, or opinions, was an ingrained part of the system. It served as a check and balance to ensure that, if a clarifying question truly needed asking, the selected speakers could not dance around the topic, straw-manning arguments or refusing to answer inquiries directly. Aware of her neighboring continent's customs, Tyene Medrana accepted the question with good grace; she turned to the man who had shouted, smiled sweetly at him, and answered.

"And on what terms would you have peace, good sir? Would you send The Board a bottle of champagne? Some chocolates, perhaps? I would even suggest a few girls - from rumors we hear across the ocean, I gather that my daughter would be especially popular with their leader - but I suspect that, in the end, our tributes would end up as ashes in the river with the rest, and we would have our war all the same."

Rory McBain was not going to be shut down so easily; at Medrana's response to his shouted question, he lurched to his feet, and pointed a finger directly at Tesla.

"WE COULD SEND HER BACK!" he roared.

There was a commotion in the crowd at these words; Tesla had been aware that this might happen, but she had not realized it would be stated so boldly. She felt her insides squirm as every head in the crowd turned in her direction, trying to get a better look; in desperation, she looked at Tyene, who was readying herself to respond to McBain's suggestion, when a much deeper voice, somehow calm despite its volume, boomed over the sudden commotion.

"You serious, McBain?"

Tyene Medrana did not say a word; she turned to look at Anton, then bowed her head in his direction, ceding the floor to the tall blond man.

Anton Molinaro got to his feet, his flat hazel eyes on the man in the crowd, a deadpan expression on his face.

"Thank you, Rory, for bringing this topic to the forefront. I had not known which of my fellow Acadians would venture to suggest that returning Tesla Mancini could somehow avert war... but from the whispers I'd been hearing, I figured someone would."

Rory McBain flushed. Anton continued.

"If I thought that delivering this young woman to the front step of The Guvna's Mansion would protect the people of Trepani, and the rest of my fellow Acadians, I would do it myself, without a second thought."

He paused.

"But that isn't our situation. It wouldn't matter if we gave her back; were I to hazard a guess, if we brought her back alive, The Director would have her throat slit, lay the blame at our feet, and put her on display for all of Kingston to see. He would hold it up as one more example of how uncouth we Savages are."

"If you have any doubts on that front, take a look at the propaganda rolling out on the Guvernment Media App down in Kingston; I assume that you've seen the garbage they're spewing down there, that the Savages broke into The Guvna's Mansion to abduct Tesla, that we killed members of the City Watch and the Capitol Guard in the process."

Anton shook his head.

"If there's any confusion - if you believed a word of that nonsense - then you should be aware of the real story. Tesla came of her own volition. There was no abduction, and no casualties during our escape; if any members of the City Watch or the Capitol Guard are dead, it's because The Board disposed of them after my crew and I showed them mercy. This whole song and dance they're doing, claiming that the war is all about Tesla, is nonsense."

"So thank you for the suggestion, Rory McBain, but returning Tesla Mancini to The Guvna' would do nothing to avert this war."

Rory McBain had sat back down by now, the color drained from his face. He offered no retort.

"Anyone else?"

When his challenge went unanswered, Anton turned to Marcus Cahn.

"Now that we've dispensed with that foolish notion, I suppose this would be a good moment for you to lay out your approach."

Marcus nodded, the pale green eyes glancing curiously between Anton and Tesla, the latter of whom sat stunned in her seat, completely unsure of what to make of her brother speaking up in her defense. Had it been in her defense? Tesla could not say, and before she could consider the matter further, Marcus was speaking.

"I empathize, McBain, with your desire to avoid war. And while everyone in attendance ought to know of the great respect between Anton and I, I would submit that desperation and foolishness are often hard to differentiate; I do not blame you for trying to find a peaceful resolution for our community, though I ultimately agree with Anton's view that this is a non-starter. There will be war; the only question is, on what terms?"

Marcus paused; he took a moment to look around at the crowd as he considered his next words.

"Kingston may become a threat to us in the weeks and seasons to come, but as it stands, their ability to press into the heights of the Cadillac Mountains remains limited. Even after the improvements from the work that won the first Elevation Upgrade Prize, the Bubble Suits still stop functioning several miles short of Turquoise Falls."

"All the more reason to strike now, I should think; we ought to wipe them out before they develop the capabilities to push further into the mountains," Tyene Medrana interjected.

Marcus smiled, and started to respond, but Rose Jones beat him to it.

"It's a much easier thing to say, Tyene, when you've no connections to the sentient beings down in the valley, but we did not part from the people of Kingston so long ago; many of them are friends, family, cousins, siblings. They are not some faceless, nameless enemy; they are captured, yes, propagandized beyond belief, but if we can't find sympathy for them, what does it say of us?"

"A fair consideration," Marcus said, picking up the thread. "And what if the Kingston Guvernment, and Dynamic Solutions, have already reached the pinnacle of innovation? What if it is impossible for them to achieve the required upgrades they desire? Ought we not leave them down in the valley, where they aren't bothering anyone? After all, they still haven't figured out a solution to their Laureate problem; why should they be able to accomplish this aim of reaching the peaks of the Cadillac Mountains? We might be waiting for, well, forever, before The Bubble Society develops the technology they need to chase us up here."

Her moment had come; Tesla looked up in the crowd briefly, her eyes finding the place where Ollie and Coreen stood watching with Carly, up on the boardwalk at the top of the Town Square. Tesla and Coreen's eyes met; with a slight nod of encouragement, Coreen confirmed that Tesla's instincts were right.

Tesla got to her feet. Marcus's pale green eyes found hers; he gave a slight nod in her direction.

"I cede the floor to Tesla Mancini."

Tesla took a deep breath, let it out, and spoke, relieved to hear her voice sound almost normal as it echoed around the Town Square.

"I appreciate your thoughts on the matter, Marcus; I have family and friends I left behind, and I do not want to see them hurt."

Another deep breath.

"But while I appreciate your desire to wait, you should throw out the assumption that The Bubble Society won't be able to realize their envisioned upgrades. In fact, were I you, I would assume the opposite… because I already figured out what they need to do."

The crowd, which had started to buzz when Tesla stood to speak, grew eerily silent at that. Tesla's eyes flicked briefly to Gavin, who was smiling at her, then to Marcus, who was looking at her steadily.

"You already figured it out?"

Tesla nodded once.

"Weeks ago. A different method entirely, but one that would produce more significant effects than what Knower Ludquist came up with. It would work in coordination with his improvements to get the Bubble Suits to the peaks of the Cadillac Mountains."

"As it stands, I'm the only one who is aware of this; I've been independently developing Bubble Suit upgrades on my own for decades, and while I did not take this past proof-of-concept experiments, that was only because the conclusions were obvious enough that I didn't think it necessary. Nor did I want to create the possibility that Kingston's Guvernment, or the folks at Dynamic Solutions, would discover traces of the experiments I would have run."

"I destroyed the evidence of my work as thoroughly as I could, but the point remains; there is a way to upgrade The Bubble Suits, and I would urge all of you to proceed on the assumption that, given enough time, and enough Knowers thrown at the problem, that The Bubble Society will reach that conclusion as well."

The silence in the wake of these words was absolute; it was Gwynivere Holt who broke it, making a small noise to get Marcus's attention, as he was facing away from her. Once he had turned to acknowledge her, Gwynivere got to her feet, and began to speak.

"It seems to me that Ms. Mancini's information seals our fate."

"The people of Kingston will come for us, one day or another. So, we will be ready for them."

"It ought to be done thoughtfully, of course. As we know, Kingston remains well stocked with artillery from the Economic Era; we are not facing some rabble armed with sticks and stones. We face a well-organized, single-minded force, and no matter how badly their physical vehicles may be failing, they have weaponry to do the job for them. We will need to be patient, find the right moment to make our move."

Tyene Medrana shook her head.

"We shouldn't wait around for these lunatics to mobilize their arsenal; we ought to strike hard and fast, before they can fully organize themselves into a wartime society."

"Why not both?"

Everyone turned to face Alabaster Minteran, a small man whose keen green eyes stood out prominently against his olive skin and thick white beard.

"The people of Kirfi side with the delegates from Giota and Alysanne; our shared roots with The Bubble Society aside, the time for tearing free of that codependency has long since passed. They may have been part of our families, part of our communities, but that was in a different world, a different time. They chose their path long ago, as did we… and in any case, we are not the aggressors. We already ran once; if we run again, it will only mean that we meet them on the shores of Alexandria, rather than on their turf."

Tesla could not quite believe what she was hearing, but all around the circle, heads were nodding in agreement. Only Marcus Cahn and Rose Jones's expressions showed any skepticism; whatever Darlene Brown might have felt, she did a remarkable job of keeping her face neutral.

Alabaster saw this as well; with a nod, he continued.

"Then I don't know there is anything more to say… Darlene, I have no wish to usurp your position, but it is not as if we had not discussed today's schedule in our preparations. Even so, if you would like to formally declare it time to vote…"

Darlene waved him off from her seat.

"Not at all, Alabaster. I think everyone knows how they will vote on both measures."

The small man nodded.

"Well then, as you all know, we have broken this portion of today's vote into two pieces. First, we will decide whether to call up a standing army. I put it to the six charged with this vote; those in favor of calling up a standing army, raise your hands."

All six hands raised in unison on this point; her insides churning, Tesla's eyes found Gavin's. She saw that he had abandoned the earlier distractions of the crowd; the discussions had his full attention now, and he looked as alarmed as she felt. Clarence, on the other hand, did not seem to share his concerns; the old man no longer had his eyes shut, but he appeared remarkably calm as he took in the exchange.

"Very well. And the second vote… we have three options on the table. We either play the aggressor, set up a position at Turquoise Lake, or simply put ourselves on alert, ready to respond if there is provocation from Kingston."

"I'll start with the first option; those in favor of playing the aggressor?"

Tesla's stomach clenched as she sat there, watching the six; when Tyene Medrana's hand went up, she felt herself shudder, even though she had expected it.

But it was when her brother's hand joined Tyene's that she felt truly sick.

She thought about her parents. Thought about her sisters.

"And those in favor of setting up a position at Turquoise Lake?"

Alabaster raised his own hand as he finished voicing the question; he was joined by Gwynivere Holt.

"Very well. Kirfi and Giota are for the position at Turquoise Lake, Alysanne and the Hunters for playing the aggressor. And, for the sake of formality, who would simply keep us at the ready?"

Marcus Cahn and Ruby Jones exchanged a weary glance before they raised their hands.

"As you will. Well, that splits the vote, and we've planned for such a contingency; given the nature of the options, all parties agreed that if we split the vote, we would take the moderate course."

Alabaster paused to let out a slow exhale.

"The Acadians - with the support of our friends from Alexandria - will take up a defensive position at Turquoise Lake. That, of course, leaves us to elect the leader of this unit; all in favor of Anton Molinaro?"

This time, the hands went up in unison, though Anton himself abstained. Coreen had warned Tesla this was the likely outcome, but even so, the reaction surprised her, particularly after the opposition that had been voiced to some of Anton's views. Despite that, it seemed that, with the decision made to go to war, nobody doubted Anton Molinaro should be the one to lead them.

"Very well. Very well."

Alabaster was breathing hard, as if he had been sprinting; those moments he took to catch his breath reminded all in attendance of what they had just decided. It was nearly half a minute before Alabaster fully regained control of himself, though nobody was bothered by this; a similar feeling of suspended incredulity was rippling through the crowd.

Eventually, Alabaster found his voice.

"Well then, it's war. And with that settled…"

Alabaster trailed off as he turned to face Clarence and Gavin.

"We need to decide what to do with these two."

BOOK 4, CHAPTER 15

"What's your problem?"

He turned his eyes on the pair that were so much like his own. The young woman's hazel eyes crackled with electricity, where he knew his own looked tired, old.

He had known, even as he made the walk along this path to the water's edge, that she was following him. He was aware that she had been watching him since Al Nierland and Brock Lukavsky had escorted Clarence and Gavin out of the Town Square, escorting them to their imprisonment in the Tower of Trepani. Ever since Clarence and Gavin had been taken out of sight, those hazel eyes had been tracking him, waiting for the crowd to disperse, intent on getting him on his own.

Even so, he had not imagined that she would confront him so boldly; if that had been her plan, he would have wagered on her doing it in front of others, somewhere public, somewhere with witnesses.

Anton was sitting on his heels, gazing out over the surface of Grand Lake; he rose to answer Tesla.

"Excuse me?"

"You heard me. Our parents, our sisters, live down in Kingston, but you were more than ready to blow the place off the face of Shurtain."

Tesla glared at him, her jaw set.

"Don't you care? How can you support something like that, as if it's nothing, as if it's not your family?"

Hot tears were streaming down her face; angry, Tesla wiped them away, but she did not take her eyes from her older brother's.

Slowly, Anton shook his head.

"No. You've got that wrong."

"My parents died years before you were born. They died the day Andrea was born."

Anton exhaled.

"I don't fault them; I can't fathom what it's like to have a child with no real future. If she were my kid, I don't think I could have dealt with it."

Tesla's expression hardened.

"From what I've heard of your kids, you couldn't have. And wouldn't have."

Anton's eyes flashed warning at that, but Tesla was past caring; she had no more to say. Anton continued.

"In any case, she wasn't my kid. And whatever Donnie and Kelli had to do, I couldn't give up my life because my sister didn't have one."

Anton met Tesla's eyes then; she thought she saw something in them, some flicker, but then Anton was speaking, and his eyes were still again, the moment gone if it had ever existed.

"We'd gone our separate ways even before The Advent, and since then… as you've noted, I've got daughters of my own to protect now. It's been a lifetime since I saw Donnie and Kelli… and until the other night, I'd never seen you in the flesh."

He shook his head.

"I won't deny we share the same blood. But don't call me your brother; I promise you won't hear me call you my sister."

He stepped around Tesla, who stood silent, watching Anton with disgust as he passed her and disappeared back up the trail, the night swallowing him up.

BOOK 4, CHAPTER 16

"I'm beginning to have grave concerns about our Head Knower."

Tarissa Cross lounged in a chair on one of The Retreat's many balconies, one leg crossed over the other, a miniature teacup pinched between the fingers of the right hand. She was surrounded by three of her fellow Board Members, who were all fussing with their own teacups, adding milk and sugar from the assortments of fixings on the tray that two Guvernment Officials had wheeled onto the balcony moments earlier. It was an absurd exercise - the milk and sugar they added to the teacups did nothing whatsoever to alter the composition of the tea they would inject into their fluid ports - but still, appearances ought to be kept up, for in The Bubble Society, appearance was everything.

"You began to have grave concerns about the Head Knower some decades ago, my dear Viceroy."

Tarissa Cross gave a false tinkle of laughter at Corwin McKenzie's witticism; Gina Townsend and Nessie Hunter joined in the laughter.

"Too true. And yet the longer the wait for the next iteration of the air filtration devices drags on, the more I doubt *dear* Mallion. I simply cannot imagine a scenario where any member of The Board would be so untimely in responding to a request."

The other Board Members responded with sanctimonious nods and muted sounds of approval. Playing off their response, Cross continued.

"Indeed, I am starting to believe we need to appoint a replacement; I have approached The Director about this, of course, but he has told me to be patient, to give Mallion time."

The others once again nodded in agreement, but while Corwin

McKenzie showed all outward signs of being on the same page, his next words were not quite aligned with the sentiment of what Cross was saying.

"Too true, Tarissa. And yet, The Director may have a point; do you not remember the panic on the night that old Ancel died, that night when we had to figure out a way to fix the fact that our Head Knower had died at the age of ninety-eight, two years earlier than should have been possible?"

Cross shrugged.

"Of course I remember, Corwin. What I remember is we found a solution, the way that The Board always finds a solution. The public believed the lies Mallion constructed about Ancel's birthdate and birthplace, and The Bubble Society continued on its way."

"Too true, too true."

McKenzie said nothing more, but doubt lingered in his eyes; what he remembered about that night was how close they had come to disaster. He had no wish to repeat the exercise with a far younger sentient being; it would be exceptionally difficult to explain the situation to the citizuns of The Bubble Society if Head Knower Mallion suddenly disappeared.

For while she did not say it, that was what Tarissa Cross was suggesting, that they dispose of Head Knower Mallion. There was no other way; how could they tell the citizuns of Kingston that the most Knowledgeable sentient being on the planet Shurtain had not been Knowledgeable enough to continue in his current role as Head Knower? It was impossible, which made the Head Knower a lifetime appointment, whether or not that was explicitly acknowledged.

But while Corwin McKenzie realized this, he wondered whether Tarissa Cross saw it the same way, or if she had become so enamored of her power that she believed Mallion was just another disposable piece, a cog in the machine. Nor was he the only one in the circle with such concerns; Nessie Hunter chimed in next.

"I understand your frustration, Tarissa; it is poor form for any sentient being to make a member of The Board wait on anything, but that is not our only route to progress; others are pushing forward with different aspects of our plan."

The group turned to Hunter, who continued to speak, her big brown eyes shimmering.

"We know that all that can be done is being done. Board Members Johnson, Garcia, and Montenegro have the Halls of Parliament firmly in hand, ensuring that we can pass any laws we see fit while maintaining our status as a Democracy. Board Member Klaus, with the assistance of Board Member Mwangi, has effectively taken control of the City Watch and the Capitol Guard; acting through their commanders, of course."

"And as to replacing Head Knower Mallion; wasn't it you, Tarissa, who instructed Board Member Delverta to go around the Head Knower, to ensure that the Knowers are working as hard as they can without any interference from Mallion?"

Cross shrugged, a frown on her face.

"It was, but I had hoped for faster results on that front."

Hunter grinned, her smile ironic.

"Faster than a day? You gave the task to Yvonne yesterday, did you not?"

Once again, Cross shrugged.

"I understand your impatience - we in this circle are certainly familiar with the frustrations of waiting on less competent sentient beings to accomplish tasks we could easily handle ourselves - yet this is what it is to lead. You're doing a wonderful job, Viceroy, and nobody could doubt it."

Cross glowed at Hunter's use of her title; McKenzie and Townsend nodded in agreement, encouraging this response.

"I only wish I still had Board Member Fernandez at my disposal; I should make good use of his abilities. Yet The Director took charge of Fernandez - without a word of explanation, I might add - and who am I to question The Director?"

For the first time since the Board Members had arrived for their meeting, an air of disquiet tinged the atmosphere. Hunter and Townsend exchanged uneasy glances; McKenzie frowned, looking at Viceroy Cross, then glancing up, as if to check whether any spirits of the air were hovering above him, listening, before he spoke.

"Yes, well. I am certain that The Director had sound reasons for requesting the services of Board Member Fernandez. He is an exceptionally capable individual, after all."

"The Director would tell you he has sound reasons for everything, including for why he has not seen fit to leave The Retreat since The Advent. Yet it seems to me that I am always the one left to carry out the plans."

Hunter and Townsend's eyebrows rose in alarm. McKenzie had a different reaction, his eyes flickering away from Cross to the emptied vial of "tea" that she had set on the table next to her; as he suspected, there was a special label on the empty vial, indicating it was laced with alcohol. McKenzie glanced back at Cross and noted the glaze in her eyes; he wondered how many cocktails she had consumed on her way in.

"Don't get me wrong; I have learned a tremendous amount from The Director over the years. His grasp of Knowledge is no doubt impressive, but as the years have passed, I have come to believe that the rest of The Board possesses a similar connection with Knowledge, an intuitive grasp of everything in the world that allows us to Know exactly how to navigate life on Shurtain, how to control our destinies."

Townsend and Hunter's mouths were now slightly open, their eyes darting around the way that McKenzie's had earlier, searching for invisible specters that might be listening in on their conversation.

"The Director played a role once, I do not deny that, but his time has passed; Kingston is ready for new leadership, a new vision. The Director is out of touch; he has been cooped up in The Retreat for too long. He has no understanding of what the people want, what the people need; for instance, do you imagine, for a moment, that he could have dreamed up tonight's event on the spot the way I did?"

Nessie Hunter and Gina Townsend exchanged a look of genuine alarm at this; for his part, Corwin McKenzie seemed to have become extremely interested in a passing cloud.

Unfortunately for them, Cross had paused her monologue; she was waiting for acknowledgement, and as the silence stretched on, the awkwardness demanded that one of the others speak up.

Townsend took the plunge.

"You mean the Celebration of Knowledge you planned as an attempt to mollify the population's outrage at the passage of Resolution 4451?"

Cross raised an eyebrow.

"Of course. What other event would I have referred to?"

Townsend nodded slowly.

"Well then, I ask you again, would The Director have had the Knowledge to dream up such an answer on the spot? Does he understand the sentient beings of Kingston well enough to find such a fantastic way, not only to mollify the population's anger about Resolution 4451, but to get them genuinely excited about the opportunity to work another half-an-hour in devotion to Knowledge? Wasn't it me who thought of the idea of a party? After all, if the people want to have a drink, let them have a drink! Let them have two, and while they're at it, let them eat cake!"

Townsend continued to nod, but her expression was still skeptical.

"It was an inspired response, no doubt. But - and forgive me if I am mistaken - wasn't Resolution 4451 your idea in the first place?"

Cross frowned slightly, looking up and to the left as she searched for the memory.

"No, not really. It was Head Knower Mallion's idea; he was the one who pointed out that he lacked the workforce hours to accomplish all of our goals, I merely found a way to rectify that. And it was Board Members Johnson, Garcia, and Montenegro, in their roles as the Speakers and the Moderator of the Halls of Parliament, who passed the law. I didn't have much to do with it."

McKenzie was now staring at Cross in frank disbelief; Townsend and Hunter exchanged another nervous glance. It was Hunter who finally broke the silence.

"Well, to your point, Tarissa, tonight's event should be truly spectacular. And if you will excuse me, I should rest for a few hours, so that I am prepared to execute my role tonight."

The others made noises of agreement as they stood; Tarissa Cross nodded and smiled, allowing her subordinates to leave her alone on the balcony, her tiny teacup pinched between her fingers as she gazed out over the city she would control one day.

—

"I can't believe this is real."

Shannon was pressed up against a window of their limousine, her eyes craned skyward as they passed the billboards that had been erected along Central Boulevard. She glanced back over to Anna and Thea, who sat across from her in the limousine, their reactions more demure.

"C'mon! You two have to see this! It's aaaamazing."

Anna and Thea exchanged a glance; Thea giggled.

"We already saw it Shan; the billboards have been up all day."

"I knoooow, but now they have spotlights on them! Spotlights on us!"

It was true; plastered on billboards across Kingston were twenty-foot images of Shannon, Anna, and Thea, dressed to the nines in the outfits they had worn for The Declaration of War. It was an exciting moment for them all; they had been pushed into the spotlight as the main attraction at tonight's Celebration of Knowledge.

For Shannon, it was her wildest dream brought to life, and even Anna and Thea could not deny that they were enjoying all of the attention; their appearance at Kingston's Declaration of War had created a certain level of celebrity for the young women, which only grew with their appearance on *Rise and Shine Kingston!*

And tonight, they would be center-stage.

—

It had all started that morning, when two members of the City Watch had marched into their lecture hall at the Academy of Knowledge to request that Anna Lindberg, Thea Lindberg, and Shannon Quinn all leave the school with them immediately; they were needed on urgent Guvernment business. All three complied with the request without hesitation, though the twins harbored a slight sense of unease as they made their way back to the main entrance of the Academy of Knowledge. It was hard not to, with the rising sense of unease surrounding anything and everything related to the Kingston Guvernment.

This unease had started with the increased presence of the City Watch in the city streets, which had remained a constant in the weeks since Knower Ludquist had been awarded the inaugural Elevation Upgrade Prize, but it was the recent passage of another slew of Guvernment Resolutions that had truly stoked the fire.

The feeling had been amplified today, for today was the first work day since the Halls of Parliament had passed Resolution 4451, the first time that they had been required to report another half-hour earlier to the Academy of Knowledge. And it had not only been the students; it was also the first day that the Knowers who taught classes at the Academy of Knowledge were forced to report at that hour, and they had decided to report, not to their classrooms, but to the President of the Academy, demanding that they either receive richer compensation or have the work schedule rolled back.

Unfortunately, the President of the Academy had no power to do either of these things - she had been ordered to report to work half-an-hour earlier as well, the same as everyone else - so while the Knowers who served as professors argued their case to the Knower who served as President, the aspiring Knowers on the campus crowded around their three fellows who might have some insight into the Guvernment's motivations, the three aspiring Knowers who had been part of The Declaration of War, and who had been appearing on their holographic screens as part of *Rise and Shine Kingston!* each morning since then.

Anna, Thea, and Shannon had no more insight into what was driving these changes than any of their peers - all they could say was that there was something strange about the morning show they were now part of - but that did not stop Shannon from telling a very different story.

"You don't have to worry, it won't last forever," she had announced to the crowd gathered around them in the campus courtyard. "They're only increasing the work hours temporarily, because they Know they are near the end of the window when they could still find Tesla. As soon as we find her - and Knowledge Knows that ought to be soon - then all of these Resolutions will be dropped, and we'll get back to living our lives."

Anna and Thea had exchanged a wary glance at this - both were aware that, unless someone had pulled Shannon aside to disclose some secret Knowledge to her, their friend was making this up out of thin air - and they did not like to think what that might mean if someone from the Guvernment found out.

So it was with some trepidation that Anna and Thea followed the Guvernment Officials out of the lecture hall. They let Shannon, who spoke animatedly to the Guvernment Officials as they exited the building, take the lead; she was quite obviously taking the opportunity to see how her flirting skills were enhanced by her newfound celebrity, and the Lindberg twins saw no reason to distract her.

As it was, the two Guvernment Officials were too old, too single-minded, to be drawn in by the superficial young woman's nonsense, but that was hardly a tragedy; as the girls were about to learn, a long list of suitors in their own age group would soon have the three of them fixed in their sights.

Tarissa Cross would see to that.

It had been Cross who was waiting for them when they arrived at The

New Capitol, Cross who had ordered Board Member Townsend to deliver Anna, Thea, and Shannon to makeup and wardrobe, Cross who had arrived in the dressing area a quarter of an hour later to bring the younger women up to speed.

"It has come to my attention that, due to misperceptions of Kingston's citizunry, a wave of discontentment has swept through The Bubble Society in response to the increase in work hours."

Anna opened her mouth to answer, but Cross did not wait for a response; instead, the Viceroy of The Board sighed dramatically before continuing.

"If only our Knowers would have been more efficient during their work hours, there would have been no need for such measures; unfortunately, there is a need, and Knowledge Knows that we can't cut back on hours with our need for an upgraded air filtration system so dire."

"So, to appease the citizunry, I have taken it upon myself to plan a city-wide celebration of Knowledge. All of the public houses and cantinas will be open past curfew, with entertainment set up all around the city."

"Now, I was going to have our dear friend Derek headline the events, but he pointed out that Tesla's former lover should be at home, out of sorts and forlorn, and once he did, I realized I had always Known that he should not be the headliner; after all, handsome as he is, he's still a man, and men are nowhere near as likely to draw a crowd as us women."

And so it was that, a few hours later, the three young women found themselves in a limousine, dressed to the nines, passing twenty-foot billboards with the three of them plastered across them.

The scene was no less magnificent when they arrived at Kingston Plaza, the square that housed Bailey's Bar and so many other establishments. The Plaza was even more decked out than usual tonight; Tarissa Cross's team had spared no expense, rolling out the red-carpet treatment. The event had been widely publicized throughout the day on the Guvernment Media App, and it showed in the turnout; as Shannon stepped out of the limousine onto the red carpet, she gasped at the sea of sentient beings waiting for their arrival, reveled in the flashbulbs of cameras embedded in the Bubble Suits going off all around her. She nearly stumbled getting out of the car in her high-heeled shoes, but caught herself, took a deep breath, and stepped onto the red carpet and into her destiny, smiling and waving in all directions as she made her way into Kingston Plaza.

Anna and Tesla followed her out. Even with their suspicions, the twins, both clad in black dresses and heels, could not help but be swept up in the moment as they stepped onto the red carpet; the cheers and excitement of the crowd around them were infectious.

Thirty minutes and two drinks later, it was hard to think about anything but the music and the young men trying to dance with them; worries about

Tarissa Cross and the Guvernment were the furthest thing from their mind.

Mo Brickson did not share this sentiment; he frowned as he wandered into Kingston Plaza behind Neville and Leonard, and it was not until Neville turned around to ask why Mo was not responding to them that Mo realized he had been ignoring the group chat on his holographic monitor.

It made sense - in the weeks since his assignment to Guvernment Surveillance work, Mo had become practiced at looking past his holographic monitor, at seeing nothing regardless of what image was projected in front of him - so it was no wonder that he could so effectively zone out the Guvernment Messaging App now. Even after Neville asked the question, Mo did not bother to look at his screen.

"I got a better question; why don't you two speak out loud so I can hear you?"

Neville and Leonard shared a quick glance; they felt for their friend, aware that Mo was required to work close to a 10-hour day, as he had to be in his seat before the Knowers he surveilled arrived at work, and he had to stay there until the last Knower had departed. It seemed unavoidable that Mo's mood would become steadily more downcast.b

But at the same time, Mo was starting to become a downer; Neville and Leonard were not happy about the extended work hours, either, but they had been excited about the news of the Celebration of Knowledge, and a chance to blow off some steam. Mo, however, had maintained an outlook that seemed to have become perpetually dour, warning his friends that they better watch for the other shoe to drop before they trusted the intentions behind this Celebration. Privately, Neville and Leonard agreed Mo might be turning into a conspiracy theorist, a revolutionist, and they did not see what good could come of that; much as Neville and Leonard loved their friend, they feared what that could mean, both for Mo, and for those who had heard him speak this way and had not turned him in.

Given their current moods, the three friends quickly separated, Neville and Leonard breaking apart to spend time with some of their old friends from Kingston High. For his part, Mo wandered through the mob, taking in the scene.

In days past, Mo Brickson would have been the first to order up a drink, but he was not interested in that tonight. Truth be told, he was not sure exactly what he was interested in anymore, but while he could not give a name to the lurking entity that had so captured his focus, he had an odd feeling that he would recognize what he was looking for when he saw it.

As he finished that thought, Mo spotted a young woman sitting off at the edge of the crowd, one leg crossed over the other, her foot tapping in time to the music, but in a fatigued sort of way. He noticed there was no drink at her side; only a vial of mineral water, half-empty. Without truly understanding why, but somehow certain this was why he had come here tonight, Mo approached the young woman.

She looked up when he was a few feet from her; obviously exhausted, she seemed not to have noticed his approach. She was very pretty; her blond hair cut short, her green eyes brilliant even through the haze of tiredness.

"Mind if I sit," asked Mo, indicating an empty seat next to her.

The young woman grinned.

"Not at all. I'm Aubrey, what's your name?"

"Mo."

"Well, it's nice to meet you, Mo. I'm sorry I didn't get up to greet you; all my friends wanted to be here tonight, and they dragged me along, but I'm too tired to do anything but sit. It's been a long couple of weeks."

Mo nodded, his expression empathetic.

"I hear ya. They reassigned me from the Department of Infrastructure to the Department of Surveillance, and I can hardly stomach it. Didn't ask for this garbage, sitting around all day, watching the Knowers at work."

Mo looked back at Aubrey, expecting some sign of agreement; instead, he found that the green-eyed blond had a sort of smirk on her face.

"What? Ya wanna trade places with me? Where they got you working?"

Aubrey's smirk shifted to a smile.

"I would *love* to trade places with you. I would have loved to trade places with you, regardless of what you do, from the day I received my work assignment from the Guvernment."

Mo started to ask what she did, but Aubrey beat him to it.

"I work at the front desk of The Villa. And lately, things there have gone from bad to worse."

BOOK 4, CHAPTER 17

Tesla sat by herself on the overlook, perched on a boulder and gazing down at Trepani.

She had left Coreen's house before dawn, assuring her training partner, the closest thing she had had to a friend in years, that she was simply ready to test her body on her own.

It was not a lie, exactly, but it was a half-truth at best.

The truth was that Tesla had barely slept last night.

The truth was that being in the same house as Coreen and her family was too much to handle when Tesla felt so torn apart inside.

The Acadians had not decided to push the action, but left unsaid was the fact that they were merely waiting for the right moment to destroy The Bubble Society. To wipe everyone Tesla had ever known off the face of Shurtain.

It was painful to think of her family; it was nearly as painful to think of Anna, Thea, and Shannon. No matter how far Tesla had drifted from her childhood friends, she still cared about them; she did not envision them retaining their friendship through old age, but even so, she wanted them to have a chance to live their lives, or whatever lives The Bubble Society would have afforded them.

She had wanted to escape, yes.

But she had never wanted to bring destruction down on her home.

And from where she sat, she could see the mechanism of that destruction gathering; at least two hundred men had passed through the streets of Trepani in the time she had sat perched on her outlook that morning. A good half of them were massed in the western bowl of the valley, where they were preparing to make the march down to Turquoise Lake.

That was not the only change; Tesla was up on a ridge north of Grand Lake, with a view that allowed her to see Trepani in its entirety - the eastern part of the city was to her left, the western to her right, the Tower of Trepani directly in front of her - and everywhere she looked, there was more activity than normal, masses of sentient beings moving through the streets with an unusual amount of urgency for the early morning hours.

Tesla could hardly believe the irony of her circumstances; she was no Coreen, but she was physically stronger than she had ever been, and she had become competent enough with the pistol strapped to her thigh to hit any target close enough to pose a physical threat, but she felt more helpless than she could remember.

As the thought passed through her mind, her gaze shifted to the Tower of Trepani, the place where Gavin and his great-uncle were being held. The rest of the Acadians might have put enough time and space between themselves and Kingston to become indifferent to those they had once called kin, but Gavin would understand how she felt; as she sat there, thinking about her family being caught up in an armed assault, or buried beneath the rubble in an artillery attack, she finally understood what had driven Gavin to try to return to Trepani. It was the prospect of heart-wrenching finality, the desperate desire to get one last look before someone disappeared forever, pulled beyond the senses and into the beyond.

"Fancy finding you here."

Tesla jumped; she had not heard anyone, or anything, approaching. When she turned, and found that it was Santino, she relaxed, though she cursed herself for her lack of awareness.

"I could say the same to you. Why aren't you down in the valley? I would have thought you would be with your cousins."

Tesla had good reason for the assumption; she had passed Nately's Public House on her way back to Coreen's the previous night, and she had seen Santino there with Bruno and Paulo. True, Santino had been on a different part of the porch, speaking quietly to a young woman while his cousins reveled with a pack of rowdy young men, but he had still been there.

Santino grinned.

"You thought wrong. I don't subscribe to the consensus regarding our possibilities; I think someone needs to come up with an alternative."

"Why?"

"Because if history tells us anything, armed military engagement almost never goes the way that either side envisions it. It's impossible to account for every repercussion of a small action, much less a mobilization of this magnitude."

He shook his head.

"Even if we took the simplest course - or what appears to be the simplest course - and wiped The Bubble Society off the map, there would be fallout. I'm not sure what that fallout would be, but I don't believe it would be good for our collective conscience as a people to wipe out an entire city; not when so many of the people are just there, living their lives without a bit of bad intent in their hearts."

Santino shook his head.

"The citizuns of The Bubble Society did not choose their circumstances; they did not choose to live in a constant manipulation. They believed the lies, yes, believed the propaganda.... but they did not create it."

Santino shifted his eyes away from the growing mass in the valley; he was surprised to find Tesla smiling at him.

"As it happens, I agree. But what I really meant is, why do you believe that? You live with your cousins; why aren't you down there with them? You talk about rowdy young men; why aren't you one of them?"

Santino laughed.

"Gavin asked me a similar question once, the first time I met him."

He shook his head before continuing.

"Did you notice that Coreen and Ollie didn't volunteer themselves for this?"

Tesla shrugged.

"They have a daughter. You don't."

"That didn't stop them both going after Gavin."

Tesla blinked; she had not considered that.

"I think, to answer your original question, that I'm not down there because I try to take the time to see the world through more lenses than others. I actively swap them out, take the time to look at the world in different colors, to see how it feels from that perspective; it's a technique I adopted from my grandfather. Coreen picked it up as well, and my grandmother is a master practitioner."

"In any case, looking at the world in this way leads a sentient being to the conclusion that there are always more possibilities than we first appreciate. There is always another way. You also start to realize that even the person with the wildest tale, the craziest story... well, that person probably had a reason to believe it."

Santino paused; Tesla watched in silence as the young man shifted his gaze to where Tesla had been looking when he initially approached her.

Towards the Tower of Trepani.

Santino changed topics abruptly.

"Coreen has told me some interesting stories about you; stories that you told her. About how you acquired a Spike, for instance."

Tesla's eyes narrowed.

"What are you saying?"

"I think I'm saying exactly what you're thinking."

Santino smiled, flashing his dazzling white teeth from behind his freshly sculpted beard.

"Any chance you'd be interested in an adventure?"

BOOK 4, CHAPTER 18

Gavin lay flat on his back, staring at the ceiling, unable to sleep.

It was intolerable; in Kingston, he could have taken any number of compounds that would force him into an unconscious state, but he had nothing like that available to him now, when it seemed this night would never end.

To add to his irritation, Gavin could hear the deep sounds of his great-uncle's breathing as the old man slept easily in the next cell, completely unbothered by their imprisonment in the Tower of Trepani.

It was more than Gavin could stomach; the old man could talk all he wanted about how things were apt to change sooner than later, but those were just words. After everything Clarence had said, the two of them had wound up imprisoned in this stone tower, a place that almost made Gavin long for his days in solitary confinement as a Ward. Gavin had taken comfort in his great-uncle's words ahead of the Acadian Summit, but his confidence in the old man had proved ill-founded; as they had sat imprisoned in Grand Tower this past week, Gavin had concluded that the reason that Clarence had not been - and still was not - more concerned about their situation was simple: he was stark raving mad.

Even after they had been dumped in this place, the only thing Clarence had told Gavin, during the one moment he shifted his attention away from his meditations to acknowledge the younger man, was that nothing had changed about their journey since their talk on Jerry and Darlene's porch, that this was merely a way-station on their path, another proof that life on Shurtain often unfolded in unexpected ways.

The conversation had occurred when they were both already in their cells, which might have been a good thing; were it not for the walls between them, Gavin would have liked to hit his great-uncle and see if he could knock some sense into the man.

If he had imagined what his friends back in Kingston would have thought of him wanting to smack sense into anyone, Gavin might have laughed, but his bandwidth was too limited to see the humor in anything at present; he just wanted to get out of his cell, out of this tower. He was tired of his mind racing, tired of the sleepless nights; after all the training he had done, his body was desperate to get out and move.

It was too much to tolerate.

He was so preoccupied with his troubles that he did not hear the hook when it caught around one of the bars in his window.

—

Tesla tested the rope twice before starting up the last stretch of the tower; it was the shortest leg of her journey, but it would also be the most difficult.

The Tower of Trepani had ledges on top of each window on its first five levels, positioned to provide some shade from the sun. When Santino's balance had proven shaky as he attempted to stand on the narrow space above the first window, Tesla had snorted derisively and told him to get out of her way.

Perching like a ballerina on a balance beam, Tesla had broken from their loosely formed plan, telling Santino to play lookout; he might not live for this, but *she* did. She would handle it.

And then she was moving, taking three hard strides and jumping up, catching a crevice in the tower's facade with her left hand, scrabbling for another hold, catching a foot, securing her right hand in a cranny, reaching for a ledge on the second story…

Santino watched with a slight sense of disbelief; Coreen had raved about Tesla's progress on more than one occasion during their planning sessions over the past week, but he had never imagined anything quite like this.

Then again, perhaps he should not be surprised; after their planning sessions, he had no doubt that Tesla would apply her overwhelming intensity to any obstacle placed in her way. He did not necessarily care for that intensity - they had only been planning for a handful of days, and it was already wearing on him - but there was no question that she was an ideal accomplice for the night's mission.

Embracing his new role as lookout, Santino glanced up and down the street as Tesla gathered herself on the ledge over a fifth-story window. It was the dead of night; Shylan and Aphrodite were mere crescents, and there were no streetlights in Trepani. Even so, an-ill timed glance out the wrong window, an insomniac in need of a nighttime stroll…

Santino glanced up, and saw Tesla extracting her grappling hook from her waist; as they had been told, the burnished bronze facade that wrapped the top level of the tower would be far more difficult to climb than the other portions of the tower.

This was far from an insurmountable obstacle, however. In fact, it was one of the reasons that Eleanor had suggested, in the many discussions that took place ahead of the Acadian Summit, that Gavin and Clarence be imprisoned in the Tower of Trepani, rather than out on Jerry and Darlene's property, if the speakers at the Summit did decide on imprisoning them.

Tesla did not look back down; once she had verified the rope was secure, she braced herself on the wall and started to climb, pulling hand over hand, until she could reach the bars on Gavin's window.

—

Gavin's heart stopped when he saw the hand appear.

The window was in his peripheral, which added to the eeriness of the scene; when the hand entered his field of vision, it might as well have belonged to a skeleton, shooting its bony hand out of the ground in a last effort to evade the grave, for the terror it caused him. Gavin rolled away on instinct, wondering what fresh hell Shurtain had in store for him tonight.

Then the second hand was there; a moment later, Tesla Mancini appeared, a black stocking cap over her blond locks, greasepaint on her face.

Gavin blinked.

Shook his head in disbelief.

Yet even as Gavin tried to convince himself that what he was seeing was real, Tesla was planting her left foot on the windowsill, then grabbing something from a pouch on her hip with her right hand as she slipped her left arm through the bars and laced it back out, hooking herself to the bar by the crook of her elbow. By then, Tesla had a vial in her right hand; she gave it a hard shake, and the solution within started to foam.

Tesla passed the vial to her left hand, pulled the cork out with her right, and then swapped the two items so the vial was back in her right hand. Reaching out, she poured some of the solution at the base of the furthest bar from her; with an audible hiss, the bar began to smoke, dissolving away to nothing.

For the first time, Tesla turned her attention to Gavin.

"Come grab the bar."

Her whisper was so quiet that Gavin half-thought he was dreaming it, but when he crossed his cell, and gripped the bar that Tesla was working on, it felt solid enough. Without a word, Tesla shifted the vial to her left hand, pulled a small brush from her hip pouch, and dipped it in the solution before carefully applying it to the top of the bar.

"There. Give it a pull, but be sure not to drop it; there's a guard on duty down below."

Gavin nodded, and pulled on the bar; the last intact bit of metal twisted apart when he did, and the rod came free in his hand.

"Good. Now set that down and grab the next one."

Four bars later, Tesla had enough space to drop into the cell. When she did, Gavin stood there blinking, hardly able to believe what was happening. It did not help that, beneath the greasepaint and slight sheen of perspiration, Tesla smelled *incredible*, some flowery aroma that he could not quite describe in mere words.

"What…what are you doing here?"

She smiled at him then, the same smile she had used when they had met in Kingston Park all that time ago.

"I'm breaking you out, what do you think?" She whispered. "But we're not done yet; you're a bonus. What we really need is your great-uncle; he's the only one who has any idea where we're going."

—

Gavin felt as if he were in a dream as he watched Tesla work.

As she applied more of her solution to the deadbolts holding Gavin's cell door in place, he took stock of all the equipment Tesla carried; she was dressed in all black, had a pistol strapped to her belt at the small of her back, and a fixed-blade knife holstered on her left hip. She had also wrapped two coils of rope around her torso in addition to the length attached to her grappling hook, which she had wound up and clipped to her belt after entering the cell.

But, hard as all this was to believe, Gavin had one overriding thought in his mind, confirmed when his cell door swung open.

Tesla knew what she was doing.

—

The four of them stood at an overlook in eastern Trepani, looking back at what they could see of the city in the little moonlight present on this night, the first hints of dawn still waiting to appear.

They had said little during their escape. Minutes after she stepped through Gavin's cell door, Tesla had the door to Clarence's cell opened; a moment later, they were crossing back to Gavin's cell, the old man's eyes alert and ready.

The two men watched in silence as Tesla shrugged off the two huge coils of rope wrapped around her torso; once she had them off, she knotted them together, then fed the two ends around either side of the last bar remaining in Gavin's cell window.

For a moment, Gavin wondered why she was doing this, but then he understood; the missing bars and the destroyed locks were dead giveaways, but they were not as obvious as a rope hanging down the side of the Tower of Trepani, which would have been visible to any sentient being passing by. With both ends of the rope reaching the ground, they could pull it down after them once they descended.

There had been no alarm raised. There was no pursuit to throw off.

That would not last forever, however; at best, they had a few hours. When the guards brought Gavin and Clarence their morning meal, it would not be hard to figure out what had happened.

"Well, no sense lingering. We've got a long journey ahead."

Tesla, Gavin, and Santino gave slight nods of agreement at Clarence's words. Then, as the burn of the coming dawn appeared on the horizon, they turned east, and walked into the rising sun.

Book 5

BOOK 5, CHAPTER 1

Clarence Barnett stood on the hilltop, basking in the glow of the early-morning sunlight, a broad smile on his face. It was a different journey - and it would take a different path - but he could not help remembering the morning when he had started that first voyage to Elysia, some sixty years ago, with two companions at his side.

Damned if life had not seemed real back then.

What was it now?

He shook his head, reflecting on all the things he had seen in his years on Shurtain.

Of how many strong people, how many wise people, how many good people had been lost along the way.

Of how the story kept going despite all that.

And how there was, quite obviously, some sort of story playing out.

Whether or not any of it was real.

—

Real or not, the sky above them was clear, the morning air crisp; they had a long road ahead of them, but they could not have asked for a better day to start.

The hilltop was the first rest they had permitted themselves since the outskirts of Trepani, where they had paused to turn and take a last look at the city, still and peaceful under the crescent moons.

But there had not been time to linger; they needed to put distance between themselves and the city before their absence was discovered.

The way was dark, but the eastern path out of Trepani was easy to follow, the bit of moonlight enough for them to make their way. Santino and Clarence walked at the head of the group, moving in silence, while Tesla and Gavin trailed behind, Tesla speaking in a low tone as she filled Gavin in on everything that happened during the week that he had been held in the Tower of Trepani.

Even at the hilltop, they did not rest for long; the sun was up by then, which meant that they could be spotted from a distance. All agreed that their absence would have been noted by then, and that there would be a pursuit, or at the very least, messengers sent to Giota, Kirfi, and Larissa to warn the other Acadian cities of their escape.

This was why Clarence meant to have them off the beaten path sooner than later; the main trail was convenient, no doubt, but it was also obvious, and he wanted nothing to do with it.

The others had been unsure on this point - Santino had pointed out that he was not aware of another route from Trepani to Kirfi, or Kirfi to Larissa - but Clarence had only laughed, and told Santino not to worry.

According to him, there were plenty of other ways to reach Larissa, and the shores of the Amphitrite Ocean.

—

"I understand why we need to get to the Amphitrite, but do we really need to go through Larissa? I can't imagine we're going to get much of a welcome there."

Clarence shrugged at Santino's question.

"Better Larissa than Giota; I can't say many things for certain, but regardless of how your Uncle Marcus greets us, I can guarantee it will be a more hospitable welcome than anything we could expect from Gwynivere Holt."

Santino started to ask a follow-up, but Clarence anticipated the question.

"Why do we need to go to any city? Well, you said you understand why we need to reach the Amphitrite; how do you propose we traverse the Amphitrite, if not by ship?"

When Santino offered no answer, Clarence continued.

"Short of building a vessel ourselves, we have to acquire one, and that means risking one of Acadia's port cities. With the rest of the continent gone to ruin, that means Giota or Larissa."

Santino nodded, a slight frown on his face.

"You thought of all this since we freed you?"

Clarence turned to look at Santino then, a half-grin on his wrinkled face, mischief in the old eyes.

"Hardly. I'd counted on this coming for a long time. The details are murky, but I've had a general sense of what would come next for some time, and prepared accordingly."

"How long, exactly?

Clarence grinned.

"Oh, sixty years, or near enough that it makes no difference. Ever since a journey I took with your grandfather… and one other. It's not that I can tell the future, or stop it coming… and the timing and details evade me, so you can hardly call me a prophet, but ever since Salomon, Theodore, and I made our first journey to Elysia, I've had a feel for what's coming, in the same way you can feel an incoming storm, or an approaching wave; it's all in the vibrations. It hasn't led me wrong so far… for better or for worse."

—

For Gavin, the whole experience had an eerie sense of unreality.

From the moment that Tesla's hand had appeared outside his cell window, his participation in his own story had been tinged with a sense of disbelief; it was too fantastic to believe.

But here he was, hours later, and it seemed that this was no dream; this was his life, and it had once again turned into an adventure. He thought that Santino and Tesla might have consulted him on the plan, but then again, he had little room to complain; until a few hours ago, the only thing in Gavin's future had been his cell.

And now…

Now they were making their way through the Cadillac Mountains, intent on reaching the Amphitrite Ocean and sailing away from Acadia itself, intent on leaving the continent, that, until a season ago, Gavin had believed was the only place on Shurtain with a city capable of sustaining life.

Yet if Clarence was to be believed, the planet Shurtain was teeming with life; if he was to be believed, sentient beings were not the only creatures on Shurtain capable of tapping into consciousness.

Santino believed it. So did Tesla; it was why she was walking beside him now. Gavin had his doubts, but even so, he preferred being outside to being imprisoned, and it was not as if he could go back to his old life in Kingston.

More importantly, Gavin was aware, on some level, that he would have followed Tesla just about anywhere. He glanced at her as the thought crossed his mind, losing track of her words as he took in the depths of her hazel eyes, which buzzed with energy despite their sleepless night. Walking next to her, without the burdens he had carried on their way to Trepani, was like something out of a dream, an all-consuming experience, pushing memories of the past and thoughts of the future into nothingness, leaving only the present, this moment with Tesla. Her intense focus had faded once they cleared Trepani's outskirts; it was replaced by a sort of giddy euphoria, the afterglow of her success blending with her excitement at what would come next.

"I still don't really understand the plan - I don't think I will until we get to Elysia, and see it for myself - but I have to do something; I can't just sit back and let my family be wiped out. So when Santino came with a plan, and it made some sort of sense, I thought it was worth rolling the dice."

Gavin nodded.

"But what did he tell you, exactly? I'm still not understanding most of this. How are we going to save the people in Kingston? We're going the wrong direction."

Tesla shrugged.

"It's hard to say right now, but Santino thinks - and I agree - that we need a different way of looking at things. That much was clear at the Acadian Summit; we aren't going to overturn public sentiment without a new argument, one that reorients our collective thinking. Santino thinks - and his uncle, grandmother, and Clarence all agree - that we might find that perspective in Elysia."

"Elysia?"

Tesla looked at him, surprise on her face, her smile holding back a laugh.

"Didn't you ever learn anything about Shurtain's geography, Gavin?"

He laughed at that; when he did, Tesla's restraint broke, and she joined in.

"Where would I have learned about Shurtain's geography?" Gavin asked, running a hand through his mop of blond hair, which had grown unruly during his week in the cell. "You went to Kingston High, just like me; all the Knowers taught us there was that other continents exist on Shurtain. The Dead Continents, they called them; nobody ever mentioned that any of them had names. The Knowers just taught us that they were grim, inhospitable places, and that any sentient beings who had once inhabited them died shortly after The Advent."

Gavin smiled at Tesla, ran his hand through his hair again.

"I'm not you, remember? I might have thought something felt off during my years in The Bubble Society, but I just thought that meant something was wrong with me; it says on page one of *The Manual for Proper Behavior* that nobody need ever question a Knower, for they have a direct connection with Knowledge, so I never questioned whether what they taught me at Kingston High, or Kingston Elementary, was true. So the continent names are new to me, ya?"

Tesla laughed.

"Fair enough. Well, Elysia is one of six continents on Shurtain, one of the two smallest. It's actually to the southeast of Acadia, so we're hardly taking the most direct route, but when Santino and I planned this out with Eleanor and all the rest, they implored us to trust Clarence if we were able to free you and get away, and Clarence says the best way is through Larissa, not Giota."

"But why are we going to Elysia?"

For the first time, Tesla frowned.

"That's the part I don't really understand. Santino and the others say that there are different types of beings living on Elysia. *Shamans*, he called them, but he didn't give me all the details."

She glanced ahead to where Santino walked with Clarence.

"Sometimes, I think you've just gotta trust."

Gavin grinned at that, shaking his head.

"You don't agree?" Tesla asked.

Gavin shrugged.

"Oh, I do, on the whole."

Gavin hesitated, running a hand through his hair again before he finished his thought.

"It's just that, I'm not sure my great-uncle is the one I'd want to trust."

Their eyes met; Tesla did not say anything, but her expression turned his grin into a whole-hearted smile. Her eyes shifted to his hair.

"We're going to have to do something about that."

Gavin laughed; he ran a hand through his hair once again, as if he had only just realized how long it was.

"Ya, it's getting to be a lot to handle. I'll chop some of it off when we stop tonight, or ask Santino to do it."

A small smile spread across Tesla's lips; she reached up, and fingered a lock of Gavin's hair.

"I don't think so; that's going to be my job. I've got some ideas."

BOOK 5, CHAPTER 2

The rooftop deck of The Lodge at The Hot Springs was as good a place as any to watch the fallout at the Tower of Trepani.

There was no need to ask what had happened; they were already aware.

It was the reason that Marcus Cahn had lingered in Trepani.

But his work was not done yet; there was one more task for him to complete before he could turn back for Larissa.

He would be the one to deliver the message to Anton.

It was not the only way - they had some communications equipment up and running - but the signal could be sketchy in the mountains, and messages often came out garbled. In any case, this was not a time to talk over radio; Marcus wanted to see how Anton would react to the news.

Would he care?

Or would he be too focused on preparing for war to be concerned?

Neither would surprise him; having established their plan to build their defenses at Turquoise Lake, Anton had shown complete ambivalence when it came time to determine Clarence and Gavin's sentence at the Acadian Summit.

On the upside, it meant that Marcus would pass through Trepani once more on his way home. He was happy that he could look forward to that day, even if it would be just a day. On that trip home, the good-byes would be hard - none more so than the one with the granddaughter who would grow so much before he next saw her - but there was no use dwelling on that.

"It's done. I suppose I ought to get moving."

He turned to face the others who stood watching the scene with him;

Eleanor, Coreen, Ollie, and Harlan, four of five others who had known the plan. The fifth who had been in the know - Marcus's youngest sister, Mykala - was downstairs with Carly, taking advantage of a last hour with her grand-niece, before she left for Larissa with most of the others.

"You're certain you don't want me to join you?"

Harlan had raised the question on multiple occasions during their planning sessions.

"I appreciate it, but there's no need. I'm well used to traveling in Nature, and besides, Ollie will accompany me down to Turquoise Lake and back."

Ollie gave a curt nod; Marcus continued.

"In any case, it's far more important that you get back to Larissa. The news of The Bubble Society's intention to expand their domain to the east, and our response, will spread to the population sooner than later. I prefer that you deliver the message, so that you can control the tone of the narrative, and perhaps instill some semblance of calm. That's the best thing we can do for now; buy time, preach patience, so that Clarence and the rest of them have a chance to reach Elysia."

Harlan raised an eyebrow.

"You're sure this will be enough? We're putting an awful lot of faith in Santino's plan here. Shouldn't we try for some other contingencies?"

The point had been discussed during their planning sessions, but it had been set to the side; at the time, what had mattered was deciding on the best way to help Santino and Tesla.

Eleanor responded.

"It's not just Santino's plan; I never thought I would see Salomon's hand at work again, not so many years after his death, but it wasn't hard to recognize, once it appeared. I was shocked that Santino could remember Salomon telling him about the Shamans, but it seems he was meant to make this journey; after all, it was a similar journey that set all of this in motion."

Eleanor paused.

"In any case, I don't see what we can do. Our people have made their decision, and I don't see any way of changing that as things stand. This is more a hope than a plan; I can't say I truly expect them to change anything, but if there is any chance that this could write an end to everything that started all those years ago, when Salomon and Clarence went on their own journey with dear old Theodore, then I think we ought to take it."

The others glanced at Eleanor in surprise; the third member of that journey had never been forgotten, but it was rare for anyone to mention the man's former name.

Not with what he had become.

After a long silence, Harlan nodded.

"Fair enough, then. I suppose there's nothing else to say; it's time to go."

—

"Gone?"

The three men stood on the eastern ridge of the valley that held Turquoise Lake. Below them, a thousand sentient beings went through their paces; half were training, drilling in general fitness and hand-to-hand combat, while the rest erected barricades and watch towers on the ridge at the western end of the valley, taking advantage of the overwhelming high ground that Turquoise Falls provided.

Marcus nodded.

Anton did not respond at first; he just stared into the distance. Ollie kept his face blank, his eyes on the men drilling below.

It was a long time before any of them spoke.

Finally, Anton shook his head.

"Good riddance. You say they've left Trepani? Then there's no sense in bothering with it. We built our defenses to prevent anyone coming up from Kingston, but we're also in the way of anyone who would try to go down, so they won't be able to get to Kingston. As long as Clarence isn't going to meddle here, then he can go wherever he wants."

"You don't think we should try to bring them in?"

Anton shook his head.

"It would be a waste; Giota and Trepani are already under strain from the resources I'm demanding down here. And it's no mean feat to track down sentient beings when they get lost in the Wild and want to be saved; running down someone as capable as Clarence, when he doesn't want to be caught, is a whole different animal, and I'm not trying to give up anyone who is capable enough to have a shot at success in that venture. Not now, when we need to get our defenses up and running. You might have used dogs to run him down, if he hadn't gotten a head start, but I'd count on him having pulled more than a few tricks to kill that trail."

"Go ahead and put the word out. I'll send messengers to Giota - we can spare a few people - and you can inform Alabaster, and the people of Kirfi, on your way back to Larissa."

Marcus nodded.

"No arguments from me. Anything else you need?"

Anton and Marcus looked at each other for a long time. Neither acknowledged it, but both were thinking of a time, decades ago, when the last request would have been accompanied by the word *brother*; it had only seemed fitting, with the relationship Anton had developed with Salomon, and in turn, Salomon's oldest son, Marcus, who was fifteen years Anton's senior.

But those days were long past.

And there was nothing left to say.

"I've got everything I need. You ought to get going; it's still early, and you can knock out a decent chunk of your voyage before sunset."

Marcus nodded, extending a hand.

"Until then, be well."

The two men shook briefly, not quite making eye contact. As they walked away, Ollie watched Marcus look back, giving Anton a last glance, an unmistakable sadness in his green eyes as he looked at the younger man.

BOOK 5, CHAPTER 3

Aubrey Draper had always made a point of ignoring the details of her surroundings at work.

She did so, not out of mean-heartedness, but at the advice of more seasoned workers, mentors who had given the young Aubrey their two cents when she received her occupation assignment after graduating from Kingston High. Aubrey's more senior peers were generous in sharing their thoughts on how to best navigate the road in front of her, advice that was sorely needed, for in Aubrey's wildest dreams - or worst nightmares - she had never imagined she would be assigned to work at The Villa.

Even now, years later, there were days when it all felt fake, days when Aubrey sat at her station at The Villa's entrance, absentmindedly staring at her reflection on the glass-topped desk, wondering if she ought to grow her short, blond hair out or perhaps go with a different color.

It was in such moments that the thought would hit her: maybe this was just a dream she could not wake up from. Maybe there was some way, some possibility, that she could snap out of it, and wake up to find herself somewhere else, anywhere else… a place where she could live a real life.

Aubrey had become practiced at ignoring these uncomfortable moments, but her years of experience were no help today; despite all that conditioning, Aubrey Draper was not calloused enough to ignore the alarming changes taking place in front of her.

Until very recently, it had been, not simply rare, but unheard of, for a Laureate candidate to be dropped off at The Villa's entrance; it was not in the usual protocol laid out on page 97 of *The Manual for Proper Behavior*, which called for a specialized branch of the Emergency Response Team to visit Laureate candidates at their homes and to transport them to The Villa in the ERT vehicles.

That was before.

The initial break in protocol had occurred three weeks ago, when a woman arrived on The Villa's doorstep, proclaiming that she believed her husband showed signs of becoming a Laureate. The man in question stood next to the woman, staring in Aubrey's direction with a vacant expression on his face.

For her part, Aubrey looked between the two people, unsure of what to do in this unprecedented situation.

Then, before Aubrey could think of a response, the woman left, turning on her heel and striding away from The Villa - and her husband - as fast as her Bubble Suit would permit.

Still unsure of what to do - and swimming with pity for the man - Aubrey had stepped outside to get George from his post. George had called a member of the Care Staff, the Care Staff had verified that the man was a legitimate Laureate candidate, and the man had been admitted to The Villa.

Aubrey had thought that would be the end of it.

Now, one of the only things keeping her sane was her sense of humor about her naiveté on that day.

She could hardly believe it had only been three weeks ago.

So little time had passed.

And yet so much had changed.

There had been a line this morning: a line of Laureate candidates.

It had been the same all week; every morning, Aubrey arrived to find a line of candidates waiting for The Villa to open its doors.

Today, there were nine of them. Three were close to Aubrey's own age; two of them turned out to be a year younger.

It gave her the creeps.

Nor was Aubrey the only one feeling uneasy; George's usual cheerfulness was fading in the face of the ever-increasing flow of Laureate candidates, and the Care Staff, already overwhelmed before this change, was looking increasingly haggard.

There were even rumors of disappearances, of Care Staff members who had started to show signs of becoming Laureates themselves suddenly vanishing, never to be heard of again.

When it had been one, Aubrey had scoffed.

But six?

And whether or not those disturbing rumors were true, the cold, hard reality of their situation remained; The Villa could handle those arriving at the entrance now, but if the pressure increased any more, they would need to hire more staff to help manage the situation, or something was going to blow. The whispers regarding disappearances might be nothing more than a wild conspiracy dreamed up by the staff, but there was no way to dispute the existence of the line out the front door of The Villa's entrance.

Even worse, the people in line were only the tip of the iceberg; a few of the citizuns arriving at the entrance had done so without consulting anyone, but many had resorted to such measures because they had tried to follow the process laid out on page 97 of *The Manual for Proper Behavior*, only to learn of the significant delay caused by the backlog of Laureate candidates for the Emergency Response Team to assess. Word was the assessments, which the Emergency Response Team had once completed within hours of a request, now had a days-long waiting list.

Aubrey had no idea what any of it meant.

Or at least, she did not like to think about the implications of what her eyes were seeing.

—

Mo Brickson could not comprehend how his job was a job.

It had been five weeks since the Guvernment, acting through the Halls of Parliament, had passed the legislation that led to Mo's transfer from the Department of Infrastructure to the Department of Workforce Surveillance. Three weeks after that, the passage of Resolution 4451 had extended the work day even further, and Mo found himself resenting the situation more with every passing day.

It was common for the general citizunry in The Bubble Society to look down upon the laborers in the Department of Infrastructure, but that had never bothered Mo; these people, who did nothing to keep the city of Kingston up and running, could have their opinions. Mo had older brothers, a father, and uncles who all did similar work, and he had a lifetime of evidence that they were good men - or good enough - sentient beings who were trying to make their way on Shurtain, looking to raise a family, and do something worth doing with their time. Mo was armed with the experience of his own reality, so whatever *The Manual for Proper Behavior* might say, he had never seen a reason to feel the shame that The Bubble Society insisted a person in his position ought to; on the contrary, Mo had always taken a sense of pride in understanding the reality of the situation, well aware that the work he did kept Kingston up and running. Mo enjoyed fixing things, he enjoyed working hard, and he enjoyed completing the tasks that allowed his fellow citizuns to take it for granted that Kingston always had, and always would, work the way that it did today.

Mo understood that his perspective was not the norm; the default for citizuns in The Bubble Society was to dismiss anything accomplished Before Knowledge, which meant that, instead of possessing a sense of gratitude for the sacrifices previous generations had made to settle the valley, Kingston's citizuns were more inclined to criticize their ancestors for doing all that work in a way that was not environmentally friendly, to curse their forebears for failing to build Kingston using theoretical technology that the Knowers of the present had yet to master.

Mo had more appreciation for it all; he could make a rough guess, from working on repair projects, of the absurd number of hours that sentient beings had poured into making Kingston what it was. He had taken pride in carrying that flag forward, in being part of the team who continually reinvested in Kingston's infrastructure, allowing the systems that allowed the city to work to continue functioning into the future.

He did not take pride in his current work; Mo could find no sense of dignity in sitting there, observing a group of his fellow citizens as they went about their work as Knowers.

Instead, he felt dirty. And Mo had a bad feeling about what would happen to any society that devoted its resources to spying on its own, rather than trusting people to engage in work that created a beneficial end product. If you did not trust that citizuns would go out and build wholesome lives on their own - if they did not possess that basic instinct - then what sort of society did you have?

Could you compel such behavior through surveillance?

Through censorship?

Through force?

Perhaps the Knowers should have been more selective when they culled the history books at Kingston High, for even Mo was aware that, in centuries past, the ground that Kingston stood on had seen the rise and fall of three separate Empires, Empires that had once ruled over the entirety of Acadia, and even more distant parts of Shurtain. So Mo was well aware that those Empires had died on this same hill, in this same valley.

To make his situation even more frustrating, Mo had yet to gain any better understanding of what the Knowers under his observation were supposed to be doing, which meant that all the hours he spent at his desk, staring at the Knowers on his holographic monitor, were a complete waste of time. All those hours that he would have been out and about, fixing what needed to be fixed in Kingston… all of them had gone down the toilet, when an attendance monitor, or time-clock system, could have verified that the Knowers arrived and departed work at the correct times without keeping eyes on them the entire day.

But while Mo had yet to figure out what the Knowers under his observation were supposed to be doing, it did not mean he was not learning anything. One thing he could see was that, regardless of the progress they may or may not be making, the Knowers appeared increasingly exhausted, an issue that had been exacerbated by the passage of Resolution 4451.

The exhaustion was not only affecting the Knowers; the problem was even more evident in Mo's peers at the Department of Workforce Surveillance, who were required to be in their seats five minutes before the Knowers were due to arrive at their offices, and to stay five minutes after the Knowers departed. In a single day, it did not seem like much; over the course of a five-day work week, it was almost an extra hour.

Many of Mo's co-workers had reacted by throwing themselves into the party scene with increasing levels of enthusiasm, but Mo did not join them; on the one occasion he did indulge, he found himself unable to engage with his thoughts the next day, and that had pushed his new job from merely unpleasant to completely intolerable.

So Mo had abstained of late, though he was almost alone in that; the majority of his co-workers in the Department of Workforce Surveillance appeared determined to make up for the life they were giving up to the utopia by throwing themselves into the evening revels, even if it meant cutting into the hours designated for dinner and sleep.

Anything to squeeze a little more partying into the evening.

After all, what did it matter if they showed up to work hungover? All they had to do was verify that Knowers under their watch were doing some sort of work; anyone could do that through a haze of exhaustion, especially with stimulants available to inject into their Bubble Suits if they started to nod off. Mo saw the deteriorating state of his co-workers, and thought it was fortunate that all they had to do was keep the Knowers under surveillance; he could not imagine what it would be like to do any sort of problem-solving in such a state, let alone come up with the sort of novel innovation that would allow someone to capture the next iteration of the Elevation Upgrade Prize.

But then, that was not his role.

And if Mo had seen some of the Knowers under his watch hammered drunk at the bar an hour after work as he sat sober next to Neville and Leonard… well, how they did their work in such a state was their business.

"Oy! All members of the Department of Workforce Surveillance, to attention!"

The sound of the booming voice over the loudspeaker nearly caused Mo to fall out of his chair; it was the first time since he had started in the Department that they had such an announcement. Before he could see what his fellow workers were doing, the voice continued.

"You are to report to the conference room on Basement Level 1. We have received an emergency request from the top; we've got a big update on the work toward the Elevation Upgrade Prizes, and we need to bring you up to speed as quickly as possible."

—

"Head Knower Mallion, I am growing weary of your excuses. I don't want to hear an explanation; I want to see a product."

Mallion took a steadying breath as he stared at Tarissa Cross. Experience told him that he needed to hold his ground, or Cross would run roughshod over the meeting.

"I don't understand what is causing the delay, if I'm perfectly honest. I have bent over backward for you. I have re-allocated portions of the workforce to your department, I have extended the working hours, and provided the surveillance you reques…"

"I didn't request surveillance."

Cross blinked.

"Then why, pray tell, did we develop a Department of Workforce Surveillance?"

"Because you thought it would be a good idea. I never said anything about it."

Cross shook her head.

"Well, whoever came up with the idea, it clearly hasn't worked. It's been almost half a season since we introduced the surveillance, and your Knowers still haven't come up with the upgrades we need."

Of late, Gina Townsend and Corwin McKenzie had accompanied Tarissa Cross to her meetings with Mallion, but today, it was Yvonne Delverta and Reginald Klaus sitting in a corner of Cross's office, nodding sanctimoniously at her words. Mallion did not miss the significance of this; he understood that these two had been brought in to convey precisely how serious the situation was.

As if Mallion might not Know.

For her part, Cross was pacing back and forth behind her desk, occasionally glancing at the chair in the middle of the office, which Mallion had declined to take upon his arrival. This was not because Mallion did not wish to sit, but because he was aware that, at Cross's request, the front legs of that chair had been cut slightly shorter than the rear, which meant that the object of Cross's ire would both feel like a schoolchild and struggle to remain on their seat during their encounter with thc Viceroy of The Board.

So Mallion had declined Cross's overly gracious offer of a chair; he felt he had enough to contend with, and did not intend to engage in any more of Tarissa Cross's mind games than was strictly necessary.

"Frankly, I'm out of ideas. Should we come up with a new name for the project? Something jazzier, a title that conveys the urgency of the situation?"

"Operation Mach One, perhaps?" Delverta suggested.

"Or Operation Wormhole Speed?" Klaus put in. "I can't imagine a project could fail to have its timeline accelerated, with such a sobriquet."

Mallion was hard-pressed to keep his expression neutral.

Knowledge help me.

"In your estimation, how would changing the *name* of the project have any impact at all on the work that needs to be done?"

The three Board Members swapped confused expressions. Then, as one, those expressions hardened; the three of them turned their ire on Mallion, Cross speaking for the group.

"Well, *Knower* Mallion, I should think that our workforce would take on that project with an increased sense of urgency. How could they not, working on an endeavor with such a grand name?"

"You don't think the workforce feels an increased sense of urgency as it is? You don't think they realize what's going on? All around them, there are signs of preparation for war, and we've got them working longer hours than ever. Not that it's doing us any good; the number of Knowers that we've lost permanently to The Villa since Resolution 4451 has caused a *decrease* in total hours worked."

"I should think that result encouraging. With more Laureates devoted to Knowledge, it is more likely that Knowledge will meet our needs. A great reward requires a great sacrifice, wouldn't you agree?"

Mallion, who was well aware that Tarissa Cross Knew the truth of what went on at The Villa every bit as much as he did, managed to keep his expression steady, but it was an effort.

"Yes, but not in the sense you mean it. A great sacrifice in terms of time on task, of thinking of new ideas, of thoroughly testing those ideas through experiment. We are creating a novel technology, after all; the process is not as straightforward as sacrificing a virgin and having Knowledge drop the solution on our doorstep."

"So you think that we should sacrifice a virgin? Why didn't you say that earlier, it can be easily arran…"

"No, I'm telling you that nothing about this is that simple. My Knowers need time on task, time to think. The sentient brain is not a blunt instrument; it works in strange ways, needs time to recharge with proper sleep and activity, if it is to come up with fresh ideas. One of the greatest minds in the history of sentientkind was known for drifting to sleep in his chair as he worked on problems. You can't just…"

Mallion stopped; he had been on the verge of telling Cross that she could not just chain the Knowers to their desks and expect that it would not negatively impact their work, but he did not like to think what she would do with that suggestion, so he changed tact on the fly.

"What I'm saying is, you need to let the process play out. I don't understand why you think that this should be straightforward."

"Because, Knower Mallion, the people of Kingston are the pinnacle of sentient evolution, the chosen people of Knowledge, the ones who navigated the degradation in Shurtain's atmosphere. All the previous generations of sentient beings lived their lives in ignorance and squalor so that we could emerge, the end product that has finally achieved a complete understanding of the Universe, a state of total Knowledge. Why shouldn't we be able to shape our destiny?"

Mallion gazed hopelessly into Cross's eyes, so fervent in their belief, and felt the fight drain out of him; there was no convincing her, and he had no interest in spending the rest of the day arguing the point.

For all the excitement Mallion had felt at his appointment to the office of Head Knower, it had turned out to be a lousy lot; he could toe the line, and keep his office and the accompanying comforts, or he could veer off and be deemed a heretic, in which case he would be snuffed out without a second thought, taken into the bowels of some Guvernment building or another, where, if he were lucky, he would be shot in the head before his body was burned, his ashes dumped in the river.

And if he were unlucky… well, that did not bear thinking about.

"Well, Tarissa, I'll leave it to you. What do you think is the best name to speed up this process?"

BOOK 5, CHAPTER 4

As Clarence and Santino told it, Kirfi had grown nearly as large as Trepani in recent years.

Like Trepani, Kirfi sat in the bowl of a valley, one of the more hospitable places in the heights of the Cadillac Mountains, but where Trepani sat next to Grand Lake, Kirfi was a river town, built out from the banks of the Eastern Grand.

Tesla and Gavin had to take their word for it; from their vantage point in the distant mountain peaks, they could barely make out the city, even with the binoculars Santino had brought along.

The going was difficult, but that was part of the routine by now; it had been true since they crossed the Grand River on the morning of their escape, wading across the flats at a spot where the river was wide and shallow enough for them to cross without too much concern of being swept away.

No trail led to that crossing, nor was there anything obvious to mark the place, but Clarence obviously knew of it; he had not hesitated to step off the main trail at his exit, following a steep slope down through the trees, signaling for the others to follow him with a wave of his hand.

Comfortable as he had become moving around in his body, Gavin took the slope at a slower pace than his great-uncle, who picked up speed as he went, leaning into the grade of the hill, aggressively accelerating down certain stretches, launching himself off anchor points to slow his progress before leaning back into the hill; Santino and Tesla moved a bit faster, though neither of them tried anything like that.

It was one more reason for Gavin to wonder where they were going, and why they were following Clarence; he continued to ponder the question until he reached the riverbank.

Then he glanced at his great-uncle, and all traces of concern left him.

Clarence had visibly changed; back in his element, Gavin's great-uncle seemed larger, more lively. He was an altogether more imposing presence; something feral had kicked on in the depths of the old man's operating system.

Clarence noticed Gavin looking; aware of what the younger man was seeing, the older man grinned.

"It's good to be back in Nature."

—

And indeed, it seemed that once he was back in the Wild, Clarence was a far more comfortable sentient being; this extended to fully divulging his plan; or at least, the portion of the plan that would get them to Larissa.

"We'll be a good while out in the mountains, but it's a cheap price to pay, given the issues we would have passing through Kirfi. I've only just escaped confinement; I have no desire to return."

Clarence did not reference the portion of the Acadian Summit that had followed the decision to go to war; the others were already well aware that Alabaster Minteran had been among the most vocal proponents of holding Gavin and Clarence in the Tower of Trepani until after the war's conclusion.

"There's also something to be said for taking the longer route; we'll have experiences we would never encounter back on the main trail. The way we're going will deposit us out of the Cadillacs a bit to the south of Larissa; it's not taking the main trail, but it's not uncharted territory, either."

Gavin felt that the view of Kirfi, distant as it might be, was one of those experiences; sitting up in the alpine, above the tree-line, and taking in the majesty of the scene around them.

They had camped in the place the previous night, taking a break from their journey to watch the sunrise over this spot, its beams turning the gaps in the peaks around them from an inky black canvas to a tapestry of pinks and purples and oranges.

Kirfi itself was a mere smudge at the edge of their vision - without Clarence, they would not have been able to make it out - and even so, it was only because Kirfi sat where a gap in the peaks opened a window into a valley, which made it easy to zero in on the place from a distance.

The scene was all the more incredible for the challenges involved in getting there; camping in the peaks of the Cadillacs, middle of Summer or not, was a chilly experience.

Yet as the days wore on, the frigid nights seemed less of a hardship; it might be cold, but that cold was exhilarating, giving Gavin a newfound appreciation of the warmth that came with the rising sun, a gratitude he had never experienced during his years living in the comfort of his climate-controlled Bubble Suit. His first journey from Kingston to Trepani had been spectacular, but this was something different, something rawer, infinitely more primal, and that was to say nothing of the views; there was a certain unreality to being up this high, to looking down on the peaks of lower mountains, to traversing Shurtain at altitudes dominated by mountain goats and marmots.

It was also true that the nights no longer felt so cold. As they stood to continue on their way, Tesla squeezed his hand; Gavin grinned, turning to catch her eye. He ran a hand through his hair with his free hand, which was as short as he could remember it being, and reflected that the nights were not so bad with Tesla in the sleeping bag next to him, adding her warmth to his own.

—

"All right, that's everything we need. Now, sit down, and stay still; I've never cut anyone's hair before."

Gavin obeyed, taking a seat on the rock he and Tesla had moved from the edge of their campsite. It was wide, with a reasonably flat surface, perfect as a makeshift seat; heavy, but not so heavy that they were unable to move it between the two of them.

Gavin was uncertain as to why they had taken so much time to find the right stone, and he was even more confused about why Tesla insisted on cutting his hair inside her tent, but he did not not voice these questions; Tesla had told him they needed something to use as a seat, so he had helped her find a suitable object, and she had told him they needed to move the seat into the tent, so he had helped her move the stone she had picked out.

Now Tesla had told him to sit down, so he was sitting down, looking up into those bright hazel eyes as she gazed at him, an appraising expression on her face, the scissors Santino had lent her in one hand, a small, sharp knife in the other.

"Mind if I try something short?"

Gavin shrugged; he had never adjusted his Bubble Suit settings to shorten his hair when he had lived in Kingston, but if Tesla wanted to cut his hair short…

"Whatever you want; you're the one who's gonna be looking at me."

Tesla smiled; Gavin took in every detail of it, the way she bit her lower lip for the briefest of moments before she flashed her pearly white teeth.

"All right, then. Let's start with the top."

It was the most relaxing experience; Gavin could not have cared less about the locks of dirty blond hair falling to the floor, or what he would look like after this. All that mattered was that Tesla's touch was magic;

when she gently ran her fingertips up his neck, or scraped the edge of her hand against his scalp to lift up a lock, rivulets of pleasure rippled through Gavin's brain, so intoxicating that he struggled to keep still.

As she continued to work, Gavin noticed that Tesla was expanding the boundaries of her touch, slipping her free hand past his neck to touch his shoulders, to pass over his chest, making the softest of grabs; when she did, all of the work he had put in with Santino and Coreen flashed through his mind, and Gavin found he was pleased with himself for how he had spent that time.

Tesla was working behind his ear now, her body positioned close to his, her face next to his own as she examined the remaining stubble and scraped it away with the edge of the knife.

"Ok," she said, her voice soft and deep, a sort of purr in his ear touched by the heat of her breath. "That's the haircut. Now it's time to clean up the stubble you call a beard."

It was said playfully, and did not bother Gavin - he knew he could not grow a beard anything like Santino's - so he only grinned at her ribbing. Thinking of scenes from some Guvernment Films he had watched as a youth, he started to tilt his head back, turning his face up to Tesla to give her a better angle.

"Nu-uh. Keep sitting up."

Gavin obeyed; a moment later, Tesla had swung herself down into his lap, wrapping her legs around his back to better secure herself, the hazel eyes dancing with mischief as they looked down into his brown ones. He could feel, from the grip her legs had on him, how strong she had gotten since she left Kingston; her body was lithe, vibrant, supple.

"Now, sit still; I'm going to need to be careful here."

She was; her touch was light, deft, the fingertips of her left hand tracing across his skin as her right handled the knife.

"All right, all done. Look at you."

Tesla leaned back to evaluate her handiwork; Gavin simply looked at her. Her eyes, which had been taking in his haircut, shifted to meet his own; Gavin saw, in that brief instant, that the mischief was gone from the hazel eyes, replaced by a fiery intensity.

"I almost forgot."

Tesla leaned in toward him.

"There's one more thing I want to do."

Then she was kissing him, and everything else went out of his mind; there was only Tesla, and her taste, and her smell, the touch and feel of her, his soft groan of pleasure as she bit down on his bottom lip, the sensation of her hands reaching down under his shirt…

—

They woke up together the next morning, Tesla's head pillowed against

Gavin's chest.

They had not slept much and did not wake early; as they came back to consciousness together, Gavin and Tesla could hear the sounds of Santino and Clarence moving around outside their tent.

"Suppose they're going to notice I didn't pitch my own tent," Gavin murmured.

"Good morning to you, too," Tesla whispered back.

The prior night had been full of surprises, but they were not over; Gavin smiled as he felt Tesla's hand touch his cheek, turning his face so she could engage him in a deep kiss. As they broke apart, she spoke.

"I don't care if they notice. I never would have imagined it, back when we first met, but I *want* you, Gavin. I started to want you on our journey to Trepani, and I knew I wanted you at the Acadian Summit."

She leaned back; their eyes met, and Tesla's smile grew.

"It tore me apart, watching you and your great-uncle get escorted out of there, knowing there was nothing I could do, not then. But even though I couldn't do anything in the moment, it didn't mean I couldn't do anything at all; it was just fortunate Santino had a plan that overlapped with mine."

"Don't get me wrong; I'm excited about where we're going, and I'm worried about my family, my friends, almost everyone back in Kingston. I'm putting my hope in this plan. But I also wanted you, so I hope they notice… life's too short not to go for what you want."

—

It did not surprise Santino to watch Tesla and Gavin as they carried a large stone into Tesla's tent. He had gotten an inkling that this might happen during his planning sessions with Tesla, and nothing since their escape had dissuaded him of that notion; Tesla and Gavin had been caught up in their own world since they escaped Trepani, and Santino had figured it had only been a matter of time.

It made him smile; he liked Gavin, whatever trouble his new friend might have caused, and he liked Tesla, in a way, though Santino had spent far too much time around Coreen to desire anything like her live-wire intensity in a potential partner. He enjoyed being around people like Coreen and Tesla in short bursts, but he also knew that anyone operating in a state of constant agitation would wear him raw.

Nor was that the whole of it; there was something else about Tesla, something Santino tried not to acknowledge to himself. In the time that he and Tesla had spent planning the breakout in Trepani, her intelligence and daring had been obvious, but that knife cut two ways; something about the young woman's ruthless, calculating nature gave Santino pause.

He could not imagine fully trusting Tesla Mancini, because whatever she said to the contrary, he did not believe that Tesla Mancini cared much at all about anyone else on the planet Shurtain; at least, not when it really came down to it.

That was not to say she did not care at all; to the contrary, their time together had shown Santino that Tesla cared about her family, cared about Gavin, cared about her friends in Kingston. But whatever Tesla said, Santino could also look at her actions in the stories she told, and observe that, when it came time for Tesla Mancini to make her moves, only one sentient being's interests were truly considered.

Of course, this was a fleeting concern; Santino had no intention of pursuing Tesla, and as a traveling companion, or friend, she was good company. But in the end, he thought she had a lot more of her brother in her than she would ever admit.

Santino had reached these conclusions as they made their plans, but saw no reason to dwell on them; in the here and now, he was simply happy to see his two friends finding connection. In any case, he had more than enough to think about without considering the interpersonal dynamics of their traveling party.

Santino did not know why he objected so vehemently to the decisions made at The Acadian Summit, but from the moment that the Council voted to go to war, and the crowd had reacted with excitement, Santino had recognized what a vast gulf existed between himself and so many others in Trepani.

The days that followed only reinforced that impression; there was an excitement, a fervor, about the idea of defending the homeland from their enemies, of marching to man the barricades and prepare for war; there were even whispers that they might reclaim the valley, retake Kingston, and extend the reach of the Acadians back to the western coast of the continent.

Santino did not think much of that idea, and felt dismayed when he heard so many of his friends, Bruno and Paulo among them, speak eagerly of engaging the enemy in battle. Nor could he overlook the fact that there was more than a tinge of vitriol in some of their words, a desire to exact vengeance on The Bubble Society for forcing the Acadians to leave Kingston in the first place.

Santino did not question that there was a time and a place for war, but while he had never served in combat, he carried the belief, instilled in him by his grandfather, that both sides always bled in war. He found it baffling to listen to so many of his peers speak of the coming war as if they would win their battles in dominating fashion, with no cost to themselves. Even without his grandfather's thoughts on the matter, Santino could not have lived the life he had, with so much time in combat training, out hunting, without recognizing that there is nearly always a price to pay in physical confrontation; the question is a matter of how high that price will be.

Yet even his cousins, who had known their grandfather, had fallen prey to this mindset. Not all of them - Coreen, for one, had seen too much of the Wild, and spent too much time with Salomon herself, to be so naive - but Bruno and Paulo had been as swept up in the popular rhetoric as the rest of Santino's friends.

Perhaps there was some possibility the Acadians would win a bloodless victory, but Santino thought it a small one; he thought it far more likely that confronting The Bubble Society in open war would mean death and destruction for all.

All of this seemed obvious to Santino, yet so few of the people around him had shared his concerns. This, in turn, caused him to question himself.

Who was he?

Why couldn't he go along with the plans like his cousins?

Did he know who he was?

In that, Clarence was more helpful. The old man did not directly address Santino's troubles - the younger man had not shared them with him - but he did tell stories about his grandfather, and on some level, Santino felt that was helping him find answers.

Even the worst stories helped.

—

"It was the longest night of my life. As that afternoon faded into evening, I kept thinking that something would happen, that Time and Space would somehow reverse themselves and correct the unacceptable error Nature had made."

Night had crept in by then, leaving the campfire to light the clearing. Santino and Clarence sat around the flames, watching the flickering light as darkness overtook the world.

"But it didn't."

Clarence shook his head at Santino's words, his eyes on the fire.

"No. It didn't."

There was a long pause.

"What happened, exactly? I've only ever heard there was an accident on a hunt. Nobody ever got into the specifics."

Clarence shook his head again, his eyes still on the fire.

"There aren't many specifics to get into. It was supposed to be one of our last hunts of this season, ahead of that first Winter. We were a party of eight; aside from myself and your grandfather, you would know your Uncle Marcus, and Anton. The other four who accompanied us then have all passed on; we lost two of them on that day, and the other two in the years since."

"I wish I could say it was some dramatic story, one that gave us an opportunity to struggle valiantly in an effort to save our friend. I say friend for lack of a universal term; your grandfather, Salomon, was so much more to each of us. A brother to me, a father to many, a teacher to more, kind to all."

Santino thought of voicing a question, but when he looked at Clarence, he saw that the old man's eyes had taken on an odd glaze; Santino kept his silence, waiting for Clarence to continue.

"We were pushing up towards the peaks of Mount Norbert, tracking elk. We had a bead on a bull moose, who was retreating up towards the tree line. Whether the old bull was that crafty, or it was just bad luck, I can't say, but he led us up a cliffside trail."

"It happened so fast; one moment, we were tracking along the trail, certain we would catch the bull and be on our way home before dark."

"Then part of the cliff wall sheared off."

Clarence paused, his eyes transfixed on the fire; Santino could almost see the memories replaying in the old man's eyes.

"Your grandfather was in the lead with two others, no more than ten feet ahead of the fourth man in our procession, who suddenly found himself on the edge of the world."

"It was so eerie. There was a sound, but nothing like you would expect; a deep rumble, the crashing of stone, and then nothing. The ravine the cliff fell into was so deep that we never saw a sign of impact; there was no sound, no plume of dust. They never had time to shout out; they were just gone."

A sad smile crossed Clarence's lips then.

"We sentient beings try so hard to control our destiny. And it's not just The Bubble Society; much as we Acadians pride ourselves on living in harmony with Nature, of our ability to live off the land in the Wild, many of us have that streak of hubris, the belief that sentient beings can overcome the world around them through effort and ingenuity, that we can somehow thwart Nature's purpose."

Santino frowned.

"But sentient beings do have some ability to change the world around us, no? I mean, through that effort and ingenuity, we Acadians steered clear of The Bubble Society, and we've built something better; maybe the folks in Kingston wouldn't agree, but they would lose a vote to the wider planet of Shurtain."

Clarence grinned.

"You assume that those events were at odds with Nature's purpose, then? No, no, it's no matter, and it's hardly the point. What I mean to say is that sentient beings can only control what sentient beings can control, and we aren't the ones who lay down those constraints, no more than the ants designed the limitations of what their species can and can't do."

"No matter what we do, what we build, what we aspire to, we ultimately do it at Nature's mercy. We do not overcome Nature; we operate in accordance with the Laws it has laid down, Laws that aren't written down anywhere, Laws that express themselves as hard rules in our physical universe."

"I cannot, for instance, separate my soul from my mind and body, cannot walk through this realm as an invisible spirit; no matter how loudly I scream about that, no matter how loudly I proclaim that it ought to be my god-given right, I have no power to change the physical rules of the sentient experience in this domain."

Clarence paused, shook his head.

"Salomon Cahn was as great a man as this planet has ever seen. Even as boys, he stood apart from the rest of us. It was always obvious that he would become a leader of great importance; after our journey to Elysia, there was nothing that I thought more certain. But in the end, he got no trial, no chance at recourse; Nature swept him off the board as indifferently as all the rest of us who find ourselves here, inhabiting Shurtain in these sentient forms."

"Every step of the way, from sperm joining to egg, to whatever that process is that allows us to pull materials from the environment around us and convert them into the building blocks that allow our bodies to grow and regenerate… the way our spirits animate those bodies, injecting life into something that will rapidly decay the moment that spirit disappears… every step of the way, we are totally and utterly at the mercy of Nature, and its decision to allow us to have this experience."

Santino sat in silence, processing Clarence's words. He was thinking about a particular detail of the story Clarence had just told; he wondered why nobody had mentioned it as they had laid the plans to free Clarence and Gavin. His grandmother, at the least, would have known.

"You traveled to Elysia with my grandfather?"

For the first time since they had gotten on the topic, Clarence's expression shifted, a wide smile spreading across his face.

"Ah, now there's a story."

BOOK 5, CHAPTER 5

They were breaking social convention, walking into a bar in the Axios District when their own residences were in the Andola District, on a night when there was no special promotion, no Guvernment-sponsored event.

But they were well past the point of worrying about breaking convention.

After all, what was the Guvernment going to do?

Force them to work even longer hours on Operation Mach One?

No, it was time to act.

And they could only think of one thing to do.

Fortunately, it was easy to find the three they sought.

All they had to do was log onto the Guvernment Social App.

—

The buzz of fame had worn off quickly.

True, their posts still went to the "Featured" section of the Guvernment Social App, and every sentient being in Kingston knew who they were, but Anna, Thea, and Shannon could not help but notice that fewer and fewer people were showing up to the locations they promoted for the social hour. Even with the Guvernment's publicity machine at their back, the events had drawn smaller and smaller crowds since The Celebration of Knowledge; now that the Guvernment was putting its focus in other areas, the interest had burned down to nothing.

It was a bummer, as Shannon put it, but secretly, Anna did not mind; she had become increasingly aware that the events that they had promoted over the past weeks had not helped any of them accomplish their true aim, or done anything close to it. They had not put it so bluntly, even to each other, but when the Guvernment made them the centerpiece of their promotions, each of the young women had hoped to leverage their fame into an attractive, successful boyfriend, a potential husband, a companion and confidant. This had nothing to do with being female, and everything to do with being sentient; had the shoe been on the other foot, they would have dreamed of finding their wives, or if they were attracted to the same sex, the wife or husband who was right for them; the details were the details, but sentient beings were crafted to love, and anyone their age would have hoped to translate their fame into a relationship.

Unfortunately, posting photos of themselves in their bikinis under the banner headline "We're at the Drunk Elephant tonight - come party!" had failed to draw the type of suitors they were seeking. Potential candidates had come to party, that was true, but most of the young ones that showed up were drunken hooligans, and the older ones were sloppy or creepy in some way or another. Worst of all, regardless of age, the men treated the three young women like a bunch of drunk bimbos, rather than as aspiring Knowers, just because they were drunk and dressed like bimbos, which they saw as a gross breach of the appropriate social etiquette outlined on Page 13 of *The Manual for Proper Behavior*.

In any case, those days were over; with Operation Mach One spun up, the Guvernment was no longer actively promoting festivities, and the partiers in Kingston had gone grassroots, spreading out across the bars and cantinas in their own districts, or simply hoarding combinations of liquor and amphetamines for home use.

All of that meant that the young women, who would have been too preoccupied to notice who was coming and going a few weeks ago, did not miss the unremarkable trio of young men who stepped through the doors of the Drunk Elephant on this quiet night.

At first, it was only Anna who noticed them: three young men, a couple of years younger than her. Anna watched the trio sidle up to an end of the bar, where they engaged their holographic monitors and tapped commands into the control panels on their wrists; as she did, it occurred to her that she might have recognized them from her days at Kingston High, though it was difficult to keep track of such things.

Anna could not be sure, but from the focus that two of the young men put on their screens - and the lack of attention they paid to the barkeep - Anna guessed they were continuing some sort of discussion on their Guvernment Messaging Apps.

She shook her head, wondering about the social norms on the other side of this seemingly arbitrary age gap.

Nobody in their year, nor the year below them, used the Guvernment Messaging App in lieu of spoken communication, but for the class after, it was as if a switch had been flipped. In the space of a single year, it became rare to see any of the younger ones talking to each other at school. The trend continued with each subsequent class that entered the school system; rather than speak to each other, the new generation of sentient beings restricted their communication to entries in the Guvernment Messaging App.

Anna's attention moved on, and she started to ask her twin a question, but at that moment, Shannon squealed in delight, causing Anna's heart to skip a beat.

"Our post got a response!"

That again.

Anna's pulse slowed back down; she could not care less if their post had gotten a response. On the first night, she had shared Shannon's excitement when the messages started to roll in, but by the twentieth response, she realized that most of it was white noise, superficial responses from mindless individuals with nothing better to do but send their thoughts out into the ether through the Guvernment Media App.

Anna shook her head, remembering her moment of realization on that night, when Shannon's mutterings recaptured her attention.

"What?... this is weird."

"What's weird?"

"I got a message that says *We're here, can you tell us about the last time you saw Tesla?* It's from someone named Leonard."

Shannon tossed her head.

"Well, forget Leonard. I'm tired of these guys showing up to ask questions about Tesla, or the abduction. As if we're just here to be storytellers. They're supposed to be interested in *us*, not Tesla. I loved her, but she's gone, and anyways, how am I supposed to know what happened to her? If this Leonard were really here, he'd come talk to us; I bet he's just sitting at home, or some other bar, messing with us... wait, there's another message... *We'll tell you about the last time we saw Gavin*... what the heck does that mean?"

Anna and Thea exchanged a glance; her twin did not appear to make the jump, but Anna did.

"There's another message being posted..."

Shannon was primed to read whatever would appear on her screen, but Anna did not wait for her friend; instead, she swiveled around on her bar stool.

"Hey! Leonard, and whoever you two are. You can come talk to us, you know."

As Anna anticipated, the three young men, whom the bartender had just approached, turned at the sound of her voice; after overcoming their initial surprise, they exchanged glances and nodded. There was a round booth big enough for ten on the edge of the Drunk Elephant's dance floor; Anna gestured toward it, then picked up her drink and led the others toward the booth. It was a better place for a real discussion.

—

"So let me get this straight. You want us to tell you where they took Tesla, because you think your friend Gavin must be in the same place?"

The young men nodded.

"Ya, that about sums it up," Leonard confirmed.

"So you think he's alive? This Gavin Owens, the one who disappeared?"

Again, the young men nodded.

Thea was asking the questions; she exchanged a glance with her twin before she continued, leaving Shannon to hover at the edge of the discussion.

"I don't see the connection. Tesla was abducted. That's what they told us, on the morning of the Declaration of War. If I remember correctly, your friend tore his Bubble Suit and disappeared."

The one who Leonard had introduced as Mo responded; he spoke in a low rumble of a voice, his tone ominous.

"So they say."

Anna, Thea, and Shannon exchanged surprised glances; Shannon bit her lip, trying not to giggle, and Thea did not seem to know what to say, which left it to Anna to pick up the questioning.

"And what does that mean?"

Mo stirred in his seat. He had not spoken much to his companions on the walk over, or for that matter, since they had learned that Operation Mach One would be put into action. He had been deep in thought - Knowledge Knew that he had more than enough time to do that in his present occupation - and despite the variety of obnoxious slogans now being pushed to his Guvernment Media App, providing the citizuns of Kingston frequent reminders to keep up the pace for the sake of the utopia, Mo had found he had less to do than ever, which gave him the space to continue asking questions, to replay all the events of the past couple seasons, sifting through the details over and over.

The thought did not hit him all at once; the first hint came during *Rise and Shine Kingston!*, as the hosts droned on about the remarkable progress the citizuns of The Bubble Society had made on the Elevation Upgrade Prize since the collective project had been rechristened Operation Mach One. Simone Collister had gone on at some length about the miracles of Knowledge that were the Bubble Suits, and how all of Kingston ought to continue to believe that Knowledge would soon bless them again, given the bounties it had been bestowed upon them in the past.

It was all too much; it would have been one thing if he could have turned the volume down, but even when he shut his eyes to it, Mo could not get away from the daily broadcast of *Rise and Shine Kingston!*, from Simone and Malachi's sanctimonious lectures that bore no resemblance to the reality Mo was experiencing.

In fact, it had gotten so bad that he wondered whether he should just tear his Bubble Suit open and have done with it, if this is what life on Shurtain was going to be moving forward.

And in that moment, when Mo verbalized the question in his own mind, things started to change, for it was in that moment when Mo started to wonder if tearing a Bubble Suit would actually have the effect everyone told them it would.

After all, Gavin had not been in any particular distress before the ERTs had arrived.

The question had hit Mo two days ago, and his mood had grown even darker than it had been in the days since. It was a source of concern for his friends, though it was an insignificant item on their mounting list of problems; much as Neville and Leonard would have like to see Mo more cheerful, what really had them worried was that Mo had stopped taking any statements from the Guvernment at face value, and they felt sick with fear at the idea of what that could mean for him, both if he was wrong, or, even worse, if he was right.

"It means I'll take what I take outta their words. Still wanna hear 'em, one way or the other, but I'll decide what they mean, whether they have any basis in truth, or if it's just a sentient being making noises with no real meaning behind it."

Thea started to respond, but Mo was on a roll.

"Look, when they passed Resolution 4433, the one that established the first Elevation Upgrade Prize, Gavin was the only one who'd gone missing. It didn't make any sense; why would they go to so much effort to retrieve a dead body? The heck would they learn from it? That sentient beings die without Bubble Suits? If Knowledge ain't Knowed them that already, it never will."

Mo paused, but nobody tried to interrupt him this time; the girls were staring at him intently, while his friends kept their eyes pointedly away from him, looking anywhere else in the room, as if that could disassociate them from the madness Mo was spewing.

"Way I figure it, they were aware, or 'least had a suspicion, that they were going after these Savages, back when Gavin first went missing. Someone had an idea that he might still be alive."

Shannon giggled, and when she did, the others could not help themselves; even Neville and Leonard joined in the laughter.

Mo was not moved; he waited for the laughter to die down, then continued.

"Believe what you want, but anyone with eyes can see that something strange is going on. I'm trying to get some idea of what that is, and whether it might mean that our friend is still alive."

Anna looked at him, her expression shrewd.

"So you think these Savages abducted your friend as well? And gave him one of these mouth filtration devices?"

"Like a test run?" Threw in her sister.

Mo turned his hands over.

"Could be. Or not. But since you bring it up, I'll ask you three, since these two," he indicated Leonard and Neville, "don't wanna answer me. If our Guvernment has the Knowledge to build these mouth filtration devices - using the technology they claim these Savages stole - then what are they doing setting up more Elevation Upgrade Prizes?"

Neville and Leonard both continued to frown, but their expressions had changed; the young women could tell they were no longer trying to distance themselves from their friend's opinions, that their discomfort now stemmed from the fact that neither of them could find a satisfactory way to reconcile the argument.

The twins shared the briefest of glances; it was all they needed to know they were in sync, that both of them saw reason for concern in what this Mo was saying.

"Look, I've had a lot of time to think about this. They got me staring at my holographic screen, watching the Knowers sit at their desks and work on their holographic screens, for hours on end, five days a week. Plenty of time to think, and I'm not saying I got any answers, but I sure got a lot more questions."

Shannon giggled again, but the others did not; the twins, whose expressions had grown much more serious, exchanged another glance. It was Thea who responded.

"Ok. Let's say that is the case; what do we do about it?"

BOOK 5, CHAPTER 6

A full day had passed since Gavin's first glimpse of the Amphitrite Ocean; despite everything that had happened in that brief time, the novelty of seeing the ocean had not started to wear off. In fact, he imagined that he could spend the rest of his life on water's edge, staring out at the sea and syncing with the rhythm of the waves.

Perhaps he would have, if the world around him did not pose so many demands.

And if Tesla did not have him so distracted.

They were together now, sitting in the sand, reveling in the adrenaline of their latest escape as they looked out west over the Amphitrite, watching as the first rays of sunlight met the ocean.

The scene was familiar, but the vantage point was new; yesterday, they had arrived in Larissa, and looked out to the east to watch the sunrise over the Amphitrite Ocean.

Today, everything was reversed; or at least, it felt that way, looking west with the sun rising behind them. It seemed as though they were in a different world, even though they had only traveled a short distance - roughly eight miles - in their escape.

But those miles made all the difference in the world.

Because they were not in Acadia anymore.

—

They had made their final approach to Larissa shortly after dawn.

They could have made it the previous night, pushing through to finish the last few hours of the journey and rest in Larissa, but Clarence had insisted on camping one last night; now, as they stood in the pre-dawn glow, the sun cresting over the ocean, they understood why.

Brilliant as the sunrises and sunsets had been in the Cadillacs, this was something different, a scene too wondrous to describe; for Tesla and Gavin, who had only seen pictures and videos of the Amphitrite, and only understood the idea of oceans as a concept, it was almost an out-of-body moment, the witnessing of a physical phenomena that could not be conveyed through words, written or spoken, a place that could only be experienced, a visceral reminder that sentient language could not express awe any more than it could articulate love.

Fortunately, Tesla thought, there were languages that could express that, languages that conveyed information faster than any spoken word could hope to; as they stood there, shimmering in the light of the sunrise, Tesla leaned into Gavin's side, and smiled when he responded by wrapping an arm around her and pulling her into him.

No need for words at all.

They stayed there for an hour, content to sit and be still for a time, to take it all in as the world around them became a shifting painting, the glowing orb of orange rising over the Amphitrite into the indigo of the night sky, inexorably pushing back the darkness, casting great swaths of pinks and blues that hid the stars above them as the world around them came to life.

The sun was well into the sky when Clarence indicated they should move; he and Santino took the lead, once again falling into conversation as Tesla and Gavin fell in some paces behind them, Tesla reaching out to take Gavin's hand as they began their trek along that last stretch to Larissa.

It was almost too much to believe; in her preparations, Tesla had embraced the idea of the unknown, understanding that she had no idea what was on the other side of what she was stepping into, only knowing that she had to get out.

She had counted on difficulties.

She had bet on adventure.

But in all her scheming, all her planning, it had never occurred to her that she might fall in love.

—

They could tell, well before Marcus Cahn and the rest of his party were in shouting distance, that they had been right to think they would find help in Larissa.

Marcus and the others had ridden out on horses, several empty mounts in their party. His brother-in-law, Harlan Brinson, rode at his side; the men who trailed after them wore nondescript clothing, but the alertness in their eyes, the intensity in their expressions, marked them as warriors as clearly as any uniform.

When the horses brought the party from Larissa within shouting distance, Harlan boomed out a greeting.

"You've later than we expected. Troubles along the road, or finally getting old?"

Clarence grinned.

"No troubles; we just took the scenic route. No particular reason."

They were close enough to speak in normal tones now; Harlan grinned as he glanced at Marcus, who picked up the conversation.

"Can't fault you on that. There shouldn't be too much trouble here; there are some in Larissa who are in favor of taking much harsher action against you, but everyone has bigger concerns at this point. It's why Anton wasn't bothered with chasing you down; as long as you don't try to pass through his position, and get back to Kingston, you'll have no trouble from his end."

Marcus paused. He looked directly at Clarence before he continued.

"Even so, I hope you don't plan on staying here long. Word will spread quickly of your presence - Larissa isn't big enough to keep such things secret - and with things so unsettled, it's hard to say what might happen."

Clarence nodded.

"We'll be in and out; only a bit of help getting on our way. Can we ride and talk? It's been a long journey, and it would be good to get to town and get a plan in place as quickly as possible; as you hoped, we don't plan on staying long."

—

Marcus and Renee Cahn rarely ate at Kelli's Shipyard, but with Clarence and the others staying in rooms on the upper floors, and Harlan and Mykala regulars at the place, it seemed an apt occasion to take a break from cooking and enjoy the evening.

Kelli's - often known simply as The Shipyard - was oceanfront property, its front patio and wraparound porch offering spectacular views of the Amphitrite Ocean, the ever-present sound of waves rolling into the coast providing background noise as they gorged themselves on mountains of seafood.

Yet even as they sat there, letting their food digest and enjoying the scenery, there was an air of unease around the table. Whatever Marcus had said, Tesla was quick to notice that more than a few people had looked at them sideways, both as they entered Larissa, and as they made their way through the city, restocking on supplies while Clarence and Harlan inquired about a ship.

There was a similar feeling tonight; nobody had approached their table with anything other than friendly intentions, but Tesla could feel something hanging in the atmosphere, a sense that danger was lurking, that this tranquil sense of calm could break at any moment.

The upside was that they would leave on the morning tide, news that came as a great relief, at least to Tesla, when Clarence delivered it. Santino seemed content to stay here for a time - he sat at the head of the table, chatting animatedly with his uncles - but Tesla had an overwhelming sense that they should move on, that they had already lingered too long.

She shifted her focus away from Santino and Marcus, looking at Gavin's profile next to her. He, of course, had a huge smile plastered across his face, one that had been present all day, and that had grown even larger as they sat at the table. Tesla reached under the table and gripped Gavin's right hand with her left, causing him to turn to her, his grin broadening when her eyes met his. She tried to tap into his flow, to tell herself they were safe, that she should enjoy the evening, but even as she listened to the others, she felt as if she were not truly inhabiting her body; her mind was full of concerns.

They spoke of Trepani as they ate, but little had changed since they had departed. The defenders were in place at Turquoise Lake, fortifying the defenses, solidifying their outposts. It was all going well, as far as such things went, but there was little surprise over that; after all, nobody had ever questioned Anton's competence.

The conversation had then turned to family, which provided some distraction; Tesla had not had time to learn much about her co-conspirator's backgrounds as she and Santino had sat plotting Gavin and Clarence's escape with Eleanor, Marcus, and Harlan, so it came as news to her that Harlan and Mykala had five children of their own.

"Five in eight years; I truly don't know what I was doing. I blame him," Mykala turned to her right, where Harlan sat. "If he would have stayed over in Alexandria, back in Alysanne, I can't imagine I would have lost my mind the way I did. Then again, we only have today, and when this guy is your husband…"

Harlan grinned, flashing his smile from behind his thick black beard.

"And of course, Diana and Abe think they're old enough to run the house now. 13 and 12, and they insisted all would be fine if we left them in charge, with the 9, 7, and 5-year old at home with them…" Mykala trailed off, rolling her eyes.

"What did you do with them?" Tesla asked.

"Oh, the neighbors kept an eye on them. Diana and Abe aren't wrong - they're responsible for their age - but if something went wrong, it would be a different story. Fortunately, our neighbors, Bob and Midge, are good people, if a bit quirky, and their daughter, Donna, left home years ago - she has a family of her own out in northeast Larissa - so Bob and Midge are always happy to lend a hand. Useful, since my sister-in-law quickly lost interest; not that it would have mattered this time, as Renee was with us when we went to Trepani."

Renee smiled as the others turned to her.

"I can't deny it; having a newborn niece, then a nephew, was exciting at first - Coreen, Sao, and Leanna were all teenagers when Diana came along - but as much as I love my niece, her extended visits were a bit much. I've been fortunate enough to filter out memories of raising my own, keeping the good and letting the rest drift away; I thought it best not to venture too deep back into those waters."

The others laughed.

"As for my mother-in-law handling that granddaughter of mine… Eleanor is a better woman than me, no doubt. I love Carly dearly, of course, just as I love Coreen, yet the house is a great deal more peaceful without anyone climbing up curtains, or on top of cabinets."

A good-natured chuckle was shared by their end of the table at this; Tesla looked at the older woman with a shrewd expression.

"I'd have thought those things trivial, given everything else your daughter went on to get into."

Renee sighed.

"Too true. I was proud of Coreen when she chose her path, but I have never known relief like the relief I felt when she told me that she was leaving the Hunters to start a family with Ollie. Call it what you will, but I wanted to know my daughter was safe; I could not have stopped her from doing what she wanted any more than I could stop Shurtain from spinning, but it was a relief when she made that decision. Carly is rambunctious, no doubt, perhaps best experienced in small doses, but there is also nothing like being a grandmother; in fact, it's the primary reason I supported your plan to free Clarence, and this one."

Renee indicated Gavin; the others turned to her in surprise.

"It's already been said, by many others, but I do not wish to see our people go to war. I do not wish to see wives and husbands, mothers and fathers, sisters and brothers, sons and daughters, friends and family, march to their deaths. Coreen and Ollie did not join this first wave, but I have no doubt of what my daughter will do if our defenses are actually threatened; Coreen has never been one to run away from the fight."

An unsettled silence fell over the table.

"Well, that's not coming tomorrow," replied Marcus, breaking the silence. "And for now, we have tonight."

"True enough," said Clarence. "But if this old man is going to be ready for tomorrow, it's time to call it a night. Cheers, all."

—

The creak of the window shutter broke the silence of the witching hour.

Gavin stiffened as he came out of his dream state; when he did, it was to find Tesla was already awake, her eyes alert, staring at the window as a figure stepped through the opening, silhouetted by the moonlight.

It was Clarence Barnett.

"What are…" Gavin started, but he fell silent when his great-uncle put a finger to his lips. A moment later, Santino followed Clarence through the window. Once he was in, Clarence gestured for Tesla and Gavin to join them at the window; they did, Tesla wrapping herself in a sheet, Gavin padding across the room naked.

At first, Gavin did not understand what his great-uncle was pointing to; then, in the gloom of the night, he saw a shadow moving on the ground level, a figure trying - and failing - to obscure itself in shadow.

"He's not the only one. There's three others outside and four in the building already. We need to go. Now."

Clarence spoke in a hushed, urgent whisper; his words prodded Gavin and Tesla into motion. They moved quickly to dress; fortunately, their packs were ready to go.

"How do we get out?" asked Tesla, her voice as hushed as Clarence's.

The old man gestured to the window.

"Santino and I have already placed our packs on the the roof - there's no lights up there, and they didn't see me moving - so my bet is we can get down that way, then run like hell to Harlan's; our best bet is to get across the sea, over to Alexandria, and if anyone's going to make that happen in the dead of night, it's Harlan. But the main thing is to get out of here as fast as possible; we need to make sure he doesn't catch up to us."

Tesla shot Clarence a quizzical look.

"Who is he? There's more than one, didn't you say that?"

Clarence shook his head, a strange clarity in his eyes, a focus that Gavin had never thought he would see in his great-uncle.

"Hired guns. Either our pursuer recruited them here, or more likely, he hired them elsewhere and brought them here with him. It doesn't matter; no matter who they are, we need to go."

Clarence started for the window; at the same moment, they heard footsteps on the staircase, climbing their way.

"Go, go, go," he urged, indicating that Tesla should be the first one through the window.

Her foot was on the sill when the crash came, the sound of a door breaking down at the far end of the hall.

"Now," urged Clarence, but Tesla did not need prodding; she was already out, scrambling across to the roof, pack on her back, Gavin close behind her. Santino followed them out, and Clarence was next, bringing up the rear as another door, closer to their own, was kicked open.

—

"Quickly, now, and quietly."

They heard shouts of anger from behind them, indignant occupants of rooms adding their voices to the sounds of the men who were moving down the hall towards Gavin and Tesla's room, knocking in each door they passed and shouting their frustration each time they found an empty room.

The noise attracted attention from below. That proved to be to their advantage; the second team put in place by their enemy, the group that was responsible for perimeter surveillance, was drawn in by the sounds, revealing themselves in the lights as they approached The Shipyard. The man on the north end went so far as to climb the stairs onto The Shipyard's wraparound deck.

It was all Clarence needed; without a word to the others, the old man dropped off the roof, catching their enemy by surprise, driving a foot into the juncture of the man's neck and shoulder, disabling his target and softening his own landing in the bargain.

Tesla, Gavin, and Santino did not need urging; they moved to the edge of the roof and dropped over the edge to the support beams, then slid down the ten or so feet to The Shipyard's wrap-around deck. Clarence checked that the man was still unconscious; satisfied, he nodded.

"Forward," Clarence whispered, his tone urgent.

They followed him down the stairs to the ground level, then crept to a corner, trying to keep their breathing under control. Clarence pointed at a path through a small grove of trees, one that would take them in the general direction of Harlan and Mykala's home.

The others nodded at Clarence; then, just as the old man started to make a run for it, one of their pursuers stepped around the corner of the building, his pistol at the ready.

Clarence was quick enough to redirect the gun, but not quick enough to stop the shot; the pistol went off, the bullet firing up and through the bottom of The Shipyard's wraparound deck.

The struggle continued; the man was trying to throw Clarence off him, to free himself, and the gun.

A second shot went off; this one ricocheted off the side of the building.

There was no time for this.

They had to get out of here.

Those were the thoughts in Santino Vincente's head as he stepped forward, fist cocked. He repeated the motions he had practiced countless times in his years of training, loading on his right foot and swiveling his hips, uncoiling his upper body, his left fist arcing up behind the full momentum of his considerable mass, his mind reminding his body to accelerate through contact.

The uppercut landed flush, slamming into the base of the man's chin and driving the top of his brain up into his skull, sending him into immediate unconsciousness.

Clarence did not hesitate to press their advantage; he disentangled himself from the falling man, then urged the others into the night, toward the trees, toward escape. The night had broken out in sound, the shouts of their pursuers coming from above as they hurried back down the stairs, in the direction of the shooting.

Then they were at the trees, and gone, but as they disappeared into the gloom, Santino took one last glance at the scene, his eyes finding the man he had struck; he knew, from the amount of blood pooling around the man's head, what he had done.

There was no time to think about it now; now, it was time to run.

—

They reached Harlan and Mykala's and knocked at the door hurriedly, trying to keep the sounds muted, but knowing that they needed to wake the residents immediately.

It was almost as if Harlan had been prepared for this; in any case, he was dressed when he answered the door, ready to lead them through the dark streets of Larissa, toward a small harbor where a few dozen fishing vessels were kept. Other ports would be watched - their pursuers had been too numerous to assume they would not have an eye on the principal harbors - but now that they had lost their trail, it would be difficult for the pursuit to track them on a small fishing boat crossing The Sister's Break to Alexandria in the dead of night.

It appeared to have worked; at least, they had not seen any signs of their enemy as they crossed.

They made their landing in a small boathouse on the shores of Alysanne, where Gavin and Tesla took their first steps onto the continent of Alexandria.

That had been less than an hour ago; now, as the others sat inside, discussing what they ought to do next, Tesla and Gavin had wandered off, jubilant in the aftermath of their escape, to find a place in the sand where they could sit and watch the rising sun.

Tesla leaned back into Gavin's chest as they took in the scene.

"There's something I've been waiting to tell you for a couple days now."

She paused, breathing hard, her face close to his, a smile she could barely contain straining at her lips, matching the glimmer in her eyes.

"I'm pregnant."

BOOK 5, CHAPTER 7

After twenty-six years on the planet Shurtain, Anna Lindberg had come to believe that she had a pretty good idea of what a sentient being could expect out of life.

Anna had entered the year 21, A.K., expecting that this year's hundred days of Summer would see her complete her post-graduate studies at the Academy of Knowledge and transition into her new role as a Junior Knower on one of the many Knowledge teams in Kingston. Then, with her career trajectory secured, she could fully turn her attention to the weighty proposition of finding the right partner, one who would meet with Guvernment approval, so their allocation of children would be expedited; they would get a boy and a girl, if Anna had her way.

Instead, the planet Shurtain - or at least the city of Kingston - had been turned on its head.

Anna had completed her studies at the Academy of Knowledge, and she had transitioned into a Junior Knower role on a team overseen by Knower Robinson - their research focused on nasal filtration systems - but at the same time, she felt her future had become more uncertain than ever. Indeed, as Anna walked into Bailey's Bar on this, the 100th day of Summer, she carried the feeling that everything in her life had gone sideways, that things that were supposed to be immutably fixed in place were not permanent at all, but ever-shifting, ever-moving, requiring constant adjustment and reassessment.

Nor was it only her life that was impacted; the same forces that had waylaid Anna's vision for her life were affecting the other sentient beings of Kingston in the same way.

To make things more disorienting, Anna had been separated from Thea for the first time in their lives. It was not a total separation, as her twin was also working on a team overseen by Knower Robinson - Thea's team was focused on oral filtration systems - so they worked out of the same building in the Center of Industry, but they were no longer by each other's side every moment of the day.

The twins were together now, making the walk from the Center of Industry to Bailey's, where they would meet Shannon and the others; for her part, Shannon had been assigned to work on a team overseen by Knower Ludquist, optimizing the upgraded design that had won him the original Elevation Upgrade Prize.

There was a certain irony in this; her chances at winning remained remote, but a season after that sunny day at the Academy of Knowledge, when Shannon had expressed her dreams of winning the Elevation Upgrade Prize, she found herself working on a team focused on implementing that solution.

On the downside, this new role had shown Shannon how crazy her dream had been. In her new position, Shannon was working alongside some of the most senior Knowers, including Ludquist himself, and the conversations she had with them, brief as they might be, had convinced her that she was quite unlikely to win either of the new Elevation Upgrade Prizes; she simply had not devoted enough of her life to Knowledge to offer the same insights as the senior members of her team.

Of course, this did not matter nearly as much as it once had; Shannon was already famous, or famous enough, and she had never had much interest in doing the actual work required to win the Elevation Upgrade Prize, just the spotlight that would come along with it.

This shift in attitude was fortunate, because as the young women were learning in their new positions, it was entirely possible that nobody would be winning another Elevation Upgrade Prize anytime soon. Their experiences on their respective teams, brief as they were, had shown the young women that even Knowers who had studied at the altar of Knowledge for decades were proving helpless in the face of this challenge.

They had also found that their fellow Knowers did not seem overly bothered by this. To the contrary, one Knower on Anna's team had gone so far as to tell the younger woman not to pour too much of her energy into any of this; at the end of the day, they would work the same hours, consume the same nutrient packets, and live in the same homes regardless of the effort they put in.

As disheartening as that had been to hear, the comment itself was far from worthless; in fact, Mo Brickson and Aubrey Draper had found the words highly intriguing. It was quite the change in circumstances, Anna thought, as she and Thea turned the corner into the plaza; here she was, a newly ordained Junior Knower, bringing the words of more senior

Knowers to Mo, who she had thought entirely crazy on first meeting him, so that he could give her his interpretation.

Such was the transformation of the Summer; strange as it would have seemed a year ago, Anna had no trouble believing the conclusions that Mo and Aubrey had drawn so far. Their reasoning was clear, their logic was sound, and they welcomed any questions that undermined their arguments, which they were happy to answer.

Inevitably, their arguments held up.

Anna and Thea turned a corner, bringing Bailey's into view. Leonard, Neville, and Shannon were already at the bar. Mo and Aubrey would be the last to arrive; the Department of Surveillance continued to keep its workers in place until after all of the Knowers had vacated their posts for the day, which meant that Mo would set out for Bailey's after the others, and Aubrey's position at The Villa left her with a longer walk than those who worked in the Center of Industry.

That was just as well, Anna thought; it gave the five of them time to organize their report.

In addition to the insights that Anna, Thea, and Shannon had gleaned in their roles as Junior Knowers, Neville and Leonard's new responsibilities at the Department of Media Production had allowed them to get another perspective of what was going on in Kingston. Neville was working in a role on the broadcast scheduling team, and got to sit in on strategy sessions where the executives discussed how and when media reports should be dispensed to the citizens of Kingston, while Leonard had been assigned to create short "pro-utopian" films profiling how fortunate sentient beings were to live in The Bubble Society. Leonard found it difficult to find creative inspiration for this project; before this year's Advent, it would have been easy, but with their access to Kingston Reservoir cut off, their work hours increased, and the continued hole left by Gavin's disappearance, Leonard was no longer feeling so fortunate to live in The Bubble Society, no matter how page 2 of *The Manual for Proper Behavior* told him he should feel.

The feeling was not unique to him; in fact, it was the primary reason that he, and the others, were bringing their reports to Mo. None of them had done anything but observe, but that was all Mo needed; he seemed to have an instinct for making sense of it all from there.

They did not have to wait long; shortly after Anna and Thea greeted the others, Mo and Aubrey appeared on opposite sides of the plaza and began making their way toward their friends. Anna knew that Mo would not want to talk at the bar, but that was nothing new to the bartender, who happened to be Aubrey's younger sister, and had a round table set aside for them in a semi-private room inside.

—

"Hate to circle back on it again, but I wanna make sure I got it right. You're telling me, after everything they told us 'bout the Savages stealing our Knowledge, that we don't have anything close to a viable oral or nasal filter?"

Anna and Thea shook their heads; Thea answered for both of them.

"Not so much as a basic prototype. We've both continued to ask around - surreptitiously, as you suggested, which is why it's taken so long - but none of the other Knowers on the team had ever heard of a mouth or nose filter before Tesla's abduction. They were obviously familiar with the Bubble Suit's built-in air filtration system - that's the one that Knower Ludquist was able to upgrade - but they have no idea at all about any other filters, oral, nasal, or otherwise."

Uneasy glances were exchanged around the table. Mo locked eyes with Aubrey, who frowned before she shared her latest update with the group.

"Another day, same story. I don't know if it can really get worse now, but the stream is steady; more Laureates of all ages rolling in every day. We're nearly to capacity, which has never been anything close to a consideration before; I don't know what the Guvernment will do if we run out of space."

"The pro-utopian broadcast schedule has picked up as well," Neville added. "*Rise and Shine Kingston!* will be a full half-hour starting tomorrow - the second half of the show will have a series of reminders that sentient beings ought to be on their way to work, as truancy has become so common of late - and every workday will now feature a thirty-minute break so all of our citizuns can view an educational film on the virtues of living in a utop..."

A crash outside interrupted Neville's words; everyone but Mo jumped to their feet, looking out of the private room's doorway, across Bailey's to the plaza beyond, where a small crowd was gathering around a cloud of dust.

"What was that?" asked Leonard, his voice strained as he craned his neck around to look through the window, where a cloud of dust was billowing up.

"Buncha' shingles fell off the roof."

The others spun their heads away from the crash to look at Mo, who remained seated, his eyes on his steepled hands.

"How do you know?"

"Cuz' I saw they were loose 'bout two weeks ago, and I been keepin' an eye on it since. It was bound to happen, if not yesterday, then one of the next few days here."

Nobody contradicted him; they were still too shocked by the crash, too distracted by the crowd gathering around the rubble. Mo, completely unconcerned by the situation, continued the discussion.

"Well, I don't got an answer, or anything close to one, but I reckon I got enough to come to a conclusion at this point."

The clamor continued to grow outside, but the others were no longer paying attention to that; intrigued by Mo's words, they retook their seats.

"This claim that the Guvernment makes - that sentient beings have the Knowledge to control Nature, to shape our destiny and create the utopia they call The Bubble Society - it's all a buncha' bullshit."

—

"It's completely unacceptable, is what it is."

Tarissa Cross's anger radiated off her as a sort of heat; Head Knower Mallion sat there, under her scorching gaze and the eyes of most of The Board, wondering if the woman would drop dead of cardiac arrest, despite the Bubble Suits being designed to prevent such maladies.

To his disappointment, Tarissa Cross remained upright, and continued to vent her displeasure.

"It has been weeks, Mallion, weeks, and if you and your Knowers don't get something figured out quickly, we will have to delay our attack on the Savages until after Winter. Do you really think such a delay is acceptable, with the strain you've put The Bubble Society under in the pursuit of this Knowledge that you find so elusive?"

Mallion exhaled.

"Acceptable? I do not know if that is the word, Ms. Cross; the delay is disappointing, the wait interminable, and yet we are trying to invent a novel technology. Who can say if we will ever invent it?"

"I can say, Mallion; in fact, I Know that The Bubble Society will create such a filter. Our success is inevitable, our future safeguarded, our control of sentient destiny an iron grip; how could we possibly fail to invent something as simple as these breathing devices?"

Mallion did not respond.

"Frankly, I think your lack of enthusiasm might be the problem. If you were on the frontlines, encouraging our Knowers on, convincing them that the solution is close at hand, then perhaps they would make better progress."

"Or perhaps they would come after me," retorted Mallion irritably. "Perhaps they would not take it well, after all the time they have spent working on these problems, to have someone come through and tell them that it ought to be easy, that they just need to have some spring in their step."

Cross considered this, then nodded.

"You're exactly right, Mallion."

Mallion blinked, confused.

"You're not the one to inspire our Knowers, much less the citizuns of The Bubble Society; that's become clear enough this season. It's time we bring the sentient beings who are equipped to do that out to center stage."

BOOK 5, CHAPTER 8

The morning air was crisp, the water in the creek cool. The buck dipped its muzzle to drink; steam rose from its snout as it lifted its head back up to glance around.

The world was changing; evergreens dominated the scenery at this elevation, but they were not the only trees in the Cadillac Mountains, and as Autumn rolled forward, taking them closer and closer to Winter, the color change was in full effect, the monolith of greens shifting to a tapestry of reds, oranges, and yellows, an ephemeral painting that the Wild put on display for a few brief days each year.

The buck may not have appreciated the artistry of this cycle as a sentient being would, but he could read the signs and understand that the seasons were changing, that Winter was fast approaching. A time to graze, a time to prepare. Soon, the eight-point rack he had grown that season would fall off; after that, grazing would not be so easy as today, when the food remained abundant, when he could drink and graze downstream of Turquoise Falls, the faint sounds of the waterfall around him.

It was those sounds that prevented the buck ever hearing the twang of the bowstring; the arrow was through him before he realized that anything had happened, a perfectly placed shot that dropped him where he stood, his hind legs on the bank, his muzzle in the water.

Anton was quick to spring on his prize. He was not the only one; as the blond man emerged from the trees, jogging with his bow at his side, three others joined him, carrying their own weapons as they ran out from their cover, intent on retrieving the buck before the Western Grand pulled him off the bank and into its current.

They retrieved the animal without issue; Anton was the first to reach the buck, and he had pulled it mostly clear of the stream by the time Al Nierland reached him to assist. Once Al was engaged, the job became easy; at a glance, Anton guessed the buck weighed four hundred pounds, but you would not have known from the way Nierland handled it.

Anton glanced around at the two younger men behind them. Bruno Hughes, one of Salomon Cahn's many grandchildren, stood closest; at a nod from Anton, he followed Al, pulling out a knife to begin the process of packing out the meat. The other young man followed suit.

As the others worked, Anton returned to the stream, briefly washing his hands - not because they would stay clean, he would return to assist the others momentarily - but because he needed to throw cold water on his face, and did not want to do it with blood on his hands.

After a season of unceasing preparations, with Winter fast approaching, even the emotions of a hunt were insufficient to keep Anton as alert as he would like to be.

"Surprised an animal that large stuck around, what with all the ruckus we're causing up at Turquoise Lake."

Anton did not respond at once; he was staring at his reflection, flickering back at him in the rushing water. His blond hair, which he had cut short after they had moved down to Turquoise Lake, had grown back quickly, and for the first time, he noticed grey mixed among the blond. His beard, in need of a trim, showed similar changes, and the transformation did not stop there; even in the ripples of the creek, Anton could see the deepening lines forming around his eyes, across his forehead.

None of it was a surprise; he had not slept well these past weeks, his mind racked with thoughts of all that needed doing, and he was well aware of the toll it was all taking on him, even if he ignored it and pushed on.

The organization of a garrison.

The construction of their defense outposts.

The positioning of their heavy weaponry.

And on top of it all, the persistent need to hunt, to prepare, not only Trepani, but Giota, Kirfi, and Larissa for the cold, hard Winter ahead.

Anton shook himself; the difficulty, or lack thereof, was irrelevant. What needed to be done would be done; he would make sure of it. Mind clear - or as close to clear as it got these days - Anton turned to acknowledge Al's words, nodding.

"I'm surprised he didn't leave the area weeks ago; we might keep a clean camp, but it's impossible for a thousand sentient beings to move into an area and not make their presence felt."

Nierland nodded in agreement, thinking back to what Gwynivere Holt had said on a recent visit.

Anton, Al, and a few others had taken Gwynivere and her contingent to a ridge of the bowl that cupped Turquoise Lake, a ridge with a commanding view of the valley below that allowed them to look down at the teeming mass moving below.

"I can see you've been busy," Gwynivere had commented, observing Anton in her periphery as she kept her gaze on the valley.

"Busy would cover it," Anton had deadpanned. "Yet nowhere near as busy as we would need to be if the sentient beings down in Kingston get their act together and figure out a way to come meet us."

"Sad, yet true," replied Gwynivere. "But perhaps that day will never come to pass. Perhaps the Knowers down in Kingston never figure out this problem, whatever your sister might say, and The Bubble Society will remain stranded down in Kingston."

Anton did not acknowledge the reference to Tesla; he simply shook his head.

"No. From everything we've heard, they're pouring too much into this project to fail. If they don't figure out the air filtration issue, they will be forced to blindly unleash their arsenal on us; my best guess is that, if they don't figure it out by Winter, they use those hundred days to make a last push. If they don't find a solution by Spring, they will resort to their arsenal; they won't have the resources to do anything else."

He paused.

"We can start winding down the garrison at the end of the week; all of the heavy lifting is done, the construction work finished. We can recall the troops if there is a threat from The Bubble Society, but something tells me that won't happen before Winter."

"Why not keep them here? Keep them ready, in case the worst happens?"

Anton shook his head.

"If I could do it without cost, I would. But I can't; wiser military minds than mine observed that a population cannot be on a continual war footing, lest they bankrupt the home front. We've avoided that so far, but there's no reason to maintain a force of this size unless conflict is imminent, not now we've got our position dug in. We're dialed into Kingston's media broadcasts; trust me, if you were watching that every day, you wouldn't doubt that they will trumpet any progress they make loud and wide. If that happens - if The Bubble Society shows any sign they might soon be ready to march - then we can get our defenders back in place before this outpost is threatened. For now, I think we can start sending everyone home to their families, and be grateful for the cover Winter will provide us."

To Gwynivere's surprise, Anton chuckled, and almost grinned, at his own words; then the moment was gone, the stoic expression was back.

"Never thought I'd hear myself say anything of the sort about our Winter."

Gwynivere gave him a sidelong glance.

"And how will you spend Winter? You might come to Giota, stay with Katarina and Mitzy; you have not asked how they are."

Anton's expression did not so much as flicker.

"Well, if you won't ask, perhaps you'll allow me to tell you that they are well, that little Mitzy is smart, strong, and growing up fast."

Anton's face remained impassive as he responded.

"That's good. If we ensure Giota's continued existence, perhaps that will continue."

He shifted the topic before Gwynivere could comment further on his third daughter and her mother.

"There is one thing that bothers me; I assume you got word of the attack on Clarence and the others in Larissa?"

Gwynivere nodded, a stern expression crossing her face.

"I don't understand why we didn't do more to capture them before they reached Larissa, nor do I appreciate Marcus allowing them to pass through; whatever his stance might have been, The Council agreed with the stance Alabaster and I championed along with Ruby and Tyene. We had Clarence and Gavin locked up, and that imprisonment was supposed to last until the war's end."

She paused.

"But what of the attack? Why should a few Acadians with some sense trying to stop Clarence and his madness bother you?"

Anton shook his head.

"They weren't Acadians," he said, his voice quiet.

He paused.

"What do you mean, they weren't Acadians?"

Anton turned to meet Gwynivere's eyes again.

"When the shots went off, it brought a crowd; they caught two of the men. Marcus questioned them; evidently, it was not difficult, as they had no loyalty to the man who had paid them."

"That man had hired them in the port of Greco, over on the continent of Thoran. Evidently, he told them little and less of his true identity, but the men he hired were no fools; they knew where their employer had come from. They saw no reason to challenge his lies - not when the coin he traded was real - but nor were they deceived by them."

"Based on everything our captives said, Theodore Bouregard has not forgotten that sentient beings don't need Bubble Suits to survive on the planet Shurtain, even if he's convinced his whole society of the opposite. The fact that Bouregard feels compelled to keep his population in the Bubble Suits, even when he wants to mount an assault on us up here, tells you all you need to know about how things are going down in the city, but right now, there is a more pressing matter."

"The people of Kingston might all wear Bubble Suits, but based on what Marcus gathered from the men they captured, Mateo Fernandez isn't bound by that constraint anymore. And if The Director has granted Fernandez that privilege, who can say what other surprises are in store?"

BOOK 5, CHAPTER 9

"That's it for today's episode of *Rise and Shine Kingston!* Citizuns of Kingston, it is our duty to demonstrate what a delightful day it is to be alive in our utopia, what a gift it is to live in The Bubble Society, the greatest society that ever has been and ever will be. Now let's get out there, and do our part for the community; as you all know, your sacrifice to Knowledge is allowing us to build a bigger and better utopia."

"The hell it is! It's killing us all!"

Jimbo Kerns was on his feet for the morning broadcast, ranting and raving as he paced around the living room. His roommate, Diego Avion, watched in mute exasperation as Jimbo nearly tripped over a chair, catching himself by shooting out a hand and leaving yet another indentation on the drywall of their apartment walls.

At least he had not punched a hole this time.

As Jimbo righted himself, Diego glanced around their apartment, taking in all the other damage - the holes in the walls, the scraped paint, the crooked furniture - that stood as testament to the frequency with which Jimbo had repeated this behavior over the past weeks.

Diego had done his best to mitigate the issue, going so far as to put in a request to the Guvernment Housing Authority for a television; he had hoped that, if Jimbo could watch the Guvernment Media Broadcasts on an external screen, he might at least stay stationary as he screamed at the people reading from the teleprompters, instead of walking around blindly and tripping over the furniture.

Of course, the requisition request had been delayed - everyone in Kingston understood that you would be lucky to get a response for a

Laureate Assessment these days, much less a furniture request - but the building's maintenance man, Curtis, had told Diego that one of the sentient beings with an external television in his apartment had recently been whisked off to The Villa, and that he would look the other way if the television got moved.

Diego had taken Curtis up on the offer; it was a simple enough task, as Kingston's apartments did not have locks on the doors, which made it easy for Diego to let himself into the vacated apartment and liberate the television.

Unfortunately, his efforts had been for naught; even with the television set up, Jimbo insisted on watching the Guvernment Media Broadcasts through his Bubble Suit's holographic monitor as he stomped around their apartment, tripping over chairs, plunging through walls, and adamantly refusing to use picture-in-picture mode, insisting that the news required his full attention.

It was enough to make Diego thankful that they only had one window in their apartment, and that there was a table blocking it off from the rest of the room. Otherwise, Jimbo would have plunged through the glass by now; Diego was certain of it.

"It's killing us, don't they see that? We gotta get help fast, or we're all in trouble."

"They can't hear you, Jimbo."

It was the first time in weeks that Diego had responded to Jimbo's ravings. Like his roommate, Diego was a member of the City Watch, but unlike Jimbo, he had never been all that concerned about the search for Gavin Owen's body, or why it was taking place. Diego's days were long enough without trying to figure out why his commanders issued the commands they issued, or why the Guvernment made the decisions that it made.

"What?"

Jimbo spun around at Diego's words, staring at his roommate with a glazed expression on his face, a side effect of looking at the world through a holographic monitor.

"They can't hear you. The people on the television, or whoever it is that you're talking to. I'm the only one who can hear you; me, and a few of our neighbors. Walls are thin in this place."

Jimbo shook his head.

"But I gotta do something - *we* gotta do something - it'll kill us all, can'cha see?"

Diego shook his head.

"I dunno about all that. But I can't do anything about it, old man Hersh next door can't do anything about it, and poor Ms. Pottmore upstairs can't do anything about it. Whoever it is that makes these decisions… they can't hear a word you're saying."

But they could.

—

Tarissa Cross's mouth tightened as the video clip cut off, erasing the image of the two men in the apartment, the one shaking his fist as he raved at thin air.

"*That* is what I am talking about, Mallion. You ask me what I mean when I say that your Knowers are undermining all that we stand for; well, this is what I mean. Your incompetence, your inability to meet deadlines, has severely undermined the public confidence in Knowledge. We need to take some sort of action, and sooner than later."

Zenus Mallion did not respond; he had an inkling of what was coming, more or less, when he had been summoned to The Retreat that morning, and there had been no surprises so far. Mallion had taken a seat in the conference room, provided a straightforward answer to the first question posed to him - *Are the air filtration devices complete?* - and been treated, along with the rest of The Board, to a fifteen-minute rant as Tarissa Cross answered her second question - *Do you have any idea how that makes me look?* - on her own.

As the silence stretched on, Mallion realized he would have to offer some sort of response. He glanced at The Director before he did - surely, the man could step in, and force some sanity into these discussions - but The Director did not appear to be paying much attention to their exchange, or to anything else going on in the conference room; his eyes were distant, his expression placid.

"I'm sorry to hear that, Viceroy. I must admit, I find it ironic that the year we have made the most significant advance in Knowledge in two decades - Knower Ludquist's Bubble Suit upgrades - is the same year that we are experiencing this public loss of confidence. I submit it might have something to do with the expectations that were presented to the public; there was no evidence to suggest we could improve the efficiency of our air filtration system in such short order, or that it is even possible to build the mouth and nose filters you requested."

Mallion saw the skin at the corners of Cross's eyes tighten at this; aware that he was about to hear more about the supposed theft the Savages had committed, he pushed ahead.

"That said, I am confused as to what this has to do with… how did you put it, how it makes you look? Your fellow Board Members and The Director surely understand it is not for you, in your role as Viceroy, to solve these problems. And by design, you are all concealed from the public - at least in your positions as members of this Board - so I don't see what impact this has on your image."

"You're wrong on two counts there, Mallion."

"First off, it makes the Guvernment, and by extension, Dynamic

Solutions, look bad, and we, The Board of the company, cannot allow that. We channel the will of Knowledge, we shape sentient destiny. We are the shepherds of the citizuns of The Bubble Society; we must not allow our flock to see us as anything less than omniscient."

"Second off, the citizuns of Kingston are about to find out who I am; The Guvna' has done well enough in his speaking roles, but dire times call for dire measures, and we have all agreed that it is time for me to step into the spotlight. We must establish, once and for all, that Knowledge is all-powerful, that the sentient beings of old were an uncouth, unsophisticated people, a mongrel race incapable of producing anything but chaos."

Mallion ignored the last remark; common as it was to hear, the sentient beings uttering that sentiment seemed to have forgotten that they themselves had lived in the years Before Knowledge. That irrelevancy aside, he was interested in another point.

"How do you intend to do that?"

For the first time in Mallion's memory, an honest-to-goodness smile spread across Tarissa Cross's face; she glowed, and for a moment, Mallion saw her beauty, the mocha skin, the black hair, the big brown eyes.

"I will give a speech, the likes of which you have never seen. It will be so captivating, so charismatic, so articulate, that the people of Kingston will be falling over themselves to follow me forward."

"And then, we will blow up The Old Capitol."

—

Kelli Molinaro stood on the highest balcony of The Guvna's Mansion, flanked by Andrea and Rachel as she looked down on the crowd gathering in Capitol Square, where a stage had been erected in front of The Old Capitol.

Kelli, Andrea, and Rachel could not see Donnie - not yet - but she knew that he, and the other sentient beings scheduled to speak at today's ceremony, would be cloistered in the entry chamber of The Old Capitol, waiting for the scheduled moment to make their procession out of the fading edifice. It was to be the most formal of occasions; after all, it was not often that a people eradicated the last traces of its historical record from existence.

They did not have to wait long; the crowd filled Capitol Square quickly, the sentient beings from the Amada District - there was not sufficient room in Capitol Square to hold the citizuns from the Axios and Andola Districts, not when the event was outside of Kingston Amphitheater - packing the place to bursting.

For the briefest of moments, it struck Kelli that something seemed off about this crowd; she had attended hundreds of functions in her role as The Guvna's wife, and had seen her share of excited crowds, but she could not recall feeling the sort of energy she felt today, the undeniable anger that simmered in the crowd.

The doors of The Old Capitol creaked open, sending thoughts of the crowd from Kelli's mind.

For a moment, she stood frozen, unable to breathe, shocked into silence by the faces she saw at the front of the delegation.

Both Kelli and Donnie had been left in the dark about exactly what would happen when he had received the phone call ordering him to report to The Old Capitol within the hour - Donnie had only been told that they would be retiring The Old Capitol, whatever that meant - and while life had taught Kelli Mancini to expect the unexpected, she would never have imagined that her husband, The Guvna', would be flanked by these members of The Board as he took the stage at a public event.

Yet there they were; Reginald Klaus and Yvonne Delverta trailed close behind her husband as he led the procession out of The Old Capitol. The presence of Giuseppe Montenegro, Astrid Johnson, and Sofia Garcia was not a surprise - Kingston's population Knew the three from their respective roles in the Halls of Parliament - but Kelli had never imagined she would see Klaus or Delverta onstage in a public setting.

Of course, nobody else in the crowd would be able to understand the significance; Donnie had only communicated the truth of The Board to her during their hours in Onyx Canyon, where such confidences could be shared. To the others, these two were strangers, generic faces with unknown backstories.

It was, without reservation, the thing that worried Kelli Mancini the most as she watched her husband step up to the podium.

—

"Ma fella' citizuns, we gatha' today fer anotha' momentous day in da history o' Da Bubble Society, another celebration o' da gifts Knowledge has bestowed upon us."

Donnie's words distracted Kelli from her musings; with no idea of what was to come in his speech, she wondered, for the briefest of moments, whether the Knowers had finally achieved the upgrades required for the Bubble Suits to function at higher altitudes. The thought put Kelli's heart in her throat; she wondered what it would mean if they had.

"Now, I can guess whatchur thinking, and no, I ain't here ta 'nnounce anything ta do with da Elevation Upgrade Prizes. Da Knowers are continuing ta work on it, so y'all can 'spect something sooner 'n later, but not today. Today is summin' different."

"Da Guvna's Office has decided, in conjunction wit' Da Halls o' Parliament, ta create a new office, one o' da greatest importance."

"In honor o' dis incredible day, we've planned quite da event - one dat is certain ta propel us ta greater heights - but I'll leave it ta our new Minister o' Knowledge ta make dat 'nnouncement. Citizuns o' Kingston, put yer hands together fer Tarissa Cross."f

Numerous as they were, the crowd's initial response was tepid - more confused than anything - as Tarissa Cross strode out from between the doors of The Old Capitol onto the red carpet that led to center stage. Then the music kicked in, surging out of huge speakers and injecting life into Capitol Square as Cross made her way to the podium, beaming and waving every step of the way.

For his part, The Guvna' wandered off to take a spot at the edge of the stage, next to Knower Ludquist, who, like The Guvna', appeared to have deliberately placed himself as far away from Reginald Klaus, Yvonne Delverta, Giuseppe Montenegro, Astrid Johnson, and Sofia Garcia as was possible. Satisfied with his position, and happy to be done with his bit in this charade, The Guvna' faced the crowd, intending to settle back and enjoy the show.

Instead, as he took the crowd in again, The Guvna' realized that something was wrong, that something about this crowd was different than your typical gathering in The Bubble Society. The differences were subtle - the anger in the eyes, the set of certain jaws - but in that moment, Donnie Molinaro knew that something had changed in the citizuns of Kingston, even if they had not yet realized it themselves.

—

"Hello hello Kingston! How are we all doing today?"

The crowd reacted to Tarissa Cross's greeting by looking at one another in confusion, exchanging quiet mutters as they tried to figure out if anyone had ever heard of this woman.

"I saaaaid, how are we all doing today?"

To salvage the moment, a stagehand set off an extra volley of fireworks; satisfied that there had been some sort of response to her question, Tarissa Cross plunged forward.

"Now, I Know how pleased you all are to have been part of the latest, greatest efforts to make our Bubble Suits all they can be; the hours have been long, but it is good to see proof that the citizuns of The Bubble Society are only too happy to work for the greater good of our utopia."

"I stand before you today to tell you that all of these efforts will soon pay off; with the unrivaled devotion that we continue to show to Knowledge, it simply cannot be any other way."

"However, I was not appointed Minister of Knowledge to stand idly by, and to that end, I believe I have discovered the reason that Knowledge has not granted us the nasal and oral air filtration devices we all desire so deeply."

The crowd took on a noticeable change at these words, their anger momentarily forgotten as they waited for Cross to continue.

"The problem, in my view, is that despite all we have done, all the efforts we have made, we still have not shown sufficient devotion to the power of Knowledge. By allowing The Old Capitol to stand, we have worshipped false idols, committed blasphemy, continued to glorify the years Before Knowledge and the sentient beings who lived back then, who were little better than the Savages, grubbing around the planet Shurtain in their own skins, at the mercy of the atmosphere for their very survival."

"You all Know how much times have changed, but we have not done enough to change with them. Even in its dilapidated state, The Old Capitol stands as an affront to Knowledge, an insult to everything we have been delivered in the past decades."

Cross paused. She was expecting a rousing round of applause - she had scripted it into her speech - but the crowd was staring at her in confused silence, trying to understand where she was going with all of this. It left a bad taste in Cross's mouth; it struck her, in that moment, that Kingston's population, even those sentient beings who lived in the Amada District, were a bunch of idiots, too stupid to react properly, even as they listened to the most momentous speech that would be delivered in their lifetimes.

But Tarissa Cross could not worry about the shortcomings of the citizuns of The Bubble Society now; those could be corrected later. At the moment, she had a speech to deliver.

"All of that will change today, the 31st of Fall in the Year 21, After Knowledge. Today, we will step into the fullest expression of our utopia; today, we will demolish The Old Capitol. We will leave no trace of anything that existed Before Knowledge, and The New Capitol and The Guvna's Mansion will shine all the brighter for it."

The Guvna' stiffened at these words; even in their backstage preparations, Tarissa Cross had not told him exactly what would happen at this ceremony, only that he would introduce her in her new, public-facing role as The Minister of Knowledge so that she could retire The Old Capitol, a phrasing he had not thought to question at the time.

Now, as Donnie Molinaro processed what Cross was saying, his eyes sought out the blue uniforms and high-peaked hats that marked the Capitol Guard, as well as the harsher black uniforms of their counterparts in the City Watch. They were there, and in considerable numbers, but it was not enough, not nearly enough, if this went the way that Donnie thought it might.

"As Minister of Knowledge, I will do the honors; our Knowers have designed the controlled demolition to go off without any danger to the crowd assembled here in Capitol Square. We built everything around those specifications, placing the stage outside of the danger zone, so that we can all bear witness to this incredible moment."

Cross turned to where her fellow Board Members stood.

"Moderator Montenegro, if you could bring me the primer?"

Giuseppe Montenegro stepped out from the group, holding a small device with a large red button, which he held out to Cross as he approached her. The crowd watched with bated breath as Cross did a little shimmy, overcome with excitement as she prepared herself to press the trigger.

The Guvna' was one of two people in attendance no longer watching Cross; Donnie Molinaro was already acting on his overwhelming instinct that something was about to go horribly, horribly wrong. He was joined by one other; as Cross had outlined the "precautions" that his fellow Knowers had taken, Viktor Ludquist had felt terror seize his insides. Fully aware of how incompetent most of his fellow Knowers were, Ludquist did not have to be asked when he noticed The Guvna' walk to the edge of the stage and jump down into the crowd; he simply followed.

Tarissa Cross noticed none of this; she was in her element, casting a final smile over the crowd before she turned sharply on her heel to face The Old Capitol. As she looked at the fading edifice, and triggered the red button, a single, distinct thought crossed through Tarissa Cross's mind.

This is your moment, T. The moment you cement yourself as the future Director.

—

It took half-a-beat for it to happen.

There was a moment of silence, of absolute stillness.

Then the rumbles came; not explosions, as some had expected, but a lower, deeper vibration, a sound at the edge of hearing emanating from deep within the bowels of The Old Capitol.

It was only the beginning; a second later, the sound hit a different pitch, and then The Old Capitol was shaking, collapsing, its walls coming down, the structure mushrooming out for the briefest of moments, then shrinking in, back toward the initial expansion.

Then there was another series of sounds, this volley far louder: the sounds of more explosives going off somewhere deep in The Old Capitol.

For the briefest of moments, in the last seconds of calm, the Knowers who had rigged the building for demolition exchanged looks of confusion, but they never got the chance to voice the alarming questions that second set of sounds had raised in their minds; at that instant, the shockwaves rippled out from The Old Capitol, and the world went into chaos.

—

The Guvna' and Knower Ludquist had been wise to move.

As Donnie Molinaro had anticipated, the hastily built stage was nowhere close to capable of surviving the controlled demolition; when the tremors reached it, the stage vibrated, cracked, and collapsed, all in the space of a second, sending the distinguished individuals who stood upon the dais sprawling through the air.

People were screaming by then, the shockwaves hitting the crowd, knocking many to the ground and sending the rest into a fury, pushing and squabbling as they attempted to regain their feet, shoving others down in their attempt to get upright.

Pandemonium reigned as Donnie Molinaro darted through the crowd, fighting his way toward The Guvna's Mansion even as dust and debris billowed up around him, engulfing the crowd in the discharge of The Old Capitol as the shockwaves, now clear of Capitol Square, rippled out in every direction.

The scene was utter confusion, chaos; The Old Capitol was gone, collapsed to rubble, leaving a sweeping view to the southeast, a view that allowed the people in the crowd to see clear across Kingston, from the hilltop where Capitol Square sat to where the Granite Bridge spanned the Grand River.

Somehow, through all the madness, the crowd's attention was drawn to the continued progress of the shockwaves; some pointed to where the ground continued to ripple in the distance, attempting to get the attention of others in the crowd.

Amidst the debris of the stage, Tarissa Cross was getting back to her feet; setting aside the shock of being tossed to the ground, she climbed to the highest point on what was left of the stage, a broken hunk of wood that slanted upwards at an angle.

It gave her the view she needed to see it all.

The shockwaves reaching The Granite Bridge.

The tremors in the ground running straight into the base of the causeway.

The vibrations in the bridge as the shockwaves passed through.

The moment when the tremors cleared, reappearing to continue on their path on the far side of the Grand River.

For half an instant, Tarissa Cross dared to hope.

And then, with the crowd's overwhelming attention on it, The Granite Bridge collapsed.

BOOK 5, CHAPTER 10

The water in the pool was warm, the room lit by a handful of candles that bathed the marble walls in a soft glow.

The man floated in the pool, savoring it all; the touch of water on his skin, the intoxicating aroma of the candle, the sound of ripples softly echoing in the otherwise silent chamber. And this was only the opening course; the main attraction awaited him, uncorked and left to breathe in The Retreat's most luxurious accommodations, one of the two master suites on the penthouse level, rooms that opened onto an expansive balcony with sweeping views of the forest around them and the city beyond.

It would come, in time… but there was no need to hurry, no need to rush. These moments were to be savored; after all, the finest vintages would soon run dry, leaving him with nothing but inferior substitutes to satisfy his desires, to indulge his imagination.

The man lounged in the water for another quarter-hour before he rose; he exited the pool, and picked up the lush towel that awaited him. He dried himself off, then made his way out of the marble chamber, into another dimly lit room, where he took a seat in a comfortable recliner. He reached out a hand to the small table on the right of the chair, pressed the button that sat atop it, and settled back, closing his eyes to await the next stage of this process.

He did not have to wait long; within moments, there was a bustling, the sounds of two others padding through the room.

The clink of glass on wood indicated that his cabernet had been delivered; the man did not open his eyes, but instead reached to the spot he knew the glass would be, took it in his hand, and brought it up to his nose. He sank his face into the expansive glass, closed his mouth, and inhaled deeply through his nose, allowing tendrils of the aroma to course through him. Then, as that feeling peaked, he took his first sip of the burgundy liquid, exuding a satisfied sigh as his pleasure centers spiked to new heights.

The man returned the glass to its place and sat back, allowing his two attendants to do their work, enjoying the sensations as they groomed him from head to toe, shaving back stray hairs, clipping his nails, powdering his feet, and, finally, touching him with two spots of a sweetly scent. Occasionally, the man returned to his glass, but he did not indulge too deeply; the wine could enhance the experience ahead of him, but too much, and he would not be in a state of mind to enjoy what awaited him.

"We are finished. Are you ready?"

The man nodded; he kept his eyes closed as the lights in the room came on. Even when he stood, his eyes remained shut; he allowed his two attendants to gown him in robes of soft velvet.

"It is time."

The man opened his eyes; seeing Cornelius and Penelope Kastner, he gave a brief nod.

Then The Director stepped through the doorway, into the master bedroom suite beyond.

—

She was gowned in the finest of silks, wore necklaces of immeasurable value, had spent days in accommodations more luxurious than she could have dreamed.

Still, the young woman appeared tense, frightened. Even with her back turned to him, her eyes on the view of the horizon, The Director could sense that.

This was not foreign to him; in fact, it was expected.

After all, it was a jarring enough experience for the Guvernment to summon you; getting cut out of one's Bubble Suit put the sequence of events in a different stratosphere of strange.

And yet, familiar as it was, it would not do; The Director knew, from long experience, that he would have to set this young woman at her ease if he were to fully enjoy what was to come. Fortunately, he was practiced at this, had honed his craft with hundreds of others during his decades running The Bubble Society, and he understood how important it was that he deftly apply his craft now. This young woman, this Ursula, was one of the last on his list who had not been grown by the Department of Child Development, and The Director was all too familiar with the shortcomings of those vintages.

Once upon a time, The Director had been excited for those girls to reach womanhood, believing that they would satisfy his tastes even more thoroughly than the women born Before Knowledge, but the newer vintages had left him wanting. Their bodies had no strength to them, no ability to engage in any sort of vigorous physical activity, sexual or otherwise. The young ones even tasted wrong; whether it was the growth process in the Department of Child Development, or simply a lifetime of consuming the nutrient paste pumped into the Bubble Suits, The Director could not say.

But he understood that such women did not satisfy his cravings.

Which made it all the more important that he make this one count.

"The staff has prepared a delicious meal for us: three courses, with a main dish of river trout. They will be bringing it in soon; won't you join me at the table?"

—

Ursula was a beauty, The Director thought: brown eyes, smooth, tan skin, black hair, and a small, sensuous mouth. Penelope had attended to Ursula these past few days, ensuring that she ate well and bathed multiple times each day. The process allowed the woman's skin to breathe, to interact with the open air, before she was put before The Director.

As Ursula drank a third glass of wine, and the terror in those brown eyes dulled away, her beauty was all the more evident. The Director wished he could keep this one - in the past, it had been his practice to hold on to favored choices for weeks, even a season or two - but he had learned that even the best of them would wilt in captivity, their spirits dying within them, making them less tasteful to The Director.

In years since, he had applied those lessons; he preferred to indulge in the young women when they were at their best, still pure, and virgin, not yet fully captured by the horror of their new reality. He would enjoy them for a few hours, perhaps a day or two, and then would move them along the procession, replacing them with a fresh vintage the next time his desires were aroused; that way, The Director only had memories of these young women at their best.

This one was not yet at her ease; The Director continued to enjoy the meal, waiting for her to broach the topic.

"What's going to happen to me?"

Ursula blurted out the question suddenly, animalistic fear returning to her brown eyes as the words passed her lips.

As soon as she spoke, she flinched away from The Director, focusing her gaze on the distant view through the windows on the far wall. The Director smiled; when he responded, it was in his most scholarly tone, a wise old professor guiding the wayward child through the uncertainties of life on Shurtain.

"Happen to you?"

Hearing the softness in the man's voice, Ursula turned back to him. She nodded, her brown eyes begging for mercy.

"Why, my dear, didn't Penelope tell you? You have been selected to join the Elite of Kingston, to live a life of unimaginable life and luxury, to enjoy all the sensual delights this planet has to offer."

"But my… my…"

Ursula groped at the tan skin of her left wrist, the fingers of her right hand pinching at the surface, as if they could still grip the membrane of The Bubble Suits.

"Ah, of course, how could I have forgotten? Well, as you can see, both you and I are healthy enough to function without the Bubble Suits. We could not survive indefinitely - nobody can - but our bodies are strong enough to withstand the perils of Shurtain's atmosphere far longer than your average sentient being."

Her brown eyes wide, desperate to accept what he was saying as true, Ursula asked the question that had haunted her since Penelope had appeared in her bedroom, a Spike in hand.

"So I'm not going to die?"

The question came in a frightened squeak. Embarrassed, Ursula looked away, but then The Director reached across the table, and took one of her hands in his; she turned back, reassured by the softness of his touch.

"Die? Why should you think we would allow that to happen to you? You, my dear, are here to be cherished."

—

They were in the heat of the act, The Director pushing the young woman's face down as he took her from behind, when the doors burst open.

The Director spun around, coming free of Ursula, searching for the source of this unexpected surprise; he found Penelope and Cornelius standing in the doorway.

For a moment, The Director remained in the same position, upright on his knees, still on the bed, looking back and forth between the two small figures. He had intended to yell at the intruder for interrupting him, but Penelope and Cornelius would not have appeared without good reason; after all, they had helped him prepare for each of these ceremonies, and understood their importance.

"What is it?" he snapped.

Cornelius and Penelope exchanged a brief glance; Penelope offered the first answer.

"The destruction of The Old Capitol has led to some unexpected consequences."

"What consequences?"

The pair exchanged another glance; this time, Cornelius answered.

"For one, the Granite Bridge collapsed from the shockwaves."

"You interrupted me to tell me that a bridge collapsed? In the middle of a vintage of this quality?"

Penelope shook her head.

"No. We interrupted you to tell you that there is a massive riot spreading from Capitol Square. The city is in chaos, and we need you in the situation room. Now."

—

Donnie Molinaro was moving before the sounds of the demolition reached him, pushing his Bubble Suit to its limits as he moved as quickly as he could in the direction of The Guvna's Mansion, all thoughts of his office gone, his mind fixed on the need to reach Kelli, and the girls, to get them the hell out of The Mansion, out of Capitol Square, before it was too late.

He could only hope that Kelli would have the wherewithal to understand what she was seeing, and to get the girls to their evacuation point; Donnie did not like the idea of being stuck on the top floor of The Guvna's Mansion with chaos growing below. He would not hesitate to ascend to the top levels to retrieve his family, if that was what it took, but he knew it would cost them precious time, and more importantly, it might leave them trapped.

The spread of the shockwaves nearly knocked Donnie to the ground, but his years in the Bubble Suit had not entirely sapped him of the balance and dexterity built over decades living out in Nature on the coast of Western Acadia; he caught himself, one hand briefly touching the ground to redirect his momentum, and regained his footing amidst the tumbling bodies around him.

He was more than halfway across Capitol Square now, past the statue in the center of the courtyard, closer to The Guvna's Mansion and Kingston Amphitheater than he was to The Old Capitol, too close to his goal to be denied; all around him, the mob rioted, those people who had regained their feet jostling and shoving each other, fighting for space, but Donnie ignored it all, weaving through bodies, set on his course.

Yet the crowd was not content to let him go; as he weaved around a woman, barely skirting her, Donnie felt a hand contact his chest, making contact just below his left shoulder to shove him back. He sensed, rather than saw, the right hand that followed the shove, a fist on a path for his chin.

Donnie reacted without thinking, instincts hardwired into him years ago taking over; his left hand swept up, hand open and fingers rigid, keeping his digits clear as his palm struck the man's forearm at the wrist, redirecting the punch past Donnie's head, causing the man to stumble as his fist met nothing but thin air.

For the briefest of moments, Donnie started to follow up on the sequence, but even as he did, he realized that the incident had not gone unnoticed, that he had not gone unrecognized. Blue-uniformed men had flooded out of The Guvna's Mansion, Capitol Guards swarming Capitol Square to add to the presence of the City Watch, and several of them had seen the man attempting to assault The Guvna'; before his attacker could recover his balance, two of the Capitol Guards were on him, tackling the man to the ground as four of their fellows surrounded The Guvna' to escort him the rest of the way to The Mansion.

Then he was through the doors, and Kelli was waiting, both girls with her. Donnie Molinaro did not hesitate; he caught Kelli's hand as he reached her, not breaking stride, letting his family match his pace as he led them to a door that opened onto a winding stairway, one that descended to the cellar.

It was by no means the only secret exit - or entrance - to The Guvna's Mansion, but it was the best for an escape of this sort, as it would put them out in a safe location, well away from Capitol Square. The Molinaros followed Donnie into a dark corner of the cellar, where he pushed through the false back of a disused fireplace and led them into a long, well-constructed tunnel.

A quarter of an hour later, they emerged in open sun, not in a riot, but in the rolling hills of The Guvna's Park, and some semblance of peace.

They had no idea of the atrocity that had taken place while they were in the tunnel, blocked off from the satellite signals that controlled the Bubble Suits.

—

Viktor Ludquist watched in shock as the Capitol Guards swarmed around The Guvna'.

He had been counting on following The Guvna'… well, wherever he was going. Ludquist had few ideas of his own, yet as soon as he saw the Capitol Guards close ranks on The Guvna', Ludquist knew he needed a different plan; he had to get away from this chaos, away from the madness.

Ludquist turned from The Guvna's Mansion; he was near the edge of the crowd now, past the worst of the mob. Moving as quickly as he could, he circled around Capitol Square, looking for somewhere, anywhere, to go, wishing his Bubble Suit would allow him to run, to act in accordance with the desperate pounding of his heart.

It was not until Ludquist's route brought him back to the smoking ruins of The Old Capitol that he saw what he was looking for; a path, or at least a slope, that led away from the madness.

He took the chance; Ludquist plunged over the edge of the hill, so thankful to be away from the chaos that he was not bothered by the steep grade, or his inability to control his continued acceleration.

At least, not at first.

Ludquist was running now, but not by choice; his Bubble Suit was losing control of his momentum as he proceeded down the hill, which seemed to stretch on endlessly. Ludquist did not know how to stop, had no way of slowing himself; by the time he realized his descent was completely out of control, it was too late. He tried to throw his weight backwards to slow himself, but to no avail; Ludquist ran on and on, keeping his feet moving lest he go rolling down the hill, until an open ledge suddenly rushed up on him.

With no way to stop, Ludquist plunged over the edge and slammed head first into the massive boulder that stood in front of the sheer wall.

—

The patrons at Bailey's watched the scene unfold in stunned disbelief.

Capitol Square was not nearly large enough to accommodate the entire population of Kingston, so those citizuns who lived in the Axios and Andola districts had received instructions to watch the ceremony at home or at another public gathering place.

Mo and Aubrey were there, with the rest of their group; Anna, Thea, and Shannon had not been made part of this ceremony, and had decided to join their co-conspirators at Bailey's.

The crowd at Bailey's watched the early scenes in much the same way they had watched the proceedings of the Halls of Parliament, back when the passage of Resolutions 4448, 4449, and 4450 had thrown their lives into such turbulence; today, there was once again a sort of suspended disbelief, though the angry mutterings that came in response were no longer so hesitant, no longer so hushed.

The sentient beings of Kingston were done with it; tired of the long hours, tired of the exhaustion, tired of seeing their friends and families ushered off to The Villa in greater numbers, and at ever younger ages. The idea of living in a utopia still appealed to them, but they were finally starting to openly question whether that was what their Guvernment was providing.

For Mo and Aubrey, it seemed like it might be too little, too late; nevertheless, it was good to see the people around them waking up a little bit, tearing back the veil that had prevented them from seeing the evidence in front of them.

But perhaps they were wrong. Perhaps there could be another way; perhaps Kingston was not destined to continue on this disastrous course, sacrificing as many sentient beings at the altar of Knowledge as was necessary to achieve their desired aim of destroying the Savages.

Until Tarissa Cross began her speech, Mo had wondered about this, clinging to the idea that his fellow citizuns might wake up before it was too late. But as Mo realized what this Cross woman was about to do, all semblance of hope drained out of him.

The crowd's reaction to the destruction was not as immediate as that of the crowd in Capitol Square, the danger not as imminent; as Mo glanced around, looking for a way out, he found that most of his fellow patrons were frozen in place, stunned by the scene unfolding on the screens.

For his part, Mo was already grabbing Aubrey by the hand, pulling her up as he spoke calmly, but firmly, to Neville and Leonard.

"We have to get out of here."

His friends responded to his words with blank stares; behind them, Anna, Thea, and Shannon were similarly speechless.

"Something horrible is about to happen. We have to move - NOW!"

But even as they did, the ripples from the demolition reached the plaza; all around him, Mo saw people thrown off balance, stumbling to the ground.

They did not see the Granite Bridge collapse - that was not broadcast on the Guvernment Media App - but they felt it happen, heard the deep vibrations of destruction. The broadcast, which showed reaction of the crowd in Capitol Square, served as confirmation, or came close enough; when the people in the plaza saw the on-lookers in Capitol Square react in a mad fervor to whatever it was they could see from their vantage point, the crowd at Bailey's followed suit.

Mo had finally gotten his friends moving, but it was too late; all around them, people were attacking random strangers. The pressure had been too much; the stress was the powder keg, this latest debacle the match.

Chaos had engulfed Kingston.

—

"Freeze the suits. All of them, dammit."

Penelope and Cornelius exchanged a glance.

"You're certain? We can only play this card once…"

"Well, if we're not going to play it now," The Director gestured at the scenes of the riot on the screen. "When are we going to play it?"

—

It was dark when he woke up.

Struggling to find his bearings, Viktor Ludquist blinked his vision back, trying to regain his focus; even in the dark, he could tell his sight was blurred. His head hurt abominably, his mouth tasted terrible, and his right wrist throbbed horribly, as if the full weight of a sentient being's body had landed on it after a fall.

It all came back to him then.

The ceremony.

The demolition.

The chaos.

His escape… and then…

Ludquist pushed himself to his hands and knees, looking up at the massive boulder in front of him, remembering his flight down the hill, and the moment when the rock had rushed up on him.

As he looked up at the boulder, he realized that something in the air smelled wrong; it was not only in the air, but in his nostrils, overwhelming his Bubble Suit's air filtration system.

Then Ludquist looked to the sky, and understood; heavy clouds of smoke hovered over Kingston, the last remains of exhausted fires that Ludquist realized must have raged in the city.

What Ludquist could not know is that in the hours he had lain there, insensate, the veil had been ripped off the The Bubble Society.

To end the riots, the Bubble Suits of the citizuns across Kingston had been frozen, leaving each sentient being stuck in place until the City Watch could reach them, either clearing them, or charging them with hooliganism.

Of course, the charges were not the least of it; the real hammer blow was the Knowledge that the Guvernment, and Dynamic Solutions, had that type of control over the citizunry.

Ludquist would learn all of this soon enough; for now, he stared up at the heavy black clouds, despondent. There had been all this change, this mad rush, Operation Mach One, and for what? It seemed that The Bubble Society would devour itself rather than give up control over one girl, one young woman, one Tesla Mancini.

Finally, Ludquist looked away; he shook his head, trying to clear it, thinking of the continued propaganda surrounding The Guvna's daughter, the frequent stories about Tesla Mancini on *Rise and Shine Kingston!,* all of the nonsense. She appeared to have been a remarkable young woman, that was true, but Ludquist could not understand why The Bubble Society was going to these lengths to retrieve her, particularly as the Savages had shown no inclination to continue picking off Kingston's citizuns one after another, as had been widely speculated in the wake of Tesla's abduction.

Realizing that he needed to find his way back to Capitol Square, and eventually, to his home, Ludquist turned around, looking for a way out of the chasm he had fallen into.

When he did, all the thoughts troubling him - thoughts of the riots, of Tesla Mancini, of his pulsing headache - all of it went out of his head.

A door stood in front of him.

It was a steel door, swung open on its hinges, evidently blown open by the explosions. As the thought occurred to Ludquist, he glanced up, and realized that the doorway must open into the basements of The Old

Capitol.

Ludquist stepped through the doorway, into the darkness. The flashlight accessory in his Bubble Suit did not immediately turn on - it seemed to have been damaged in his crash - but with a few good whacks, Ludquist got the light to flicker on.

He did not have to go far down the hallway; Ludquist paused at the first door he reached, turning to his right to study it. Ludquist found, to his bewilderment, that this door also appeared to have been blown outward; Ludquist could see where the deadbolt had torn through the doorframe. He ran his fingers over the spot, wondering.

After a long moment, he lifted his eyes from the broken lock.

Holding his breath, Ludquist stepped into the room.

He had not expected to find anything; by all rights, this old, gutted-out room, which had been left forgotten for years in the bowels of The Old Capitol, should have held nothing but cobwebs.

But Ludquist could sense that there must be something more to the story; he could tell, somehow, that *someone* had been here, inhabiting this place, much more recently than that. He also thought he could smell the scents of an explosion in this very room, as if it had been rigged to go off, inadvertently triggered by the charges put in place for the building's demolition.

Knower Ludquist moved slowly through the room, casting his flashlight over every inch of its contents, at the wreckage of what had formerly been desks and chairs, at the burnt remains of hookup ports behind shattered monitors, at some of the connections that had been drilled into the walls.

It hit him all at once; in a moment of insight, Viktor Ludquist understood what this room had been set up for.

And he suspected that, once he understood *why* it had been set up, a great many things would become clear.

BOOK 5, CHAPTER 11

The place had been named The Gateway before living memory: three miles of open water, separating two continents that had once been one, the space between the southeastern corner of Alexandria and the southern tip of Olympia.

Three miles that would become four, then five, as the continents continued to drift apart.

Their journey had not lacked for wonder; they had taken the long way, departing Alysanne through the Sister's Break, crossing from the Amphitrite into the icy waters of the Larean, the northern ocean surrounding Shurtain's arctic circle. Clarence assured them it was well worth their while, going around the northern side of the continent; it was the long way, and it would be cold, but the priority was losing their tail, and for that, the northern route was the best way to go. It might not be the end of it, but Clarence thought it most likely that their pursuit would fall back, and look to prevent their return to Acadia, rather than chase them to the edges of Shurtain.

They had traveled east on the Larean, sticking as close to Alexandria's northern shoreline as possible; the change in conditions was harsh, but for a group that had recently hiked the peaks of the Cadillac Mountains, the cold was not enough to keep them cowering in their cabins, even as the days marched toward the official beginning of Winter.

For Gavin and Tesla, it all had a sense of wonder, the frozen world around them: the lazy snowfalls melting into the ocean or piling on the coast, the walruses they spotted, the spout of water from a whale not half-a-mile in the distance, the white-tailed eagle that landed on the prow of their ship and traveled with them for an afternoon.

The two were rarely far from each other as they took it all in, sitting with one another and staring out at the beauty around them as Clarence navigated the ship. It all felt too perfect to be true, at least in the here and now.

Yet even as they sat there, talking, dreaming, being, there was a sense of anxiety, even guilt, that intruded at times. For while they might be safe - or as close to safe as they could be - they were all too aware that things were very different back in Kingston.

They wondered about their friends, the ones Tesla had drifted away from, and the ones Gavin had been close to. They talked about their families, the one Tesla had wanted to get away from, and the one Gavin had not wanted to let go of.

But more than anything, Gavin and Tesla spent their time thinking, and talking, about the transformation to come, that tiny being growing within Tesla who was already changing both of them so much.

For Gavin, it had created a new sense of connection, something to hold onto in a world where those closest to him had already gone.

For Tesla, it was something very different, a well of emotions she had never dealt with before.

There was the unbridled excitement, coupled with unreality, when she thought of herself, holding her child.

There was the undeniable fear, tied to that same sense of unreality, when she thought of what had to happen to get to the other side of that vision.

And there was the deep sense of regret, tinged by something very close to guilt, when Tesla thought of her own mother, and what it must have been like.

In her visions, her child was never sick.

In her visions, her child never left.

Tesla tried not to beat herself up over this, but for her, that was easier said than done. She tried talking about it with Gavin, hoping that it would help her to say that she would have done things differently, if she had known how it would feel now.

"But I'd never felt this way before. I'd only felt the way I had; I could never have imagined seeing life this way."

Gavin helped - he certainly did not fault Tesla for anything she had done - but he could only help so much, because he had never struggled with anything like what Tesla was feeling. He was sympathetic, but he could hardly be empathetic; after all, he had spent his life ignoring instructions from various teachers and Knowers who insisted he needed to pay more attention to the outcomes of his actions. For Gavin, those instructions - or demands - had made little impression; he had always just moved on, often entirely forgetting what had been said to him. He could not imagine what it would be like, having any sort of criticism playing on loop.

On that front, Santino had more in common with Tesla, but he did not want to interrupt the soon-to-be parents with his troubles, dark as they were.

Santino did not mind the cold, but troubled as he was, the confinement was unwelcome; he would have loved something, anything, to distract him from the thoughts eating him within.

Clarence helped; the two spent long hours together, speaking of life, and death, and all that had happened to Clarence and Salomon in their years together, both on their journey to Elysia, and afterwards.

"Salomon would have understood. Your grandfather was not a violent man, but nor did he live in a fantasy world. There are forces in this realm with dark intentions, who want nothing more than to control and exploit the world around them, and as long as they exist, there will always be a need to fight back. To resist. You did not go looking for a fight, did not do what you did out of cruelty, or spite. You did it out of necessity; your grandfather would have told you to find that truth within yourself, and to hold on to it."

Santino had only nodded. He understood what Clarence was telling him - he even agreed with it - but he also knew that it had not penetrated him, had not been accepted by his being as truth. Unable to sleep, he found himself spending long nights alone, awake in the frigid cold, staring up at the stars, and wondering.

Whatever the upside of their northern passage, all were pleased to reach the far side of Alexandria, relieved to see that first horizon where the land started to fall off, curving as the continent's coastline turned south. Subsisting on fish, plentiful as they were, had grown old; it would be a relief to reach the first port city on the far side of Alexandria, where they could resupply.

Days after that, the cold started to abate, an indicator that they had crossed out of the Larean Ocean, that the waters they now traveled were officially part of the Tunisian Ocean.

A week later, when their southern course diverted southeast to get around the jut of land known as Humphrey's Hump, they caught their first glimpse of Olympia, a blurred darkness at the edge of their vision, far out to the east.

For the rest of their journey, they sailed between the two continents, making their way through the Khana Gap, Olympia coming in and out of view until it became a consistent part of the horizon.

Yet as spectacular as it was to reach The Gateway - and to see the open waters of the Marean Ocean to the south - their destination was beyond, in a different sort of place.

And the story Clarence had told them, starting on that morning in Alysanne, had Santino, Gavin, and Tesla far too preoccupied with their final destination to suggest stopping at The Gateway, magnificent as the place might be.

—

"The direct route will be watched, without a doubt. Their focus will be on ensuring we don't return to Acadia, but if we take the straight shot down the Amphitrite to Elysia, there's a chance they intercept us on the way. They know where we're going, after all. So, we go north, and around Alexandria."

It had been early morning, just after sunrise, on the day of their escape from Larissa. Harlan had led them north from where they had initially landed, to a harbor with much larger ships than the one they had crossed the Sister's Break on. He was arranging their passage now; it was fortunate they had a native with them, as the residents of Alysanne might not have reacted kindly to strangers knocking on random doors, trying to find someone who could spare a ship, at such an early hour.

"And how," Santino started, "Would they know where we're going?"

Clarence shook his head, glancing from Santino to Tesla to Gavin, then back again to Santino. He saw no reason to conceal the last bit of the story any longer; they had come too far, and needed to understand.

"Because The Director is coordinating their pursuit; it's the only way that someone would be permitted to strip off their Bubble Suit and venture out of Kingston into greater Acadia. There are precious few who are even aware that it's possible, which means that I don't just know who sent the pursuit; I've got a pretty good idea of exactly who Theodore sent after us."

"Theodore?"

Clarence nodded.

"That's what his name was, back when he and I accompanied your grandfather to Elysia. Back before he met the Shamans, and started down the path to become The Director."

"That's how he'll know where we're going; The Director - and the two Shamans who left their homeland to join him - will not have forgotten about Elysia, no matter how many years it's been."

—

"We never should have gone. But we were young, careless, and I don't think anyone, sentient being or Shaman, understood what was lying in wait on Elysia."

The air around them was frigid; ice clung to the northern shores of Alexandria, but this far south, the Larean Ocean itself was clear of ice, or at least, clear enough.

"You see, your grandfather broke a covenant, bringing us along. He was an only child, and while many of the others whose families prepared them for such an Initiation had peers around their age, Salomon did not."

"Under the circumstances, it was natural for him to form bonds outside of those circles. But he did not understand the necessity of the preparations his family, and those other families, had put their children through, preparations to ensure they would not abuse what they would learn on their journey, or the validation process he had undergone before he was deemed ready. At least, he did not understand it then."

"As far as we knew, Theodore was a good enough fellow. His parents - his father, in particular - ran in different circles than either of our parents, but we never thought much of that at the time; we were friends, good company, young and wild. Too young to consider what really drove us in life, when it came down to it."

"And that was the problem, at the end of the day. What drove Theodore; that, and the fact that there were a pair of Shamans who had been waiting for such a sentient being to arrive on Elysia."

"Whether Theodore carried whatever it was inside him, and woke the two Shamans up to their base desires, or if the two Shamans were waiting for someone they could corrupt, or something in between… I don't suppose we'll ever know, unless they can tell us. But however it happened, it all went wrong."

"We went to Elysia to go on a vision quest, the transition to adulthood that the Cahn family had embraced for generations. The vision quests were known to awaken dormant powers, to allow sentient beings to be more present, more connected, with the fabric of the reality around them, and the fragility of it all. In the right conditions, it creates a sort of recognition of the fleeting nature of all of this, allowing you to reconnect with the wonder of it all, to have realizations that would not occur in any other state."

"But every experience is different, and not all powers are light. There are great darknesses in this realm, and that darkness will channel itself through any willing vessel."

Clarence paused then, staring out, shaking his head.

"Even on our return journey, mere days after we had gone through our experiences, it was obvious that something had shifted in Theodore. I sensed it more acutely than Salomon, perhaps - I sensed all such things more acutely after my first experience with the entheogens - but this was not a hard thing to sense. I was raving about how the entheogen had tilted my reality by a few degrees, just enough to open my mind to an entirely different perspective of the Universe, one I never wanted to leave; Theodore insisted that he was could not tell whether the experience had any effect on him at all, or if he had even had an experience of the sort I had described."

"We returned home, and Salomon and I started seeing less and less of Theodore, who had informed us that he had reached adulthood, and must devote his focus to learning the family trade. The Bouregards owned Kingston's major railways and its premier banking institution, and it was his responsibility to carry those institutions forward; the days of his boyhood were over."

"It was not until years later, when Salomon and I decided the time was ripe for a return journey to Elysia, that we learned the awful truth. Less than a year after our departure, the two Shamans who had led Theodore on his vision quest had disappeared from Elysia."

"None of the others knew where they had gone, or even if they had gone - it was possible they had been the victims of an accident - but the Shamans were not inclined to believe that, as they had never found their bodies."

Clarence had paused again then, staring out at the waters of the Larean.

"Their names were Penelope and Cornelius. And as time revealed, there was no accident; they've been at The Retreat, with Theodore, all these years."

BOOK 5, CHAPTER 12

Viktor Ludquist sat alone on his balcony, gazing up at the stars as he ran calculations in his mind, checking every step ten times over, asking whether he had learned everything he needed to know.

The last six weeks had passed in a whirlwind, both for Ludquist, and for Kingston's general citizunry. The changes Ludquist had experienced were nothing like the changes the rest of Kingston's citizunry had endured - his could even be described as pleasant - but that did not make his reorientation any less dramatic.

The night was cold - particularly at two in the morning - and while the sky was clear tonight, Ludquist need only look at the coating of snow on the sentinel trees surrounding The Retreat to be reminded that this was no short-lived chill; Winter had arrived.

For most involved with Operation Mach One, that arrival brought with it a sense of failure; even if they invented a novel air filtration device now, it would be Spring before they could test it.

Ludquist was immune to this reaction.

He was too consumed by the thread he had started to pull on, down in the basement of The Old Capitol.

It had not been long before he had enough to share with Knower Robinson, and then, Head Knower Mallion. Ecstatic to learn of Ludquist's discovery, Mallion offered him every resource The Bubble Society had to offer, the services of any Knower that Ludquist believed might be able to assist him as he completed his quest.

At the time, Ludquist turned it all down. It was a job for one person, unraveling the story of what had happened down in the bowels of The

Old Capitol, of why somebody had gone to the trouble of constructing a computer lab in an age when the average citizun only interfaced with computers through their Bubble Suits.

The trail was nearly dead, but not quite; as Ludquist breathed life back into the smoldering embers, the glow of a path began to emerge.

The girl had been good, no doubt; brilliant, even. She had scrambled everything, but there were times when she had to interact with Guvernment servers, and the records remained, even if they appeared random at first glance.

Of course, nobody in Kingston's Guvernment ever would have bothered to check these logs; even if they had, there would have been no reason to think that all of the random entries came from one source. In fact, Ludquist ordinarily would have drawn the opposite conclusion; had he seen the records in a vacuum, he too would have written them off to a system error.

But he was not looking at the records in a vacuum; he was working on the assumption that one individual had been interacting with the system regularly for years.

So when he found those seemingly random records, it seemed worth his while to see how far back he could go.

It was then that things began to open up.

Because Tesla Mancini had not always been so fastidious in her habits.

Ludquist slipped a pack of cigarettes from his pants pocket, extracted one, and lit it; an image of the young woman filled his mind as he savored the first drag, reflecting on the amazement he had felt when he lined up the dates, and realized the reason that the girl had not originally been concealing her location, back when her family had lived in the Andola District, was that she not yet five years old.

Of course, Tesla's identity was the least of what Ludquist had learned; with that information in hand, he had pushed his investigation forward, going through each of the requests to the Guvernment's servers in order.

It was an imperfect process; Tesla had pulled a wide variety of files from the servers, and while he could glean some insight from that, it was not as if she had written her thoughts out for anyone to read. Her uploads to the Bubble Suit software repository were easier to understand; the work was anonymous, hidden away in dark corners of the code base, but once he found it, Ludquist had no doubt as to the author.

He had taken time to linger over the code that ran Tesla's Bubble Suit upgrades, but it was the files and reports that she had pulled that truly caught his interest. It took weeks of piecing together the clues Tesla had left behind, of trying to trace her line of thinking, her reason for pulling all of this information.

For if Ludquist was certain of one thing, it was that Tesla Mancini had a reason for doing everything.

After devoting so much time to the task, it felt strange when the insight hit him; in a single moment of clarity, he suddenly understood what it all meant.

And in that moment, the craving for a cigarette, a desire he had not felt since his second year in a Bubble Suit, became quite overwhelming.

That insight also led Ludquist to circle back on Head Knower Mallion's offer, though not in the way that Mallion had expected.

Ludquist did not request any resources; at least, not from Mallion. Ludquist merely wanted the Head Knower to facilitate a conversation. Of course, Ludquist should not have Known this individual existed, but Ludquist had not simply asked for a meeting, or even if the man existed; he had *told* the Head Knower that he must speak with The Director, as soon as it could be arranged.

As a result, Ludquist now had accommodations that were quite to his liking; in this place, Ludquist could do as he liked, work at his leisure, smoke when he pleased, so long as he continued his work on the air filtration system, the work that was coming together so neatly as Ludquist got deeper and deeper into the hints Tesla had left behind. He had reached an understanding with The Director, who, as it turned out, was well aware that the Bubble Suits were completely unnecessary.

Or at least, completely unnecessary for their stated purpose.

But as The Director explained to Ludquist in that pivotal meeting, as far as their real purpose went, the Bubble Suits had always been - and would always be - absolutely essential.

—

Mo Brickson stepped through the open doors of Bailey's, scanning his wrist at the turnstile as he passed it.

"Thank you for checking into Bailey's, Mo Brickson. As a Level 3 member of Kingston's Surveillance Team, you are permitted to participate in recreational activities for the next forty-two minutes; please mind the time, and ensure you are able to check in at your home at your assigned time."

The scanners had been installed all over Kingston during the week after the riots. Mo half-ignored the tinny, robotic voice, but he could not forget what the scanners represented.

No more than he could forget the first week after the riots, when The Bubble Society had been on complete lockdown.

After that hellish week, any change was welcome, even if that change was a life with significantly greater Guvernment restrictions on movement and behavior.

As part of the overhaul, the Guvernment announced that the Department of Surveillance would double in size, allowing them to keep, not only the Knowers, but the full citizunry, under constant watch. They had also doubled the Capitol Guard and the City Watch; the pairs of black-clad figures walking patrols on the streets, even in the plaza where Bailey's sat, ensured that no citizun in Kingston would forget that.

As for the Department of Surveillance, the sudden influx of so many new members had created a need for leadership. Given his general sobriety - a rarity in the Department - Mo was promoted to a managerial role.

Mo did not care for his new position any more than his last one - he still felt his talents would have been better used out in Kingston, where he could be rebuilding the Granite Bridge, or reinforcing Kingston's two remaining causeways - but the powers-that-be felt differently, and as long as they did, Mo was not going to waste the advantages of his new role.

The Guvernment might count on their surveillance system being fool-proof, but in his new position, Mo had learned certain things, such as the fact that the Bubble Suits did not transmit out of certain cellars or vaults.

Cellars like the one in Bailey's.

These places could not be used for too long, or too regularly; the Department of Surveillance did not have the bandwidth to follow up every time a citizun's Bubble Suit lost its signal, but if the problems lasted too long, or a specific Bubble Suit transmitted errors from the same location on a regular basis, then someone from the City Watch would be dispatched to investigate.

Despite these inconveniences, the dead spots still created the opportunity to speak freely, and that was reason enough to take the risk; every day, as the Guvernment tightened their control of The Bubble Society, the sentient desire for freedom became more pronounced, fighting back, testing its ingenuity as it wriggled desperately, making a last gasp before it was all too late.

It was that desire that had caused their underground network to form. It was not a standard black market - the Guvernment continued to supply the necessities of life - but in terms of trading information, it was the only safe place to go, assuming your information did not come straight out of *The Manual for Proper Behavior* or off of *Rise and Shine, Kingston!*

That dead spot was why Mo was at Bailey's, but he had time before he was expected at the meeting spot; he made his way to the bar, planning to get a drink so he would blend in with the crowd.

As he sat there, he wondered why he bothered with all this, why he could not give up the subterfuge, the cloak and dagger deception, and simply accept that his life was the way that it was, that The Bubble Society was the greatest society that had ever been or would ever be, and get on with playing the role assigned to him.

He supposed it was because he could not reconcile that this would be how he spent his opportunity to possess sentient consciousness, his chance to be part of this reality, this experience, whatever that was. His very existence was a miracle, the fact that he was here, able to move around the planet Shurtain with his consciousness and personality intact even as his physical body moved through time and space. It seemed too beautiful a gift to waste on… this.

Perhaps these little meetings were a waste of time, the games of mice facing an insurmountable force, a power that few understood, that few could fix down. In the face of that thought, Mo thought of abandoning it all.

Then he thought of who he was here to meet; at the thought of Aubrey, Mo felt the corners of his mouth turn up, felt a warmth in his chest that was quite distinct from any other sensation, though every bit as pleasant.

If the Kingston Guvernment had their way, Mo would never feel such things; he would be compliant, he would do what they told him without complaint, he would accept that answers could not be questioned and that questions would not be answered.

So if all that was left to them were these little moments, these minutes where they could speak their minds without fear… well, then Mo would live for those moments, because life without anything to live for was no life at all.

—

Donnie Molinaro shifted; they had been in the rock alcove nearly an hour, and pleasant as Kelli's body might feel against him, he could sense parts of him going to sleep.

"Not thinking of leaving, are you?"

Donnie grinned.

"Not hardly. We get another snow like da last one, and it'll be another season before we can come back here. Fortunately, Da Board's got more'n 'nuff problems without wondering where I dis'perred ta fer a couple hours, so long as I'm out here. Down in da middle o'da city, that'd be a different matter."

Kelli shifted against her husband, pressing her weight into him through their Bubble Suits, the closest they had been able to come to physically connecting during the past twenty years.

"It's not going to get better, is it?"

Neither of them had stated it so plainly until now, but as Donnie reflected on his wife's words, he realized that belief had been there for a long time, unspoken.

"I dunno. I'd like to hope, but…"

"It's hard to hope when you see the people in charge are just sentient beings, and vulnerable to the failings of sentient beings, first-hand?"

Donnie nodded.

"Oughta jus' speak fer me; always in tune wit' what I'm thinking, and always say it better."

For half a beat, Kelli smiled, but the grin melted quickly.

"What will happen? Now that they've discovered how to upgrade the air filtration systems, I mean?"

Donnie chuckled.

"Well, Tarissa Cross officially moved Operation Mach One from product development ta manufacturing, but it's too late ta get it done before Winter; s'pose you can guess how she's taking dat. Throw in da fact dat dey did it through da air filtration system, and not da air'n mouth filter… well, dat's been it's own sorta entertainment, fer one thing."

Kelli shook her head.

"I can hardly imagine; it wouldn't surprise me to hear she demanded Head Knower Mallion figure out a way to control the weather, stop the snows from coming until The Board can send our army after these Savages."

"Oughta' start gambling, 'lil lady."

"If it wasn't illegal, like everything else in this damned city, maybe I would be."

Kelli shook her head.

"It would be funny if it weren't so serious. Tarissa Cross, and all the rest of them. They've never accomplished a thing in their lives, yet they expect everyone surrounding them to perform miracles, to create new inventions at the drop of a hat. And despite their ineptitude, they presume to make decisions for the rest of us, demanding that we bow to their form of leadership, no matter the results."

"I wish she had to spend one day with Andrea. I wish she had one day where she had to face what real hardship, real pain, feel like, what life looks like then. But she gets to hide away in the Amada District, and enjoy luxury with all the rest of The Board up at The Retreat, congratulating themselves as the society they run crumbles beneath them."

Donnie did not say anything - it did not seem there was anything to say - so he nodded instead, touching his chin softly to his wife's head.

After a moment, Kelli turned around, looking into her husband's blue eyes with her green ones.

"Donnie?"

He did not nod this time, but she saw the acknowledgment in his eyes.

"I'm afraid."

BOOK 5, CHAPTER 13

The snow fell thick around Anton Molinaro as he stood on the ridge, taking a final look down at all of the structures they had erected.

The barracks.

The watch towers.

The barricades.

Next to it all sat Turquoise Lake, an icy sheen on its surface, the rays of the sunrise highlighting the steam evaporating in the early morning air. The ice would burn away in the daylight today, but it would not be long before the surface grew thick enough to survive the day's sun; the Western Grand might continue to flow through its depths, but the surface of Turquoise Lake would freeze with everything else.

Nearly all of the troops who had built the defenses had already departed, and the rest would need to leave today, their heavy artillery in tow, and Anton at their head, to wait out Winter in Giota. Those who would spend the time in other cities - Trepani, Kirfi, Larissa, even Alysanne - had left in the preceding weeks; the snows had already started to fall by then, and the people in Trepani and Kirfi would be breaking out the shovels to carve out paths through the streets.

Al Nierland and Brock Lukavsky had been two of the last to depart up that trail; they had remained as long as they could, both to ensure there were no unexpected surprises, and to support Anton in his leadership duties, but in the end, Nature left them without another option, and all three men had seen too much of the Wild to tempt fate in these conditions.

Anton had not thought twice about it at the time, but in the days that followed, as he issued orders and maintained the defenses, playing out the thread, he had realized, with a sort of grim acceptance, precisely how alone he was in this world. The planet Shurtain might be home to millions of sentient beings, yet there was nobody he could trust, nobody he could share his thoughts with, no reason to speak at all, save to keep up the trivial pleasantries that maintained the superficial connection between him and his troops.

He also thought that he should be grateful for the time ahead, grateful for the fact that they would all have more time to live.

But somehow, he could not do it. Could not find it in him to look forward to sitting around, his ultimate purpose delayed. It did not matter whether he spent the time in Giota, or went off on his own, into the snows, to test his skills in the worst of conditions.

No matter what, he would be restless.

And in that restlessness, the thought of spending time with Katarina and Mitzy rubbed his nerves raw. It was not that he did not love them, would not do anything in his power to protect them, but life with small children demanded a certain pace, a certain rhythm, that Anton had no intention of tapping into.

He would fight for them, yes; he had always fought for his people.

But sitting with them, being still and present as they hurdled towards the abyss?

That sounded like something out of someone else's life.

Anton shook himself; whatever it sounded like, there was nothing for it.

Winter had arrived.

BOOK 5, CHAPTER 14

Tesla had never imagined sand so white, water so clear, as the beach that they landed on in Elysia.

Eight days had passed since they had crossed through The Gateway and entered the Marean, the southernmost of Shurtain's five oceans.

More than the others, Tesla would have loved to stop back at The Gateway; she had read the old histories of Shurtain, archived away in the Guvernment servers, early in her teenage years, so she had heard of many of the landmarks they passed, but seeing them in person was infinitely more incredible, and The Gateway was the highlight. Even from their vantage point on the water, Tesla could appreciate the stunning architecture of the cities of Caliad and Enox, the two cities that now stood opposite one another on Alexandria and Olympia. Two cities that had been one, back before the continent split, if legend could be believed.

Maybe, one day, she would come back.

For now, they could not linger.

There were places to go.

And time was running through the glass.

In fact, it was as they passed through The Gateway, Tesla standing at the ship's prow, nestled in Gavin's arms, his right hand resting protectively on her swollen belly, that she realized, for the first time in her life, her desire for adventure had been overwhelmed by something else.

She wanted to feel safe.

At least for a little while.

She had not been certain whether that was possible anymore, given the way the past year had played out.

Yet now, as they rowed their way toward the white sand beaches of Elysia, their ship anchored in the middle of the crystal-clear lagoon behind them, she was starting to believe. When Gavin jumped over the boat's edge, and turned back to help her out, Tesla felt her body start to relax; when he set her down in the knee-deep water, a palpable shudder ran through her.

Tesla smiled; only now, as she felt her muscles uncoiling, did she realize how tense she had been. She looked back at Gavin, who was smiling at her reaction, and briefly leaned into him before she turned to greet the little group that had pulled their boat to shore.

Tesla knew what the figures in front of them were - Clarence had told them all about the Shamans on their way to Elysia - so she did not mistake them for small sentient beings, easy as the mistake would have been to make without Clarence's primer.

Three of the five who had come to greet them were female; when Tesla turned to look at them, she realized that they were all looking at her, smiling approvingly. Tesla suspected she knew why, but the oldest of the women confirmed it, approaching Tesla and taking both of the young woman's hands in hers.

"Please, be welcome. Visitors are a rare t'ing now'days; 'tis a special delight ta have'ya come ashore, carrying the miracle of life."

Tesla reddened slightly, but smiled at the same time. She had not known what to expect of the female Shaman's voice - she had thought it might be high-pitched - but the woman spoke in a pitch similar to her own, albeit at a calmer, more measured pace.

"I'm Anabelle. Allow me ta introduce t'others."

She released Tesla's hands and turned, holding her left hand in the general direction of her companions.

"Mariana. Selena. Hubert. Winston. We be knowin' Clarence, of course, but who you others be?"

Tesla handled the introductions, leaving Gavin and Santino free to take in the scene; Gavin was simply smiling, looking at the Shamans and waving as Tesla said his name, but Santino took in the new faces with a more critical eye, and did not miss the glimmer in Winston's eyes when their gazes met.

Santino did not have to wait long to discover the reason for this; as soon as greetings had been exchanged, the thin Shaman, whose shock of white hair stood out brilliantly against his black skin, addressed Clarence.

"So, mah' ol' friend; how be Penelope and Cornelius these days?"

Book 6

BOOK 6, CHAPTER 1

Tarissa Cross strode purposefully down the hall, her Bubble Suit set to project a navy blazer, an effortlessly elegant look fitting of Kingston's next Director.

Enough was enough; it was time to act.

Winter had not been kind to The Board, nor to The Bubble Society, whose citizuns were becoming increasingly disaffected as the weeks dragged on. Tarissa Cross might not have cared about this, if business was proceeding as usual, but it was not; the lethargy that had taken hold of the population during the Winter had dragged productivity down to an intolerably slow pace.

Before, the citizuns of Kingston, content in their utopia, had done their work with a certain indifference; now, with the population's health in an undeniable decline, the city under surveillance, and the Knowledge of what their Guvernment could do to them front and center in everyone's mind, the citizuns of Kingston were showing a widespread resentment towards life itself, even as they checked the box by reporting for their daily labor obligations.

Head Knower Mallion had attempted to explain this to Cross, but she was not interested in excuses, she was interested in results. Yet, to her great dismay, Cross had found that imposing increasingly harsh punishments was ineffective, even counterproductive, in a city that was already sorely lacking for effective workers.

Cross placed the blame for all of this at The Director's feet; if he had made a more decisive move to bring the citizunry into line, they would not be facing these problems, but instead, she and the rest of The Board had been left to manage the situation without full authority to do what she - and everyone else - could see needed to be done.

It was frustrating beyond belief, the way that The Director would arbitrarily bind her hands. The latest example of that had sparked today's plan; when Cross had suggested that the citizuns of Kingston might fall into line if they started each episode of *Rise and Shine Kingston!* with the public execution of a dissident, The Director had cut her legs out from under her, turning those maddeningly calm eyes on her and responding with a simple "No" before the rest of The Board could say a word on the matter.

The Director might have dismissed her idea, but Tarissa Cross Knew that the majority of The Board would have sided with her; she would just have to do something about The Director. The man was too old, too soft, too unwilling to do what needed to be done; once, he would have had it in him, but it was clear to Tarissa that The Director had grown too weak to man his post. And putting loyalty to him over loyalty to The Bubble Society would have been an abdication of her duty, that responsibility she had been entrusted with when the The Director had appointed her to The Board.

As Cross turned down the hallway that led to the Dynamic Solutions Boardroom, she saw the scene playing out in her mind one last time. It would be difficult, no doubt, to speak the words, but she was up to it. The atmosphere in the room would be uncomfortable; even now, as she made her approach, The Director would likely be wondering why she was late, and why so many members of The Board seemed apprehensive, but Cross would not let any of that stop her. It was even possible that she was wrong in assuming that she would meet this feeble resistance; The Director was old, and of late, he had seemed preoccupied during their meetings, disinclined to pay any attention at all to his subordinates. His time was done.

Cross would be sympathetic; at first, The Director might protest, try to claim he was still up to the job, but Cross had assurances that the majority of The Board would take her side. It had taken time, but she had flipped them in the end, securing her position when she had convinced Corwin McKenzie that her side must win. There were still holdouts, but Cross Knew they would go whichever way the wind was blowing; Board Member Fernandez was the exception, but they had not seen Fernandez since the morning after Tesla Mancini's abduction, and The Director had summarily ignored all inquiries into his whereabouts, which left the rest of The Board to conclude that the man must be dead. There was no reason to think that Fernandez would do anything to bar Tarissa Cross's ascent.

No, the only thing left was to work out the succession plan; The Director would see that quickly enough. Once he did, he would accept, perhaps even applaud, Tarissa Cross's takeover; after all, he had appointed her as his second-in-command, made her the Viceroy of The Board at Dynamic Solutions.

She had reached the end of the hall.

She took a deep breath, gripped the door handle, and pulled it open.

She stepped over the threshold, and into her destiny.

—

She saw that something was wrong the moment she stepped through the doorway.

Many of the signs were subtle; Yvonne Delverta, the most important of the allegiances Cross had secured, looked furtively away when Cross sought her gaze, and Nessie Hunter and Gina Townsend mirrored the behavior. As for Corwin McKenzie, he was staring straight ahead, conspicuously making no reaction whatsoever when Cross entered.

One sign was not subtle; for the first time in seasons, Board Member Fernandez, a man of average height, with a wide face, broad shoulders, and a strong jaw, was back at the table, in his usual seat at The Director's right hand. To Cross's dismay, Fernandez was not merely looking at her; he was leering, protuberant black eyebrows slanted down toward his bulb of a nose, a half-smile coming out behind his thick lips, his brown eyes taking Cross in with an obvious sense of amusement.

As for The Director, to Cross, his face appeared impassive, utterly neutral, but for some reason, a shiver went up her spine when she met his gaze.

Finally, The Director broke the silence.

"Welcome, Tarissa. I believe you have something to say to us?"

Before Cross could respond, The Director tapped on the wrist panel of his Bubble Suit, prompting the conference room's sound system into action.

Tarissa Cross stood with her mouth half-open, abject horror rooting her to the spot as she heard her own voice played over the room's audio system, delivering the speech she had so carefully rehearsed for this moment.

—

The very idea of hope had become taboo; in the wake of what had happened to the citizuns of Kingston during the riots on the day that the Guvernment had demolished The Old Capitol, expressing as much as a hint of optimism felt sacrilege.

Still, during the long season of Winter, some found that sentient nature demanded that they continue to dream, that they find a way to believe that somehow, someday, something might get better.

Even if their default network utterly rejected the idea.

Despite that, while left unspoken, it was there, that distant, feeble, glimmer of hope that Spring might bring something different, that life could change for the better.

But how could life get better, now that they understood what they had thought they Knew was not true?

Nobody, not even the most senior Knowers, had Known that the Bubble Suits could be frozen, much less that they could be frozen en masse.

The group sitting at the outside bar at Bailey's had discovered this truth during the long Winter; even under the new threat, Mo, Neville, Leonard, Anna, Thea, Shannon, and Aubrey had continued to probe, to ask questions.

They had stopped for a time after the riot, and they were more circumspect now, but as things stood, they were still living, still having an experience, and as long as that was true, they had to do something; none of them would accept living as a blank slate, a robot of The Bubble Society with no past, no present, and no future, save for their identity as a worker in what the Guvernment called a utopia.

When they did resume their inquiries, the task proved less difficult than they anticipated; as weeks passed, and they got further and further away from the horror of that day, the initial terror faded, and slowly, but surely, the citizuns of The Bubble Society started to talk about what everyone wanted to talk about: what had happened on the day of the riots.

That desire to talk allowed the co-conspirators to collect a wide range of unique accounts of what happened on that day.

Knowers, both from the Center of Industry and the Academy of Knowledge.

Members of the Department of Workforce Surveillance.

The discontented among the City Watch and Capitol Guard.

Sentient beings who filled roles at the Department of Media Productions and The Villa, even a few individuals from the Department of Infant Development.

Citizuns who spanned the spectrum from the Andola District to the Amada District.

From what they had gathered, not one of them had Known the truth: that the Bubble Suits could be frozen at the drop of a hat.

That Kingston's Guvernment had that sort of control over them.

Even the members of the City Watch and Capitol Guard, whose Bubble Suits had remained unfrozen so they could sort out the trouble on the day of the riots, felt the chilling effect; all but the dimmest of the officers understood that while they might be the ones enforcing the rule of law now, this feature of the Bubble Suits could just as easily be turned against them.

The effect had terrified the citizunry into some degree of compliance during the Winter, casting a dark shadow over the city in a season when energy was already low; the Bubble Suits might prevent the people from feeling the cold, but the deep snows around them, and the cloudy skies above them, did nothing to brighten the mood.

The snows went further than impacting the mood of the place; already short-handed, the Department of Infrastructure was hard-pressed to keep the roads between the various districts and The Center of Industry cleared. Even if the place was open, the route up Riverside Parkway to Kingfisher Reservoir would have been left blocked, while projects such as the reconstruction of the Granite Bridge had been pushed back to future seasons, perhaps the Summer, or the Fall to come.

Whenever the Savages were defeated and Kingston's future as a utopia was re-cemented; then they could fix the city.

Of course, that did not mean the citizunry sat idle; to the contrary, there was plenty of work to do, though it was not quite the work that the recently closed Department of Air Filtration Construction had expected. As Knower Ludquist's latest invention did not require mouth or nose filters, there had been a mass reassignment from the hastily formed Department to the newly formed Department of Re-Engineering, where technicians, working in tandem with the Department of Manufacturing, were training to install the new Bubble Suit upgrades, preparing for the moment when the project was cleared for mass deployment.

The citizuns of Kingston understood that they would get this upgrade whether they wanted it or not. They understood they were one breath away from being frozen in place, seized by some unknown entity that could, at an instant's notice, take away a sentient being's ability to move, that sacred capacity bestowed upon them by Nature.

The citizuns of Kingston still did not Know who had done it, or even where the capacity to freeze the Bubble Suits existed; Shannon, Anna, and Thea had made efforts to tread into that territory with the most senior Knowers on their respective teams, but when they managed to find opportunities to ask their questions without too much risk, they discovered that even the senior Knowers Knew no more about the matter than they did.

And while nobody had been frozen since the day of the riots - nobody that they had heard of, at least - and the high-strung anxiety that gripped the population had dulled to a low pulse, they could not forget. The people now realized the type of control they had handed over, finally understood why the heretics who had died in the Aeronbald Volunteer Experiments had insisted on making their attempt. For many, the thought of a quick end, even a painful one, seemed more appealing than this endless cycle of waking and working, of extended labor hours and restricted leisure time, all enforced by the City Watch and Capitol Guard, which had seen their ranks swollen by reinforcements throughout the Winter. Armed guards were a constant presence in the streets, in the parks, in all the public places; even now, as the co-conspirators sat at the outside bar of Bailey's, they could see eight black-clad figures spaced around the plaza.

There was one thing that had not changed; nothing had been done to stem the increased flow of citizuns becoming Laureates, though nobody, except those few still determined to conform to every letter in *The Manual for Proper Behavior,* believed that The Villa was what the Guvernment said it was. This awakening had made for no shortage of heartache, for what was a person to do? It was no easy thing living with a Laureate candidate, yet the citizuns of The Bubble Society were now terrified to turn their loved ones over to the clutches of The Villa.

All of it put an increased strain on the rest of their society; in recent weeks, Neville and Leonard had seen the ranks thinning out around them at the Department of Media Production, their former co-workers transferred to backfill the ranks of the City Watch or the Capitol Guard, or to swell the numbers in the Department of Re-Engineering.

Yet, even amidst all of this, these seven, and so many others, could not reconcile the thought that things would be like this forever, that this was all life had to offer.

It was then, as they sat together in dejected silence, saying none of this and thinking all of it, that an alert came on, forcing itself onto every citizun's holographic monitor.

The citizuns of The Bubble Society shifted their eyes to their screens. Many of them expected to see Tarissa Cross - she had become a fixture in their lives with her regular appearances on *Rise and Shine, Kingston!* - but they did not.

It was The Guvna'. He started speaking immediately.

"Ma fella' citizuns, da day has finally come; we are ready ta upgrade da Bubble Suits. All citizuns are ta report ta Da Center o' Industry, where'ya will be directed t'yer particula' upgrade site."

"Da City Watch will oversee da process, wit' assistance from Da Capitol Guard; afta y'all are done, Da Watch and Da Guard will get da upgrades demselves."

The Guvna' paused and looked directly into the camera. He was still handsome, still had color in his hair, but it was undeniable that The Guvna' looked a decade older than he had just a year ago, the lines in his skin deeper, his transition to grey accelerated.

"Y'all Know what dis means; once da upgrades are complete, we'll be ready. Ready ta confront da Savages, and ensure our survival. It's da first time you'll hear dis, but it won't be da last: ta ensure da defense o' Kingston, it's essential dat we obliterate da rest o' Shurtain. And dat's exactly what we'll do."

The Guvna' nodded, his eyes still on the camera, his expression stern.

"It's a terrible burden - da burden o' da Knowledgeable sentient beings

- but it's da burden Knowledge has placed on us. And now dat Knowledge has granted us da tools ta carry out its will, we have no otha' choice; we must put da Savages down, and show da world da power o' Knowledge."

—

Donnie Molinaro stepped out of the broadcast booth into the main room. The Director was there, sitting in a throne-like chair, flanked by two of his personal guard as well as his perpetual companions, Penelope and Cornelius.

Donnie Molinaro had never known what to think of the latter pair, not since the evening when he had become The Guvna'.

That was the night when he had been introduced to The Director and his two companions.

The road to The Guvna'ship had been a whirlwind, but nothing on his journey had stunned Donnie Molinaro more than that first meeting with the trio who revealed that they had carefully plotted Donnie's ascension to his current position, pulling one string, then another, year after year.

But it had always been less The Director, and his story, that bothered Donnie; it had always been the two minions who troubled him most.

"A fair job," The Director assessed.

The Guvna' shrugged.

"Nuthin' else fer me?"

The Director shook his head; The Guvna' turned to leave.

"I must say, it fascinates me. Even now, as we prepare to lead our people to war, you ask no questions, inquire about nothing, when I call you here."

The Guvna' turned around. He looked The Director up and down, wondering what had provoked the comment; the two of them had been meeting for decades, and during that time, The Guvna' had never asked about the why of anything he was told to do. That had never been a problem, never been questioned; Donnie Molinaro noted the intensity in The Director's eyes, the sheen of perspiration on the man's forehead, and supposed that the totality of the day's triumph must have uncorked something in The Director.

"Dunno what'ta tell'ya 'bout dat; you and I are different fellas, though. I mean, ya talk 'bout *our people*, like ya got ownership over 'em, but far as I'm concerned, dey ain't *my people*, unless ya mean in da sense o' bein' ma fella' sentient beings."

He paused.

"Even if I did see it yer way, I'm just anotha' cog in da machine. A more visible cog, but an entirely replaceable one. As you 'splained in our first meeting; ain't my place t'ask questions, or set policy. All I'm here ta do is create da illusion dat da Guvernment is accountable ta its citizuns, dat some sorta transparent process exists. So I do whatcha ask, and don't ask questions. Don't expect you'd answer 'em if I did."

The Director nodded.

"All true. And you've done a brilliant job in your role; it's why I've gone to such efforts to keep you in your position, constructing new reasons, new precedents that allowed you to continue in your role. I couldn't dream up a sentient being better suited to the job, an individual who is both an exceptionally gifted orator, and compliant in carrying out our plans. I'm grateful for that; Knowledge Knows I've had more than enough problems with non-compliant subordinates this Winter."

Donnie Molinaro stirred, but an image of Andrea flashed through his vision, and his impulse dissolved; he continued to look at The Director, his expression placid.

"Others in your position might want to be in on the plan, might make demands based on their position, but you have shown discretion; in return, I have decided to let you in on a little secret; the story of what today's events truly represent, the plan, laid so long ago, that is so near completion."

The Guvna' frowned; he glanced from The Director to Penelope, and then to Cornelius. Somehow, he sensed that what he was about to say was wrong.

"The completion o' da Bubble Suit upgrades?"

The Director shook his head.

"No. The completion of the Bouregard family's vision for Kingston, Acadia, and the planet Shurtain."

BOOK 6, CHAPTER 2

Gavin stared down at the tiny being in his arms, breathing slowly as they rocked back and forth, the ropes of the porch swing creaking as they moved.

Ethereal beauty surrounded him, the sun casting early evening light over rolling hills that gave way to the ocean on the horizon. Gavin paid that little mind; his attention was all for the slumbering face of the tiny girl he held, his focus on her closed eyes, patiently awaiting that moment when the lids would open, when those hazel eyes would find his, and his daughter would smile.

Before Elysia, Gavin could not remember patiently waiting for anything.

How life had changed.

—

Their time in Elysia had passed in a haze, the days unrolling at a languid place, the Universe allowing their experience to continue, giving them the opportunity to take one step, and then the next.

For four weeks, those steps had been on an ascent; Santino, Tesla, Gavin, and Clarence had traveled from Elysia's eastern coast through the Tungsten Mountains in the company of the five Shamans who had greeted them.

They were on a course for Indica, Elysia's principal settlement, which rested on the northern side of the continent, on the other side of the highest peaks in the Tungsten Mountains.

For others, that might have posed difficulties, but after their time in the Cadillacs, the Tungstens felt downright hospitable; even with her growing belly, Tesla had no problems following the well-worn trail through the mountains, which felt more like big hills when compared with the raw peaks they had traversed in the Cadillacs. Besides, it was warm in Elysia, and as they traveled northwest, closer and closer to Shurtain's equator, it only grew warmer.

They had set an easy pace, at least by sentient being standards; the Shaman's limited stride lengths forced Clarence and the others to keep their own pace in check. Even if the Shamans had the legs to push the pace, they might have gone at the same speed; Hubert had said as much - quite cheerfully - when Gavin asked if there was a faster way to get there.

"This is da life we live; why hurry tru' it? A sentient being ain't a bird, and we ain't sentient beings, so we go one step atta time, and we get where we're going all da same."

Like the other Shamans, Hubert was short, no more than five feet tall, but where Winston was rail thin, Hubert, was stout, with broad shoulders, and a belly that hung over his loose canvas shorts. Like Winston, Hubert's skin was a deep, onyx black, but his black hair had yet to go to grey, one of many signs that Hubert was a good deal younger than his companion.

As to the women, they were roughly the same height, an inch or so shorter than their male counterparts. Annabelle was the oldest of them; she was thin, with dark brown hair going to grey and darker brown skin. Mariana had bronze skin, brown hair, and piercing green eyes, while Selena looked like a younger, female version of Winston; she was not quite so thin, and her hair remained black where the years turned Winston's grey, but her skin was the same onyx black, her eyes and face similarly shrewd.

The Shamans were a cheerful lot, and after their time at sea, Santino, Tesla, and Gavin realized they needed that; they had put it aside, done their best to enjoy the journey, the day in front of them, but there was no denying that a certain tension had gripped them during their weeks on the ship, the constant question of whether they were still pursued, of whether they would reach safe harbor in Elysia, or be taken before they reached their destination.

Clarence was harder to read, but whatever his feelings had been during their journey, he seemed more or less content to move at this measured pace, though he did override Hubert on the second day when the Shaman suggested they stop for a second morning meal.

"She's managing well enough now, Hubert, but I think it might be better if we reach Indica before Tesla has the child; at least, I gather that was Annabelle's intention."

His words had brought a chuckle from the other Shamans, and a frown from Hubert, though his response indicated he was not much bothered.

"Eh old man, maybe you eat a bit more, get a bit more meat on dem bones, be strong 'nough to go more hours."

"Of course; I've failed so many times on the rugged trails of Elysia."

Tesla spoke up at that.

"Is the trail this good across the whole continent?"

Annabelle nodded.

"Most o'dem; there only a few routes on da eastern half o' da continent, but dem trails be far more extensive on da western side of Elysia. No mountains o'er there, which make it easier. Dis path connects wit'em, at its end; all you hafta do is keep on dis trail, and it'll take'ya 'cross Da Narrowing Bridge."

"The Narrowing Bridge?"

Mariana answered the question.

"The eastern 'n western halves o' Elysia are still connected by a land bridge. For most o' time, weren't halves o' our continent - t'was a single, intact body o' land - but o'er time, the Marean Ocean pushed into a small inlet on the southern side o'da continent. In time, it carved out an inlet, den a gulf. It continued o'er da centuries; years later, we started referring to da emerging halves as Western and Eastern Elysia, but it weren't for hundreds more years dat we start up calling da remaining stretch o' land connecting da two halves Da Narrowing Bridge. You were alive den, weren'tcha, Winston?"

Mariana's eyes sparkled as she made the last comment; the older Shaman grinned.

"Ah, not hardly, and y'know if that was da case, Annabelle woulda been 'round too. But den again, it wasn't so far off; da eventual outcome became clear maybe t'ree hundred years ago, something 'bout dat."

Mariana nodded.

"Someday, da ocean will break all da way thru, and Elysia will break into two continents, same as Alexandria and Olympia. Should be, maybe a thousand years more, but dat's up to Shurtain in da end, ya?"

"Any case, trail'll stay easy all da way to Indica. No fear on dat count."

As their journey progressed, the adventurers intermingled more and more with the Shamans, Tesla gravitating toward the females, who would assist her with her child's birth, Gavin attaching himself to Hubert, who shared his sense of humor, and Santino connecting with Winston, who knew far more about him than Santino ever could have imagined.

"Ja, you were 'bout two, maybe t'ree, when I last heard tell o' you. Salomon told me all 'bout you, you, and your cousins, all his children, when he'd come here. Dat was the last time I seen 'im; since then, it's only been Clarence coming from Acadia. Thought Marcus, or Nadia, might come back with summa da others, but it neva' happened."

Santino stopped for a moment, brought up short by the mention of his mother's name.

"My mother came here?"

Winston nodded.

"Oh ya, she was here dat last time with Salomon. Not everyone wants to take da journey, and many times, motherhood itself is a powerful 'nuff transformation. But Nadia, she want to go deeper, and da Cahn family always encouraged its own to come back here, try'n get some perspective on 'et all. Salomon passed da tradition along to his children, like his father, and his grandfather before dat; he was even gonna bring dat Anton, afta da move up'ta dem Cadillac Mountains was over."

Santino blinked, taken aback once more.

"He was going to bring Anton?"

"Oh ya. He say dat young man need it worse'n anyone afta' da work was complete. But 'et neva came'ta be."

Santino nodded.

"What would you have done with him, if he had come?"

Winston had turned, showing every one of his teeth in a broad smile.

"Dat, young fellow, is 'xactly whatcha gonna find out."

—

"Dis da place."

They stood at the mouth of a cave, a gentle breeze the only disturbance in the afternoon air. Santino and Winston had hiked for hours to get here, setting out before dawn so they would arrive with plenty of daylight remaining. They would be here for a day, but that was not so long; both of them recognized that the time would slip away if it were not used consciously.

Still, there was enough time to stop and appreciate the place. They were not here to enter the cave - it was the wrong time of year to harvest - but to be present in the surroundings, and to honor a family tradition; his grandfather, his mother, and his uncle had all traveled with Winston to this place for their first experience with the entheogens.

It had been carefully planned. They had arrived in Indica two days ago; since the morning meal the day after their arrival, Santino had seen little of Tesla and Gavin.

The Shamans had different ideas for all of them.

And Clarence had departed the morning after they reached Indica.

Indica could not quite be called a city, but nor was it some ragtag settlement; with cold an occasional challenge but heavy snow unheard of, the Shamans of Indica lived in yurts spread out across a valley in the northern Tungstens. There were a handful of larger structures, wooden halls built to accommodate gatherings in poor weather, but only a handful. Indica, with its high desert climate, was not built with poor weather in mind; instead, the Shamans had poured their efforts into their outdoor gathering places, the rows of seats carved into the red sandstone that faced out toward an archway, the common cooking space in the center of the yurts, where huge cook-fires lit up the nights.

Enthralling as it was to enter these new surroundings, Santino remained preoccupied; it was not that he did not appreciate seeing how the Shamans lived, or the beauty of Indica, but that he was too concerned with the experience awaiting him to devote much attention to anything else.

Yet now that it was time, he felt a sense of unease; he was about to cross an invisible barrier, to step out of this experience and into something new, something that, as Winston put it, he had to experience to understand; there were words to describe it, but they could never do it justice.

"Ready?"

Santino turned back; as he had stood there, lost in his thoughts, the thin Shaman had prepared a small altar on a nearby rock.

Santino took a deep breath, then nodded; as he sat down next to Winston, his mind returned to the conversation they had around the fire, some nights before they arrived in Indica, about the entheogens.

—

"It's not the only reason to come here - the Shamans can tell you I've been here many times for more ordinary visits - but certainly, it's a reason that many sentient beings travel to Elysia."

"You can't do this anywhere else?" Tesla had asked.

Clarence shrugged at her question.

"Oh, you can, but the potential complications are endless, and it's well established that the best source materials grow in the caves of Elysia. You could take an entheogen with you, or concoct one abroad, but even for the most skilled, the experience won't be the same. The Shamans are far more practiced; they've been experimenting for centuries, have a deep understanding of how different entheogens will affect different beings."

He shook his head.

"I've experimented with it myself - the Shamans have taught me more than a bit about their arts over the last half-century - but while I can create an experience for myself, I'm not the right person to do it for anyone else. I won't live long enough to acquire that level of mastery; it's much better to find the right Shaman for the right individual."

Tesla frowned.

"But you said The Director's roots are here, in these experiences; what makes you so sure this is a good idea?"

Annabelle answered.

"Dat t'was a curious case, but unfortunate as 'et was, we learned a great many lessons from 'et."

She paused.

"Da darkness was 'en dat one dey called Teddy. From da moment he arrive on Elysia, we all sensed it - we Shamans, I mean - but none o'us seen what a cause fer concern it be. No more'n we realized dat two among us been waiting for such'a person to come along."

She shook her head.

"What 'et was happened wit' Penelope and Cornelius… we neva' did figure where exactly dey went wrong. We understand what grew inside 'em, know what'ta look for now, been much more careful about… not investigating one another, but encouraging everyone to share our frustrations with dis life we live. Nowa'days, we even encourage da Shamans ta seek out adventure, if da urge is there. Before, we'd just expected everyone would wanna stay; 'et was dat rare anyone expressed any otha' desire."

"Our life here, it passes slow and easy."

"For some, dat'a dream. For others… et's not so good. Dey want adventure, drama, intrigue… things Elysia don't provide so much as da rest'o Shurtain."

"Maybe if we seen 'et coming, maybe things woulda been different. But that's just 'et; nobody can see everything coming. Hard enough to explain what be happening right now. We do our best… and continue to live."

Annabelle smiled then.

"We can't guarantee anything, but I don't think'ya need'ta worry; I ain't seen a hint of what I seen in Teddy in you folks."

—

Back in the present, Santino shook himself; his eyes found Winston's.

"Let's do it."

—

Tesla still did not know quite what to make of this new version of Gavin.

He was not that different - her apprehensions on that front had proved unfounded - but there was one aspect that stood out: that sense of guilt for the mere fact of his existence, that undercurrent of anxiety that had been so at odds with his relentless optimism, was gone.

They had been in Indica for two weeks, taking their new world in, when Gavin had first broached the topic.

"Nobody says I have to, or even should, but the perspective Hubert talks about, understanding myself more, feeling more connected to the world around me… I'm interested."

They were sitting together on the floor of their yurt, backs to the bed behind them. Tesla smiled.

"Well, you've got your choice. I guess I made mine seasons ago, even if I'm only realizing what I committed to now that I'm spending time with Annabelle and Mariana. Motherhood wasn't exactly something we talked about in Kingston, but everything they've told me has me more excited, on the whole."

She paused, looking deep into Gavin's eyes before she continued.

"I love you… well, just because, and you don't need to change anything for me. But I also realize we aren't going to be the same people by the time this kid of ours is grown; we're going to grow into different versions of ourselves. I'm changing now, and as Annabelle told me, the physical changes are more than just the child growing in me; the wiring of my brain is changing, and it's going to change even more during the birthing process."

As she said this, Tesla took Gavin's right hand and laid it over her belly, then covered his hand with both of hers.

"They say you'll get some of that, since you're here and present with us, but as they say, it's not the same; it can't be the same, because as much as you're here with me, you're not the one with a child growing inside you. What we got to share, the first time you got to feel kiddo kick, was… perfect. But what I felt on my own - getting kicked from the *inside* - I mean, I can't share that with anyone. It's something you have to experience."

She grinned.

"At the end of the day, I trust you'll be with me through my changes, and if you want to pursue something you believe will help you grow, I'm going to be there for you."

Tesla took her hands off Gavin's and turned herself around, then pulled him in for a kiss.

"Just don't stop being you, ok?"

He had been gone for two days.

And when he returned, he had not stopped being him.

In fact, he was more himself than ever; Gavin acted the same, but he no longer twitched as if someone were applying shock therapy when he did something that was blatantly at odds with *The Manual for Proper Behavior*. It had been an unconscious tick, hardly noticeable - Tesla had only picked up on it after their relationship started - and it had never prevented Gavin from doing anything, but now, his subconscious appeared free of that grip.

Tesla loved it. She had her own experience coming, and did not plan to follow in Gavin's footsteps, but even so, on the night he got back, she could not help asking.

"So; what was it like?"

—

Santino's eyes flashed back open, the night sky filling his vision once more. He could not have detailed the movements of the stars, but he could tell how different they were; it was one sign of the time that had passed.

"Didja see anything?"

Winston sat with his back to a rock a few yards away, solemnly observing Santino.

Santino nodded, unwrapping himself from a blanket as he sat up.

"A lot, actually. That was way different than the other times."

Winston mirrored the nod.

"Ya'mon, closed-eye, inactive, very different den open-eye, active."

Santino shrugged.

"It was strange, though. I found myself on a mountain pass, working to cross through. I couldn't find the way, even though I know it is there, that it must exist."

"I ought to have felt panicked - the snow was falling fast and thick, threatening to bury me alive if I couldn't find my way out - but for some reason, I felt calm, even though my brain was telling my body it ought to feel panicked. It was as if some part of me understood that I don't need to get there today… but I need to get there someday."

He paused, looked over at Winston.

"Does any of that make sense?"

Winston smiled, running a hand over his thin chin.

"You tell me, 'mon. The entheogen interacted wit'chu to cause da vision; 'et was for you'ta interpret, not me."

Santino nodded.

"Well, I suppose we do have time; we're here until Tesla gives birth, at least, and perhaps until Clarence returns. Assuming he ever does."

Winston chuckled.

"Oh, I be counting on dat. When he comes and goes, dat's past telling, but dat one always find his way back."

They had been in Elysia for nearly a full season - ninety days had passed since their arrival - but between Tesla's pregnancy, and the fact that it was the dead of Winter in Shurtain's northern hemisphere, they had no plans to leave anytime soon.

As to Clarence, he had not bothered to tell anyone where he was going, except to say that he needed to handle the problem waiting for them back in Acadia; their pursuer would not have given up on them, so Clarence could not forget about him. That was all he had said before departing, going back the same way they had come.

Santino nodded.

"We will have to go back though, with or without him. We rolled the dice, and got lucky, but the stalemate in Acadia won't last forever; the war will come."

Winston shrugged.

"You say so, den maybe 'et so. Be darned 'ef Penelope and Cornelius dinnit work dat magic well; forty years to divide a people into two civilizations, and twenty more to push 'em to war. Oceans might blush, if dey could; y'know how many hundreds o' years 'et take dem waves to divide a continent?"

He shook his head.

"Den again, a continent can't think, and while thinking have its wonders, I see'n 'et as a double-edged sword, with sum'o'dem people cutting em'selves more often'n anything else. Ain't strictly sentient beings, seeing as two o' my kin be stirring 'et all up, but coming up, we had a saying, dat for every problem sentient thinking solved, 'et created a hun'red more. A few o' dem problems end up in da world round 'em, dat world o' illusions, but a great many more live in their own heads."

"So maybe yer right, thinking dis war must come. Maybe there's no turning back time, but I'm old 'nuff to remember when you was all one tribe, one city. Sentient beings on either side o' dis divide were family, not so long ago. But 'et always seemed sentient beings were ripe for division; convince'em they gotta pick a side, and dat another side's da enemy, and dey be off'ta'da races."

He paused.

"And if you say da war gotta come… well, long as da thinking stay dat way, I s'pose dat's true."

—

Santino had not stopped pondering Winston's words in the weeks since that night.

Tonight, he sat alone, his back to the cave mouth, his eyes on the shifting hues of the sunset, but even as he took in the beauty, his mind lingered over the wonder of his most recent days in Elysia.

Tesla and Gavin's child was not the first newborn he had held, not the first infant he had met on its inaugural day on Shurtain, but after accompanying them on this journey, watching Tesla and Gavin together all this time, the child growing inside her, holding their daughter, mere hours after she had come into the world, was something different.

He thought back to the Gavin he had met on the outskirts of Trepani, to the Tesla he had gotten to know in those days they had planned Clarence and Gavin's liberation. Those people were still there, but the afterglow of their daughter's birth had transformed them; Gavin appeared content to sit with his child until the end of time, and all the cunning and calculation fell away from Tesla's expression when she held her little girl.

Santino knew this was not fixed, that certain traits would remain when the tides receded; the ebbs and flows of the days and years to come would return them to their natural rhythms, but they would be changed, evolved.

What about him?

He knew that he was changed, as well.

And if the end of his last experience held any truth, he was about to be changed again.

Perhaps, this time, he would see the last piece of the puzzle.

Santino slipped the lozenge in his mouth, tightened the blanket he had secured around himself, and laid back on the ground. He closed his eyes, and let the journey take him.

BOOK 6, CHAPTER 3

"The traps you put in place are sufficient?"

"I'd think so; they are four returning on a single ship. Whether they try to land in Giota, or make the long run back to Larissa, we will be waiting to intercept them. There's nowhere else to go; if they land anywhere else, the war will be over, our victory secured, before they get back to Trepani, or Turquoise Lake."

The two men stood on The Director's balcony, taking in the night air and view of the city beyond. It had been a long day - Tarissa Cross's planned coup attempt had demanded an early start - but that was nothing in light of the overwhelming victory they had secured.

The Director nodded.

"I hope so. We have come too far to allow Clarence Barnett to derail us."

Mateo Fernandez shook his head.

"We won't. It was sheer luck that allowed him to escape me in Larissa, and coming back won't be near as easy as running away."

The Director nodded.

"Even so, these mercenaries of yours; you trust them?"

Fernandez shrugged.

"As much as anyone should trust any mercenary. But what else would you suggest? I can't keep eyes on both ports by myself."

"I could reassign units from the City Watch and the Capitol Guard to your command."

Fernandez frowned.

"And what would we do with them after? Even if we sent them to watch the route to Giota, and kept them in their Bubble Suits, they would see Clarence and the others operating in open air. What would come after that? How would they react? How would we ensure their silence?"

The Director turned to Fernandez, genuine bemusement on his face. Fernandez understood.

"In that case, I think I'll stick with my mercenaries. I don't want to go into the field with a bunch of troops who believe you need a Bubble Suit to live on Shurtain; Knowledge Knows how they'll react if they encounter evidence to the contrary. I'd rather deal with potential treachery; that, at least, is predictable."

"Understood. Well, it has been a long day, but a productive one; I assume you will want to get back south to your command."

Fernandez nodded.

"As you say."

Fernandez turned and made his way back into The Retreat; as he walked through the doorway, Penelope and Cornelius Kastner passed him, on their way to join The Director on the balcony. Fernandez glanced back before proceeding; he looked at the two small beings, now standing on either side of The Director, and for a moment, he wondered.

But wondering would not get him anywhere; Fernandez shook himself, and pushed through the doorway.

—

"So close."

The Shamans did not respond to The Director's words, letting them float in the chill night air.

"All these years, all this work, and it comes to this. An intoxicating experience, no?"

"A heady brew," supplied Cornelius.

The Director nodded.

"It still amazes me, how a vision established generations ago can play out so many years in the future. How we have reached the precipice of success, that total control my great-great-great-grandfather dreamed of when he laid down Acadia's railroad system, all those years ago."

He shook his head.

"That those first steps could have led to all this… it amazes the mind. Yet there it is; those moves gave our family control of commerce across the Acadian mainland, and the advantages necessary to dominate the money-lending that financed the many ventures relying on those rail lines, which, in turn, led to the creation of the First Bank of Bouregard."

Cornelius and Penelope nodded. They were well familiar with the story - after sixty years in each other's company, there was nothing new left for them to discuss with Theodore Bouregard - but they listened intently all the same.

"And yet, it all might have been for naught, were it not for the two of you, and your ability to bring me to that critical realization, that understanding that it would never be enough to control a people's movement and means of exchange. For total control, we would have to go further than my ancestors ever dreamed."

Cornelius and Penelope exchanged a smile; it was Penelope who responded.

"We were only too happy to do it. We've benefited greatly from our side of the swap; we needed some way to get away from Elysia if we wanted to see something interesting happen on Shurtain. All that peace and calm, living in the present as they let the future come… it was interminable. A sentence to live and die in a dream world."

"We wanted more," added Cornelius.

The Director nodded; as he gazed out into the night, he recalled his voyage to Elysia, landing on the white sand beaches, Salomon introducing him and Clarence to those strange beings, the Shamans, whose differences in appearance were nothing to their differences in customs.

On his second day, he met Penelope and Cornelius.

Or perhaps it was better said that Penelope and Cornelius had met him; on that first night, as their people discussed the new arrivals, and the dark aura that surrounded one of them, the pair had known they had their target, the vessel they had waited for all these years.

They set about charming him, taking the necessary steps to gain his trust.

They had not breached their true aim until after they had used the entheogen to send Theodore on his first journey; instead, they seeded the idea as the experience occurred, taking it in turn to whisper the thoughts to the young man's unsuspecting self, encouraging that desire for control that was so evident in him, feeding the beastling, and transforming it into a monster.

Once they were done, it was Theodore who broached the discussions.

After two more journeys - and hours of planning - it was Theodore who proposed sending a ship once he had returned to Kingston; a ship that would land in the dead of night in a cove on the western coast of Elysia, one that would take Penelope and Cornelius away, to rendezvous with Theodore on the western coast of Acadia, where he would be waiting for them in the city of Quincy.

From there, they would get to work.

And as Penelope so wisely pointed out, if the Bouregards wanted to realize the vision of their forebears, they would need to go much further in their quest for control.

Theodore agreed with this readily enough; after all, he had often listened to his grandfather, and father, bemoan the current state of affairs, the limitations of their power, in many discussions, both around the house and in more formal quarters. However, despite their complaints, the elder Bouregards had resigned themselves to their limited power, accepting the fact that there was only so much one could impose upon a population before they would revolt.

Penelope had smiled when Theodore shared that with them; she and Cornelius exchanged a coy look before she responded.

"Of course they will. That's why we're not going to impose anything; we're going to tilt the conditions until they hand over control willingly. By the time we're done, they'll be ready to revolt if we *take away* the control we impose on them."

Theodore Bouregard blinked.

"How?"

Cornelius answered.

"We won't call it control; we'll call it protection. We'll convince the people that it's for their own good; we'll convince them that our interventions are the only thing keeping them alive."

From there, their first objective had not been difficult to identify.

They needed to create the conditions that would allow them to provide salvation.

And for that, they would need to destroy Acadia.

But not just destroy Acadia; find a way to poison it from the inside out, bringing the people to their knees, to the point where they were so fearful and desperate that they would accept any solution that solved their problems, no matter the downside.

It began with sabotaging the rest of the cities on the continent, undermining the flow of resources on the railways, slowly, but surely, breaking down the structures of those cities, ensuring their eventual collapse; if their plan was to work, then there could be no other power center in Acadia, no city that could harbor a resistance to Kingston's eventual control of the continent.

In that, the Bouregard resources had proven useful; with control of the railways, it was easy to create shortages, to have portions of the track sabotaged, and trains delayed, to make it altogether more difficult to live anywhere west of Kingston on the main portion of the Acadian continent. It meant losses in the short term, but the Bouregards could survive that, given the windfall it would bring in the future.

These first seeds of the plan had years to develop; in the meantime, Theodore had kept up appearances, taking up his expected apprenticeship at his family's bank, learning the necessary lessons to prepare for his eventual role as the top executive. For their part, Penelope and Cornelius moved into rooms in Theodore's personal home on the Bouregard estate, which contained no fewer than five full-sized houses scattered across the gated property in addition to the mansion itself, which stood as the crown jewel of the many stately homes west of Capitol Square in Kingston. But while they spent much of their time there, hidden away from public gaze, plotting with Theodore, the two Shamans also left for weeks, even seasons, at a time, traveling the continent of Acadia, using their wiles to remain in the shadows, learning more about their targets without alerting anyone to their presence.

As for the friends he had traveled to Elysia with, Theodore saw less and less of Salomon Cahn and Clarence Barnett as the years waned on. Theodore had initiated this, telling his old companions that the demands of his family, his inheritance, must be put first, an explanation that his friends understood; after all, they were changed since their own voyages to Elysia, and it had always been impossible to miss the gravity of the Bouregards in Kingston's landscape, even if Theodore had once done his best to set that aside, and blend in with his friends during the years of their youth.

All things considered, they had parted on good terms.

It was more than a decade later, when Theodore's old friends started to get an inkling of what the Bouregard family resources were being used for, as Theodore took more and more control of those powers, that they changed their tune.

By then, Theodore and the Shamans had gone well beyond interfering with rail schedules.

They were actively poisoning the food supply.

It was a great deal more complicated, of course, a labyrinth of agreements between chemical manufacturers, corporate powers, and the Guvernment of the day. And they did not say they were poisoning the food supply, at least not openly; they claimed they were finding ways to produce food more efficiently, so that Acadia might feed the many starving peoples living around the planet Shurtain.

But as complicated as the structure was, and whatever legal protection the agreements might afford those at the top, those who looked hard enough, dug deep enough, could determine who the agreements benefited.

Doing something about it was a different matter; striking at the Bouregard family, and the other families who comprised the oligarchy that controlled Kingston during the Economic Era, back Before Knowledge, was no easy matter.

Not when they owned the judges.

Not when they wrote the laws.

No, the difficulty in fighting back was not a lack of courage; it was a lack of organization. The forces aiming to seize control had laid their plans for years; they had the bandwidth to actively seek out threats to their interests, to disband them before they gathered any momentum. Their opponents did not enjoy these luxuries; they were the people, obliged to attend to their daily tasks, to make a living and put bread on the table for their families. The intrigues of the families who determined Kingston's policies, the processes that determined how they came to agree on new laws, new actions, was a black box, carefully hidden from public view, which only made the people's task more impossible; how could they divert the course their overlords had set for their civilization, when the true motives and actions were carefully hidden from them?

Still, it was not enough; it was not the end.

Theodore Bouregard had seen that, in his visions on Elysia.

The families that made up Kingston's oligarchy were too public, too well known. It might take a Herculean effort, but if their enemy organized against them, they would be overwhelmed.

So if he wanted to ratchet up the control, Theodore Bouregard thought he had best take steps to further insulate himself.

It was a gradual process; another decade passed before everything was in place. But by the time his father passed away, leaving the forty-one-year-old Theodore as the sole controller of the Bouregard Estate, he, and his two co-conspirators, were ready to push the plan into overdrive.

Theodore began by ending the family's iron grip on Thc First Bank of Bouregard, renaming it The First Bank of Kingston on the same day that he distributed shares of the bank to a dozen other influential families in Kingston. The Bouregards still held the largest share of the company, and Theodore would remain in place as The Director, but the bank's decisions would now be a matter for The Board.

From there, the moves followed fast and hard.

The strain of Theodore's sabotage of Acadia's railways and food supply had long since started to strain the people at this point; whole cities in Central and Western Acadia had already been abandoned, and those that remained were following a similar trajectory. To add to their troubles, a steady uptick in all manner of diseased states was causing concern across the continent, as well as in Kingston itself.

But it was not until The First Bank of Kingston began to aggressively acquire new companies, adding huge corporations to its portfolio, that matters were pushed past the breaking point.

Of course, nobody saw the issue at the time, or at least, nobody with the power to do anything about it. After all, why should the acquisitions be a problem? They were, after all, made by The First Bank of Kingston, an institution put in place to benefit the city the bank was named after.

Once again, there were people - many of them - who could see through the machinations, get past all of the misleading documents and explanations, the legalese, and see, to some degree, what was going on, but few of them were able to connect the actions of the bank - and Theodore Bouregard - with the collapse of society across Acadia, because nobody except for Theodore, Penelope, and Cornelius understood the full extent of what had been done.

It was the same reason it was not questioned when Theodore

Bouregard, the bachelor who was the sole surviving member of his notable family, announced that he would be donating a large portion of his wealth - which had grown considerably as The First Bank of Kingston's acquisitions increased - to found a new organization committed to ending the health crisis in Kingston, an organization named Dynamic Solutions.

By then, those few in Kingston who understood what was happening had started to spread the word, alerting as many people as they could of the impending danger, but this proved difficult. For one, it was not safe to spread this tale, which had been deemed heresy. For another, it was difficult to make people believe that such a complicated, deranged scheme could really have been put into action.

At the center of the resistance was Salomon Cahn, who had been among the first to recognize what his one-time friend was up to. Salomon had not been certain where Penelope and Cornelius had disappeared to, when he had first learned the news from Winston on a return visit to Elysia, but he had his suspicions, and as the years wore on, and Salomon saw the subtleties behind his old friend's plans, he came to his own conclusions.

But Salomon Cahn came from a lineage of wisdom, rather than power, and he lacked the means to fight back openly against the resources that Theodore Bouregard marshaled.

Yet while he could not overthrow the powers-that-be, he did not have to submit to their control.

Theodore had not seen Salomon's move coming; nor had Penelope, nor Cornelius. By the time they realized what had happened, on the first day After Knowledge, it was too late; Salomon, and the others, had slipped the trap.

It had long been a sticking point for The Director, and matters did not improve when he received the reports that his old friend had died; he was not pleased to find out he had been deprived of the pleasure of seeing that happen, now that he understood the steps Salomon had taken to resist him.

But perhaps he would encounter Clarence Barnett, one last time, and witness that old friend's final moments.

For so many years, only Penelope and Cornelius had known the full extent of what he had done; even Fernandez, who was as much in The Director's confidence as anyone, had not been told anything close to the true story, and the rest of The Board had only been told what they needed to Know.

Those long years of secrecy had made it immensely satisfying to tell Donnie Molinaro the full story; Theodore Bouregard had worked too hard not to let a fellow sentient being appreciate his work. The Guvna' had not disappointed, his expression turning more and more incredulous as The Director told him the full story of The Bubble Society, and how the world that they existed in had come to be.

"Of course, it will not do for the public to learn any of this - the citizuns of The Bubble Society must be kept ignorant for our utopia to thrive - but I'm not concerned about you sharing any of this. You've shown you can keep a secret, and if we hear you spreading the story, then we can always remove you from the picture."

The Director paused to meet The Guvna's eyes before he delivered his last warning.

"Don't forget, freezing the Bubble Suits is the least of the power we can exert on the sentient beings within."

The Guvna's stare had hardened as The Director told his story; The Director thought he could even see hatred in the depths of Donnie Molinaro's blue eyes. But no matter; like every other citizun of The Bubble Society, Donnie Molinaro would thank him, once their utopia was secured; he simply did not have the Knowledge to see it yet.

The Director wished there was a simpler solution, a way to deploy their large-scale weaponry against these Savages, but whatever the official stance of The Bubble Society might be, Theodore Bouregard understood that sentient beings were still dependent on Nature for some things, and the Grand River was one of those things; without that lifeline, Kingston would collapse, no matter their technology, or Knowledge.

So The Director had no desire to carpet-bomb the Savages, not when his intelligence indicated that their main outpost sat on the banks of the lake that fed the Grand.

This would be better, simpler.

The Bubble Suits would be upgraded.

They would march.

And they would slaughter anyone who stood in their path.

—

Anton Molinaro stood in his place on the ridge, observing his troops as they cleared paths through the snow that remained in the valley next to Turquoise Lake.

The Winter had offered an opportunity for rest, but somehow, Anton left it more exhausted than he had entered.

It was his own fault; he could not handle the restlessness within during these prolonged periods of inactivity, and once again, he had left the town he had wintered in to the shrill sound of a pregnant woman reminding him he would need to come back, to be there for the child's birth.

Al Nierland's voice shook him from his troubled thoughts.

"How long do you reckon we have?"

Anton shook his head wearily, glancing between Al and Brock Lukavsky, who had arrived with at the head of the bulk of their forces, troops sent from Alexandria, from Larissa, from Kirfi, and of course, from Trepani.

"A few days, I think. It's hard to get a handle on precisely what happened - the powers-that-be in Kingston have ensured that - but they installed their upgrades to the Bubble Suits the other day in a mass deployment. The latest we've heard is that they're massing in Capitol Square; I can't think of any reason for that, except to send their military against us."

Al and Brock exchanged a glance.

"On that point," started Brock. "We had some talks on that front in our time in Trepani. We expect that The Bubble Society will reassign the Capitol Guard and the City Watch… but beyond that, who is going to make up this army of theirs?"

BOOK 6, CHAPTER 4

Neville could not believe it was real.

The armor they had attached to his Bubble Suit during the latest round of Elevation Upgrades.

The rifle they had placed in his hands.

Or the thousands of troops that stood in lines in Capitol Square, rank upon rank, facing the stage that had been erected in front of The Guvna's Mansion, ostensibly being inspired by the rally in the Square as they awaited their next order.

But if it was a bad dream, Neville could not wake up from it; Leonard and Mo stood to his right, similarly equipped, and they, like the thousands around them, were as helpless as Neville.

That portion of the population assigned to the First Army of Kingston had not been allowed to return home after they reported to the Center of Industry to get their Bubble Suits upgraded; instead, they had been shuttled along to the recently building that had been the Department of Air Filtration Construction, which had been hastily converted to a sort of barracks, with camp beds strewn in every conceivable place, filling up hallways beneath the many monitors that continued to run mock-ups of the imagined mouth and nose filters on loop.

In the three weeks that followed, they had been put through an accelerated training program, led by the former members of the City Watch and the Capitol Guard, whose ranks had been drained to fill roles in the newly formed Army.

Their trainers assured them they would be well prepared for the moment, that the leaders of the City Watch and the Capitol Guard were the finest warriors the planet Shurtain had to offer, and that Neville and the others could not wish for more competent teachers.

Neville was not so certain; no matter how many times his instructors assured him they were among the elite, their inability to consistently hit the targets they were shooting at on the range did not inspire much confidence in anything else they were being taught.

Lost in his thoughts, Neville did not register what it meant when he saw The Guvna' step out onto the terrace of The Guvna's Mansion. But when the man raised his arm, and the trumpets blew in response, Neville understood the time had come; in lockstep with the other troops, he began to march, on a course across the Stone Bridge, up Riverside Parkway, and toward war.

—

Kelli Mancini had pressed herself against her husband's chest, her arms wrapped tight around him.

In days past, when they had first arrived in Kingston, she would have kissed Donnie when they broke apart, then straightened his tie before telling him she looked forward to seeing him that night, channeling magic wherever her fingers touched.

That had been Before Knowledge; since The Advent, there had been no ties to straighten, and no matter what attempts the Knowers made to emulate the sensation of kissing another sentient being, attempting the act through the Bubble Suits had never become more than a pale imitation, a mockery of the connection once available to them.

And today, Kelli Mancini did not know if she would see her husband that night, if she would see her husband again. The troops massed outside The Guvna's Mansion in Capitol Square told the story; The Bubble Society was ready to march, to bring justice down upon the Savages, and to rescue Tesla.

Kelli Mancini did not hold out much hope for any of this; all she felt was dread, a gnawing pit of despair in her guts that told her it would all go wrong. She could not imagine what would come, could not reconcile the idea of moving forward without Donnie, could not think what she would do for Andrea if things did not go to plan, or even worse, if they did.

She said none of this; Donnie knew it all already, and if he was going to return, he would need all his wits about him, would need to focus on the moment, the task at hand, so all she said was, "I love you. Please come back to us."

Donnie nodded; he reached around, gently took the back of her head, and leaned in so their foreheads touched.

Then the moment was over; they broke apart, and Donnie Molinaro walked out of their bedroom, toward the stairway that would take him to the ground floor of The Guvna's Mansion.

—

"You will appear to be the leader, working from the front. I will command from the rear. It would not be proper for me to reveal myself, but nor can I take this in remotely, not with so much on the line; I need to be on the scene."

Donnie Molinaro nodded once, his blue eyes cold as they met The Director's brown ones. Even now, he was hard-pressed not to throw himself at the man who, he now understood, had engineered the events that culminated in his oldest daughter's perpetual illness.

Yet what good would it do, when the man he faced held the power to freeze the very Bubble Suit he wore, held the power of life and death in his hands.

Even so, Donnie Molinaro believed in providence; he believed in justice, that on a long enough timeline, the arc of the Universe would reassert itself.

So he would wait.

And he would watch.

For in time, even the humblest of men could find their opportunity.

With those words in mind, Donnie Molinaro shifted into Guvna' mode; he met The Director's eyes, nodded, then turned and crossed the foyer of The Mansion to take his place at the head of the troops massed in Capitol Square.

—

As they put the finishing touches on their makeup, Anna, Thea, and Shannon could not help but glance askance in Tarissa Cross's direction.

They had been told that Cross was still in charge, and the woman was still ordering them around as they prepared to deliver a final rallying cry to Kingston's Army before the troops marched, but something about Cross was, not just off, but broken. Despite the dislike they had developed for the woman during their interactions, they could not help but feel bad, or at least concerned, about the change; they might prefer this version to the old, but they could not imagine what could possibly have happened to cause such a dramatic change in Cross's demeanor.

For Cross, the reality was much worse than the appearance; she shuddered whenever she remembered the events that had followed the attempted coup.

That first morning, when she had been cut out of her Bubble Suit and left in a cold cell, naked and alone.

The moment when The Director had arrived, late that afternoon. He had stood in silence for a time, staring at her; then he informed her that she would be turned over to the pleasure of those who had proved more loyal.

Cross cringed when she thought of the feel as, first Fernandez, and then that odd creature, the one they called Cornelius, had used her.

But it was the memory of what the last one - the female named Penelope - had done to her, day after day, that tied her stomach in knots.

When The Director had returned, weeks later, to tell Cross she would be put back into a Bubble Suit to take up her role as Viceroy, she had no idea what to think. There was relief - any reprieve from her suffering was welcome - but she did not imagine it would last for long, and did not want to think what horrors awaited her when it was over.

Still, she was managing; as Tesla's forlorn lover, Derek, finished up his speech, Cross signaled to Anna, Thea, and Shannon, who stepped onstage as Derek walked off.

Utterly drained, Tarissa Cross sank into a chair, staring blankly ahead as The Guvna' stepped out from the front doors of The Mansion; she was too lost in her troubles to follow what was going on as The Guvna' smiled at Derek, and sidled up to the young man.

"Understand you were 'bout to be my son-in-law."

Derek felt heat rise to his cheeks; unsure of what to say, he shrugged.

"Don't wurry, jus' yankin yer chain. Afta' all, if we can't smile in da face o' death, did we ever actually recognize da price o' livin?"

Derek stared at the man.

"Death?"

The Guvna' shrugged.

"Dat's what I figger's waiting at da end'o dis march. Don't you?"

—

Aubrey Jenkins stood on The Villa's rooftop balcony with several of the caretakers, watching as their city's army made their progress across the Stone Bridge.

Things were quiet at The Villa; most of the care staff remained in place, but the ERTs and security guards had been reassigned to the Kingston Army, where they would do the greatest good for Knowledge.

It left a haunting feeling, so many of the lucid disappearing, leaving behind a skeleton staff, and the Laureates.

Aubrey would have had her own fears about being assigned to the Army; she knew that Mo, and all the others, faced grave danger, wherever it was they were marching.

Even so, she wished she could have been with them; she wanted to be with Mo, that was true, but it was not the only reason.

The real reason is Aubrey could not face, did not want to even imagine, what life in Kingston would be like if they did not come back.

BOOK 6, CHAPTER 5

They stood on the bluffs overlooking the eastern side of the Narrowing Arm, staring out to where Elysia's northern shores fell away to the Amphitrite Ocean.

It was twenty days into Spring, and they knew that, up in Acadia, the thaw would be happening in full force, melting away the chrysalis of Winter and bringing the continent back to life.

One way or another, they were going to be part of it.

And they were not going back alone.

Winston stood next to Santino at the head of the group, looking out over the scene. Behind them, Gavin and Tesla stood together, Tesla holding Lilyann, Gavin with a hand around her waist as they waited for Winston to give some sign he was ready to proceed.

There still had not been any word from Clarence, and they did not know what dangers awaited them between Elysia and Acadia, but that was immaterial; the only choice was to return, and if they did not act now, the chance might disappear forever.

"Shall we move on? It's a good view, I agree, but we can't stay here forever. We need to reach this ship you arranged, if we're going to sail on the morning tide."

Winston nodded at Santino's words, but showed no inclination to move. A frown crossed his face as he glanced up at the sun in the sky; it was a cloudless day, and it shone bright, casting few shadows at high noon.

"Winston? What do you…"

"Ah, der 'et 'es."

The old Shaman smiled as he pointed back to the east, where a large, triangular sail had appeared on the horizon.

"Who is…" Santino started, but before he could finish his question, several more sails had appeared behind the first; as they watched, a third line appeared behind the second, twice as many ships again.

Winston only grinned.

"Who you think 'et 'es? Where else Clarence been all dis time?"

—

"I figured if Tyene Medrana, and the rest of the Alexandrians, were willing to raise an army, they might lend us a few ships."

Clarence stood with his five passengers at the prow of the lead ship. He paused to smile at his companions.

"Fernandez is waiting for us; there's no doubt about that. But he'll be expecting a single ship, not an armada."

"And Tyene Medrana wasn't exaggerating when she said her people were ready to join us; I was overwhelmed by volunteers, and most of them joined the troops that were preparing to leave for Larissa. It seems to me that the free people of Alexandria, and the planet Shurtain, are done with The Bubble Society."

BOOK 6, CHAPTER 6

He gave the signal when the sails appeared on the horizon.

Mateo Fernandez watched as his captains carried out the orders, pulling up anchors and unfurling their own sails, eager to move after so many days of inactivity. They had anchored in a cove of rocks some miles off the southern tip of Acadia's southeastern peninsula, far enough from Giota to avoid attracting attention, but close enough to have an eye on anyone approaching from the south. Unless Clarence and the others had looped out into the Amphitrite Ocean, and come back at Acadia from the east, they could not reach Giota without passing Fernandez and his men.

They had not done that; after a season spent waiting, Fernandez finally had his targets in his sights.

He and his men were ready for it; Fernandez had doubled down after the disaster in Larissa, quadrupling the number of mercenaries in his hire. He had two-thirds of that number with him now - the rest were in Larissa, monitoring that potential destination - and while his troops did not share Fernandez's motivations for wanting to end all this, they were itching for a fight after so many days of inactivity.

It looked like they were going to get it.

Fernandez shouted for them to max out their speed, though it was unnecessary; the sailors had already stretched every sail to its limit.

Yet, strangely, they did not seem to be approaching their target any faster.

By the time Fernandez realized that this was no illusion, that the effect had appeared because their target had stopped its progress, it was too late.

The rest of the sails had already appeared, bringing up the lead ship's rear.

—

Tesla sat on the elevated platform of her ship's second deck, watching the takeover with Lilyann in her arms and Gavin at her side.

Once, she might have insisted on joining Santino and Clarence on the lead ship, demanded that she be among those who would first board the enemy's vessels.

These days, there were other priorities.

Even so, it appeared that she would have been safe enough if she had been part of the landing party; once they had seen what they were facing, the mercenaries from Thoran had lost all interest in fighting, and willingly turned their employer over.

Now Fernandez was tied up and under watch, and the mercenaries were sailing southwest, on their way home. It was one more obstacle out of the way, brought Tesla one step closer to reconciling the knot in her stomach, that burning desire that had flamed up in the aftermath of Lilyann's birth. Before Lilyann, Tesla had hoped that the people of Kingston would live on, that her parents, sisters, and friends could go their own way, whatever that might be, and fulfill the paths their lives were meant to take.

But as content as Tesla had felt she held her daughter on that first night, propped up on the cushions Annabelle had arranged for her recovery, she could not lie to herself.

Something was missing.

In a tiny corner of her mind, Tesla knew she wanted to share her daughter with her parents, to reconnect with her mother, to say all the things she had never thought to say before she left.

She did not share this with anyone, save Gavin; she did not want to appear ungrateful, not with her daughter healthy and good friends around her, but nor could she keep it to herself.

Gavin understood; he did not hold out much hope, but if his parents had survived the Winter, he wanted the same, whether or not Lilyann or his parents would remember it.

"We'll just have to see. We have to hope we were right in hoping things would wait until after Winter, and then… I guess we'll find out."

Tesla remembered those words as they stood on the deck.

"Looks like we'll get to see Acadia again."

She turned to look at Gavin, a brilliant smile on her face.

"How about that? Did you ever imagine your daughter would be born on a different continent?"

Gavin laughed.

"Of course. Being a father was always part of the plan, living back in

Kingston; always Knew I'd get to find out what a wonder it all would be."

Tesla leaned into him, shifting Lilyann in her arms. She looked up, and held his gaze.

"It's not quite what I imagined, either. I couldn't guess what I would find, leaving The Bubble Society behind, but I never thought it would be this."

She stopped, smiled.

"Whatever's coming next… thank you. For helping me feel alive… even if this taste is all we get, I'd do it again in a heartbeat."

—

It all seemed to be breaking their way, Gavin thought, as they rowed the small boats into the rocky cove at the base of Giota.

What they would find at the end remained in question, but he was starting to think they would make it there. The woman at the head of their welcoming party was the latest stroke of fortune; they had expected to see Gwynivere Holt, and had been uncertain as to how she would handle the sudden reappearance of Clarence Barnett and Gavin Owens.

But Gwynivere Holt was not there to greet them; the delegation that appeared at the top of the stairway carved into the cliff face was led by a different woman.

Gavin could not make out Santino's face from his vantage point, but when his friend jumped from the boat, rope in hand, and turned back to tie it off, Gavin saw he was smiling. Once Clarence had joined him on the shore, Winston clinging to his back as they stepped off the boat, the trio turned to greet Eleanor Cahn.

"Eleanor; I didn't expect to see you here."

Eleanor smiled.

"We had a hint you might be coming; Tyene Medrana did more than approve the ships that brought you along. She arrived at the head of some ten thousand days ago; they are at Turquoise Lake now, part of the defense. It appears that conflict is imminent; The Bubble Society is on the march."

Santino nodded.

"In that case, I can't stay for long. The three of us," he indicated Clarence and Winston, "Need to get to Turquoise Lake."

—

Anton sat at the head of a long wooden table, taking in the faces of the captains he had invited to join him in the hall.

"You know why we are here. The Bubble Society's army has marched past Kingfisher Reservoir, and is set to camp well past the old Elevation

Limit. It depends on when they wake, and how hard they push, but they could be here as early as mid-morning."

"From what we can gather, they've decided to have this fight face-to-face, on the ground. As to the tactics they will use, that's more difficult to say. Even if they aren't using their heavy artillery, it doesn't mean they won't have a few toys with them."

He nodded toward Al Nierland and Brock Lukavsky, who sat on his left.

"Fortunately, we'll be ready for that. I believe we've prepared for all possible contingencies; if they resort to toxic gases, or any other attempt at an airborne attack, we have masks at the ready. But I don't think they will; I can't say whether they were ever confident in their Bubble Suits' ability to withstand such an attack, and given how recently they rolled out these upgrades of theirs, I'd think it unwise to stress a new system."

Anton paused; this time, he glanced from Marcus Cahn to Tyene Medrana, from Gwynivere Holt to Alabaster Minteran, then from Coreen to Ollie Jokofski.

"We will prevail, but survival is not guaranteed; we have a difficult road ahead of us. But that is what it is; life is hard, and as long as I have breath to draw, I'm prepared to fight for…"

Anton trailed off; the door to the hall had been thrown open. Bruno and Paulo Hughes stepped into the room, breathing hard. Half the table rose at their appearance.

"We need you all outside," Bruno managed to say.

"Clarence is back. And he's not alone," Paulo added.

—

The five figures were descending into the valley when Anton and the others emerged from the hall.

Even from this distance, Anton could see that his youngest sister was holding something - someone - in her arms. She walked at Gavin Owens' side, close enough for the young man to have his arm around her.

Next to them were Clarence Barnett and Santino Vincente. Anton shook his head; it was all too fitting that Clarence would show up at this moment.

But it was the fifth figure who had his attention: a small figure, too short to be a sentient being, and rail thin, though from the way he walked, it seemed he was strong enough.

A growing silence filled the valley as the little group approached Anton and the others. There was no panic in their movements, no sign they were concerned someone would throw them back into custody. They appeared perfectly calm, sure of what they were doing.

"What's all this?"

Anton asked the question when the new arrivals were in speaking distance; if it was directed at anyone, it was directed at Clarence, but the answer came from the small, thin figure.

"Ya'mon, yer ol' friend, Salomon, he tell me you'd be comin'ta see me years and years 'go now. Den dis young fella come 'long; he thinking you waited too long, so he bring me ta' you."

BOOK 6, CHAPTER 7

His eyes opened.

He blinked, looked around, confirming he had returned.

It was like waking from a dream, but no dream had ever felt so real.

Anton reached out his hand, stared at it. He moved a few fingers, then scaled the test up, directing his consciousness to engage his body, to instruct it to stand up.

It worked; his body responded to his intentions seamlessly. Anton was back on Shurtain, and everything about his physical experience seemed to be consistent.

Even if his perspective of it all had transformed.

He knew what to do next; he had woken with a certainty in his being, words from the darkest chambers of his journey echoing through his mind, flashes of the things he had seen hovering at the edge of his consciousness.

He walked slowly out of his tent.

—

Anton could not say, even now, why he had agreed to go with Santino and Winston.

Perhaps it was Winston himself; the Shaman, as he called himself, exuded an eerie calm wildly at odds with the atmosphere around him. Anton might have chalked this up to indifference, but he did not; he could sense that it was something deeper than that.

But whatever his reasons had been, Anton had made his decision, and he could not forget what he had seen, what he had heard, as he had moved through that dark place, stumbling along, blind, running his hands along the walls as he searched for a way out.

It was not there.

Finally, accepting the futility of his situation, he had stopped.

And once he stopped, he heard the voices; faintly at first, then louder.

Was he hearing them?

Or were his thoughts producing them?

It was hard to say in the dark.

What was not hard was to hear what the voices had to say.

Or more specifically, what the one voice had to say, once he had filtered out the noise around it.

Where was he?

In the pitch blackness, Anton was no longer certain who he was asking the question of; himself, or the stranger?

All he could do was accept his situation, and listen to the message.

I was not trying to survive.

I was trying to build a place where we could continue living.

There were aspects of survival, but that was never the point.

Because in the end, we will not survive.

You will not survive.

So we take the time we have.

And live the best we can.

What comes next will come next.

And death will not forget you.

Whether you lived, or survived.

—

An unsettled feeling shrouded the hall.

With Anton absent, Marcus Cahn had taken the seat at the head of the table, but he was reluctant to make a move until time forced his hand. Still, someone needed to do something, to show strength, and while it was not his natural role, Marcus Cahn recognized that his life had reached an impasse; whatever he might have liked for life to be, it was demanding that he be a warrior, a leader. They already had word from their scouts, who had descended the Cadillacs to get eyes on The Bubble Society's army, that the enemy had woken early, and was well on their way.

If conflict was what life demanded, so be it.

Marcus got to his feet, ready to rally the troops, to send the commanders out to their respective units.

At that moment, Anton appeared in the doorway.

—

The younger man approached the older.

Anton stopped in front of Marcus; for a time, they said nothing, only stared, the rest of the tent watching carefully.

When he spoke, Anton did not flinch, did not look away; Marcus credited him for that.

"I think there is a different way to look at all of this."

Marcus gave the slightest of nods, his green eyes meeting the hazel ones.

"Ever since The Advent, I have regarded the people of Kingston, the citizuns of The Bubble Society, as our enemies."

"I see now that we only have a handful of enemies. There are a few individuals, determined to retain control, who are driving these actions. And then there are the rest of Kingston's people, who are just along for the ride."

"Sentient beings might be capable of leading themselves, but the hard truth is that most of society doesn't want to lead themselves. They don't want to deal with the reality of our Universe, don't want to face the fact that nobody knows where Consciousness emanates from, that nobody knows why we're here, or where we're going; it's so much more comfortable to believe there is someone, somewhere, who does understand what's going on, who can convince us that we aren't wandering in the dark through parts unknown… even if that's precisely what we are doing."

"But that desire to have answers cuts both ways; if we can shift the collective consciousness of the citizuns of The Bubble Society, wake them up to the truth of what's going on, we could write a very different ending to all of this. My guess is, the way recent events have gone, they're more than ready to wake up."

Marcus smiled.

"You have a plan?"

Anton nodded.

"It's simple enough. I know who will be leading them, and I know what I have to do. All I need is a Spike."

"We'll still want to keep everyone at the ready; if I fail, you need to be prepared to strike hard and fast. Ultimately, we have to defend our people… but that doesn't have to mean war, unless the other side forces things."

Anton shook his head.

"I only wish I had more Spikes; we have a few down here, but I never imagined we would need more than that. It'll still work, but I saw more… way more."

A heavy thud, followed by a loud clatter, caused Anton to turn around.

He found Clarence Barnett standing there, two bulging sacks dropped at his feet. Anton looked down at the sacks, and smiled when he saw the metal objects spilling out of them. He glanced up at the older man; Clarence spoke through a wry grin.

"I was starting to wonder when you'd get here; you're damn near too late."

—

Donnie Molinaro had some memory of what he would see, once he heard the sounds, but he still felt awe when he came over the ridge that brought Turquoise Falls into view.

It had been a long time since he had been to this place, or any place like it.

But he had not come to appreciate the beauty today.

He came as The Guvna', with an army marching behind him, and an understanding that they would meet the foe today; their intelligence seemed suspect, because early reports were that there were far more Savages than the rugged Cadillac Mountains could possibly support, but by all appearances, their enemy was waiting for them, massed on the other side of the waterfall.

The Director had told The Guvna' all of this, in a dead-of-night meeting with the rest of The Board, where The Director detailed his plans for the morning's battle, and what he expected would happen in the day to come.

It appeared that the Board Members were as certain of The Director of their coming victory, sure that the upgraded Bubble Suits would allow them to overrun the paltry rabble that no doubt faced them.

Donnie Molinaro had no idea what to expect - he was nowhere near as certain as the others that their foe would be so underwhelming - but whatever he expected, he felt a great sense of hopelessness as he stood on the ridge, looking at Turquoise Falls, preparing to cross the meadow between him and the switchbacks, hoping that their enemy would not take him out as soon as he appeared on that open range. The Director had told him he need not worry, that their enemy lacked such capabilities, but Donnie Molinaro understood this was nonsense; if he did go down, it would not be a tragedy, not from The Director's perspective. The Guvna's death, at the head of the column, would serve as a rallying cry, a noble sacrifice to motivate the rest of the troops to charge their enemy.

But Donnie Molinaro did not find a bullet waiting as he crossed the meadow beneath Turquoise Falls.

Instead, he found an eerily calm landscape, the Grand River pooling at the base of the Falls, then continuing on its way, flowing down to Kingston.

The place was almost empty.

Almost.

On the other side of the meadow, two figures were approaching. One figure Donnie did not know, though he could see what he must be.

The other he knew all too well.

Donnie Molinaro dropped his weapon, but did not slow his progress; he continued into the meadow as fast as his Bubble Suit would permit, on a course to meet his son.

—

The Director thought they might hear something as soon as The Guvna' cleared the ridge and entered the meadow; if not, it would happen after they climbed the switchbacks next to Turquoise Falls, and entered the valley where the Savages had erected their defenses.

He stood in the rear, Cornelius and Penelope at his side. The three briefly exchanged glances, but as more and more of their troops crested the ridge, they assumed that the Savages had decided to wait until The Bubble Society's troops were on the switchbacks.

When he reached the ridge, The Director thought it would be a chance to reassess, to regroup.

Instead, he found a scene more horrible than his worst nightmares.

Two figures had come down from the switchbacks; they were crossing the meadow, calmly walking to meet The Guvna'. Their lack of Bubble Suits was conspicuous; this was evident in the way the frontline troops hung back, trying to halt their progress.

Unlike the troops, The Guvna' did not seem bothered by the fact that the two figures approaching him were not wearing Bubble Suits; in fact, he seemed eager to meet them, was stretching his strides as far as he could.

At that moment, recognition came; The Director stopped in his tracks, exchanging panicked glances with Penelope and Cornelius, searching for a way to force the action, to avert this catastrophe.

—

Donnie Molinaro stopped a few feet short of his son, blinking dazedly as he took in the hazel eyes, the lined face, so similar, and so different, from the face he had seen on the morning of The Advent.

He smiled. Then he took in his son's full appearance, truly appreciating the fact that he was not wearing a Bubble Suit for the first time.

"Wouldn'ta believed what I'm seeing right now, a few weeks back."

Anton arched an eyebrow.

"Got da full story round den; apparently, Da Director couldn't help 'imself, once he thought da victory was secured."

Anton nodded.

"Guess we'll have to see about that."

Anton's left hand had been concealed behind his back; now he brought it out in front of him, holding a Spike out to his father on an open palm. The two men looked at the Spike, then at each other.

"It's up to you. It always has been."

Donnie Molinaro paused; decades of conditioning, of praising Knowledge for delivering his oldest daughter to a safer fate, all of it hit him now, demanding that he turn away, that he run from this heresy, this twisted reality that his son lived in.

Then he looked past Anton, up to the top of Turquoise Falls, and saw a wall of sentient beings - the Savages - gathering there, looking down into the meadow, none of them wearing a Bubble Suit. A sense of calm came over him.

Donnie Molinaro reached out for the Spike; he took it from Anton, and with a deep breath, started to make long cuts along his Bubble Suit.

The Bubble Suit fell away from his torso, leaving The Guvna's upper half exposed and naked.

Behind him, The Bubble Society's Army drew in their breath as one, waiting for something terrible to happen.

Donnie Molinaro glanced back at them, then turned to his son; Anton was now holding out a folded robe for his father, who took it, tossed it over his head, and finished stripping off the Bubble Suit.

The two men stood there, staring at each other.

As the seconds stretched to minutes, the hushed silence of The Bubble Society's Army gave way to angry mutterings; chief among the voices was Mo Brickson, who gestured animatedly in the direction of the Savages as he spoke to his friends.

Anton smiled; he glanced down at Winston, who whistled, then raised his fist in the air.

The rumblings were immediate; Donnie Molinaro looked back to the top of the ridge, where the Savages were now pouring down the switchbacks. Then he glanced back; as he expected, the soldiers of his army were staring ahead in disbelief, or muttering to their comrades.

The Guvna' turned back to his son, ready to ask what they should do next.

He found that Winston had already taken charge; the Shaman had raised his thin arm, and was pointing to where The Director stood with Penelope and Cornelius.

—

Theodore Bouregard stood rooted to the spot, as if the thin old Shaman's hand was freezing him in place.

All he had worked for.

All he had sacrificed.

It could not fail now.

But what could he do?

Freeze the Bubble Suits?

What good would that do?

He turned to Corwin McKenzie.

"Give the order to charge. Now."

McKenzie blinked at him, his mouth agape as he glanced back and forth between The Director and the Savages.

They were at a distance, but McKenzie could not see any mouth filters, any nose filters, and The Guvna' had certainly not put one on.

All McKenzie saw was sentient beings, breathing open air.

And The Guvna', standing there, still alive.

As if to confirm what he was seeing, the Savages began to march past the spot where The Guvna' had gathered with the two figures, toward The Bubble Society's Army.

They were not carrying weapons.

Instead, each Savage carried a bundle, topped by a thin, silver Spike.

McKenzie stood mute as he watched the Savages approaching their soldiers, watched The Bubble Suits being cut, watched their forces stepping free, covering their nakedness with robes and staring around in disbelief.

It all happened slowly, as if in a dream.

But eventually, all of the soldiers had cut their way free.

The only ones left in Bubble Suits were the members of The Board, standing on the ridge with The Director, and his two companions.

For a few long moments, the valley fell silent, the soldiers of The Bubble Society's Army turning back to look at their leaders.

The first war cry of the day, so long expected, finally rang out.

EPILOGUE

Tesla Mancini got to share Lilyann with her parents.

In the days and weeks that followed the events beneath Turquoise Falls, the events that ended Knowledge, the Acadians reconnected with their old neighbors, the one-time citizuns of The Bubble Society.

Amelia and Brent Owens were not among them; as Gavin would learn, the two had passed away within days of each other, the very same week that Gavin had tried to return for a final visit. However, this was not the blow it might have been; he was content with his life, overjoyed with Tesla and Lilyann, and he had come to believe his parents might well be in a better place, one where their consciousness could express itself once again, rather than being trapped in the broken physical vehicles that had confined them to The Villa.

Andrea Mancini died three years after the End of Knowledge. There was no specific cause, but with the link between her consciousness and her mind as damaged as it was, she had continued to require constant care, and eventually wasted away, unable to understand why she needed to feed herself, unable to fully express the spirit her family saw in her eyes. She passed away surrounded by that same family, living in Trepani.

Anton Molinaro was there when his sister died, with all four of his daughters; having all four of the mothers in the same place remained an imperfect situation, but Anton could not change his past, and he was doing a far better job of living his life since the End of Knowledge. The four mothers could agree on that, at least.

Donnie and Kelli Molinaro moved to Trepani with Andrea and Rachel. After so many years, he and Kelli accepted that Andrea, like everyone else, would not live forever, and they ought to focus on making the time she did have the best it could be, rather than fixating on what she might lose if she did not live as long as her siblings.

As to Dynamic Solutions, and The Bubble Society, both had gone up in smoke with the deaths of The Board Members, The Director, and the two Shamans on that fateful day in the Cadillac Mountains.

The rest of Kingston took time to recover, but recover it did, as it had after the collapse of so many other empires. Kingston, and the planet Shurtain, still had a great many stories to tell.

AUTHOR'S NOTE

The world changed a lot between the time I wrote the first "sketch" of this book, and the time I published it.

This then-unnamed title was one of five candidates to be the next project when I finished *The Legend of Tucker Wilson* (which, at times, seemed to be on track for "never"). I can't recall the precise date that I came up with the idea for this story, but I can recall where I was living at the time, and from that, can say that it would have been during either 2016 or 2017.

The initial inspiration for *The Bubble Society* came from a relatively offhand line in George R.R. Martin's *A Dance of Dragons*, the fifth book in his acclaimed *Game of Thrones* series. I've included the (paraphrased) quote below; this comes from Lord Wyman Manderly in a conversation with Ser Davos Seaworth in Chapter 29 of the book.

"… I am too fat to sit a horse, as any man with eyes can plainly see. As a boy I loved to ride… but those days are done. My body has become a prison more dire than the Wolf's Den."

That idea stuck with me, the idea of being a prisoner in one's own body, and I started playing with how I could push on that thought in a story.

Of course, as I wrote, life happened, and unless you were under a rock for the last decade, you will be aware that quite a bit happened in our world between the time I had this initial idea for a book, when I finished *The Legend of Tucker Wilson* in the Spring of 2022, and when I completed this book in the Spring of 2025.

This is true on both a global and personal level; I'll get to the global level next, but on a personal level, when I first had the idea, I had not yet met the two individuals who became the inspiration for Gavin and Tesla's characters… that's a story for a different time, but suffice to say the writing process is truly something else.

On a global level, we lived through COVID, and, for many, these years, and the fallout, caused a complete reorientation of what we believe about the world around us and the structures human beings have put in place.

I would be lying if I said that everything that has happened - or at least, my perspective of everything that has happened - did not influence this book. After all, that's what writing is; I can try to put myself into my character's shoes as much as I want, but at the end of the day, these ideas are all flowing through me, even if I am diverting them from somewhere else. Like any other writer, my life experiences help to fuel the fire that, for whatever reason, drove me to devote my mornings, for nearly three years*, to bringing this particular story to life.

As to what it all means about my thoughts on what we lived through… ultimately, it's left to the reader to interpret that. After all, this is fiction… but at the same time, I won't run from the fact that many of the core beliefs about life expressed in this work reflect lessons I have learned - or think I have learned - in my own journey to find meaning and connection in this experience we call life.

And the Knowers?

I won't deny I have met some exceptionally intelligent human beings… as far as human beings go.

I have yet to meet an omniscient person.

I have yet to meet an infallible person.

And I have yet a person who was not a human being, and subject to all the good and bad that makes up human nature.

So, take that for what you will; if you dig this topic, I highly recommend reviewing the thoughts Socrates offered on the matter in *The Apology*. And if you can't believe words that dated could be relevant to someone in the modern day, you might enjoy taking some time to read Marcus Aurelius's *Meditations;* from my perspective, it offers (among many other things) a rather convincing argument that human beings have always been human beings.

*On the three years, big thanks to all the great musicians I spent the time listening to… won't get every artist here, but my Spotify year-in-reviews showed a lot of Morgan Wade, Zach Bryan, Dylan Gossett, Sam Barber, Shane Smith & the Saints, Caamp, Bob Dylan, R.E.M. and Tom Petty… also should acknowledge Dashboard Confessional's *Hands Down* (early lyrics: Breathe in for luck, Breathe in so deep, this air is blessed, you share with me) and Dispatch's *The General…* two songs from my teenage years that came back into my life for this story.

ABOUT THE AUTHOR

Steven Clinton was born in Morristown, New Jersey, in 1988. He moved to Colorado at the age of six and has spent most of his life in the state. Clinton enjoys all things outdoors and can usually be found somewhere in the Western United States.

Clinton's first book, *The Legend of Tucker Wilson*, is available as a single volume as of 2024; look out for his next book, *The Life and Times of Aaron Adessi*, in 2026.

To learn more about his writing, and all the other things Clinton loves to get up to in life, check out his website OneManExperiment.com

Made in the USA
Monee, IL
21 May 2025

17597558R00280